THE RISE
AND FALL OF THE
FIFTEENTH CALIPHATE

THE CIA GIVETH AND THE CIA TAKETH AWAY...

BY CARL DOUGLASS
NEUROSURGEON TURNED AUTHOR WRITES WITH
GRIPPING REALISM

PUBLICATION
CONSULTANTS
We Believe In The Power Of Authors

PO Box 221974 Anchorage, Alaska 99522-1974

books@publicationconsultants.com, www.publicationconsultants.com

ISBN: 978-1-59433-895-3
eBook ISBN: 978-1-59433-896-0

Library of Congress Catalog Card Number: 2019951701

Manufactured in the United States of America.

DEDICATION

"I extend my deepest gratitude to our Armed Forces and First Responders serving both at home and abroad in the war against terrorism."

–John Doolittle, Member of the U.S. House of Representatives from California's 4th district

The present author wholly endorses that sentiment and dedicates this book to all of those genuine heroes past, present, and future.

AUTHOR'S COMMENT:

This book attempts, in semi-historical form, to tell the story of terrorism and terrorists in the Middle East, and most particularly in Iraq and Syria where the Islamic State took root. It is also–by necessity–an exposition in fictional form of the culpable and also heroic involvement of the United States Central Intelligence Agency in the rise and fall of several terrorist organizations in the region. While a serious attempt is made to present the antecedents of the Syrian debacle, the complexities of the situation–as it has evolved and as it now exists–already fills libraries of nonfiction attempts. Those efforts were brilliantly written to bring some semblance of clarity to the confusion. It would be beyond hubris for this author to assert that he has been able to make of all simplicity and understandability. Rather, this is a partial—but hopefully accurate and insightful, albeit limited—explication of what has gone on and what is going on that has drawn the world into a kaleidoscopic condition blighted by such evil. No claim is made to this novel being a complete explanation of the interaction of the many warring factions, their supporters from the local and international communities, and the changes of allegiance and providers in this continuing unfortunate drama.

Obviously, all the death, destruction, and dislocation, are almost beyond comprehension and worthy of a worldwide period of mourning, somehow dedicated to the proposition that the terrorism must be stopped, the widows and orphans granted asylum and safety, and the world brought back to its senses as it has done after the legions of wars of the past. All this book intends is to tell a story which can provide an education and yield a concern for those hapless victims and their tragic nations while engrossing the reader in a good yarn.

DISCLAIMER

This is a book of fiction based loosely on real events and real people, some of whom are included by name since they are part of the underlying real history. However, the characters who are allowed to think are fictional and are entirely a fabrication of the author's imagination. If you are very familiar with the actual events, you will note that the author has taken liberties with times, places, dates, real characters, and their utterances. On the whole—however–a serious effort has been expended to have the historical research match the story woven in this novel.

AUTHOR'S NOTE
ABOUT THE STRUCTURE OF THE NOVEL WITH ASSISTANCE PROVIDED FOR THE READER:

There are three prologues to help the reader to understand the patterns of behavior which elucidate the history of the involvement of the United States in regime change around the world and how that pattern led either directly or indirectly to the formation of the Islamic State. There is an appendix divided into six parts: Cast of Important Characters, Glossary of Terms, a Timeline of Terrorism, a List of Abbreviations and Acronyms, a carefully selected List of Suggested Reading, and a brief Nonfictional Narrative about Terrorism, terrorists, the rise and fall of terrorist organizations, and the contributions made by the American CIA to both the rise and the fall of organizations and governments in the Middle East and the consequences of the decisions made by the real players in the unfolding historical drama. It is possible that you will run into a few of the author's own opinions in that section. The author strongly recommends that the reader take advantage of the appendices in order to keep the terminology, translations, and characters, straight.

CONTENTS

PART ONE

PART TWO

PART THREE

APPENDICES

PART ONE

PROLOGUE I

"Illegal immigration is not a new problem.
Native Americans called it…White People"
–Anon

BANANA WARS 1

CHAPTER ONE

Second *USS Kearsarge* (BB-5), Anchored off the Pearl Islands, Gulf of Panama Bay, August 12, 1903

Six enlisted men of the United States Marine Corps, GCE of the II Marine Expeditionary Force, 8th Regiment, 2nd battalion, eighth marines, Delta Battery, 3rd Platoon, 6th rifle squad, sat anywhere they could find the tiniest bit of shade. They drank copious amounts of Hamm's Beer–"Born in the Land of Sky Blue Waters"—and listened to a minor league game on the ship's radio which featured the up and coming pitcher, Three-Finger Brown, who was poised to pitch a no-hitter. The cloying humidity and tropical heat were inescapable. The men were shirtless and dripping with sweat; even their fatigue trousers were wet. To escape the omnipresent boredom of ship life, the marines played a desultory game of lowball poker using tattered and worn cards. They were playing the 2-7 triple draw variant. Their current hand was aces low and flushes and straights high.

Their semi-stupor was interrupted by the ship's radio with an important announcement: "Now hear this, now hear this, be advised that Mordecai Peter Centennial Brown, better known as Three-Finger, or Miner, or Brownie, by you fanatical fans of baseball, has jist pitched another no-hitter. He is headed to the majors; ya kin take it frum me, boys. For y'all from another planet who ain't heard of Three-Finger, I'm agunna enlighten y'all. He went and had a farm machine accident when he wuz a kid; he lost most of two fingers on his right hand. A bit later, he broke his middle finger; and the quacks set it wrong; so, it come out crooked-like. But, he's a real go-getter. He didn't let that stop him, nosirree. He went and developed a new kinda curveball, which broke funny jist before reachin' the plate. Not only did it curve, he made it curve and drop at the same time."

Every man on board the *Kearsarge* was a baseball fan. They had their preferred teams, but they could not be choosy about what came over the ship's radio on any given day. They cheered uproariously for Three-Finger's great feat and—for a moment—forgot the heat and their boredom.

The next announcement an hour later caused a collective groan: "Now hear this. Now hear this. Sweepers man your brooms on the after deck. Moppers man your mops on the quarter deck. That is all."

This time there was a collective sigh from the men. However, even sweeping and mopping were better than the soul-numbing boredom; so, everyone got up grumbling—as sailors always do—and set about to do their assigned tasks. The *USS Kearsarge* was a flawless mint condition navy vessel even before the morning's cleaning and somehow a brighter and a more ship-shape battleship afterwards—and great source of pride to the ship's officers and crew. The ship's brass gleamed in the bright tropical sun, and its white hull was a thing of beauty as it rocked gently in the calm gulf waters.

In the officers' mess for his daily briefing, Captain Joseph Newton Hemphil crowded the ship's forty officers and ten marine corps officers into the small space for drinks. The only noncoms were marines Master Gunnery Sergeant Orville Cramer from Berryville, Arkansas, Sergeant Major Jethro Amos Rider from Tuscaloosa, Alabama, and navy MCPO [Master Chief Petty Officer] Joe X. Tyler from Norfolk, Virginia, and CMDCM [Command Master Chief Petty Officer] Neal Bradley Dastrup from San Francisco, California. The Filipino mess boys served *ron ponche, saril*–a drink mixture of sorrel sepals, ginger, cinnamon, cloves, sugar, water, and a splash of rum–a corn beer nonalcoholic variant of *chicha–chicha de jora*, and coffee.

The seated men stood for the captain as he took his place at the head of the conference table.

"As you were, Gentlemen," Captain Hemphil said, his demeanor unusually sober. "Our orders have come in from the CNO. We depart Panama Gulf at 0230 tomorrow to go up-coast to an anchor site just off Point Mala on the Azuero Peninsula. We'll disembark the marine force by putting down almost all sixteen smaller boats. That includes the forty-foot steam cutter, the 33-foot steam cutter, both of the two thirty-three-foot launches, all ten of the 30-foot boats, the four cutters, the Admiral's barge, and the Captain's gig. For safety's sake–in case of an accident–we'll retain the two whaleboats which can serve as big lifeboats, the two twenty-foot dinghies, and two eighteen-foot catamarans for the same purpose. Questions?"

Marine colonel, George "Bully" Breckinridge asked, "What about the marines' orders, Sir?"

"I have been instructed to withhold them until we are at anchor off Point Mala."

"When do we inform the men, Captain Hemphil?" asked the CMDCM.

"Just before time for the smoking lamp to go out. Anything else?"

There were no more questions or comments.

"That is all, then. Keep the men busy and then get them ready for action at eight bells of the dog's watch."

"Aye-ayes," were heard from all the officers and enlisted.

There was the intention of secrecy before the disembarkation, but there was also the ever-active grapevine source of information/ misinformation. A rifle team is the basic element of the GCE [Ground Combat Elements] of the marine corps. It consists of four Marines: the team leader, a sergeant [E-5], one rifleman, rank of Pvt/E-1, one assistant automatic rifleman, rank of PFC/E-2, and one automatic rifleman, rank of LCpl/E-3. They ate together, marched together, and fought together. Today they reasoned together.

"We are gonna attack tomorra," Pfc. Carter said. "I got it from my usual accurate source."

Sgt. Snyder snorted, "Nervous Nelly. The quartermaster's office crew has the straight skinny. We are on our way back stateside. We have just shown the colors, and the spics have caved-in to Roosevelt's big stick."

Pvt. Gabler put in his two cents worth, "I heard that we are goin' to go ashore, but just to make them beaners wake up to reality—who's in charge. They'll see us boys marchin' along their streets, and they'll decide that peace and obedience is the way ta go. Then, we'll march right back to the *Kearsarge* and go back to port.

"Fat chance of that," staff sergeant Moss from the platoon said dismissively; and since he was of such an elevated rank, that pretty much ended the erudite discussion.

It became obvious at five bells of the morning watch that something real was afoot. The two 3-cylinder vertical triple-expansion steam engines and five Scotch boilers, connected to two propeller shafts began to rumble. The lead ship began to wheel to the north and to get into motion. The forty officers and five-hundred-fourteen enlisted men of the ship's crew, and the fifty officers and eight hundred enlisted men of the marine contingent observed that all the ships—destroyers, destroyer tenders, heavy-hull repair ships, and general-stores ships–in the *Kearsarge's* squadron were moving apace. The early hour and determined progress meant that this was more than a drill, but less than an attack from the sea. The *Kearsarge* propulsion system was in peak condition; and soon, the battleship was producing 8,705 kW of power and moving at nearly seventeen knots. This was serious; all the men realized that they were in for something of importance.

Meals were special that day—heavy on the protein—which further heightened the tensions of the crew. By the end of supper, it was clear that they were going to battle; and it was likely to be a long, hard deployment.

At eight bells of the dog watch, the sound system called out: "Now hear this; now hear this; all hands on the afterdeck. Be prompt about it and line up in squadrons."

The ship's and marine contingents moved swiftly and in an orderly fashion into their assigned positions aft. They had drilled endlessly for this exact maneuver.

Captain Hemphil stood on the short podium at rigid attention.

CMDCM Dastrup barked out the first command, "Attention on deck! Captain's on the after deck. All hands give heed!"

The battleship's captain spoke into his microphone, "The CNO has communicated our orders, and we will obey them to the smallest detail. Tomorrow in the dark of night, we will disembark our marines onto the shores of Panama for the commencement of a strategic mission designed to protect our Panamanian allies against their Colombian dictators. We will establish a permanent base to protect American interests. All navy hands will aid the marine deployment and set aside their own interests until that is accomplished. Marines will make preparations for disembarkation and a three-week march tonight beginning at eight bells of the dog watch. New jungle uniforms, boots, weapons, and kit, will be issued in an orderly fashion after which there will be an all-marine inspection in the enlisted men's quarters. Final inspection will be done at the time of disembarkation. At that time, all bunks will be ship-shape, breakfast will be over and policed; and marines will depart with the help of naval crew ready for battle. That is all."

The only items for question left to be answered was where they would land, and when they could expect the shooting to begin.

The marines lined up in squads as soon as the word was given after the eight bells chimed. Each man was given a new jungle uniform, olive-drab underwear and tee shirts, socks—pre-treated to prevent fungal infections—puttees to close off the pant leg; so, dirt, bugs, chiggers, and sharp grass seeds, wouldn't get into the marine's boots, socks or pants–and canvas rubber soled boots tested by the navy's quartermaster's scientists for resistance to jungle rot. Short pants replaced the marine regulation khaki trousers. Blouses were short sleeved. Each man was issued a brand-new kit: light-weight, tough cotton-canvas webbing M-1902 backpack and carrying pack—in truth, despite their requirement in the field, the packs being the marine's home, holding everything for their comfort, survival, and efficiency–they were little more than uncomfortable bags with straps on them, a source of constant inefficiency and griping.

Each "home-away-from-home" consisted of a belt, suspenders, sliding clip fasteners, entrenching tool carrier, ammunition cases, canteen cover, pouch containing first aid, and sleeping bag carrier. Weapons for the packs included a USMC combat tactical knife [designated USN Mark 2 Utility Knife], double-edged boot knives, and a Gerber Epic Knife–a small, snub nosed utility knife with snap in sheath—and a separate small canvas pouch for personal items such as soap, razors, tooth brushes, candy, and emergency hard tack rations.

"Pretty sharp new gear," Pvt. Gabler observed.

He had grown up poor and had had to share hand-me-downs until he enlisted. This new clothing and kit items were the best he had ever seen in his life. He had found the marine way-of-life to be his cup of tea. He intended on being a lifer like the sergeant-major he idolized.

Once the new kit was divvied out, marine Master Gunnery Sergeant Orville Cramer called the warriors to attention, "Good, efficient work men. Take your kit back to your bunks; change into regulation battle gear; and return on the double to the quarter deck and form up by squads. That is all."

The men gave an appreciative chuckle.

An apparently chaotic scene with blurs of movement ensued as the eager marines suited up, carefully situated their gear into the packs, and moved at a trot to their assigned places.

"Not fast enough," Gunny Cramer carped with a slight smile, which was returned by his subordinates.

Then Sergeant-Major Jethro Amos Rider, barked out an order in his basso-profundo voice: "Count off by twos. Form up two columns with the ones on the right and the twos on the left."

That took only a minute for the well-practiced marines to accomplish. They stood at attention.

"You will march in an orderly but brisk fashion to the armory where you will receive your weapons for the upcoming battle. Column Right, forward march!" and after a few moments, "Column Left, forward march. Get a move on jarheads!"

The grunts were all issued a fresh new M-1903–an American five-round magazine fed, bolt-action service repeating Springfield rifle–which supplanted the Krag-Jorgensen rifle, a source of appropriate griping by the seagoing warriors. The legendary M1903 Springfield rifle–which quickly became affectionately known to marines as the "'03"–would become one of the most revered battle rifles in marine history. They were also issued leather ammunition cross-belts and three hundred 30.06 cartridges. All marines—officer and enlisted–received two new Colt Navy revolvers

The larger men who qualified as machine gunners received a Colt M1895 "potato digger" machine gun. Snipers obtained coveted Marine Corps M1903A1 sniper rifles with pistol grip stock and Unertl 8x scopes. These guns were marked as M1903 despite the obvious differences in the two rifles. The Marine Corps was reluctant to adopt the M1903A1 due to a difference in cost compared to the M1903. They simply ignored the Army's nomenclature and regarded—officially, at least–all M1903 rifles as such, regardless of stock types, sight types, and longer barrels.

Sixteen heavy machine guns were Benet-Mercies and Colts. They served the forces by being mounted on the flat cars and on the roofs of the boxcars of the train rolling through Panama from Cólon after they were requisitioned by the Corps during the first day of the Panama battle. The Marine Corps had recently adopted the Benet-Mercie light machine gun or–as its operators came to know it–the "machine rifle." .303 British Light machine guns used in cavalry units and swift moving units–which used readily available .30 caliber rifle cartridges—were liberally distributed to the many squads. It was light, clip fed, and shoulder fired. It could be supported by a front mounted thin bipod and in the rear stock with a butt-mounted, screw-thread monopod. Tired and not particularly strong men could use the gun; so, it contributed an increased measure of security to the grunts who were only paid $100 a month to put themselves in danger; it made them feel more important as well as safe.

Major-General Bullard Henry Lewis arrived on board the ship sometime during the night, and his ship also delivered a full load of mules and mule-drawn tank wagons and military stores wagons. He assisted the process of arming his marines, then declared the project ready for landing that morning.

CHAPTER TWO

"So, he went on, tearing up all the flowers from the garden of his soul, and setting his heel upon them…"

"…and the wild beast rose up within him and screamed, as it had screamed in the Jungle from the dawn of time."

—Upton Sinclair, *The Jungle*, Doubleday, Jabber & Company, February 26, 1906

Azuero Peninsula, On the march towards Parita Bay, Panama, August 13, 1903

When the last marine, muleteer, and cook, had offloaded from the USS *Kearsarge*; and every wagon, every piece of military equipment, pot and pan; horse, pig, and steer; and reserve store was lined up on the rough narrow track leading away from the coast, Gen. Lewis pronounced the expedition ready to proceed on its "God-ordained" mission.

Sergeant-Major Jethro Amos Rider from Tuscaloosa, Alabama shouted above the cacophony of the preparations and the beginning of the day's rain, "Ten-hut!, ten-hut!, all hands, listen up. Marines form two parallel columns facing east. Equipment managers bring in your animals and wagons behind the marines. Animal wranglers bring your animals into position behind the wagons."

The senior officers rested on their cavalry mounts while the hustle/ bustle of Rider's orders was carried out.

SGM Rider reported to the officers, "General Lewis, Sir, the company stands ready and awaits further orders."

"Move the columns forward, Sergeant-Major."

Rider's voice boomed over the heads of the quiet standing marines, "Column right, move out on the right. Column left, move out on the left. Forward 'harch!"

Like a giant centipede, the marine force and its equipage began to move its serpentine way forward over the now muddy track. It was raining in pelting sheets, and it was pitch black on a moonless night. The going was slow.

The scouts had been up all night traversing the uneven hillside to determine the best route for the columns to follow. They agreed at the onset to proceed five miles forward, then to return and to mark the way with pastel colored stakes at prescribed intervals. As the columns advanced through the hostile darkness, the man behind put his left hand on the shoulder of the man ahead. They inched along keeping to their close-order drill—one movement, one sound, one mind, the essence of the Marine Corps. They stumbled along in the dark as best they could singing in a near–piano softness the jodie calls they had learned by rote:

> Your left, your left
> You gotta go home on your left.
> Left, right, left, right,
> You gotta go home on your left,
> Sound off, one, two,
> Sound off, three, four,
> Sound off one, two, three, four
> One, two, three, four!

> You had a good home, but you left, Your right
> You had a good home, but you left, Your right
> Jody was there when you left, Your right
> Your baby was there when you left, Your right
> Sound off! 1, 2

Sound off! 3, 4
1, 2, 3, 4, 1, 2 ... 3,4!

There ain't no use in going back,
Jody's livin' it up in the shack,
Jody's got somethin' you ain't got,
It's been so long I almost forgot
Sound off! 1, 2
Sound off! 3, 4
1, 2, 3, 4, 1, 2 ... 3, 4!

Talkin" to my daddy on his dyin' bed,
With a smile on his face this is what he said,
When I came out of my mother's womb,
I found myself in the delivery room,
All bloody and white, I rappelled to the floor,
Cut the umbilical and crawled to the door,
Cruised the ward and I'm lookin' good,
Baby little marine like I should,
Khaki diaper, shiny brown baby shoes,
Butter-knife sword, and baby dress blues,
Troop truck stroller, tricycle tank
Three diaper pins on my collar for rank,
Down the hall I heard some crying like heck,
Walked right in called attention on deck,
Listen up wimps, I'm in command,
All your cryin' and your snivelin' I will not stand,
They said "Aye, Aye, Sir; and I had it made,
I was the commandin' officer of the baby brigade.

Hundreds of cadence songs, dozens of miles, sore feet, blisters, gripes. On they went until 1000 hours when the Sergeant-Major called halt. The giant fiery tropical sun was in full flower, and the heat and humidity were oppressive and sapped a man's will to go on.

The cookies started breakfast, brunch, actually—cream-chipped beef on a shingle, rafters of bacon, scrambled dehydrated eggs, and coffee that tasted like tobacco juice—the usual bivouac fare. Morale was good;

the view was magnificent. It was a brilliantly sunny day now that the rain had stopped, and a marine could see forever out over the cobalt blue Pacific Ocean. The highlands and igneous rock mountains swept down the emerald foothills to the golden strands of the beaches. The contours were rough and uneven which added to the attractiveness of the mountains and the numerous headlands and tree covered bays. In the far distance, they could see Parita Bay, their destination for the day. The scouts reported no sightings of people or villages and did not have any indication that the marine column had been seen.

The officers received their orders from Gen. Lewis as they ate their breakfast—fresh pork chops, poached eggs, toast with butter and Oregon blackberry jam, freshly squeezed orange juice, and hot blueberry muffins.

"Our ultimate goal for this mission is to capture and control Panama City and to establish permanent possession of the proposed Canal Zone, including a five to ten-mile strip on both sides of the canal once it is completed."

"When might that be, Sir?" asked Col. Breckinridge.

"Don't know, Bully. President Teddy says a coupla years, but that means we have to get the French out of the canal business; we have to cut Panama free from Colombia; and just incidentally, the powers-that-be must get the blinkin' thing built."

"Like getting Rome built, eh, Sir?"

"Yeah, like that. Right now, we have to get the land for the good old U.S. of A. That's where us marines get involved. So, our part of the plan to get the process on the road is to march as fast as possible to where the railroad is finished; take control of it; then march on to Panama City; capture it and the country; and to establish an occupation force. The railroad is crucial; so, we can move fast; and so we can capture the communications systems before the government in Colombia can be alerted and send in an army. In short, Gentlemen, we must accomplish a *fait accompli* before the Colombians know what hit 'em."

Bully started to interrupt, but Gen. Lewis held up his hand.

"Here's how we do this thing…exactly. Bully, you take two-thirds of the grunts and most of the heavy equipment with you and start a quick march west to Panama City. The rest of us will probably catch up, but if we don't, hold up before launching the attack. Understood?"

"Understood, General."

"All right. The rest of the grunts will get on the train with me and get control of everything along the way back east to Colón. It is imperative that we cut off communications from Colón to the capital city of Santa Fé de Bogotá, or we'll have a war on our hands instead of an "incident." My men and I will rely on small arms, machine guns, and grenades; so, we can travel light and fast. I'll send a rider back with a message as soon as it is possible."

Gen. Lewis went through the ritual of packing, tamping, and lighting his pipe and began to taste the smoke contemplatively. He was a physically powerful man—big, tall, and muscular–with a ruddy bluff complexion. He had the face of a thug–scarred from thirty years of battle and furrowed from days facing the sun—and wore an habitual scowl. His purposes were serious, and his thoughts were both somber and important. He did not countenance interruption when he was thinking. The general's uniform was always full-on spit-and-polish, seen to by his Filipino aide-de-camp—except when he was in battle.

Lewis was not an armchair general; he was in the thick of things, sweaty, dirty, sunburned, and taking more risks that his marines who would march barefoot over hot broken glass for him. He wore two-stars on his collars, an infantry emblem over his heart, but no battle ribbons other than the blue and white medal of honor award ribbon, lest anyone doubt his courage and accomplishments. Gen. Lewis was not a handsome man; he was every bit a warrior. His eyes were hard blue, his nose bulbous, and his face was always regulation clean-shaved even in battle conditions whenever his aide—Ferdinando–could corner him long enough for the twice-daily shave required to keep him an example for his men.

Marine colonel, George "Bully" Breckinridge, Gen. Lewis's second-in-command, was a handsome man, tall and slim, with clearly defined tree-branch hard muscles. He had ginger hair and a closely cropped sandy mustache—regulation size and shape. His nose was patrician, his lips full and attractive especially when he smiled and laughed, which was often. He had a lantern jaw and a hard-cleft, strong, butt chin, and high cheek bones, like an Indian. Where Gen. Lewis had something of an olive complexion beneath his bronze tan, Bully had fair skin with a similarly deep tan, but his facial color was softer, more gold than bronze. Like his general, he was a spit and polish marine from head to toe; and he prided himself in having brightly shined shoes even in combat conditions. With

Gen. Lewis as an example, the colonel could not sit back and watch to direct a battle, he had to be right there in the fray as sweaty and dirty and with the same harshly profane vocabulary which his men loved and copied.

Sergeant-Major Jethro Amos Rider was taller, straighter, stiffer, and more muscular; than any other marine in the expedition force; that is why he was the sergeant-major. He looked better in his uniform than the generals, better than the Mid-City New York gym muscle builders in the shower, and bigger than the devil himself when viewed by a cringing enemy. The Latinos called him "*El Diablo Él Mismo.*" He could run carrying a machine gun in each hand, hold up the tongue of a tank wagon, and screw on lug bolts using only his fingers. He could out eat, out drink, and out shoot, the best in the corps.

Rider had jet-black kinky hair that would not tolerate a comb, an in-grown hair problem on his face which required him to get an exception from the clean-shaven face rule; so, he had a gorgeous shiny curly black beard and five-inch long mustachios that women could not resist. His nose had been broken twice and repaired once by a medic in the Philippines. He was not handsome, but devilishly attractive. His voice was basso-profundo and commanding even when he whispered.

Master Gunnery Sergeant Orville Cramer was from Berryville, Arkansas. He was a racist; his father was a racist; his grandfather was a racist; and his great-grandfather was a slave-owner. Cramer made no bones about his attitudes and found them fairly general and welcome in the Corps. No one censored his epithets; no one around him suggested integration of the Corps. He had a thin, bitter face. His mother–like all mothers–had told him that if he frowned all the time, his face would become a permanent frown. She was right. Sun had made a topographical map of his face and gave him a squint in his eyes that made him look constantly suspicious. He had one flaw in his dress. He insisted on wearing a small American flag embroidered on his sleeve which his grandma had made. The officers gave up on trying to get him to comply with tradition.

His hair was light brown and fine in texture. He had a rapidly growing occipital bald spot which was advancing forward and backward. The monk's tonsure part of his hairline was long and fluffed out under his helmet. He wore a hat at all times—even during mess and enlisted men's dress ceremonies–to hide the baldness which humiliated him.

The four jarheads of Delta Weapons battery rifle squad, USMC—Sgt. Mark E. Snyder, Pfc Rodney Wayne Carter, Pvt. Glen Gabler, LCpl. Nephi Muhlestein, and attached medic Danny NMN Broadhead–were very similar in appearance above and beyond the sameness of their uniforms, their kit, and their weapons, which seemed almost to be parts of their bodies. That was none too surprising since they all came from the small town of Thistle Crossing, Utah where there was rumored to have considerable consanguinity. The branches of the military in that day made a concerted effort to enlist young men from the same community and to keep them together to take advantage of the camaraderie already part of their lives. It was presumed that they would work together more easily than if they were strangers.

They were fairly short, as marines go; and they had tough, wiry, farm-boy physiques. They all had pale complexions and had never been able to lose their farmer-tans—face, neck, forearms, and hands indelibly darker than the rest of their bodies despite the recurring sunburns and suntans of their backs, chests, and lower legs. They all had almost square heads—hence earning them the forever title of "jarheads"—thick features, and interesting faces suggestive of both innocence and toughness. Owing to insufficient access to medical care, their skin was pocked and scarred from poorly treated acne, measles, and small-pox in two of them. Unlike the officers, none of these grunts had been formally schooled beyond the sixth grade except for the education afforded them by the Corps.

General Lewis and Colonel Breckinridge got up from their siestas and began to get the noncoms up and to move the men out quietly. There was now a proscription against making noise of any kind, including singing jodies. The centipede rose to its feet and began an orderly march with all legs hitting the ground—left, right, left, right, repeat—with numbing precision and regularity. They had short uphill treks, and longer downhill trots, moving them farther and faster than the trailing equipment wagons and stock. Originally, they were expected to get to the railhead well after dark. Now—at their present pace—they would arrive in broad daylight. The sergeants passed the word to slow down. The way down became wetter, denser, and harder to traverse. Roots snarled the men's feet and the horses' hooves. Branches inflicted small blows, a plethora of scratches, a definite opportunity to try out the men's worst vocabularies.

Finally, SGM Rider called a halt to avoid the entire column being detected by the citizens of the hamlets and villages the marines were now passing through. It was siesta time, and people were sound asleep in windowless huts trying to escape the cloying heat. No one called out an alarm. Private Glen Gabler slipped into the dense underbrush to take a leak into the wide murky creek. It was to his great credit that he did not scream or shout when a middle-sized crocodile splashed into the opaque water beside him. He back-pedaled furiously and spread the word to the rest of the gyrenes. SGM Rider passed along orders that all urination was to take place in open areas; so, no snakes, or crocs, or things-that-go-bump-in-the-night, could appear and excite cursing, and cause an inadvertent general alarm to be sounded.

It was still light even though the sun was setting somewhere out there in the sea by the time the remainder of the troops and their gear pulled in behind the advance coterie. Now, the tired marines had time to rest before launching their attack on the train. The officers ordered double sentry duty and company silence. The men were issued cold sandwiches and large vessels of water—no alcohol. They slept well, knowing this may well be the last good sleep they would enjoy for days.

CHAPTER THREE

"Beyond the Chagres River
Are paths that lead to death
To the fever's deadly breezes
To malaria's poisonous breath!
"Beyond the tropic foliage,
Where the alligator waits,
Are the mansions of the Devil
His original estates.
"Beyond the Chagres River
Are paths fore'er unknown,
With a spider 'neath each pebble,
A scorpion 'neath each stone.
"'Tis here the boa-constrictor
His fatal banquet holds,
And to his slimy bosom
His hapless guest enfolds!
"Beyond the Chagres River
Lurks the cougar in his lair,
And ten hundred thousand dangers
Hide in the noxious air.

-James Stanley Gilbert, *Beyond the Chagres*, from the book, *Locks,*
Crocs & Skeeters, 1898

The Panama Railroad Bridge Crossing over the Chagres River at Barbacoas, Panama, August 15, 1903

Beginning in 1903, President Theodore Roosevelt oversaw the realization of his dual long-term goals: building a trans-isthmian Panama Canal, and defeating the French goals of accomplishing the engineering effort before the United States. A railroad had been built previously—finished in 1855—and served the meager needs of the time fairly well. However–by 1898—the railway showed significant signs of wear, and by 1903–shortly before the marines arrived–the need for a major renovation exceeded what could hope to be accomplished by maintenance effort alone. The U.S. engineers dedicated to building the canal determined quickly that they first had to build a well-functioning railway from Cólon to Panama City. There was no real other option because they had already made a firm choice to use locks and to create an artificial lake [Gatun]. The choice of those options objectively required that the old railway route from 1855 be changed because it traveled through the Chagres River valley, which would be flooded by the lake.

When the marines were looking at the Barbacoas Bridge over the Chagres River that August morning in 1903, they were looking at the terminus of the railroad of the moment. Effectively, the entire railroad was scrapped; and the huge project of rerouting and rebuilding the line was underway beginning at the Cólon end. Sgt. Rickie Sanchez–a native Spanish speaker–walked around the small settlement of Barbacoas, twenty-three miles west of the Atlantic terminus in Colon and about half-way across the isthmus towards Panama City on the Pacific terminus.

There he struck up conversations with several Panama Railroad employees and learned two things of importance: first was that the train could go no farther west and had to turn back the way it came after crossing the massive wrought iron structure–more than six hundred feet in length and rising forty feet above the river on stone piers—spanning the three-hundred-foot wide Chagres River. Second, he learned that the road was not terrible from there to the west along where the old tracks had been and would support wagons and horses without much danger or even inconvenience at that time of year.

Gen. Lewis declared the next day, August 17, to be the start of the attack. Very little happened in the small town below them throughout the steamy day. Everyone took a two-or-three-hour siesta, and then simply forgot about any more work. The town closed-up at dark, and the streets emptied. The ready units of Lewis's marines slipped down the hillside though the torturous undergrowth and secreted themselves along the road into town, and among the pilings of the bridge. The main force moved into position as close as they thought they could without being seen in the dim light of the few remaining city gas lamps.

The huffing and puffing steam train could be heard from about five miles to the east as it chugged slowly along the moderate ascent from the jungle. The scouts stationed at that point galloped along ahead of the train, which was no great feat, given the glacial celerity of the old iron engines. With the timing in their favor, the marines waited patiently for their ambush. The scouts reported that the tops of the train cars had soldiers stationed with machine guns, presumably to defend against banditos. They could hardly have imagined what lay in wait for them.

Gen. Lewis and Col. Breckinridge held their men in check in the humid darkness until the train engines were switched onto sidetracks and around to the back of the train in preparation for the return to the east. The early rising passengers began to board the passenger cars; and the freight started to be carried aboard by a combination of Indian and Chinese railroad workers, temporary Indian free man labor, and slaves. The morning was already almost smotheringly hot; and the train workers, passengers, and marines, had trouble keeping the salty sweat out of their eyes. It was fifteen minutes before midnight.

With a nod from the two senior officers, two buglers sounded the fearsome *To Arms* on their regulation soprano bugles staccato fortissimo three-four time in the key of G. "*Ta ta ta ta tatata tatata tatata tatata tatatatata… Ta ta ta ta tatata tatata tatata tatata tatatatata…*" like the sound of screaming eagles. The marines howled their war-cries and dashed up the hill, over the side of the bridge, and down from their bush enclosures. The sequence of *To Arms* was bugled out twice and then was followed by two chilling loud calls of *Fix Bayonets*.

Most of the machine gunners atop the trains had been sound asleep slumped over their guns. The bugle calls, the howling banshees, the clatter of the wheels on the tracks, and the hissing outcries of the steam engines, along with the panicked frenzied shrieks of the passengers and the laborers, was a rude cacophony from hell, as it was intended to be for the gunners. They could not function for precious seconds; seconds they could not afford.

Nimble marine fighters swept up the steps of the cars, up the steel bar rungs of the ladders, and to the tops of the twelve cars and engines of the old train. The marines were upon the gunners before they could move their guns into effective positions. There was pandemonium as Panamanian and Colombian boys toppled away from their heavy Benet-Mercie and Colt machine guns—purchased by the Colombian army from the United States–almost before they fully realized that an attack was in progress. The marines could not get to the top of two of the passenger cars, and the Colombian soldiers had time to wheel their guns into position and to begin to fire a steady stream of bullets in the general direction of the oncoming marine chargers.

Ten marines were dead before the first passenger car top was pacified. The dead littered the curved surface, and several bodies rolled over the sides. Three machine gunners on the most frontal of the train cars were effectively holding off the marines and making it possible for the engineers to get the train chugging into motion. At first, forward progress was slow; but gradually, it began to pick up.

"Get those gunners, or we've lost the battle," Gen. Lewis hollered at the top of his lungs.

Two more marines perished in the attempt. The train wheels began to screech forward, faster and faster.

Marines fell off the side, and it was clear that the train was going to speed away to safety and to be able to warn the troops in Cólon. If that happened, it was possible that the marine expedition to retake Panama from Colombia would be an expensive and lethal failure.

Major-General Bullard Lewis did not allow a place on his planning sheets for failure. He often referred to himself as being stupid about things like that, or that his vocabulary had gaps in that regard.

To the utter amazement of the marines around him, Col. Breckinridge leaped from his horse and into the space between the last two cars. He steadied himself on the draw gear of the Janney coupler, adjusted his machine gun sling on his right shoulder, grasped highest steel bar rung on the back of the car, and began to climb up as fast as his muscular limbs could propel him.

He could hear the staccato chattering of a light machine gun coming from the top of the car, and he could not be at all sure whether the gunner was his or theirs. He popped his head up and heard a stream of bullets screech past him for his trouble. It made him angry because the shooter was one of his own. He was not a man to accept being killed by friendly fire. It was unmanly to his way of thinking.

"Hey, you stupid devil-dog, it's Bully. I'm comin' up. If you shoot me, I'll have you up on charges. DO YOU HEAR ME??"

He could have been heard in Panama City even over the clatter, clash, and banging going on around the two men.

Corporal Emil John Franklin had attained control of the roof of the car Bully was trying to mount. When he heard the famous colonel bellow, he could not help himself; he began to laugh out loud.

"Sorry, Colonel, c'mon up. I promise not to shoot you this time. You and I can be unfriendly fire together."

Bully did not waste a second. He pulled himself up and ran straight up as if he were in a race. As he passed Cpl. Franklin, he gave a small friendly salute and a smile.

"Hey, Bully, keep yer head down. Them guys up front ain't so friendly."

Bully had been in situations like this before, and he ignored the well-meant advice that any sane man would consider completely reasonable. His legs pumped up and down like machine pistons as he covered the ground between himself and green uniformed soldiers on the cars in front. They looked at the powerful marine hurtling towards them like a raving maniac as if he were some kind of gringo demon who was immune to bullets.

Bully did not think about bullets as he forged his way thoughtlessly towards the three gunners waiting for him. He could not have been sure what they were thinking; but, somewhere in the back of his mind, he must have known how unnerving he appeared to them. Hundreds of bullets flew past him, over him, and into the steel floor below him. On he came.

He leaped across the opening of the two cars separating him from the Colombians. Then—to the consternation of the machine gunners—he suddenly dropped to one knee and whipped his machine gun to his shoulder and began to spray bullets on full auto at the astonished defenders. Two of them went down during the next two seconds. The third soldier was more seasoned and brave, and he held his own. He shot off Bully's favorite campaign hat and scorched a hole in his right blouse sleeve. Bully rolled to his side and fired off his last two rounds, killing his enemy before he ran out of ammunition. Three Benet-Mercie and Colt heavy machine guns lay quiet on the steel floor.

The marines hanging on to the sides of the train cars witnessed the whole thing and cheered when the last defender went down. Bully's reputation was indelibly imprinted into their brains for as long as they lived. That would not be long because the train had picked up speed at full throttle which meant that they would be in Cólon in less than half an hour if Bully could not bring another rabbit out of his hat to stop the train.

Things got more complicated. Colombian soldiers—who had been hiding in the caboose—now climbed up to the tops of the roofs of the cars. They crept up behind Cpl. Franklin before he was aware of the threat. The Colombians were able to put two rounds into Franklin's left leg, and he fell to the steel below him. They rushed him to administer the *coup de grâce*. He was in agonizing pain, and his consciousness seemed to be fading in and out. From somewhere deep down inside his marine wired brain, he summoned up the fortitude to turn and fire his machine rifle in the general direction of the rushing Colombian soldiers.

The first two shuddered from the thudding .303 bullets. They fell face forward like felled trees. The intrepid marine corporal sat down on the floor and faced his attackers. A dozen of them closed in on him in two haphazard columns firing as they went. Franklin was hit again, this time in the left arm. It was excruciating to hold his gun up, but the marine did it. He squeezed the trigger one last time and held the stock as he swung the barrel back and forth. .30-06 bullets came at him seemingly from all directions.

In truth, however, they were helter-skelter. None of the soldiers could aim. Death dressed in khaki was too close, and the rounds from Franklin's machine gun were coming all around them. They began to fall when they got to within fifteen yards of the only partially conscious marine. He was still holding his automatically firing Benet-Mercie light machine rifle when he became unconscious. The last attacker fell dead less than a foot from Cpl. Franklin.

The train had to be stopped. Bully raced–without a moment's hesitation or thought—towards the Mogul locomotives, which had two leading wheels and six drive wheels. Special distinctive features of the locomotives selected for the rough and twisting railbeds were the long low sloping tender, designed for greater ease in reverse running, and that they were also designed to avoid toppling over because of that unevenness and roughness. No one was in the first engine; so, he leaped from it to the forward iron horse. The engineer was oblivious to anything except his gargantuan task of keeping the train roaring along at top speed. He was doing the work of an engineer, the fireman, and the support crewman. His shirt was soaked, and his bib blue denim overalls were black with soot. His face was so black, he could easily have been mistaken for a negro.

For a moment, Bully watched the engineer rush methodically to stoke coal into the furnace, then tip water into the fire-tube burner from the pannier tanks on the tank car behind where the two men were standing. At frequent intervals, the nearly exhausted engineer raced to shovel coal from the shoot and into the coal box. His breath was coming in ragged gasps.

Bully chose his moment. The trainman had just set his scoop shovel down and wiped a filthy drag across his blackened face.

"Don't move, *Hombre*," Bully said, yelling over the crashing and banging and hissing of the machinery in the engine room.

The man nearly leaped out of his skin. Nevertheless, he had the presence of mind to pull an ancient revolver from his belt. Bully had planned for this moment. He threw himself into the man's bulky round frame and twisted the gun from his hand. He held it pointing at the man's mid-forehead.

"*Sentarse!*" Bully commanded."

The humble trainman had the heart of a warrior, and he threw himself towards the powerfully built marine. Bully shot him in the mid-chest once, and the man's heart exploded. He died a hero; but he died to facilitate the American marine mission; and Bully did not give him a thought.

What he did think was, "*I missed the class in train driving at Quantico. Now what do I do?*"

He looked at the handles, dials, meters, knobs, and gears. Nothing came to mind. Gulp.

"*I suppose it'll stop when I run this thing into the Caribbean in about half an hour, I guess,*" he thought aloud.

CHAPTER FOUR

{French}*"Mon climat intérieur est tropical aujourd'hui : il y a de la pluie, du soleil, des odeurs fortes, et un sentiment de pourriture végétale flotte dans l'air débilitant."*

{English}"My inner climate is tropical today: There is rain, sunshine, strong odors, and a feeling of plant rot is floating in the debilitating air."

–Simone et André Schwarz-Bart, *Adieu Bogota*, 2017

Cólon, Panama, mid-afternoon, August 15, 1903

Colonel Breckinridge need not have given much thought to the gadgetry of the engine room of the train. He could not have known about the dead-man switch. The train surprised the tired marine officer to his core by slowing gently to a stop over a quarter of a mile. If he had been a praying man or if he had any truck with miracles, he would have thought this was one of those. He shrugged and chalked it up to just one more of the things in the world that he would never understand. Besides, he had work to do.

As soon as the escaping train had gone too far from the Chagres River for the main body of marines to catch it, Gen. Lewis called a halt.

"Sergeant-major!"

"Sir?"

"Have the men form up, on the double."

"Sir, yes Sir."

He made smart about-face and boomed, "Companies form your ranks, double-speed. Be quick about it or I'll have your livers for lunch."

The men, even the medics and cookies were glad to have someone taking charge and to have order return to the ranks. General Lewis would handle this. The sooner they got going with discipline, the sooner they would get after that rebellious train and Bully.

"General, the men have formed their ranks, Sir."

"Men, we will capture that train in short order. It cannot have gone far. All officers and enlisted sergeants and above meet the sergeant-major and me. On the run!"

No one had to be told twice. The officers and non-coms gathered their weapons quickly and raced to where the two leaders stood.

Gen. Lewis had his emergency plan well in mind by the time the rest of the leaders stood at attention in front of him.

"Gentlemen all, you will see to it that every man is armed—every man, including docs and cooks—and form them up ready to ride or to run. Wranglers bring up every horse, mule, and piece of saddle-tack, and ready the mounts for the race of their lives. Medics ready all you need to treat the anticipated wounded. Any questions?"

There were none,

"Then, move out. Double-double time," boomed out the authoritative voice of SGM Rider.

In every battle and every war, there are times which can only be described in time-honored military terms...snafu.

The horse wrangling, saddling, and bridling process, could best be described as comic-opera by civilians and a general snafu by soldiers, sailors, and marines. Most of the horses and only a handful of mules were broken to saddle. A rodeo commenced with a wild melee to get control of the balky, unbroken SOB potential mounts. Two and three men were required to subdue the majority of the horses and mules enough to get them saddled and bridled. The unfortunate riders assigned to those totally uncooperative beasts were on their own to fast-break them enough to have them able to provide a useful ride. Horses and mules reared up on their hind legs, kicked with their hind legs, and rolled over on their backs, and thrashed their legs. Even the officers—all of them—entered into the dust cloud and helped get some control of the intended mounts.

By the judicious use of colorful marine Corps language, main-strength, and awkwardness, a motley cavalry of sorts was standing at the ready. With curses and threats the officers and non-coms got the rank-and-file to cease and desist from laughing at the hilarious rodeo circus that was swirling around them. Finally, something of calm and order was achieved.

"Follow me, men. We are going to save Bully and the rest of the boys, and we are going to commandeer that cursed train. We are on our way to Cólon!"

"Keep order and discipline and stay close to the general, everyone," shouted Sergeant-major Rider over the din caused by the angry horses and mules.

Fat chance of that.

As soon as Rider shouted his order, the rodeo recommenced and the forward progression of the improvised cavalry became a whirling circle moving only more-or-less in the desired direction. Gen. Lewis cursed the mounts, the riders, the weather, the dust, and everything and everyone in general. Even the lifer sergeant-major picked up a few additions to his vocabulary from his esteemed leader.

At long last–after what seemed like an eon–a semi-disciplined, but atrocious appearing, cavalry unit began to gallop down the sides of the railroad tracks in the direction of Cólon and the missing train. Now, nature played a beneficial role. All horses and mules love to run, even those less than an hour broken enough for brave men to mount. In what was more like a unidirectional stampede than a dignified cavalry charge, they began to gallop for all they were worth. This genuine equine enthusiasm began to make up for the comic preparation fiasco.

Bully Breckinridge sent two grunts back towards the Chagres River Bridge to seek help. Then, he gathered fourteen marines who were either not wounded or only had minor flesh wounds to do emergency temporary holding care on the seriously wounded—seventeen men. It was an integral part of the marine training to perform first-aid, and the survivors were at their best that day. Tourniquets and bandages were applied, and every man—dead or alive—was moved off the train car roofs as gently as humanly possible. Still, there was screaming.

Bully himself took personal charge of getting the gravely wounded Corporal Emil John Franklin off the roof. On the rail car top, he and his two assistants put pressure bandages on seeping wounds, and tourniquets above spurting ones. Franklin's last words were the regiment's mottos.

He whispered, *"Non Sibi Sed Patriae"* [Not for self, but for country… Front Towards Enemy."]

Sympathetic as he was, Bully was glad to hear Franklin moan and occasionally cry out in agony. He was alive. No one could ask for more for the time being. By employing their most careful main-strength and awkwardness, the three intact marines lifted their brother down off the roof and onto a contrived shady patch of grass. He was still alive. Pvt. Michael O'Reilly from squad 8 made the sign of the cross and kissed his personal cross for emphasis.

Harry Cohen, a Jewish boy from Crown Heights, Brooklyn, and lapsed Hasid, wanted to add his religious help.

"Hey, Mike, I ain't all that religious, and probably my Jew background wouldn't help poor Franklin here much. Think you could teach me the right way to do the sign-of-the-cross stuff. Maybe it would help God to get our message. Whatta you think?"

"Can't hurt none," O'Reilly said—what did he know? "This is the way youse remember how to do it."

He repeated his previous movements, but in slow-motion.

"It's like this: Spectacles, Testicles, Wallet, and Watch." He demonstrated the movements of his hands. "Get it?"

"Got it."

The two boys gave Franklin–a Southern Baptist—all the help the sign-of-the-cross could provide by a dozen repetitions until Harry got it down pat, much to the suppressed amusement of Bully.

"Bully, I hate to mention it, but do you think we should give poor Franklin here an improvised set of the last rites?" O'Reilly asked cautiously.

"I'll have none of that, men. Franklin is a genuine hero. He is going to get the Medal; and he is going to get it standing up before the president and his family, so help me, God…besides, he isn't even a Catholic."

The entire isthmus of Panama is only about forty-seven miles wide at the point where the railroad and the canal were under construction. The bridge over the Chagres River is less than twenty-seven miles from the Caribbean terminus. The train had come to a stop six miles from the bridge; so, the filthy and completely engaged cavalry and racing ground troops were able to eat up those miles as fast as humans, horses, and mules, could possibly do.

SGM Rider and Gen. Lewis were the first to arrive on the scene at the train. They leaped from their horses, tied them to metal railings, and moved into action. The two men ran to the nearby thicket and cut branches to create six makeshift stretchers.

"Found your field hat, Colonel," Rider said. "Hole in it but I thought you looked out of uniform without it."

"Thanks, Sergeant-major. Bravo Zulu. One can't go out without his cover."

He accepted the well-worn 1899 field hat with its broad hard brim, 'fore and aft' crease at the top of the hat, round screen vent, three rows of stitching that strengthen the edge of the hat's unfolded brim, and still intact USMC's distinctive Eagle, Globe, and Anchor, cap badge and heavy coat of dust and grime with a grateful smile. He put it on and gave the enlisted man a small friendly tip-of-the hat salute.

Shortly, the rest of the men arrived at the train and leaped from their mounts—those who still had mounts. A considerable number of rider-less horses and mules straggled in and wandered around the open area surrounding the tracks. The wranglers had their work cut out for them to round them up. Some locals helped in the round-up by leading their fine horses and mules off into trails in the underbrush.

Captain Robert Jacobsen and his medical staff efficiently set up an emergency treatment center in a shady area and began treating the wounded. Col. Breckinridge directed four marines to carry Cpl. Franklin to the aid tent. They gingerly lifted their brother onto the makeshift stretcher and winced every time he moaned or cried out.

"Put him here on the operating table, Boys," Captain Jacobsen said.

"Is he gonna make it, Doc?" Pvt. Gabler asked, showing the concern of the entire Corps.

"Can't say yet, Son; but we'll do everything we can. We know what he did for us; so, we'll give it our all."

"We trust you, Doc. Thanks for taking care of us."

Doctor Jacobsen and two medics began to strip Franklin and to wash him off. He had bullet wounds in both of his left limbs and one in his chest and had lost a significant amount of blood. The doctor started two intravenous lines and pumped in three liters of saline water and started several bottles of plasma. He was gratified to see the corporal begin to pink up and to breath more easily.

"Let's do a trach first," the doc said, and proceeded to put a tube into Franklin's windpipe through a small incision in the front of his neck.

"Good, now we've got control of his airway. I think we need to do a thoracotomy first, what do you think, Lieutenant Thompson?" he asked the head nurse, a twenty-five-year veteran of the service, and a woman whom the doctor trusted as much as he did his own judgment.

"I do agree, Bob, but we have to get a move on. His left leg wound is still putting out a lot of blood, and the tourniquet has been on long enough."

"Tom and I will get the thoracotomy underway. Get Sergeant Gunderson to assist you and get down into that wound to expose the bleeder. You know, Marie, you should be a doctor."

"Any idea how hard it is for a woman to get into medical school?"

Doctor Jacobsen made his incision along the upper margin of the seventh rib.

"I do," he said. "It's stupid. As stupid as the denial of the rights of negroes to serve the Corps in combat roles."

He cut out the sixth rib and placed rib retractors to widen the opening. The left chest cavity was full of blood.

"Give me a bunch of sponges, Mike."

The surgeon rapidly sopped out copious amounts of clotted and fresh fluid blood until he said, "I see BRB. I'm getting close to the bleeder. Here's the bullet—a .30-06." It clinked as it dropped into the metal pan. "And here's the bleeder…posterior intercostal artery, ribs six and seven. Clamps, Mike."

The bleeding stopped immediately.

"Mike, wash it out, then close it up. Put in a big chest tube, all right?"

"Yes, Sir."

Mike had assisted in hundreds of surgeries, and Doctor Jacobsen had full confidence in his abilities.

"All right, Marie, let me see what you have."

The leg wound was open, and clamps were in place above and below the opening in a badly torn femoral artery.

"Good job, Nurse Nightingale," he complimented her. "Let's see if we can close this thing."

The two surgical partners opened a new surgical incision in the proximal area of the right leg and swiftly removed a ten-centimeter segment of greater saphenous vein to use as a graft.

Doctor Jacobsen laid the vein end-to-end next to the proximal open end of the artery. The size differential was considerable.

"Think it'll stay patent, Bob?" Marie asked, her face in a frown.

"It'll have to. We have to get blood flowing. There will be plenty of pressure and flow. My concern is about getting a good seal on the closure. It will be tough, and it'll be a close one."

It took them forty-five minutes to make an end-to-end anastomosis which remained dry once flow was re-established by unclamping the artery. The vein bulged and strained with the blood flow it had never before had to endure, but it held.

"Close up the two wounds, Marie, I'll check the arm. Doesn't look good."

The thoracotomy wound closure and placement of the chest tube had been done well by the chief corpsman, and he was now assisting on the several other more minor injuries in the tent.

"Good work, Mike," the doctor called over to the next table.

"Turn't nuthin,'" Mike answered and continued to put a plaster cast on a fractured tibia.

Doctor Jacobsen uncovered Cpl. Franklin's left arm. It was nearly black even though the tourniquet had been removed nearly two hours ago.

"Ruined," the doctor said. "It'll be gangrenous before morning. It has to go."

Since the limb was almost completely devoid of blood flow, the above-the-elbow amputation went quickly—twelve minutes.

"Not a record, but pretty quick," Marie said sadly.

Bob nodded. It was always a defeat to have to amputate. There was no time to waste on angst. The doctor had more wounded who needed care, and he went immediately to them.

Graves registration assignees put toe tags on the feet, and ID tags around the necks of their brothers-in-arms and bagged the dead marines for future transshipment home. They dragged the corpses of the Colombian soldiers to a shallow pit they had prepared beforehand. They threw the enemy soldiers into the hole without ceremony, poured liberal amounts of gasoline on them, and lit the funeral pyre. It was 1600 hours when they finished.

General Lewis surveyed the scene which had finally become orderly.

"On the train everyone except the wranglers and the stock. Let's take Cólon!"

CHAPTER FIVE

"Here's the way to destroy your life in sixty seconds or less;
convince yourself that something is 'right' simply because
you want it to be, and then go act on it."

–Craig D. Lounsbrough

"Cold, still and merciless
Death comes visiting
With absolute finality"
–Neena Verma, *A Mother's Cry…*
A Mother's Celebration, 2016

Cólon, Panama, late evening, August 15, 1903

The train began to move briskly ahead in the direction of the Caribbean terminus of railroad. A new Yankee engineer, the fireman, and the support crewman, were in control of the behemoth. The marine officers and senior non-coms bent over topographical maps of Panama and City of Cólon to plan the surprise attack on the unsuspecting citizens and garrison of the key city.

"How many in the garrison, Sergeant Sanchez?" Col. Breckinridge asked.

The lead sergeant of the scouting unit answered, "Somewhere in the neighborhood of a hundred, Sir, give or take."

"Give me your idea of their mettle, will you, Sanchez?""

"Metal, Sir?"

"The word is 'mettle'; it means character or determination."

"Maybe like 'backbone, Sir?"

"Yeah. What do they seem like as men? Are they any match for us?"

"They're not. Most of them are young. Not long ago they were farmer boys, dirt-poor share-croppers at best. They were dragooned by the Colombian military and stuck out here in the sticks, paid a near-starvation wage, and treated like coolies. I think they would respond to talk, to a parlay that gave them a chance to work for a decent government and to have some pride. Think how we are in the marines. It's the place for a man."

"If we talk to them, we let the cat out of the bag, don't you think?"

"Maybe, but it could also end in a very quick and bloodless surrender; and we could be on our way to Panama City with a victory under our belts and no more dead marines."

"I don't know. Maybe it could work, but I can't afford a catastrophe; none of us can."

Gen. Lewis was listening intently.

"Let's give it a try," he said. "We can have our spies keep watch, and if things go into the tank, we can start our attack before they have a chance to turn on us."

Col. Breckinridge had a decidedly dubious expression on his face, but he gave in to his superior officer and nodded his head.

The plan became an arrangement of marines to surround the garrison building at midnight and for Sgt. Sanchez and two of his fellow scouts to make the offer to the executive officer of the garrison force.

Sanchez made the arrangements. The entire garrison was asleep except for executive officer and his bodyguard.

"*Capitaine*, we have very little time," Sanchez said, coming directly to the point. "My friends and I are with the United States Marine Corps. Our mission is to take over the garrison, the ports, the railroad, and the canal, for a new, independent Panama. We know it would be much better for you and your men. We hope you see that. We promise you full protection."

Capitaine Guillermo Rodriguez looked at Sgt. Sanchez as if he had just spoken in Chinese or pig latin or anything other than Spanish. The shock that registered on his face was so deep and indelible, that he could not fathom any other course of action than what he did. He pulled out his .38 Cal pistol and pumped three shells into Sanchez's chest, then shot and killed both of the other scouts, who had not had a chance even to think about defending themselves.

Before the *capitaine* could make another move, the ring of marines closed in and began an attempted slaughter of the sleeping men in the garrison, beginning with Rodriguez. The Colombians were not as passive and meek as the attacking marines had presumed they would be. A battle raged in the close quarters of the barracks until sunup resulting in thirty-two Colombians dead, and three marines joining them in the long sleep. Sixty-nine defeated—many wounded—green uniformed men surrendered.

Gen. Lewis and Col. Breckinridge were infuriated. They had presumed—inaccurately, as it turned out—that the meeting would be viewed as having been conducted under a flag of truce. The marine officers were unshaken in their conviction that the Colombians had murdered those particular marines who occupied an important place in the men's hearts–in cold blood–an unforgivable betrayal of universal military code. They had the terrified citizens and defeated soldiers rounded up and placed in the center of the city's humble plaza. The citizens of Cólon stood shivering in the furnace heat of the morning sun, certain that they were about to die for no reason they could understand.

Gen. Lewis ground his teeth, thinking. All eyes turned towards him.

Dr. Jacobsen was a medical doctor and knew his place. In his twenty years in the corps, he had never spoken up on a matter of military logistics. This time he did.

"General Lewis, Colonel Breckinridge, I was a witness to the conversations that our scouts had with the garrison officers. I know–and you know–that there was no flag of truce and no communication that our marines were here for anything but to force a surrender by threat. These men surrendered; killing them would be to commit the unthinkable. What we have done through the night is barely pardonable. However, to massacre these defenseless citizens would be mass murder of innocents and a violation of the spirit and the letter of international law. It would be a huge black mark on the honor of the United States Marine Corps that we could never live down.

"I here to inform you that—should you commit this crime—I will report all that happened here to a board of inquiry conducted by the chief of naval operations. The only way to stop me is to murder me here and now. Add that to the charges you will eventually face."

Doctor Jacobsen was very popular among the officers and the rank-and-file. He had helped a good many of them and their buddies when they were in extremis. Now, he stood stolidly facing them, stiff and erect. He kept his hands at his sides to demonstrate that he posed no threat and that he would make no effort of any kind to protect himself.

A large portion of the marine contingent stood as silently as the Easter Island statues glowering as they observed the proceedings. They were witnesses; and every man drilled the officers with hard, unyielding gazes. The United States Marine Corps has served in nearly every conflict in United States history. Gen. Lewis feared that he was no more than a few seconds away from a mutiny, the first in marine corps history. The longer the impasse lasted, the more brittle the gap was between officers and men. The men struggled with their commitment to the concept of *semper fidelis* versus what decent men knew was right. It came down to a lethal question of who was going to blink first

General Lewis blinked.

"Sergeant-major, select a force of ten good men and establish a detention center in the St. Mary and St. Joseph Church. Keep them safe and comfortable until the rest of us establish a Yankee Strip along the railroad and canal zone.

"All officers and non-coms line up with your men and board the train to Chagres River Bridge. We will begin our march to Panama City from there and will accomplish that march in no more than thirty-six hours.

"Wranglers, round up all your animals and begin herding them to Panama City. Do so with dispatch. That is all."

The general then turned his back on the marines facing him and—with the rest of his officers—marched into Cólon City.

The city and its surroundings were not quite so easily pacified as the interchange among the marines would suggest. No sooner had they begun to disperse, than a sniper fired three rounds in the direction of the marine force.

The marines dived for cover. Apparently, the sniper was a poor shot; or he was firing from a difficult location, because no one was hit.

Bully yelled, "Find that sniper and any other positions of resistance. Look lively now!"

Squads began zig-zagging and dodging their way into the city, bayonetted rifles at the ready. Bully Breckinridge selected the sergeant-major and two marine privates at random and conducted his own search and destroy mission.

Cólon–the "town on Manzanillo Island"—was called by the haughty residents of Panama City "*El Otro Lado*" or now more often by locals and newcomers "Aspinwall" in honor of the founder of the Panama Railroad Company. Even for the tropics and the rest of Central America, it was most accurately referred to as "a pest hole." There was no fresh water, sewage disposal system, or means of drainage; garbage and refuse were dumped into the unpaved streets; that and animal and human feces made passage through the town tricky. Citizens covered their faces with perfumed handkerchiefs or held their breath as long as they could.

Carrion birds—oblivious to humans—gathered in flocks to tear at cadavers both animal and human. The birds were large, emitted a ghastly odor, and frightened any but the most hardened denizens of the city.

"These must be some of the finest vultures on the planet," Bully observed as he ran from one point of self-protection to another.

"Nice town," said SGM Rider.

"Gives us another delightful day in tropical paradise," griped Staff-sergeant Kendall T. Moss from Utah.

"Until just a little while ago, Cólon was little more than land built up around a swamp—Manzanillo Island. Look over there; most of the foundations of the buildings are under water—the whole town is below sea level. The place hasn't got a chance of survival. Lots of the buildings are plain rotten."

What dry land existed in the city was brought there and dumped as fill and was never compacted or secured. Wet vegetable garbage and sewage were a majority part of what passed for soil. It rained almost every day which kept the putrefaction active and fast. Open-topped wooden tanks–catch basins—were set on the roofs of some buildings. They were the sole source of water, what the citizens hoped was clean water. The tanks had to catch enough water during the rainy season to tide the town over the four-month dry period. Many building owners kept live fish in the tanks as an easily accessible food supply. Some tried to keep the water clean, but most allowed the catch basins to become murky aquariums full of tadpoles, frogs and serpentine water plants. This water was peddled as "pure, clean water for drinking and washing" in the street from moldy carts, or large cloudy glass jars by water carriers to make a living.

There was not a paved street in all Cólon, the men stepped carefully over decrepit old furniture, leather molds, and rusty iron frames. The putrid soil emitted putrid gases. Every marine could see himself falling victim to the pollution and foul air.

Another shot was fired at Bully, Rider, and Moss. They took cover behind some shipping crates.

Moss pointed to a discarded boiler tank half a block away, "There's a rifle barrel poking out of the boiler's metal wall."

"Moss, go around the block and get behind the tank. Drop a grenade in some opening. The shooter had to have gotten in somehow."

The tank exploded as hoped, and fragmented body parts of two men scattered throughout most of the block. Instead of stopping the shooting, the explosion seemed to have awakened the hidden Colombian soldiers and their town supporters to action. Shots began to ring out from everywhere in front of them.

Bully ordered Rider, "Sergeant-major, go back and bring the troops. We've got ourselves a real battle here."

Gen. Lewis headed up the scores of marines who came to the defense of his three men. He was anxious–overanxious–to get revenge on the town in a fight that would not bring criticism down on him and his gyrenes.

Bully and Gen. Lewis conferred for a few minutes then separated and gave their men a series of quick orders. In a few minutes, U.S. marines surrounded the three-block area in front of Bully and Gen. Lewis. They cautiously began to close in the perimeters in ten-foot increments, then yard-by-yard as the resistance intensified. The poorly trained Colombian soldiers and untrained civilians were no match for the machine line precision of the advancing gyrenes. They were passing through a bordello section of the polluted city. Most of the prostitutes—women from all over the world—worked inside filthy stalls along a particularly muddy street called Bottle Alley.

Ordinarily, pimps stood outside in almost ankle-deep mud soiling their colorful boots to hawk the claims of their "lovely, clean, young," girls and to herd incautious drunks bodily through the swinging doors of the stalls. They made an exception on this day because of the terrifying racket of gunfire. As the marines drew closer to Bottle Alley, men in green uniforms began to panic and to dash out of the stalls. They paid no attention to the marines' orders to halt, fired off a few desultory rounds, and found themselves receiving crossfire from three sides. They fell stacked up in the mud of the putrid street, including blood to create an abattoir quality to the already loathsome scene.

The remaining Colombian fighters dwindled down to a handful, and they wisely fashioned white flags from their underwear and attached the flags to sticks.

"Drop the sticks," ordered the first two marines they encountered.

The enemy soldiers complied with remarkable alacrity.

Cpl. Dominguez arrived to translate.

"Hands behind your heads. Interlock fingers. Kneel down. Lie on your bellies."

That took two minutes.

"Now, put right hands behind your backs."

The marine privates clamped hand cuffs on the men's right wrists.

"Now, put left hands behind your backs close to right hands."

The marines finished clamping the handcuffs. That was good because they only had enough for this group.

The perimeter of intent marines closed down to less than ten feet and only drove three more POWs into the center. An experienced sergeant ordered the enemies to remove their shoes and socks. He removed the shoelaces and tied their thumbs and great toes together. All the soldiers—who were now POWs—were herded into the same circle.

SGM Rider and three of the enlisted men from Thistle Crossing, Utah arrived to move the POWs back into the main plaza of the town to incarcerate them in the church with the previous internees.

Rider sought out the mayor of Cólon from among the frightened town's people.

"Are you the mayor?" he asked.

"Si, Señor. I yam him."

"I am Sergeant-Major Jethro Amos Rider, United States Marine Corps, Sir. What is your name, *Señor?*

"I yam Don Adolpho Miguel Rodrigo-Pomposo, *Señor*, and *el alcalde de la ciudad*, at your service."

A priest stepped up beside the city's mayor and introduced himself, "*Señor Jefe,* I am the bishop of Cólon. I would like to be of assistance as well if there is anything I can contribute to stop further bloodshed. My *nombre* is Padre Juan Pablo Martinez."

His English was better than the mayor's but both did better than Rider did with his Spanish. He made no further attempt to use Spanish.

He explained what was expected of them and of the townspeople and the POWs.

With regards the POWs, Rider said, "A squad of well-armed and well-trained marines will remain here when the rest of us leave. I will make it simple. If any of them is hurt or killed, I will return and kill all of you. If they report to me that you were disobedient and uncooperative, I will take you to the prison in Panama City and lock you up for all your lives. If anyone attempts to communicate with the garrison in Panama City in any way, I will bring my marines back to Cólon and put all of you in front of a firing squad. If you do not bring trouble, you will be well treated and released after we have accomplished our mission. I am a man of my word, Amigos. Both for punishment and for reward."

The men—including the POWs—abjectly bowed and scraped crying out their willingness to comply to the smallest detail.

Rider reported to Gen. Lewis, "Sir, the townspeople have been placed under house arrest; and the mayor and the priest have sworn to be responsible for our POWs. I think they are thoroughly cowed and won't be a problem."

"I hope not for your sake, Rider. Now, let's take advantage of the growing darkness and get the men and gear onto the train. We have urgent business sixteen-and-a-half leagues from here. Move out." [A league is a unit of length, three miles. It was common in Europe and Latin America at one time, but in older marine parlance it was sometimes used to describe the distance a man could walk in an hour.]

During the battle for the inner city of Cólon, the cookies and wranglers had impressed a number of young citizens to assist in the loading of the train and of several mule carts to get the regiment on its way without further delay.

Gen. Lewis gave a final set of orders to the men of the occupying force, "This place is the devil's playground. Remember, the devil does not have your best welfare in mind. The fallen doves here all—and I mean all–have the clap or a case of the bad blood. Bottle Street is off limits. The MPs will patrol regularly. Get arrested on that pestilential street, and you come up on charges. Get the clap or any of those Mexican or French diseases, and you will be cashiered out of the marines. It cost too much to train and outfit you to have you throw yourself away because of an incurable disease. You'll be court-martialed, and you will be kicked out for "conduct unbecoming.""

The consumption of alcohol along Bottle Street was considered horrendously large even for the infamous Yankee Strip. Over the years of construction, so many empty liquor bottles were tossed into the street that they created a solid layer of compacted glass beneath the mud. Future pavement contractors found it unnecessary to put down a gravel foundation because the thousands of bottles buried there served the purpose of a solid foundation. And the general was right about the incidence of sexually transmitted diseases. There was no useful treatment for syphilis; and the strain of gonorrhea that developed there, was immune to all known treatments.

General Lewis and SGM Rider were glad to be on their way to a good clean fight.

It was certainly no picnic being left behind to man a garrison and to keep the peace for the United States' in the Panama intervention. The new residents—the marines—soon shared with the long-time citizens the sight of death daily and inevitably grew calloused to it. Death most often came from violence. The corpses of murdered men and prostitutes were found almost every morning lying face down in the bay or in the mud of some obscure alley.

The railroad owned the bodies like they did everything else in the Zone; so, most of them were stripped of all clothing and jewelry and delivered to the several Cólon morgues. Ever attuned to the opportunity to make money, the railroad executives had the living workers and slaves collect the corpses—most of whom were unidentifiable—and to put them into barrels full of alcohol and pickling spices. They then entered into a profitable–but seldom admitted–trade in cadavers for medical schools up and down North and South America.

The several local barbers were an industrious and business-savvy bunch. They set up shops right in front of the prostitutes' stalls on Bottle Street. There they cut hair, took over the body pickling business, built coffins and barrels, and made all arrangements with the medical schools. A few people died of natural causes, were identifiable, had money, and therefore were eligible for embalming and a decent Christian burial. The barber/undertakers took good care of those bodies and of their families, should they be available. Given their capacity to see profit, they also treated the clap for a sizable fee.

It came as no particular surprise to anyone–marines included–that cholera visited Cólon once a year, sometimes more often. Nor were the medics surprised when the marines came to them complaining of an assortment of abdominal maladies. It was a pleasant surprise for the medics and the MPs that the marines learned by observation that the professional girls were not a good idea for them to frequent, and not a single marine came down with a drip or a frank case of the clap.

When the couriers returned from Panama City with a set of orders to leave the country forthwith, they marched out of Cólon with zest and boarded the *Kearsarge II* with alacrity.

CHAPTER SIX

"The number of revolutions, rebellions, insurrections, riots, and other outbreaks in Panama was 53, within the space of 57 years."

–President Theodore Roosevelt, *Third State of the Union Message*, December, 1903

Panama City, Panama, late evening, August 17, 1903

For all the effort of suffering through a long hot march and a battle carried out in a pestilential town in the tropics, the train ride to the stepping off point for the major battle ordered by President Roosevelt and the marine brass was quick and uneventful. The expeditionary force disembarked on west side of the Chagres River at Barbacoas, and the noncoms herded the well-rested marines off the train and onto the rudimentary road to Panama City and into a more or less orderly marching formation.

Gen. Lewis, Col. Breckinridge, Lt. Hiram Smith, Sergeant-major Rider, and Master Gunnery Sergeant Cramer, were in the first rank followed by the non-coms and their marines lined by squads. The column moved out at a brisk walk towards their goal, Panama City. Seven miles away from Barbacoas, they encountered a grizzled man in a worn and patched set of railroad coveralls walking determinedly in their direction.

Gen, Lewis held his hand up to let the column rest and spoke to the man who was viewing the marine force with obvious curiosity.

"Sir," Gen. Lewis asked from his horse, "*Hablas Inglés, Señor?*

"*Si, General,* but Ah speak American a good deal better, if ya'll don' mand."

The general laughed and got down from his horse.

"Good to have a chance to palaver with a guy from home. Let me guess. Georgia or West Virginia, am I right?"

"Close enough, Sir, Ah'm a free West Virgin-i-a eer."

"What's a mountaineer doing way down here in Panama, if you don't mind me asking?"

"Buildin' the railroad 'til we all got laid off fer a tam."

"I think our presence will hasten the day for you to return to work."

"And, if ya'll don't min' me askin,' what ah all a ya'll doin' in this green hell that ain't fit fer man nor beast ta live in.?"

"You a tried and true flag waving American patriot, Mr…?"

"Alby Prentiss, and Ah certainly am. Whatever y'all ah doin' hyah, God be praised."

"Well, Alby, I'm Major-General Bullard Henry Lewis, USMC. Pleased to meet you. Alby. "I've never been to West Virginia, what's good about your state?"

"We have a sayin' in West Virgini': One Big Happy Family, Really!"

It took Gen. Lewis a couple of minutes, and then he began to laugh so hard he almost fell off onto his knees under his horse's belly. When he got back his control, he asked the West Virginian with the dry wit,

"I have a question for you as a man who knows these parts. How far do you reckon it is to Panama City from here?"

"Mebbe three far-sees, not even that fer. Take y'all couple hours at the worst."

Gunny Cramer–a life-long Yankee from New York—turned to the general and asked, "Could you interpret for me, General? How far's a far-see?"

Gen. Lewis laughed, "Well, it is not an exact distance like a furlong or a fathom, but it relates to that far point in the distance which is as far as you can see from your present location. Alby here says we'll go as far as we can see from here, then do that twice more. Then, we'll be there."

"And, I thought I had the English language down pat," Gunny Cramer said.

"Always something more to learn, Gunny, never forget that. And, Gunny, let's move 'em out."

As they passed by him Alby Prentiss gave a small but courteous salute and received a reciprocal nod in return.

The marines moved as quickly as the old West Virginian had suggested. This was in part because they did not have to march through mountains as they had when they first entered the country at Point Mala. Low mountains run through most of the country, leaving a gap in the center– the region of the isthmus, the future "path between the seas"–that is nearly at sea level. It is relatively flat which facilitated movement of the large contingent.

They approached the outskirts of Panama City as the sun was just beginning to set. Gen. Lewis decided that the marines could not risk showing themselves before they were entirely ready and had a careful battle plan. They moved to the left into a narrow copse of guaiacum trees on the banks of the Chepo River and made a temporary, cold camp—no fires, no lights, no noise. Sentries made sure that no one came in or went out of the camp. Scouts wandered around in the outskirts of the city to ascertain if the populace was aware of their presence.

A pair of Pfc signal men was sent to the beach to alert the *Kearsarge* that the expeditionary force was in place and ready for an attack by land in the very early hours of the coming day. They were able to establish a clear radio frequency signal which they would use to coordinate the land and sea attacks. Captain Hemphil gave a short message and set of orders in Morse code from him to the marines: "we came here not just to win, but to make Panama a de facto dependent state on the U.S., not an enemy to be pounded into oblivion. Tread lightly."

The attack began at 0430 with a landward bombardment from the *USS Kearsarge*. The shelling purposely fell on the beach away from buildings which had the desired effect of terrorizing the citizens and government officials living along the coastline. The marines raced through the dirt streets towards the power center of the city. They bypassed the cattle ranches and farms of the elite, and their cowering slaves. Outside the city walls, they ran double-time through a neighborhood of free blacks living in thatched huts. The negroes looked on in bemusement and curiosity but did nothing to draw attention to themselves. The first challenges to the oncoming marines came from the city guard who acted as sentries around the base of the walls. One sentry was bayoneted, and the rest threw down their arms, recognizing futility when they saw it.

Citizens—awakened by the naval bombardment—stood on the rampart walls staring at the beach. They scarcely realized that their real danger was the enemy at their gates. A walled bastion on a rocky promontory to the west surrounded the handsome stone and decorative stucco buildings of the Spanish colonial administration and the elegant two-story mansions–the *Casco Viejo.* The men of the mansions—owners and servants—poured out into the bricked streets wielding swords, machetes, and an assortment of long-ago useless firearms. A portly, mustachioed, self-important, Colombian grandee fired a rifle bullet somewhere in the direction of Gen. Lewis.

The general spurred his horse and galloped directly at the grandee, who dropped his rifle, turned, and began to run. Gen. Lewis pulled his English bulldog revolver from his belt, fired a single round from his handgun and dropped the erstwhile leader in his tracks. A few skirmishes engaged the overwhelming force of marines with brave but foolish challengers, and another four fatalities brought the homeowners to heel. The government of Panama City, and the colonial Colombian administration surrendered without further bloodshed.

"I am Don Hipolito Antonio Ricardo Guitáin-Doloraso, at your service," a voice called out from the crowd in educated accented English.

"Come forward," Gen. Lewis ordered from his warhorse, Devil's Mount.

A tall, dignified, white-haired, man stepped forward from the onlookers and saluted the marine general. His face was lean and his look serious. He had a perfectly and freshly trimmed white Van Dyke mustache and beard. There was a short, thin dueling scar on his left cheek. Don Guitáin-Doloraso wore a starched and pressed white shirt with pearl buttons, separate collar and cuffs, matching vest with a large pocket watch on a gold chain, a heavy gold Roman Catholic cross, a long, thin, scarlet tie, a four-button double-breasted suit coat and trousers, beige-colored braces with gold stripes running down both edges of the suspender straps, and pristine white gloves. Because shoes and boots were regularly machine made–even in the tropics–he wore fitted white lace-up shoes.

"I am Major-general Bullard Henry Lewis, USMC, Señor Guitáin-Doloraso, are you a man of authority here?"

56

"General, I am the Governor of Panama for the Nation of Colombia. Until this moment, I was the most senior administrator of Panama. I hasten to tell you that I am a member of the separatist movement. If you have come to the Isthmus to assist us in the separation, I am your man, Sir."

Historical records indicate that the period leading up to the American marines entering Panama to ensure separation from greater Colombia, there were forty administrations of the Panamanian department of Colombia's Panama, fifty riots and assorted rebellions, five attempted and failed secessions, and thirteen interventions by the United States, acting under the provisions of what was known as the Bidlack-Mallarino Treaty. Partisan clashes and foreign intervention exacerbated racial antagonisms and economic problems and intensified grievances against the central government of Colombia. There was a large and growing percentage of separatists in the Panama Zone by 1903, including leaders like Colombia's governor of the Panama section, Governor Guitáin-Doloraso.

"Governor, we believe that all of our best interests are served by having a peaceful settlement of this matter. You can be of material assistance, if you are genuine in your support of the separation."

"I am at your service; what can I do to save my fellow Panamanians?"

"Consider this plan. Use your loud-speaker system, Governor, and start with the national anthem. When that is finished, make an announcement that we have a *fete a compli* here. The garrisons of Panama City and Cólon have come over to the Panama side and support separation from Colombia. They will fight on the side of the United States Marines sent by President Roosevelt to help the Panamanians to achieve their freedom. All citizens lay down your arms. Law and order will be supervised by the marines and naval services in conjunction with the police forces of the capital city."

In case the governor failed to memorize the entirety of Gen. Lewis's statement to his citizens, the general's secretary had had the foresight to draft a large-print version in both English and formal Spanish.

In short order, the *Hymn of the Isthmus* blared out over the loudspeakers located around the city—three times in succession. The governor's voice was scratchy since the equipment was not the latest available in the States; but with several repetitions in both English and Spanish, most of the population was aware of the sudden and crucial changes that had occurred that day in their city and newly created country.

Sgt. Snyder, LCpl. Muhlstein, Pfc. Carter, and Pvt. Gabler, were among the marines gathered in the *Casco Viejo* to hear the message that they had just won a war without a shot being fired by the 6th rifle squad of the 3rd platoon.

"I suppose it'll be tough going around the town to sample all the wares," LCpl. Muhlestein said and flashed a wry grin.

"Tough work, but somebody has to be the occupying force," Pfc. Carter agreed.

The meager amount of dust settled; and Gen. Lewis divided forces up to keep the peace in aristocratic Bella Vista, in the densely populated perimeters of the city, in the farther inland working-class tenements, and outside the city proper in the rural farm and rancho areas.

The 6th rifle squad of the 3rd platoon was sent to the area of the city just east of the beach and wharf areas which were to be supervised by navy personnel. Throughout the city, acceptance was at first grudging on the part of some Panamanians, but most were closet separatists at heart waiting to be able to celebrate their freedom. Panamanians were the most diverse of any people the marines had ever seen, even in the Philippines.

During the five months the marines policed Panama City, they dealt with Spanish *Panameños,* the mixed population of Creoles, mestizos, European immigrants, Africans, indigenous Indians; *interioranos* [interior people—the Hispano-Indians]. The mestizos—mixed European and native Americans–considered themselves the real Panamanians, unlike the *cholos* [a pejorative term for the lately acculturated native-Panamanian-Americans]. The *cholos* were rather haughty and referred to themselves with pride as *naturales.* By the time the marines boarded the *Kearsarge II* for the homeward voyage, almost no Panamanians considered themselves to be "former Colombians."

The date for formalization of the separation was set for November. To convince the government and other citizens of Colombia, Gen. Lewis sent an article announcing the separation as an agreed upon *fait accompli* to the major Colombian newspaper, *El Tiempo.* The White House sent a telegram to the president of Colombia:

> "Be informed, as of this date, the United States Government
> has recognized the de facto Government of Panama. Stop.
> The Department of State has instructed Mr. Beaupre, the
> United States Minister at Bogota, to inform the Colombian

Government, and Mr. Ehrwen, the Consul at Panama, to notify the new Panama Government of the fact. Stop."

Colombia reacted violently. The military intervention by the U.S. marines in Colombia's affairs was the last straw. President José Manuel Marroquín dispatched an army from the region of northern Panama known as the Calovébora. The government deployed troops from the Tiradores Battalion from Barranquilla under Generals Juan Tovar and Ramón Amaya, and instructed the commanders to take over the functions of the Governor of Panama.

The United States learned of Marroquín's orders and communicated with him that the U.S. Navy would descend in force on Barranquilla if the Colombian battalion did not return to its base. Marroquín knew that he and his military forces were no match, and he backed down. The Colombian force on its way from Barranquilla and–in addition–the forces already stationed in Panama and Cólon—a total of 460 men–left the Isthmus zone in the mail steamer *Orinoco* without a shot being fired. That left the former Department of Panama completely in the hands of the hated revolutionary traitors.

Panama declared its independence from Colombia on November 3, 1903 in the *Parque de la Independencia* in Panama City, and the *de jure* recognition came on November 13 giving the United States everything it asked for in the establishment of the independence. Construction began on the U.S. Panama Canal project in 1904. Colombia did not recognize Panama as a legitimately separate nation until 1921, when the U.S. paid Colombia USD $25 million in what was called "compensation." Provisions of the Canal Treaty–Hay-Bunau-Varilla-Treaty of 1903–were repeatedly misused as a pretext for armed intervention by the United States. In addition–in many cases–the U.S. Marines were actually requested to provide protection and enforcement by the Panamanian elites themselves, in order to get rid of political opponents.

BANANA WARS 2

"In Hispaniola, bluejackets and marines took on the task of civilizing the tropics. In the late 1920s, with an imperial force largely of marines, the American military waged its last banana war in Nicaragua against a guerrilla leader named Augusto C. Sandino."

–Lester D. Langley: *The Banana Wars: United States Intervention in the Caribbean, 1898-1934* Rowman and Littlefield Publishers, January 28, 2002

CHAPTER SEVEN

Headquarters, Third Battalion, Third Regiment Marines, Camp Lejeune, North Carolina, December 12, 1915

The call to HQ Third Regiment came to Sgt. Harry Chandler, who knew everyone and everything worth knowing about the Marine Corps. He was a forty-five-year lifer and would like to remain on duty until he died of natural causes. His present MOS was aide de camp to Brigadier General Stephen Morgan Price, the commanding officer of the third of the third. Price and all his officers and gyrenes were bored with camp duty and drills at Camp Lejeune. Price was becoming concerned about reports coming in to HQ from the MPs regarding a rising incidence of alcoholism, arrests of his jarheads for bar fights, drunk-and-disorderly trips to the brig, and incidents of domestic violence—all clear indicators that his warriors needed to get back to what they did best, killing people for the U.S. of A.

"HQ Company, third marines," Sgt. Chandler answered the ring telephone crisply. "I am instructed to inform the caller that this is not a secure line."

"Sergeant, get General Price on a secure line with me PDQ."

"Sir, may I ask who is calling?"

"No."

There was such a definitive tone of unquestioned authority in the caller's voice, that Sgt. Chandler answered, "Aye, aye, Sir."

He marched into Price's office without knocking. The general was playing solitaire and listening to a gramophone record of *It's a long, long way to Tipperary* by John McCormack, a rising star on the stateside popular music scene.

Price liked it because it hinted at the days the Corps had spent in London. It was one of those catchy, hum-along kind of songs.

"Sir…"

Gen. Price held up his hand for silence; and no one, but no one ever interrupted when he did.

Price turned up the volume for the last verse:

That's the wrong way to tickle Mary,
That's the wrong way to kiss!
Don't you know that over here, lad,
They like it best like this!
Hooray *pour le Francais*!
Farewell, Angleterre!
We didn't know the way to tickle Mary,
But we learned how, over there!

"Sir, I hate to intrude…"

That hand sign again.

"The president's man, Colonel House, is on the line. Seems urgent."

"Who'd you say, Sergeant?"

"Edward M. House, Sir. The man himself."

"Why dint' you say so to begin with, Chandler? One more screw-up like this and you'll be working in the laundry.

Sgt. Chandler remained standing.

"What, now?"

The man wants to talk on a secure line, Sir."

"Oh, fer cryin' out loud, Sergeant, make it happen."

Five minutes later, Gen. Price said, "Hello, Col. House. Hope you didn't have to wait too long. It took a bit to be sure that we had an altogether safe line. Now, what can we do for you and the president?"

"General, much as I enjoy chatting with you, I have a very precise message that I will read to you, then it will be delivered by courier."

House began to read the short message:

To: Brigadier General Stephen Morgan Price and the Third Battalion, Third Regiment USMC
From: Woodrow Wilson, President
Subject: Orders for deployment

Internal disorder and revolution in the Republic of Haiti has become critical, jeopardizing American lives and property, and creating a disruption to commerce and good order in the Americas. The third of the third marines will deploy to Cap-Haïten to become part of the now forming Advance Base Brigade with the 1st Regiment to bring order to Haiti. The 1st Regiment, the fixed defense regiment, is currently in place.

You will protect and deliver a shipload of heavy motorized equipment, tanks, and artillery, to supplement the men and materiel already in country: eight additional companies, including four 5-inch gun companies, a searchlight company, a mine company, an engineer company, a fire control unit, and an antiaircraft company.
Depart first light, 4 January, 1916

Signed:

Woodrow Wilson

Thomas Woodrow Wilson, POTUS, on this, the 12th day of December, 1916

"Colonel House, please convey my answer to President Wilson. The third of the third is honored and prepared to serve him and the people of the United States by complying with this set of orders."

It seemed like a decade of planning and drilling was going into the marine contingent's state of readiness. By the required date of departure—4 January, 1916—every detail had been hammered out to a practical state of over readiness. The six-thousand strong third brigade boarded the *USS Montana* in Miami, Florida headed for Cap-Haïten, Haiti full of "wim, wigor, and witality" as its field commander, Col. Oscar Wallace Peterson, put it, and ready to live up to its motto, *Fortuna Fortes Juvat* [Fortune Favors the Bold].

The island of Hispaniola is located 675 miles from Miami. It is the part of the Greater Antilles Caribbean island group and is the second largest island in the Caribbean. The marines arriving in 1915 were not the first, nor would they be the last. On December 3, 1914, the Advance Base Brigade was reorganized with the 1st Regiment–the fixed defense regiment—deployed and transported to Haiti on the USS *Montana* on January 27, 1914. In December, urged on by the National City Bank in the U.S. and at the explicit request of the National Bank of Haiti–already under foreign direction–the U.S. military seized the Haitian government's gold reserve. The navy took the gold to the National City Bank's New York City vaults "for safe-keeping."

In February, 1915, Jean Vilbrun Guillaume Sam–son of a previous president of Haiti–established a dictatorship with the approval and assistance of the United States because American business interests were fostered by the dictator and his regime. Five months after he was "elected" to be president for life, President Sam faced a serious resurgence of the simmering anti-American revolt. His response was to order the massacre of one-hundred-sixty-seven political prisoners who had opposed his promotion to the leadership of the island country. All the defenseless victims were from prominent Haitian families–mostly members of the better educated and wealthier mixed-race population with German connections. In response, President Sam was detained and later lynched by an enraged mob in the capital, Port-au-Prince, when they learned of the wholesale massacre.

President Wilson and his cabinet publicly stated that the revolt against President Sam was an "intolerable anti-American revolt" and as such, was a threat to American business, to the Monroe Doctrine, and less publicly considered the revolt to be a specific threat to the U.S. owned HASCO [Haitian American Sugar Company]. On July 28, 1915, President Wilson ordered 330 U.S. Marines to occupy Port-au-Prince, still a fairly measured response given the affront Haiti had caused America, Wilson thought.

The final straw for President Wilson came shortly after the assassination when the *caco*-supported anti-American Rosalvo Bobo was named the next president of Haiti. The *cacos* were peasant guerrillas from the north who resisted forced labor and the theft of their lands by greed-driven overlords, the corrupt Haitian government, and the powerful Americans. President Wilson and his government determined that American economic dominance was under imminent threat, and he acted decisively to regain control by adding an additional contingent of six hundred marines. The president acted robustly by dispatching a new contingent of marines—the third of the third—to the troubled island nation to quell the disturbances once and for all.

The battleship, *USS Montana* [BB-67]–slower but larger, better armored, and with superior firepower, than the predecessor Iowa ships—arrived in the small port of Gonaïves on the northeastern shore of the Gulf of La Gonâve of western Haiti and disgorged the thousands of marines, their support squads, and enough military equipment to carry on a major war for more than a decade.

With only enough time to have breakfast, the marines formed up in four columns and marched across the fertile Artibonite Plain northeast towards Cap-Haïten 100 km away. It was sweaty work, but the men and their animals were in good condition. The march took five days, although it should have taken only three.

The delay resulted from time expended to repel Haitian attackers. The attacking rebels—local militia men–pejoratively called "*cacos*" by the U.S. Marines–strongly resisted American control of Haiti. During the first period of the occupation, they received considerable support from the German government and the entrenched German-Haitian elite. They were well armed, well uniformed, well-fed, and fought with the deeply entrenched ideological conviction that they were the saviors of Haiti from its northern invaders.

The 3rd regiment of marines had explicit orders from Washington and Port-au-Prince that Haitians carrying a gun were to be shot on sight.

"Battle-positions, Jar-heads," ordered Col. Peterson. "Commence firing on my command."

The marines took defensive positions behind bushes and low inclines. Front ranks knelt on one knee, their rifles at the ready. Behind them stood riflemen and snipers in standard three-quarter frontal position, rifles all with chambered rounds. Machine gunners flanked the rifle mens' lines.

The *cacos* began running from about one hundred meters away on a downhill slope.

"Commence firing, marines. Fire at will. Halt when you hear my side-arm fire."

A deadly fusillade began with the *cacos* coming to within seventy meters. The *cacos* were brave—overly brave. They kept coming across the open grassland despite many of them falling around them. The machine-gunners held their fire to allow the bulk of the *cacos* to have a chance to surrender; but the Haitians kept coming, oblivious to the carnage among them.

Col. Peterson pointed at the flanking machine gunners who responded by opening a withering cross-fire. The *cacos* had been able to get off an occasional shot, none of which hit a marine; but now they were beginning to topple like macheted corn stalks. The rear ranks were stumbling over the haphazardly lying corpses which prevented them from being able to aim. In a few minutes, every *caco* was either dead or dying. The American marines had turned a battle into a massacre.

"Sergeant Sneldon, come forward," Col. Peterson ordered.

"Sir, yes Sir!"

"Sergeant, take your squad and Sergeant Cosgrove's and dig a pit."

"Aye, Sir."

Col. Peterson next called the sergeant of the sixth squad.

"Sergeant Zimbrowski, it's your squad's turn in the barrel. Use mules to move the enemy dead to the pit and dispose of them."

Sergeant Zimbrowski was none too eager, but he nodded his head.

The process was lengthy owing to the hard, rocky soil and the large number of corpses needing disposal. The dead men had no dog tags or other unit identifiers; so, they were pulled into the pit without being recorded. The marine chaplains were displeased, but they made no protest about the body disposals that were to take place without a Christian ceremony.

The bodies were laid out in neat serried rows and covered with a mixture of water and potassium hydroxide [lye] to create what the natives called *pozole*.

The three squads on graves' detail that morning drew lots and three men lost the draw. They were required to remain behind the main body of marching marines to allow time—about three hours—for the bodies to decompose, then they sloshed gasoline over the rows of gelatinous corpses and lit an inferno. After that, the three marines raced to catch up with the relatively slower moving body of marines.

There were two more minor skirmishes before the unit marched through the rear gates of Cap-Haïten and established their camp.

Sergeant Henryk Zimbrowski's squad was the last to arrive, and the most needy for water, food, and sleep—in that order. The sergeant was a bluff, freckled, red-head, with striking sky-blue eyes. He had the rotund shape of a heavy-weight lifter, except that his muscles were the product of hard work, both before enlisting from farm work, and after, from living up to his reputation as the strongest man in the Corps. Zimbrowsky, the Pole, was assigned three Italians from Chicago's Little Italy neighborhood on the near-west side. Cpl. Luigi Russo, Pfc. Emanuele Bianchi, and Pvt. Floriano Messina, were curly haired, olive-skinned, and slight of build. They were all handsome and knew it; so, they were a clear danger to unsuspecting maidens. They were jokers and flashed easy smiles or easy sneers depending on the situation. They were among the most popular marines in the third regiment.

Colonel Peterson was one of a long line of marines. His cousin, Glen Gabler, was a lifer who had served three missions to Central America and was a font of knowledge for his more illustrious younger cousin. The two men did not look at all alike. Peterson was very tall, very skinny; and his face was aquiline in comparison to his cousins and friends from Thistle Crossing, Utah who all appeared to have come from a cookie mold that produced shorter, tougher, lighter skinned, and coarser looking men.

All the marines in Col. Peterson's family and acquaintanceship had several things in common, and nothing much to do with their physical appearance. They were all dyed-in-the-wool, pugnacious, semper-fi, rule-obeying, lifer marines. Col. Peterson was looking forward to the first real combat in Haiti, and he was not going to have to wait long.

CHAPTER EIGHT

"Talk softly and carry a big stick...The Duties of One Citizen
to His Neighbor Not more Important, However, Than the Duties
of the United States as a Nation to Other Nations."
    —Vice-President Theodore Roosevelt, speech at the
        Minnesota State Fair on September 2, 1901,
            Minneapolis Tribune Headline

Forward Camp,

Cap-Haïten, Haiti, May 14, 1916

After only six weeks of the occupation, U.S. General and newly appointed High Commissioner, John H. Russell, Jr. seized control of Haiti's customs houses and administrative institutions, including the banks and the national treasury. Under Russell's control, forty percent of Haiti's national income was designated to repay debts to American and French banks. After that, relationships with the Haitian people deteriorated to barbaric levels.

Caco guerrilla ambushes killed marines and cooperating Haitian authorities and often mutilated the corpses. Marines and U.S. soldiers outnumbered and outgunned the *cacos* most of the time and gained significantly one-sided victories. The blood lust reached a point that machine guns were turned on crowds of unarmed natives, sometimes by mistake but sometimes not. Early in the occupation, the governance of Haiti was one of continual bush warfare.

To avoid public criticism, especially in the U.S., President Wilson frequently claimed that the occupation was a mission to "re-establish peace and order and to rewrite the Haitian constitution…" He insisted that the occupation by U.S. forces and its temporary involvement in the management of Central American countries "… has nothing to do with any diplomatic negotiations of the past or the future, or with any eye towards profit."

The third regiment spent its days patrolling well into the interior of Haiti on search and destroy missions against the *caco* bandits. Almost every other day, Peterson's marines encountered *cacos* who attacked from ambush. Sergeant Henryk Zimbrowski's squad was first up for battle duty, given that they had had to perform the odious burial duty on the way to Cap-Haïten; so, their new assignment was a reward.

One of the last holdouts was Fort Rivière. Several sorties had been sent to test the security of the perimeter, and none of them could find a substantial weak spot. Most of Haiti was pacified, but Washington was not satisfied. Col. Peterson received a terse communique from General Alexander Archer Vandegrift, Commandant of the Marine Corps:

> Message:
> From: Office of the Joint Chiefs of Staff, United States Armed Forces—Directive of the Commandant, USMC
> To: Field commander, Central American Theater, HQ Company, 3rd Marines
> Date: 18 May, 1916
>
> Subject: Hostilities against American forces emanating from enemy base at Fort Rivière, Haiti.
>
> Col. Peterson: command is dissatisfied with progress to dislodge the *caco* rebels from their stronghold in Fort Rivière, Haiti.
> Sir, you have the means and the manpower. Whether due to procrastination, sloth, or fear of a determined enemy, there

is no excuse for further failure to secure full pacification of Fort Rivière and any other remaining nests of insurgency.

You will commence an all-out attack on or before 20 May, 1916 with completion of action in no more than five full days, or a replacement will be sent from Washington to get the job done.

No reply necessary.

Gen. Alexander Archer Vanderegrift

Signed, Alexander Archer Vandegrift, General and Commandant of the United States Marine Corps, 18 May, 1916

The scolding letter from the chief of the marines galvanized Col. Peterson into action. He reminded himself of the long history of the marine corps as winners, not just occupiers. He was angry—not at his men, who he knew were doing their best—at himself for failing to live up to the credo of winning. He asked himself if he was holding something back because maybe he could not quite accept the concept that marines should fight wars to further the ends of big business in America. He came from blue-collar people for generations back—most of the men had been coal miners or share-croppers. He was the first person he knew of in his family to have finished high school, let alone to have graduated with honors from an ivy league university.

"I will get that socialist nonsense out of my head, and get the job done!" he yelled silently at himself.

He put down Gen. Vandegrift's message and shouted at his aide-de-camp, Major Richard D. Adams, "Maj. Adams, schedule a meeting of every officer and every ranking non-com in my office today at 1300 hours. Full dress uniform with medals. Inspection will be part of the meeting; so, warn them ahead of time!"

Maj, Adams knew something serious was afoot because Col. Peterson—usually "Oscar" or "OW" to him–was being unusually formal. He was never called "Major Adams" in private. This could not be good.

Maj. Adams spread the word—both with strict formality and with friend-to-friend informality—that this was important and a meeting not to be taken lightly or, heaven-forbid, skipped altogether.

That the gathering was not a social one was immediately clear to every man when it was apparent that no food or drink was to be part of the arrangement.

Chairs were set in precise rows and not around tables. Every officer and noncom—uncomfortable in the starchiness of his formal uniform in the wet inferno heat of the day—took a seat and from past experience with such meetings, sat stiffly.

SGM Thomas Cartwright III stood at full stiff attention in front of the crème de la crème of the marine corps in Haiti and barked out a command, "Attention on deck! Oscar W. Peterson, Colonel and commander is arriving on deck!"

Grim faced men sprang to attention.

Col. Peterson walked stiffly among them, commenting here and there about flaws in this officer's shoeshine or that non-com's less than precise tying of his tie knot. More than half a dozen red faces resulted, and the effect of focusing the officers' attention was gratifying to the colonel.

"At ease. Be seated, Gentlemen," the colonel ordered. "We have been in-country too long not to have achieved complete pacification of the rabble *cacos* and to have achieved a society characterized by law-and-order, respect for American values, and complete protection for the business interests of our citizens. Today is the last day that we will see in this two-bit country where such lawlessness persists.

"Maj. Adams and Sergeant-Major Cartwright have prepared a copy of your orders collectively and individually for your companies, platoons, and squads. You will memorize your orders and those that apply to the corps as a whole.

"Fort Rivière stands as an insult to you. This insult shall be erased over the next week, or I will resign my commission as a failure and give way to a better man. I am that serious about this mission. Tomorrow, the entire Haitian corps will march out of Port-au-prince and Cap-Haïten and will launch an attack on that devil's castle such that the people of Haiti will never forget.

"We march at 0600 hours. A handful will be left to mind the garrisons; but every other marine, soldier, cook, and wrangler will be there. Every mule and pack animal will carry our weapons of war, and they will be used to a merciless end. We shall be victorious. Remember the Spartan mothers who told their sons, 'Return with your shield or upon it!' That will be our motto for this mission.

"*Semper Fi!*"

"OORAH!!!" came the response from the officers and enlisted who were ready for battle as winning marines.

The marine garrison of Port-au-Prince traveled the 251 km to Cap-Haïten—also known as Le Cap and Au Cap–arriving three days later. The combined garrisons marched along the dusty streets out of Cap-Haïten making a cloud that obscured visibility of their exit. A very few citizens of either city cheered them on. Col. Peterson now commanded a field expedition of six companies—roughly 700 men. Marines and sailors on the *USS Connecticut* BB-18 stood on the deck of their ship awaiting orders to join Peterson's marines.

From Cap-Haïten, the march was only thirty-two kilometers over easy-going grassland to Fort Rivière. The vexatious last stronghold of the *cacos* was a mountain fort on the summit of Montagne Noire, on the north coast of Haiti, located just to the south of Grand Rivière du Nord. From a distance, especially with the enhanced vision of telescopes, Fort Rivière was seen as an old masonry fort built atop the relatively steep 1,680 meter high, Montagne Noire.

The fort itself did not appear to be a particularly difficult target, and Col. Peterson and his marines and LCdr Emil Buracz–who had come ashore from the battleship *USS Connecticut* with his seamen and marines to participate in what everyone was coming to realize was going to be a very important battle in the War with Haiti—were in agreement that Montagne Noire was going to be more of a problem than the fort itself. Fort Rivière's front was reachable only by a steep slope with uneven loose rocks underfoot; the other three sides fell away at such an acute angle that an approach from those directions was considered to be impossible even for trained mountaineers. There was no artillery in or around the fort, and spies had informed the Americans that they would only encounter about 300 *cacos* in the fort.

The marines and sailors had moved stealthily through the undergrowth and along the course of the river until they fanned out around the base of the frontal slope of the aptly named "Black Mountain" [*Montagne Noire*].

Owing to the small garrison force in the fort, the *cacos* were unable to send out scouts or spies; and, consequently, they were unaware of the relatively large force of marines and navy men who were surrounding them, for all intents and purposes.

Col. Peterson assessed the condition of the fort itself, "The place was built in the eighteenth century by the French. It has long since fallen into disrepair with its masonry walls beginning literally to fall down. The parapets are overgrown with trees and brush to the extent that sentries would not even be able to walk around them to see us coming. They are totally unusable as defensive positions during a fight, all of which is to our distinct advantage. Our scouts checked out the northern face of the fort which used to have a usable and defensible entryway, but that has fallen in so much that the entrance is clogged with dirt, building stones, and rubble. It is not passable.

"That leaves us and the *cacos* only one entry way into the fort. Short of outwaiting them and starving them out, our only access—and therefore only battle plan—is to go through a small passage the *cacos* dug out. They are small, undernourished people, and they made the passage only large enough for two of their men to walk through. Practically speaking, that means that our forces will have to enter one man at a time. The first marines in will be like sitting ducks in a shooting barrel.

"So, here's the plan. Lt.jg Corey Hamilton and Sgt. Meeker from the ship and Cpl. Luigi Russo and Pfc. Emanuele Bianchi, from Sergeant Henryk Zimbrowski's 3rd of the 3rd's squad are the best artillery men. We will set up the guns around the base and try and move them up the slope if they don't encounter too much resistance. LCdr Emil Buracz has carte blanch to select a force of three companies to do a feint up the north slope under the artillery covering fire.

"I will take three companies of the most experienced devil-dogs up to the tunnel entrance under cover of darkness. We will move through that…tunnel and into the main open area of the fort. My supply of curses over that tunnel is inadequate, forgive me. I'll take Zimbrowsky because he has a cool head and is a good man under fire, but also because he is the strongest human I know. Maybe he can just scare those little *caco* weasels into dropping their guns. He works well with his squad; so, Zimbrowsky and I will enter first, then his squad will come behind and secure the entrance into the open area inside the fort. Once we have at least captured the first defenders' attention, the three companies will move into the parade ground area as fast as possible. Any questions?"

There were none.

"All right, we'll start at 1900 hours tonight with the artillery. Everything moves after you hear my whistle. Lt.jg Hamilton and his big guns will pound the walls away from the area of the tunnel. At 1945, LCdr Buracz and his assaulters will start up the slope. I don't have to say that we don't need heroes. They are to draw attention to themselves, not to win posthumous medals. They are to go slow, hide well, and move with caution. They get to shoot their guns a lot. My contingent will go up to the tunnel opening on the west slope as soon as it's dark and will wait until the noise gets the weasel *brigands'* attention. Oorah!"

The response was a subdued but intense, "OORAH!" in reply.

CHAPTER NINE

Surrounded by twenty-two Chinese Divisions, "Chesty"
Puller told his men, "They are in front of us. They are behind
us. We are surrounded 29 to 1. This simplifies the problem!
No matter where we aim, we will hit the bastards! They can't
get away from us now!"

–United States Marine Corps Lieutenant General Lewis
Burwell "Chesty" Puller, No known attribution.

At the base of Montagne Noire, Haiti, May 20, 1916

Col. Peterson fidgeted nervously as he walked around the area where
his marines lay hidden. He kept his hands clasped behind his back
so that none of them would realize that the myth of his imperturbability
was contrived. Time crept by like the movements of a climbing two-toed
sloth. By 1820 hours, the ambient light was dim enough for him and
his three companies of marines to work their way up the western slope
toward the entrance into the narrow tunnel. The way became ever more
difficult due to the overgrowth of vines, roots, and low-hanging branches.
Peterson secretly hated both snakes—of all kinds—and spiders—of any
kind—and the thoughts of entering that dark tubular prison cell became
increasingly more daunting.

"*Get a grip,*" he muttered soundlessly to himself.

He and Zimbrowsky knelt in front of the opening. It was 1850. Ten more minutes. Everyone in his contingent was in place and waiting for the plan to unfold to include him.

1900. Col. Peterson blew three quick blasts on his whistle.

Instantly, the six artillery guns began to fire. They sounded as if they were on the far side of Montagne Noir. Almost immediately, shots began to come from above the two men aimed at the apparent positions of the howitzers.

Peterson cupped his hand over Zimbrowsky's ear and harshly whispered, "In we go. You first."

"Lucky me," groused Zimbrowsky, but in he went in a slow squat-walk.

Two-thirds of the way into the twenty-five-foot long semi-dark tunnel, two rifle shots range out; and the bullets ricocheted off the roof of the tunnel.

"Hit the ground, Big Z," Peterson hissed.

Zimbrowsky fell forward into a prone position. Peterson sucked in a deep breath and held it for three seconds while he sighted down the barrel to the new 1903 barrel sight. He squeezed the trigger and sent a blast across Zimbrowsky's back and down the tunnel. The *caco* dropped to the floor of the parade ground adjacent to the inside entrance.

"Get 'im?"

"Uh, huh."

"Let's motor," Peterson urged.

They went single file towards the opening of the tunnel into the parade area. Just before they got to the end of the tunnel, gun shots came generally their way, some short, some to either side, and quite a few zinged off the ceiling of the tunnel. Peterson and Zimbrowski stood beside each other in a three-quarter frontal shooting stance and began to fire off rounds as fast as they could pull their triggers and reload. Visibility dimmed with the accumulating cordite smoke, but they could tell that the *cacos* were falling all around the entrance. Their barrel bursts created enough firelight for the marines to be able to see to aim. The marines' shots were deadly and could hardly miss given the narrow confines of their shooting range.

The pile of bodies grew so deep that the *cacos* could not find a position where they could take a shot. That gave Peterson and Zimbrowsky time and room enough to move forward with some sense of security.

They reached the opening, climbed over the corpses, and peaked into the dimly lit open area.

More than two-hundred *cacos* stood with their rifles pointed at the tunnel opening.

"Split up, Big Z, we have to let the jarheads behind us to get in here."

"Good plan, Sir. Wouldn't want to hog all the fun."

The two men log-rolled into the parade room and began shooting off rounds from the standard marine prone firing position.

Incredibly brave marines from the 3rd of the 3rd's squad began forward rolling into the room firing as they went. Two machine gunners made their way in and began a controlled crossing fire fusillade. The Americans then charged the *cacos* with fixed bayonets. The *cacos* emptied their rifles erratically at the marines, then charged the massively larger enemy force. Many of the *cacos* were–by then–armed only with improvised clubs, machetes, and rocks.

There ensued a deadly, but rather short, hand-to-hand melee. By the time nearly two hundred *cacos* had been killed, the entire three companies of marine and navy warriors had made it into the open area and began a leveling fire that the *cacos* could not withstand. They began to flee in all directions. Many dropped in their tracks as they ran. More turned to fight to the finish and perished in what had become a grossly unfair fight. Many of the small Haitians tripped over collected debris and large protruding roots causing them to hesitate and die. Rebel resistance crumbled.

Shortly, there were no more *cacos* left in the large cluttered former parade ground. The place had taken on the appearance of a smoky, dark, murky, hell-hole. Combatants stepped on and stumbled over dead bodies—enemies' and friends.' The wounded and dying screamed out their last breaths. The ground was slippery with blood.

The seamen and marines who entered the uneven parade ground last ran after the fleeing *cacos* who seemed to have a pre-planned escape route. It was slow and difficult going because of overgrowth with high grass and bushes. The *cacos* made their way pell-mell towards the north parapet section. Before they made it to the wall, fifty-sixty of them were killed. At the wall barely two hundred made it to the crest of the parapet, and they found themselves in a position where they had no place to go.

They tried to climb down the many trees that had overgrown the dilapidated parapets. They began to jump off the front of the fortress.

It would have been likely that they would have been killed by falling, but most of them were under very heavy fire. It was a shooting gallery with human targets and nearly two-hundred sharpshooters. The great majority of the jumpers were dead before they hit the ground. No prisoners were taken.

In the immediate aftermath of the battle for Fort Rivière, the naval and marine officers assessed the action. Of particular interest to the professional warriors, was the fact that *cacos* were such woefully poor marksmen. They found that the defenders were armed with rifles, machetes, swords, knives, sticks, and rocks. Only a very few Americans were hit with bullets; more suffered wounds from thrown rocks. They determined that the *cacos*–not knowing what the gunsight on their rifles was used for–typically threw down their weapons in order to defend themselves. Given their personal discretion many of them rejected their poorly functioning rifles and armed themselves with stones when closely threatened by Marines. They were ignorant; and many of them behaved foolishly; but they were not cowards. Even when overwhelmed by sheer numbers while fighting well-trained marines, they fought ferociously hand-to-hand and used rocks against firearms and bayonets.

The following morning, a small detachment of motorized marines raced back to Cap-Haïten, loaded up a ton of dynamite, and returned to the scene of the battle. For the remainder of the daylight hours, the marines strategically laid down sticks of dynamite all around and inside Fort Rivière. They marched away as the explosions went off, turning the fort into a disorganized pile of rubble.

Major Smedley Darlington Butler, First Sergeant Ross Iams, and Private Samuel Gross, were awarded Medals of Honor for actions taken during this engagement.

The longer-term legacy for the United States and for Haiti was that the American occupation of Haiti lasted from 1915 to 1934 and created an in-bred hatred for America and all it stands for to the present day. The U.S. administration set out to improve the Haitian constitution—the American public was told—but ended up overhauling it to the point that it was essentially dismantled for perpetuity. The constitution was already very shaky, and when revision of the constitutional system was complete, the Americans had reinstituted what it euphemistically termed "civil conscription"–impressed labor–for building roads, and established the National Guards which became a nearly perfect model for corruption in Central and South America for many decades to come.

To America's credit, the United States collected taxes and reinvested them in massive improvements of infrastructure: nearly 2,000 km of roads became usable; just under 200 excellently engineered bridges were constructed; many irrigation canals were rehabilitated; hospitals, schools, and public buildings were repaired and maintained; and a good many new ones were constructed. In the main cities, drinking water became safe to drink.

The United States military forces were regularly involved in civil wars in Haiti and other nations.

As a result of the occupation by the United States [1915-1934] there were several direct and indirect significant effects on Haiti. An early period of unrest culminated in a 1918 rebellion by up to 40,000 former *cacos* and other members of the opposition. The scale of the uprising overwhelmed the Gendarmerie, but U.S. Marine reinforcements returned to Haiti to help put down the revolt. The assassination of rebellion leader Charlemagne Péralte in November, 1918 solidified U.S. Marine power over the *cacos*. An estimated 2,000 Haitians were killed in that uprising, one of many during the occupation. In 1934 under President Franklin Roosevelt, the marines left Haiti, turning power over to the authority of the *Garde d'Haïti*.

The elite Haitians–who were mostly mixed race with higher levels of education and capital—acting in concert with wealthy American business people and the American government–continued to dominate the country's bureaucracy and to strengthen its role in national affairs.

"Not much has changed. Today, as Haitians attempt to create an alternative to debt, dependence, and the indignity of foreign domination, the attacks continue. Since the election of President Jean-Bertrand Aristide in 2000, the United States has moved to sabotage Haiti's fledgling democracy through an economic aid embargo, massive funding of elite opposition groups, support for paramilitary coup attempts, and a propaganda offensive against the Aristide government... Since 2000, the U.S. administration has effectively blocked more than $500 million in international loans and aid to Haiti. This included a $146 million-dollar loan package from the Inter-American Development Bank (IDB) intended for healthcare, education, transportation and potable water. Under the terms of the loan agreement, Haiti paid fees and interest totaling more than $5 million long before seeing any money. Since December, 2001, the Haitian gourde has lost 69% of its value and Haiti's foreign reserves have shrunk by 50%, largely due to the embargo."

–The U.S. War Against Haiti,
Haiti Action Committee, World Traveler,
www.haitiaction.net, March, 2004

BANANA WARS 3

CHAPTER TEN

"I spent 33 years and four months in active military service and during that period I spent most of my time as a high-class muscle man for Big Business, for Wall Street, and the bankers. In short, I was a racketeer, a gangster for capitalism. I helped make Mexico and especially Tampico safe for American oil interests in 1914. I helped make Haiti and Cuba a decent place for the National City Bank boys to collect revenues in. I helped in the raping of half a dozen Central American republics for the benefit of Wall Street. I helped purify Nicaragua for the International Banking House of Brown Brothers in 1902-1912. I brought light to the Dominican Republic for the American sugar interests in 1916. I helped make Honduras right for the American fruit companies in 1903. In China in 1927 I helped see to it that Standard Oil went on its way unmolested. Looking back on it, I might have given Al Capone a few hints. Best he could do was to operate his racket in three districts. I operated on three continents."

–U.S. Marine Corps Major General, Smedley Butler, *War Is a Racket*, 1935

Corporate Offices of The United Fruit Company, Corner of Hancock Street and Dorchester Avenue, Boston, Massachusetts, May 15, 1954

Communiques from such diverse places as the old offices in New Orleans, the headquarters of The Banana Farmland in Quetzaltenango Department in Guatemala, from the dictators Marcos Pérez Jiménez of Venezuela and Rafael Trujillo of the Dominican Republic whom the UFCO had put into place and kept there at considerable expense, and several from Presidential House, Guatemala City, had been pouring in to the corporate office of Andrew W. Preston, President of the United Fruit Company. On a day-to-day basis, Bradley Palmer—the corporate attorney and director–was United Fruit; but the dynamo was in Santo Domingo putting out a few little brush fires the commies had started.

First, Preston called the Old Senate Building in D.C.

"Senate Office Building, how may I direct your call?"

"Get me Joe McCarthy," he demanded.

"I will inquire of his office to see if he is taking calls."

"Don't inquire. Tell Joe it's Andy Preston. I need to talk to the man, PDQ."

She shrugged her shoulders and gritted her teeth almost audibly enough to be heard over the phone.

"Yes, Sir."

The operator connected with Room 2251 and listened to Ruby Jenkins, McCarthy's receptionist, "Senator McCarthy's office from the great state of Wisconsin. Who may I say is calling?"

"Ruby, this is Linda at communications office. I have somebody named Andy Preston on the line. He acts like he's somebody or someone who knows somebody. He said that the senator would take his call. Maybe's he's just a crank. I'll unplug him if you want."

"N-n-no, no, this is the UFCO. We'll take it."

"I guess so. I'll put him through."

The senator answered himself, "Andy, hello there. Good to hear from you, my friend. What can I do for you?"

"Look, Joe, my people down south are getting pretty jumpy. The commies are coming out of the woodwork. We're gonna see real trouble down there and soon. We have good friends of ours and the U.S. of A. Looks like they can't handle it alone. If the commie tacos get a real fire going down there, the lid'l blow of the country. Árbenz has personal ties to some members of the communist PGT, and they're talking. We can't have that. Look, Joe, you have Ike's and Allan's ears. The White House and the CIA really have to get off their duffs. And they have to do it pronto. Get back to me when you have something."

Andrew could have said that Joe owed him and UFCO plenty for their generosity in the last close election, but he did not do it. Right now, he needed McCarthy's enthusiasm—to get some of that anti-communist fire working for the right people…like Andrew Preston. He decided to save the iron fist for later if it became necessary. For the moment, the velvet glove would have to suffice.

Preston's calls to Marcos Pérez Jiménez at his presidential *Palacio de Miraflores* in Caracas and Rafael Trujillo at the *Palacio Nacional* in Santo Domingo went as expected: "Greetings my friend, sorry I could not reply immediately to your call. I was at the White House having preliminary talks with the president and Allan Dulles from the CIA. The talks were encouraging. That is about all I can tell you at this point."

Reply: "I know you are trying, Amigo, but we are getting beyond the point where trying will be enough. We have been pretty firm down here with the PCV [*Partido Comunista de Venezuela*]/DPSP [*Dominican Popular Socialist Party*]. They are gaining strength to the point that we expect open fighting in the streets. Perhaps the Venezuelan/Dominican governments will fall. It is in the hands of the *Estados Unidos* and our friends in the CIA now. That communist Árbenz has to go in the next few weeks–maybe a month–or we all get into a bloodbath. I don't need to tell you at the UFCO how bad that is for business or how much the U.S. values its profitable relationship in our nice little countries."

"Of course, you do not need to tell me, of all people. This is what we are going to do: I meet Ike and Allen this week. You keep the lid on that simmering pot of yours for now. I am quite sure the CIA has been trying to convince Ike to act. I know our good friend, Senator McCarthy, has. It is only a matter of time, and I will do what is necessary to make it a short time. Say hello to your fine wife for me."

Oval Office, White House, Washington DC, PDB [President's Daily Briefing], May, 16, 1954

Meeting recorded and stamped "TOP SECRET, EYES ONLY, POTUS, Dir. CIA, and Secy. of State.

Present: Dwight D. Eisenhower, POTUS; Allan W. Dulles, DCIA; John Foster Dulles, Secretary of State; Richard B. Russell, Jr. (D-GA); Chairman House Defense Appropriations Subcommittee, Members: H. Styles Bridges (R-NH), J. Chandler (Chan) Gurney (R-SD), Leverett Saltonstall (R-MA), Millard E. Tydings (D-MD), and Harry F. Byrd (D-VA), Senator Joseph R. McCarthy (R-WISC), and invited guests; Bradley Palmer (corporate attorney and director, United Fruit Company), and General Carlos Castillo Armas (Guatemalan military officer and politician).

Date: May, 16, 1954.

Subject: Emergency appropriations for covert action in Central America.

Summary of findings and decisions:

I. History of U.S. involvement in Central American activities.

- There have been multiple occupations, police actions, and interventions on the part of the United States in Central America and the Caribbean beginning with the Spanish–American War in 1898 under President Theodore Roosevelt, and later by almost every succeeding president usually under the aegis of the Good Neighbor Policy in 1934. When direct military action has become necessary to protect the American sphere of interest under the Monroe Doctrine and vital American economic interests, military interventions were most often carried out by the United States Marine Corps and—at times–with the Navy providing heavy naval artillery support.

- After the history changing major victory of the U.S. over Spain, the Treaty of Paris required Spain to cede all control of and to grant independence of Cuba, Puerto Rico, and the Philippines under the patronage and oversight of the U.S. To maintain good order and to protect U.S. economic interests, the U.S. military was obligated to conduct interventions in Cuba, Panama, Honduras, Nicaragua, Mexico, Haiti, and the Dominican Republic—in several of those nations, more than once. The series of conflicts appeared to have ended with the withdrawal of U.S. troops from Haiti in 1934 under President Franklin D. Roosevelt.

- Due to the repeated inability of the tropical countries below the U.S. southern border, it became necessary for the U.S. to maintain vigilance over the entire western hemisphere (see Monroe Doctrine). The U.S. became the de facto police force to protect our interests, to reconcile warring differences, to correct lawless and corrupt governments and societies, and to exert authority over expanding tropical trade.

- In almost every instance, U.S. help was requested by democratically established governments to defend against actions of ungrateful workers—especially banana workers—who falsely alleged maltreatment and abusive working conditions—as an excuse to mount unlawful and dangerous militant labor movements. In 1913, for example, tropical fruit consumer organizations, the United Fruit Company, and the U.S. government, were obliged to counteract high import duties imposed by communist leaning governments with the populist assistance from labor movements. In this instance, as in many others, the successful protective actions prevented widespread unrest and the overthrow of governments acting with the best interests of the United States of America in mind and in practice. In other instances, similar communistic associations protested the consumption and commerce in tea, coffee, chocolate, and the export of tropical fruits such as bananas at fair prices, as being aristocratic in nature, and causing elevation of prices for the oppressed poor in the growing countries. Such socialistic fantasies were contravened by U.S. influence. Such attitudes, discourse, and corruption rife in Central and South American societies is what prompted repeated U.S. influence and—at time—interventions.

- One of the most notorious strikes by United Fruit workers occurred in November, 1928 near Santa Marta on the Caribbean coast of Colombia. Lawless and murderous strikers provoked defensive measures on the part of the Colombian government. On December 6th, embattled Colombian Army troops under the command of General Cortés Vargas, defended themselves by engaging in a deadly firefight with a crowd of violent strikers in Ciénaga. According to government sources estimates of the number of casualties totaled forty-seven in contrast to the inflated rebel estimate of three thousand. The military and the government rightly justified this and other actions because the strikers were subversive, and its organizers were Communist revolutionaries. The United Fruit Company was once again helpful for the Colombian government's efforts and protective of U.S. interests. U.S. army units stood poised to intervene if it became necessary to protect American personnel and the interests of the company. Socialist and communist agitators in the U.S. protested the involvement of America in what they deemed to be a Colombian issue.

- Exemplary beneficial and altruistic interventions have included the request by the nation of Guatemala in 1901 to employ the United Fruit Company–an invaluable U.S. owned and operated international conglomerate—to manage the country's postal service and again in 1913. Pursuant to that contract, the United Fruit Company created the Tropical Radio and Telegraph Company. By 1930, good business practices enabled the company to absorb more than twenty poorly managed local rival firms. As a beneficial result for the company, the people of Guatemala, and the commercial interests of the U.S., the UFCO acquired a stable capital of $215 million USD and saw it become the largest employer in

Central America—a credit to its nation of origin–the U.S.–and as a successful promotor of healthy economic growth in Guatemala. UFCO's policies of acquiring tax breaks and other benefits from host governments enabled a furtherance of the benefits the company is able to provide for cooperating nations. Unfortunately, certain elements in Guatemala–mostly communistic in their ideology–particularly those partial to the influence of the current sitting president, Colonel Jacobo Árbenz Guzmán, nicknamed *"El Chelón"* [The Big Blonde] and *"El Suiso"* [The Swiss] take a dangerous opposition point-of-view.

- Finally, there is the matter of land ownership in those so-called banana republics. By dint of its business acumen and vigorous business practices, the UFCO has accumulated significant land holdings which are used to provide employment and profit for the country, the people, the company, and America. The communists deplore the ownership as corrupt, heavy-handed, and unequal, land holding opportunities for the company. Those communists similarly disdain the governments which offer such inducements and concessions to the company to further economic development within their nations as "servile dictatorships." It has been considered a responsibility of the company, their host governments, and the U.S. government, to educate the citizens about the value of such capitalistic and democratic practices.

Conclusions and orders by POTUS:

- Communist agitation in Guatemala has escalated to the point that American intervention is necessary and is deemed to be overdue.
- President Col. Jacobo Árbenz Guzmán–under the Monroe Doctrine—is deemed to represent a clear and present danger to the interests of the United States and must be removed under the maximum prejudice policy

to prevent further agitation by this individual and other like-minded officials.

- Since diplomatic efforts and other nonaggressive measures of persuasion have failed and are unlikely to be effective in the future, it has become necessary to consider that a state of emergency exists which requires direct intervention by United States military forces. A sufficient contingent of U.S. Marines shall be dispatched to regain order and to protect U.S. interests.

- The CIA shall participate in early interventions in Guatemala to guarantee a presidential coup and successful results for the overall operation. DCIA Dulles shall effect the organization of a top-secret infiltration group to be led by Carlos Castillo Armas–code-named "*Calligeris*"— with an initial force total of 480 individuals divided into four separate operating groups at the discretion of General Armas.

- Two separate lists shall be developed: individuals whose actions are so egregious and their influence for wrongdoing so pervasive that only executive action will suffice, and individuals with lesser complicity and/or influence selected for incarceration or exile. In certain special cases, because of the likelihood that they will be released or helped to escape, those individuals may be transported to the United States for incarceration.

- The operation shall have the top-secret code name of "Operation PBSUCCESS."

Signed:

[signature]

Dwight D. Eisenhower, POTUS; May, 16, 1954.

CHAPTER ELEVEN

"The forest did not tolerate frailty of body or mind. Show your weakness, and it would consume you without hesitation."
—Tahir Shah, *House of the Tiger King: The Quest for a Lost City*, published by John Murray, 2005

"The Fruit Company, Inc. reserved for itself the most succulent, the central coast of my own land, the delicate waist of America. It rechristened its territories as the 'Banana Republics' and over the sleeping dead, over the restless heroes who brought about the greatness, the liberty and the flags, it established the comic opera... Perhaps this war will pass like the others which divided us leaving us dead, killing us along with the killers but the shame of this time puts its burning fingers to our faces. Who will erase the ruthlessness hidden in innocent blood?"
—Neftalí Ricardo Reyes Basoalto, [pseudonym Pablo Neruda], Chilean poet, winner of the Nobel Prize for literature in 1971, written while in exile for supporting communist causes.

Puerto Barrios, sole Guatemalan port to the Atlantic Ocean, and drop-off point for Operation PBSUCCESS June 18, 1954

The CIA armed, funded, and trained, a force of 480 hand-picked men led by Gen. Carlos Castillo Armas for Operation PBSUCCESS. They were conspicuously not an American military force—no spit-and-polish, medals, creased pants, shined boots, or scrupulously and tenderly treated firearms. The men came in all sizes, ethnic backgrounds, religious affiliations (including none), colors, and dispositions. What they all had in common was a passionate hatred for communists, each for his own reason. They were—by nature and training not talkative men—fighters used to keeping secrets to the death.

Armas divided them into four groups varying in size from sixty to 198 men each. The divisions suited Armas because he knew every man for his skills, ability to work in a team, and what frightened him—which was usually not very much. He knew their faces, their physical forms in dim light, and could recognize every man by the back of his head.

There were Poles, Germans, Lithuanians, Czechs, American Indians, Colorado ranch hands, mercenary soldiers fresh from the French Foreign Legion, former recon marines, blacks, Jews, and a smattering of unrepentant nazis. Every man was issued clothing and equipment that came from anywhere and everywhere except the United States of America.

The assortment of men received miscellaneous used clothing with tough short sleeve olive drab canvas button shirts and cargo shorts from old South African border patrol troops, tough African buffalo hide lace-up boots with rubber soles from a local Kenya Regiment that spent weeks in the bush hunting Mau Mau rebels during the previous year. Bush hats originated in Algeria. They had been used by FLN fighters opposing the French. Curved kukri knives came from Pakistan; FN Five-seven semi-automatic pistols were designed and manufactured by FN Herstal in Belgium; and Swedish Automatgevär m/42 semi-automatic rifles which were purchased on the black market. They had an untraceable United Nations mix of materiel, but nothing from North America.

The PBSUCCESS clandestine agents were transported from Fort Lauderdale, Florida aboard the Italian World War II troop transport ship, the *Angelina*, which was specifically refurbished and refitted for the mission. What it lacked in creature comforts, it made up for in speed and quiet passage through even rough waters because of its slender hull. The voyage was uneventful. The crew ate as well as sailors on U.S. naval ships of the line, listened to the recorded music of Johnny Cash—*Ring of Fire*–Webb Pierce—*There Stands the Glass*—Jim Reeves—*Bimbo*—and Loretta Lynn—*The Coal Miner's Daughter*. The *Angelina* dropped anchor in the warm, calm waters off Puerto Barrios, a rich farming area almost wholly owned by the United Fruit Company, which made it a nearly perfectly safe harbor from which to commence PBSUCCESS.

The ship emptied its warriors via inflatable rubber rafts developed by the French Zodiac company. The Zodiacs came about from work on rubber-coated fabrics for the airship industry. The rafts slid silently to the white sand beach, and the warriors slipped away into the nearly impenetrable darkness. When every man was accounted for, Armas told them to follow him to the first hiding place where they would wait until the coming of first light.

The invasion of Guatemala had actually started three days earlier with a massive CIA psychological warfare onslaught. With its usual and extraordinary thoroughness, the W.O.M.S [Wise Old Men in Washington] had created their own radio station to broadcast a steady barrage of anti-President Col. Jacobo Árbenz Guzmán and his government propaganda. Old Argentine bi-planes dropped leaflets predicting doom, gloom, and defeat, for an enemy attack that had not yet even happened. Posters nailed to telephone poles screamed abuse in Spanish against socialism, communism, Árbenz, and the Russian triumvirate of Marx, Stalin, and Lenin. Others lashed out with epithets and disgusting caricatures of Pablo Neruda, Che Guevara, Carlos Marighella, Edith Lagos, and Carlos Altamirano, being tortured, hanged, and being used as *piñatas*.

The effect on the Guatemalans on the street was electrifying and horrifying. The simple people were becoming terrified of invading Americans, Russians, Japanese, and things-that-go-bump-in-the-night. The heavy-handed criticism and effort to marginalize and isolate Guatemala extended throughout Latin America and was spreading internationally. All of this was communicated to the innocents of Guatemala that these military events—favorable to the rebellion–were genuine news. Companies like the United Fruit Company had a vested interest in keeping their Central American plantations stable, and to them, anything that contributed to that end was moral. To the citizens of Guatemala, the world had turned upside down and was rapidly coming to an end.

The primary goal of the PBSUCCESS clandestine agents and their masters was to capture and control *La Ciudad de Guatemala*. The four groups of agents broke up and moved separately to their pre-determined initial sites of action before all four re-grouped for the attack on the capital.

Ed Campbell, Jackie Hendricks, Henry Zslowskiwiez, and Tom Dastrup had become friends—and more importantly—mutual defenders, and confidants, during the training period for PBSUCCESS, and were selected to be part of the Zacapa attack. Zacapa was the Guatemalan army's largest frontier post and was considered to be the most difficult assignment for Castillo Armas' raiders. Armas, himself, was the leader of the Zacapa raid.

Ed was a lean, sinewy man with a thatch of unruly blah brown hair, bushy eyebrows, ear hair, and nostril hair. He wore long side-burns ala the new singing sensation, Elvis Presley, and went around humming the music to Presley's popular song, *Jail-house Rock*. He spoke only rarely—so much so that many of the commandoes initially thought he was a mute. When he did speak, he revealed his university education in history and the humanities. He was generally respected as a brain, and because he was the best hand-to-hand fighter in the 480-man team, Ed literally commanded respect.

Jackie was the class clown, always inflicting practical jokes on team members and making up lyrics to silly ditties. He had a round, open face and an easy infectious smile. His nose was rather bulbous and red, giving him a clown-like appearance which enhanced his comedian persona. He should have had flaming red hair to complete his picture; but instead, his German ethnicity blessed, or cursed, him with straight dirty brown hair as unmanageable as that of his friend, Ed's. His solution was to keep it in a very short, fitted-to-the head bulldog cut. He was the only one of the entire 480 commandoes to have a tattoo. Fortunately for his selection to the PBSUCCESS team, the tattoo was of a generic over-developed Nordic cutie which could have graced the deltoid of any European or Scandinavian sailor.

Henry with the unpronounceable Polish name had long since given up trying to tell friends how to pronounce, let alone spell it. First grade had been a nightmare. He went by "Z" as his only name. Z was quiet and retiring. He had purposely avoided drawing attention to himself by making sure that he did not achieve the scholastic acclaim he deserved, the military honors he might have been given, or by speaking in public on matters he often understood better than those who occupied the limelight. His humility belied his intellectual and physical prowess.

He was a large man—huge, actually—standing six-seven and weighing three-twenty with no apparent fat. He had a bland, kindly face; but his formidable size made him a man to avoid nevertheless. Z's hair was balding—which embarrassed him—so, he shaved himself to a cue-ball slickness every morning. He had two deep dimples in his cheek and a butt chin. No one would have considered him handsome, and he remained aloof and diffident to girls and women all his life as a defense. The thing that made him stand out was action, not words. He was a fighter whom his mates respected, and his many enemies over the years feared.

Tom was one of those guys who never got an "A" in school and bragged about his gentlemanly "C"s. He had an entrepreneurial bent that made this stint in military and spy activity definitely temporary. He intended to be a big businessman and admired the UFCO above all others in his pantheon of heroes. He grew up not "wanting to be just like you, Dad" but instead "to be just like Bradley Palmer, the United Fruit man." He considered his present gig to be a stepping stone to that end. He was no coward; he wanted to survive; nor, was he hero material. He wanted to stand out as a producer; and if other men wanted to become dead heroes, let them do it.

Tom had a strong, earnest, believable face. With that useful attribute, he could have been a successful con-man. Instead, he was assiduously honest and was highly respected by everyone for that. He had a regular face, regular physique, and the gait of a common man. He did not stand out in a crowd, and he never purposefully attracted attention by talking out loud, giving his opinion unless he was asked, but prided himself in knowing everything and everyone connected to his current enterprise.

The going was difficult to get from Puerto Barrio to Zacapa due primarily to being bogged down by the weight of the tons of supplies and a lack of appropriate transportation. It took the rebel forces several days to reach Zacapa and the other three targets. Along the way, the four friends in the Zacapa group had a small event to rejoice about. One of Armas' planes blew up a bridge after the unit had passed over it. The gendered enthusiasm was short lived, however, because Armas and the W.O.M.s in Washington D.C. had made a fundamental mistake. It is a time-honored dictum that a fighter should never underestimate his enemy. The Zacapa frontier post was more heavily fortified, had more defenders, and was a more professional military establishment, than the Wise Old Men—with all their ingrained prejudices—had bargained for.

Tom was the first to make his way through the perimeter fence that first night. He grumbled to himself and repeated his personal mantra that his "*mama didn't raise no heroes, and would give me a good spanking if I come home in a box.*"

He and Jackie used heavy-duty wire cutters to open the chain-links sufficiently to give him access to the outermost entry to the base, which was an open grassland at that point. He silently killed two sentries on his way to the communications building the planners had assured him was right there in front of him, maybe a hundred meters away. That was the first mistake in what would shortly look like a genuine snafu. It took him forty-five minutes and a long belly-crawl to get to the edifice, only to find that it was nothing more than a half-empty light equipment repository. Tom was determined to salvage something of value from all his efforts. He angled to his right and hugged its rough brick walls to make his way through the deep shadows to the next adjacent building.

Tom saw a sign which read, "*Edificio de la Espiritual Comodidad por Todos del Miembros del Ejército.*"

"*Looks like maybe something important, HQ or Communications or Planning or Logistics,*" he thought.

It perhaps would have been better had Tom been able to read any *Español*. He spent three hours investigating. With some effort, he was able to break in as the sky began to turn grey instead of India Ink black. That was illuminating. He found crucifixes with Jesus impaled and bleeding hanging from them, priests' vestments, Spanish language hymnals, and Spanish language Bibles.

"*Oops,*" he muttered angrily to himself. "*Time to make like a tree and leaf.*"

When he crossed back through the fence, he was met by Jackie, Z, and Ed.

"So, what's it like? Any good info to take back to the *jefe*?" Z asked.

"Nope. All I could feel there in the dark were some administration type buildings. We are going to have to go in guns blazing in daylight. Too dangerous to use a flashlight."

The men all sighed. There was nothing they looked forward to less than a daylight–all parts exposed–assault.

Gen. Armas agreed, but said, "I'll have to give it some thought."

One of the things all the men in PBSUCCESS teams agreed upon was that they trusted Gen. Armas had their welfare to be paramount in all the planning and actions of the group. He was anxious, knowing that time was fleeting. Surprise for the whole operation was becoming a diminishing hope with every minute that went by.

"Get me radio coms," he ordered.

A radio man was constantly nearby, and he made himself known.

"Need to send an encrypted radiogram to the *Angelina*," the general said.

PO1 George Fitzgerald held his pen and writing pad at the ready.

"Send this," the general ordered and proceeded to dictate.

Fitzgerald quickly set the message to encryption and sent it via his SCR radio set:

- Decrypted outgoing message: 19/05/1954 0822. Operation PBSUCCESS. Unable to make progress at pre-determined Zacapa site. Require naval artillery and marine participation. Over.
- Decrypted incoming reply: 19/05/1954 0855. Operation PBSUCCESS. Granted. Expect USMC reinforcements in five hours, complete with artillery and heavy equipment. *Angelina* will commence firing on location after Marine major's communiqué. Out.

Lt. Goeffery Lander Ryan and four hundred marine enlisted were led into the PBSUCCESS secret pre-action camp by closely following their comics [maps made by military intelligence] and for the last mile by CIA scouts. They marched into camp at 1410, slightly ahead of schedule. They brought with them two M24 Chaffee light tanks, six 1954 M-37 Dodge military Power Wagon pick-up trucks with machine gun mounts, twelve M16A4 grenade launchers with scopes, six M240B 40mm medium truck-mounted machine-guns with 10,000 rounds of ammunition, six 1954 USMC M37 Korea War gun trucks with 50

Caliber machine guns mounted in place. The marine platoon with its add-ons included two LAR [Light Armored Reconnaissance] squads and three MOS 0331—Marine Corps Infantry Machine Gunner squads [MOS: Military Occupational Specialties]. They came loaded for bear.

"When do you want to launch the attack, General?" Ryan asked. "We essentially came ready to go. We'll be squared away for take-off at 1600. Okay with you?"

"*Muy bien,*" the general said with an anticipatory smile.

The marines hurriedly rechecked their packs, the mechanical operation of their weapons, and each choked down three dicks of death [links included with beans] with two pints of iced tea. They were hot to trot and ready to roar.

CHAPTER TWELVE

"We find in your houses and courts nothing but sparkling pomp and showy dress, boldness, and presumptuousness of heart, insatiable avarice, hatred and envy, backbiting, betraying, harloting, seduction, gaming, carousing, dancing, swearing, stabbing, and violence...The pitiful moaning and misery of the wretched men does not reach your ears. The sweat of the poor we find in your house, and the innocent blood on your hands."

–Menno Simons of the Netherlands, the original
Mennonite, *Foundations of Christian Doctrine,* 1539

"Thy wee bit housie, too, in ruin!
It's silly wa's the win's are strewin!
An' naething, now, to big a new ane,
O' foggage green!
An' bleak December's winds ensuin,
Baith snell an' keen!

Thou saw the fields laid bare an' waste,
An' weary winter comin fast,
An' cozie here, beneath the blast,
Thou thought to dwell-
Till crash! the cruel coulter past
Out thro' thy cell...
But, Mousie, thou art no thy-lane,
In proving foresight may be vain;

The best-laid schemes o' mice an' men
Gang aft agley,
An' lea'e us nought but grief an' pain,
For promis'd joy!"
–Robert Burns, *Ode to a Mouse, Kilmarnock volume*, 1786

Perimeter of Camp Zacapa, Guatemalan Frontier Post, 1600 hours, June 20, 1954

At 1500 hours, Ed, Jackie, Z, and Tom, led the way for ten marine sappers and twenty highly trained saboteurs to their positions preceding the onslaught. The saboteurs spread out around the perimeter to be situated at key roads, railways, telegraph lines, and airfields, with the aim of violent disruption of entrances, exits, and communication portals. This would be the modern and small-scale equivalent of a siege around a castle. The sappers–aka combat engineers–were a special breed: First of all, they were on exchange duty from the 6th Engineer Regiment, combat engineering unit of the 9th Light Armored Marine Brigade. Second, they all wore full face beards, an historical tradition handed down from multiple countries and many generations of American sappers. Third, although they had full training as fighting marines, the officers and noncoms of the regiment had extra training to conduct demolitions missions, to clear minefields, to construct and breach trenches, tank traps, and an assortment of fortifications.

When necessary, the men with the MOS of combat engineer, built bunkers, bridges, and roads. The other part of their MOS consisted of the destruction of the same things. They laid or cleared land mines, depending on the circumstance. They had the dubiously desirable specialty of combined arms breaching—an area of endeavor that Tom Dastrup especially eschewed because its high likelihood of producing heroes. They wore British ghillie suits. After a few minutes, the sappers with all their gadgetry slipped into the variegated green jungle and were lost to the view of the CIA agents.

At 1600 hours, the saboteurs and sappers were heard from: two dozen or more bombings took place all around the unsuspecting frontier post. The effect—even for the prepared and initiated—was formidable. For the intended recipients, it was not nearly so benign. The effect was intimidating and stupefying, even before the first wound was inflicted. Immediately upon the cacophony produced by the saboteurs and sappers, artillery fire came from the marine M198 155 mm Medium Howitzers, and M252 81 mm Extended Range Mortars. The garrison of the camp was demoralized and softened-up before the actual marine and CIA attack commenced.

Four bugles sounded "*To Arms.*"

A horde of PBSUCCESS CIA agents, overly wrought-up young marines, and an ill-defined collection of local rebels, began a hell-fire terrifying attack preceded by a protective steel and explosive shield of the two M24 Chaffee light tanks, six 1954 M-37 Dodge military Power Wagon pick-up trucks with 50 cal. machine gun mounts, big men yielding M16A4 grenade launchers, the six M240B 40mm medium truck-mounted machine-guns and six 1954 USMC M37 Korea War gun trucks with 50 Caliber machine guns mounted in place.

Suppressive fire for the running devil-dogs and CIA riff-raff was provided by M249 Squad Automatic Weapons, and runners carrying 240B machine guns. The 240s weighed twenty-seven pounds and required a strong and fit marine. The young men that day positively relished the chance to run, to sweat, and to shoot hundreds of rounds.

The going was easy, and no rebel or marine casualties had occurred during the first twenty minutes of the onslaught. The path was fairly narrow but clear. The sappers had cleared the Guatemalan mines using a specialized Caterpillar D9 armored bulldozer. Then, along the sides of the cleared area, they planted some of their own T-48 mines in their own secret pattern.

Immediately after the mine field was altered, a withering crossfire began coming from two large buildings on opposite sides of the open field of the camp that Tom Dastrup had reconnoitered two days previously. Marines and rebels began to topple over. Some fell into the sides of the cleared area and were blown up by "friendly grenades." Fourteen died.

Tanks moved into play almost immediately. Both camp buildings— including the church—were reduced to rubble in a matter of minutes with considerable loss of life on the government troop side. Medics rushed to the wounded to give life-saving help. They marked the bodies of fourteen dead marines for later transport home.

The government troops had nowhere safe to go after fleeing from the bombarded buildings. They gathered in the parade grounds in front of the headquarters building that was still standing. No officer was able to unite the troops into any semblance of an orderly military unit. There was talk of retreat, but it became obvious that it would be easier to herd a bunch of cats than to get an orderly retreat in motion.

As the marines, rebels, and CIA operatives, appeared from in between the still standing buildings, several government officers began to organize a safe surrender for themselves and their men. One of the soldiers—frightened and distracted by the approaching juggernaut—began firing wildly in the general direction of the oncoming enemy.

The marine response was horrendous. Government soldiers dropped on top of one another as the marine machine gunners cut them down like rows of corn stalks. When it was all over, 234 government soldiers were dead; fifty-eight were seriously wounded; and over a thousand fell to their knees and begged for surrender. The marine sappers hastily erected a barbed wire enclosure to serve as a POW compound. The surrendering men underwent the indignity of having their weapons confiscated, even their Swiss army knives. They were stripped down to their underwear, had a very thorough body search performed, and then herded like so many sheep into the enclosure.

A marine sergeant-major yelled at Ed, Jackie, Z, and Tom, who were standing around with nothing particular to do, "You lazy good-for-nothings, get over here and move these W.O.G.s into their new home."

The term W.O.G. originated as a pejorative term for Latins and other people who are not white who worked on the Suez Canal project. They were required to wear a uniform stenciled on the back with "Working On Government"—project–on it.

In practical fact, the military operations connected with PBSUCCESS could hardly have been considered to be a success. The battle at Camp Zacapa–the Guatemalan Frontier Post–was the closest the Americans came to a military victory. The largest force was concentrated to attack the Atlantic harbor town of Puerto Barrios. It was an outright failure. Some of the others—like Esquipulas–took on the quality of "Keystone

Kops" adventures. The action against Jutiapa never happened because the sixty-man force was arrested and jailed by Salvadoran policemen before it got to the border, and the CIA operatives spent the period of the regime changing action of the United States in a Salvadoran jail. Castillo Armas' CIA/rebel forces wasted several days to reach their targets. That gave the cities time to prepare and often to turn away the rebel approaches.

The final "attack" on Guatemala City was more psychological than actual. The invasion provoked a brief panic in the capital, which quickly decreased as the rebels failed to make any striking moves. The pre-attack psy-ops actions by the CIA were so effective that the terrified citizens of the city and the intimidated army—fearful of a major American invasion—demanded the surrender and the arrest of President Jacobo Árbenz Guzmán almost immediately after a brief naval bombardment commenced. The Árbenz army refused to fight; Árbenz then tried unsuccessfully to recruit a civilian militia supportive of him and his policies. Casualties were minimal.

Árbenz resigned on the twenty-seventh of June. General Carlos Castillo Armas became president of Guatemala ten days later, following negotiations in San Salvador headed by the United States.

Similar banana war outcomes took place throughout Central America, South America, and the Caribbean—Brazil, Colombia, Costa Rica, Cuba, Dominican Republic, Ecuador, Haiti, Honduras, Mexico, Nicaragua, Panama, and Philippines–during the years of power of the United Fruit Company. The term, "banana republic," became popular and positively portrayed the United States as a police force that was sent to reconcile warring tropical countries, lawless societies, and corrupt politicians, while establishing a reign over tropical trade that enhanced and cemented U.S. domination for generations.

In truth, the banana wars began because oppressed laborers working for U.S. international conglomerates such as the United Fruit Company, Henry Ford's "Fordlandia," and Charles Goodyear's rubber companies, were rife with cruel–even murderous–injustices, corruption, creation of lawless societies, and escalating labor abuse in Latin America. Banana workers began what was an early civil rights movement in the tropical fruit and rubber trades. The struggles led to outright wars in tropical countries with labor movements being put down by dictators with conspicuous American assistance. The discourse and corruption facing

Latin American people and governments prompted the United States influence and intervention to protect its own commercial domination and regime change as that became necessary. Massive counterinsurgency campaigns by U.S. supported dictators left tens of thousands of people maimed, massacred, or missing.

MIDDLE EAST I
CHAPTER THIRTEEN

"The March 30, 1949, coup by Syrian Army Chief of Staff Col. Husni al-Zaim was one of the first covert actions that the CIA pulled off since it had been created in 1947."
–Douglas Little, Professor Department of History, Clark University, *1949-1958, Syria: Early Experiments in Covert Action*, May, 2003

Office of The President, Shukri al-Quwatly, Presidential Palace Mount Mezzeh, Damascus, Syria, March 20, 1949

President Shukri al-Quwatly stretched out on the office's huge arm-chair and placed his silk-stocking feet on the ottoman. He gave a hearty sigh of satisfaction, surfeit from his splendid *mjadara* Damascene gourmet dinner: chicken shawarma, *besni tava yapilişi,* and *barak bjebnee, znoud al banat*–Biceps of Ladies–salad with pomegranate and spiced with sumac. He had enjoyed his favorite Syrian desserts, *Baklawa*–pistachio filla wedges in rose water syrup with fragrant Aleppian dessert syrup and *Kanafa*–unsalted cheese layered with fine phyllo pastry, baked and topped with homemade orange blossom syrup. He belched, one of the privileges of his rank; he could do whatever he wanted; and nobody dared complain or criticize. Legislative elections held on July 2, 1947 put him in office. President al-Quwatly was re-elected by the Chamber of Deputies on

April 18, 1948. Being the darling of the American CIA guaranteed his longevity in his position. He had been president for two years, something of a record in Syria.

Shukri had to smile at his good fortune. He was powerful, feared, fawned over, able to indulge his every hedonistic whim, and fat—in a region where obesity was a mark of wealth and success. His rank was the equal to any historical khan, sultan of the House of Osman, or Grand Vizier. Shukri had the distinction of being the first president of an independent Syria, a convoluted achievement that finally took place in 1943.

It had not always been the case. In the late 1930s and early 1940s, he had been a rod-straight slender figure in stiff, dark French civilian mufti with a high fez. He looked and acted like hundreds of other low-level French colonial administrative officials. His unsmiling thin face graced as many official photographs as he could manage. His only identifying characteristic at that time was a small, thin, Hitlerian mustache, which was popular in Vichy France at the time.

Fortune–it seemed to observers—smiled on Shukri. He, however, gave due credit to his own cunning and ability to cultivate useful associations among the French colonials who became the power behind the throne of the Kingdom of Syria in 1920. When the kingdom was established, Quwatli became a minor civilian government official. He was not ordinarily a brave man and regularly allowed other men to become heroes—more often than not–dead heroes. However, he overcame his venality due to a deep disillusionment with monarchism and went well out onto limb to co-found the Republican Independence Party.

As he expected, Shukri Quwatli was almost immediately sentenced to death by the French occupiers as they asserted their control to suit their own interests and to curry favor with the Syrian tribal warlords. Ever ahead of the game, Shukri quickly moved to Cairo where he served as the chief ambassador of the Syrian-Palestinian Congress—a rather grandiose position given the small numbers of members. He was cunning enough to cultivate strong ties with Saudi Arabia, a prescient and forward looking decision.

He used these connections to help finance the Great Syrian Revolt in 1925, which should have sealed his doom at the hands of the vengeful French government. However, to the great surprise of everyone in Syria–not the least of which was Shukri himself–the French authorities in the Middle

East pardoned Quwatli in 1930. Thereafter, he returned to Syria, where he began to work on cultivating political allies and frenemies and gradually became a principal leader of the National Bloc. He was elected president of Syria in 1943 and oversaw the country's independence three years later.

Shukri became a well-known gourmand, even among the rich food loving Parisians. He hired famous chefs from around the Arab Muslim world and from France itself. He worked at packing on the pounds and soon became rotund enough to draw attention to himself as a quintessential rich and pampered Arab potentate and dilettante gourmand. By 1949, the man was enormous. He weighed nearly 400 pounds and stood 5'11." He was short of breath at ten steps, wheezed when supine, and had developed a mildly cyanotic complexion—what his doctors called "a blue bloater" behind his back. Despite losing his previously fit and active physique, he remained secure in the knowledge that he had a tight hold on the reins of the Syrian body politic.

The potentate liked to look like one. He–like most affluent Damascenes–dressed very conservatively, stylishly, and fashionably in public outside his sumptuous personal quarters. However, given his choice in private, Shukri much preferred tent-like traditional *keffiyahs*, with a traditional Arab red and white or black and white checkered headscarf, very loose-fitting Nile Valley *gallabiyah*—prompting critics to say that their president's tailor was Omar, the Tentmaker. At times he wore white robes with gold piping along the edges, old-fashion toes-up Moroccan leather slippers, and a gold tasseled and burgundy-colored wool American-style Shriners' fez embroidered with a heavy gold scimitar, crescent, and ornate words, *"Al Malaikah"* given to him by the veteran CIA agent, Miles Weston Howard II.

Oval Office, White House, Washington DC, PDB [President's Daily Briefing], March, 22, 1949

> Meeting recorded and stamped "TOP SECRET, EYES ONLY; POTUS, Harry S. Truman; Director CIA, Frank G. Wisner; Secy. of State, Dean Acheson
> Present: POTUS, DCIA, Frank G. Wisner, Secretary of State; Dean Acheson Secretary of Agriculture; Charles F. Brannan;

Chairman House Defense Appropriations Subcommittee; Rep. Erik Norton Clyde (R-CA); Special Agent, COS [Chief of Station, Damascus] Miles Weston Howard II, and invited guests; CEO Marcus Denali, Arabian-American Oil Company (ARAMCO); Major General Mohamed Ibriham al-Sham, Colonel Abdullah Faid ibn Nagib [Syrian Arab Army officers. Col. Nagib is with the special forces]

Date: March 22, 1949.
Subject: Trans-Arabian Pipe Line (TAPLINE) from Saudi Arabia to the Mediterranean. Problems with right-of-way through Syria.

Summary of briefing and decision of POTUS

- DCIA explained the fundamental difficulty with dealing with the president of Syria, his cabinet, and especially his cabinet. The problem appeared to stem from the current president, Shukri al-Quwatly's, pathological inability to make decisions, especially regarding issues which he deems to include choices on his and the Syrian government's part when the U.S.S.R. offers something of an alternative option. His choice is almost always to be neutral, which he considers to be the safe choice.
- Case in point for the PDB of May, 22, 1949 is the application by ARAMCO for right-of-way passage for the company's proposed TAPLINE [Trans-Arabian Pipe Line] across the Middle East. To date, Lebanon, Jordan, and Saudi Arabia have been cooperative and— for a consideration—have granted the right-of-way; and ARAMCO is prepared to begin breaking ground except for the recalcitrance of the Syrian government and parliament.

    CEO ARAMCO discussed the difficulties the company is having: there have been violent anti-U.S., anti-Israeli, and anti-ARAMCO, demonstrations throughout the country but most violent in the capital city, Damascus, for the past year. The current regime will not listen to reason or even to offers of favorable treatment.

- Gen. al-Sham, and Col. Nagib declared the total willingness on the part of the SAA to gain and to maintain control. However, Col. Nagib pointed out, only a vehemently anti-Russian president backed by equally pro-U.S. military can accomplish that mission. Gen. al-Sham pointed out that any usurpers would need financial, political, and military assistance from the United States to complete the great tasks ahead to secure democracy and working capitalism in Syria.

- DCIA and COS Agent Howard concurred with the Syrian officers and indicated that the agency was ready and willing to direct the necessary covert actions to accomplish the goals set out in the PDB.

POTUS decided:

The buck stops at his desk, and he ordered under a presidential executive action for the CIA to move ahead with dispatch to complete all necessary covert activities to aid in the smooth transition to a new, more pro-American regime in Syria.

Sufficient funding for covert operations with use of USMC forces to enforce the actions as becomes necessary.

Depts. of State, Defense, and Agriculture will receive orders commanding compliance. Agriculture will funnel funding through its secret accountancy apparatus.

Signed:

Harry S. Truman

Harry S. Truman, POTUS

Miles Weston Howard felt a combination of jet lag and hangover after his flight back to Damascus. In could have been much worse. He could have had to fly first class on one of the commercial airlines, or even back in steerage—as he always referred to the cheaper seats way back in the economy section. It was unthinkable that he might have caught a Space Available military flight in a drafty puddle jumper that would have taken a couple of weeks and a lot of backaches before he got to his destination. Instead—because he was the station chief, and his mission was important and time sensitive—he was able to fly directly from Andrews Air Force Base to Al-Dumayr Military Airport 40 km northeast of Damascus on Airdale, the CIA airline fronted by USAID at the time. It was comfortable enough—too comfortable with too much free liquor—and he unwisely let himself become hungover. Now, he was paying for his indiscretion.

He was always prepared for the oven blast of the desert when he stepped down out of the plane, but that did not make it any better. Of all the things he hated about the Middle East, the furnace heat and undulating mirages of the desert floor were the worst. The meeting he was about to attend was a must—a make-or-break—for his career, to say nothing about the reputation of the United States which he was committed to serve. Miles was thirty-four years old—going on sixty in his mind—but still having to keep in good enough shape to perform as well as a fit thirty-year-old.

He really was not so bad, he had to admit to himself once the initial blast furnace effect wore off. Miles Howard was born and reared in Butte, Montana, and was raised to be a cowboy on an isolated ranch. He tired of that when he turned ten and wrangled a move to Las Vegas, Nevada to live with a maternal uncle until he left for college. His parents regarded his departure as one less mouth to feed.

He never quite lost the ranch-boy mind-set; and he remained as tough as he had needed to be fighting with the local grade-school boys in Butte, and on the football field of Las Vegas Clark County High School, located on the dusty arid crossroads of 4th and Clark Streets. Fighting was a way of life. His uncle and aunt were too poor to feed another mouth; so, Howard had to work at one casino or another doing odd jobs to earn his keep. Survival required learning how to fight better or to run faster than the men who thought they could slap him around enough to get him to fork over his week's pay.

Miles grew up quickly and learned to fight well. One of his fights happened to capture the attention of the primo mob boss Tony "The Ant" Spilotro—who preferred his other nickname of "Tough Tony."

The Ant had heard a little something about the middle school spit fire. Since Miles was in the favorite age for mob recruitment, Tony took the tough kid under his protective wing. Howard grew up by the time he was seventeen. He was six feet two, two hundred pounds, and had a leathery brown complexion from exposure to the Las Vegas sun. He had a reputation, and The Ant promoted him to be one of his main bodyguards. Howard learned several skills that he would never talk about but which stood him in good stead when he became a U.S. agent.

He was handsome, charismatic; and the girls liked him—probably because of his "bad boy" rep–and he did not act overly modest about it. He had dark brown heavily curled hair which made him look something like a Sicilian, but his size gave him away. Unlike his boss, Tony, Miles preferred to remain in the background and to use the menace of his size and his reputation to get his way instead of the theatrical murderous antics of The Ant. Along the way, Miles gained a few knife and bullet wounds, a crooked nose, some unpleasant facial scars, and considerable wisdom during his education as a junior mobster.

He was saved from a life of crime and its almost inevitable consequences—Tony Spilotro was gunned down—by his first arresting officer, Danny Wiseman, a detective third grade in the LVMPD.

"Sit down, you punk," Wiseman said, and pushed the boy into a hard, straight-back metal chair in the interrogation room after his arrest for punching out an angry pimp who believed The Ant owed him money.

Instead of behaving like a punk, Miles sat down without protest or tough-guy theatrics, and said, "Yes, Sir."

Wiseman studied the young man's tough face for a few minutes, then said, "Listen, Kid, you wanna end up like the rest of these nogoodniks—in the lock-up, have VD, get shivved in prison or shot in the back of the head because some big-shot crime boss thinks you might have ratted?"

Miles pondered for a moment, "Not really, Sir. But what's a have-nuthin' kid like me gonna do…be a punk for some mutt…be a professor at a Ivy League University, maybe?"

He did not ask his question as a usual sardonic and sarcastic up and coming gang banger would. It was more ironic than actually sarcastic, more a genuine question than a comeback.

"That about sums it up, Kid. You go down for this beef, and you'll end up dead in alley with nobody to care the least bit."

"No other choice, right?"

Wiseman drew in a deep breath; and for the first time in his long career in law enforcement, he decided to take a chance.

"Tell ya what, Miles…okay if I call you Miles?"

"Sure, thanks. It's my name. Besides I haven't been a mobster long enough to get a handle that has stuck."

"And that's good. I am willing to take a chance on you. I don't file the arrest and LVMPD felony incident report. You and me, we walk outta here and go to my place for a nice home cooked meal made by my wife. You agree to quit this crap life of yours, and I help you get a decent one. That sound okay with you?"

"I don't know what to say. I was gettin' ready to go into the night's holding cell and have to fight off a bunch of pervs or rival gang bangers. Anything's gotta be better'n that, right?"

"Look, Miles. If all you want is to get out of one line on your record and a free meal, I really don't have much to offer. Think, Boy. I am offering you a way up and out. Make up your mind. Out with me, or back to your nice friend, The Ant. Which is it?"

That decision turned out to be final and live changing. Tony Spilotro and his small gang never learned what happened to their up-and-coming boy. Miles fell in love with big, soft, sweet-hearted Levina Wiseman and the Wiseman's three children. He moved into their spare room, and—for the first time in his life—he became part of a family. He made straight A's his last year in school despite having to make up for the junior year he missed altogether. The Brotherhood of Las Vegas Detectives chose Miles Howard as their project for that year and used their fairly considerable influence to get him into the University of Nevada, Reno on a full scholarship.

The Second World War was approaching, and it took all the influence the BLVD could muster to get him a deferment, a place in the Army ROTC, and with his stellar record, a draft placement as an officer. His first assignment was to attend OCS, and that is where he first encountered the OSS [Office of Strategic Services]. Gen. Donovan himself visited the U. of Nevada on a recruitment mission for his nascent organization of spies and saboteurs.

CHAPTER FOURTEEN

Like all government agencies, the CIA was not created over-night and functioning at full capacity the following morning. In fact, there were various renditions of an intelligence agency for 6 years prior to the formal establishment of the Central Intelligence Agency. At the beginning of World War II America's first peacetime, non-departmental intelligence organization was created. That organization moved and morphed and changed names and ownership, was dissected and dismantled before President Truman signed the National Security Act of 1947 creating a permanent Central Intelligence Agency.

–United States Central Intelligence Agency Web Site Home Page

United States Embassy, Damascus, Syria, March 22, 1949

The OSS was originally formed as an agency of the JCS [Joint Chiefs of Staff] to coordinate espionage activities behind enemy lines for all branches of the United States Armed Forces during WWII. Day-to-day OSS functions included the use of propaganda, subversion, assassination, interrogations, and later, post-war planning. For the duration of World War II, the Office of Strategic Services conducted intelligence collection by spying, turning Nazi personnel into spies against their own country and its military organizations—by inducements, threats, and traps—performing acts of carefully selected sabotage, waging propaganda war, organizing and coordinating anti-Nazi resistance groups in Europe—which is where lieutenant and finally Lieutenant Colonel Miles Howard was largely posted–and providing military training for anti-Japanese guerrilla movements in Asia. At the height of its influence during World War II, and at the approach of the war's end, the OSS employed almost 24,000 people. Miles Howard—by dint of his work ethic, ruthlessness, native intelligence, and modus operandi of personal continuing education—became one of the senior field agents and an important trainer of agents.

Miles learned how to develop an overview of America's enemies. His last posting as an OSS agent was in North Africa and the Levant. He acquired very useful working knowledge of the region, its religions, its main players, and its languages; Arabic—including the Levantine and Mesopotamian dialects, Farsi [Persian], and the North African version of French. He learned and then taught the elements of technology acquired from the Germans to supplement his growing fund of knowledge about American technology and especially American weaponry.

By 1947, when the OSS was officially morphed over to become Truman's Central Intelligence Agency, Miles Howard was in a perfect position to serve in the highest echelons of the emerging overall intelligence service. He knew the ways, means, and people, of the spy world, and was the recognized expert on the labyrinthine clandestine world of the Middle East. He knew where the bodies were buried, who buried them, and what the political machinations were going to be for the next decade.

With all that expertise, Miles was made the chief of station in Damascus under the cover assignment as assistant military attaché–the plum assignment–and probably the most complicated one in all of the spy world in the first two years of the CIA's existence. He knew Shukri al-Quwatly extremely well, including his soft spots. Miles put him into the office of president of Syria, and he could take him out. He and his fellow-agents in the Middle East shared a saying with their counterparts in Afghanistan: "The CIA giveth, and the CIA taketh away. Blessed be the name of the CIA."

He also knew Major General Mohamed Ibriham al-Sham and Colonel Abdullah Faid ibn Nagib of the Syrian Arab Army on both a personal and a professional basis. They shared a mutual distrust and interdependence with one another. For that reason, COS Miles Howard was back in Syria for a crucial meeting with the two Syrian officers who were about to change the direction that Syria was taking.

The meeting in Damascus had been scheduled after the visit of the two Syrians and the ARAMCO CEO present in the PDB. For both convenience and security purposes, the meeting was scheduled to take place in the barracks building of Col. Nagib's special forces unit on the air force base. He had ordered every man in the unit out for the day to set up the stage for a *coup d'etat*.

It was 1030 hours on Tuesday, March 30, 1949. Mike was impressed by the lack of traffic on the streets, and the dearth of military personnel in and around Al-Dumayr Military Airport that morning. Although he knew full well what was afoot, he felt a certain chill that one gets knowing that something eventful is about to take place. The barracks building was empty of its usual army special forces operatives, and the only people present were those involved in the top-secret discussion.

Miles saw Gen. al-Sham and Col. ibn Nagib, CEO Marcus Denali of the Arabian-American Oil Company [ARAMCO] and a small assortment of assistants and secretaries. The only surprise was seeing U.S. Assistant Secretary of State George McGhee, which underscored the importance of the conference.

Gen. al-Sham greeted each member of the group with a warm handshake and a greeting which included a small bit of otherwise unknown intelligence about each man or his family. Thus, he established himself as the leader, and the chair of the coup committee. He had to know that his overt action in making himself the titular leader placed him in lethal danger if the coup should fail.

"Gentlemen, I will dispense with the usual custom of Arab courtesies and will get down to the business at hand since time is running out. As nearly as I can determine, all is in readiness for the regime change. We have six tanks—U.S. M24 Chaffees and newer M41 Walker Bulldogs–on station around Damascus and a wide and significant assortment of materiel from our U.S. allies at the ready. Special forces units are presently moving quietly about the city taking control of key positions including military, governmental, and communications buildings. I have two battalions of loyal regular Syrian Arab Army soldiers in ready reserve in four locations around the periphery of the city. So far, all of this has been entirely secret.

"It is our intent to make this a bloodless *coup d'état*; so, secrecy remains paramount. However, I and my soldiers have both the means and the will to shed blood and take lives as necessary to complete our mission, as Allah wills. The agenda is as follows: Col. ibn Nagib, assistant military attaché, Howard, and I will enter the presidential residence and announce to the weak and shameful al-Quwatly that the coup has been accomplished and offer him to opportunity to save his life and to leave his post immediately. We have military transport ready to escort him away.

"If he attempts to resist or to have his minions resist us, we will take necessary measures. We will all meet back here at the conclusion of the day's events."

No one else felt the need to speak. All actors spread out to play their roles.

Miles and the two army officers traveled directly to the presidential palace and walked in as if they were invited. Four guards started to move forward but stopped and stood at attention as the senior general and well-known army colonel and the frequent visitor to the palace, Mr. Howard, walked past them with a perfunctory nod.

They walked into President al-Quwatly's office without knocking.

The room was empty of people. The beautiful ornate furniture–handcrafted walnut wood and traditional Arabic decorative 19th century Syrian Moorish Mother-of-Pearl *intrasia* ornamentation fitted into hollowed out, dried, and polished walnuts side tables, console, desk, table, throne, and chest, were clean and free of any papers or other documents. The president was gone. The three men looked at each other in bemusement. Had their best laid plans gone agley?

Gen. al-Sham was livid. He stormed out of the office and accosted the palace guards.

"Where is the president? Do not lie to me. Do not inconvenience me. It is imperative that I see him immediately!"

The guards were thoroughly cowed and responded quickly, "He is in hospital. Heart attack or something, Great General."

There was only one hospital in Damascus worthy of consideration—the Khaled Ibn Al Walid. The plotters moved across the city in record time. Cars, lorries, cabs, and pedestrians, fled in all directions from the juggernaut of military vehicles. They had seen this before and knew when to become absent or invisible.

The three men rushed into the hospital.

"Where is the president?" demanded al-Sham peremptorily.

The timid little receptionist shrank back into her hijab and ran her fingers through the pages of admissions.

"He was admitted to room 114, Sir," she managed.

The plotters ran headlong past her, down the hall, and barged into room 114.

President Shukri al-Quwatly was mildly sedated to quiet his heart and had been napping. The commotion at his doorway awakened him abruptly and he sat bolt upright in his over-sized hospital bed. That was a ponderous process given his size and poor physical conditioning.

"Wha…What is the meaning…What is going on?"

He blinked and finally recognized the intruders.

"General al-Sham, what are you doing here? Have you not been informed that I am ill…that it may even be critical? This infernal excitement could do me in. Explain yourself, General; and the explanation had better be a very good one."

The three intruders closed ranks and stood shoulder-to-shoulder for emphasis.

Gen. al-Sham dropped his bomb.

"Shukri," he said deliberately being dismissive and disrespectful. "You are nothing more than Citizen al-Quwatly. You are hereby informed that you have been deposed by *coup d'état*. The army will form an interim government until national elections can be held; this should take place within the year.

"Resistance is futile. Transportation awaits you and will deliver you to your Misr Airlines flight to Cairo. You will be seated in the economy seats and will be served commoners food. Do not come back."

Six rugged special forces noncoms marched into the room and surrounded the stunned former president. Dr. Aymenn ibn Isias rushed into the room and pushed aside the soldiers.

"What is the meaning of this outrage? I am a heart specialist, and this sick man is my patient. He has a bad stomach ulcer and a heart condition. If you drag him out of here, his death will be on your shoulders. I would say on your conscience, but I doubt that you know about such a thing."

Col. ibn Nagib hit the slightly built bespeckled doctor across the face with a vicious backhand so powerful it lifted the defenseless man off his feet. He crumpled to the floor and was rudely kicked out of the path of exit for the former president. A nurse wheeled in an over-sized wheelchair.

"Climb in it, Shukri," Gen. al-Sham ordered, a wicked and threatening glint in his coal black shark's eyes.

Al-Quwatly struggled with only partial success to get to a seated position in his bed and fell back twice before succeeding. He was unable to get to a standing position.

"Throw him into the wheelchair," Gen. al-Sham ordered the senior of the soldiers, SGM Abu Bakr ibn Haq.

Ibn Haq gave a slight nod in the direction of the other noncoms in the squad. They smartly marched to the bedside and ceremoniously lifted the obese man in a chair position and plopped him into the wheelchair.

On his way out, the former president encountered CIA COS Miles Howard and Assistant Secretary of State George McGhee.

Miles gave a him a wan smile and shook his head briefly.

"I warned you Shukri. You chose the Russians. You chose neutrality, and you chose to deny your country a highly valuable petroleum pipeline. Ponder all of that while you bask on an Egyptian beach."

McGhee merely nodded.

Al-Quwatly's parting words–largely lost in the tromping of combat boots and the squeaking of the chair's wheels—were directed at general, "And, Gentlemen, let us all try and guess the name of the next president."

At 0530 hours the following morning, immediately after *muezzin* sounded the *aazan* for the call to *salat* and intoned the *fajr* [the dawn prayer], the citizens of Damascus were treated to a shrill, all-consuming fire emergency level siren that split the air for three minutes. The second the siren's screaming died out, the Syrian national anthem, *"Ḥumāt ad-Diyār"–Guardians of the Homeland,* blasted their ears three times in close succession. Immediately following that series of wake-up calls, the unmistakable voice of Major General Mohamed Ibriham al-Sham filled the airway.

"My brothers and sisters bonded in blood and loyalty for our beloved al-Sham, and in the name of God, the Compassionate, the Merciful, who has forbidden oppression to Himself, and made it forbidden among His servants, and may blessings be upon his Prophet SAWS—[*sallallahu alayhi wa salaam*–may God's prayers and peace be with him], I announce with humility and respect that I, Major General Mohamed Ibriham al-Sham, have answered the call of the people and the parliament and cabinet to become president of the great nation of Syria. I pledge to you a new day of peace, prosperity, and security. We will draw ever closer to our good friends and stand against those who would oppress us. Very soon, we will bring a visible economic miracle to pass for all our citizens. Rejoice my friends, the tyrant has fled to his chosen homeland of Egypt. We will not see him nor his like again."

The full speech was repeated on a rolling sound tape for the next twenty-four hours. Syrian Arab Republic Radio played it most of the day only interrupted by the anthem and laudatory national and international figures including congratulations from the U.S. Ambassador and a short comment by President Truman, himself. The state-controlled newspapers had two-inch headlines and the entire paper was dedicated to printed articles praising the new "savior of Syria" and the "great new clean breath of the nation."

On May 16, as promised, Ibriham al-Sham approved ARAMCO's TAPLINE. Two weeks later he outlawed the Communist Party and banned all activities and propaganda speaking in favor of the U.S.S.R., its leaders, or news coming from or about the communist nations. Al-Sham next arrested and jailed hundreds of left-wing dissidents and sympathizers and executed dozens for anti-Syrian activities. At the end of June, he abolished the parliament and his cabinet and garnered all power to himself. In July, he signed a Syro-Israeli armistice to the hurrahs in the Zionist, European, and Israeli media. A promise that the U.S. Congress would grant swift approval of $200 million dollars in military and economic aid came from his old friend, Miles Howard, who was speaking for his "higher-ups."

However, on August 14, al Sham was overthrown by Col. Sami Hinnawi. and summarily executed. On December 19, 1949, Col. Adib Shishakli ousted Hinnawi in Syria's third coup in nine months. Chargé d'affaires Harold Cunningham cabled Washington in late November reasoning that "if the U.S. is to profit from the results of the latest coup, it will be necessary...to show Shishakli how and when we can help him." The State Department and the seventh floor of the Langley CIA building collected a mountain of testimonies and objective evidence and finally won Pentagon approval. The decision was admittedly political, not military, or security based. It was even questionable if it was wise in terms of American economic interests.

It often takes the DOD and the Pentagon weeks or months to decide difficult and complex matters; but within mere days of consultations in late December, DOD signed off on an early delivery to Syria of a useful, but limited amount of selected military materiel which would not arouse the ire of the rest of the Middle East or of our allies. The absolute goal was to walk close to the edge, but to avoid even the most remote chance of open conflict. The Cold War was in full swing; the Korean war between American and Russian surrogates was like water for chocolate—likely to boil over at any moment.

Finally, in late 1952, Harry Truman and his administration pressed the World Bank to expedite Syria's request for a $200 million loan. Things were going swimmingly and just about to be finalize to the satisfaction of all signatories. Before they could reach a date to sign a formal deal on an arms package, Col. Shishakli was overthrown in still another army-orchestrated coup on February 25, 1954. The Communist Party–whose membership had been decimated down to half its numbers before Shishakli appeared on the scene, and whose leaders had been driven underground by the ruthless dictator—correctly saw the coup as the first step toward a national front with the Ba'athists and others opposed to Western influence.

On August 12, 1957, the Syrian Arab Army surrounded the U.S. embassy in Damascus despite the announcement on September 8, 1944, by Syrian Minister of Foreign Affairs, Jamil Mardam Bey, that Syria fully recognized and would protect existing rights of the United States and its nationals. The 1957 affront to the United States came directly from the Chief of the Army claiming that his army had aborted a CIA plot to overthrow the neutralist President in the last few minutes before the disastrous coup could be finalized. Once again, the army came to the rescue of the country—the army said.

The generals installed a new regime under Syrian Chief of Counter-intelligence Abdul Hamid Sarraj. He promptly expelled three U.S. diplomats, jailed dozens of American and pro-Western Syrian officers, and made highly visible moves to bring the country closer to Moscow. By the end of August, the U.S., Turkey, and Iraq, considered taking an action that could have escalated into a full-scale, Soviet-U.S. confrontation.

Although wiser heads in all those countries finally prevailed, great damage was done to American/Syrian and more general Middle East relations. This fifth abortive CIA coup plot in eight years capped nearly a decade of covert U.S. meddling in Syria.

The Arab Socialist Ba'ath Party patiently awaited its turn. Hafez al-Assad became the secretary of the Syrian Regional Command of the party in 1970 and Secretary General of the National Command in late 1970. His son, Bashar al-Assad, became the Regional Secretary of the party in Syria after his father's death in 2000 which gave him the same dictatorial power enjoyed by his father until his death. Opposition to Bashar al-Assad helped to lead to the current ongoing Syrian Civil War, the growth of a multitude of Islamic extremist entities, and finally to the establishment of the Islamic State—the much-vaunted Caliphate. The United States remains committed to its original reason for involvement in Bashar's Syria—to effect regime change.

The legacy was like that in Central and South America: decades of creating "Banana Republic Leaders" around the restive and poverty-stricken world, imposition of American business greed on struggling developing countries, and lasting hatred for America and Americans even though many of the ventures attempted by Americans were well-meaning. The key to the failures was the atmosphere of secrecy that ruled the behavior of U.S. diplomats, soldiers, intelligence agencies, and missionaries.

In each case of failure, the CIA's involvement was spread abroad, and the agency became a hiss and a byword in Syria ever afterward. In October, 2010, *Reporters Without Borders* ranked Syria 173rd out of 178 countries in the world on the *Press Freedom Index.*

PROLOGUE II

Viet Nam: The 1ˢᵗ Indochinese War [the French War; Franco-Vietminh War, the Anti-French Resistance War]

CHAPTER ONE

"Die Luft der Freiheit weht." [better rendered in Latin, *"Videtis illiam spirare Libertatas auram*—the wind of freedom blows."]
–David Starr Jordan, First president of Stanford University. Motto on original Stanford seal. The German version prevailed when the seal was standardized and made official in 2003.

Oval Office, White House, Washington D.C., United States of America, March 12, 1945

President Roosevelt returned from the exhausting eight-day Yalta Conference—some called it the Crimea Conference, and in the secret files, it was code-named the Argonaut Conference—in the Crimea. The travel itself drained the ailing president, but the cerebral and verbal jousting with the other two great egos in the meeting—British Prime Minister Winston Churchill and U.S.S.R. Premier Joseph Stalin—had sapped his energy down to the dregs. The president had not touched his favorite dish, scrambled eggs and fish chowder—the old Fairhaven recipe. He sat with his aides and full-time loyal staff of men and women devoted to domestic and foreign policies—Assistant to the President and Personal Secretary, Marguerite "Missy" LeHand, The Gate Keeper; his Secretary of State, Edward R. Stettinius, Jr.; his Secretary of the Treasury, Henry Morgenthau, Jr.; Roosevelt's old friend, Chairman of the

Joint Chiefs of Staff, Admiral William D. Leahy; and his close personal friend and adviser, "Deputy President" Harry L. Hopkins, intermittently squeezing his temples with his fingers, stroking the ears of his favorite Scottish terrier, Fala–Murray the Outlaw of Fala Hill–and working for breath. His doctor, Admiral Dr. Ross McIntire, had diagnosed him with hypertension—but assured him and the American public that a man of his age needed that much blood pressure to push blood through his atherosclerotic arteries, and that he was only suffering from fatigue, nothing a short vacation in Warm Springs, Georgia wouldn't set aright.

General of the Army, George C. Marshall, reported on recent events and decisions related to the partition of Europe, the encroachments of Stalin from the East, and the continuing nagging complaints from France's egotistical new president, Charles de Gaulle.

"Mr. President, the issue with President de Gaulle is coming to a head. You did not invite him to the Tehran Conference, or to the Argonaut Conference. The Berlin Conference of the Three Heads of Government of the U.S.S.R, U.S.A., and U.K. is coming shortly. He is very angry and feels hurt that he has not been included in the meetings. He insists that his exclusion is personal on your part and that France is being disrespected."

President Roosevelt was too tired to prevent his anger and grouchiness from surfacing.

"So, let's be open about it. I do not like that arrogant sniveler— Charles André Joseph Marie de Gaulle."

Roosevelt fairly spat out the French President's name in a sarcastic mincing tone.

"He wants to be invited to the Moscow conference and to have a revision of the two preceding ones to which he was not invited. He wants his fiefdom in Indo-China returned to him with American military help. He is not going to get either. Those people in Cambodia, Viet Nam, and Laos have had enough of colonization. Let them be free, I say. There is an old saying from Rome; I forget the author, "*Videtis illiam spirare Libertatas auram*—the wind of freedom blows." I won't contribute a penny or a Frank or a single American soldier, to France to keep them in their overlord position. That is final," the president said in his rather unique half-English/Yankee mid-Atlantic dialect common among members of the U.S. diplomatic corps and senior level older people at the upper crust levels of his well-to-do Eastern social set.

"Do you not fear the Communist threat, Mr. President, the domino theory, in the region?"

"Of course, I do," the president barked irritably, his famous tenor voice rising in decibel and pitch to near strident soprano, "Maybe I dislike de Gaulle some less than I do Stalin, but I still have no intention of the French returning to the status quo in Indochina. I intend to shore up the Vietnamese government and to get the best people in the country to leave the North and move down to Saigon. In fact, I have found just the man to do it for us. He is in the intelligence department; and likely, none of you have heard of him. His name is Parker Leary Granston. He is an air force intelligence officer who served in the OSS [Office of Strategic Services]. He comes highly recommended by General William J. Donovan from the OSS and General John W. O'Daniel. We are going to win the hearts and minds of the Vietnamese, and we are going to do it quietly. This the very man for that project."

President Roosevelt was too weary to argue with anybody, especially his formidable wife, Eleanor.

"Franklin, we are going to Warm Springs, Georgia forthwith; or I am convinced you will not live out the month. Even Harry and Bess think you are in serious need of a rest and recuperation vacation. I won't take no for an answer."

Roosevelt smiled at his determined dynamo of a wife and said, "Yes, Boss-Eleanor, I believe you are right. Let's leave the first of next week and stay a month."

"Wonderful, King-Franklin, I have already made all of the arrangements."

"Of course you have, my dear, Lady Bountiful, of course you have."

The vacation trip to the Warm Springs Little White House did not go well. First of all—at the president's insistence—Eleanor's secretary, Lucy Mercer Rutherfurd, a beautiful and refined woman—in contrast to Eleanor's famous lack of good looks—who was also Roosevelt's great long-term love, came along over Eleanor's protests. She was there despite Eleanor having long before found incriminating letters that had passed between the two illicit lovers and Franklin's promise not to write to or see her again.

His health deteriorated steadily, until he had to take to his bed. Despite every effort to bring him back to his former vigorous, arrogant, purposeful self, Franklin Delano Roosevelt suffered a massive cerebral hemorrhage after sitting for a watercolor portrait and died on April 12, 1945 at the age of sixty-three.

Harry S. Truman became president of the United States on the same day, amidst profound concern throughout the political world about his capacity for world or even national leadership. He was—according to the prevailing attitude among American commoners, and politicians—untutored in foreign affairs and knew nothing about the complex diplomacy of his great predecessor.

For Vice-President Harry Truman–who inherited the presidency–it was a shocking and unwelcome experience. He inherited all the burdens Roosevelt had borne in his secretive mind. Truman, for example, learned of the Manhattan Project for the first time upon "The Boss's" death. Truman was no shrinking violet for all his quiet acceptance of the obscurity of the vice-presidency. He had a sense of humor and appreciated what one of his predecessor's, Thomas Marshall–the twenty-eighth vice president, who served under Woodrow Wilson from 1913 to 1921–had to say about the vice-presidency: "Once there were two brothers. One ran away to sea; the other was elected vice president of the United States. And nothing was heard of either of them again."

Truman rose to the occasion, at the Potsdam Conference—as the Berlin Conference was renamed–which he attended in occupied Germany along with the Soviet Union, the United Kingdom, and the United States, represented respectively by Communist Party General Secretary Joseph Stalin, Prime Ministers Winston Churchill, and Clement Attlee, and Truman, and conspicuously, not by de Gaulle. In the lovely pre-war mansion, the heads of the allied states decided how to administer Germany. The defeated Nazi nation had agreed to unconditional surrender nine weeks earlier on VED, May 8, 1945. The original goals of the conference also included the establishment of postwar order, peace treaty issues, and countering the effects of the war—none of which were fully recognized or implemented later.

Truman decided that Roosevelt–for all his prodigious brilliance, creativity, and stern patience, during the horrors of the depression and the war–was overly romantic and soft in some areas, especially in Indochina, despite his strong resistance to de Gaulle. He summoned Lt. Col. Parker Leary Granston to his office.

Col. Granston was ill-at-ease with his call to the White House. He especially did not relish any job with high public exposure. He was at heart a spy–after all–and one who wanted nothing more than to do his job and to work his magic behind the lines and away from the cameras where his specialty of ingratiating the native insurgents could take place without interference from the W.O.M.s of Washington. At the appointed hour—the appointed minute, in fact–Matthew J. Connelly, the punctilious appointments secretary, showed Granston into the Oval Office.

"Have a seat, Colonel. I'll be right with you after I sign a few more of these infernal pieces of paper-work," the president said from behind the seven-foot-long, time-worn, fire-scarred, and repainted, Theodore Roosevelt desk.

While President Truman grumbled and signed, Granston looked with amusement at the sign on his desk, "The Buck Stops Here."

There were two other men seated in the room. The younger of the two sat silently and expressionless on a padded armchair, his feet fixed flat on the floor. He was thin and had advanced balding which created a wide cleavage of still dark-brown hair down the middle of his scalp. His wide-set intelligent eyes took in the newcomer at a glance then resumed their blank forward fixation, indicating that he was deep in thought. He wore a faintly striped grey three-piece suit, a perfectly starched white shirt, and his Princeton University school tie which was tied in a perfect double Windsor knot. Like the other man, George Kennan, he wore recently polished black wing-tipped Florsheim shoes.

The older of the two other men in the Oval Office with Granston was immediately recognized by him. He was Edward Reilly Stettinius Jr., President Truman's Secretary of State, and apparently the younger man's superior in rank. He sat with his legs crossed in a relaxed posture. Stettinius was a robust handsome man in a rugged sort of way. He had heavy black eyebrows and a full head of snowy white hair—prematurely so. He wore a tailored grey pin-striped suit with unfashionably wide collars, a white shirt, and a polka-dot dark-blue tie with an asymmetric single knot tie. He took brief notice of Cranston, gave him a brief nod of recognition, and went back to his own thoughts.

President Truman looked up from his work, set down his pen, and stepped out from his desk to introduce Lt. Col. Granston to the diplomats.

"Colonel, I have the pleasure to introduce my secretary of state, E. R. Stettinius and George F. Kennan, the smartest guy in the room and one of Secretary Stettinius's 'Wise Men.' He is deputy chief of mission in Moscow. He has some very interesting opinions. I would like you to hear him out, because his concepts are pretty much what I want you to carry out on the ground in the new position I have in mind for you.

Kennan shook Granston's hand, then began to speak.

"French Indochina, as I am sure you are well aware, includes Cambodia, Laos, Tonkin, Annam, and Cochin China. All attention has been been centered on the ghastly world war—which has just come to an end. Gen. Patton predicted that Stalin and his communist bloc would become our enemies for World War III, and there is real truth to that prediction. It is my studied opinion that the bulk of our efforts as a country must be to put a stop to Stalin's avaricious drive for world domination. We must not make the same mistake we did in underestimating Hitler back in '36 and '37. Nor, Gentlemen, should we underestimate Mao Tse Tung, Stalin's counterpart in China. While I am not so sure that China wishes to have complete world domination as did the German, Hitler, and now the Russian, Stalin; but he does intend to dominate all of Asia and to turn it into a communist sphere of interest. It is of paramount importance that we do all in our power to keep any of that from happening.

"Contrary to the opinion of our late and revered President Roosevelt, we must use the French to hold back the Viet Minh and therefore the march of communism down the Vietnamese peninsula. The French are almost at the end of their tether there. Without us, they will crumble; and we can't let that happen. It is my opinion—and that of my university and political confreres—that we should employ a long-term enervate and weaken approach to the problem, unlike the set battle mind-set of the recent great war.

"First, prop up the French. Second, enhance the strength of the odious—but useful—Diem regime in southern Viet Nam to hold back the onslaught of the Chinese and Russian supported northern Vietnamese factions. Third, we must not appear to be overtly thwarting the Chinese or Russians, but rather to be supporting the rightful government of Viet Nam and the French armed forces who are already entrenched in that unfortunate land. While I share our late president's aversion to the French as politicians, I believe it is in the best interests of America to support de Gaulle and to do it clandestinely.

"You come highly recommended, Lieutenant Colonel Granston. We believe you and your crew of CIA operatives can be of inestimable help. Elections are coming to establish a new presidency for the country. We will have the old malefactor–Diem–be elected, by hook or crook. We want you in country to help make that happen. We also need for you to counter-mand the beginning fall of the dominoes—so's to speak—in Cochin, China by going off to Hanoi, but only in a very quiet and unheralded way."

Granston interrupted, "Sir, exactly what would my marching orders be."

President Truman answered that question, "First, you will be dropped into the Hanoi area where you will get people from our side of the ideological spectrum living there–especially the Catholics–to leave the north and make their way back south in time to vote for the right candidates. The election is coming soon; so, you have your work cut out for you. Ho Chi Minh has to see the Catholics flocking down into the south. Diem is a catholic, and we can count on them to vote for him. The result may be a divided country, but anything is better than a completely communist one. Do you accept the assignment, Colonel?"

"Yes, Sir, Mr. President. Will I have free reign?"

"Pretty much. You will answer to Rear Admiral Sidney Souers, head of the CIG [Central Intelligence Group], destined to become the first Director of Central Intelligence in 1947 when the agency is created, and to me of course, but find a way to get the job done and do it. I won't get in your way."

Truman was a man of his word, by moral suasion and by pragmatic necessity. After abruptly being thrust into assumption of the presidency, the new president asked all the members of Roosevelt's cabinet to remain in place. For a president with all the power and prestige appertaining to that office, the man from Missouri informed the sitting cabinet members that he would remain open to their collective and individual advice. While his door would always be open to them, he made it clear that there was a central principle of his administration: he would listen to all sides of questions; but he would be the one making decisions; and they were to support him in unity. The secret appointment of Lt. Col. Granston was one decision that only he and a couple of other men would know about for decades.

Granston replied crisply, "Aye, aye, Sir," and was dismissed.

The following day, he boarded a pre-production Y-R4D-Douglas navy transport plane for Tan Son Nhut Republic of Vietnam Air Force facility in Saigon along with a small, tightly knit coterie of hand-picked fellow spies and an impressive load of equipment he deemed necessary to complete his assignment.

Four days later, he and his men occupied separate rooms in the small Flowers of Springtime Hotel overlooking Hanoi's Ba Dinh Square.

CHAPTER TWO

"Your statesmen make eloquent speeches about . . . self-determination. We are self-determined. Why not help us? Am I any different from . . . your George Washington?"
–Ho Chi Minh, a comment to unnamed
U.S. OSS agents, Mid-July, 1945, Paul Mus,
Viêt-Nam: Sociologie d'une Guerre, 1952

"I can conceive of no greater tragedy than for the United States to become involved in an all-out war in Indochina."
–President Dwight D. Eisenhower, Press Conference,
February 10, 1954

Hanoi, Viet Nam, September 5, 1945

In early march, 1945, an OSS agent—whose name is unknown–met Ho Chi Minh in Kunming, China. Since their short-term goals were very much the same, the American and the Vietnamese negotiated only briefly over fragrant rice and Shaoxing, a strong flavored, caramel-colored, Chinese rice wine used to make savory dishes like drunken chicken. Given the fact that the two men came from opposite sides of the planet, had two different and diametrically opposed world views and sociopolitical ideologies, it was more than remarkable what they achieved. They struck a simple and implementable deal. The OSS agreed to equip the Viet Minh with radios and some light arms. Ho's Viet Minh agreed to give the OSS intelligence, harass Japanese forces, and try to rescue

American pilots shot down over Viet Minh-controlled territory to the degree possible.

Lt. Col. Granston met with Ho at the communist leader's request.

"President Ho, it is an honor to meet with you, Sir. How may I be of assistance?"

Ho was sick: feverish, had shaking chills, and his eyes were sunken. He shivered uncontrollably.

"Mr. Smith, I have been given your particulars. I need to have your OSS to parachute in a load of supplies. The Japanese are harassing us severely around Lao Cai. As you probably know that beautiful little city is located in the mountainous northwest, at the intersection of the Red and Nanxi Rivers just across from the Chinese border. You can well imagine that the proximity to our friends–the PRC–makes this something of a delicate matter."

"Certainly, Mr. President. I will make the communications. If you don't mind me saying so, you appear to be unwell. With your permission, I will have doctors, nurses, and medicines flown in as well."

"That would be most kind and most appreciated, Mr. Smith."

Granston returned to his hotel and had his radioman, Clem Atkins, convey the message, indicating it was urgent since Ho was in danger of dying from what was obviously advanced stage malaria. Less than a week later, twenty-two OSS agents parachuted into the beautiful mountains near Lao Cai in an obscure location on the Nanxi River. Granston met them and used his facilities to rush quinine–an ancient drug used to treat malaria from as early as the seventeenth century made from the bark of the cinchona–quina-quina—tree to Ho. It was introduced into Viet Nam by the French and was known to the Vietnamese as "Jesuits' bark," "cardinal's bark," or "sacred bark." The OSS and the Viet Minh—led by Ho Chi Minh, whose health returned to normal–fought side-by-side and drove out the Japanese from their last remaining stronghold.

Granston's next visit with Ho in early September found the wispy wraith of a man to be back in the peak of health, and the leader of a nation that had defeated the Japanese and had driven the hated Nipponese from the peninsula. Ho was at one of the peaks of his long struggle against outsiders who would occupy and rule his country against the will of nearly every Vietnamese person in the country. His popularity was soaring.

"Mr. Smith," said Ho—who knew perfectly well that "Smith" was a clumsy *nom de guerre*—I have you and your country to thank for my good health and for the assistance in ridding our land of the hated Japanese."

"You are most welcome, Sir."

"Mr. Smith, I am indeed grateful, but you must always remember that I am a Vietnamese first and always, a communist second, and a friend of America's as long as my country is treated in a friendly and respectful way. Because of your help and personal concern, let me say this with emphasis: if America elects to support the French against my country, you must leave immediately. I will not be able to guarantee your safety if you insist on staying here."

Granston knew full well that Truman was going to support the French because the president's overarching policy was to halt the progression of communism everywhere. Viet Nam was the latest and most obvious center of that attention. In August, the Japanese surrendered unconditionally to the Allies, and vacated Viet Nam to the control of Ho Chi Minh and his Viet Minh forces. Bao Dai–the puppet of the Japanese, and the last emperor of Viet Nam—abdicated; and Ho, and his guerrillas moved into Hanoi. On September 2, 1945, Ho and his communist followers established the Democratic Republic of Vietnam with Hanoi as its capital. Lt. Col. Granston and his CIG cadres remained in Hanoi just long enough to witness the creation of the new nation and the attendant jubilation among the long-oppressed populace.

Granston understood the takeover of Hanoi to be only the beginning of the communist onslaught; so, he and his men left Hanoi in the middle of the night and headed for the Catholic enclaves in the south. They had good intel gleaned over their months in the northern half of rapidly dividing Viet Nam. The main crew hurried to the Catholic concentrations in Hai Phong, Hung Hoa, Lan Son, Cao Bang, Phat Diem, Thai Binh, Thanh Hoa, Vinh, and Ha Tinh. They spread a gospel of approaching doom for Roman Catholics and for the oppressed priests.

The oppression began as far back as the early 1800s when Emperor Minh Mang placed restrictions on Catholicism which he considered to be a quasi-occupying force from France. The emperor enacted "edicts of interdiction of the Catholic religion," and, in fact, on all forms of Christianity which he branded as heterodox doctrine. A revolt resulted which was quelled with draconian measures by the imperial government.

Christian towns and villages and their religious buildings were destroyed. The personal possessions of the citizens of whole cities were confiscated. Families were violently broken apart. Many of the devout were subjected to branding on the forehead with *ta dao*, [false religion]. More stringent restrictions were imposed; missionaries were hunted mercilessly; and missionaries and priests were executed—often in vengeful and dire ways—in order to eradicate what he considered to be a source of division in his peaceful country. 130,000 to 300,000 Christians died in the various persecutions of Minh Mang, and he became the archetypal bogey-man ever afterwards.

Granston's men hurried from diocese to diocese spreading alarm among the already fearful Catholics. Ho Chi Minh became the new Minh Mang, and he was once again relentlessly seeking out the long-suffering Catholics. They sometimes dressed as priests and told the quavering congregations in the chapels and cathedrals that priests and nuns were being murdered, crucified, or burned at the stake in a sweep coming from north to south towards the very town in which that day's speech was being given.

South Vietnamese soldiers dressed in peasant clothing and mingled among the already frightened people telling them that "Uncle Ho's" godless communists resorted to making a pact-with-the-devil–Vietnam's traditional mortal enemy China. Even as they were having this conversation, two People's Liberation Army divisions had been invited to invade the north from across the Red River. Even more shocking to the simple and innocent peasants was the fabrication that the oncoming Chinese heathens were doing their raping and pillaging with the open approval of the traitorous north Vietnamese communists.

Granston, himself, sneaked across the 17th parallel and was picked up by a U.S. army convoy and taken to Saigon for several days of clandestine meetings with the U.S.'s choice to become South Vietnam's next prime minister–Roman Catholic Ngo Dinh Diem–from among others vying for the lucrative position–the three sects—the Cao Dai, the Hoa Hao, and the Binh Xuyen, each of which had its own army. The most prominent and vexing was the prominent general Trinh Minh Thé. Diem was an ingratiating sort; and he and Granston quickly took to each other; but like two attorneys shaking hands with crossed fingers on the unseen hands nullifying any promises. Ngo—patriot that he was–sipped several glasses of sugar cane Mekong whiskey, and Granston settled for a Coke and a couple of Butter-finger candy bars which had not been available to him for months.

After the requisite inanities about the sweltering heat in the city and especially in the Mekong Delta and about the recent tasty gourmet imports from Paris, Granston felt it was finally time to get to the point.

"Ngo, my friend, how goes the election preparations? Are the devils gaining on you?"

Ngo pondered the question for a moment.

"It is far from a sure thing, Parker. I'm sure you know that. Do you have anything to suggest, my friend?"

"Are you seeing any influx of Catholics across the DMZ—enough to make a difference at the polls?"

"Some of my co-religionists are dribbling across, but not nearly enough. What more can we do?"

"I think the Company might be able to help. We need some printing done. Can you push your government printers to get out some materials we have been looking at? We think we have an information program that has promise."

"A little printing is no problem. Hold on, and I will get hold of my secretary."

Ngo made two calls, then turned back to Granston.

"Done. You make up the materials you want printed, and you will have them at the end of the day ready for travel."

Although Granston was able to keep any smile of his face, Ngo caught a glimpse and began to laugh.

"You had everything ready to go, didn't you, Parker, you wily rascal? Well, I'll get back to running my part of the country; and you can get your "information" materials to the printer. Here's his address."

Granston left. He walked out of Diem's office thoughtfully chewing on his second Oh Henry bar of the day and got a pedi-cab back to his hotel. He gathered up the templates that had been so carefully made by the counterfeiters in Langley three weeks previously and got another ride—this time to the Nguyen Family Printing Enterprise.

That evening while Granston, Ngo Dinh Diem, and French Generals Andre Trancart and Christian de Castries were enjoying a sumptuous

French dinner in the Hotel Continental, the eldest son of the Nguyen printers family approached their table deferentially.

Granston looked at the man and cocked his left eyebrow.

"Materials ready and in family warehouse, Great Sir."

"Thank you. I will pick them up early tomorrow morning."

There was no discussion of payment. That would have been grossly impolite. Granston had a very good reputation—one that greased the skids in many of his clandestine deals in Viet Nam. Trust made things so much easier, a lesson Granston had learned early in his covert career.

By the light of a hand-held lantern the next morning, Granston inspected what he had commissioned. There were real appearing Viet Minh leaflets giving the communist soldiers instructions on what to do when dealing with the subjugated peoples with whom they were dealing. First, they were to have the head of the family write out a comprehensive list of all the family's material possessions.

The pamphlets did not state in so many words that the list would make it simplicity itself for the communists to expropriate all the family's goods with minimal effort—the further unstated goal of fomenting peasant anger and sense of futility that would persuade one more Catholic family to abandon the north for the south of Vietnam. Other pamphlets looked more formal and less indirect: they were orders to the NVA soldiers to take possession of all the belongings of persons deemed to be Catholics or other persons known to be in opposition to the government.

There were folksy pamphlets from the Central Evacuation Committee in Haiphong—a secretly American-funded group claiming that for those who left the north to live in the free region of South Vietnam, the cost of living would be three times less and that there would be welfare payments and free rice lands for the first five years after emigration. That particular pamphlet concluded that "If you and your family remain in the Wicked North you will soon come to know famine as never before. The Holy Church directs you to leave as soon as you possibly can. If you do not, the Church will damn your souls. Leave now, my Catholic brothers and sisters!" Other leaflets purported to be secret news transmissions from far northern families to more southerly—and more Catholic—families that Chinese PLA soldiers were using mass rape as a weapon and hunting down priests, deacons, and nuns like so many rabid dogs in order to exterminate them.

Granston and his fellow spies evaluated the results of the propaganda campaign and found that within three weeks the names of families registering with the Central Evacuation Committee in Haiphong almost quadrupled, despite everything in the pamphlets being complete fabrications by the CIA.

Lt. Col. Granston returned to the Cao Bang and Phat Diem sectors of what was now all but formally known as North Vietnam—technically, the Democratic Republic of Viet Nam—as covertly as he had left the region two weeks earlier. He and all his agents donned priestly frocks and began distributing the pamphlets in earnest and were gratified by the effect that the falsified information was having. Knowing the division into north and south Vietnam was soon going to be a reality, Granston energized his spy group to hasten the exodus to as large a level as could be achieved in the time remaining.

Ho Chi Minh's victorious assumption of power in Hanoi proved to be short lived. In December, 1946, the French reoccupied Hanoi, and turned an unpleasant and difficult relationship between the French and the Vietnamese communists into an all-out war that lasted eight grueling years. The French and Ho Chi Minh's followers looked at the same facts with diametrically opposite conclusions.

From the French point of view, they were the loving benefactors of a benighted country. Largely through the persuasive efforts by French Catholic missionaries starting in the mid-nineteenth century, the French vigorously worked to introduce and to integrate Western culture, education, and the Catholic religion. They were the first to bring Christianity to what they considered to be a backward pagan country. Although they benefitted from their introduction of modern capitalism by creating a vigorous exportation of tobacco, indigo, tea, and coffee, France maintained a net negative profit balance over the years of colonialism. Frenchmen from time to time requested of the government that the nation leave its Cochinchina colonies as unprofitable.

By then, Viet Nam had become very nearly a French province. Aspiring bright young Vietnamese attended local French controlled schools in the colony, and they were freely accepted into French universities for advanced educations. When insurgents complained that they were being dominated and badly treated by the colonizing and occupying nation of

France, the proponents of continuing colonization—most notably Charles de Gaulle—were affronted that their altruism was going unappreciated.

Viet Nam had endured a thousand years of occupation and domination by Imperial China which left an indelible social and cultural imprint on Vietnamese culture. Nevertheless, the Vietnamese were inherently nationalistic and proud of their own culture. They finally drove out the hated Chinese. Communist nationalists/insurgents felt very much the same way about domination on the part of France.

Contrary to the French opinion about their colony being managed as an altruistic gift of France, the nationalists took painful note of the many brutal incidents associated with disagreements which took place with growing frequency by the French provincial government. These practices included citizens often being held in prison for long periods without being charged, where they died from malaria, tuberculosis, or malnutrition. The French became infamous for such barbarities as roping dissenters together and throwing them into the sea to drown.

The Second World War unhinged the *Ancien Régime* and greatly weakened France. The war invited Japan in as a new and extraordinarily vicious and brutal dictatorship and heightened the movement among even noncommunists to be free once and for all from foreign domination. The French *Armée coloniale* returned to a much more nationalistic oriented country. The *Armée* lost its long-maintained reputation as a strict professional armed force providing law, order, and security, for the citizens of Viet Nam, and gained a reputation of sadism and arbitrary favoritism for the rich French plantation owners.

U.S. President Truman and his successor, Dwight D. Eisenhower, favored the French position over that of the insurgents, mainly because of the strongly held opinion that Ho Chi Minh and his Viet Minh rebels were communists who represented a future existential threat to America. Neither president—however—had much in the way of affection for the old European colonial system, especially that of de Gaulle's France. American assistance to France was limited, sporadic, and generally parsimonious. The government and citizens of the United States became increasingly less enamored with the French position during the First Indochinese War as the French slowly lost to a peasant army. With all its complexities, the culmination of eight years of war came in 1954 in a small city in the hill country of northwestern Vietnam—Dien Bien Phu.

CHAPTER THREE

"Underestimation of nonconventional units or a guerrilla enemy by regular forces is a cardinal military sin."

–Howard R. Simpson, *Dien Bien Phu: The Epic Battle America Forgot*, by Hardcover, Brassey's, Inc., May 1,1994

"I should lay it down that the existence of secret agents should not be tolerated as tending to augment the evil against which they are used...But in the sphere of political and revolutionary action, relying on violence, the professional spy has every facility to fabricate the facts themselves, and will spread the double evil of emulation in one direction, and of panic, hasty legislation, unreflecting hate, in the other. However, this is an imperfect world."

–Joseph Conrad, *The Secret Agent*, Methuen Publishing, UK, 1907

French Embassy, Boulevard Gambetta, Hanoi, Viet Nam, February 3, 1954

Lt. Col. Granston was the only American and the lowest ranking person in the banquet hall of the French Embassy in Hanoi that February evening. The occasion was the celebration of the birthday of the most recent commander of the French Union Forces in Indochina, Henri

Navarre. After standing and saluting the Tricolor while the *Marseilles* was performed by the regimental band, the highly decorated *Général de corps d'armée* Navarre—holder of two separate *Croix de guerres*, the *Médaille de la Résistance* with rosette, and the Distinguished Service Cross from the United States, was toasted with several rounds of Veuve Clicquot. The expensive champagne was served from a gala of wide coup glasses by the mayor, by General Charles Piroth, the artillery commander, and lastly by Granston, who—by default–represented the United States of America. This evening was the first time Granston had worn his full-dress air force uniform complete with medals in over a decade.

After three rounds of *hourras*, Navarre rose to speak.

"Gentlemen, I will be brief in keeping with the joyful occasion we are enjoying here in this beautiful and quintessentially French old colonial building. I salute Mother France."

There were more "*hourra!, hourra!, hourra!*s from the standing and saluting officers.

Navarre went on, "I have been given a precise mission by Premier Mayer: create military conditions that will lead to an honorable political solution. I interpret that as being to leave Vietnam with pride and honor and not in defeat. In order to do that, we must establish—once-and-for-all—respect for French might and will."

He then set forward his tactical plan: find a single defensible location with the appropriate qualities and lure the Viet Minh army into a classical set-battle similar to those by which France had defeated the Nazis in World War II.

"My scouts at the suggestion of Major General René Cogny–the commander of the Tonkin Delta–proposed Dien Bien Phu, which has an old airstrip built by the Japanese during World War II, and with the help of our American friend here, I have made the final selection of Dien Bien Phu as that location. After dinner, we will retire to see on the map where that small city is located and why it was selected. We will begin in earnest to develop a defensive battle plan which will so cripple the Viet Minh that they will be unable to prevent our graceful and honorable departure from this troubled land. We will avoid asking for assistance by our stubborn allies—the Americans—unless we find ourselves in extremis. Then, once again, we will make use of the remarkable resources of our friend here the "military attaché."

The men chuckled quietly. Everyone knew that Granston was the chief of station of the CIA even if no one from the U.S., France, or Viet Nam, said it out loud.

The dinner would have been sumptuous anywhere or at any time. Given the wartime conditions, it was nothing short of extraordinary. It began with lovely Vietnamese girls floating through the room in body-hugging white *ao dais* to deliver Vietnamese delicacies as appetizers. On silver platters, there were small cups of Hanoi's rich culinary traditions. The embassy culinary staff had gone to considerable lengths to present many of Vietnam's most famous dishes: *pho bo* and *pho ga, cha ca, banh cuon,* and *com,* which originated in Hanoi, and Granston's favorite, *bun cha*–a savory dish consisting of charcoal roasted pork served in a sweet/salty soup with rice noodle vermicelli and lettuce.

That course was served with a pale ruby colored Bordeaux claret, the best Granston had ever tasted.

The entrée was served by waiters imported from Paris for the occasion, indicating the high regard with which Premier René Mayer held Gen. Navarre. The soup was *pot-au-feu* brought out in a huge steaming cauldron carried on an ornate litter by four waiters manning the poles. As required by Escoffier, the meat and vegetables were perfectly fresh. Women had risked their lives; so, the *dignités* could enjoy this particularly French soup at its perfection. Grey liveried waiters hefted ladles full of the hearty brew to the delicate white tureens of the guests, each of which bore the embassy crest. Cranston worked to contain himself because he knew what was to follow. He also minimized the alcohol he consumed because he had a full night's work ahead of him, and he would need his wits to be fully intact.

The fish was *darne de saumon royale* with *sauce périgueux.* Next came *escsargots a la bourguignonne* and *grenouilles sauteés aux fines herbes.* The meat was *tournedos chasseur* with *chaudes de foie gras* and truffles. The poultry was *faisan* à *la bohémienne and canards sauvages.* The pheasants and ducks were grown on the chef's property for such grand occasions. On each plate was a mix of the freshest *braisage des légumes* in pork fat and separately, *lentilles au beurre, truffles à la serviette,* and *riz* à *la créole.*

The entrée wine was a smooth, but manly, Sémillon white Bordeaux– not the best in Granston's memory–but remarkably good given the war time scarcity conditions.

Next came the palette cleansing light lemon sorbet, which brought back memories of home and better times from his boyhood.

Dessert was the triumph of the meal since the ingredients had to be brought in at peril by military transport. A large round platter was placed in the middle of the long mahogany table. On it—for the choices of the *dignités*—were *beignets soufflés, biscuits à la cuillar, flan cuite à blanc, crème à l'anglaise,* and the piece de resistance, *sacher torte la madeleine* baked by chefs imported from the Hotel Sacher in Vienna. The dessert wines included an assortment of sauternes, Beerenauslese Riesling, Cremant French sparkling wine, and Uroulat.

The *dignités* ate until they were surfeited and had drunk enough alcohol to dim their wits for a day. Lt. Col. Granston made himself small and obscure; so, no one missed him in the cursory battle planning after dinner meeting or saw him slip out of the embassy onto Boulevard Gambetta in the French Quarter. He took advantage of the heavy darkness resulting from inadequate funding in Hanoi to maintain streetlights properly. He quickly hurried down the boulevard past the Grand Palais and turned left into a neighborhood that had seen better days, to say the least. By Hoàn Kiem Lake, he thought he saw some one out in the gloom; so, he wandered aimlessly in the old quarter neighborhood until he was sure he had not been noticed or followed. Tradecraft was so ingrained in him that he could not have avoided the sudden stops, looks in shop windows, double backs, and sudden bursts of speed down side streets.

Granston ducked into a dark, debris-strewn alley off Hàng Bạc [silver stores street] and climbed a rickety and rusty fire escape ladder to the third floor of a decaying red-brick apartment building. He knocked on a bedroom window in a pre-arranged code.

The window opened suddenly and silently, and Granston found himself facing the snub nose of a sawed-off shotgun. He could not see the person holding the gun; so, he spoke in French.

"Easy. It's Granston. Let me in before we're spotted."

A gloved hand reached out and assisted the tall man through the narrow window into a room as dark as a mine shaft.

"Parker?" a familiar voice whispered.

"Neal?" answered Granston.

"Yes. Follow me."

Neal pulled Granston down a labyrinth of hallways in the pitch blackness, feeling his way along familiar walls. Neal Dastrup turned a doorknob and helped Granston to get inside. Neal closed the door, then switched on the single overhead lightbulb by its long chain. As soon as his eyes adjusted to the dim light, Granston took note of the room. The three windows had been painted over with black paint. There was a filthy couch, a Spartan wood table, and two unmatched straight back chairs. In the corner of the room, there was a single socket for a plug-in for the electric hot plate. There was no source of running water and no bathroom facilities. There were eight lumpy old mattresses spread around on the floor, each with a thin olive drab army surplus blanket. On each of the mattresses sat one of Granston's CIA agents. They all looked at him for what the next move was to be.

Granston shook hands with everyone and greeted them by their first names.

Glen Gabler III asked, "So, what does our esteemed world traveler have to report?"

Granston said, "The French are going to hell in a handbasket. They have had a string of failed attacks and necessary retreats from Cambodia, through Laos, and all the way down from the north of Viet Nam. I attended a dinner at the Hanoi embassy tonight, and I saw the pitiful state the French Union Army is in. The dinner was grand, as grand as anything you might see on the Avenue des Champs-Élysées in Paris at the Place de le Concorde end on Bastille Day.

The French leaders here in Viet Nam are pathetically out of touch. They want to leave the north and remain in charge of the prosperous south. They won't consider negotiating a surrender with Ho to save the remnants of their army. They have never figured out how to fight guerrillas, and now they want to make a last stand World War II kind of great nose-to-nose battle, all to take place over the period of a week or so."

"Well, that's plain nuts," said Glen shaking his head. "When and where do they expect to hold this inevitable disaster?"

"Probably March this year. That's not certain, but the place is—Dien Bien Phu, up north."

"What do the W.O.M.s want to do?" Neal asked.

"For now, Eisenhower and Dulles are holding the line that the U.S. will support the French; so, that we can prevent the domino effect all the way down the peninsula and beyond."

He shook his head.

"Don't they know that ship's already sailed?"

"You know, I'm not sure what the W.O.M.s really want. I know there's no love lost between de Gaulle and the heads of the government in Washington. Right now, Ike has promised to support the French Union Army. Is he willing to enter into a quagmire war with the Viet Minh and their proteges, the Viet Cong, in the south? I can only speculate on that."

"What's our immediate goal, then Parker?"

"I have thought it over carefully. Tonight, we vacate this detestable dump and head south. I think we have been pretty successful in getting the northerners to move down towards Haiphong because they have been receiving some frightening and miserable treatment at the hands of Uncle Ho and his commies in addition to our nudging efforts. We need to concentrate on the remaining Catholic strongholds. One thing I can say about Ike and the W.O.M.s is that they are ready to do just about anything to get the old crook Diem into office. I think all of us regard him as the worst of the worst except for all of the other wanna-be premiers battling for the premiership.

"I have some more pamphlets. You'll love them. The basic plan is to get the papists to be afraid enough to abandon the property where they buried their ancestors and lose all their investments. We have to convince them that life in South Viet Nam will be better—a lot better. Capiche?"

The nine CIA operatives spread out among the Catholic concentrations in Ba Ria, Bac Ninh, Ban Me Thout, Bui Chu, Can Tho, Da Lat, Da Nang, Hai Phong, Hung Hoa, Konum, Lang Son, Cao Bang, Long Xuyuen, My Tho, Nha Trang, Phan Thiet, Phat Diem, Phu Cuong, Quy Nhon, Thai Bionh, thanh Hoa, Vinh, Viknh long, and Xuan Loc. They ran most of the way all day every day to get the word out. When some Catholics balked at the idea of moving or protested that they were unaware of any communist anti-Catholic activity, the operatives convinced the real priests and nuns to spread the alarm and to chasten the members who did not move quickly enough by saying that such people had their heads in the sand.

There was an impetus to the propaganda effort as word filtered in of grievous French losses. The operatives took to wearing the standard priestly garb—cassock, clerical shirt, and a detachable clerical collar–all the time now. They abandoned any attempt at rational and objective presentations. Instead it was a propaganda psy-ops campaign now in high gear.

Soothsayers were bribed to predict disaster under communism, and prosperity for those who went south. They distributed tens of thousands of pamphlets with slogans telling the religious and superstitious Catholics that "Christ has gone south," "the Virgin Mary has departed from the North," and gory doctored photos showing unspeakable anti-Catholic persecution under Ho Chi Minh. Nuns from all the targeted areas told of horrible rapes of innocent nuns, crucifying and castrating priests, and of Viet Minh cadres carrying precious religious icons out of cathedrals.

Posters showed the communists—men with leering faces and vampire like teeth—closing cathedrals and driving parishioners into the streets, beating them with bamboo canes. One particularly effective poster showed a congregation of weeping Catholics being forced to pray to Ho. The caption on that vividly colored poster was in large red letters with flames streaming from the edges of the letters read, "MAKE YOUR CHOICE" or "LIVE CATHOLIC IN THE SOUTH OR LIVE AS A COMMUNIST SLAVE IN HO'S NORTH," and "SET OUT FOR THE SOUTH NOW."

One of the most outlandish pieces of propaganda showed "captured" documents that purportedly came from the People's Republic of China intended for Ho and his minions, that the PRC was preparing to drop atomic bombs on the Catholic cities below Hanoi. Other documents stated that the government in Washington would launch an attack to liberate the north when all anti-communists had fled south. The only way for good Catholics to avoid death in a nuclear holocaust was to move south and to do it as soon as possible. To punctuate that claim, the artists in Granston's team created pamphlets that vividly showed Hanoi with three circles of nuclear destruction superimposed on it.

Diem himself was smuggled into the Hanoi and Haiphong area on five occasions between February and March of 1954 while the French were still able to keep a tenuous hold on the territory. He presented himself as the savior of the Catholics. The priests were particularly persuaded by the silver-tongued politician. Granston's campaign finally began to resonate with the northern Catholic priests.

"The anti-Christ Ho strives to end freedom of worship and all religious worship with Ho becoming God, and communism the only religion permitted. We must leave to save our souls and the Holy Roman Catholic Church. So, we decree that sacraments will no longer be given in the north, and anyone who stays behind after these warnings from God, the pope, and all the saints, endangers his or her very souls. Children and parents will be excommunicated," the priests announced.

Granston's men acted on recommendations from Neal and Glen to implicate the Viet Minh in terroristic and ghoulish acts against Catholics. They took nine fresh corpses of Viet Minh soldiers and dressed them as local peasants or priests. While the bodies were still fresh enough that the blood could still flow sufficiently for the operatives' purposes, they hanged them head down from tree branches near the gates of cities. Each man had a large sign nailed to his chest reading in large Vietnamese script, "OUR VAMPIRES WILL BLEED EVERY CATHOLIC WE FIND." CIA saboteurs poured sugar into the gas tanks of Viet Minh vehicles, slashed their tires, and fashioned trip wire bombs to assassinate senior Viet Minh officers.

Granston and his men gathered large numbers of men and women who were convinced of the CIA's message and had them distribute rice, chopsticks, fresh leafy vegetables and nourishing bean sprouts, sautéed vegetable mixes, bowls of salty sauces—especially the national favorite, *nouc mam,* and gave credit to Diem and his family and the Catholic dioceses in South Viet Nam. To appeal to men–who seemed the most reluctant to leave their property behind–the operatives distributed the traditional male foods, dog and snake.

Granston and his CIA cadres had expected to encounter considerable difficulty and a slow pace of Catholic exodus; but by the end of February, drib-drabs of Catholics moving into the Haiphong Harbor area were becoming a torrent which tested the ability of the locals to accommodate them. Granston contacted his boss, Allen W. Dulles, who quickly supplied the funding. He and the rest of the Washington W.O.M.s were overjoyed with Granston and his operatives' work. They were certain that the out migration of Catholics would swell the ranks of voters who favored Diem and would overcome the strong Buddhist majority that presently existed. With U.S. funding, and CIA organizing, the Central Evacuation Committee in Haiphong was well prepared to begin Operation Passage to Freedom if or when the French finally lost their hold in Viet Nam.

Oval Office, White House, Washington DC, PDB [President's Daily Briefing], February 7, 1954

Meeting recorded and stamped "TOP SECRET, EYES ONLY; POTUS, Dwight D. Eisenhower; Director CIA, Allen W. Dulles; Secy. of State, John Foster Dulles; Chairman of the Joint Chiefs of Staff, Admiral Arthur Radford
Present: POTUS, DCIA, Secretary of State, CJCS, Special Agent, COS [Chief of Station, Hanoi]

Date: February 7, 1954

Subject: U.S. military intervention to shore up French Union Military forces in Viet Nam

Summary:
- CJCS assessed the situation in French Indochina as dire with collapse likely to occur in a matter of months if not weeks. He stated that the only real way to alter the course of political and military events in Viet Nam would be to launch atomic bomb attacks on key cities and installations in northern Viet Nam. His analysts reckoned that a ground war by the United States would prove to be extremely lengthy and costly in humanitarian terms, loss of American lives, and American treasure.
- Secy of State stated that he reluctantly agreed with CJCS despite the initial world-wide condemnation that would almost certainly result. That outcome would likely be relatively short term—a matter of months to a year or two and would be preferable to entering into a prolonged ground and air war. Even victory would be unlikely to change the sociopolitical climate in Southeast Asia. The Secy stated—for the record—that it was his studied opinion that the so-called "Domino Theory" was highly overrated.
- COS Hanoi's opinion was that the U.S. had an obligation to assist refugees to leave North Vietnam and to make every effort to assist Ngo Dinh Diem to become the next

premier of South Viet Nam. When that is accomplished, the U.S. should exit the country as soon, as honorably, and as gracefully, as possible. Continued or escalated "boots-on-the-ground" would almost certainly lead to protracted war and an outcome not favorable to the United States. He based his analysis on his many years of dealing with both north and south Vietnamese citizens, military officers, and political figures.

- POTUS stated that he was firmly opposed to the nuclear option and equally firmly in favor of preventing a communist takeover of Cochinchina. He did believe in the Domino Theory and was determined that Asian communism would not make a clean sweep of the region. That would favor the PRC's domination of the region which would profoundly alter the world social, political, economic, and military, situation, and was unacceptable to him or to the United States. He emphasized that he had confidence in Truman's gradualist concept: build up capitalism, democratic institutions, and a professional military force, in South Viet Nam to a point of deterrence to the communists. Then, gradually move against the north to clear the peninsula of the communist menace. At least for the time being, it would remain U.S. policy to assist the French to keep law and order in the region.

Signed:

Dwight D. Eisenhower, POTUS

CHAPTER FOUR

"In 358 B.C. Philip of Macedon met the Illyrians in battle with his reorganized Macedonian phalanx and utterly defeated them. The Illyrians fled in panic, leaving 7,000 dead–three quarters of their whole force–on the battleground." It was said further, that Philip's wife looked on the agonies and deprivations of the departing refugees and asked her husband if they could help alleviate the suffering of those unfortunate Greeks. He replied, "No, let this be a reminder to those who would challenge us, this is what defeat looks like."

–Attributed to Thucydides

Battle of Dien Bien Phu, Mountainous Northwestern Viet Nam near the border with Laos, March-May, 1954

By the end of 1953, it was apparent to Lt. Col. Granston and his CIA operatives that nothing short of a miracle from on high would save the French. A succession of commanders been proven incapable of suppressing—let alone defeating–the insurrection of Ho Chi Minh's Viet Minh. The French were fighting for honor, for their far-away homeland and its prestige, for their leaders in France to be able to continue the status quo of colonization. Without saying it out loud the most important thing for the men with boots on the ground was to desert Indochina with their reputations intact, even if frayed. Ho was fighting for independence;

his most senior general, Vo Nguyen Giáp, was fighting for communism and to aid in the spread of communism throughout Asia. The Viet Minh had proved that time was on its side.

That was not so for the French army. Through the last half of 1953 and the first half of 1954, The French Union's French Far East Expeditionary Corps strove feverishly to strengthen their defenses in the Hanoi delta region and to prepare for a series of offensives against Viet Minh strongholds/ staging areas in northwest Vietnam. They set up fortified towns and outposts in the area, including Lai Châu near the Chinese border in the north, Nà San west of Hanoi, and in the Plain of Jars in northern Laos. Battles there were defensive, and—for the French—failures.

There were no successes that staved off the apparently inexorable forward progress of the peasant army of Ho and Giáp. Granston and his spies told the French generals, the colonels, and the captains, that Giáp's thousands were coming—through the trees, along the hillsides, and wading through streams. They traveled by night in December and January. As the French made their all-too-obvious way towards Dien Bien Phu–deserting their posts as they moved on–Giáp's men and women moved during the day as well, through friendly villages as they went south.

The Viet Minh became stealthy as they neared Dien Bien Phu; and with gargantuan human effort, they managed to move the bulky weapons of war through terrain that the French presumed was impossible to approach. They dismantled the guns—the weapons were largely thanks to China and to a lesser extent the Soviet Union. In all they had twenty 105mm guns, twenty-four 75mm mountain guns, heavy mortars and anti-aircraft guns. They transported them on rafts and dragged the parts on skids through roads they hacked out of the jungle. Giáp had his army move with stealth up the rear slopes of the mountains all around the French positions, to dig tunnels through the mountain, and put into place their artillery pieces overlooking the French encampment–the monsoon drenched valley below.

The relative positions made it like the proverbial "shooting fish in a barrel" for the Viet Minh; the French infantrymen called it "the chamber pot." This positioning by the genius general and his indomitable peasant army made them almost impervious to potential French detection or attack. The heavy machinery of war—tanks, artillery, stockpiles of ammunition, heavy trucks, anti-aircraft guns, etc.—and the thousands of soldiers began to take up positions encircling Dien Bien Phu in the valley below. With French *hauteur*, the generals ignored their Vietnamese peasant spies. Granston bristled at the blind stupidity he saw and heard.

Granston, Glen Gabler III, and Neal Dastrup III (both grandsons of former CIA operatives), collared every officer they could and told them the truth—the same truth the peasant cadres had been trying to convey.

To General Charles Piroth, the artillery commander, Granston said bluntly, "General, my men and I have seen with our own eyes—that the V Minhs are moving into the hills around the valley and are settling in. They have gotten heavy artillery in without your sentries being the wiser. You are in peril, Sir."

Gen. Piroth wore pince nez spectacles on his prominent nose, and he looked over them in an intentional gesture of disdain.

He said with finality, "I have the best artillery pieces and the best artillerymen in the world. I do not worry about the rabble and their pea shooters."

Granston wanted to scream, but he just turned away and rolled his eyes.

He next cajoled the aides-de-camp of Generals Jean Gilles and Jean Dechaux–the ground and air commanders—to get their commanders to give him a hearing.

The two men were impatient.

Gilles said bluntly, "With all respect to your country, Mr. Granston, we have the finest general in the world in command here. We have a plan for luring that peasant commander and his *culs-terreux* into a modern-day open battle. He will see the folly of his ways as we scythe down his peasants like ripe wheat. We have it under control. You can tell your spy masters that they need not fear for the French Republic. It is secure."

Granston tried one last time to convey his message, but before he could get out more than a sentence, he was dismissed. He had seen up close and from afar what Giáp's "country bumpkins" can do. During the time Granston spent begging the French commanders to listen, the French Lai Chau garrison was abandoned, and 2,100 men left for Dien Bien Phu. Of those, 185 made it to the final French position, the rest having been killed, captured, or had deserted.

Also, during that two-day period, the 316th Viet Minh Division finished its emplacement in the surrounding hills and took up favorable positions, completely unknown to the French. Granston did know, but he had no patience left to waste his breath on the hubristic French. He left Dien Bien Phu for the surrounding forests to be an observer with pity for the French.

General Navarre appointed Colonel Christian de Castries over the three generals who outranked him which markedly diminished morale down in the fish barrel. The man was a vainglorious old-school cavalryman in the 18th-century tradition. Navarre made the appointment because his grand plan for this ultimate battle called for it. Gen. Navarre's plan visualized a dramatic mobile set-piece battle. Because of the officers' ignoring their spies, they failed to be able to adapt to War I-style trench warfare. Col. de Castries was uniquely unsuited for that method of warfare, and he lacked the patience to enable his army to dig in for a long siege.

Navarre's grand plan included: Dien Bien Phu was to be held at all costs; draw the Viet Minh into a pitched mobile battle on the valley floor; bring in French paratroops as a surprise just as the battle began; utilize the superior French artillery to batter the Viet Minh troops who would not be able to bring in heavy guns through the impenetrable jungles; insure the safety of the troops under his command; and either withdraw with glory and live to fight another day or to withdraw from Indochina in honor.

In the end, not a single one of the elements of the plan was accomplished. Navarre was not a fool; he was not an ignoramus; nor was he blinded by ambition for himself. He was blind to facts that he should have known because he underestimated the effectiveness of the peasant army in the extreme. He was no coward; he was self-sacrificing and brave, but with other men's lives. The goals he set could be easily seen to be impractical, even impossible. He ignored the fact that many of the goals were in direct contradiction to others. Those flaws cost him his victory, and France its pride.

For several months, Giáp had conducted a desultory and ineffective artillery bombardment of Dien Bien Phu to underscore the inadequacy of the Viet Minh artillery. During late February, however, the Viet Minh bombardment increased until it was constant but still comparatively light. The effect on the French was more than uncomfortable but not serious. Col. de Castries took it as a positive indicator: "if that's all you have, we can wait you out and then come and destroy you."

Things got worse. Resupply flights found it difficult to land on the bomb pocked runway. When the pilots found a way to negotiate the rough terrain, Giáp's artillerymen began to pick off the incoming flights using old, crude, but effective, 37 mm automatic air defense gun M1939s. Shortly, there were no more French Union paratroop replacements dropping from "Flying Boxcars." That gradually—but effectively—began to eat away at the morale of the French soldiers. Still, de Castries was able to argue that the so-called "siege" by the Viet Minh was going to wear itself out with French forces still almost entirely intact.

The French had no real idea of who and what they were up against. Giáp—the eminent Commander in Chief of the PAV—was the hardest and most brilliant of fanatical communists facing them. In 1945-46, Giáp was put in charge of liquidation of the opposition in the nationalist government, the so-called 'internal enemies of the regime.' Noncommunists were referred to simply as *viet-gian* [traitors to Viet Nam]. These so-called 'traitors' included leaders of religious sects, mandarins, and intellectuals. Giáp–like his ruthless enemies, the French, and the members of the militant religious sects–often eliminated antagonists by such methods as tying the condemned into bundles with logs and then floating them down the Mekong while the victims slowly drowned. The practice became sardonically known as "crab-fishing."

On March 13, everything changed in the Battle of Dien Bien Phu. Bombardment began in earnest, with intense, focused artillery attacks. For the French, it was something they could never have imagined awaiting them. French M24 Chaffee light tanks–supplied by the United States–held for an hour or so but were rendered harmless by the advancing Viet Minh artillery. Recognizing his profound error of underestimation and the inadequacy of his own artillery, General Charles Piroth–the artillery commander–killed himself.

From his relatively safe observation post on a hill to the west of the town, Col. Granston radioed Saigon and was patched through to Washington, D.C. He relayed the situation with terse but adequate reality and told his superiors of the pleadings of the French Union Army commanders for American intervention to save the day. He waited for an hour as the French were being decimated.

The reply was terse: "President Eisenhower has decided that the situation is too far gone. He has ordered no action to be taken to aid the French."

Granston sent his best runner, Neal Dastrup, to zigzag down the mountainside to convey the final blow to French hopes.

Col. de Castries said laconically, "Then all is lost."

On March 13, the attack in chief on Dien Bien Phu began with a vengeance. The French garrison numbered about 13,000-14,000 men; the Viet Minh massed more than 40,000-50,000 men. Those men swept down the mountain sides as soon as the Viet Minh artillery bombardment ended. The assaults were furious.

The concentric circles of French perimeter protections extended out 250 meters, but they were breached by the sheer numbers of Viet Minh soldiers pouring out of the mountains and forests. One by one, French positions began to fall; and the French fell back to the next circle of embankments. Giáp's men used each abandoned French position as a defensive post. Giáp established trenches through the valley moving the Viet Minh positions ever closer to the heart of the French last stand.

Finally, the last French position on the periphery of the town was still capable of mounting a defense. Giáp surprised the demoralized French by launching the remainder of his full infantry force against that fortification and the trenches that surrounded it. The final epoch of the Battle of Dien Bien Phu began on May 6.

There was no lack of courage, determination, or will to fight or die on either side. The fighting was ferocious beyond anything the hardened French Union Army soldiers could have imagined. During that long horrible day, the French realized that they were beaten.

Col. de Castries likened their condition to that of the *Bataille de Camerone* in 1863 which lived in the hearts of all Frenchmen. French Foreign Legionnaires made a heroic, but futile, ten-hour last stand against the Mexican army in Camarón, Mexico. It was a surpassingly courageous but useless expenditure of men. In 1892, a monument commemorating the battle was erected on the battlefield containing a plaque with the following inscription in French:

> *Ils furent ici moins de soixante opposés a toute une armée sa masse les écrasa la vie plutôt que le courage abandonna ces soldats Français, Le 30 Avril 1863.-A leur mémoire la patrie éleva ce monument."*

[English:
"Here there were less than sixty opposed to a whole army. Its numbers crushed them. Life rather than courage abandoned these French soldiers on April 30, 1863. In their memory, the motherland has erected this monument."]

"My beloved French warriors, let us likewise make such an heroic last stand."

He left out the word "futile," but every soldier knew that it was so.

There was a very brief period during which the magnificent French held off the apparently limitless and irresistible Viet Minh infantry by employing their machine guns. As more Frenchmen died, the guns fell silent. The Viet Minh advanced. The last hours of the Battle of Dien Bien Phu became an animalistic brutal mano-a-mano conflict, literally hand-to-hand when the opposing sides were too close to use weapons. The killing fields were the trenches and the bare toppled ruins of the fortifications. As evening drew nigh on May 7, the horrendous battle was finally over. Nothing remained of the Great French Union Army except a relative handful of soldiers with thousand-yard stares, one nurse, and the stench of death all around.

1,600 French troops were killed; 4,800 were wounded; 1,600 were MIA; and–on the 8th of May–the Viet Minh counted 11,721 prisoners. The survivors–including the wounded–were forced to stand for an extended period of time even though they were exhausted, and then to begin a march into captivity on a group of roads which became known to the history of France as the Highway of Sorrow. As an act of submission and as a torture, the soldiers—who were known to the Viet Minh by the pejorative, "Big Noses"–had rings shoved through their nasal cartilages; so, they could be led and jerked along like balky oxen.

They marched in hunched over positions because of the pull of the nose rings 250 to 400 miles in daily stages of 15 to 25 miles. They were under heavy guard by men whose hatred knew no limit. The prisoners were forced to march over mountainous muddy terrain, still exhausted from the long conflict. The Viet Minh refused medical attention to the prisoners and forbad fires, hoping not to attract attention. The prisoners died by the hundreds from exhaustion and wounds as they were mercilessly marched. They were kicked into ditches off the sides of the road. When they reached their internment camps, the treatment was even worse.

France came to see Indochina as *"la sale guerre,"* the "dirty war."

CHAPTER FIVE

[On 24 July, 1954] Commenting on the Geneva Accords and U.S. objectives in Vietnam, Secretary of State John Foster Dulles said "The important thing...is to seize the future opportunity to prevent the loss of northern Vietnam from leading to the extension of Communism throughout Southeast Asia and the Southwest Pacific.'

–Spector, Ronald H. *United States Army in Vietnam: Advice and Support: the early years, 1941–1960* Washington, D.C.: Center of Military History, 1983

[On 12 August, 1954] President Eisenhower and the National Security Council decided that the U.S. would provide assistance for military training in South Vietnam "working through the French only insofar as necessary." The U.S. Joint Chiefs of Staff were reluctant to undertake the training mission as they believed conditions in South Vietnam were too unsettled to make training the South Vietnamese army feasible. The decision to train the South Vietnam army, in the opinion of one historian," set in motion a chain of events that would prove irreversible."

–Spector, Ronald H. *United States Army in Vietnam: Advice and Support: the early years, 1941–1960* Washington, D.C.: Center of Military History, 1983

Haiphong Harbor, on the Cam River where it empties into the South China Sea, North Viet Nam, 1954

The mass exodus of people fleeing the abject defeat of the French at Dien Bien Phu began several months before the cataclysmic end of France's colonial reign. The work of Air Force Lt. Col. Parker Leary Granston and his CIA cadres succeeded beyond their wildest hopes and even their imaginations. The fall of Dien Bien Phu opened the flood gates for people to pour into the countryside around Haiphong in northeastern Viet Nam. Most of them were Catholics who feared for their rights, their livelihoods, and their very lives. Within days, a hundred thousand of them clogged the port begging to be ferried out aboard the *Battleship Richelieu,* and the *Jean Bart* operated by the *Marine nationale* [National Navy]–the maritime arm of the French military.

Two days after witnessing the defeat in Dien Bien Phu, Granston got a ride aboard one of the few basic French patrol boats still in service and headed for the Port of Haiphong. The patrol craft–an 82-foot *vedette patrouille*–was an unarmored motor launch equipped with two 20-millimeter (mm) cannon, two .50-caliber machine guns, a light mortar, and a .30-caliber machine gun. On the deck was a brilliantly polished plaque containing the motto of the French Navy, *"Honneur, patrie, valeur, discipline"* [Honor, Fatherland, Valor, Discipline] as it was on the deck of every ship in the French fleet. The craft was well built—a good thing—because it was jammed as full as the space available with fleeing soldiers of the defeated French Union Army.

Those relatively unscathed fugitives had been lucky enough not to have been in the vicinity of Dien Bien Phu, but their French officers had evacuated the troops from Bui Chu and Phat Diem. They had been ordered to reinforce the area between Hanoi and Haiphong but were now part of the great flight to the south. The ranking army officer ordered the ship's captain to take all the fleeing men on board. The captain was all too happy to comply because he and his crew would have a legal reason to head for the south and safety. They stayed well away from the coast because as they came in too close, they took enemy fire. Granston, Gabler, and Dastrup helped man the machine guns, and fired until the barrels turned red.

They were not prepared for the crowds they encountered as they sailed into the estuary of the Cam River.

Gabler said, "Boss, this looks like Hitler's crowds at the Nuremburg rallies. I have never seen anything like this many people jammed into one place at the same time."

Dastrup agreed, "I'd bet we're looking at well over a hundred thousand people here. We'd better get some order, some food, some clean water, and some way to deal with sewage, or we will have a humanitarian crisis on a catastrophe level."

"Let's split up and try to ward of our disaster. Glen, you look into getting tents or something for housing and get some latrines dug. Neal, you get the flow into the ships going at the most efficient level possible. There are nowhere near enough ships or planes here to make a dent in these crowds. I'll see what I can do about that."

"And, Boss, you know that this is mostly our fault."

"Hummh, some truth to that Neal. But give the defeat at Dien Bien Phu credit where credit is due."

Glen headed to the wharf where an American Seabee ship lay at anchor. He requested to be allowed to come aboard. The bos'n piped him aboard, and he was escorted to the bridge.

"Welcome aboard the MSTS *Knudson*, Sir. What can we do for you?"

"You are the Seabees, the 'Can do' people, right, Captain?"

"We are that, if we can get a chance to do our stuff."

"I take it you are running into some desk jockey who won't let you get onto French property. That about right?"

"That's it in a nutshell. Do you bring a solution?"

"A strong suggestion, at least, Sir."

"And that is?"

"Ignore the weasels, especially the French weasels. They're done here, and the pencil pushers just don't know it yet. You, Sir, are the United States Navy. I'll have a word with the clerk. Why don't you start rolling out your equipment and make decisions about how to clear up this mess. Take guns."

The captain laughed, "This may just be your chutzpah speaking, but you're right. We'll start rolling now."

Glen told—didn't ask—the French official that he was going to sign off on the U.S. Navy coming into the environs of Haiphong to build and provide. And that was that. The tired civil servant saw the need and the compelling logic, and he signed the permission document that Glen had hastily contrived.

It was, of course, not strictly kosher—most of what Granston's agents did failed to fit into that category. Under the Geneva Accords between the French and the Viet Minh, there was an agreed upon three-hundred-day grace period during which people could travel unarmed south or north as they desired without fear of attack. Another condition held that there could be no addition of any kind of troop reinforcements or military personnel. The officious and snooty French viewed the Seabees' road, tent city, and pier construction, as an onshore activity by a foreign military unit which was banned. They effectively stopped any construction by not allowing the Seabees to unload their building materials on the beach—their beach.

Not entirely mindful of French sensibilities and sense of obligation, the MAAG [U.S. Military Assistance Advisory Group] overseeing the operation, ordered ACB 1 and 2 Seabees immediately to begin construction of a 15,000-person capacity refugee camp near Haiphong. French authorities objected. After working on the camp for just one day and making significant progress, the Seabees were again recalled to their ship due to objections about landing of foreign military personnel and equipment in Vietnam.

Seabees are a stubborn bunch and a tough bunch. There was an imperative set of logic for them. It was built into their motto: "Can Do." There was a job to do, and the rugged fighter-builders were straining to get started. The French could not get the job started, let alone done. Due to the ever-increasing number of people moving through the port at Haiphong during what was now being called "Operation Passage to Freedom"—an American name–there was an obvious need for refugee camps and all that entailed in the area. The local French forces lacked the heavy equipment needed for the immense clearing and construction operations. The stiff and conservative French knew they would have to bow to the inevitable.

Despite being firmly directed not to do so by the French, the Seabees sneaked ashore with two heavy bulldozers to start with. In an effort to remain incognito and to save face on the part of the dejected Frenchmen, the Seabees removed all military identification from their equipment and from their uniforms; to the casual observer, they looked more or less like civilian construction workers rather U.S. military personnel. Under this ruse, the Seabees set to work.

In short order, they began to work their miracles. These were the engineers and builders who carried Tommy guns to work—the same fearless U.S. Navy men who cheerfully left signs on Pacific beaches for the landing marines to see before they began another island hopping battle for dominance in the Pacific Theater: "Welcome, marines, this island compliments of MCB 2." Within a day, three more CB teams were out building runways, leveling areas for setting up tent cities, digging sewer trenches, laying pipe, and laying out boundaries for a temporary city. U.S. Navy military police began to bring order—lines for chow, for distribution of tents, and for those who needed proper clothing.

There were corps waves who distributed baby diapers and feminine napkins, tooth brushes, deodorant, toilet paper, and soap—lots of soap. Everywhere the American navy stood was calm, happiness, and the comforting knowledge that someone knew what was going on and had a plan to get the families out of the chaos. The Seabees completed all the necessary site work for the refugee camp within five days and returned to their ship ostensibly undetected. The French capitulated, and within ten days, CB units were buzzing around the harbor area and over to Cat Ba Island where thousands of people had traveled by ferry just to find a place to lay their heads.

Neal's task was more difficult. There were only two French ships. They could transport about three thousand souls each for the minimum six-day round trip to Saigon. That would not do. Everyone with any sense realized that the movement of people had to be on a colossal scale. The French did not have the wherewithal to do even a hundredth of what had to be done. Neal spoke flawless French, and he used his linguistic skills to offer an argument to the senior French authorities to break the logjam that was building towards a preventable disaster.

"*Mes amis*," he began, "we cannot go on like this. We will have an international humanitarian disaster of epic proportions if we cannot move these French protected people to safety and prosperity in the south. With your permission, I can alert U.S. Navy authorities to bring in air and sea transports that will assist you in your important venture."

It actually took very little persuading. The French had become wide-awake pragmatists since that awful day in Dien Bien Phu. With precious little of it left, the proud Frenchmen acceded to the reasonable suggestion made by the American agent, Neal Dastrup, even though his title and authority remained a mystery to them.

Granston had been busy making Neal's plan come to fruition. He told more than a few white lies to convince MAAG generals that the political way was cleared for the U.S. Navy to begin what was to become the greatest mass evacuation by sea in the history of the world. The Americans rushed to accomplish what had to be done. Over the life of the operation, the U.S. put 109 ships into service including fifty-nine from its amphibious forces.

Officially, the U.S. Navy answered the French government's call to "assist" the French in evacuation of the hundreds of thousands of Vietnamese and ethnic Chinese who had lived in Viet Nam for generations who chose to make the abrupt change to live in the safe, secure, democratic, and non-communist south of the Vietnamese peninsula. From August, 1954 until the end of May, 1955, the U.S. Navy formed an evacuation unit–TF-90–[Task Force 90], acting under Operation Order 2–54–and every ship and boat the French and cooperating Vietnamese could muster mounted the massive sea lift project to move huge masses of refugees from the port of Haiphong to Saigon.

All pertinent branches of the government of the United States provided emergency food, medical care, childcare, clothing, shelter, and security at reception centers created and built by the Seabees and the Army Corps of Engineers in Saigon and several other areas in the south of Viet Nam. Volunteer sources from all over America donated ninety-seven percent of the necessary funding and donations-in-kind through the USOM [United States Operations Mission]. The Navy Seabees built the fine "Freedom Pier" from which most refugees embarked for the trip south. Granston and his CIA operatives contributed baskets full of excellent photographs for news organizations to help them show the world the accomplishments of America during the time of need of the unfortunate refugees escaping from the tyranny of communism.

The U.S. Pacific fleet concentrated seventy-four LSTs [tank landing ships], and a considerable number of attack cargo ships, LSDs [dock landing ships], and many other ships from the vessels traveling in the South China Sea for the operation. In addition, the Navy's MSTS [Military Sea Transportation Service] contributed thirty-nine transports.

They shuttled between North and South Viet Nam supplying and replenishing necessary materiel obtained from the Logistic Support Force, Western Pacific. That U.S. force provided oiler, cargo, provision, repair, salvage, and hospital, ships stationed at the midway point in Danang Bay. USCG and Merchant Marine ships were drawn into the immense operation.

All those goods and services helped considerably to ease the suffering of the Vietnamese refugees temporarily living in Seabee built camps along the transit route. Granston's operatives made their contribution by providing excellent black-and-white photographs of kind American sailors assisting children and the elderly in the camps and on the ships. The *USS Knudson* where Granston sailed back and forth was an integral part of the operation. At the end of his part at the north Vietnamese portion of the operation in October, 1954, Granston, Gabler, and Dastrup, transferred back to the *Knudson* and went up the Cam River to assist Dr. Tom Dooley as he prepared refugees from his inland service area for the trip to Saigon.

The results of Operation Passage to Freedom were staggering. The French military got on board with an altogether competitive contribution. They transported 214,000 people, making 4,300 trips by aircraft. A total of 555,000 passengers successfully made it to the south in five hundred 1,600 km, three-day, one-way voyages, 388 of which were by the French. The U.S. made 109.

It took considerable persuasion to get the policy sticklers in France to allow civilian evacuees to travel on trains from the countryside to Hanoi or Haiphong because of their priority to evacuate French military personnel and equipment. There was a built-in frustrating slowness to the project as a result, and also as a result of many peasants leaving the area temporarily because it was rice harvesting season. The educated people among them were business-minded, and they waited around to finish as many business deals as possible before leaving in the Lunar New Year.

Several thousand people who had worked for the French and Vietnamese administrations in the North were also included in the successful migration of Operation Passage to Freedom. An additional 110,000 people traveled into the south by their own means, some leaving late enough to arrive beyond the 300-day statute of limitations period. Most of those people crossed the river that divided the zones on makeshift rafts, sailed on improvised watercraft into a southern port, or trekked overland through the jungles of Laos. The agreements allowed a 300-day period of grace, ending on May 18, 1955. In total, 600,000 to 1,000,000 northerners moved south seeking freedom and land. Only somewhere between 14,000 to 45,000 civilians and approximately 100,000 Viet Minh fighters moved in the opposite direction into the dreary land of communism, as the Western news media described it.

Beyond the movement of human beings to safety, Operation Passage to Freedom moved 88,000 tons of cargo, and 8,000 vehicles. For the United States the operation was a giant world-wide public relations coup. This was especially important because it came during the Cold War, and the news media compared the slaughter committed by the Vietnamese to the humanitarian accomplishment so unselfishly produced by the United States. Overall—including Operation Passage to Freedom—the United States funded eighty percent of the cost of the French war against the Viet Minh from its onset. Communism looked bad, and American capitalism and democracy never looked better. Col. Granston and his CIA agents were not given due credit for the magnitude of the favorable world response that they engineered in part.

Dien Bien Phu can be considered a metaphor for the French colonial occupation of Viet Nam and the inevitable outcome of such occupations. The exodus from Haiphong—Operation Passage to Freedom—highlighting the ignominious exit of a defeated power, is an even more accurate metaphor. The final date for direct involvement in Vietnamese affairs was April 30, 1975. Like the French, the Americans could have and should have foreseen that day from the very start of the Second Indochinese War.

CHAPTER SIX

Viet Nam: Second Indochina War, The American War; CIA Phoenix Program

"You and your like are trying to make a war with the help of people who just aren't interested."

"They don't want Communism."

"They want enough rice," I said. "They don't want to be shot at. They want one day to be much the same as another. They don't want our white skins around telling them what they want."

"If Indo-China goes . . ."

"I know that record. Siam goes. Malaya goes. Indonesia goes. What does 'go' mean? If I believed in your God and another life, I'd bet my future harp against your golden crown that in five hundred years there may be no New York or London, but they'll be growing paddy in these fields, they'll be carrying their produce to market on long poles wearing their pointed hats. The small boys will be sitting on the buffaloes. I like the buffaloes, they don't like our smell, the smell of Europeans. And remember–from a buffalo's point of view– you are a European too."

"They'll be forced to believe what they are told, they won't be allowed to think for themselves."

"Thought's a luxury. Do you think the peasant sits and thinks of God and Democracy when he gets inside his mud hut at night?"

–Graham Greene, *The Quiet American,*
William Heinemann, London, 1955

Embassy of the United States, 39 Hàm Nghi Boulevard, Saigon, South Vietnam, March 30, 1965

David Broadhead presented his credentials as a new military attaché officer and asked directions to the appropriate embassy office. When he had walked out of sight of the embassy reception desk, an attractive young woman and a middle-age Filipino in a U.S. navy uniform met him, as if by chance. The woman introduced herself as Barbara Robbins and flashed David a broad welcoming grin. Lieutenant commander Manolo Jesús Antonio Visayas told David that he was the deputy director of the specialized skills office.

"We are the people you have come to see," he said, "Please follow us."

None of them spoke another word until they had wound their way through a minor maze of halls and stairways. They entered a door marked with a small brass name plate which—in barely readable print—read, "Naval Information Office."

"Have a seat, David. We have been expecting you."

The speaker was a tough looking, no nonsense, sixty-or-so-year-old man dressed in rumpled olive drab jungle fatigues. The pockets of his cargo pants were stuffed with papers and small items of equipment including a handgun and at least one battle knife. His long sleeve, two pocket, jungle shirt and his jungle jacket slung carelessly over a straight back steel chair had no rank insignias. The man's clothing could have been from any of a dozen different countries or back street pawn shops in Europe or North Africa.

David recognized the wiry man—who seemed to be perpetually incapable of smiling–as "the colonel" from his training days in Camp Peary, Virginia, where he learned to be a Paramilitary Operations and Specialized Skills Officer. Like "the colonel," David had learned by careful habit never to carry any objects or clothing–including military uniform apparel–that would associate him with the United States government.

"Good trip?" "the colonel" asked by way of small talk, which was not exactly his forte.

"All right."

"Have you been briefed?"

"No, Sir."

"Good. Then, I won't have to correct some crap you got from a know nothing."

He spread out a map of Indochina and pointed at a dot in Cambodia.

"This is Sihanoukville, a port in Cambodia. For the past year, we have been gathering intelligence that tells us that Sihanoukville is of some importance to the Victor Charlies. One of our librarians—you met her, name of Barbara Robbins–compiled a good study. Read it today in your quarters, then destroy it. What we pretty much know is that Charles [VC] has been in Sihanoukville to supply its members in South Vietnam and in Cambodia. Barbara examined traffic coming in and out of the port. She identified Chinese ships that visited Sihanoukville and got some of our SOGs to confirm that they were delivering arms and military materiel to Charles and have been successfully bypassing customs and immigration.

"Mind you, plenty of U.S. border watchers and all the Military Assistance Command Vietnam with their heads collectively stuck in the sand debate the importance of those same Chinese ships to the Viet Cong. That is despite of all Barbara's real-world evidence. My SOGs have wasted a good many visits to Sihanoukville, and we have no doubts. There are army and navy brass who genuinely challenge our findings. I have no fight with them. However, there are W.O.M.s in Washington–especially from State–who still fight to disprove the truth of our reports. It does not fit the story that Cambodia, and especially not the Chinese, are involved. That would be a sticky wicket.

"You, my boy, are going to take care of the problem. You are going to do so without getting caught, and you are going to do it without implicating The Company. You clear on that?"

"I am. Any instructions on how I should accomplish that mission, Sir?"

"Yeah, I'll fly in some weaponry. You can pick it up at the dock. You travel by slow bus from Koh Hong to Sihanoukville, then take a day trip to Koh Rong Island and check in at the Traveler's Heaven beach side bungalows. You are Tom Smith to them. The town is nothing; and it's not safe; so, you need to stay in your room at the dump. Most of the island is unexplored and covered by dense jungle. There are a lot of uglies out there in the dark. For that matter, be sure to take a can of Raid for the cucarachas, the monster scorpions, and bed bugs. Raid is going to be your best friend here in the paradise of Viet Nam.

"The island is something like six or eight miles from Sihanoukville. The port city is surrounded on three sides by the Bay of Thailand and has an extremely busy harbor. Your cover is that you are a Swedish Red Cross officer looking into reports that American or Australian troops captured in the delta are in a prison camp in the area, and you are here to see to it that they are treated well.

"Somewhere around o-dark-thirty you'll get a little rap on your door."

He tapped out, "da dada dum," repeated three times.

"Don't look through the peep holes. You just might see the inside of a gun barrel, and that'll be the last thing you ever see. Be careful; be careful; be careful. Those are the three main safety and security rules.

"You will meet a remarkable guy, and he will give you the straight skinny about what we have planned. He is not your boss, but he has been around long enough to be a good guy to have watching your back. Be careful; do your job; try not to stand out; and report back to me in the Hôtel Continental on Tự Do Street, which used to be the Rue Catinat in the old days. Look for me in the ground-floor bar—the Continental Shelf–when you get back. Ask anybody where that is. Good hunting."

The "colonel" looked back down at his papers, and David deduced that the meeting was over.

David slung his duffel bag over his shoulder and carried it to a cubicle-like room where he was to spend the night. He was famished and wanted to get a glimpse of the fabled city of Saigon. He decided that he might as well take a short walk to the Hôtel Continental for their famous afternoon tea—reputedly among the best dinners in the country. He put on an embroidered white-on-cream Guayabera shirt, a pair of freshly pressed linen slacks, and recently shined penny loafers; so, he would look presentable. He looked in the mirror and was satisfied; so, he walked down the embassy stairs to the front door.

His months in Camp Peary had made him hypervigilant, a quality that annoyed his friends and acquaintances who knew nothing of his involvement with the CIA. He saw busy people rushing about taking care of their daily business. His eye caught a peripheral glimpse of a car having some sort of engine trouble directly in front of the embassy gates, but it did not look like any kind of threat; so, he ignored it. He saw Barbara Robbins and Manolo Jesús Antonio Visayas walking ahead of him having an intense conversation, but they were smiling. It seemed friendly enough.

Well ahead of him, a Canh Sat officer—government policemen were called the "White Mice" because of the white gloves they always wore—moving towards the stalled automobile—an old French Citroen. The White Mice annoyed American servicemen because they interfered with a weekend's fun and relaxation in one of the gin bins or with a pliable professional girl. They enforced what the Americans considered to be ridiculous laws by demanding that the man produce a "cohabition permit" which would allow their vehicle or taxicab to proceed to their chosen place of assignation. It was an illegal form of harassment designed to blackmail the American into giving a bribe to be able to get on with his evening. Most of the Americans had witnessed the excessive police brutality the "White Mice" employed during arrests and investigations.

Nevertheless, David thought it was time for the police to do something about the car loitering right in front of the embassy. So did Barbara and Manolo. They now hurried towards the Citroen, looking concerned. The Canh Sat officer began to argue with the driver, gesturing to him that he had to vacate the place where his car was sitting. It was illegal for anyone to park there, even if he was having car trouble. It was time to get out of there or receive a ticket and a trip to Canh Sat headquarters. Barbara and Manolo now moved quickly to see if the officer needed assistance. A looky-loo crowd began to gather and surrounded the officer and the driver who refused to budge. Barbara and Manolo walked up and stood beside the officer who was now starting to write up a violation notice. More than two hundred onlookers had gathered as tempers began to fray.

Seemingly from nowhere, a second car—this one a vintage green and white 1964 Ford Fairlane—drove towards the scene at a high rate of speed. David was now sure that there was something wrong—dead wrong—about what was transpiring. His impulse to run towards the scene was cut short when the occupants of the Fairlane drove past the Canh Sat officer and opened fire with an AK-47 on full automatic. The policeman died instantly. In less than two seconds, the Citroen erupted in a ball of flame and shrapnel from three hundred pounds of plastic explosives hidden on the floor of the back seat and in its trunk spread death and mutilation in the form of millions of razor sharp splinters.

In less time than it takes to say it, Barbara Robbins, Manolo Visayas, an American tourist, and nineteen Vietnamese onlookers were dead, shredded into fragments by the bomb that had a killing load far in excess of what would have been needed to wreak havoc and memorable destruction. 183 other people–mostly South Vietnamese people going about their daily business–were severely injured. Emergency services were overwhelmed.

David Broadhead was knocked off his feet and hurled backwards by the concussive force of the explosive device and rendered momentarily unconscious. He was otherwise unhurt, although he was temporarily confused and had a peculiar hearing loss that made everything seem like he was hearing it from the far end of a narrow tunnel pipe. He was powerless to render assistance, and instead had to be helped back into the embassy. Within minutes, the scene was flooded with "White Mice," army MPs, and a company of marines. There was pandemonium, screaming, bleeding, and agony. It was a Stygian scene with gore and mangled body parts scattered everywhere.

David rested on a stretcher and thought, *"this is the first half of my first day in country, what is the rest my tour going to be like?"*

The "colonel" appeared by his side barking orders.

"Get this man out of here. He has a room at the BOQ [Brink Bachelor Officers Quarters]. He'll be safe there. Send a unit of marines to close the Brinks off to everyone except people who have clearance to be there."

A marine lieutenant colonel who knew who the CIA officer was and what he did, gave out a calm and systematic set of orders to secure the embassy, to triage the casualties, and to set in motion a rapid moving investigation of the killers and any accomplices. The commander of the Army 46th Quartermaster Graves Registration Company saluted the Lt. Col. and reported for duty—to do the job no one in the military wanted to do, but the job that had to be done.

Five ARVN [Army of the Republic of Viet Nam] medical evacuation BTR-152 APCs [armored personnel carriers] stopped at the scene of carnage, and ARVN and American medical personnel began a systematic triage and first responder set of emergency treatments. The "colonel" collared one of the ambulance drivers and ordered him to transport David Broadhead to the BOQ. The driver looked at his superior officer who shrugged and gave a quick hand signal for David to be transported forthwith. The BOQ was less than a mile away, and David quickly found himself tucked into a bunk in a safe place, for which he heaved a great sigh of relief. It was 1730 hours, and David had had a long day.

He fell into a deep and dreamless sleep; so deep that he was not troubled by nightmares of the dreadful scene and experience his first day in Viet Nam had foisted on him. He awakened at 2215 with a powerful thirst, a full bladder, and a sense of being out of place. David's three issues had nearly resolved themselves when heard a tremendous roaring explosion and felt the second floor where he was staying give a convulsive shudder.

All the way down the hall, he watched in horror as that part of the building separated from his and fell away exposing the night sky and a great fire coming from below. He had the silly–but fleeting–feeling that he was going to miss the special dinner for newcomers that would be starting in an hour with comedian Bob Hope as the featured entertainer. People were screaming; fire klaxons were blaring; and his second-floor hallway now declined at a forty-degree angle. He had to back up to get his footing. His hands clutched at a door frame behind him. They were slick with sweat; despite the heat of the evening, he was in a cold sweat.

Men yelled, "Building unsafe! Get out while you can. Move! Move! Move!"

David had not taken time to unpack his duffle bag. He hoisted it over his shoulder and began to run in the opposite direction of the bomb damage and fire. At the end of the hallway, everything was still intact but was leaning at an obtuse angle. He tried the door to the stairwell, but it was wedged shut. With his pent-up adrenaline in full force, he kicked down the door and moved cautiously down the stairs which had assumed a decidedly catawampus angle. He leaned against the wall in order to avoid falling and slid along in the darkness towards the next floor.

He found that the first floor had been driven ten feet away from its moorings to the floor above and now extended out over the street with nothing supporting it. There was no access to the bottom floor from there. He kicked open the stairway window that looked out onto a small trash strewn street. Below him, and looking back, David could see there was virtually nothing left of the bottom floor, just piles of rubble and hanging wires that hissed and snapped angrily as they dangled and moved with the sway of the building.

Fearing that the rest of the building would come crashing down any second, David looked for a way out of his predicament—any way. He reckoned that it was no more than ten or fifteen feet between him and the side street below leading to Duong Lam Son Street; so, he decided to jump. The risk of getting broken legs was not as great a concern as that of dying when the whole building collapsed in on him.

The jump was not nearly as painful or injurious as David had anticipated. The distance had been reduced by the cave-in to less than fifteen feet. It was less than the free parachute training jumps that he had practiced in the military and at Camp Peary. He hit the ground with both feet and reflexively did a tuck and roll which absorbed most of the impact of landing. He shook himself off, did a three-second assessment of his condition, and pronounced himself none the worse for wear.

He saw a group of uniformed Americans standing near the front entrance of the BOQ, and he made his way through the rubble and the crowds to where they stood without announcing his presence. He looked for a familiar face and found one in the person of the "colonel."

The "colonel" was naturally—and by training—highly observant. He looked around him at the crowd, hoping to get a clue about the perpetrators, or to see one of his agents in need. His eyes met those of David Broadhead. The "colonel" made a small nod of his head in the direction of the armored cars behind him and began to edge in that direction. David walked away from the "colonel" making a wider arc at a more rapid pace until the two men met in the shadows behind an armored personnel carrier.

"Are you okay?" the "colonel" asked.

"Pretty much."

"Busy day, David. Welcome to beautiful downtown Saigon, the Paris of the East."

Both men laughed.

"We'd better get you out of here, before another bomb goes off…not that I'm blaming you," the "colonel" said, expressing the nearest thing to a joke David would ever here from the taciturn old spy.

David was glad to be quit of Saigon, for all its attractions. The latest bombing had killed two American servicemen, an officer and an NCO. Sixty other people constituted collateral damage. An additional loss was that all the U.S. bomb-detection equipment had been stored inside the BOQ and was destroyed in the attack. The U.S. was forced to transport in more devices because the rest were mere fragments.

CHAPTER SEVEN

Recommended Courses of Action

A. The Special Committee wishes to reaffirm the following recommendations which are made in NCS 5405, the Special Committee Report concerning military operations in Indo-China, and the position paper of the Special Committee, concurred in by the Department of Defense, concerning US courses of action and policies with respect to the Geneva Conference:

    1. It will be US policy to accept nothing short of a military victory in Indo-China. . ."

–Report by the Special Committee on the
Threat of Communism, 1954

Traveler's Heaven Beach Bungalows, Koh Rong Island, Sihanoukville, Cambodia, April 1, 1965

David's second day in Indochina—Cambodia–passed peacefully. He checked into the Traveler's Heaven Beach Side Bungalows—one of perhaps a dozen low budget strip motels stretched out along the otherwise uninhabited beach. No one raised an eyebrow when he gave his cover name, Tom Smith. He had the feeling that he was neither the first nor the last "Tom Smith" to sign in. His cumulative fatigue hit him as soon as he entered the room and saw the bed, lumpy and not overly clean though it was. He decided to have a little rest, laid down for just a minute, and slept until 1800. After his restorative nap, David was fully awake; so, he strapped on his weapons and went out to find a small restaurant which had fairly clean food. Fortunately, he only had to walk about a quarter of a mile until he found a place that was open.

He filled up on *Banh xeo*—a savory crepe made from rice flour and yellow turmeric powder stuffed with pork, shrimp, and bean sprouts—*banh mi*—"bread" served as a sandwich made of a variety of pork products with pickled vegetables stuffed into a toasted baguette, and a small side bowl of *nuoc cham* fish sauce without which it would not have been a real Indochinese meal. He had two cans of the local Indochinese beer—called *Ba mui ba* ["333"]. He had heard that 333 was adulterated with formaldehyde, but he did not catch a whiff of any odor or taste of that poison; so, he enjoyed it. Back at the bungalow, he had another nap. This one lasted until 0230 when his nice dream of wahines in Hawaii was interrupted by a knock on the thin door.

Da dada dum, da dada dum, da dada dum. The sound finally penetrated into David's dreamland. The tapping on the bungalow door was soft but insistent. He rolled out of bed, pulled his Makarov PMM out from under his pillow and crept to the dirty little window that looked out onto the wooden plank porch. The moon was half crescent, just enough to cast a little light. He saw two smaller man standing directly in front of his door and a very much larger one behind them. The "colonel" had given him a heads-up about the large man; so, he took the risk. He stood so that the door would open with him behind it and quickly pulled it open. He kept his Makarov hidden behind his back while the three men entered his room.

There were two tough looking Vietnamese men dressed in olive drab shorts, old French army short sleeve shirts, and Ho Chi Minh rubber sandals. Their skin was as bronzed as an African's. David pulled the string on the overhead light. One of the Vietnamese smiled. His teeth were filed to points, and they were precisely colored with shiny black lacquer. David managed a return smile but was a little afraid of the specter the black-toothed man presented.

The large man said, "You can put away your gun now; you are among friends."

David slipped the Makarov into his rear waistband.

"I'm David."

"Karl Isaacson."

They shook hands, and David took care to shake the hands of the Vietnamese.

"This is Y'Yool," Karl said, indicating the black toothed apparition. "He is a Montagnard, and a PRU/O."

Y'Yool and David nodded to one another.

The Montagnard was small—well under five feet tall. His body fat could not have exceeded one percent. He had deep chocolate brown skin, black irises, and assorted intentional tribal scars on his chest, back, and face—all of which added to the sense of menace one gained upon seeing the taut man whose impact on an enemy's psyche far exceeded his diminutive size.

"This is Sergeant Le Duc Bach. He's a former Kit Carson. Now he's another PRUC like the rest of us."

Another set of nods.

Le—his family name—was obviously of Southeast Asian tribal extraction, but not easily categorized. He was a little taller and a little heavier than Y'Yool but had the same wiry physique that made him look as if he were about to spring as the Montagnard did. He had puncture scars on his nostrils from piercings long ago discontinued. He also had ragged unequal slit scars on both cheeks, the result of a spear thrust when he was a teenager just starting his life as a warrior. He habitually wore a loin cloth and knee-high string sandals; no one made comments on his manner of dress or about his face. People who encountered him were immediately aware that he was not the kind of man to mess with.

"Care to spell out the acronyms, Karl?" David asked, sure that he should already know, but it was better to learn now with a little embarrassment that later when it might be a problem.

"Of course. Sorry. We get way too used to using the letters as if everyone was privy. Montagnard is a native of the highlands of Vietnam and Laos. A Kit Carson scout is a guy who the marines captured and turned. They then became intelligence scouts for American infantry units. Now, he's a PRUC. Okay, PRUC is Provincial Reconnaissance Unit

Cadre. More about that in a minute. Another thing you need to know; it's kind of new to all of us, is about CORDS. That's Civil Operations and Revolutionary Development Support, a mouthful that we almost never say. With all the R's it's kind of hard for the Vietnamese to say. We are part of that because we are CIA, and our job is to run the rural development cadre, like Le and Y'Yool. The cadre were *Chieu Hoi*, VC [Victor Charlies=Viet Cong] who defected or were "assisted to defect"— the ralliers, or turncoats, those who "rallied to the correct side—who are now officially working for the Saigon government. *Chieu Hoi* in Vietnamese means "those who have returned to the righteous side."

"We call ourselves PRUC or PRUC/O instead of CIA; so, people don't get so bent out of shape. Try and think of yourself that way."

"Okay."

"Look, I hate to ask, but would it be okay for us to use your shower? We have been out in the bush too long, and our socks are rotting."

David laughed, "Sure, go ahead."

After showering and shaving and putting on some of David's Old Spice deodorant, the three men were much less threatening. Sergeant Le gathered up all his and the other PRUC's clothes and took them outside. He threw them into the fifty-gallon used oil drum sitting outside the front door, poured in a cupful of gasoline, and lit the drum on fire—so much for anonymity.

An hour had passed since the three men had knocked on David's door. Karl started to pull on a plain tee shirt he had purchased from a street vendor in Hanoi—no American markings. As he did, David took note of several things about the man. First, he was younger than he had thought when he and his cadres first walked in. He must have been twenty-two or twenty-three, but the world's cares and bad memories had lined his handsome Nordic face. Second, he was not just a big man; he was the biggest man David had ever seen. He was all muscle and weighed at least 280 pounds and stood close to six eight by David's quick assessment. Third, he was hirsute, but his chest hair did little to hide his scars. Karl had more battle scars than anyone David had seen or even heard about. The scars alone would have been sufficient to make him easily identifiable to friend or enemy. Fourth–and more than that–he had the largest tattoo David had ever seen. It extended from the top of his left shoulder, down his back, and ended halfway around his powerful chest.

The tattoo was of a huge raptor appearing bird—somewhere between a peacock and an eagle–with extravagantly multi-colored plumage. In its beak—situated on the top of Karl's shoulder—held a scrolled document with the words "Black List." Its outspread legs had exaggeratedly cruel talons which held a banner reading "*Sat Cong*" [Kill Cong] in *chu nom* lettering. The bird's outspread right wing covered most of the left side of Karl's thoracic back, and the other wing spread out across his left chest. Above the wing, and just below his clavicle, were emblazoned the words, *"Phuong Houng"* referring to the mythical bird of Vietnamese folklore which was regarded as a bird of peace. In Karl's case–and in the case of the CIA program that bore the bird's name–it was a threatening reversal of the original meaning. That fact was not lost on anyone who came in contact with men like Karl or fell into the clutches of the Phoenix Program.

Karl saw David looking at the impressive tattoo.

"That bit of ink leads us to a comment on the Phoenix Program because you are about to become one of us in the program, David."

He pulled on his tee shirt.

David's appearance was in stark contrast to that of the conspicuous mountain of a man talking to him about the Phoenix Program. David was tall and slim in comparison to the remarkable height and bulk of Karl. David had mousy, unruly brown hair cut short in military style. His face was lean and nondescript with an unexciting thin-lipped mouth, small nose, hazel eyes, and chestnut eyebrows. There were no defining marks on his face or body. He did not have the powerful full muscle look of Karl, but he did have a very muscular body—each muscle cut and defined, a washboard abdomen, and prominent jaw muscles.

"A lot of us have been involved in the Provincial Reconnaissance Unit action, and our successes have led the great ones in Washington to devise an advanced program of record keeping and methods of getting Viet Cong to switch sides. They call it the Phoenix Program, which is more appealing to the Vietnamese than any tough sounding military program. The gist is to concentrate action on behind the scenes capture of Charlies based on information gleaned from all sources. We work in secret…absolute secret. We have places to take the people we collect and methods to get information, to get them to inform on their misinformed friends, and to come over to the good side as active Vietnamese citizens— to become ralliers, to use the French term.

"This weekend, you will get your first taste of how it all works; then, with some OJT, you will recruit your own unit, like mine. There aren't many of us…maybe a hundred; so, what we do is very important. Maybe the most important thing anybody does to win this war."

"And, I take it that us being here in Cambodia–in Sihanoukville—is related to this Phoenix Program and that I am going to be directly involved," David said.

"You are one very smart man, David," Karl said with a grin.

Karl's face was at its best when he smiled. He had almost luminescent blue eyes—piercing, according to men he faced as an enemy—and distracting hair. It was snow white, the color of an old man's hair, but absent the color, it was thick and young looking in accordance with his age. Later on, during the adventure in Sihanoukville, Bach told David that Karl's blond hair began to turn white after he was captured and tortured by the Viet Cong two years ago.

"This is the problem, and we have the plan. Chinese ships are bringing in military supplies to the VCs here in Cambodia. The VCs offload it onto small boats or haul it overland by truck to the Ho Chi Minh trail where it works its way into South Viet Nam to kill Americans and our good Vietnamese. We know about a Chinese ship coming in tomorrow night; we know the Charlies by name who are in charge of the transfer; and we know how and where they plan to take the materiel."

"That's pretty impressive. How do you know all that?"

"David. This may come as a surprise to you, but we are spies. It is our business to know stuff like that."

The two PRUCs laughed out loud at that bald statement by their boss.

"Of course, you are," David said with a shrug.

"So, here's the plan. You are a businessman visiting the Central Asian Cooperative Marine Machine offices. You will make yourself scarce when it gets dark and will meet up with Bach at a dive on Wharf Street. Can't miss it. There'll be a brawl going on in front of the bar. If one doesn't happen spontaneously–as usually happens—we'll get some spies involved. You two will move around like shadows keeping to the shadows and meet Y'Yool and me on the dock near the *People's Merchant Carrier* vessel. Then, we'll go hunting, silently, and nonlethally. Let me emphasize: we don't make noise; we don't let our presence be known; and we don't fail to get our two Victor Charlies. It might just happen that the ship meets with a mishap later that night. Never can tell in these treacherous waters."

David nodded his understanding. It was what he had trained to do.

"We have the necessary gear. Just get yourself to the church on time."

"Aye, aye, Sir," David said, which was enough said.

CHAPTER EIGHT

"I like to see good people win."

–Mac Miller

"The intent of Phoenix is to attack the NLF with a rifle shot rather than a shotgun approach to target key political leaders, command/control elements and activists in the VCI."

–MACV Directive 381-41

Port of Sihanoukville, Mooring Slip of the *People's Merchant Carrier*, April 2, 1965, Midnight

David and Bach met as planned in the milling crowd watching a bar fight that had spilled out onto the wharf. The bar was called Ding and Joe's Bar and Grill. A neon light with several missing segments blinked with such annoying frequency that a person afflicted with epilepsy would have a grand mal seizure if he or she were to be exposed to the flickering for more than five minutes. Above the hubbub, there was a dizzying stench of urine, polluted sea water, vomitus, and stale bodies. The place was perfect. Two more or less tough characters elicited no attention from the crowd who were enjoying the free-for-all.

The two spies left the crowded fight venue separately and melted into the shadows between the streetlights of Wharf Street. In five minutes, they were squatting together in the shadows of a Dempsey Dumpster enjoying the sweet-sick smell of rotting fruit and vegetables, cheap beer, and an assortment of uncertain organic odors. At 2345, Karl and Y'Yool joined them.

Karl wore a sailor's knit cap to cover his white hair, but nothing could reduce the impact on an observer of his great size.

"Anything stirring?" he asked.

David and Bach shook their heads.

"They'll be here. Be patient," Karl said.

They waited…five minutes…fifteen minutes…half an hour.

Then, the sleepy men came to full alertness when four Asian men in rough work clothing padded down a pathway that led to the slip where the *People's Merchant Carrier* lay at anchor gently rising and falling with the slight movements of the port's waters. Y'Yool and Bach moved casually from their squatting positions and walked slowly towards the gangplank of the ship where their quarries were headed. The two Phoenix agents were seemingly lost in conversation. No one on the wharf would have understood a word of what they were saying since they were speaking a Montagnard dialect. Furthermore, they made sure that their conversation was boring everyday chitchat.

Y'Yool and Bach reached the gangplank a second or two before the four men who intended to walk up it and into the ship. At that very instant, the harbor lights along Wharf Street all flickered twice then went out leaving the port in darkness except for the side lights along the hulls of the ships. Karl and David moved swiftly and silently through the relative darkness to within less than a foot from the four workmen. In an instant, Karl and David threw hoods over the two men of Vietnamese extraction and Y'Yool and Bach hooded the others. Each hooded man was so taken by surprise that he did not have time to react. Each spy clamped a large gauze sponge soaked in chloroform over the covered nose and mouth of the man he controlled. There was a brief but futile moment of silent struggle followed by limpness, then the unconscious victims were thrown across the shoulders of their attackers and disappeared into the now almost unmitigated blackness. Less than a minute had elapsed before the streetlights came back on to bathe a peaceful setting in soft light. Even the bar fight had burned itself out.

"Pay the harbor master," Karl said, "then get back here. We have to get our people on the *People's Merchant Carrier* and ready to unload the

Viet Cong bound cargo fast enough to be gone before the Chinese figure out what happened."

The limp figures of the Viet Cong cadres kidnapped that night were carried to a fishing skiff and ferried away from the harbor in less than ten minutes. Their eventual destination was Can Tho in the delta region of Viet Nam where they would be reeducated, rallied, and convinced to turn against their Viet Cong comrades. Or they would face unthinkable alternatives.

Because they would stand out as if they were wearing sandwich board advertisements identifying them as spies, Karl and David had to observe from a distance. For the same reason, the CIA did not employ negro people for the work in Indochina; they stood out as Americans. Racism, per se, did not factor in.

The PRUCs had hired Vietnamese laborers to pose as Viet Cong workers well before the night of the actual diversion of the ship's cargoes. They looked like poor, uneducated, menial laborers because that was what they were. They were paid to lift and carry, not to talk. If asked, they would respond that they were "*cong san Viet Nam*" [Vietnamese communists]. The peasants chosen adapted rapidly and easily to their role-playing tasks. After all, the Americans paid well. They were lined up to begin the cargo transfer well before the crew of the Chinese ship arrived to give them orders.

A rust bucket of a trawler with a broad and empty main deck pulled up alongside the *People's Merchant Carrier* and attached itself to the large Chinese ship with spring lines. Maritime law required that ship-to-ship cargo transfers take place outside the limits of ports to prevent time and money consuming accidents. Both the Chinese and the Vietnamese were well aware that they were breaking the law; so, they worked with haste, no one worrying over much about the bona fides of the workmen. They all looked pretty much the same anyway.

The STBL [Ship to be lightered or Mother Ship] was the Chinese *People's Merchant Carrier*, and the receiving or daughter ship was the CIA's adopted vessel, The *Phoung Houng* Petroleum Trawler, which bore Hanoi registry markings. The STBL had the cranes, forklifts, and tractors to move the heavier machinery and large crates. The *Phoung Houng* provided the labor and handled all union and payment issues. The CIA was a good employer. Paying well and on time kept lips zipped, they had learned that it also kept down the complaints and outside interest.

The transfer was complete before dawn, and the *Phoung Houng* was able to move out of the harbor before any customs officials or shore patrol were up for the day and in service. They made port six days later in Cam Ranh Bay, a deep-water bay in Khanh Hoa Province. It was located at an inlet of the South China Sea situated on the southeastern coast of Vietnam. From there, the cargo was distributed to ARVN forces throughout the south. This was the first such "transfer," and the Phoenix Program cadres promised that it would not be the last.

"David, I have my hands full with matters up north—Danang and just below Hue—so this has to be your baby. Get yourself to Can Tho and My Tho and take charge as if you had always been a powerful PRUC/O. Watch what the old hands do and learn. You'll pick up the details quickly; they're not all that hard. Turn 'em or kill 'em, is the main thing you need to know."

Can Tho Re-education Center, May 23, 1965

The Center looked like most other prisons or concentration camps. It was a sprawling complex surrounded by razor wire fences. There were three large parade grounds, and six barracks-like buildings. One of those was for "reeducation"—constant hectoring rote repetition of pro South Vietnamese political slogans and anti-Viet Cong and anti-communist doctrine. That building was reserved for men and women who had seen the light and were considered to be well on the way to reenter service of the true country, *Viet Nam Cong Hoa* [Republic of Vietnam]. The most advanced of the turncoats served as junior staff instructors for the new ralliers and were given instruction in how the Phoenix Program functioned and exactly how they were to work within it.

By a shrewd combination of coercion, fear, humiliation, and financial, sexual, and political inducements, most of the ralliers accepted into the advanced classes were true patriots for the Republic of Viet Nam and zealots who exceeded the original South Vietnamese who were the founding members of the program. Nothing exceeds the zeal of a convert was a motto that held cache among the PRUC/Os. It would have surprised the communist North Vietnamese to learn how many were newly baptized Roman Catholics by the time of their graduation.

David spent most of his time with that reeducation group by his own choice, and soon began to develop four units that he trusted and would use in the field. He tended to avoid the other two barracks buildings and to eschew the tactics employed there, although he knew those tactics were as much a part of the reeducation process as what was going on in the more civilized unit he preferred. Of necessity, David had started out in the middle-level retraining center in order make him a convert just like his ralliers.

It was a grim task to supervise activities he found abhorrent and have to maintain a non-tell poker face all the while. In his four-month tour in that middle building, he saw stubborn men and women reduced to whimpering beggars after being subjected to humiliations such as walking around naked, being sprayed with cold water, or having latrine buckets dumped on their heads. He knew he would never admit to what he saw and did there, but he would never be able to erase the scenes from his memory.

Nice David Broadhead from an upscale Episcopalian neighborhood in Poughkeepsie watched and participated in multiple beatings, assorted forms of rape—including object and gang rape, and introduction of eels and snakes into orifices–water boarding, bringing in vicious half-starved dogs to maul the detainees, and a process everyone called the "Bell Telephone Hour." Ralliers who had rejected their communist history the most vehemently were trained to attach bare electrical wires to vulnerable areas of a stubborn Charly's genitals, tongue, and inside the rectum, and to taunt the prisoner before administering a shock. The shocks were graduated in intensity; some proved fatal. They seldom produced converts, which frustrated the captors no end.

David especially detested what the guards called "the airplane persuasion." The most hardened of the prisoners had their arms bound behind their backs, then a rope was looped over a hook on the ceiling. The victim was slowly suspended in midair. Most times the man or woman's shoulders dislocated causing excruciating and persisting pain. If that was not enough to bring about a willing conversion, the Charly would be beaten with rubber hoses, bamboo canes, or leather whips brought in from cattle ranches in Texas. The fellow prisoners–who were there to be indoctrinated and to become good citizens of South Viet

Nam–were obliged to watch. If they turned their heads, they received a jolt from a cattle prod.

Despite all those efforts, most of the communists remained stalwart and endured to the end without informing on their comrades or renouncing their allegiance to their country as a communist nation. In frustration, the worst of the worst were simply executed. A few who were believed to have valuable knowledge that they refused to divulge were sent off to the Con Song Island prisons—a fate worse than death.

David made only occasional visits to the third barracks even though he was nominally in charge of the entire camp and despite the fact that that barracks had the highest rate of sincere turning of the communist cadres. It was the camp infirmary. Incongruously, there was kindness and gentle professional care by trained and certified health care workers. They treated the wounded bodies and souls and pleaded with them to give reasonable consideration to joining the great effort of the Republic of Viet Nam.

A substantial minority gave in to the kindness who had resisted all other persuasions. David's role was to assess the genuineness of the conversion and to invite them to join the successful ralliers in the first barracks where the food was good, the treatment comradely; and the chance to repent fully compelling. He established himself as their leader in the environment of the infirmary. His reports to his superiors about the effectiveness of the kindly persuasion methods went unnoticed or unheeded.

He was glad and relieved when the DDCIA decided that it was time to put the full PRUC program in effect to interdict the activities of the Viet Cong once and for all. David Broadhead was delighted to get out of his odious camp duties and to move his well-trained cadre units into the action for which the Phoenix Program was created.

CHAPTER NINE

From ghoulies and ghosties
And long-leggedy beasties
And things that go bump in the night,
Good Lord, deliver us!
–Traditional Scottish poem

Que viene el Coco ["Here Comes the Bogeyman/The Boogeyman is Coming"]—the classical painting by Goya (Francisco José de Goya y Lucientes. c. 1797) stuck fear into the hearts of misbehaving children. "However, the Spanish American bogeyman does not resemble the shapeless or hairy monster of Spain: social sciences professor Manuel Medrano says popular legend describes *El cucuy* as a small humanoid with glowing red eyes that hides in closets or under the bed. "Some lore has him as a kid who was the victim of violence... and now he's alive, but he's not."

–Cited in Xavier Garza,
Creepy Creatures and other Cucuys, 2004

"This is the patent age of new inventions for killing bodies, and for saving souls, all propagated with the best intentions."
–George Gordon Byron, 6th Baron Byron FRS [Lord Byron], quoted as the frontispiece epigraph in Graham Greene's, *The Quiet American*, Op Cit

Hoa Phu, Strategic Hamlet, June 28, 1965, 0300

The strategic hamlet of Hoa Phu–a dot on the map of South Viet Nam just north of Saigon–did not exist six months before the PRUCs gathered in its shadows that night. It was the creation of the United States Agency for International Development to shield the innocent villagers from the scourges of the wicked Viet Cong. Just over 200 families were moved to a strategic location for security purposes. They were given about twenty dollars in compensation as well as a new property in a fertile rice-producing region. The people, their pigs, their tools, and their treasured belongings, had been transported en masse to a place entirely foreign and new to them.

U.S. and RVN workmen rebuilt the thatch roofed dwellings, duck ponds, and rice paddies, to accommodate the new arrivals. A deep circumferential pit was dug around the tiny hamlet and a sharp-pointed bamboo palisade was put into place with the sharp-ends pointed outwards to deflect enemies. Their previous villages were then burned to the ground. Most of these people had originally come to the RVN to escape the ravening communist Viet Minh. All but a handful of those who moved to Hoa Phu were forced to do so at gunpoint.

David Broadhead and his PRUC cadres received a briefing from CIA and Vietnamese Special Branch operatives—acting as detectives rather than soldiers–working in the HIP [Hamlet Informant Project] that one of the villagers—a secret agent in the employ of the CIA—had evidence that a prominent citizen of the hamlet–ostensibly a Catholic–was a VC double agent. Nguyen Giang was in contact with VC in the area and was plotting to destroy Hoa Phu and surrounding hamlets to destroy the efforts by the United States and the South Vietnamese government to pacify the area. A second informant accused a neighbor, Phan Cao Thanh, of being part of a VC terrorist unit that executed bombing attacks in Saigon City.

It was to be their first raid, and the PRUCs had gone over every detail ad nauseum to be sure they got it right.

David whispered, "This is Nguyen's hooch. Binh, Chi, and I will take him. Duc, you take Tuan and Vien to get Phan. No collateral damage. Remember that, no family members are to be injured."

"Frightened?" asked Chi.

"Very much part of the mission. Make it memorable, but not reportable."

David, Binh, and Chi, crept up to the single entrance to the hut. There was no door which made silence an almost guarantee. David pointed to Binh for him to stand outside as a watch, and he and Chi slithered into the pitch-black darkness of the humble little hut. They were dressed entirely in black including gloves and balaclavas. Vision was rudimentary, but possible because the men had newly issued night-vision goggles. Everything appeared in a ghostly green misty color.

They slid up to the sides of the Nguyen's mattress. David held a washcloth soaked in chloroform at the ready.

"Now," he whispered, and clamped the cloth over Nguyen's face with an iron hand.

Chi clamped his hand over Mrs. Nguyen's mouth and hissed, "Shh, shh. No sound or you and your family die."

The husband was unconscious, and the wife was too paralyzed with fear to move or make a noise. Mr. Nguyen was portly–an unusual condition for a Vietnamese farmer—which made it something of a struggle to get the man into position to hoist him over his shoulder. With another two gestures—a finger to the mouth and a throat slitting motion—Chi relinquished his hold on the man's frightened wife. It was only then that the two agents became aware that two children were standing on their little thatch mat watching them mutely, their eyes unblinking and full of abject terror.

Chi asked, "What to do with them?"

"Nothing," David said, "let them spread the word tomorrow. The villagers will figure out that they had crossed the government, and that is not done. It will be a good lesson all around."

With that, they slipped back into the night, leaving the dark silent hut behind them. None of the other villagers was the wiser of the event that had just occurred.

While David, Binh, and Chi were busy accomplishing their mission, Duc, Tuan, and Vien had been able to kidnap Mr. Phan. They did encounter a hitch. Mrs. Phan awakened and started the first sounds of what was going to be a high soprano scream. Tuan cut that short—literally. He whipped his razor-sharp knife across her throat so that all that came out was a gurgle. She became one of those "collateral damages"

David had warned about. The three men—former Can Tho Re-education Center internees—decided it would be better if David did not learn of this mishap; so, they lied in their report to him.

The PRUCs had a considerable amount of evidence against the two men they had abducted. The CIA informants were only paid if the people they accused confessed to being part of the VCI [Viet Cong Infrastructure]. They laid it on thick in their pre-raid reports to ensure their own success.

The two captured men were first taken to the nearest PIC [Province Interrogation Center] where they joined other political leaders, outspoken students, left-leaning union members, and free-speaking journalists, in a round-robin course of questionings over the next month. Phan was bewildered at the accusations leveled against him. He told David everything he knew about the VCI in the region with some obvious embellishments.

"I am a small merchant in Hoa Phu. I sell eggs and chicken meat to people in the area. My wife makes rice cakes to supplement our income. Mr. and Mrs. Nguyen—who live on the northern edge of our hamlet are our competitors, and they have often threatened us with being reported to the authorities for being VCI. Ask anyone about Mr. Nguyen's jealously of our success. They will tell you."

Everything Phan said came entirely voluntarily without even needing a threat of torture. David sent cadres to check out Phan's story and found it to be true. They also learned that Mrs. Phan had been killed during the abduction and that made David determined to right as much of the wrong as possible. He sadly related to Mr. Phan that the Viet Cong had murdered his wife and that he was terribly sorry. Mr. Phan was released and driven back to Hoa Phu, at least what was left of it. In the interim while he was gone, the Viet Cong paid a visit to the hamlet and told the villagers to destroy everything that was built and to burn the rest. That was what Mr. Phan found. The wires of the enclosure were unraveled and strung out for three-quarters of a mile around the perimeter.

The roads and rice paddies had been bulldozed. The meeting house, post office, and small store had literally been torn to pieces. There was nothing left of the huts except mounds of ashes blowing in the wind.

The message was clear: this is Viet Cong land, enter at your peril. Dozens of signs were planted haphazardly around what was once a functioning hamlet. They read: "Death Area" or "*Mins.*" Yards of trip wires were scattered around and poked into the ground. No one dared to investigate whether not a specific wire was active or fake.

Mr. Nguyen was the diametrically opposite sort of man to Mr. Phan. He was as polite as Mr. Phan and apparently as willing to talk freely. However, he conveyed no information, admitted no guilt, and would make no promises. He was beaten, water boarded, and his feet were thrashed with a cane until they were bloody. He maintained a stoical flat expression throughout his ordeal. He never whimpered or begged or relented. Finally, he was driven in the back of a pig hauling truck to Can Tho Re-education Center and interned in barracks number two.

David followed up a year later and learned that Mr. Nguyen died in one of the fetid Can Song Island cells. His family was branded as traitors to the republic and imprisoned in army's notorious Long Binh Jail–called LBJ by the prisoners–on the outskirts of Saigon. They were housed in rehabbed shipping containers as jail cells. During the monsoon months it was stifling hot, but in the dry summer months the containers became ovens. Both Nguyen children died of heat prostration. There is no record of what became of Mrs. Nguyen.

David Broadhead became very skilled and efficient in his role as a converter of VCI over the next three years, exceeded in stature only by the famous or infamous "White Ghost," Karl Isaacson. David got better at triage—determining whether a captive was a hard-core VCI and needed to be retrained in the second barracks, or was a malleable person who had been brain-washed or coerced into becoming part of the Viet Cong and should have only a short visual education of barracks 2 and then be moved up to the privileged barracks for the *Chieu Hoi* Program. He learned early on in his career with the Phoenix Program that the absolute, violent, and impossible to reach men and women, needed to be shot after the first attempt at an interview. It was a most efficient method, and David was praised by his superiors and rewarded with promotions for his accomplishments.

The crown jewel in his list of successes was when he gathered the intel and arranged for the kidnapping of Ho Chi Minh's Inter-zone V [northern South Vietnam] region VCI commander Nguyen Van Bac headquartered in Danang. Nguyen had recently been promoted to commander of the B-5 Front Quang Tri Border Zone. Nguyen was directly responsible for trucking from Cambodia to Viet Cong bases near the border along the Sihanouk Trail. It was in early 1968, and the three-star company grade officer had become rather lax with regards his personal security. A CIA operative, Nguyen Dai Xuan, was carrying a backpack full of C-4 explosives towards the Ho Chi Minh Trail nervously watching for U.S. bombers overhead. Nguyen Van Bac paused for a rest in a security bunker along the way and was enjoying a cold 333 beer with his subordinates as Xuan passed by. The conversation was loud and excited. No one noticed a lowly coolie pause to adjust his backbreaking load.

"The end is near, my friends. Do not let this be spread abroad, but Ho himself has assigned General Vo Nguyen Giáp to mount the final offensive during Tet this year. This will be the largest offensive in our glorious history, and the filthy Americans will have to bid us goodbye. I have been honored to be chosen to plan all movement of materiel to the selected locations, and Chairman Ho has selected Hue as the centerpiece of his historical operation. We will begin this very week to move everything necessary for the capture of Hue. I expect nothing but the utmost effort for our great cause. Be silent, and be vigilant at all times, men. There are spies all around us. This must be the greatest secret of our careers."

Nguyen Van Xuan trembled with excitement. What he had learned was a secret almost too important for one man to bear. He forced himself to move methodically up the trail as he and the other backpackers always did. At the first fork on the trail, he slipped off to the side into the brush as if to answer a call of nature. He made certain that no one had seen him, then he shed his load and retained only enough rations and water to make the hazardous trip to Hue to warn his PRUC masters of what was impending.

Nguyen was exhausted, feverish, dehydrated, and malnourished, when he approached the secret mountain headquarters of the Provincial Reconnaissance Unit. The guards were ready to send him away until David walked by and overheard the breathless outpouring of information that came from the exhausted man. Nguyen had been one of David's best successes during his time in the *Chieu Hoi* recruitment operation in Can Tho. Although the poor man was barely recognizable, David recognized a small familiar tattoo on his left wrist.

"Nguyen, my brother, what is it you are saying?"

Nguyen almost fainted with relief when he saw the PRUC/O.

"I have very important and very private information for you, Sir. Please take me to a place where we can talk without being overheard."

"First let me get you something to eat and drink, then we can talk."

Nguyen nodded gratefully.

He gobbled food as if he had forgotten what it looked like. He drank half a carton of milk, then burped contentedly.

"Sir, I have overheard a very important conversation; and for that reason, I left my place on the trail to come to you."

"You were right to do that, Xuan. And you have suffered greatly and took serious risks to help the right government to prevail. Tell me your news."

Xuan related what he had heard verbatim. When he finished, the tired man looked to his senior officer for confirmation.

"PRUC Nguyen, I believe you, and our PRUC unit will act on it immediately. Have you a reasonable guess where Leader Nguyen Van Bac is now or where we could find him sometime in the near future?"

"He is a vain man, Officer Broadhead. He is to have a celebration of his sixtieth birthday in one week in the Hanoi Metropole Hotel—nothing but the best for the great military leader. Great in his own mind, at least."

"Do you happen to have a good idea where the hotel is located in Hanoi, Xuan?"

"Sorry, such as I do not frequent such as Metropole Hotels."

"Touché. We will find it. We have librarians for that."

The headquarters analyst—"librarian"—found the exact location and all about it after a five minute study of her topical map of Hanoi and its environs.

"Hope I didn't keep you waiting too long, Boss," she smiled smugly.

He laughed, "Great work as usual...for a librarian."

"Here it is," she pointed, "15 Ngo Quyen Street, Hoan Kiem District [French Quarter], Hanoi. This is the opera house next door. Here, on the west is Hoan Kiem Lake. It is heavily forested and should provide good cover."

"What about escape routes?"

She took out a translucent yellow marking pen and traced a fine yellow line from the front door of the hotel and wound it out towards the east where the least traffic was known to exist, especially at night. The PRUCs shook their heads in unison and murmured to themselves, "*too risky.*"

The librarian smiled her enigmatic—and know-it-all—smile and made a second trace. This line exited from a rear window—which she marked with the notation, "2ⁿᵈ"—and drew the line straight out to the woods to where a thin path was drawn on the map which none of them had seen before that moment. Her yellow line took a long circle, most of which seemed to be in the wrong direction until it returned in the direction of Saigon 1139 km away to the south. The line she drew was pretty much in tiger country all the way.

"How feasible is this escape route away from the hotel and around to Hoan Kiem Lake?" David asked Nguyen Van Xuan.

"I, myself, did grow up in a little fishing hamlet on the banks of beautiful Hoan Kiem Lake. I am very familiar with all the trails. There are more than show on this map. But…it is feasible, I say, but carries some risk because it is too wide, too well cleared, and too heavily traveled. There are clusters of huts all along, and the PRUCs would have to be silent and have to be sure that Nguyen Van Bac remains unable to make any sound."

"The stakes are high," chorused Vu Caden and Dao Xander.

"It is war," replied David indicating how well he understood the risks and also the potential benefits.

"I wish to go. I can be a good guide. You will just have to feed me a bit," said Xuan.

Everyone laughed.

While they were talking, the librarian produced a blueprint of the floor plan of the Hotel Metropole. For the next two hours the librarians and the PRUCs scrutinized every square centimeter of the blueprints until they came up with two plausible escape plans, both of which had them exiting through the window the librarian had first proposed.

"Not to be pushing into the areas where I do not have standing," said Xuan, "but, we must leave here tomorrow in order to be in good hiding from the guards."

David mused for a moment then added, "Or in good places out in the open."

Caden nodded and said "Masqueraders, like spies, no?"

"Yes, like spies. Librarian friend, can you produce proper attire for wait staff at the hotel?"

"Overnight, yes."

"Then, why don't you get your people started. The rest of us will arrange transportation, weapons, provisions, and camouflage. Let's all get a move on. We can sleep tomorrow during the day, because most of our travel will be under cover of night."

David chose as the kidnap force, himself, Xuan, and Vu Caden. And after a moment of concentration, he added Karl Isaacson and his two main PRUCs.

"The giant with the white hair?" asked Vu.

"He has been in country for years doing this sort of high-stakes undercover action. He can be invisible. You know that it is very difficult to see elephants in a forest even when standing next to them. Most people do not look up, and all they see is straight ahead or to either side. The elephant's body is so large and tall that it as if one were looking into a deep forest. Isaacson is a master. He was the winner of every escape and avoidance maneuver at Camp Peary, and that is saying a lot."

"I'll contact him. I'm sure he'll want to be part of this," said the librarian.

"Ah, she wants him because she is sweet on the big man," joked Caden.

He was rewarded with a disdainful glower from the young woman. She did not have a sense of humor about missions, and she certainly lacked any humor touching on any possible love life she might have or aspire to.

By dint of remarkable effort coupled with professional efficiency based on experience, the team was ready to go. They would meet Karl and his two cadres just south of the DMZ. The ever useful librarian gave each team member a good quality color photograph of Leader Nguyen Van Bac and a personal map of the routes of travel and the area of Hanoi and its surroundings. David nodded his congratulations on a job well done. They planned to leave when it was still dark; so, that gave them a scant two hours to catch a nap.

The team traveled to the DMZ during the darkness and did a HALO parachute drop into the one safe area on either side of the demarcation line between North and South Viet Nam. Both sides of the combatants had mine field maps showing where a man could travel safely if he was very precise about where he put his boots on the ground. The quality of their parachuting was tested to the enth degree, and their long arduous training paid off that night.

They disposed of their silk, donned night vision glasses and their heavy packs, and set out to the north and Hanoi. They walked at night with Xuan acting as guide, and rested under cover during the hot, humid days, sweating and thirsting all the time. The third day's pre-dawn light had just begun to appear as they crossed into the territory of Hanoi city. They found an old barn that had been refurbished for southern spies like them and had never been discovered. They rested, drank copious amounts of clean water, and ate some freeze-dried food—generally disliked and called "wood chips" by the LRRPS [Long-Range Reconnaissance Patrol] scouts who had had to be the guinea pigs to first test the new rations out.

The men selected to be fake waiters suited up in the fresh new liveries with authentic monograms on the left chest for the Hotel Metropole Hanoi. They slipped out of their hiding places in the woods and weaved their way into the crowds walking and bicycling to work that morning—just fish swimming with the rest of the fish. Karl, David, Xuan, and Vu Caden, had to wait until darkness returned before making their separate ways to the Hotel. They had decided during their hiking that they would enter the hotel the same way they planned to leave it—through the second-floor rear window.

Because of their study of the blueprints, they knew that the window led into an old and seldom used storage room. They threw grappling hooks through the window and pulled themselves up with ease—again owing to their rigorous and exacting training. Once inside they hid in a corner and took a chance to flash a small light on the blueprint to find the room where their intel had told them that Nguyen Van Bac was using for the night. Good fortune smiled on them.

The leader's room was on the same floor. He had reserved a full ten rooms, and those suites were being set up for an extravagant gala party, no expense spared. One of the cadres—dressed in a hotel uniform—reconnoitered the layout and preparations on the floor.

"Boss," he reported to David and Karl, "security looks lax. Lots of booze, and a floozie a minute is checking in."

David gave Karl a look.

"I'd like to go in well after dark to give them time to get good and drunk, and well distracted by the ladies brought in as birthday presents."

"I agree completely. What's to keep some nosey security guy from checking into this storeroom?"

"Disinterest, mainly. We can lock the door from the inside. That should discourage further attention on the part of a guard who has other things to occupy his mind and other parts, don't you think?"

"I sure hope so. But, all the same, we need to have our guns ready if they get onto us."

"Of course. But, by the same token, we need to silence any intruders instead of banging away with our guns."

"That would certainly be the first line of defense."

"And offense…"

The daylight hours inched by slowly. The room was small, dark, dusty, musty, and smelled of rodent feces and mold. It was too dark to play cards, too dangerous to talk out loud, and too hot to move about except to stretch occasionally. Whispering became boring; so, they simply turned to their own thoughts to get through the boredom of the minutes and seconds that passed with glacial celerity. The greatest effort was to avoid sneezing.

By mid-afternoon, it probably would not have mattered if they sit off firecrackers in their oven of a room. The partygoers had gathered in droves and were whooping, hollering, and celebrating, with abandon. They were setting off strings of large Chinese firecrackers everywhere on the second floor, and no one from the hotel staff came up to protest. Two of the fake hotel workers slipped out of the storeroom at 1600 for another quick reconnaissance. Half-way down the hall, a couple of NVA security guards–who were more than one sheet to the wind—hailed them and offered them some champagne.

Who were they to refuse the generosity? They looked over their shoulders to make sure no imaginary employers or employees of the Metropole could see them, then sheepishly accepted the flutes full of the lovely pale beige expensive champagne and enthusiastically enjoyed its tiny bubbles. They thanked the guards effusively and parted as new best friends.

Elegant Asian girls in a variety of form revealing dresses, traditional tight-fitting long dress *Ao Dais*, French evening gowns, and apparel that failed to provide adequate coverage, moved freely in and out of the several occupied rooms on the floor. They paid no attention to the lowly hotel servants and giggled their way from one pleasure dome to another.

The report from the mini-reconnaissance mission was received with something that approximated glee by David, Karl, and the rest of the PRUCs. In other circumstances, they would have jumped up and down and shouted out their pleasure. As it was, they settled for wide grins. It was good joss. Then, it was back to waiting.

The partiers became more boisterous; the speech in the eight tonal Vietnamese of the north became increasingly incomprehensible as the evening wore on. By midnight, there was less shouting and talking; and it seemed that there was less shuffling up and down the hallways of the second floor. The rest of the hotel seemed to be totally asleep according to an up-to-the-minute walk-around by the trusty pseudo-hotel-employees.

By 0200, there was relative silence. David opened the storeroom door a crack and took a listen. Aside from some enthusiastic snoring and an occasional tell-tale sound from a girl in one of the rooms, there was nothing. A Vietnamese PRUC stepped gingerly out into the hall and saw nothing but good news. Two sentries in front of room 2023—where Comrade Leader Nguyen Van Bac was supposed to be spending the night—were dead drunk on the floor on either side of the hotel room door.

"Let's do it," David said.

They left one guard in the room, and the rest of the PRUCs slipped silently out into the hall. They were heavily armed and carried bottles of chloroform, plastic flex-cuffs—which had just become available that year–and ropes to secure Leader Nguyen if all went well. They were fully ready to use their knives on any other occupants of the room to ensure silence if it became necessary.

David softly–and as silently as humanly possible–pushed on the door. As ridiculous as anything he could imagine, the door was unlocked—not even fully closed. The open door gave way to sounds of a man snoring like a helicopter rotor, and the smell of booze and cheap perfume. He did not have to adjust his vision to the dim light in the room. David and the rest of the PRUCs were wearing their night-vision glasses.

They pushed stealthily into the large suite, taking all due care not to trip over anyone or anything or to knock anything over that could make a noise. Xuan pulled on David's elbow and whispered.

"That is him. That is Leader Nguyen Van Bac. I am absolutely certain."

On the bed with Nguyen were two women, neither of whom was dressed, and both of them wreaked of liquor and sweat. There were two couplings on the floor; two men and two women lying semi-comatose in apparent alcohol overdose induced blackouts. None of them posed a threat.

David took out his chloroform and started to pour the clear colorless liquid on a fresh gauze pad. Karl put a hand on David's to stop him.

"Could kill him. Better just to gag him and get out of here," he whispered directly into David's left ear.

David nodded his understanding and returned his brown glass bottle of chloroform to his pocket. He put his ear to Nguyen's nose and mouth and ascertained that he was passing air through both. To say that he had halitosis would make one the master of understatement.

Karl handed him a roll of matte olive drab "duck tape," and David tore of two lengths to cover Nguyen's mouth and eyes. The man did not move a muscle other than his very healthy snoring muscles. Fortunately for the PRUCs, Nguyen was a typical short, thin Vietnamese who was easily carried by one strong man. Karl assumed that assignment and lifted Nguyen out of bed as easily as he would a four-year-old child.

Agents checked out the hallway and found it empty. Nguyen and his newly acquired entourage slipped silently into the hall and made their way towards their storeroom escape route.

"*Tạm dung lại*! [halt] came a harsh order from the nearby stairwell.

An entirely sober NVA sergeant who had obviously realized what was happening stepped out of his chosen security guard post and confronted the PRUCs. Nguyen Tram, made a lightening quick move and threw one of his personal throwing knives. It stuck the NVA soldier in the center of his throat cutting off his windpipe. The stricken man threw up his hands to get at the terrible pain in his throat that cut off his voice and his ability to breathe. Tram's second knife embedded itself in the man's heart, and he died without another sound.

David rushed to the man, ascertained that he was indeed dead, and kicked his body back into the darkness of the stairwell. Now, the PRUCs moved with lightening efficiency. In a matter of seconds, they fashioned a rope harness to lower Leader Nguyen safely down from the second-floor window to the ground. David and two of his PRUCs took charge of that task, and Karl and his two men, Y'Yool and Bac, stayed behind as a rear guard.

The second-floor hallway suddenly became alive with combatants. Karl and his men leaped through the storeroom door and into the hall and began cutting down the sentries with sound suppressed PAVN MP-40s taken from captured Viet Cong cadres. The PAVN soldiers continued to rush them despite suffering terrible losses of comrades and receiving serious wounds. The last few minutes were hand-to-hand knife fights.

The PAVNs—though brave and well trained—were no match for Karl and his men who had honed killing to a master level art.

After checking for any other threats, Karl and his men rushed into the storeroom and out the window. David, Leader Nguyen, and the rest of the PRUCs, were nowhere to be seen, which was expected. Karl, Y'Yool, and Bac, knew the escape route by heart and ran as fast as their legs could carry them in the direction of the trail. They caught up with David, and each man took a turn carrying the inert Viet Cong leader. It took an hour before the Hotel Metropole Hanoi lit up and a small PAVN and Viet Cong army began pouring out of the building. They ran in all directions, having no clues about the escape route of the kidnappers. It was nearly two hours before they decided to follow the trail that wound around Hoan Kiem Lake to the west. Darkness and the lack of night vision glasses hampered their progress.

After two days of night running and daytime hiding, the PRUCs were back safe in South Viet Nam, well below the DMZ. Only then did Leader Nguyen Van Bac begin to come out of his alcoholic stupor sufficiently to realize the dreadful position he was in. He was aware of what went on in the Con Song Island prisons, since he had witnessed first-hand what the French did when they had control. He had no desire to perish as a tortured hero.

"I have information, American," he said to David without being prodded to do so.

"Truth only, Nguyen," David said with a ring of deadly threat.

"Of course, of course. I can tell you of troop movements, hiding places of arms caches, the names of spies who have infiltrated your ranks."

"In due time. Right now, and I mean this very minute, you begin by telling us the PAVN and Viet Cong plans for attacks in the Republic of South Viet Nam during Tet."

The question stunned him. Only a small handful of men and women knew anything about such plans or that they even existed. He paused. Xuan kicked him hard in the groin.

"I overheard you. I am a spy. I heard it all. Talk, or I will cut off your manhood and serve it for dinner."

Leader Nguyen believed him, making his terror complete. He spilled his guts, every detail. The PRUC unit could hardly run fast enough or find vehicles quickly enough to get their treasure trove of information back to the headquarters of the Phoenix Program.

CHAPTER TEN

"The enemy's greatest success was achieved in the historic city of Hue, where Communist armed forces moved into the imperial citadel and held out for 26 days. During their occupation, they brutally murdered a great many innocent people. More than 3,000 bodies were later discovered in mass graves. Many victims had been tortured and others had been buried alive. Enemy forces paid an extremely high price for this adventure. Of the estimated 84,000 men the Communists sent into the attacks, about 45,000 were killed by the end of February, including some of their most experienced cadre. Thousands more enemy soldiers were wounded or captured. The Tet offensive was, by any standard, a military defeat of massive proportions for the North Vietnamese and the Vietcong."

–Lyndon B. Johnson: *The Tet Offensive,*
New York Times, October 24, 1971.

"I warned a group of Congressmen at a meeting in the Cabinet Room late in the summer: "Ho Chi Minh thinks he can win in Washington as Ho did in Paris."

–Lyndon B. Johnson, Cabinet Meeting,
summer, 1967, Op cit, above

"[The Tet Offensive] failed because we underestimated our enemies and overestimated ourselves. We set goals which we realistically could not achieve."

–PAVN General Tran Van Tra, writing in 1978,
as quoted in, Lorell, Mark & Kelley, Charles, Jr.,
Casualties, Public Opinion and Presidential Policy During the Vietnam War, 1985

The General Offensive and Uprising of Tet Mau Than, Citadel of Hue, Viet Nam, January 30, 1968

The official North Vietnamese and Viet Cong name for the Tet Offensive of 1968 was The General Offensive and Uprising of *Tet Mau Than*. The directors of the war in Hanoi also referred to it as *Tong Cong kich, Tong Khoi Nghia* [General Uprising]. In South Viet Nam it was known simply as the "Tet Offensive." Knowing the plans for Tet from the debriefing of Nguyen Van Bac, all sectors of South Viet Nam were better prepared, even though many American generals and officials in Washington thought it highly improbable that the VC could pull such a major offensive off and tended to ignore all warnings from the PRUCs.

In concert with the almost purposeful ignorance on the part of high officials of South Viet Nam and the United States was the almost willfully ignorant determination on the part of the generals of the PAVN, the leaders of the VC, and the government of the DRVN to ignore the very real possibility that one of their ranking military officers would have turned over his information about the plans for the Tet Offensive. As a result, the offensive began on schedule. Even knowing that it was about to take place, ARVN and the U.S. forces were surprised to their core about the massive extent and audacity of the strike.

During the week before January 30, David and Karl gathered all their PRUC unit cadres into the Citadel of Hue and—along with ARVN brigades–stocked in as much water, food, ammunition, and shoring of the defenses as thoroughly as they could do. Hue is set on a plain backed

197

by foothills of the *Chaîne Annamitique* and is situated eight km from the South China Sea coast. Hue is traversed through its center by the River of Perfumes [Huong River, or Hue River]. On the left bank of the river sits the Chinese-style Vietnamese imperial citadel, *Dai Noi*.

At 0630, the "surprise" attack began. General Giáp threw his forces in centripetal lines from his base in the Parrot's Beak area of Cambodia, located barely thirty miles from Saigon. The audacious plan was a campaign of surprise attacks against military and civilian command and control centers throughout South Vietnam. The offensive was countrywide and well-coordinated. The supposed surprise was calculated by Ho and Giáp to coincide with the middle of the Lunar New Year [Tet] and in violation of a truce agreed upon by both sides. Even with the heads-up from Leader Nguyen's information, David and Karl and their agents were shocked at the sheer ferocity and magnitude of the offensive.

From seemingly nowhere, the north eventually sent in over 80,000 North Vietnamese and Viet Cong troops. Almost simultaneously they struck more than 100 towns and cities throughout the Republic of Viet Nam. As Nguyen predicted, this well-organized assault included three-fourths of the forty-four provincial capitals, five out of the six autonomous cities, a third of the district level towns and villages, and the capital, Saigon. The offensive was the largest military operation conducted by either side up to that point in the war by far. Hue was a major objective, and the artillery attack was like nothing any of the PRUCs had seen before. They huddled in fear behind improvised shelters and tried to wait out the artillery barrage with their psyches still intact. They were all brave men, but they were afraid. The test of their mettle and courage was that they endured it all and were still able to function.

After the artillery barrage ended, thousands of screaming communists assaulted the Citadel. They were beaten back again and again with heavy losses on both sides. The PRUCs received orders to leave Hue and to regroup back in Saigon after two weeks of unsuccessful fighting by both sides. It was feared that the capital would fall, and the end of South Viet Nam as a viable nation would occur in short order.

The PRUCs knew they were needed in Hue; so, they did the best they could to procrastinate the day of their departure. Finally, they received absolute orders to leave; and during the night of February 28, they slipped into the tunnel built for that purpose and melted into the night. From Saigon, they hunkered down to endure the fight and to plan the counterattack which was part of Washington's and especially the CIA Phoenix Program's strategy from the time the spies brought in the invaluable informant.

The attack on Saigon–which occurred while David and Karl and their subordinates were quartered in the city—included a disturbing Viet Cong suicide attack on the American Embassy compound. Fanatical VCs dressed as ordinary peasants blasted a hole in the wall of the grounds and entered the handsomely landscaped area in significant numbers screaming and firing their AK-47s and B-40 grenade launchers wildly at no specific target. Later, it was said that they were high on drugs. A determined set of defenders—military police, marines, volunteers from the embassy staff, and the PRUCs, prevented the VCs from entering the embassy building itself. The defenders adopted a "take-no-prisoners" policy and ended up killing every single one of the attackers, a harbinger of things to come.

The battle of Hue lasted another two weeks with no let-up in its intensity, during which time the Viet Cong occupied the Citadel. Viet Cong forces around Hue included six main-force battalions, with an additional two PAVN regiments operating in the area. When David and Karl returned after the NVA and Viet Cong troops faded back into the countryside, the two PRUCs were dismayed at the level of destruction in the venerable old city. Half of it was destroyed beyond repair. Corpses had not been properly buried. The old imperial city was severely injured.

Hue was first established in 200 BCE, when it served as the seat of the Chinese military authority in the kingdom of Nam Viet. It survived occupation and revolts and persisted in a formal setting that drew the important people of the time to it. In 1802, Emperor Gia Long—founder of the Nguyen dynasty which controlled southern and central Vietnam from the mid-16th to the mid-20th century–moved the capital from Hanoi to Hue in an effort to unite northern and southern Viet Nam. He built the Citadel which that day in early February, 1968 still hung on in a sickly and weakened, but persistent, way as the PRUCs surveyed it.

French colonial forces responded to an insurrection by Vietnamese nationalists in 1885 by storming the Citadel and–out of sheer spite– burned the magnificent imperial library and confiscated every object of value. The emperors stayed in Hue but were weak. They were puppets who were excluded from events of any national importance. After the Japanese were ousted at the end of World War II, the imperial dynasty came to its inevitable end.

American marines, PRUCs, and ARVN soldiers, began mopping up the stragglers of the Viet Cong and PAVN forces who had not evacuated the plain soon enough. No prisoners were taken. The VC and PAVN bodies were dumped in pits and burned. There was a deep and pervading hatred of the northerners by the ARVN soldiers. Nearly 6,000 civilians lost their lives during the battle; of an original population of 140,000, 116,000 were left homeless. And then there were the mass graves discovered as the soldiers combed the area. The 2,800 victims unceremoniously dumped into trenches and pits had either been clubbed or shot to death or simply buried alive.

From witnesses who survived the massacre, it was learned that the PAVN had quickly begun to round up people they had already identified, and—under the guise of "re-education"—to line them up for extrajudicial execution. The murder victims were people—even whole families—believed to be potentially hostile to communist control. The unfortunates taken into custody included South Vietnamese military personnel, present and former government officials, local civil servants, teachers, policemen, and religious figures—a systematic "ethnic" cleansing.

It is said that "hell hath no fury like a woman scorned." Whoever coined that phrase never met the ARVN colonel who first discovered the mass graves. That discovery set the tone for what was to come over the next two or three months. After Tet, several military elements contributed to the advantage that the South had over the invaders from the north. The offensive was largely centered in the northern and central provinces of South Viet Nam, whereas, the RVN strengths were mostly centered in the southern half of the nation and were not severely weakened.

Information gleaned from PRUC, South Vietnamese, and U.S. military sources including ralliers like VCI commander Nguyen Van Bac, lists of VCI suspects gleaned from the PIC torture chambers in all provinces of South Vietnam built by the American Pacific Architects & Engineers Company, from the PRUC captives—abducted political leaders, students, trade unionists, suspect villagers, and journalists harboring communist ideologies, made a massive hit list for the hunters.

The information produced an estimate of North Vietnamese and Viet Cong forces in South Vietnam during January, 1968 that totaled nearly 325,000 men. There were 130,000 PAVN regulars, 160,000 VCI, and 33,000 service and support troops. They constituted nine divisions composed of 35 infantry and 20 artillery or anti-aircraft artillery regiments. There were 230 infantry and six sapper battalions.

The Thieu government, the U.S. government with all its involved agencies, and especially the CIA's PRUCs, went after those remaining enemies with an extraordinary level of vengeance. It was no longer a professional military or counter-intelligence action. It could no longer be ignored as "the American War." This was personal; and the majority of South Vietnamese civilians turned against the VCs, now considering them to be murderers and violators of the soul of Viet Nam for having cast down a monsoon storm of horror during the universally recognized and beloved peace period of Tet.

CORDS held an unprecedented meeting in Saigon in mid-February. All 120 CIA officers who ran the Phoenix Program and the 2,000 PRUCs whom they managed, U.S. and RVN special forces officers from all branches, and certain civilian contractors who served in secret capacities, were there. The message was simple: *Sat Cong*. The mission for all was to destroy, to eliminate in toto the Viet Cong forces of South Viet Nam from the face of the earth. ARVN and RVN special forces officers joined in the brief discussion. An organization developed with lists of suspects assigned to each unit throughout the country.

It was largely unsaid, but the tenor of the meeting was that this was not going to be a police action; there was not going to be the usual daintiness of evidence collection, legal charges, prosecutions, courtrooms, verdicts, appeals, or hand wringing. They all knew that many of the people they would round up and eliminate could be innocents—collateral damage—some of whom would be the victims of petty village grievances, family squabbles, jealousies, and revenge seeking. It could not be helped. The scope of the demand was too great.

If David Broadhead had any qualms of misgivings, he kept them to himself. When he got back to his temporary headquarters in Hue, he assembled his PRUCs and told them:

"We have been given the green light. We have a list from the CORDS meeting and our own list of suspects we either were not sure of or didn't have time to process. Now, we split up and bring them in or kill them wherever and whenever we can. They will panic as soon as they realize what is happening; so, we have to move as quickly and quietly as we can. No hint of what is going on is to come from us. My estimate is that we have a month, maybe three, to clean all of this up."

He waved a large handful of papers to punctuate his message.

It was a time to delegate and to relinquish full authority. He appointed his ten most trusted PRUCs to be PRUC/Os with himself retaining over-all command and veto power. Each of the PRUC/Os was assigned eight to ten men under his authority, and each was given a list of several hundred names and a bio for each, including last known address or location.

The remarkable efficiency and usefulness of the information was largely obtained or at least collated by the use of computers. Some of the earliest computers were made for the military, and the Phoenix had been using the machines since the establishment of the organization. Military requirements for portability and ruggedness led to some of the earliest transistorized computers, such as the 1959 AN/MYK-1 (MOBIDIC), the 1960 M18 FADAC, and the 1962 D-17B; the earliest integrated-circuit based computer, the 1964 D-37C; and all of them were available for use in the Phoenix Program at one point or another.

The work was done quickly and with remarkable efficiency given that it involved the abduction and detaining of human beings—people who, for the most part did not have street addresses.

An example was that of the apprehension of a half-French communist named Pierre Pham, a well-to-do planter with ties to the Chinese triads. The problem for David was to avoid alerting either the triad chieftains in Cholon or their target. That was complicated by the fact that none of the PRUCs had any idea where his plantation was located, and the computer information contained only his biographics of birth date, place of birth, name of spouse, name and location of his eleven children. Time was of the essence.

The 1964 D-37C was able to answer the question of where the many children lived and worked. Three younger children had "Pham Plantation" as their place of residence. One older child had a precise street address: No. 372 Vo Van Tan Street, near its intersection with Cach Mang Thang Street. It was a fifth-floor walk-up. He lived there with his wife. They had no children. No place of work was listed.

David and Nguyen Van Xuan did a bit of preliminary work designed to save them wasting time hunting and persuading the man, Pham Pierre Do. They sent a pair of librarians to get photos, and they obliged by getting excellent shots of Pham and his wife Kym. They knocked on the Pham's apartment door ready to strike with paralyzing force if needed. No one was home. As they turned to leave, they saw a man walking away from the apartment building headed west. He was somewhat too far away, but David was sure that he was their quarry. They followed him at a respectable distance using careful tradecraft techniques to avoid being detected prematurely.

Pham paid no attention to them or to anyone else. He had a book in his hand and wore an old canvas messenger bag as his carry-all as did many Vietnamese men. He walked into a sidewalk café, waited a couple of minutes for a table facing the street, ordered, and opened his book. David and Xuan walked past the entrance to the café once, then rounded back to ensure that they had not been followed or recognized. Pham was intent on his book but seemed to be enjoying his cheap breakfast of *banh mi* [bread] and *opla* [eggs] with a large glass of deep amber colored *tra da* [iced tea].

David and Xuan entered the café separately and found tables on either side of Pham. They ordered coffee and a beignet, waited, and watched. They had only allotted half an hour to surveillance; so, they checked everything in and around the café and took note of anyone who came anywhere near Pham or even looked at him. He seemed to be a loner and a reader, and not much else.

David stood up, check in hand and started walking towards the cashier's desk. Xuan pushed back his chair and walked to where he stood by Pham's chair. He bent down to tie his shoe which brought him to Pham's attention. Pham gave Xuan a cursory glance and returned to his book. Xuan sat down at Pham's table across from him.

When Pham gave him a rather startled look, Xuan asked politely, "Is this place taken, Sir?"

"Well, I guess not…but there seem to be several other places that are unoccupied."

"That is so, but this table is special for my friend and I. Here he comes now."

David walked briskly to the table and pulled back the third chair. Pham looked bemused.

"I beg your pardon," he said, "but I was enjoying this table in privacy. Why don't you move to another table?"

"Because," David said with ice in his voice, "you are the one we have come for."

Pham's face became a mask of fear. He had heard something of the recent spate of unexplained kidnappings, and this struck a disquieting chord.

"We are going to take a little walk to the Binh Tay Market to have a chat. You are going to stand up and walk with us as if we were old friends. Understand?"

Pham was almost paralyzed with fear. He did not consider that he might have a choice in the matter. These men were strangers, and they did not look like men who made trifling requests…demands, really.

Pham started to ask a question, but Xuan put up his hand to silence him.

"Stay quiet and cooperative, and you will be home with your wife, Le, before lunch."

The mention of his wife's name felt as if an icy hand had reached into his chest.

The three men walked to the large market where the PRUCs maintained a vendor stall for quiet discussions. No one ever asked them anything about their business. In Cholon, one did not ask unless invited to do so by the proprietor. Triads and VC had stalls there, and they did not like to have idle chats.

"Mr. Pham, I am sure this is all very confusing. We only want one thing from you. Tell us, and we will be on our way. Refuse, and you will find this to be a day you will remember with regret," David said by way of introduction.

Pham looked at David intently, waiting for the question.

"We are business associates of men who work with your father. We need directions to get to his home. We need to see him this evening. Please do not lie to us. We have ways of knowing, and we will have to have you accompany us to our office until our business with your father is concluded. Are you understanding me so far?"

"I think I understand…"

Xuan interrupted him, "You are about to ask why. We do not answer "why" questions, and we do not give out information. What is your father's address? Give us directions to get there. Be quick and be brief. Where is he now?"

Pham had no idea who or what these men were, but he was sure that he could not fail to comply. 1968 was not a year to appear to be uncooperative with the authorities, and these men seem to be authorities of one sort or another. He quickly and quietly answered all their questions and that made him feel less anxious for some inexplicable reason. His relationship with his father was very strained; the man was belligerent and domineering. Pham did not feel that he owed Pierre Pham very much—certainly not his life.

"You have done well, Mr. Pham. We are going to the U.S. Embassy where you will wait for a time. It will probably be tomorrow morning before we return. You will be treated well.

David, Xuan, Binh, and Chi, took young Mr. Pham to the embassy where he was assigned to a small bedroom which had a bed, table, chair, table lamp, and five books extolling life in the Republic of Viet Nam under the Diem regime and now under the Thieu presidency. It would be a long wait.

While Binh got Mr. Pham settled in, the other three arranged for an armored car, bullet proof vests, and an assortment of weapons. It took them three-quarters of an hour to reach the Pham Plantation. It was not yet mid-day. David and Xuan walked cautiously to the front door, and Binh and Chi hurried around to the back and waited for David's signal. He knocked on the heavy door. Then he knocked again. After another brief pause, the door opened; and an elderly Chinese woman servant greeted them politely.

"Very good mornings, Sirs. May I know of what is your business here at Pham Plantation?"

"We are here to see Mr. Pham. Is he in?"

"What is the nature of your business?"

"Government," David said and pushed past her taking care not to push her or to frighten her.

"Take us to him, now, please, *ba tot* [good grandmother]," Xuan ordered as gently as he knew how.

Somewhat flustered, the *nguoi hau* [servant] made a shaky about face and led them through the beautiful old French colonial house. They walked over the somewhat chipped and fading red tile floor and out the back door to a wide screened-in veranda. The porch looked out over an expansive lawn which had a tennis court and *manège* riding arena equipped for serious dressage training. Beyond that lay the untended remains of what was once a flourishing rubber tree plantation. The servant led the two PRUCs to where a sixty-plus-year-old white-haired man sat drinking a nostalgic 1789—a favorite sweet cocktail invented in Paris which includes white wine, whiskey, and Lillet; a sweet and citrus flavored French aperitif. He gave the two PRUCs a languid and bored look.

"I have seen your two comrades skulking over there in the coffee Arabica trees. You might just as well have them join us," the autocratic older man said tartly. "Can I offer you something, a *rhum et citronade* or some 1789, perhaps?"

David gave a small hand signal to Binh and Chi, and they walked towards the veranda, hands resting casually on the handles of their pistols.

"What is this about, young man?"

David was not in the least cowed by the imperious behavior of their subject for arrest.

He said, "Mr. Pierre Pham, I presume?"

"And who else would I be?"

"You are to come with us to the United States Embassy. We are officers of the Provincial Reconnaissance Unit here in the eastern Saigon district."

"That means nothing to me, young man. Whatever you are and whatever you do, you have no business here ordering me around. Bring your superior if you wish to have any further communication with me."

Maybe it was what he said, or maybe just how he said it; but Xuan and Binh stepped up behind him on the lounging chair, hooked their hands underneath his armpits and sat him up as fast as a jack-in-the-box. Mr. Pham's hauteur diminished some with that movement.

"What is this about?"

"We will discuss that at the embassy. Come along."

David took hold of the lapels of Mr. Pham's recently pressed white linen afternoon coat and drew him forward.

Suddenly, in a move that astonished all four of the PRUCs, the older man spun about knocking all the hands touching him off. He pulled a snub-nosed revolver and shot Binh in the left arm with it. Before the PRUCs could begin moving, Mr. Pham dashed off across the open lawn area towards the tennis court equipment building. Xuan and Chi both shot the fleeing man in the back, and he pitched forward on his face, stone dead.

The servant screamed.

"Shut up, old cow!" Xuan said, and she turned off any further sounds as if an electrical switch had been flicked.

David told her to go back in the house and not to say anything to anyone about what had just happened. If she did, they would know and would come back for her. Chi ran to the body and removed his identification cards from his coat to use as evidence of the righteousness of their mission and its results. Late that afternoon, young Mr. Pham reportedly suffered a fractured neck in a freak accident at the embassy.

That case was not very different from many thousands of others that dealt with VCI operators and sympathizers throughout South Viet Nam during the months of late January through April. PAVN and VCI forces paid an extremely high price for their General Offensive and Uprising of *Tet Mau Than*. Estimates of the combatants that served the cause of the north—agreed upon by both sides—were 84,000 men. Of those, the Communists sustained losses of 45,000 killed by the end of February, including some of their most experienced cadres. Tens of thousands more enemy soldiers were wounded or captured.

The Phoenix program rounded up and eliminated most of the remaining Viet Cong in South Viet Nam. The Tet offensive was—therefore, in the judgement of both sides—a military defeat of massive proportions for the North Vietnamese and the Vietcong. Militarily, Tet changed everything: fresh determination was exhibited by the Thiệu government. On February 1st, Thiệu declared a state of martial law; and on the 15th, the National Assembly passed his request for a general mobilization of the population. That resulted in the induction of 200,000 largely willing draftees into the armed forces by the end of the year—an unprecedented political victory for the RVN.

However, also on February 1st, General Nguyen Ngọc Loan, chief of the National Police, publicly executed VCI officer Nguyen Van Lem, a spy captured in civilian clothing. Unfortunately for the South, the execution was captured by a famous Western photographer, Edward T. Adams, and a film cameraman. That small piece of photo journalism went to press entitled *"Saigon Execution."* It won the 1969 Pulitzer Prize for

Spot News Photography. When the American War was chronicled years later, that piece of photography was—and still is—widely seen as a defining moment in the Vietnam War. Because of its influence on public opinion in the United States, it became known as "the picture that lost the war."

Adding to that, many of the victims of the CIA's Phoenix Program were in fact innocent. By 1972 Phoenix operations were responsible for more than 81,000 Vietcong and 26,000 prisoners otherwise 'neutralized'— some whose crime was only to have become unpopular with village headmen or CIA informants.

After the stunning military victory by the West, the war dragged on for two more desultory months without changing the status quo. However, the North Vietnamese were able to prolong the Paris Peace talks interminably until American public opinion sapped all the energy for prolonging the talks out of the weary Allied negotiators; and, on April 30, 1975, the United States evacuated as many of its combatants and sympathizers as possible. The news media and the American public were able to snatch a colossal defeat out of the jaws of a clear-cut and decisive victory. Psychologically and politically, it was a disaster. It was an ignominious defeat and a chaotic evacuation entirely reminiscent of that by the French after Dien Bien Phu in 1954.

> "The reality of the 1968 Tet offensive was that Hanoi had taken a big gamble and had lost on the battlefield... Our powerful air force and navy air resources were poised and ready. We could have flattened every war-making facility in North Vietnam. But the hand-wringers had center stage, the anti-war elements were in full cry. The most powerful country in the world did not have the willpower needed to meet the situation."
> –USN Admiral, Ulysses S. Sharp, Pacific Fleet commander, *We Could Have Won in Vietnam Long Ago*. Reader's Digest, May, 1969

... "The difficulty...was summarized by a newspaper editor in the western film, The Man Who Shot Liberty Valance. Deciding not to publish the truth of an explosive political story, the editor justifies it by saying, 'When the legend becomes fact, print the legend..."

–John Marini, Professor of Political Science, Adapted from Hillsdale College, *Politics by Other Means: The Use and Abuse of Scandal,* Imprimis, Hillsdale, Michigan, March, 2019

"You can kill ten of our men for every one we kill of yours. But even at those odds, it will be you who will tire of it; and you will lose; and we will win."

–Ho Chi Minh

PART TWO

PROLOGUE III

Afghanistan

CHAPTER ONE

Away out here they've got a name
For rain and wind and fire
The rain is Tess,
The fire's Joe
And they call the wind Maria
Maria blows the stars around
Sets the clouds a-flyin'
Maria makes
The mountains sound like folks was out there dyin'
Maria (Maria)
Maria (Maria)
They call
The wind
Maria
— *They Call the Wind Maria*, Lyrics by Alan J. Lerner
and music by Frederick Loewe for their
Broadway musical, *Paint Your Wagon*, 1951

Reglan Desert. Southwest Highlands Plateau, south of Central Highlands, Afghanistan, October, 1981

Four men sat on a barren hill overlooking a desolate dun-colored wadi, their faces covered with a heavy cotton cloth to keep out the blowing sand. Their clothing—*Perahan wa tunban*, *patkay* turban, and heavy wool shawl, all the color of the omnipresent sand that flurried around them and invaded their skin pores, finger and toe nail beds, and crotches—identified them to anyone who might have passed them by, as a nomad, a farmer, or a Pashtun mujahideen. It would be a highly unlikely event for their presence to be noted out there in the vastness of the desert which was as inhospitable as the dark side of the moon. Like all desert men, each of them had an AKM-74 slung over his shoulders, a skin bag for water, and a wide belt around his long tunics and baggy folded trousers holding a wicked looking recurved slender *Pesh-kabz* stabbing knife.

Despite their heavy beards, aquiline noses, and brown skin complexions, fluency with Arabic, Urdu, and Pashto, none of them were natives of Afghanistan or the Middle East. None of them were Muslims. None of them were religious–let alone fanatics–like the men around them. These four men were special agents of the United States Central Intelligence Agency serving in the National Clandestine Service as operations officers. All four had at least ten years of field service on their records—most of which was served in various locations and with several different specialties throughout the Middle East. All of them were hand-picked for their current positions by U.S. Congressman Charlie Wilson, Democrat, of the 2nd District of Texas and his man in Afghanistan and Pakistan, GS-12 Gust Lascaris Avrakotos and with the full–but unacknowledged—approval of the Seventh Floor at Langley.

These four men were as secretive as it is possible for men to be. None of them even knew the full or real names of the other three. Bill Edward Campbell was known among the four as "Ball"; Jonathon C. (NMN); Hendricks was "Crank"; Harvey Edward James O'Dwyer, was "Three," and Robert Emmanuel McDonald, was "Bob." The requirements for their having their GS-11 ratings and for being chosen to suffer the heat, frustration, and deprivation, of their NCS posting in Afghanistan were: to be at least eighteen-years-old, a United States citizen, must possess a bachelor's degree with an overall average minimum GPA of 3.0–have at least a college bachelor's degree—two had master's and two were PhDs—be a fluent polyglot.

It was required that each man have a history of traveling or living abroad, have a proven sensitivity to other cultures, have excellent physical and psychological health, be in an excellent level of physical conditioning, be able to prove that they are energetic and have a high degree of endurance, street sense, and good intuition. It was vital that the prospective agent be able to cope well under stress, and be willing and prepared to spend most of his Careers working overseas; orphans and bachelors were given high preference.

In addition, Wilson and Avrakotos required that the men have no tattoos or piercings, be hirsute and present themselves for their recruitment appointment in a long full face beard and scalp uncut for at least three months, have excellent vision unaided by glasses, be able to shoot eight out of ten bulls-eyes at eight hundred yards, and that they be proficient with knives, unarmed hand-to-hand combat, and able to use a plentiful variety of large and small weapons.

The agents had fairly similar backgrounds, educational and military experiences, and duration of service in the Central Intelligence Agency.

Bill Edward Campbell—"Ball," was a handsome young man—twenty-nine-years-old with dense brown hair which was now frizzy, greasy, and totally unkempt, like that of the other carefully chosen members of his team. He was slender with very strong and agile musculature. He had hazel eyes with a mere tint of green, not that different from many of the mujahideen with whom he fought. He bore a diagonal facial scar from a bayonet slicing from hand-to-hand fighting he sustained during the waning years of the Viet Nam conflict; and for which, he received the Silver Star. Jonathon C. (NMN) Hendricks, "Crank," was the group's jack-of-all-trades in electronics, mechanics, and resourcefulness, as well as a great man to have on your side in a fight. He had an olive complexion, brown hair the color of mud, large nose, full lips, and a perpetual scowl.

Harvey Edward James O'Dwyer, "Three," was lanky and looked like he was all elbows and knees without his clothes and despite his voracious appetite. Had it not been for the proscription against alcohol for the duration of the unit's time in service, Three would have been a confirmed alcoholic even at his young age of twenty-five. He had deep brown eyes, very heavy eyebrows and beard without a hint of grey.

Robert Emmanuel McDonald, "Bob," was the only man among them whose code nickname matched his birth name in any way. Bob had ginger hair in copious amounts all over his body. In that, he was not so different from many of the mujahideen who sported red hair and green eyes. His face was pockmarked from untreated adolescent acne. He was so fond of his first name that he refused to lose it even for the clandestine service. He was a member of a bizarre organization entitled "Bob's of the U.S.," a twenty-thousand-member group which included fourteen women. He was from Texas, and willing to fight if anyone should make the mistake of disrespecting the great Lone Star State or that greatest of football schools, the University of Texas Longhorns in Austin. He was a stocky, tough, superstar, tight end whose football career terminated when he fractured his left hip in the Texas-OU game during his senior year in 1973. Twelve players and two coaches went to Parkland Hospital with significant injuries that afternoon, and 412 inebriates associated with both schools passed through the emergency rooms of that world's busiest ER that night. Every intern, resident, and surgically inclined medical student, and not a few nursing students, were dragooned into service as they always were for the famous yearly Texas/Oklahoma brawl.

The four agents had several things in common besides their fairly similar physical looks: they had all been in special forces; all had served at least briefly in the recent unpleasantness in Viet Nam; all four trained in the grueling CIA special "dark agent" program at "The Farm" in Virginia and did not wash out; and finally, they all were seconded to service in the infamous CIA Phoenix Program. They were good men who could be mean as junk yard dogs when they had to be.

The wind began to pick up as it always did at sunrise in the desert.

"The wind is gonna blow the dirt off our guys if it gets any worse," Crank muttered.

"Won't matter, anyway," Ball said. "The dust'll be so thick we won't be able to see to shoot from here anyway."

He checked to see if his favorite rifle was still free of the infiltrating dust. He kept his personal treasure in a camo duffle lined with oil cloth. The 1963 Soviet Dragunov semi-automatic marksman sniper rifle and its 7N14 ammunition developed for snipers were maintained assiduously against the corrosive fine sand. Ball had a good supply of the original Soviet 151 grain projectiles that travel at 830 m/s with a sharp hardened steel core service ammunition. Like the rifle, it all felt smooth and clean. Ready. The rifle had been in perfect condition when it was removed from the dead hands of a Red Army sergeant a year ago. The only improvement by the CIA ballistics lab had been to add a genuine Soviet quick-detachable PSO-1 optical sight with improved lenses and to add thermite to the cartridges for more explosive heat and incendiary power. They would still be able to make the necessary shots if the targets—three

BTR-80 personnel carriers—would only get there in the next fifteen minutes before the weather socked in.

The wind velocity was increasing, and visibility was decreasing. Another ten minutes and they would not be able to see far enough to have the required accuracy. Dust devils began to form in the distance and were moving towards the agents' position. Ball knew that he would be unable to see his mujahideen's hidey-holes in a few minutes. That was not all bad; neither would the Sovs.

Bob took his customary prone position as the spotter while Ball readied himself and his weapon for his shot. It would have to be 36 and ¼ centimeters high to account for the distance and wind drift. He picked out a rock by the side of the ragged gravel road and sighted in. Visibility was all right, not perfect; but it would do.

Bob asked, "Hey Ball, do you know what the real miracle was when Moses saw the burning bush in the Sinai desert?"

"It was pretty much a miracle to see a burning bush way out there in this sand pit, I'd guess."

"Nah, the real miracle was that there was a bush to see."

Both men chuckled, and Ball said, "No chance of seeing a bush out here in the Reglan Desert of Afghanistan."

Three squinted through his binoculars at the western distance.

"Sovs in sight," he said, his voice gravelly from the dust in the back of his throat.

"Got 'em," Bob said.

He began to follow the vehicles' approach through his spotting scope.

"Three minutes tops," he estimated.

"Got 'em in my scope," Ball said. "Can you see the mujs?"

"I see a few fuzzy humps in the sand. I think its them."

"Pray they don't get riled up yet."

"See the little red ribbon by the rock?" Bob asked Ball.

"Yeah, just."

"Everybody on it?"

They all said they could see it.

"When the first Ruskie truck goes past it, hit the detonator, Three. Ready?" Bob asked.

"Like we haven't gone over it fifty times," Three snapped.

"Twenty seconds and counting," Bob said and began to count backwards.

As always, his visual estimations were spot on.

Three BTR-80s came into full view and approached the red ribbon at speed.

"Hit it!" Bob ordered, and hell broke loose.

Three detonated the DIED immediately in front of the first personnel carrier, and Crank detonated the IED behind the third truck a second after the first explosion. The BTR-80s slammed on their brakes and began to move about in the confined space in the trap as if it was going to be possible for them to escape. The donkeys that had hauled in the IEDs brayed in donkey terror.

"Target locked on," Ball said and slowly squeezed the trigger.

A quiet throaty whumpf noise came out of the end of the Dragunov sniper rifle; and in two seconds, the driver of the first troop truck was dead. He fired three more times, and after the third round exited the Dragunov's barrel, all three drivers were dead from precise head shots.

"Missed. Had to shoot twice at the middle one," Ball said by way of self-criticism.

"You're slippin' old man. You can see the other side of life's hill comin' towards you." Bob ribbed Ball.

Ball ignored his friend. Both of them knew that Ball was barely twenty-nine and was still one of the best sniper shots in the world.

"Let's get down there," Ball ordered and began to put away his sniper equipment.

All four men took up their *modernizírovanny Avtomát Kaláshnikova* [AKM-74s], fixed the type I bayonets, and began to trot down the hillside, slipping and sliding over the sand dusted rocks.

As they started their descent, the mounds of dust below them came alive, and from each a ragged, bearded, robed, desert phantom appeared and began running towards the terrified Red Army regulars.

They were screaming their ages-old battle cry and adding *"Allahu Akhbar!!!"* every few steps.

The Soviets were confounded, startled, and beginning to panic as they saw the wild mountain-men rushing towards them heedless of any of the desultory protective fire coming from the vaunted Russian army. A jackal and a pair of foxes scattered away from the screaming horde. In less than a minute the mujahideen were on the Soviets, and it was a slaughter. The four CIA agents arrived too late to be able to exert any kind of control over the blood lust and savagery roiling before them.

Recognizing the futility of trying to reason with the mujahideen, Ball, shouted, "Let them get it out of their system. Nothing we can do about it. This poor bunch of Sovs is going to pay for the slaughter in the Chindawol uprising on June 23, 1979. The ruling Khalq-PDPA communist government–propped up by the Soviet Red Army—massacred men, women, and children; and the mujahideen never forgot or forgave. It was not in their nature. Just hope it happens quickly."

The "battle," such as it was, lasted less than ten minutes. Soviet infantrymen–even those who begged–were bayoneted, garroted, beheaded, stabbed, and shot to death. Their corpses were mutilated. Bodies were disemboweled, heads smashed with gun butts, and sledge-hammers, and pieces of Russian soldiers were taken as trophies.

The four battle-hardened U.S. intelligence agents who thought they had seen everything, finally had to turn their heads aside.

Then the plunder began. The four agents fought to bring about enough order to see to it that the weaponry, documents, and the vehicles were saved for future use. The mujahideen stripped the Russian soldiers of their shirts, trousers, boots, belts, side arms, and knives. Their women swept in behind the men to finish off any survivors and to extract gold teeth and ears, and brass belt plates as trophies for body counts.

"They're lucky none of them survived to learn about the tender mercies of the Afghan women," Three said soberly.

"Let's get this stuff back to base," Ball said, and the four men split up to give orders to the headmen of the mujahideen to get the trucks loaded down with booty and driven to the desert camp for distribution to the deserving tribes.

"Another quiet day at the office," Crank said, his voice strained.

"Welcome to sunny Afghanistan," said Ball as he swung his muscular frame into the driver's seat of the forward BTR-80.

CHAPTER TWO

Office of the Director of the Central Intelligence Agency, 7ᵗʰ Floor OHB, CIA Building, Langley, Virginia, May 12, 1981

Meeting recorded and stamped "TOP SECRET, EYES ONLY, Director and POTUS

Officers present: DCIA, ADCIA, WH Chief of Staff, Don Thomas Regan, Rep. Hon. Charles Nesbitt Wilson, Special Agents: Bill Edward Campbell, code name "Ball"; Jonathon C. (NMN) Hendricks, code name "Crank"; Harvey Edward James O'Dwyer, code name "Three"; and Robert Emmanuel McDonald, code name "Bob."

Presenter: DCIA Wm. Casey

Subject: Urgent covert action ordered by President Reagan under 1981 Executive Order 12333 to be employed against the Soviet invasion of Afghanistan.

Summary:
1. Illegal Soviet invasion of independent and sovereign nation of the Democratic Republic of Afghanistan from December 24, 1979 to the present day to sure up the pro-Communist government of Parcham leader, Babrak Kamalin. CIA noted growth of Soviet domination as far back as 1973. It was noted

with alarm and followed closely by covert agents that leaders in the Kremlin were hoping for a rapid and complete military takeover that would secure Afghanistan's place as a Middle East exemplar of the Brezhnev Doctrine, which held that once a country became socialist, Moscow would never permit it to return to the capitalist camp.

2. President Reagan determined that the Brezhnev Doctrine would never be applied successfully in the Middle East, but the president and the intelligence and military services were determined to avoid direct conflict with the Soviet Union that could plunge the two major powers into a thermonuclear war.

3. The president orders that the CIA send agents to Afghanistan to infiltrate its military, governmental units, diplomatic corps, and to disrupt the Soviet dominated agencies to the greatest degree possible without implicating the United States as being involved. The DCIA is ordered to provide agents to assist the mujahideen freedom fighters in any way possible. Sufficient funding is set aside to provide for inducements, payment of patriots of freedom to obtain intelligence information and to set up training and arming of insurgents against the communist regime and the Soviets, and to encourage guerilla fighters to link up with other tribal units with the goal of developing a unified fighting force to drive out the Soviets. Agents in place will direct CIA activities vis-à-vis the mujahideen and to act as the action arm of U.S. involvement, in deepest secrecy.

4. Rep. Charles Wilson will act as the liaison between the agents, the CIA directorate, and the federal government, including the executive and legislative branches. He will be key in seeing to it that funding is available as needed. Mr. Wilson described his criteria for selection of extremely secret and highly trained agents to be employed in Afghanistan. To quote the Honorable Mr. Wilson, "I do not want knuckle-draggers who want to perform heroics behind the lines. They all have to be team players but also be individuals capable of being strategic thinkers and weapons experts. I look for Green berets, men with NATO experience studying the Soviets up close, and those fully prepared for guerilla warfare. They are required to demonstrate essentially native-born fluency in at least

two languages, esp. Russian and Soviet satellite languages, Urdu, Pashtun, and Arabic. Arabic is critical. I demand that they be well-trained in HA-LO parachuting, mountain climbing, demolition, effective at ambushes and kidnapping, and rappelling. I look for nerdy nondescript-looking bookworm guys, good at dating the prettiest of Texas girls, good at kicking ass in a bar fight, and are boring grinds. I try to get ethnics of one sort or another, guys who are unemotional and can give bloodlessly precise responses to questions about arms, strategy, and killing—especially killing. Each of them has to have studied guerrilla warfare like other men study medicine or engineering. Above all else, my dirty dozen has to believe that there is no reason why the mujahideen cannot win. No dumb geniuses for me. Let me explain that. My guys often performed mediocrely in school but, in fact, have very high IQs. Genius IQ is generally considered to begin around 140 to 145, representing ~.25% of the population–1 in 400–and all my guys fit into that category. Finally, they have to pass the fifteen-month CIA training course at Camp Peary.

5. The first four in-country operative agents will be known by code names: Ball, Bob, Three, and Crank. In keeping with June 23, 1982 Intelligence Identities Protection Act which bans publication of the names of covert intelligence officers, under no circumstances are the true identities of these men to be divulged, the number of agents involved, or that American operatives are present in Afghanistan. If captured or killed, the identities of the men will remain secret, and the CIA and the United States Government will deny any knowledge of such agents or any covert activities on their part.

6. Given the extreme importance of this mission, it is anticipated that this operation will become one of the–if not the–largest covert operations in the nation's history, and the level of secrecy will rival that of the Manhattan Project and other similar crucial actions. The most severe of penalties will apply to anyone for any divulgence of information about what will be officially—and secretly–called Operation Cyclone, even if accidental and nonpurposeful. By seeing this document, the reader is committed to absolute secrecy under the Official Secrets Act.

Special Agents were administered the oath.

Rep. Wilson responded: "Gentlemen, it is immediately obvious that four men–although they are superb agents—constitute an insufficient number to operate successfully in a hostile war situation in a country covering 250,000 square miles of territory with some thirty-six and a half million warring people. It is aptly known as the 'Graveyard of Empires.' I have a list of a dirty dozen agents ready to go, and they will need to be vetted quickly. We will need a ton of money, and I will see to it that the appropriations committee gets off its duff. This is the most important operation ever started by the United States, and I am going to see that we add the commies in Russia to the graveyard."

CHAPTER THREE

"The guerrilla fights the war of the flea, and his military enemy suffers the dog's disadvantages: too much to defend; too small, ubiquitous, and agile an enemy to come to grips with."
—Robert Taber, *War of the Flea: The Classic Study of Guerrilla Warfare*, The Citadel Press, New York, 1965

Tunnels in the Sodyaki Ghar Mountain, Paktia Province, near the Mujahideen logistic base situated at Zhawar Kili Al-Badr Camp, six kilometers from the Pakistani border, October 12, 1983

Five operations officers of the U.S. Central Intelligence Agency–who looked more mujahideen than the mujahideen–sat in a cave deep in the system dug out in the Sodyaki Ghar Mountain waiting for the Pakistanis and a man known to them only as an extremely secretive "Tactician." He was touted as a charismatic guru of sorts able to win men to the jihadi cause. The Paki ISI agents arrived first and acted as a security phalanx for the men coming in a later convoy. The electrical lighting system in the cave belied the inky blackness of the night outside. The "Tactician" only traveled by night, and no one was ever given his schedule or route of travel.

It was over an hour beyond the expected time of arrival, and the tired CIA ops agents were becoming antsy.

The lead agent, Gust Avrakotos, said, "Calm down. He'll get here when he gets here. I have met him several times when Charlie and I brought in arms shipments for his jihadists. I only know him as Tim Osman, but—as you will see—that's as fake as your own silly little names. Don't act surprised if he gives some different name. I can tell you this. This Osman guy is completely unpredictable and may or not come today or in a few days. He is worth the annoyance, believe me. We need the guy. Try and play nice."

The other four shrugged and withdrew into themselves and sucked on their weak and unpleasant tasting Tuartara-APA pale ale bottles smuggled into Afghanistan from New Zealand. Another hour passed before the signal was received that the Pakis were entering the cave. The arrogant ISI agents greeted Gust with bear hugs and triple cheek kisses and began a hushed conversation in Pashto explaining when Osman would arrive and what he expected of the CIA agents.

The ISI leader, Col. Awan al Malik, pointedly ignored the other agents, speaking to Gust as if they were not there. Col. Al Malik was short, rotund, but very muscular, and bow-legged. He had the requisite Muslim bushy full beard covering a generous portion of the pock-marked skin of his bronze colored face. He had exceedingly full eyebrows and tufting hair sprouting from the tragi of his ears like a goat and his flaring nostrils giving him something of a comical look. The cruelty of his eyes overshadowed any humor a man might feel glancing at his hard face.

Al Malik threw off his turban and woolen shawl revealing his Inter-Services Intelligence officer's uniform with its battle ribbons and paratrooper insignia and his weapons—standard issue FN 57, and two hand-guns from his web-belt, a Heckler & Koch USP [*Universelle Selbstladepistole*] and a Glock 40 semi-automatic. He left his massive Bowie knife—a gift from Charlie Wilson, whom he considered to be his counterpart in the America CIA–hanging from his belt as a reminder. He wore snake-skin cowboy boots, also a gift from the flamboyant Texan.

Shortly thereafter, twenty-five-year-old Tim Osman quietly entered the cave room. He was slim and tall–6'6" tall and weighed 160 pounds–more like a Saudi than an Afghan. He had a long, thin face, a full-face beard and scalp hair down to the base of his neck of thin stringy black hair with touches of premature gray. Osman's eyebrows were thick and jet black without the stringy quality of rest of his hair. Like the Prophet, he plucked his pubic and axillary hair, a fact that was revealed when all the men took a communal bath. His skin was dark brown, as much from his years in the Middle East sun as from his genetics. His brown eyes were large and active, seemingly taking in everything at once. Osman—nobody called him, "Tim"–had a patrician and uninviting face. He never smiled. Although he was in the home of Afghans, and in the presence of his putative employers—the CIA–his air of superiority dominated; and he seemed to take for granted that he was the man in charge. No one seemed inclined to challenge that presumption.

Osman wore a well-seasoned olive drab coat and pants and had a relatively clean turban that was wrapped around the locally favored tight white skullcap. Like most Pashtun men, his turban was tied so that one end of the cloth hung down across his chest. He habitually wore a military-style wrist-watch on his right wrist, with the face of the watch protected on the underside of his thin wrist. The CIA men considered most of his apparel to be rather a costume, and especially the flair of the turban with the long end hanging down to catch the wind and the west German affectation of the right wrist bearing the signature watch. They kept such thoughts strictly to themselves.

Three silent women in burkas served the men *naan* and *manto*, carefully folded dumplings with *halal* sanctified minced meat inside, steamed in a cooker with onions. As soon as that course was cleared, the ghostly black-garbed serving women reappeared with a platter filled with fried rice with chunks of carrots, onions, *lahm maa'iz* [boer goat meat], raisins, and mixed special dried herbs.

Osman inquired, "Was the *dhabiha* performed in accordance with the Holy Book, Brother Hajii?"

"I supervised the mullah myself, Brother Osman," the Afghan host, Hajii bin Muhammad al Khost, said nervously. "A single cut was made to the four *awdaj* [tracts]–the jugular, the swallowing tube, the great artery of the head, and the windpipe."

"The dedication was to Allah?"

"Of course, Great Leader."

Osman nodded his grudging consent. The women attempted to serve a special drink—iced chai.

Osman announced with his usual self-designated authority, "I forbid it. None of my followers may partake of iced water. It is a western innovation which is not spoken of in the *Qur'an*."

He also forbade the playing of music. The women bowed their heads and scurried away with the offending drink and substituted it with goat's milk. The musicians disappeared silently as well.

For dessert, the men were given *haft-mehwah*, a mixture of seven fruits and nuts symbolizing spring, an optimistic gesture since anything approaching spring was nine months Away. It was not a given that any of these perpetual warriors would still be alive by then. After they were surfeited from the large meal, they indulged in a hot soaking communal bath.

After the meal, Osman was eager to get down to the business at hand and the reason he and his brethren had traveled so far and at such risk.

As he settled into the steaming water, the "Tactician" turned to the sweating Col. Al Malik and said, "Praise be to God the Lord of the Worlds, and prayers and peace be upon the noblest of those sent, his family, companions and whoso has followed them with *ihsan* to the Day of Judgment. Some of the dear brothers asked me to offer their congratulations on your efforts of late—both you, on your blessed Islamic country, and on ISI, where you serve. You are recognized at this time of the history of our blessed jihad, and God Almighty is the Guarantor of Success for us all. Beloved brother, Awan, your prowess as a warrior of Allah is known far and wide for your daring capture of two American agents of the Crusader RAND Corporation who were supplying tactical information about the movements of the mujahideen to the hated Soviet atheists."

Col. Al Malik bowed in humility for such high praise indicative that it came from a great leader, which mystified the four CIA agents. Avrakotos seemed to accept the idea without even showing his usual skepticism at inflated rhetoric.

Osman continued, "We cannot rest on our laurels, as the ancient Greeks were fond of saying. No, it is time that we find good brothers to carry out a particularly important set of missions. As you all know the hated Soviets are gradually bringing together equipment and forces to launch an attack on the major mujahideen base at Zhawar, situated in Paktia Province. Our scouts indicate that it will be very soon. We lack the heavy armor and powerful weapons possessed by the Crusaders. We must correct that imbalance within days.

"I have a plan and a method to carry it out. You must supply the brave fighters and every ounce of their daring. We will move by night on the DRA base in the west border of the Paktia province. Our fighters will enter the compound by night. Our brothers within the compound will arrange to leave the keys in the ignitions of two M-55 Soviet tanks. They will be filled to capacity with ammunition. We will have trailer trucks waiting two kilometers away on the road to Zhawar. We will drive the tanks onto the trailers and transport them to our base. When the crusaders come to attempt to conquer our supply base, they will be totally surprised to find the tanks aiming at them and will be beaten and destroyed, so help me God! the Merciful and the All-Powerful."

Avrakotos asked, "Who among the mujahideen can drive such machines, General Emir?"

Osman gave a brief quiet laugh, "Why, Brother of the Book, that is why you were ordered to bring your operatives with you. We have intel that at least two of them are altogether facile with tank operations. Is that not so?"

"It is so. Nice of you to inform me at this late date."

"Not so late, Brother; we have nearly three days before the attack. Is that not enough time for your intrepid fighters?"

Avrakotos raised his hands in mock surrender.

He turned to Ball and looked him square in the eyes.

"Who me, boss? I am only a diplomatic analyst. It says so in my official papers on file in Rawalpindi."

"Humility ill becomes you, Ball. You and Three can do this caper without breaking a sweat," Avakotos said and smiled.

CHAPTER FOUR

The most deserving of people in wealth are the mujahideen in the path of God so that sufficiency may be realized even if infants, children and the hungry die, because preserving the religion is of greater priority than preserving life.

–Official Statement of the Armed Islamic Group

Tunnels in the Sodyaki Ghar Mountain, Paktia Province, near the Mujahideen logistic base situated at Zhawar Kili Al-Badr Camp, six kilometers from the Pakistani border, October, 12, 1983 later that night

After Osman and the mujahideen left the communal fire, the five CIA agents sat silently until they were sure that they were the only people still awake. Ball and Avrakotos crept around the perimeter of the fire pit and checked into all the shadowy nooks and crannies. Confident that there was no one–not even women or children–to hear what he was going to say, Avrakotos brought his men close to him and whispered.

"Look, you guys, I know you think something is pretty fishy here, and you deserve to know what is going on. Thanks for keeping mum while the conversations were going on. The first thing is, do any of you know who our "Osman" is?"

There was a unanimous shaking of heads.

"I recognize the man from some photos I've seen, but I can't place him for the life of me," Crank said.

"Good. Enough of secrets. I am going to tell you one of the greatest secrets in the U.S. You have been sworn to guard all classified info with your lives, and this is one of the most important ones you will ever learn. Like "Tim Osman" is a *nom de guerre* that only the Firm and a few hand-picked mujahideen are privy to. Only the man himself, me, and Charlie Wilson, know his real name, background and purpose. Not even the DCIA himself. Osman is a Saudi whose real name is Usama bin Laden. You may hear Osama, but our linguists insisted on the "U."

"Here is the short version of his background: His father was a very rich and powerful Saudi privy to the royal family's thoughts and decisions. His name was Muhammad bin Awad bin Laden meaning that he came from a seriously aristocratic lineage. Muhammad was an immigrant from Yemen who was known to be both brilliant and ruthless. By dint of his extreme work ethic, he founded a multi-billion-dollar construction conglomerate–The Saudi Binladin Group–and made himself the richest man in the Muslim world except for the Saudi family.

His son–Usama bin Laden–the seventeenth of some fifty-eight children—was born March 10, 1957. Usama received an ultra-elite, Western-style, education—the best available in Saudi Arabia–then attended a Christian Quaker school in Lebanon for a finishing year. His father—Muhammad—had at least twenty-two wives and fifty-eight children. Son Usama has had at least five wives, and probably several concubines, and is said to have been the father of twenty-four or likely more children himself. They are fairly well known but have been kept away from his jihadist activities for their protection.

"Bin Laden graduated with a degree in civil engineering in 1979 from King Abdulaziz University in Jedda, Saudi Arabia. He first came to Afghanistan that same year and used supplies from his father's company to help support his jihadist movement against the Soviet Union's invasion—several million dollars-worth. Son–Usama Bin Laden–inherited between $25 to $30 million when Muhammad died. Usama invested very wisely and built his holdings up to the billionaire level, I'm informed. He turned the whole potful over to his jihadist activities in Afghanistan. So, at present, he is the *capo di tutti capi* of the jihadi mafia."

"How in the world did that secret remain secret?" Three asked.

"People died who learned it. For his followers, it is more than their lives are worth to leak to the press or otherwise."

"I've got a pretty good idea, but, Gust, what is he to us?"

"Simple: the enemy of my enemy is my friend. Capiche?"

"Sure, but how does that work?"

"Good and timely question. Also, a simple answer: bin Laden serves up the fanatical jihadist soldiers to die for our mutual cause; and we provide the money, equipment, and weaponry for our beardy brethren to fight against those devils, the Sovs. Make no mistake. When the Sovs are beaten—and they will be—our relationship will do a 180° turn; and we will face our own weapons in a new and long Afghan war."

"Jeez," Crank said. "Is the CIA always involved in stupid things? I remember the Phoenix Program in Viet Nam; that was another ill-thought-out shamble."

"But remember, my comrade and brother-in-arms, ours is not to question why; ours is just to do or die. And, besides, that's why we all make the big bucks, right?"

The five had a good, albeit quiet, chuckle.

"I have a bit more intel you need to know. Before the Sovs and the DRU make their attack on Zhawar, Charlie Wilson and I will bring a multi-million-dollar cache of weapons and gold from Pakistan to Zhawar by mule and camel train along with beaucoup more fighters for the cause. In fact, I will not be part of the raid on the DRU because I am heading back to Paki tomorrow to get that show on the road."

"Crap," Ball said, "We were counting on having you."

"Like I said, 'yours is not to question why.'"

It was good that Avrakotos could not see the collective set of frowns on his agents' sober faces in the darkness.

CHAPTER FIVE

"But this US and western habit of playing with jihadi groups, which then come back to bite them, goes back at least to the 1980s war against the Soviet Union in Afghanistan, which fostered the original al-Qaida under CIA tutelage.

"It was recalibrated during the occupation of Iraq, when US forces led by General Petraeus sponsored an El Salvador-style dirty war of sectarian death squads to weaken the Iraqi resistance."

–Kenan Malik, *Terrorism has come about in assimilationist France and also in multicultural Britain. Why is that? The Guardian*, November 14, 2015.

DRA [Democratic Republic of Afghanistan] Army Outpost, Near the Pakistan Border, October 16, 1983.

The DRA base sat in the middle of a wide green valley protected by high mountains all around. Entry and exit to the valley were via narrow canyons at both ends of the valley over rough, rutted dirt roads which were impassable in the winter. Although the snow-pack was minimal that year–the freezing cold and icy winds rendering the perceived temperatures to well below zero–this was likely the last week in the year when the roads would be passable before the heavy snowfall locked the valley from intruders.

The base was manned almost entirely by newly conscripted soldiers of the Democratic Republic of Afghanistan whose enthusiasm for the Soviet puppet state and its imposed Marxist-Leninist and atheist ideology of government was shallow at best and forced upon the people and the soldiers by brutality. Forward scouts of the mujahideen brought back intelligence indicative of generalized sloth and indifference among the putative protectors, and frustration among their Russian officers.

The night was pitch black owing to overhanging dark clouds and a slit-size crescent moon. The Russian smoking lamps went out, and the camp closed down for another freezing and fitful night of poor sleep. The scouts and the forward mujahideen positions urged that the mission begin now.

Ball, Crank, Bob, Three, and ISI leader, Col. Awan al Malik, gathered close together and each nodded his assent without speaking.

The four CIA special agents silently separated from the main body of the mujahideen fighters and stealthily crept to the perimeter chain-link fence.

"Make the opening big enough to run two men in at a time," Ball ordered.

Crank wielded the metal cutters and made a large U-shaped opening which could be closed behind them and not be immediately evident to the guards. Then the agents ducked through the opening and stood on the sides of the opening to help their eight mujahideen cohorts through. Using silent hand signs, Ball and Bob directed the rest of the men into the compound. The most telling signs were raising two fingers and pointing in each of the four directions around the DRA camp followed by an unmistakable throats-slitting motion. It was not necessary to put their forefingers to their lips. Silence was a given if they were to survive the night and to complete the mission.

They went in two-by-two to be able to watch each other's backs. Each time they saw a guard, one slipped silently up behind the young soldier and dispatched him without a sound. Some guards made the mistake of smoking, in part to keep their fingers warm in the chill of the advancing night. Some DRG soldiers were half asleep and not adequately aware of the dangers lurking around them. Some were locked in conversation with a comrade—a discussion which would never matter again. Some were garroted; some stabbed in the kidneys which created such sudden and severe pain so that they could not cry out; some had their throats slit—a cut so deep that they were nearly decapitated—with a single *dhabiha* type cut through the jugular vein, the trachea, the esophagus, and the common carotid artery—which rendered the victims silent and unable to struggle in less than a second. There was not a single gunshot or outcry. The entirety of the external security corps was wiped out without any Soviet officer or enlisted man knowing it had happened.

Ball whispered into the ear of the nearest mujahideen in Pashtu, "Go back to the fence and fetch the rest of the brothers. Bring them to me here."

In five minutes, twenty-eight rough-hewn bearded wraiths emerged out of the gloom and reported to Ball for instructions.

"Three and Crank take two mujs each and get into the garage holding the tanks. Bob, get us four mujs to get the front gates open. Ibrahim, take the rest of the brothers and break into the barracks as soon as you hear the first shots from Bob and me. Three and Crank, take out the guards around the tanks silently if you can, but with however much noise you have to make in order to be certain that you two can drive the tanks out of the garage and towards the front gates. When Ibrahim and his men are ready, they will move into the guard houses and officers' quarters. Kill everyone, but especially make certain that the signal corps is put out of business before any radio or telegram signal can be sent to DRG HQ.

"Questions?"

There was a quick series of whispered, "nos."

"Then, go."

Ten minutes later, the first shot rang out. It came from the garage. Two more came from the same location, followed by simultaneous cacophonous fusillades from the two sets of barracks and the sentry posts. Within seconds fires erupted in five different places, and then the rumble of the two huge Soviet M-55 tanks could be heard coming from the back of the base towards the front.

A brief firefight erupted from the officers' quarters which resulted in the loss of six mujahideen freedom fighters and the superficial wounding of Crank.

When the brief furious shooting stopped, Ball squat-walked over to where Crank was lying on the frozen ground.

"How bad is it, buddy?"

"Just a flesh-wound, like Monty Python would say. No problem."

"Where?"

Crank looked around as if embarrassed, "Butt."

"Seriously? Tell me, are you really hurt or is it just your pride?"

"Deep scratch on one butt cheek. Probably enough that some of those nice ghost ladies in black will have to tend to it. You know how rigid they are about that general area of anatomy. Makes a guy worry, what with their jealous and over-zealous husbands hanging close around."

Confident that the Soviet officers had been neutralized, and there was no more threat to him or his men, Ball started to laugh.

"You old horn toad, I think are looking forward to having a little secret tryst with one of those lovelies. And, here, I was actually worried that you were hurt; and we would have to drag you to one of the tanks."

"Thanks for all of your tender caring, Brother. I'll walk to my tank and drive it out. Think how heroic I will appear to the ghost ladies."

"Here, Crank, let me help you up. Do you really think you can drive the tank? I'm serious now."

"I'm okay, Ball. I'll sit my sore cheek on a pillow, and I will be able to make it just fine. I only ask that you stand by when those ladies come at me with their knives; so, they don't forget who're the good guys and who the Sovs are."

"I'll watch your back—no pun intended, Brother."

"Swell."

Ball helped Crank to his feet. Crank screwed up his face in pain for a minute or so, then indicated that he was going to be all right. Ball helped his co-agent to the tank and up to the entrance port. When it was obvious that Crank was up to the task, Ball walked back into the center of the compound.

Umar Muhammad bin Khost and Ibrahim walked up to Ball. "We probably done here, Boss. You think?"

"Mostly, Brother Umar, but we need to make sure none of our nice government or Soviet friends are playing possum and can sneak out a call to the main HQ."

"What means, 'playing possum,' Boss?"

"Sorry, Brother. Is American funny talk. It means, acting like dead; so, we will not pay attention to him."

"Ah, Boss Man. Mujahideen have a solution. Also, we need to take a record for Al-Qaeda and other mujahideen boss people. Leave whole thing to me."

"Thank you, Umar. Take two or three men and check things out. I'll take the rest and start the convoy with the tanks to get them back to Zhawar. Good work today."

Umar nodded, pivoted about-face and headed back to where the fray seemed to have stopped.

Ball knew perfectly well how things would be handled, but it was not his country nor his army. His job was to make sure the mujahideen and their 'boss people' created and maintained an effective fighting force against the Soviet Union and its puppet regime in Afghanistan, no more.

Before he could get all the way into his tank, he began to hear several sources of screaming. Mujahideen yelled "Live free or die"–their national motto–and "*Allahu Akhbar*!! as they shot or stabbed to death any enemies still remaining alive. Then, Ball knew, the mujahideen would hurriedly collect a single ear from each of the dead enemies. And, he also knew that some of the unfortunates would be a little less dead than some of the others as they were being mutilated.

CHAPTER SIX

"I like to see good people win."

–Mac Miller

Pakistan Border Country, Near the Khyber Pass through the Spin Ghar [Safed Koh] Mountains Between Pakistan and Afghanistan, October, 16, 1983

Avrakotos was exhausted by the time the ISI vehicle in which he was riding arrived at the designated gathering site for loading the camels and mules. The sheer size of the operation was bewildering at first to Avrakotos who was second-in-command to the U.S. representative who was the actual leader. He hoped with all his mind that Charlie was going to be there since he was the only one who knew the whole picture. He and General Muhammad Zia-ul-Haq and defense minister General Abu Ghazala were in the vehicle with him. They would never admit it, but they were uneasy about the entire mission because it could be regarded as a CIA "bandit" operation.

By the time the operation was in full flower, the entire Pakistani involvement in aiding and supplying the mujahideen in the neighboring country of Afghanistan had come to be called "Charlie Wilson's War." If any portion of the planning and arranging went south, the sitting president, Gen. Zia, and his entire staff, perhaps even the reigning figures of the PPP [Pakistan People's Party] would go down to ruin. Zia could not be implicated in a CIA operation of any kind—his very life depended on it. The Islamists of Pakistan would destroy him; they were, in fact, looking for any excuse to bring the arrogant general/president to his knees.

Zia demonstrated his sense of ill-at-ease by fidgeting in his seat; Gen Ghazala clenched and unclenched his fists; and Avrakotos was sweating profusely. As the presidential motorcade pulled into the vast open valley they were struck by three things: there were thousands of camels and mules being loaded down with paniers full of ammunition, AK-47s, mortars and mortar rounds, uniforms, rations, and winter gear. There were hundreds of mujahideen gathering on the periphery as if they were about to attend a majlis with some sort of great Saudi chieftain in his opulent tent in the desert. Finally–and to the great relief of everyone–Charlie Wilson stood on the top of his Pakistani NIMR AJBAN—4X4 SOV-ISV [special operations vehicle] holding what looked for all the world like a political re-election rally.

Charlie was exuberant and full of enthusiasm. He welcomed the generals and Avrakotos as if the entire country was his own. He plied the generals and their staffs with copious amounts of hard liquor even though it was a crime even to transport the fine amber liquids across the nation.

"Hey, how is my favorite general?" Charlie greeted Zia who smiled and basked in the glow of Charlie's attention.

"Couldn't be better, my friend. What could be better than fifty-million-dollars-worth of military goods to defeat the atheist fiends from Russia who have come to our world to attack Allah's true religion?"

"Nothing, I can think of except maybe some Stinger missiles, and they are next on my agenda before the Senate Appropriations Committee. Incidentally, Mister President, you will really need to make a state visit during the time of that meeting to clinch the deal," Charlie said with his usual effusive gusto.

Zia became serious, "Charlie, that has to happen soon. The Soviet Hind Mi-24 helicopters are slaughtering us."

Charlie said, "Gust and I have been working on the Oerlikon Company to bring down the costs and bought beaucoup boxes of AK-47 ammo from them at $50 bucks a round to get their attention. We also have close to a thousand antiaircraft guns going into the paniers right now which should help kill at least a few Hinds."

"Charlie, you know that is not good enough," Gen. Ghazala said. "The Soviet Mi-29 Hind flying gunship is the Soviet's super weapon which to this date is invincible. You have never heard one as it flies in. It emits a blood-curdling sound that is designed to frighten our mujahideen out of their wits. Without the Stingers, the mujahideen will be finished in a year, and the Russians will run Afghanistan and will begin attacks on our sacred Pakistan soon after that. You need to get it done, my friend."

"I know, Abu, and have I ever failed you or the cause? It is like trying to turn a battleship to get secret funding out of Congress. I'll do it, though, and before the Sovs are too successful. That I promise."

Waiters brought in a small desert feast fit for princes to soften the concerns of the great wheeler-dealers meeting on the Pakistan plain—sweet tea with cardamom, a variety of soups, lamb, rice dishes, kabobs using spices and rich sauces common in Indian and the best Pakistan dishes, lentils and a beautifully fashioned inlaid wood tray covered with almonds, pistachios, and *toot* [dried berry snack]. Charlie had even managed to find dried oranges and blackened bananas—a rare treat from Pakistan.

Charlie knew that Zia was America's best ally in the region, and that he had to be mollified. He made every effort to avoid showing his concern. The day before he boarded his Air Force plane for Peshawar, he had been flatly turned down by the appropriations committee chair. The stakes could not be higher. The men watched the loaders pack the precious commodities onto the camels and mules. Charlie and Gust marveled at the speed and efficiency with which the expert cameleers and muleteers carried out their work.

When the animals were loaded, and the drovers were in full readiness, the lead cameleer approached the officers and informed them that they were ready to begin the march. Charlie had a weird sense of timing, almost a self-defeating psychological trait. When things got going well, he could always find a way to spoil things. He chose that moment to have a classical heart attack.

He clasped his right hand to his chest, and his skin turned an ashen pale.

He cried out in pain. "Pain in my chest, under my breastbone. Down my left arm!"

Zia yelled for a medic. Gust helped his boss and partner to the floor. In a matter of a few minutes, an ambulance arrived at Charlie's tent; and he was whisked away to Peshawar to the world-class Peshawar Institute of Cardiology off Post Office Road.

There in the broad and now crowded Peshawar Valley of the PashtunKhwa Province of Pakistan, all eyes turned to twenty-five-year-old Gust Lascaris Avrakotos. Gust knew what was at stake and what he had to do. First of all, he had to appear to be both fully competent and also confident, or these senior militarists would disband the entire project and leave the Afghan mujahideen to the tender mercies of the Soviet army and its lackies in the PDPA.

"*That must not happen*," he screamed to himself.

"Gentlemen, it is sad, even discomforting, to see Charlie have serious trouble; but it is time for this great military and humanitarian effort to get on its way. I know everything Charlie knows, and he has full confidence in me. I want your blessing, Generals; and I will get this show on the road."

He smiled, and that broke the ice. The generals laughed at his audacity since it was so like Charlies.' They did not ask if Gust had the same access to the U.S. congressional money and power. It was a good thing they did not do that because Congress had never heard of Gust Lascaris Avrakotos.

Gen. Zia nodded his assent, and the operation had all the permission necessary to get going.

Gust called Ahmed—the chief cameleer—and the great, noisy, odoriferous, and disorderly, caravan slowly began to move towards the Pakistan entrance at the summit of the Khyber Pass. Gust was not a praying man; but, if he were, he would have called on God, Jehovah, Allah, or Buddha, or all four, to grant favor to this endeavor.

After half an hour, the great caravan began to move in something approaching an orderly fashion. Gust and the senior mujahideen boarded the British Khyber Pass Railway from Landi Kotal town at the Pakistan entrance into the fabled pass. That mode of travel was slow but comfortable. The highway through the pass was in poor condition and slow going for the caravan which plodded along. Throughout millennia of history, the pass was a crucially important trade route between Central Asia and South Asia and a vital strategic military choke point.

Charlie had already paid the bribe/toll to the Paki Afridi tribesmen and the Shinwaris on the Afghan side who considered the pass to be their private property and that they had the right to impose an exorbitant toll. Over centuries of strife, Afghan mountain men had accepted the position of protectors of the Afridi and Shinwari rights which added cost but resulted in a fifty-five-kilometer passage free of fighting and time wasting.

After arrival in the Jamrud Valley, the lowest point of the Khyber Pass—Kipling's "sword-cut through the daunting jagged Safed Koh Mountains"–and the official entrance into Afghanistan, it was time for a rest. The pass was "no-go" region for the DRA and the Red Army; so, after a respite for the men and beasts and a refurbishment of food for both, the caravan began to move at the brisk pace developed through a region hallowed by millennia of movement of trade along the Silk Road. They had over 400 kilometers to go to reach the tunnels in the Sodyaki Ghar Mountains and only a few days in which to do it.

CHAPTER SEVEN

"It is better to be feared than loved."
    –Niccolò Machiavelli, *De Principatibus/Il Princip,*
    [The Prince], Publisher Antonio Blado d-Asola, 1532

Tunnels in the Sodyaki Ghar Mountain, Paktia Province, near the Mujahideen logistic base situated at Zhawar Kili Al-Badr Camp, Khost Province fifteen kilometers from the Pakistani border, October, 24, 1983

Gust Avrakotos arrived at the mouth of the tunnels late in the afternoon with a massive accretion of men, equipment, mules, and donkeys, that had been secreted into Khorasan—the name the mujahideen used for the Afghanistan/Pakistan region. The plan had been to enter Afghanistan from Pakistan through the dangerous Khyber Pass, and that was accomplished without the secret coming out–*Alhamdulillah.*

Gen. Abu Ghazala flew in on his official ISI aircraft to be present when the largesse from America arrived and–in all humility–to take credit. Mujahideen from forty nations had linked up with the caravan as soon as they heard about the looming battle with the Russians and their puppet army. By nightfall, there were over 2,000 jihadists cramming into the cave system. The materiél was hauled into the labyrinthine caves and tunnels; the camels and mules were hidden in stables near the rear of the caves; the tanks and heavy artillery were stacked in the garages dug out for that very purpose.

The intent and purpose of the Soviet Army units and their putative allies in the Democratic Republic of Afghanistan was to capture or destroy the mujahideen logistic and mustering base located at Zhawar near the Pakistani border. They had several obstacles to overcome in order to carry out that purpose: First, they had to get a superior force of soldiers, tanks, heavy equipment, artillery, and resupply routes. Second, they had to be able to set up main bases and front-line bases in order to begin and to sustain an assault against a nearly impregnable natural and man-made fortress. Third, since there was no hope of incorporating an element of surprise into their plan, they had to strike fear into the hearts and minds of the defenders.

The 12th and 25th divisions of the DRA supported by Soviet air power–all under the command of Jalaluddin Haqqani and Yunis Khalis– expected a force of less than a thousand mujahideen which was lacking heavy guns, tanks, and air power, to constitute the defense force all but guaranteeing an easy and quick victory. Nevertheless, the DRA wanted to score a decisive win that would seriously discourage the ragtag untrained mujahideen and their foreign masters into accepting a highly unfavorable cease fire treaty and willingness to lay down their arms and become citizens of the new Afghanistan. Their spies had informed the Soviet and DRA generals that the best mujahideen leaders could not make it to the area in time for the upcoming attack. The fools were making the Hajj and were presently in Mecca.

The first attack concentrated on capturing outlying villages in order to prevent resupply for the mujahideen and to strike fear into the observers hiding in the caves. The overwhelming communist forces swept into Lezhi, a small village. They had an unexpected piece of good fortune. One of the main mujahideen commanders was captured by some of the least capable of the DRG soldiers which gave great zeal to the rest of the soldiers.

To generate fear, the Soviets allowed the DRG fanatics to hang the mujahideen commander by his ankles from an entrance arch at the gates of the village. He was then beaten to death by soldiers driving by at high speeds and hitting the man with bats, pipes, and steel bars. When that bit of sport was done, the corpse was no longer recognizable as a human being. Women were raped; men were rounded up into the town square and machine-gunned; children were chased about with pick-up trucks and run over.

Five teen-agers were allowed to go free to tell the mujahideen in the caves what had transpired. They carried a message from Gen. Haqqani that no further atrocities would take place if the fortress garrison surrendered immediately.

The CIA agents and the three mujahideen commanders listened to the five surviving and extremely distraught teenagers with hard and unmoving faces. They reported to the main force of the mujahideen soldiers exactly what had happened.

A blood curdling war whoop went up from the men for whom family was second only to their faith in Islam. The piercing outcry of anguish and fury could be heard well into the ranks of the DRA soldiers. Many of them cringed, knowing that their wild mountain brethren were undeterred by the atrocious gesture in the villages. They knew these were men who would die during torture with a fixed sardonic smile on their faces. The Soviets ordered an all-out attack on one of the heavily fortified mujahideen passes. The battle raged for ten days with terrible casualties on the part of the DRA but minimal losses on the part of the jihadists. The battle turned in favor of the attackers only after Soviet airpower overwhelmed the defenders.

Buoyed up by their two successes, the DRG and Soviets advanced. This put them in a position high in the pass; so, they could fire artillery shells into the main camp of the mujahideen. Once again, the Soviet general sent a peace cadre to the caves. Shortly after the soldiers disappeared into the caves, they reappeared laid out on a cart pulled by pigs. Every man had been decapitated, castrated, and disemboweled.

This–of course–enraged the Soviet allied forces, and they rolled out their howitzers and began making range testing shots, all of which fell short.

Ball and Bob drove their tanks to the mouth of the cave and waited until acrid smoke from the Soviet artillery caused temporary invisibility. The two T-55 tanks thundered out of the cave opening and began hurling deadly counter fire into the totally surprised DRA forces. Mujahideen poured out of the caves screaming their battle cries and firing with lethal accuracy into the hated enemy lines. The Soviets and their allies sustained huge losses and quickly fell back in disarray. The DRA expected reinforcements from Pakistan, but when those commanders learned of the failed attack and the terrifying counterattack, they refused to join their allies, turned around and headed back home through the pass. The mujahideen held off any further attacks and returned to their cave hideouts relatively unscathed after more than forty days of fighting.

The DRA removed the first general from his command and replaced him with the best commander in the government's forces, Mohammad Nabi Azimi. Gust, Ball, Three, Bob, and Crank, agreed on an audacious plan and presented it to Gen. Abu Ghazala and the three mujahideen commanders—Sulaiman Abu Bakr ibn Muhammad, Amr Hajji Abdel Noir, and Murad Wardak al Sham. The CIA agents and the mujahideen commanders came to an agreement. The mujahideen commanders were pleased to the point of being amused when they thought about the idea. It was just crazy enough that it might work. At worst, it had to be better than hiding in holes in a mountain until they were pounded to pieces by artillery or worse, until they starved.

The plan was explained to 200 mujahideen in ten minutes. Fifty-four men, including the four agents, slipped out of the side entrance to the main cave complex and crept silently over rough, rocky terrain in near total darkness the four-and-a-half kilometer distance to the forward DRA scout camp. The inexperienced young Afghans and their officers in camp were over-confident and careless. They talked out loud; some smoked; some noisily used the latrine facilities.

The mujahideen stood among trees within five meters of their enemies. Ball gave the signal—three sharp clicks of his mic—and then they began to kill their quarries as noisily as possible, rending the night air with their marrow chilling battle cries.

The Soviet officers gained their equilibrium fairly quickly and began to bring their troops to a sort of rough order. The DRG enlisted men formed up into ten-man units and began firing back at the hated mujahideen. They were gaining ground with greater success than they might have hoped for; so, the officers drove their troops forward to contact the mujahideen who were obviously now in disorderly retreat. Their screaming battle cries were becoming more distant; cries of their wounded were becoming more and more distant with every passing minute.

The lead staff captain shouted, "Move out! Now! This is our chance to cut them down before they get back to their holes."

He led the charge, and the now enlivened government soldiers ran towards the fleeing and totally disorderly mujahideen horde. The jihadists made no effort to fight back. It was evident to every Soviet and government soldier that this was a rout; the mud people had made a terrible miscalculation. The officers ran along telling the rank and file that the mujahideen were cowards and could no longer put up a credible defense. They had attacked a target too large for the men they had available for their mission. They were fools. They made too much noise. They turned and ran presenting their backs as inviting targets, and it would only minutes before the vaunted Red Army closed in on them for the kill. The officers could almost taste sweet victory.

Three was very pleased with himself. All his long, lonely, morning runs were paying off. He was running for his life and winning. Crank mentally kicked himself for sleeping in so many mornings. He was puffing, and his chest was heaving. Ball, Bob, and their hand selected mujs, had hardly broken a sweat as they loped along. Ball held up a hand to indicate to the men to slow down, to breathe hard, to complain loudly about being out of breath and exhausted. The advance contingent of DRAs reported back to the main body that the mujahideen were wearing out and were ripe for the kill.

The angry Soviet officers formed up their men into three columns—one to hit the motley band straight on, and the other two to outflank them and bring death by pincer movement to finish off every last country bumpkin.

"Fix bayonets! Advance at full speed! Take no prisoners," the overheated colonel screamed.

"Kill, kill, kill!" the frenzied young men yelled as they ran forward, driven by their adrenaline and blood lust.

Bob watched them come from his vantage point ten meters in front of the rushing phalanx.

He shouted at Ball, reverting to his boyhood Texas drawl, "Y'all, git a move on. This here's gonna be a genuine south-of-the-border-knife-fight-in-a-ditch!"

Ball blew three shrill bursts on his standard issue whistle. He was gratified when he saw his entire front-line wheel and run as fast as frightened men could run towards the safety of the tunnel opening. The DRA now ran heedlessly and recklessly forward towards the backs of the helpless mujahideen.

Ball's whistle signals also caused the next phase of his audacious battle plan to erupt. The caves above and in front of the fleeing mujahideen served them as a training and command facility. The mujahideen had dug out accommodations for a hotel, a mosque, a medical installation, and a garage to house the two T-55 tanks that had been captured from the DRA.

The camouflage of the cave openings parted and 2,000 mujahideen came out of nowhere and descended towards the nearly exhausted DRG forces, who outnumbered the mujahideen surrounding them three-to-one. The Russians and their allies were outgeneraled and outmaneuvered. At this critical juncture, the troops defending the base brought forward their D-30 howitzers, several BM-21 multiple rocket launchers, five ZPU-1 and five ZPU-2 heavy machine-guns—all unknown to Soviet intelligence before that moment–and began pounding the advancing Soviets and DRA into human pulp.

In addition to the claimants to the caves as their homes, other Mujahideen groups were active in the area; and they now participated in the defense of the base. These groups were part of various movements including the *Hezbi Islami*, the *Hezb-e Islami Khalis*, the *Harakat-i-Inqilab-i-Islami* and the *Mahaz-e-Melli*, under the authority of regional commander Bashir Khan.

The cannibas inflamed and merciless mujahideen swept over advancing Soviet coalition, annihilating the survivors of the cannonade and cut them down almost to the last man. They stepped back and made a simple "come-hither" gesture, and their women finished the work the men had begun. For half an hour the screams of the wounded being mutilated rent the air. The Afghan irregulars and their women were content with their night's work but did not believe that this one battle satiated their core need for vengeance.

The classical ambush which the five CIA agents only knew about from cowboy and Indian movies had worked perfectly. The CIA and its agents could do no wrong after that. Despite the common knowledge that they were westerners—Christians at that—their heroism became part of Afghan folklore and song as the Men of the Book who saved the day for the Soldiers of God.

CHAPTER EIGHT

Oval Office, White House, Washington DC, PDB [President's Daily Briefing], November 18, 1983

Meeting recorded and stamped "TOP SECRET, EYES ONLY, Director and POTUS
Officers present: Ronald Reagan, POTUS; William Casey, DCIA, Chairman House Defense Appropriations Subcommittee; Joseph Addabbo, (D) New York; Rep, Charles Wilson, (D) Texas

Subject: Emergency appropriations for covert action in Afghanistan and Pashtunistan Region.

Summary:
DCIA: Although there are several areas of interest throughout the world, we will focus on our relations and issues coming from our involvement in the northwestern portion of Afghanistan and the border areas of Pakistan. We have some good news to report, which may come as something of a shock to some. Late last month, our agents–and the mujahideen they supervise–fought two engagements with the Soviet/DRA coalition which opposes democratic changes in one of the poorest countries in the world. The battles were fought to protect the most major ammunition dump and arms depots in the hands of the mujahideen. Zhawar is an area with small

villages but has an extremely significant military site. Our agents and a group of hand-picked freedom fighters staged a late-night raid on a DRA military camp, killed the entire garrison and captured two M-55 tanks and several large truck loads of armaments. Subsequently, several battles were waged by the Soviets and their Afghan communist coalition to take the mujahideen stronghold in the tunnels and caves in the Sodyaki Ghar Mountain. Our people turned that attack into a chaotic retreat which ended in a rout. The Soviet forces have left the area and returned to Kabul.

The emergency we must address is that those heroes among the mujahideen lack sufficient funds to pursue the Soviets to their defensive positions and to bring about an end to the genocide that is taking place in that poor country. Our last shipment of arms and supplies was valued at $50 million and was not nearly enough to counter Soviet airpower. Our conservative estimate of the amount needed to end this war in our favor is $1.5 billion…a year. This year, as an emergency measure, we must have $500 million; or we must leave the theater with our tails between our legs.

There is good news. I have personally negotiated with King Faud of Saudi Arabia, and he has pledged $250 billion, available when we request it. There is also bad news. Congress has to–this point–refused to increase the intelligence or defense budgets sufficiently to meet our half of the coalition's needs. We must leave here today with a $250 billion transfer of defense department funds or pack up and leave Afghanistan.

POTUS: It will be done, Director. I campaigned on a promise of defeating the Russian Soviet communist empire. The most important moment in my presidency is now. We will drive the Soviets out of Afghanistan and break their backs financially as we do it. I will draft a presidential order as soon as we leave this meeting.

Rep. Addabbo: President Reagan, perhaps you haven't grasped the magnitude of this request. These reckless rogues in the CIA are requesting an amount of funding equal to the entire defense budget. They are talking billions with a "B." Remember the profound statement by the late, great Estes Kefauver about billions…

POTUS (interrupting): I knew the man well. Incidentally, it wasn't him who said that; it was Ev Dirksen. I also knew him. We don't have time for that now. More importantly, I also know that we will defeat the

Soviet Union, or they will gobble us up. I say, not on my watch. Today, we will take advantage of the opportunity that has been afforded us by our heroes on the battlefield. And, remember. Everyone, this is as Top Secret as the Manhattan Project, and the same penalties apply.

Signed: POTUS

Ronald Reagan

CHAPTER NINE

"Remember that all through history, there have been tyrants and murderers, and for a time, they seem invincible. But in the end, they always fall. Always."

–Mahatma Gandhi, *Gandhi: An autobiography*

Q "And this I'm particularly proud of: behind the headlights stinger missiles."

James Bond "Excellent, just the thing for unwinding after a rough day at the office."

Q "Need I remind you 007 that you have a license to kill not to break traffic laws."

–Movie, *GoldenEye*, 1955

Office of the Director of the Central Intelligence Agency, 7th Floor OHB, CIA Building, Langley, Virginia, November, 18, 1983, late afternoon.

Director Casey asked Gust Avrakotos, Gen. Zia—who was in Washington to receive a Congressional award—Gen. Abu Ghazala, the most important on-the-ground senior Pakistani fighting officer, Charlie Wilson, and Mike Vickers—Wilson's number two—for an exacting discussion of what the huge sums of money President Reagan was going to provide were to be used for. The president was present in the room and seriously interested; it was one of his 'special projects.'

"Don't all speak at once," Casey said after a moment of silence following his question about disposition of funds. "I need to put something down here under the line that reads "Budget Line Items."

Charlie was never at a loss for words; so, he jumped right in.

"Okay, Director, do you have a pencil and note pad ready?"

Casey was not a man with a sense of humor, and he was not smiling now.

"We need the Weapons Upgrade Program..."

"You mean 'The Charlie Wilson Personal Afghan War Chest..." interrupted Gust and laughed.

"Whose side are you on, young man?" Charlie said crossly, "As I was saying, we also need Casper Weinberger's approval for the defense funds. We have to get rid of all the usual red tape; we don't have time for it. We have to get things done. We can't function without an increase in the exotic weapons program."

"Ten million a year isn't enough?" asked Casey.

"Not close, not by half," barked Charlie.

"I'll continue. With all respect, Director, if the CIA can't see its way to fund us, then I will go to the Pentagon. My relations seem to be warmer there. I want a thousand more Oerlikon antiaircraft guns—at least—to shoot down Soviet Hind helicopters, and I want them yesterday morning."

Mike Vickers interrupted Charlie this time, "Look, Chief, you are putting too much stock in those guns. A little science lesson—they haven't been actually useful as a matter of fact. At the risk of seeming to be too forward, my assessment...my strong personal opinion–after a couple of years dodging bullets over there, is that we have to have Stinger Missiles. The Oerlikon antiaircraft gun alone is not enough to shoot down Soviet Hind helicopters. What we have to do is to convince the Soviet pilots that there were too many weapons attacking them for them to be able to complete their missions. No one tactic can suffice. We have to make them believe that they are unable to determine which countermeasure in their armamentarium will work in any given situation before it's too late. The Stingers would force Soviet pilots to fly higher and inevitably to be far less effective at terrorizing the mujahideen on the ground."

The DCIA raised his voice to break in, "What on earth is a Stinger Missile? How come I haven't even heard of it?"

"Exotic and secret weapon, Sir," Vickers answered.

Charlie Wilson interrupted, "We already have them under production, Director Casey. We are all convinced that the Stingers are the answer to all our problems. Anyway, I blundered ahead; and I'm glad I did. The tests are nigh onto perfect. So, I have them being produced at the level of World War II efficiency in building 600 in Rancho Cucamonga, California, under a secret General Electric contract to run the stinger missile construction plant."

"How did you do that?" the DCIA asked pointedly.

"Shifts around the clock, mainly manned by slim blond women."

Everyone laughed at Charlie's usual chutzpah.

"Married with children, lots of concessions like special air-conditioned areas and sterile workers in Ebola safe outfits, They manipulate tiny fine wires and work on fine gyroscopes and miniature motors, that kinda stuff. We found that only such women had the patience and dexterity to do such exceedingly detailed work. The finished products—thirty-five-pound Stinger Missiles—have proved to be very durable. For use in Afghanistan, we have established that the missiles can be frozen for years, exposed to the dust and prolonged desert heat of the Afghanistan plains, dropped on the ground from a two-story building, or stored for ten years or even more and still be usable."

"They sound like they have to be very technical and the recipients and end-users are still those ignorant mountain mujahideen country boys," said Casey.

"No, Sir. They are altogether simple to use even for ignorant but otherwise capable people. They can be carried by one man or woman and are durable and light enough to be transported by camel or donkey—a crucial requirement over there."

"Incidentally, I am not taking notes, but you are being recorded. Tell us the rest of your wild dreams, Charlie, we're all ears," the director said.

"Well, Sir, in all humility, the inventive scientists in our circle of the Weapons Upgrade Program work wonders. We know them as 'the sewing circle.' They've already invented drones for surveillance and to act as unmanned bombers. We want a bunch of them, Sir."

"There has to be more. Out with it, Charlie."

"Just a little more," Charlie said, "We plan to use empty C-5A transports to ferry in assorted supplies to mujahideen camp. Our guys will land at night and offload half a million pounds of supplies—boots, tents, blankets, medicines, uniforms, winter parkas, sniper sights, walkie talkies, rifle grenades, pistols, AK-47s, Stingers, and cooking utensils. We take off early the next morning. For security and diplomatic purposes, Pakistani ISI is going to be given all the credit.

"And one last thing…I promise…you know that we are spending beaucoup bucks to fly injured Americans and Afghans back to the U.S. for treatment and then fly them back to country empty. What we aim to do is to use those C-5As is to ship the wounded and save money. Isn't that efficient and conservative of me, Mr. Director and Mr. President?"

The president and the director tilted their heads in relative amazement, knowing that the Texas tornado was going to blow them over one more time.

Nevertheless, Director Casey was determined to get in the last word, "It's a lot of money, Charlie, Mr. President. We should remember Senator Everett Dirksen—the Grand Chameleon's—pithy observation: 'A billion here, a billion there, and pretty soon you're talking about real money.' I just learned that recently from a wise and well-studied scholar."

President Reagan laughed.

CHAPTER TEN

"Life is too short, time is too precious, and the stakes are too high to dwell on what might have been."
                              –Hillary Clinton, Concession Speech, 2008

"Don't be afraid to make mistakes. But if you do, make new ones. Life is too short to make the wrong choice twice."
                              –Joyce Rachelle

Russian Shindand Air Force Base, Herat Province, Northeast of City of Shindand, Western Afghanistan, May 1, 1986

The Russians began to regret their decision to become deeply involved in Afghanistan's tangled politics after 1982; and General Secretary Leonid Brezhnev, Head of the CPSU [Communist Party of the Soviet Union], had serious doubts about the wisdom of having ever invaded the strife-torn tribally-divided country. He and his generals constantly complained of "those incorrigible tribalists." He started discussions with the Politburo about disentangling the USSR from the entire region. None of the ranking Soviet civilians or military wished to be seen as having failed there, but Russian citizens were feeling the pain and beginning to grumble more and more audibly. Brezhnev died in 1982, and his successors came to characterize his regime as "the period of stagnation."

Black Tulips—(Soviet airplanes) ferried dead Soviets back home after they died in combat. Emblematic of the despised Russian war in Afghanistan, they became a familiar and hated sight. Quietly, in hushed conversations in cafes, the war became known everywhere as the "Bear Trap." Try as the government authorities might to keep the devastation a national secret, the families of the dead spread the grim message.

After Brezhnev died in 1982, his successors–Yuri Andropov in November and then Konstantin Chernenko for a year from February, 1984 to March, 1985—continued to push the Brezhnev Doctrine–but half-heartedly–knowing that it was time posthumous to withdraw, even if they were going to lose face in the world. The concerned Soviets in 1985 began to discuss in earnest whether to launch another huge invasion or to get out of Afghanistan altogether.

Their private discussions began to compare their efforts to convert the Afghans to communism to the foolhardy belief in the domino theory leading to their entrance into Viet Nam by the gullible Americans and their proclivity to add huge numbers of troops every time things went badly for them. It began to seem to be the lesser of evils to pull up their stakes in Afghanistan and stop the hemorrhage of blood and money, neither of which they could afford politically. Yet, despite knowing the end should come, they stubbornly kept on for another three years.

Robert Gates, Casey's executive assistant, and Mohammed Yousef–the Pakistani ISI brigadier general who was the chief for Afghan operations—and President Zia, agreed that they had the Russians on the ropes; and it was time to press the war activities of the mujahideen with increased assistance by the U.S. and Pakistan to hasten the end. Gates called Charlie Wilson and set the battle plan into practical action.

Charlie informed Gust Avarakotos, Mike Vickers, and Gen. Mohammed Yousef, that he had a green light for a much more concerted and advanced war and that the money and supplies were going to be forwarded within the week. The Department of Defense was now fully on board so long as the war was not conducted by U.S. boots on the ground. A key meeting held in the DOD heard the blunt opinion by Walter B. Slocombe that "there is value in keeping the Afghan insurgency going, thereby sucking the Soviets into a Vietnamese quagmire. The whole idea is simple: if the

Soviets decide to strike at this tar baby—Afghanistan—and we think they will, we have every interest in making sure that they get stuck."

When the mujahideen leaders got that strikingly positive good news, they immediately began to plan for a dramatic strike against the Soviet air force base at Shindand in Herat Province. The cross-border smuggling program accelerated exponentially; the CIA got permission to provide the ultimate Hind helicopter killer–the thirty-five pound General Dynamics surface-to-air Stinger missile. Gust and the four agents on the ground gathered in Pakistan Border Country, near the Khyber Pass through the Spin Ghar [Safed Koh] Mountains in Landi Kotal town at the Pakistan entrance to the pass. Even they were awed by the massive accumulation of men and materiel.

There were thousands of rough-hewn mountain men carrying an assortment of rifles, more camels and mules than men, and the nervous animals were being loaded down with paniers full of ammunition, AK-47s, mortars and mortar rounds, uniforms, rations, and winter gear. Mike Vickers had been able to buy a remarkable assortment of weapons suitable for mountain guerilla warfare: bicycle bombs, wooden cart concealed bombs, limpet mines, screaming meemies, trip mines, mines that popped out of the ground, and wire mines. Before the end of the war, both sides would plant millions of mines which made village life extraordinarily dangerous.

Vickers had been incredibly ingenious in his purchases and thefts to be able to create plausible deniability on the part of the Americans: he had delivered to the loading field, Russian Katyusha 122mm rockets which had a ten-kilometer range—and equally important–a huge screaming terrifying noise. Those Russian rockets could not be traced back to Israel, NATO, or the U.S.; the mujahideen were very familiar with and afraid of them. They said it was like being in an earthquake. Vickers had bought all those captured by the mujahideen and all that were available on the black market, which included Russian surplus at a price of tens of thousands of dollars each and $700,000 total worth by the time the caravan was being loaded.

Charlie Wilson had been able to drive the prices down on things the CIA wanted to buy. He did not care a whit when Gust informed him that his and the CIA's project in Afghanistan was running a Muslim jihad, or that their project would come back to bite them in the future. He also arranged for a dizzying amount of Israeli 2.75-inch rockets disguised as

Soviet manufacture with free ammo, huge C-130 cargo planeloads of military cargo, and thousands of trucks and helicopters. Somehow, he and Vickers were able to buy thousands of mules and horses.

And not least, the planes delivered millions in baksheesh. Charlie had learned the shortcuts necessary in the process; he learned to use a certain Pakistani arms manufacturer as a contractor to supply arms and ammunition, and suddenly things went much more smoothly. As a result, the CIA sent hundreds of millions of rounds of ammo constantly by air and sea to Pakistan and on to the Afghan rebel forces.

Charlies' workers included Chinese communists, tinkerers, and Mohammed's Egyptians. Charlie paid for all the gear, military equipment, etc. by "reprogramming" Pentagon weapons. He glibly argued that no one was hurt by the loss of the money; no project was eliminated or significantly curtailed; and no one became aware of or cared about the expense because of that. It had become an increasingly expensive jihad.

Delivery of the camels, horses, and mules was more difficult; all of them had to be sent by sea; and many sickened and died en route and had to be constantly replaced. Director Casey and Vickers hired men to scour livestock markets all over the world to buy mules to replenish those that were lost. Learning of the Americans' difficulties, Egyptian marketeers sold mules at massively inflated prices–$1,300 each—and insulted the Pakistanis by granting each mule a visa when it went to Pakistan. As a result, the easily offended Pakistanis would not allow any more Egyptian mules into the country. It cost time. Overall, it took months to establish the final mule supply lines. Congress was appalled when it learned that the mujahideen were eating some of the fine Tennessee Mules. A sane man would have gone crazy, but many said that Charlie was already there; so, the process continued relatively smoothly despite all the hurdles.

DCIA Casey personally met King Fahd in Riyadh, Saudi Arabia to obtain a firm pledge and then actual transfer of the Saudi's portion of the money to support the mujahideen jihadists. The meeting was one of those prolonged and annoying chit-chats over fruit juice, grapes, and succulent medjool dates before talking about the incredibly annoying and stubborn Israelis, then the vicious and murderous *kaffir* Iranians. Finally, after enough American and Middle Eastern gossip had been laughed about, Casey was able to secure the highly necessary $600 million by sweet-talking to the king as the "keeper of the faith."

Ball, Three, Crank, and Bob, visited Syria during the period when money and equipment was being accumulated for the mujahideen. They were responding to a request from an AID [Agency for International Development] doctor who communicated with the CIA.

Ball introduced his CIA comrades, "Thanks for inviting us, Doctor Edmunds. We actually had minimal trouble getting to you, thanks to your excellent directions. This is Crank, Three, and Bob."

"Glad to meet you guys. Let me guess, *noms de guerre*, no?"

The four nodded.

"No problems with the directions, Ball. All of us old smugglers know the ropes and the roads. Oh, have to be careful. Routes and schedules change all the time."

"So, what do you have to offer the CIA, Dr. Edmunds?"

"Come on, us Border Bandits have to stick to first names, right? I'm Kent."

"Kent, what do you have for us?"

"I'm the head honcho of aid distribution here, guys. I think the president likes me because he sent me six million dollars obtained extra from the aid money for Syrian refugees. He made some suggestions about how that money could be most profitably be spent—no need to return the overage. I took the liberty to buy hundreds of new four-wheel Toyotas and trucks that can be presented to the mujahideen commanders. By lucky chance, I have unprecedented access to the mujahideen leaders that the CIA is not allowed to meet.

The nice Mr. President and his friends at the Firm made up a good program that was very cleverly concealed, and I am only permitted to tell you a little about that. This I can tell you: the nice presidential program is ready to provide $100 million a year. It is nice because it is specifically set aside to win the hearts and minds of the Afghans. At the moment, it is set aside for getting enough food and medicine to induce the humble and helpful Afghans to stay in their villages where we need them

"Be advised that any weapons the CIA brings in will be of Soviet manufacture, and they will be provided via the Pakis. Shame we good Americans will never be able to take our well-earned credit, but it comes with the territory owned by the Firm. Those of us worker-bees like to say that we are involved in the "greatest well-intentioned smuggling enterprise in history."

"Kent, we can presume that you a fellow Firm member, right?"

"I can only say that we in the AID program can neither confirm nor deny such statements—for me or for my fellow workers in this special program."

"Touché," said Bob, and the other three agents of the Firm smiled and nodded in agreement.

A week's dawn-to-dark work with extra rations, time-and-a-half pay, and considerable brow-beating saw most of the goods sorted and ready for loading on the massive herd of pack animals. Mike Vickers flew in from Peshawar to join Gust Avarakotos and his four agents to witness and to supervise the final loading and to control the overanxious mujahideen fighters who had already spent too much time in one place for their peace of mind. General Muhammad Zia-ul-Haq and defense minister Abu Ghazala were on board for the final Pakistan element of this CIA "bandit" operation in Afghanistan that they sanctioned and from which they personally profited so greatly.

The agents and the generals acknowledged each other with perfunctory nods.

A C-130 touched down and disgorged more than enough wheat knowing that the mujahideen would sell it to get money to keep in the fight. The wheat was followed by trucks, cash, gold, sniper rifle sights, pens, seals, and letterhead stationery from Congress and the CIA, ten-gallon hats and several truck-loads of deer meat from Texas—courtesy of Charlie Wilson. There were bales of humanitarian aid supplies, cadres of combat doctors from Europe, the U.S., Saudi Arabia, and Jordan. A large platoon of spit-and-polish Pakistani special operations cadres alighted, led by their American Army Special Forces advisors and instructors. All the crates, boxes, and duffle bags were marked "GIFT OF YOUR FRIENDS FROM THE ARAB LEAGUE" and "HUMANITARIAN AID PRODUCTS."

Two large troop trucks roared up to the leaders. The end gate opened to disgorge seventy-five of Vickers's paramilitary operatives dressed in *shalwar kameesis* with beards and Chitrali hats. They trained mujahideen in Pakistan border training center camps. Like their students, the Americans rode horses to work, but they did not actually go into combat. They trained the Pakistani military cadres who did the actual training of the mujahideen.

Many of the Pakistani instructors were ISI who received their training in the American Special Forces school and the Sabotage School in Fort Bragg. Their great benefit to the jihadi enterprise came from the fact that they were blood brothers of the Afghans; they spoke Pathan and Urdu; they were fundamentalist Muslims themselves; and they—like their mujahideen brethren–had no compunctions against selective targeted killings, assassinations, kidnappings, and torture. Only their women were worse. The Pakistanis willingly accepted bounties including Soviet soldiers' ears and brass belt buckles to receive money and arms, or to line their own pockets.

Gen. Zia laughed and took a hearty swig of twenty-year-old bourbon, also a gift from Charlie as the general viewed the huge military spectacle.

He said, "I love Charlie. He is my best friend...most of the time. I especially love his motto: 'Don't pay too much attention to the rules.'"

"It's how we get the necessary work done. We couldn't have gotten where we are without you, good friend," said Mike, knowing that Zia loved high praise almost as much as he loved booze, women, and money—in no particular order of priority.

Zia gave him a smart salute accompanied by a toothy smile, for which he was famous. It was the same smile he gave to men he was sending off to execution.

When they were alone and free from jihadi and Pakistanis, Bob asked, "Think the Pakis are really OK with us running the show?"

Mike put it succinctly, "Doesn't really matter, they know that 'them as has the gold, makes the rules,' which is a defense appropriations committee aphorism which lets our military officers and our Paki friends know who makes the working rules."

CHAPTER ELEVEN

"Afghanistan is a notoriously difficult country to govern. Empire after empire, nation after nation have failed to pacify what is today the modern territory of Afghanistan, giving the region the nickname "Graveyard of Empires," even if sometimes those empires won some initial battles and made inroads into the region."
–Akhilesh Pillalamarri, *The Diplomat*, June 30, 2017

Tunnels in the Sodyaki Ghar Mountain, Paktia Province, near the Mujahideen logistic base situated at Zhawar Kili Al-Badr Camp, Khost Province fifteen kilometers from the Pakistani border, May 31, 1986

Despite the difficulties entailed in delivering men and supplies to the Zhawar Camp, thousands of mujahideen were pouring in from all over Afghanistan. A fire in the guts was becoming infectious, and the mountain fighters were becoming ever more convinced that the Russians were in real decline and were dispirited. The mujahideen in the camp area were well aware of the tremendous amount of military and living necessity materials that were arriving every day via the huge American C-130 and C-5 cargo planes, and overland with camel, donkey, and horse, caravans. To facilitate movement of men, equipment, and ammo, the CIA and its mujahideen labor force built warehouses, garages, repair centers, corrals, barns, and feeding stations, for the incredible number of beasts of burden. They painstakingly upgraded railroads, maintained tracks, and provided thousands of trucks, and more thousands of mules and horses every week. There was a shortage of animal caretakers; so, finally, the male chauvinistic mujahideen had to admit that women were perfectly capable of caring for the animals and could do so very well. After all, they had been doing so for as long as Afghanistan had been peopled by humans and their domesticated animals. That problem was solved with some adroit persuasion by the CIA agents.

None of it was easy: winds and sandstorms sometimes halted air traffic for days on end. The Russians were aware that weaponry and reinforcement fighters were on their way somewhere and needed to be interrupted. The Russians and their loose coalition of Marxist Afghans placed great priority to killing long mule trains. They came after the long strings of animals and their human protectors with a vengeance, recognizing an existential threat to their enterprise and lives.

Ball, Bob, Crank, and Three, took turns leading platoons of mujahideen fighters out of the cave system every day to ride security on the animal trains. They were highly effective leaders of soldiers, and their presence began to pay off with dividends. They trained their men in the tactics of stealthy guerilla surprise attacks. Over the month of travel of the several successive caravans, they ambushed more than a dozen Soviet patrols and eliminated them.

The goal was not just to kill the patrols, but to intimidate future ventures by the enemies. This they did by inflicting gruesome mutilations and tortures on the defeated soldiers. They allowed one or two men from each patrol to witness the horrors and to live to spread the word. Most of the released survivors made their way back to Soviet bases missing arms, ears, noses, or genitalia. That served as mute testimony that mountain country in Afghanistan–like Indian country in the old Wild West of America–was not a place any sane man would go willingly.

The result was a great increase in Soviet desertions, even including deserters going over to the freedom-fighter side of the mujahideen where they received with open arms as misguided brothers who were returning to the family—like the Biblical Prodigal Sons. The use of more powerful Chinese anti-aircraft guns and later the highly vaunted Stinger missiles kept the Soviet Hind-24 helicopters from flying over rural mujahideen villages and hideouts and finally forced the Soviet coalition army to desist from overland incursions entirely. Their tactics changed from brutal offensive operations to nonproductive defensive stances that, even the Soviet hierarchy in Moscow, came to realize was one more indicator of the approach of ignominious defeat.

On 30 May, the great leaders of the mujahideen war effort gathered in the Sodyaki Ghar Mountain caves for a grand consultation about the upcoming decisive battle. The CIA was represented by Ball, Bob, Crank, Three, and Mike Vickers. Gust Avrakotos was conspicuously absent.

"Where is he, Mike?" asked all the in-country agents, almost as a chorus.

"The simple truth is that I don't know. What I do know is this: President Reagan has a bee in his bonnet about the contras in Nicaragua who need money and military equipment to fight the communist Sandinista government. The president is as passionate about the contras and the so-called Iran-Contra affair as Charlie is about the mujahideen in Afghanistan. What I heard is that Gust committed the unpardonable sin. He argued against Congress setting aside money for the contras. He made a formal protest to the DCIA, and maybe he even sent a coded message to the president. Reagan told Casey to fire him on the spot and to put out a burn notice on him. He's gone."

"A burn notice???" said Ball. "He doesn't deserve that after everything he's done for the CIA, for America, for crying out loud. He won't even get a pension let alone the promotion he should be getting. We oughta do something. Send a protest note…something!"

"I guess you apparently didn't hear what I said. Reagan ordered it. Gust talked naughty about the president's pet anti-communist policy of the moment. Gust was crucial; what do you think would happen to any of us if we were to squeak up, huh?"

"I still think it stinks. It certainly grates on me."

"Listen, you guys, I feel exactly the same way," Mike said, completely sober now. "In fact, I might as well tell you myself before you have to learn from someone else. I am headed back to DC as soon as this confab with our hairy friends is over, and even before the big fight starts. I am ordered to get with Charlie to smooth Casey's ruffled feathers and then to go hat-in-hand with Charlie to plead our case to Reagan. Pity me, all right. Right after that, I am quitting and going into academia. Enough of this BS."

"What're we supposed to do?" asked Crank.

"Good question, Crank. You guys might wanta give it some real thought."

The grandees of the mujahideen world entered the tent where the CIA agents had been talking. It was a serious gathering of tribal leaders and military geniuses who had scarcely ever been able to talk to each other, let alone agree on anything. The fact that they had come from such great distances and at such personal danger spoke volumes.

The great ones gathered in a *majilas*-type circle. Leaders from a diverse and disparate group of mujahideen included: Gen. Abu Ghazala, defense minister of Pakistan, Ismail Khan, Gulbkuddin Hekmatyar, Bashir Khan, Mohammed Nabi, Naqib Alikozai, Abdul Rahim Wardak, Fazal Haq Mujahid, Burhanuddin Rabbini, Chen Zhāng Liú representing Chinese interests—largely regarding the use of their weaponry–and Michael G. Vickers representing the U.S..

By common unspoken consent, Gen. Ghazala spoke first, indicating that he was considered to be the chairman of the warrior group for this day.

"Brothers, Praise be to God the Lord of the Worlds, and prayers and peace be upon the noblest of those sent, his family, companions, and whoso has followed them with *ihsan* to the Day of Judgment. Allah has willed that we are about to engage in a great battle—that future historians will compare favorably to the Battle of the Wells of Badr, Muhammad's Great Victory in 624. The accursed Russians–who infest our beloved land of Pashtunistan–have employed a scorched earth policy to deal with our people. As a result, the atheists have killed a great many innocent people—men, women, and children.

"Tomorrow, our band of brothers will begin the destruction of those servants of *Shaytan* in the name of God who has forbidden oppression to Himself, and made it forbidden among His servants. My brothers, God's Army will move to the west and by great stealth, surround the Russian Shindand Air Force Base, in Herat Province. By another week, we will have annihilated all the *kufrs* in that unfortunate province; and within a year, we Afghans will once again own and rule our country. I promise you and every noble person that we will tear out their roots even if we offer thousands of martyrs!

"*lā 'ilāha 'illā llāh muḥammadun rasūlu llāh* [There is no god but God. Muhammad is the messenger of God.]!!!" Gen. Ghazala shouted.

"*Allahu Akbar* [Allah is the Greatest]!!! *Allahu Akbar!!! Allahu Akbar!!!*" the assembled mujahideen shouted as a knee-jerk response their fists pumping in frenzied unison.

Gen. Ghazala finished his exhortation with, "And the establishment of the religion is one: a *Qur'an* guides, and a sword gives victory. For our jihad will be by the sword, the spearhead, proof, and evidence. The atheists and crusaders will regret the day they were born."

CHAPTER TWELVE

"It's only an eye for an eye. An eye for an eye only ends up making the whole world blind."

—Mahatma Ghandi

Russian Shindand Air Force Base, Herat Province, Northeast of City of Shindand, Western Afghanistan, June 22, 1986

It was not until the mujadiheen hordes had surrounded Shindand Airforce base that the sentries became aware of their presence. No advance scouting units had reported the approach of the fearsome mountaineer fighters. Late in the investigation of that fact, it was determined that the reason for the absence of reporting came about because there was no record of any scouting unit having returned from their surveillance missions during the months of May and June. The Soviet leadership gathered a plethora of evidence that mujahideen capture-and-kill units patrolled the hinterlands in well-disciplined high numbers. For the previous three months, the Soviet commander of the base, General Lieutenant Ivan Abramovich Yekenovoral had ordered that no Russian coalition troops conduct sorties in the rural areas or villages. Nonetheless, the arrogant Russians doubted that the rough and ignorant mujahideen were capable of conducting a serious and united attack.

The four CIA agents, and the four tactical battle leaders of the mujahideen—had arrived by airplane two days ahead of the Pakistani Special Forces units and five days in advance of the rank and file. The entire army traveled with absolute secrecy and employed draconian measures on the men who were foolish enough to make loud noises, even loud and excited vocal utterances. No fires were permitted within two hundred kilometers of the air base. The men grumbled about the dry and bland rations, but all of them agreed that it was a necessary protection. Morale was high.

Gen. Abu Ghazala, Fazal Haq Mujahid, Ismail Khan, Gulbkuddin Hekmatyar, and Ismail Khan, conferred one last time with the tacticians who would lead the battle for the strategists. Ahmad Ahmad Chagharzai, the colonel in charge of the Pakistan special forces, who—along with the CIA agents—were to serve as the spearhead of the attack, was the only senior general to enter the blood and dirt of the actual fighting.

Ball, Crank, Three, and Bob, slept very little that night as they always did before an important mission or big fight. None of them had the slightest doubt about the severity of the danger they faced. They were up, dressed, had breakfast, and cleaned their rifles and handguns one more unnecessary time, before the Paki commandoes joined them. The Pakis were in their best combat uniforms—starched shirts, knife-sharp pleats in their short pants, and hair and beards and mustaches newly trimmed and waxed. Col. Chagharzai appeared last and was even more spit-and-polish stiff than his men. Even he was thirty minutes early.

The colonel grilled all the men about their readiness, going over his checklist with each man individually. He also required every man to demonstrate that he had—on his body or in his combat pack—all the things on the checklist and that every item was in perfect ready working order.

When he was satisfied, the colonel—a famous and highly vaunted hero in Pakistan—addressed his men, "Gentlemen, it is an honor to serve with you. I am fully aware of the rigorous training you have endured and of your service up to this point. We shall succeed as fighters and brothers. May Allah, the all-powerful, guide your steps and protect you as you fight in his holy name. You are brothers, comrades in arms; protect each other as you do what you must in His name to conduct a successful mission. You are all men of the Book; act accordingly. Protect your brothers. Understood?"

Every man, CIA and commando alike, nodded his head.

"Any questions?"

There were none.

"Then, into the darkness with me. We are winners."

At bedtime on June 21, Airforce Col. Yvgeni Nikoliavich Sammarand–commandant of the Shindand Airforce Base and its security forces–met with Shindand City Militia Commander Aymenn Hafs al'Aishat for their nightly report.

Sammarand was a fifty-six-year-old career Red Army Airforce administrator who had less than a year to go before retirement. He was tall, Rus Nordic in appearance, and arrogant. His uniform was changed twice a day and always looked recently ironed and his boots recently shined by his aide-de-camp. Commander al'Aishat was a tough-looking squat weightlifter whose blouse was strained by his over-developed muscles. His pudgy face appeared to have been born with a perpetual scowl. Even with twice daily shaves, he always seemed to need another shave. His uniform could use a brush-down to rid it of sand, and its rumpled appearance annoyed his Russian counterpart.

"Simple report from me, Aymenn," said Col. Sammarand, "all is clear inside, and the hatches are battened down for the night. How does it look outside?"

"Secure, Colonel. My staff and I drove the entire perimeter in one of our BMP-1 [*Boyevaya Mashina Pekhoty*] tanks and saw nothing amiss. The circles of bunkers were the same sturdy concrete ones that were there and intact last night; and the men were alert and bored, having seen no action for a good three months, maybe more."

"And, that's a good thing, no, Comrade Aymenn?"

"I'll take 'bored' over fighting those hairy apes from the north any day. I'm sure you agree."

"Certainly, My Friend."

"I think we are getting good control in the country, and this wretched conflict will finally come to an end," Aymenn observed, not noting the quick hint of doubt in the colonel's brow. "Just curious, how much longer do you have on this tour of duty, if I may ask?"

"A month and a half. Seems like forever. I haven't seen my wife and the three children for more than two years."

"Good for you, Yvgeni. I won't keep you, rest well, Brother."
"And you, My Friend."

The CIA agents and six hand-picked mujahideen wore NVDs [Night Vision Devices] which gave them a very significant advantage over their city militia target soldiers, along with the important element of surprise. They were able to approach the city limits undetected. They silently bypassed several sentry bunkers where most of the guards were dozing. They separated from Col. Chagharzai and his rangers who concentrated on the air base.

There were a few lights in the town coming from buildings including homes and government facilities. That enhanced their optics to the point of being almost as good as seeing in early morning. They had the best the U.S. military could provide: Third generation night vision systems maintain the MCP from Gen II, but now used a photocathode made with gallium arsenide, which greatly improved image resolution. In addition, the new GenIII MCP [Micro-Channel Plate] was coated with an ion-barrier film for increased tube life. The light amplification had improved to around 30,000-50,000x. The new MCP also had an S-25 photocathode, which produced a far brighter and clearer image–especially around the edges of the lens–a feature lacking in all Soviet NVDs. Any city onlooker would have been hard put to be able to see the agents, let alone identify them as enemy agents.

Ball, Three, Bob, and Crank, all carried military-grade carbon steel cross bows with short very stiff spined arrow shafts and tangs and razor sharp four-way cutting blades. After months of practice, the agents were excellent cross bowmen. They employed their silent weapons with deadly accuracy. Men fell over dead next to comrades who were unaware of what had happened. There were very few guards out in the town, and most of them were dispatched with lethal arrow shots. Some were ambushed and killed with ranger methods honed over centuries of use and study. Every corpse was moved quietly out of the light, as the agents moved swiftly towards their objectives.

They split up at the barracks and administration buildings where the officers were housed. Ball's task was to neutralize the communications centers; Crank and Bob were assigned the enlisted barracks, with Crank's primary duty to keep the soldiers away from their armory; Three had a simple task: kill as many soldiers as possible as soon as the first shot was heard from his co-agents.

Ball jimmied the padlock to the stairway leading up to the communications center. It was ridiculously simple—a large old-fashion Sledge key lock which was eminently pickable. He was wearing rubber-soled black shoes, and he was able to ascend without making a sound. The entry door was ajar. Ball very slowly pushed it open. Three men sat in observation chairs looking out over the city with binoculars, ignoring—for the time being—their phone systems. The three died in as many seconds from 9 mm rounds from his silenced Glock 40. None of them knew that they were killed, and neither did anyone else except their killer.

He exited the way he came in and made a beeline to the admin building to take care of the officers and any communications they might have.

Crank and Bob entered doors at each end of the barracks. They stood quietly in the shadows waiting for Ball's signal. Crank stationed himself at the locked gates of the armory. Ball ran to the admin building and forced the locks as silently as he could and trotted to the well-marked doors of the commandant, his adjutant, and the sergeant-major who served them. He guessed—correctly, as it turned out—that the commandant would be the one who would be sleeping the most soundly. His door was unlocked, and Ball slipped in. He slit the tough old soldier's throat with his KBar knife, and the man was among his ancestors before he felt a thing. Ball slipped down the hallway to the adjutant's room. The portly assistant was standing at his urinal when Ball slipped up behind him and stabbed him through a point on the left side of his thoracic back and transected the man's thoracic aorta cleanly. He exsanguinated in a few seconds without uttering an outcry. His last sounds were a gurgling from his throat.

Ball was considerably more careful with the sergeant-major, knowing the reputation for fighting skills and self-discipline the Paki ranking enlisted enjoyed. Ball entered the room stealthily enough that the muscular middle-aged soldier remained asleep. Apparently, Sergeant-major Murbeen Uloomi slept with one eye open. He leapt from the bed awake and prepared to fight. In an instant, Ball decided that the quiet approach was no longer necessary, and he shot the Paki twice in the chest and once in his mid-forehead—the so-called Moroccan trio—causing a noise that would have awakened the dead, since Ball had removed his silencer before entering the room.

The other three agents recognized the three-shot signal and opened a withering fire on the sleeping enlisted DRA men. Some tried, but none of them succeeded in getting to the handgun under his pillow. Crank killed two men who were in the latrine, and who ran for the armory. The gunfire in the city aroused the citizens, the nearby air force base, and the perimeter guards.

Col. Chagharzai and his rangers swept the base in a running gridiron pattern shooting and killing anything that moved. One ranger was killed by base commander, Col. Yvgeni Nikoliavich Sammarand. The colonel, in turn, was shredded by light machine gun fire from a ranger who was enraged that his buddy had been cut down in the prime of his life. The colonel died before he could be saddened by knowing that his dreamed of return to Russia and his family was not to be.

The general pandemonium awakened the freezing and nervous mujahideen from their torpor. It was as if the very ground disgorged its denizens when the six thousand screaming, drug-crazed killers erupted into a swiftly running mass. The foot soldiers followed light and heavy tanks, armored vehicles and heavy troop trucks, and pick-up trucks carrying W.O.G. [Working On Government–circa 1900s British Empire acronym stenciled on shirts of laborers assigned to government projects] native forces and cargoes of Stinger Missiles. Behind all of them—at a safe distance–came the sheikhs and mullahs of the ragged mujahideen army: Abu Hafs al-Kurdi, the Kurdish leader, Abu al-Hassan al-Jazrawi, Abu Abdullah al-Urduni, a Jordanian, Abu Hakim al-Australi, an Australian, Bahraini cleric Turki Binali, Abu Bakr al-Urduni, Abu Hakim Shekau, Sheikh al-Nu'aman al-Belaidi, Mujahid Sheikh Abu Qutaiba al-Shinqiti, Sheikh Abu Hamza, Ismail Khan, and Abu al-Hassan Rashid.

It was more like a set-piece World War II attack—more orderly and on a grander scale–than the usual mujahideen guerilla operation. The great buffer-shield of armor moved rapidly and inexorably towards the defenses of the base. The armor shield included Soviet and Polish T-55, older Soviet T-54, and Polish PT-76 light tanks, Soviet T-62M main battle tanks, bridging tanks to cross antitank ditches, BRDM-mounted Sagger anti-tank missile carriers, SU-100/152 World War II vintage self-propelled guns, BTR-70 and 80 APCs [Armored Personnel Carriers]. Most of the wall of armor was captured from the DRA forces or purchased from the Israelis after their multiple Soviet sponsored and funded wars with the Arabs.

Behind the shield, the front ranks transported RPG-7 antitank weapons, and the AT-3 Sagger anti-tank guided missiles, portable and recoilless anti-tank weapons, and APCs which had once threatened Israeli flanks. Then came the drug-maddened human fighters infused with bloodlust and a thirst for revenge that propelled them along heedless of the dangers. They looked like some sort of fearsome ghosts or terrible *jinns* sent by *Iblis,* the *al-Shaytan.*

They came from regions where formations of Soviet Hind gunships had swept overhead like flocks of black birds killing entire villages of 500-1000 people. Those were wounds that would not heal, and this attack on Shindand was the chance to bring some sense of balance in the horrific death-for-death-tit-for-tat world that was Afghanistan.

The Stingers proved to be the weapon that early-on turned the tide in the mujahideen favor. Twenty-two MiG-15s and forty-one Hind-24 helicopters managed to get off the tarmac to attack the oncoming hordes. They were handily dispatched by the men firing the Stingers before they could fire a single shot. For the mujahideen there was a deep thrill to watch the impact from the Stinger as it blew a soccer ball-sized hole when it hit. It did not even matter very much whether it was altogether accurate.

The fear factor of the Stinger's screaming noise was enough to cause a strong man to freeze in panic. A single mujahideen fighter became able to blow out electricity pylons and to begin to kill electrical service in a large portion of Shindand. More importantly, that same warrior was able to make airplane landing fields incapable of having planes land on them. Had they not blown planes out of the air, the landing field damage alone would have shut down the air force.

Two huge Antonov transport planes attempted to leave the field with ranking local citizens and officers of the town and the air force. With defenses in the air neutralized, with the great advantage of complete surprise, and with the soul-paralyzing screams and total lack of humanity inculcate in the warriors approaching them, most of the perimeter guards abandoned their bunkers and ran towards the presumed safety of the air base. They were unaware of the wreckage and carnage that raged on the streets and in the buildings of the much-vaunted air force bastion. The Antonovs never got off the ground.

The entire battle went on for three days, but the outcome was evident in the first six hours. When it was over, the mujahideen fired thousands of rounds of American supplied ammunition into the air in celebration.

CHAPTER THIRTEEN

Aftermath

"I have decided to kill Americans and enemies of religion in order to help the God's religion and venerate the blood of my brethren. By God, we will never forget the blood of my brethren which has been spilled by the treacherous Jews, the sons of pigs and monkeys, who are brazenly supported by the leader of the world infidels. The religion of my Lord will not be assisted until through spill of bloods and bodies tearing apart. O God! Take our bloods to be satisfied. O God! Don't allow any tomb or soil to enshroud our bodies, or a headstone to cover those bodies until our bodies are promised the Paradise in the Day of Resurrection."

–Author unknown.

Russian Shindand Air Force Base, Herat Province, Northeast of City of Shindand, Western Afghanistan, June 22, 1986

The battle was over even though a few stubborn defenders seemed not to realize it. The mujahideen moved ruthlessly and relentlessly through the city and the base killing anyone of the survivors who was foolish enough to attempt to resist. Most of the citizens sat dazed in their homes or wandered aimlessly along the roads looking into the distance with a 'thousand-yard stare.' The fighters were exhausted, and many of them simply lay down by the roadsides and went to sleep. Viewers of the macabre hellish scene afterwards reported open truckloads of hacked up bodies of soldiers who had surrendered being hauled to a dump site.

The CIA agents watched with benumbed fascination.

Only Crank could manage a comment—in the form of a ditty he had learned from someone, somewhere:

> "Well, tain't no sin,
> To take off your skin,
> And dance around in your bones."

The three others were too exhausted and dispirited to comment or even to produce a wan smile.

Mikhail Sergeyevich Gorbachev–the general secretary of the Communist Party of the Soviet Union–addressed the Politburo in a very unusual ultra-secret emergency session a week following the horrific defeat in Shindand.

"Comrades, this is not the first time, I have spoken of this; and it probably will not be the last. It would be if I could persuade you. As most of you are now aware, our forces in the Democratic Republic of Afghanistan have suffered a most disappointing and costly defeat in both manpower and gold. We are bleeding to death, Comrades; and there is no end in sight were we to come out victorious or even break even. We must look at this as the warning we have needed, as the beginning of the end. Our choice of sending in a hundred thousand or even two hundred thousand more troops is unthinkable. The other alternative of handing over our figurative swords to the dog people in Afghanistan and Pakistan and the evil Americans is unimaginable. Let this be the most important request of my tenure as chairman: Remove the Red Army from Afghanistan, and don't go back…"

The war was not over, not quite, anyway. However, in Shindand, it was. 15 Russian MiGs, twenty Antonov-12 troop transporters, 1,100 light and heavy tanks and armored vehicles, 600 trucks, 1,200 automobiles, nearly 1,000 small arms, and 100,000 rounds of ammunition, along with every governmental building, mosque, store, and business office, 2,000 homes, 500 apartments, and all of the roads were liberated or destroyed. The loss for the Russians from the MiGs alone was $150,000,000. The loss of animals and human lives was never accurately counted, but conservative estimates are that nearly 6,000 men, women, and children, perished. The loss in terms of Soviet prestige in the country and on the world stage was incalculable.

By the time of the Shindand defeat, the war in Afghanistan became a quagmire for the Soviet Union reminiscent of America's Viet Nam experience. The difference for the Russians was that by the late 1980s the USSR was disintegrating. Overall, the Soviet Union spent over two billion dollars. The Soviets suffered about 15,000 killed and scores more injured and maimed, with the never-ending expenditures for their care which kept the losses accumulating.

Despite having perpetrated thousands of atrocities–the Soviets used their air power to deal harshly with both rebels and civilians, leveling whole villages to deny safe-haven to the mujahideen which in the end came to naught. They went around the country destroying vital irrigation ditches, and laying millions of land mines which remain active to the present day. All that even in the face of having failed to implement, to protect, or to maintain a sympathetic and effective regime in Afghanistan. In 1988, the Soviet Union signed an accord with the United States, Pakistan, and Afghanistan and agreed to withdraw its troops.

On Feb. 15, 1989, a column of armored personnel carriers rolled across the Friendship Bridge, the last of a Soviet army that fought a 10-year war in Afghanistan. After losing more than 15,000 troops in the quagmire, the Soviet Union pulled back, defeated and demoralized. Later that year, the Congress of People's Deputies, the first semi-democratically elected representative body of the U.S.S.R., passed a resolution that condemned the war. The Soviet withdrawal was completed on February 15, and Afghanistan returned to its prior nonaligned status. One million Afghans lost their lives in that conflict, and their country's wars were not yet over.

Poor Afghanistan. Almost immediately after the Russo-Afghan War drew to its ignominious close, the country hurtled into civil war, one of the worst in history.

As to the CIA agents involved in the fighting, they were instrumental in mujahideen insurgents obtaining all the captured Russian war materiel and all the materiel left behind that was brought in by Charlie and all his dirty dozens. In 1985 President Ronald Reagan signed the National Security Decision Directive 166 which significantly increased covert military aid to the mujahideen, making it clear that the secret Afghan war had a new goal: to defeat Soviet troops in Afghanistan through covert military action. By that year, the Afghanistan project received fifty percent of CIA's entire operations budget. One year later, it rose to seventy percent. 1985 became the bloodiest year for the Soviet forces since they invaded Afghanistan on Christmas Day, 1979.

Of more lasting effect, the CIA and its operatives were instrumental in the creation and growth of a little known organization called the Taliban Jihadists during Operation Cyclone. The United States and Saudi Arabia agreed to match funding to jihadi groups in 1991, when over $400 million was given to what would subsequently morph into the Taliban.

Pakistan's ISI (Inter Services Intelligence) wanted to turn the Afghan jihad into a global war waged by all Muslim states against the Soviet Union. Pakistan was base camp for Afghan jihad. Pakistan–a nearly 100% fiercely Islamic country–became the third largest recipient of U.S. foreign aid. Charlie Wilson and the CIA beat back the argument growing in Congress that Pakistan was building an atomic bomb, the only way to defend against the militarily superior India.

With the active encouragement of the CIA, nearly 35,000 Muslim radicals from forty Islamic countries joined Afghanistan's fight between 1982 and 1992. Tens of thousands more came to study in Pakistani madrasahs where they were recruited into jihadism and supported by American money which was ignored by everyone involved on the American side. Eventually, more than 100,000 foreign Muslim radicals were directly influenced by the Afghan jihad and became part of the Global Holy War that persists to the present day. Afghanistan became the starter supply house and training ground for global war jihadists in Afghanistan, Pakistan, Iraq, Iran, Libya, Egypt, Algeria, Yemen, Sudan, and Palestine. Arms, ammunition, artillery, vehicles, tanks, and every sort of military paraphernalia, made its way out of Afghanistan to the terrorist countries—all bearing the indelible stamp of America either directly or by proxy. In partnership with the Muslim Brotherhood, Al-Qaeda, Al-Qaeda Iraq, ISIS—with the final iteration as the Islamic State–Global Jihadist War became a primary factor in all politics and military planning around the world.

The Afghanistan debacle can be visualized by one last vignette of the struggle which directly involved Americans, Russians, and the DRA.

No one–not even the mujahideen—ever accused the Soviet Army or its client army of the Democratic Republic of Afghanistan of being cowards. On the last day of the Shindand conflict, one surviving unit of DRA soldiers commandeered a Toyota pick-up truck with a full tank of gas and loaded with weapons—AKMs, grenades, and grenade launchers, two fifty-caliber machine guns, and several Soviet Union S-75 Dvina SAMs, and began a weave-and-bob circumferential killing spree around the Shindand airbase. The shouted *Dushman! Dushman!* [enemy] as they shot at their victims. They somehow evaded every pursuer and sharpshooter.

A frantic young mujahideen ran up to the four tired CIA agents and breathlessly gasped, "Bossmen, killers are killing our people. Need help! Go quick after those dogs."

So, the agents took deep breaths and found a Russian BTR-80 APC with its engine still idling. Mujahideen gathered around and excitedly pointed to where they had last seen the evasive killers. The agents raced away from the base compound and immediately saw the armed Toyota truck dashing around the outer perimeter of the base. They moved as fast as their old vehicle could go and made a diagonal vector towards where they judged the Toyota would be. They were correct in their assumption and calculation and almost ran into the pick-up a kilometer away.

Things did not go well for anyone from that point on. The BTR-80's left rear wheels hit a hastily planted donkey-carried IED which stopped the vehicle dead in its tracks. None of the agents was seriously injured, and they tumbled out of the vehicle holding their AKMs.

The Toyota spun to a stop to face the CIA *Dushmen* side to front and pivoted in the truck bed to bring their machine gun to bear. Three fired his AKM on automatic and killed the machine gunner and two of his DRA comrades. The DRA began shooting wildly at the agents who were standing out in the open firing back. It was a twentieth century non-Hollywood recreation of the 1881 shoot-out at the OK corral in Tombstone, Arizona.

Although it was almost the equivalent of a shootout in an elevator car, only one CIA agent, "Three," was wounded. Unfortunately, that was serious. Anger, practice on the shooting range, fortitude, or maybe dumb luck, protected the other three agents. They killed the remaining Soviets in what they termed a "mad-minute" shooting action.

Immediately the agents turned their full attention to Three. He was gasping for breath; blood seeped from his abdomen and chest; and he could not move his legs.

"We have to get him out of here, now!" shouted Crank, who began to pull at the dying man's legs.

Three screamed in agony and begged, "Leave me be…please. I want to die in peace. You will never make it if you monkey around with me."

Ball knew he was right. They would be dead men walking if they moved as slowly as they would have to by helping their comrade-in-arms, who was dying anyway.

"No man gets left behind," begged Crank.

Just then, the situation became even worse. About seventy-five meters away, a mob of women in their traditional and daunting black burkas came trotting briskly towards them screaming high-pitched ululation trills as they advanced. The women waved large hacking knives; some used steel sharpener rods as they ran. They had torture and slaughter on their minds and were heedless of any danger to themselves.

Ball turned to Three, who moaned, "Go, go, go, this is your only chance. Let my death be of some use and dignity, I beg you."

Ball looked at Bob and Crank who hung their heads.

"He's right, you know. Ten minutes from now we will all dead heroes if we stay. We have to go and live to fight another day."

The truth was glaring them in the face. In a few seconds, the three agents bade their dying brother one tearful last good-bye and took off running the 5,000 meter race of their lives.

The black ghosts came relentlessly nearer. Agent Three prepared to die.

He waited until the ghosts were within fifteen meters of him, then he quickly rolled to his side—a desperate motion of agony—took out two grenades and quickly pulled the pins out with his teeth which broke off all four incisors. The women were ten meters away and brandishing their wicked knives as Three shoved one grenade under his low back and the other under his neck and waiting in terrible piercing agony the necessary four seconds.

The blood-lust crazed women were less than three meters away when the two grenades exploded simultaneously turning CIA agent Three into a pink mist and shattering the front lines of the women.

Two years later–in a simple ceremony in Langley, Virginia–a black star for valor was posthumously awarded in secret to Harvey Edward James O'Dwyer. It would be more than thirty years before his name and the award he was given could be made public.

> When you're wounded and left on Afghanistan's plains,
> And the women come out to cut up what remains,
> Just roll to your rifle and blow out your brains
> And go to your God like a soldier.
> –Rudyard Kipling, The Young British Soldier,
> Departmental

Ditties and Ballads and Barrack-Room Ballads, 1899

Halwaua-e-Aurd-e-Sujee is a delectable dessert, which is popular in Afghanistan. The dish is made with sugar, Ghee, coarse semolina, blanched pistachio nuts, blanched and slivered almonds, and ground cardamom. After the sugar is combined with water in a saucepan, it stirs occasionally until dissolved. Then hot syrup is added into semolina, and nuts, cardamom, and rosewater are added. Halwaua-e-Aurd-e-Sujee is beautifully decorated with nuts and is cut into squares. It may be served warm or cold.

Recipe:

Halwaua-e-Aurd-e-Sujee

Ingredients
- 1 cup of sugar
- 2 cup of water
- ¾ cup of ghee
- 1 cup of coarse semolina (farina)
- ¼ cup of pistachio nuts - blanched
- ¼ up of almonds - blanched and slivered
- ½ tablespoons of ground cardamom or to taste
- 1 tablespoons of rosewater
- oil

Directions:
1. Combine sugar and water in saucepan and stir occasionally until dissolved, over medium heat.
2. Bring to a boil and boil briskly for 5 minutes without stirring.
3. Remove from heat and leave aside in pan.
4. In a deep heavy pan heat ghee and add semolina.
5. Stir over medium heat for 5 minutes. Semolina should not color.
6. Pour hot syrup into semolina, stirring constantly.
7. When smoothly blended, reduce heat and leave to cook, uncovered, until liquid is absorbed.
8. Mixture should be thick but still moist at this stage.
9. Stir in nuts, cardamom and rosewater to taste.
10. Cover rim of pan with a cloth or 2 paper towels, put lid on tightly and leave on low heat for 5 minutes.

11. Turn off heat and leave pan undisturbed for 10 minutes.
12. Spread halwau on a flat, lightly oiled platter and decorate with nuts.
13. Serve warm or cold, cutting pieces into diamond shapes or squares.

PART THREE

THE RISE AND FALL OF THE FIFTEENTH CALIPHATE:

The CIA Giveth, and the CIA taketh away…

CHAPTER ONE

He will stretch out his hand against the north and destroy Assyria, leaving Nineveh utterly desolate and dry as the desert. Flocks and herds will lie down there, creatures of every kind. The desert owl and the screech owl will roost on her columns. Their hooting will echo through the windows, rubble will fill the doorways, the beams of cedar will be exposed. This is the city of revelry that lived in safety. She said to herself, "I am the one! And there is none besides me." What a ruin she has become, a lair for wild beasts! All who pass by her scoff and shake their fists."

–Holy Bible, Old Testament, Zephaniah 2:13-15

"Show the world your strong compassion: Give your voice to voiceless Yazidi girls!"

–Widad Akrawi

Sinjar Village, Nineveh Province of Northern Mesopotamia, part of the disputed territories of northern Iraq, May 5, 1993.

The Nineveh plain is not an inviting place geographically or socially. The land is dry and unforgiving to farmers. The diverse population is much the same. There is a mix of peoples that would be staggeringly difficult to rule if that was the purpose of your political group. There are scattered and unfriendly groups of Yazidis, Christians, Turkomen, Kaka'i, Shabak, Roma, Chaldeans, Mandaeans, Armenians, Shi'ites, a small community of Iraqi Jews, and much larger settlements of Sunnis. They have markedly disparate religions and cultures, ethnic backgrounds, languages, and attitudes. In 1993, there was relative peace in the province because the people found one common ground, commerce. Religion and politics were absent from conversations among people doing business; and that was a good thing, if not entirely friendly. It is into that mix that a Yazidi girl of exceptional intelligence, beauty, and questing for knowledge, came into the world.

Khatoon Yazidi was born on May 5, 1993 in a mud hut in the mixed village of Sinjar, not far from the sacred mountain of the same name. Her aunt Nadia served as mid-wife. The house had a single tandoor oven which served for cooking and for heating—usually inadequately—during the cold winters. Khatoon was a lovely, cuddly, baby girl who won the hearts of the entire family even though she was only a girl. The Yazidi's attitude toward girls was only a step better than that of the surrounding Sunni Muslims. Khatoon had particularly striking, but not entirely rare, curly blond hair and silvery blue eyes, which set her apart from the majority of girls. It was a relatively healthy and prosperous time for the Yazidis, who numbered somewhere near 600,000 in Iraq with most of them in Nineveh province.

Like all other Yazidi girls, the baby began to learn her place in the patriarchal society and about the elements of her culture which were quite different from the surrounding cultures, especially the Muslims. By the time she was two or so, she had mastered her own culture's Kurmanji language, Kurdish–the "enemy" language as defined by President Saddam Hussein, but critical to commerce–and Arabic, in order to avoid conflicts with the Muslims who outnumbered the minority populations by overwhelming percentages. Her mother was a decent seamstress; so, she was able to make Khatoon and her sisters their allotted one dress per year, even though she lacked a sewing machine.

The religion was significantly different than all others, especially the Muslims, in the Nineveh plains. Yazidism is an ancient monotheistic religion which is something of a mixture of similarities to Judaism, Zoroastrianism, Mithraism, and Islam. Polygamy is permitted–even encouraged–in some villages. Devout men stand out in a crowd because they wear their scrupulously clean and oiled black hair in long braids. They cover their faces with a white cloth.

Traditionally women wear gauzy white dresses, veils, and headscarves, just like those of their mothers and grandmothers as far back as anyone can remember. Women have few rights, especially when a marriage ends. Honor killings are not rare. *Qawwals*–traveling religious teachers—are a significant part of the religious practices; and the men who achieve that level of veneration are important religious, social, political, and educational, authorities. Peacocks are deemed to be holy symbols.

Khatoon and her siblings learned the intricacies from the *Qawwal* Hajji al-Hawrani, a dynamic and spellbinding orator and debater.

"My dears," he said, "before God made us—mankind—he first had to create seven divinities, which we often call "angels" as do the Christians, but that is not quite what they are. They are really God, himself; but separate manifestations of his being. God did his work energetically making the universe as we know it from fragments of a broken spherical pearl. Next, he sent his number one angel—Tawusi Melek—to his earth in the form of a peacock. That is—of course—why we reverence peacocks. The graciousness of God was to paint the bird's feathers in a brilliant and shimmering array of colors to add beauty and variety to our world.

"Tawusi was sent to meet the first man created by God, and created to be perfect, all good, and immortal. But Ṭawusi had a rebellious streak; he challenged God's decision in making such a man. He told Adam that he must reproduce, but to do so he must become somewhat less than perfect. Tawusi offered the man wheat, a forbidden food. Watching from his place in the heavens, God made a dramatic decision. Instead of becoming angry with his angel for his rebellion, he told Tawusi that he would put the fate of the world entirely in his hands. Tawusi insisted that Adam eat the wheat which the weak-willed man did. The result was that Adam was expelled from his paradise and procreated which resulted in the appearance of the generations of Yazidis on the earth. Because of his brilliance and his strong association with God, he has been made our link with God and his heaven. So, of course, it is Tawusi Melek to whom we pray."

Khatoon accepted the *Qawwal's* explanation as simple, logical, and straight forward truth, and remained a dedicated convert from that day forward, doubting nothing. She helped her family and other Yazidis to decorate their houses with brilliant images of multi-colored peacocks. It reminded her and the other adherents that we all owe our existence to God, and we should show our undying devotion and love for him all our lives.

In the culture, Yazidis who marry non-Yazidis are automatically considered to be converted to the religion of their spouse and therefore are not permitted to call themselves Yazidis. Interfaith marriage is frowned upon but not outright condemned. For the Yazidis, Mt. Sinjar–sixty miles away to the east–is a holy place, and a place of refuge, which had been used several times for that purpose. Yazidi New Year is in April, and all Yazidis who are able, visit or do a formal pilgrimage to the mountain.

When Khatoon turned seven, her father took a second wife over the determined resistance of his first wife. The new wife—Lalish–was young, sexy, and not the least bit shy about offering Elias Yazidi overt displays of affection in public, something that was just not done in polite society. At the young wife's insistence, she and Elias moved out, leaving the first wife and her seven children the mud hut. He built the new wife a fine house using the best cinder block and metal for the roof. Other than to bring by an occasional morsel of meat or some vegetables, Elias paid almost no attention to his early family. He did occasionally scold Khatoon for trying to seduce men with her looks; she was seven-years-old.

2003 was a very eventful year for the Yazidis, and especially for Khatoon. That year, her father died. Mourning is long and involves the whole village. Businesses shut down; people are sad. No TVs or radios were allowed during mourning. Khatoon was secretly glad he died because he had become unpleasant and overly critical of her as his marriage to the young girl soured. Lalish disappeared into the home of a wealthy merchant as his second wife. None of the family attended the funeral.

In 2003, the Americans invaded Iraq in Operation Desert Storm; and the world turned upside down. Coalition forces planes flew over Kocho and Sinjar on their way to Baghdad. It was the first time Khatoon had ever seen an airplane. The power and influence of Al-Qaeda Iraq waned significantly as they faced the daunting American military force. For the previous ten years, Muslim animosities and moderate level attacks escalated. As AQI influence diminished so did the incursions against the Yazidis. For that, at least, Khatoon was grateful for the American presence. The death of the ruthless dictator—Saddam Hussein–at the hands of the Americans resulted in something of a truce among the different peoples of the Nineveh planes. He was universally hated there for his Operation Anfar when he ordered his air force to drop terrible poisons on whole defenseless villages as a sort of Hitlerian ethnic cleansing against the Kurds and the minorities.

To celebrate "The Liberation" as the Kurds dubbed Saddam's death, they sponsored a week-long celebration. Even the most far-right Muslim extremists joined in. For the Yazidis, it was like a second New Year celebration in a single year. Friends and families traveled considerable distances feeling safe to visit and to sight see. The majority–including Khatoon and her family–performed an old fashion pilgrimage to the top of Mount Sinjar. They wrestled their prize lamb into the bed of their old Ford truck and jounced their way to the sacred mountain. Shortly before they reached the top of Mt. Sinjar, they joined several thousand Yazidis and a fair number of nonYazidis who just wanted to share in the fun.

Khatoon was a graceful sprite of a ten-year-old who delighted in performing and teaching the largely forgotten art of Yazidi dancing. Family members, neighbors, old, young, Muslims, and even a few Jews, joined hands and danced away hours spinning in a wide circle. The older men slaughtered the lamb, bled it well, and cooked it on a spit for hours. Tired, and a bit drunk, the hive of active people sagged to the ground enjoying unusually pleasant weather and slept in the luxury of peace and security.

Beginning that same year, great changes began to occur in Sinjar and nearby villages like Kocho and Solagh. Miracles of American technology and services entered the area rapidly. Where previously there was little to excite a traditional society, there were now: cell and television towers, satellite dishes, and an increase in jobs in security, military forces, construction, hotels, and restaurants, and the pleasures attendant upon having enough money to lead a more than hand-to-mouth existence. Yazidis and other minorities with their newly acquired financial security began to own their own land. They did not have to work for the Muslim landlords for a pittance anymore. The U.S. Army Corps of Engineers teamed up with Iraqi engineering and construction firms and built paved roads, even all the way to the mountain. Saddam's Ba'athist Sunnis lost their jobs, their power, and their influence due to American occupation.

Both American and Iraqi soldiers made good will tours throughout Iraq. A group of six Americans traveled from Baghdad to as far away as Nineveh province. They passed out gum and candy to children and took instant photographs with polaroid cameras. For people who could not afford to have a mirror, those photos were the first time they had ever seen their own faces. Americans were overwhelmingly popular in the villages.

Khatoon would never forget the first time she encountered an American. He seemed very young to be a soldier and was different from the rest. He was tall–the tallest person she had ever seen. He had curly blond hair and striking blue eyes, again something she did not know existed. Her own blond hair had become light brown with age. He had a square jaw and fine features. In particular he had a nice, small, symmetrical nose, unlike the swarthy, craggy faced men she had lived around her entire ten years of life.

He smiled frequently and easily which showed large, even, very white teeth. He was clean and clean shaven; even his clothes—simple as they were, had just been laundered–another significant difference between him and her family and clan members and their neighbors. She liked that he did not smoke or chew tobacco like many men she knew. He chewed gum, and his breath smelled sweet, like peppermint. If she had known about such things, she would have decided that she had just experienced love at first sight.

Avery Daryl Challenger was technically not a soldier. He was a CIA agent on his first assignment. His uniform was simple camouflage like everyone else's, but he had no identifying insignias of force affiliation or rank. He was the youngest officer in the CIA covert service, having lied about his age to get in.

Avery and his partner Al Lee—a descendant of those American Lees—visited selected homes in Sinjar Village, including the Yazidi family to which Khatoon belonged. To have Americans drop by on a friendly visit was truly incredible to the family. Yazidi neighbors were generally standoffish, and Muslims had become overtly hostile.

They brought an interpreter. Through her, Avery—who did most of the talking and the smiling—introduced himself, first to the lady of the house.

"Hello, Mrs. Yazidi, thank you for inviting us to your nice home."

After the interpretation, she smiled and told him her name was Safaa.

"Thank you for coming so far to see us. You must be very busy. We would not like to take much of your valuable time."

"Not a problem," Avery said. "We are here to learn and to help if our help is needed."

The children stood in a stiff row behind their mother with the tallest boy on the agent's left and in descending order of size down to the smallest, a five-year-old boy named Naif, who looked rather undernourished. Avery was polite and shook each child's hand, but when he came to Khatoon, he paused, taken in by her beauty, her obvious curiosity, and her sense of humor.

He introduced himself to her, "Hi, I'm Avery."

She struggled for a moment then shyly repeated, "Aviary."

The interpreter corrected her and added what an aviary was.

She blushed, but instead of withdrawing in shyness or awkwardness, she began to laugh at herself.

"So sorry, Great Sir, I do not think you look like an aviary," the last word carefully enunciated.

Avery laughed. He laughed hard enough to have to wipe a few tears. It had to do with the opportunity to laugh in a world were little laughter was heard, and less of it expected in the future as the radical Islamists were gradually tightening their nets.

There was one large group of people who were not laughing–Saddam's Sunnis who lost their jobs, their power, and their influence due to the American occupation and continuing presence. The concept of living peacefully in a country with diversity—of thought, of religion, of culture—did not resonate with the Sunnis who believed that their God meant for them to have control over everything in their country and in the entire world eventually. Al-Qaeda's lure became increasingly more enticing as the Sunni *ummah's* declined. Al-Qaeda morphed into AQI and became the lasting and serious enemy of the American occupiers.

With a certain prescience and with a keen eye to the world that the jihadist insurgents were intent on creating, Avery recognized the existential danger that the minorities like the Yazidis faced. Despite knowing that it was none of his business and would have drawn serious censure from his secrecy minded superiors, he approached the Yazidi family patriarch—Khatoon's paternal grandfather–and matriarch, Lydia.

"You have been most inviting and kind to me, Mr. and Mrs. Yazidi. I would like to do something for you in return. I think it is important. As you know, I work for the United States government; and I see a large part of your great country. What I have been seeing in the past year since we have been here, is a growth of Islamic fighters and their power. They are gaining new people from the ordinary population all the time. My superiors and fellow workers and I see a pattern of intolerance and hatred spreading, and with it, an increasing number of violent incidents against minority peoples like the Yazidis. Are you aware of such a change?"

Mrs. Yazidi replied quickly, too quickly, "No, Sir. No. We have lived together as neighbors for a very long time; and although some Muslims don't like us because we are different, we have trouble..."

Her daughter-in-law, usually meek and submissive, interjected with feeling, "No Mother Lydia, I see it whenever we go into the city center or to the Muslim neighborhoods to sell our goods. Many people turn their backs on us. Some of our oldest customers now refuse to buy from us. They say mean things, like, 'those Yazids, they're like the Jews. They're dirty, and they smell bad. Their produce and things they make may have disease in them,' and they call us names even when they know we can hear, things like, 'dogs and pigs.' They say our children are the 'spawn of pigs and dogs, and they come from the mud...'"

Mrs. Yazidi silenced her outspoken daughter-in-law with a glance.

Avery feared for the nearly defenseless Yazidis like Khatoon, who became fixed in his mind as a person worth saving; so, her people were worth saving. That fixation would determine much of his future as a CIA agent and as a man. At the moment, it emboldened him to make a recommendation that he knew would not be received well.

"Please, Mrs. Yazidi, let me help you to leave here. I have access to land near Baghdad where you can be safe. Where the government will provide security. It would come at little cost for you, and your family can live there for many years without fear. Khatoon and your other children deserve to have a chance to live their lives in peace and away from people who do not like you and might even do you harm. I can make arrangements for a move even today."

Khatoon was a snoop, and she overheard everything. She was shocked at the idea of moving away from everything she had ever known. She knew better than to speak up one way or the other.

Lydia Yazidi was adamant.

She said politely, but firmly and with finality, "Our fathers and grandfathers have lived in this valley in the shadow of the sacred Mt. Sinjar for generations. We will stay here. We can defend ourselves if we must. You are a pleasant young man, and we believe you mean well; but you are new here. You cannot know what we Yazidis know about our people and about those who live around us. You think you can trust the government we have right now in Baghdad, but you lack experience. Do not presume to instruct us or to persuade us to move.

"My good family, and I, and our daughter-in-law, see that you show great favor towards our little, Khatoon. Do not even think that you could take her away from us to your world, Mr. Challenger. We will never allow it, and she will never permit it. She is a daughter of the Yazidi people, and here she and all of us will stay."

Mrs. Yazidi continued, "Yes, Mr. Challenger, we know how much you care for our Khatoon. We have watched and believe your intentions are pure. She is a pure girl and will remain so. To violate her would have to happen over our dead bodies. We have fears of what would happen if she were to go away with you."

"Please, Mrs. Yazidi, I have no desire to offend her or you. I care for her as I would a daughter. But I do fear for you and for her. Should you ever change your minds, you can contact me through the United States Embassy in Baghdad. I will respond. I have a question: since I have asked for you to make a great change, and you have decided against my suggestion, am I still welcome in Sinjar to visit you?"

"Yes. We will chaperone our children as our culture dictates; but as long as you come as a friend, you will be welcome to share our home, our food, and our shelter."

CHAPTER TWO

"...Islam was never a religion of peace. Islam is the religion of fighting..."
    –Quoted in, *Islamic State Releases al-Baghdadi Message*,
    BBC, May 14, 2015

Theater Internment Facility Camp Bucca, Umm Qasr, Iraq, February 4, 2004

Ibrahim Awwad Ibrahim Ali Muhammad al-Badri al-Samarrai, son of Sheikh Awad Ibrahim Ali, was born into the Al-Bu Badri tribe, in the Saladin Governorate, near Samarra, Iraq, on July 28, 1971. He was the third of four sons in the Sheikh's family which made him less favored than his two elder brothers. Young Ibrahim's father and his uncle were farmers and were pillars in their community's religious life and wanted the third son to do that as well. Ibrahim was not a strong boy and was not really suited for the rigors of farm life; so, his father allowed Ibrahim to follow his religious inclinations. Many devout Muslim families were pleased to give over a son to the study of Islam instead of pushing them into work for which success is unlikely.

Sheikh Awad sent his older sons to work in the fields and expected them to be serious helpers in the family business. Ibrahim, he encouraged to go about the village as a teacher of various subjects in the family and community's faith; and boy developed some enjoyment and exhibited a modicum of skill and popularity in delivering the messages and in getting the children to follow him around the neighborhood reciting passages aloud for the enjoyment of the citizens and passersby. As a youth, Baghdadi had a passion for *Qur'anic* recitation and was meticulous in his observance of religious law. His family nicknamed him "the Believer" because he often chastised his relatives for failing to live up to his stringent standards.

His friends reported that he was a rather soft boy who lacked the stamina and strength for sports and that he was the type of boy who never got chosen to be on a team of his peers when they picked teams for ball or other sports. Later on, he did develop enough skill to be able to gain some favorable mention for his efforts in that universal sport of football, but he did not keep up with the game as the school years went by. The area of life where he felt most comfortable was in studying the *Qur'an*, the *Hadith*, and the writings of scholars–particularly the lawyers who specialized in Sharia law.

In his early teenage years, Ibrahim strove to become an *huffaz*, since they were well respected in any community. To do so, Ibrahim would have had to memorize the *Qur'an* and to be able to recite it verbatim without making mistakes. To have the title made official, Ibrahim would have had to pass a verbal test given by three test masters who chose *Qur'anic* verses at random for him to recite. He failed to pass, which was apparently a definite let down and a blow to his self-esteem.

His interests and activities did not help him to make friends; so, through high school and university he was pretty much a loner, seeking but seldom finding compatible companions and never a true "I've-got-your-back" kind of a confidant. Where his father was a domineering and unsupportive man, his mother—whose name is unknown to anyone in any record—was loving, kind, and encouraging. She told him that he was handsome and bright and that he would go far, maybe even become a great cleric. Neither parent could be said to be fanatical or even excessive in their pursuit of Islam. They were content to be average and rather innocuous. Ibrahim had ambition to be more than that, but the opportunity never seemed to come. He slowly seethed with anger during his school years.

Ibrahim did not excel in formal schooling. He did not do well enough to get his certificate of graduation from Samarra High School. He nearly failed his English course. He had to suffer the ignominy of having to repeat the testing in 1991 which resulted in a mediocre performance. Apparently, he did not actually graduate from high school. His high-school transcript was not good enough for him to be admitted to study his preferred subjects: law, educational science, and languages, when he applied to matriculate at the University of Baghdad.

He admired his uncles who served in the Iraqi army and one who served as a bodyguard for Saddam himself. One of his brothers became an Iraqi Army officer and another who died the Gulf War while serving in the Iraqi military. Ibrahim longed for the prestige that could be gained from the military, but it appeared that a military career was just another door that was closed to him because he was deemed to be unfit due to his severe nearsightedness. It made him angrier.

Ibrahim did not find friendships in the areas he wanted to because of all the disappointments. He was shy, unimpressive; and he avoided the violence that was all around him. He again pursued a course of scholarship, rather than engaging in an active life—he never had an actual job in all his life–and became steadily more introverted and angry. His anger needed some sort of outlet; and thus far in his life, he was unable to find one.

He was ripe for recruitment, and ready when it came along while he was studying Islamic Law and the *Qur'an* at the Islamic University of Baghdad. During his period in graduate school, his paternal uncle–Ismail al-Badri–persuaded him to join the Muslim Brotherhood which turned out to be a significant step in the direction of militant jihadism. With that beginning, Ibrahim quickly gravitated toward the jihadist Salafis whose strict creed led them to call for the overthrow of rulers they considered betrayers of the faith. Under the influence of those radical Salafis, Ibrahim immersed himself in the writings of those Muslim Brothers who had embraced jihadism. Under their tutelage and influence he grew steadily impatient with the Brotherhood mainstream, which he felt was made up of what he referred to as "people of words, not action."

He supported himself by doing odd jobs. Over the next ten years–until 2004–he lived alone in a room attached to the small local Sunni [and Salafi] Haji Zaydan mosque in Tobchi, a poor neighborhood on the western fringes of Baghdad. The neighborhood included both Shi'a and Sunni Muslims, and there were very few incidents—especially of the violent variety. He despised the Shi'ites but ignored them as they did him. At some point he became a minor cleric in the mosque. He gained a reputation as a dogmatic and unpleasant zealot. He had a temper that was often displayed when he saw what he considered un-Islamic behavior. On one occasion, for example, Ibrahim became extremely upset when he witnessed members of a wedding party engaging in activity that was appalling to him. He shouted at the people he considered to be acting as the *kuffars* and the Shi'ites did.

"How can you men and women dance together in public in such an unIslamic fashion," he shouted at them.

He would not relent and finally forced the wedding party revelers to stop and to disperse.

The breaking point for Ibrahim came when the ultimate provocation took place. The United States of America conducted a lightening attack and invasion against Iraq. Ibrahim gathered with his few friends and; after the U.S. invasion of Iraq in 2003, Ibrahim helped found a very militant and ambitious group called JJASJ [*Jamaat Jaysh Ahl al-Sunnah wa-l-Jamaah*] in which he served as head of the *sharia* committee. Apparently, Ibrahim Awwad Ibrahim Ali Muhammad al-Badri al-Samarrai had found his place. He never looked back.

He was so enchanted with the jihad and with his part in it that he experimented with changing his name. With the help of his friends—rather tame jihadists—he tried out multiple iterations before finally settling on the one that warmed him the most. For brief periods, he went about as: Dr. Ibrahim `Awwad, Ibrahim `Ali al-Badri, Ibrahim `Awad, Ibrahim al-Badri al-Samarrai, Ibrahim Awwad Ibrahim al-Samarra'i, Dr. Ibrahim Awwad Ibrahim al-Samarra'i, Abu Du'a, Dr. Ibrahim, Abu Bakr al-Baghdadi al-Husayni al-Quraishi, Abu Bakr al-Baghdadi al-Husseini al-Qurashi, and Bakr al-Husayni al-Baghdadi, before finally settling on Abu Bakr al Baghdadi.

Most scholars—even his detractors—agree that he did get a bachelor's degree and a master's degree in Islamic Studies and the *Qur'an*, one of 30,000 such degrees created by Saddam Hussein using state funds. His tedious master's thesis was a commentary on an obscure medieval text on *Quranic* recitation. Ibrahim set out to reconcile various versions of that manuscript. His contribution involved no exercise of imagination and certainly no hint of questioning of the content. It was a perfect project for a budding dogmatist. He claimed to have obtained a doctorate in that period, but scant evidence of that exists.

Like most populist leaders, Ibrahim had only a nodding acquaintance-ship with the truth; and he came to love violence because of its effec-tiveness for Islam, and because it was a core necessity to re-secure stolen rights and security for Muslims everywhere. As his career as a jihadist, a terrorist, a mass murderer, and an Islamic politician, evolved, he settled on a love affair with violence for its own sake.

Others–who were his subordinates–insisted that al-Baghdadi earned a doctorate for Islamic studies in *Qur'anic* studies from Saddam University in Baghdad. According to a biography that circulated on extremist inter-net forums later, he obtained a BA, MA, *and* PhD in Islamic studies from the Islamic University of Baghdad. Another report says that he earned a doctorate in education from the University of Baghdad. He never laid claim to having been awarded *two* PhDs. Being mostly unrecognized–even in his own organization–Baghdadi was known to be nicknamed at a later time, "the invisible sheikh" and "*Al-Shabah*" [the phantom or ghost].

He changed some of his names to include the family honorific of al-Quraishi. His use of that surname came about because of his unyielding claim of being directly related to the Prophet through the Quraysh Tribe on his paternal side. Muhammad was also known as a member of the family of Hashim on his mother's side. The kings of Jordan lay claim to their divine right to be monarchs because they are Hashemites. The Jordanian jihadi brothers scoffed at Ibrahim's temerity. The jihadists with whom Ibrahim associated were neither deep thinkers nor serious scholars; so, no one else posited a question as to evidence of his link to the Prophet.

Ibrahim came to the notice of the government of Iraq and of the United States as a result of his inflammatory public rhetoric, but more particularly for several rather minor terrorist acts he either planned or participated in or both. He played a minor role in the founding of *Jaysh Ahl al-Sunna wa-l-Jamaah* [Army of the People of the Sunna and Communal Solidarity], a Salafist insurgent group that fought a few skirmishes with U.S. troops and their local allies in northern and central Iraq. CIA agents identified him as a criminal and told their employers in America where he could be found—which was at the home of an old friend. U.S. forces arrested Baghdadi in Falluja, Iraq and sent him to a detention facility at Camp Bucca, Iraq where he was held for ten months (February, 2004-December, 2004) under his name "Ibrahim Awad Ibrahim al-Badry."

The camp was known among its inmates as "The Academy" because so many of them were teachers, scholars, and students. Ibrahim was a mid-level prisoner—a "civilian internee." His detainee card gave his profession as *"administrative work"*—secretary—and that is what he spent his very small amount of work time doing. He served his time in Compound 6, a medium security Sunni compound mainly pursuing his Islamic scholarly interests and having chats with the other jihadists interned with him. Ibrahim led prayers, preached Friday sermons, and conducted religious classes for other prisoners which earned him something of a reputation as an up and coming leader, if not altogether charismatic.

Camp Bucca was an infamous prison camp among prison camp systems and was hardly a country club. However, the newly anointed Abu Bakr al Baghdadi by his preference of names, came into his own in that prison. He received an education in jihadism from the greatest professors of the ideology; and he learned about their politics, their motives, and their modus operandi, about how the war was being carried out. Baghdadi ingratiated himself with both the Sunni inmates and the Americans, looking for opportunities to negotiate with the camp authorities and mediate between rival groups of prisoners and gaining at least grudging respect. The prison was full of famous Islamic heroes including the second tier of founders of AQ. Al-Baghdadi spent long and profitable hours in conversation with such luminaries of Al-Qaeda. He also developed a significant—and well-paid–relationships with the CIA operatives who were so helpful to him.

On May 23, 2003, the Iraqi Army and intelligence services were disbanded by an order from Paul Bremer III, head of the Coalition Provisional Authority in Iraq. That resulted in hundreds of thousands of well-armed men flowing into the streets and into jihadist history. The order—coupled with an earlier decision to purge Ba'athists from the government—had serious lasting repercussions throughout the country and the world. Most of the 24,000 inmates at Camp Bucca were Sunni Arabs who had served in Saddam's military and intelligence services.

When Saddam fell, so did they, a consequence of the American purge of the Ba'athists and the new ascendency of Iraq's long-oppressed Shi'ite majority which antagonized the ardent and vengeful Sunnis. If those men had not been jihadists when they arrived, most of them were by the time they left. Radical jihadist manifestos circulated freely under the eyes of the watchful but clueless Americans, and al-Baghdadi composed many of them. Each new Sunni internee left the prison as a fire-breathing radical made in the jihadist factory of Camp Bucca. Al-Baghdadi intended to be the most explosive of those flames. Camp Bucca was the seed bed for the future Islamic State and all the grief surrounding it.

It was a ten-month concentrated education for al-Baghdadi. Ayman al-Zawahiri would live to become AQ'S chief ideologue. He was an ophthalmologist who helped found the Egyptian militant group Islamic Jihad. His career was on a steep rise; he was widely speculated to be bin Laden's successor if or when the great leader was no longer in his post.

"Abu Bakr, *As-salam alykum*. I am well, praise be to God," Ayman said.

"*Wa-alaykum as-salam*, the sycophantic al-Baghdadi dutifully replied.

"My brother, you are the new blood we so badly need. We have preserved the memories of too many martyrs. I am sure that your joining us and bringing your expertise will bring us success over the Great Satan and the Little Satan, as well."

"Is brother Abu Mus'ab al-Zarqawi an internee here?" Abu Bakr asked, hopefully because he had long to meet the great noble man.

"He is close. The devils have him interned in Abu Ghraib. You know of that place by reputation. He may be transferred here in a matter of days. He loves to teach, and you are likely to reap the benefit of that opportunity, my brother."

Abu Mus'ab al-Zarqawi—regarded by his western captors as a Jordanian hothead—was transferred to compound 6 ten days later, and al Baghdadi was able to sit at his knee and to receive his wisdom.

"I am hardly worthy of being allowed to learn from you Brother Zarqawi, Praise be to God the Lord of the Worlds, and prayers and peace be upon the noblest of those sent, his family, companions and whoso has followed them with *ihsan* to the Day of Judgment. I count you as one of those."

Apparently, there was no level of fawning that would be so excessive as to oblige al-Zarqawi to turn away. He acknowledged it with a slight nod of his head.

Al-Zarqawi replied equally effusively—a jihadist cultural pattern, "Praise be to God who has fixed the causes by their causes and made faith in Him, reliance on Him, and working to obey Him the strongest cause in realizing happiness and attainment in this world and the Hereafter and for their every essence, and has granted His allies truth in dealing with Him; so, they have reaped its fruits. I praise Him–the Exalted–for the secret of His pleasures and abundances of His blessings that man cannot count, and I bear witness that there is no deity but God alone with no partner for Him in His lordliness, divinity, names and qualities, a true complete witness by its necessities and meanings.

"And I bear witness that Muhammad is His servant and Messenger who broke the system of profits by his miracles whose signs appeared in the revelation of the great *Qur'an* and the Mi'raj, splitting of the moon, life of inanimate things, the pebbles' glorification of God, and complaints of the animal to him by themselves. Oh God, bless Your servant and Messenger Muhammad, his family and companions, the people of truth and resolve in matters, and straightening what was bent from the path, and making clear its customs and obligations. And may He grant many salutations on them and upon you, oh, Brother al-Baghdadi. We feel that you have been anointed as one of the leaders in these, the last days."

"I pledge all I have and all I am to Allah's holy jihad," al Baghdadi said, "I accept the great obligation and challenge to correct the *ummah* to return to the right fold. I understand from your noble writings that obligation by whose absence the Muslims all sin on account of the words of the Messenger of God [SAWS] [the acronym stands for the letters referring to Muhammad "*sallallahu alayhi wa salaam*" may God's prayers and peace be with him].

"I shall consider myself to be privileged to follow you to the ends of the earth. I swear to uphold Brother Usama's dedication to join him and you to attack Saudi Arabia, to rid the "head of the snake," those innovative, profit seekng, and assembled "guests"–corrupt 'heads of the snake,'" al-Baghdadi added, knowing that it would be taken as favorable by the great leader.

He was surprised when al-Zawqari replied back brusquely, "No, Good Brother, I have even argued with Usama on this matter. Before we go after people of our own kind who have gone astray, we must...and I repeat, we must cleanse the earth of those *kuffars*, the Shi'ites, in Iran. Like the Noble Book says about the despised Jews, we must hunt them down and destroy them to the last man, woman, and child, before we turn our attention to the Saudis, the Wahhabis, or to the Great Satan and his wicked minions in the West."

Al-Zawqari was trembling with the passion for which he was famous. Al-Baghdadi knew it was the better part of virtue to avoid a reply to al-Zawqari's unpopular fixation.

Assuming al-Baghdadi's agreement with his passionate hatred of the Shi'ites, al Zawqari went on, "Then, together we will erupt volcanoes of jihad until we encompass the whole earth for the glory of God, the Merciful, and we shall ever act in the name of God, the Compassionate, the Almighty; Praise be to God the Lord of the Worlds, with no enmity except against the oppressors, and the outcome is for the pious. And God's blessings be upon our Prophet Muhammad and all his family and companions. May we one day be accepted into his company in Paradise."

"*Amin*, Brother, *amin*," al-Baghdadi replied, his voice cracking with emotion.

In honor of Abu Musab al-Zarqawi's being able to join the cohesive group in compound 6, Ayman al-Zawahiri, called in all the favors he had accumulated, including some of the markers he was owed from his enthusiastic cooperation with the CIA agents. He sold out seven of his AQ rivals to show good faith to the Americans.

Al-Zawahiri asked the guard to allow him to meet with the chief of station for the American spies alone.

Sgt. Morton was skeptical, "Why would he? For that matter, why should I give you anything you want, you old snake?"

"Just contact him and tell him that Agent X1 has a message."

Reluctantly, Sgt. Morton called the U.S. Embassy and gave the correct daily code.

"Yes, Sergeant, what is wanted?"

"I have to have a secure line chat with the COS, and I need it to happen now."

Not even her superiors in the State Department or the men and women everyone assumed were Nordic-looking spies, considered refusing or interfering with any message the COS needed to give the senior embassy staff.

"I will work on it, Sir."

"Work fast. I do not have all day.

He held the line for five minutes. When a voice came back. It was that of a senior officer who had been part of the original planning for the Phoenix Program in Viet Nam.

"Yes, Sergeant Morton, this is Cunningham. Please repeat today's code."

Sgt. Morton did.

"What is your message?"

"I have an inmate here at Camp Bucca, Compound 6, who calls himself Agent X1. He insists that you talk with him. I discouraged him, but he doesn't discourage easily."

"I'll talk to him. I need to do a bit of reconnoitering out there anyway to see what our current and future enemies are doing. Say 1030 hours tomorrow, your office?"

"I'll make it happen."

The result of that conversation between al-Zawqari and COS-I Dwight R. Cunningham, Jr. was a party the likes of which no guard at Camp Bucca had ever attended in or out of the prison camp. Apparently, it was some new policy of the American brass that "You catch more flies with honey than you do with vinegar," they thought; but they weren't paid the big bucks to make policy; so, they just went along.

The "guests" were assembled under strict security guard. They were brought in from all areas in Camps Bucca and Ghraib. The Islamists had been adjudicated to be of the minor league rank and therefore not particularly a cause for concern. They included Abu Mus'ab al-Zarqawi as the putative guest of honor, and: Seyed Qutb, Khalid al-Habib, Abd al-Hadi al-Iraqi, Lashkar Tayyebah, Hassan al-Turabi, Abdullah Izam, Abdul-Rasoul Sayyad, Abu Muhammad al-Miqdisi, Saif al-Adel, Suleiman Abu Ghaith, Mustafa Hamid, Abou Mossab Abdelwadoud, and Hassan al-Turabi. Truth be known, not much was really known about most of the assembled "guests" by the CIA.

Lesser inmates served the "guests." The fare was grand in comparison to the daily boredom of rice and beans, beans and rice, and mullet mush. It included: *Biryani*, a traditional rice and meat dish; *Bamia,* stewed meat with okra; *Timman Ou Keema*, minced meat; *Kubam*, fried meat patty appetizer; and the unanimous dish among meat lovers who had been deprived of it for months, Iraqi Kebab–succulent grilled meat with spices. They drank iced tea and ice-cold freshly squeezed orange juice and lemonade. Organic juices and fruit juices were very scarce in Iraq, and none of the men had acquired a taste for them; so, no effort was made to provide them. It would have been an insult tantamount to offering pork to these Believers even to suggest alcohol.

The meal concluded at 1900 hours, and then the almost obligatory period of speech making began. Seyed Qutb and Khalid al-Habib—men relatively unknown to their CIA jailers—gave the primary lecture—a discourse in fundamentalist Muslim culture. COS-I Cunningham wrote down the speakers' names, presuming that they could be more important than first believed.

Outb spoke without preliminary or greeting, "These are the elements of The Faith that all true Believers must possess: First know that the ultimate goal of Al-Qaeda ideology is establishment of a jurisprudential and Salafi form of rule whose political system would be a mix of monarchial and aristocratic systems. We seek to revive the glorious days of the Umayyad and Abbasid caliphates and are against democracy, capitalism, and polytheism, in any form. You may write down this list and take it to heart: We fundamentalists value argumentative wisdom only for extracting truth out of the Holy Book and traditions and only in limited instances from followers of religious stipulations and traditions. i.e, are loyal to sharia law and jurisprudence.

1. We consider the above instances as being unchangeable and eternal. It is imperative to aim to establish a society where sharia law and jurisprudence are enforced in their most complete forms.
2. Since non-religious governments are an obstacle to realization of the above goals, we try to overthrow such governments.
3. We endeavor to establish governments based on sharia law; Sharia law is cast from the words of Muhammad, named "*hadith*," his actions, named "*sunnah*," and the *Qur'an,* which he dictated. The Sharia law itself cannot be altered but its interpretation, "*fiqh*," by muftis—properly chosen Islamic jurists–is given some latitude.
4. We do not believe in religious and political plurality. There is but one true God and his True Religion, Islam. We consider religion

as having answers to all human needs both for this world and the Hereafter. No other sources–but Salafi and Wahhabi jurists–are qualified to issue fatwas and pass laws to run social affairs.

5. Making laws on the basis of human wisdom is rejected.

6. Freedom of conviction cannot be accepted because it would lead to blasphemy and innovation [*shirk*].

7. Rulers derive their legitimacy from God, and leaders of different societies should be authorized by The One True God and religion; rulers who act otherwise are anathema. Freedom of expression is not acceptable because it may lead to insult against God and divine rules.

8. Religion is not separate from politics and government.

9. Political parties are not supported by Islam because they pave the way for activities of non-religious elements.

10. It is not allowed by Muhammad for a Believing man to be killed except for three offences: fornication after chastity, apostasy from Islam, or killing a Believing life without a life.

11. The most deserving of people in wealth are the mujahideen in the path of God so that sufficiency may be realized even if infants, children, and the hungry die, because preserving the religion is of greater priority than preserving life. That is a true statement of the Armed Islamic Group."

There was a standing and thunderous ovation. Even the hardened CIA agents and prison guards had never seen such an expression of enthusiasm on the part of the jihadists. For Abu Bakr al Baghdadi, it was little short of rapture. He was a changed man that day—a completed convert and a zealot.

On October 9, 2004, he was released as a certified low-level prisoner after being recommended for a release by the Combined Review and Release Board. As he walked out the door, al-Baghdadi carried with him a comprehensive compendium for reconnecting with his newly acquired co-conspirators and protégés. All of them they had written each other's telephone numbers and other vital personal information in the elastic of their underwear.

CHAPTER THREE

President's Daily Briefing
Oval Office, White House, Washington DC, PDB
[President's Daily Briefing], March 28, 2007

> Meeting recorded and stamped "TOP SECRET, EYES ONLY"; POTUS, George W. Bush; Director National Intelligence, John Michael McConnell; Secy. of State, Condoleezza Rice; Secy. of Defense, Robert Gates; Chairman of the Joint Chiefs of Staff, General Peter Pace
> Present: POTUS, DNI, Secretary of State, Secretary of Defense, CJCS, Special Agent, COS [Chief of Station, Iraq], Dwight R. Cunningham, Jr.
>
> Date: March 28, 2007
>
> Subject: Proposed withdrawal of United Armed Service personnel from Iraq

Summary:
- CIA Chief of Station reported conditions in Iraq, particularly with regards AQI and ISIS—a breakoff faction from AQI. He shared logistical information from the generals in Iraq, from sources in the jihadist community, and sources from the civilian noninvolved

segment of the population. There is concurrence that the jihadist movement–especially AQI–has been decimated to the point of being almost impotent. It is the estimate of the DOJ and the intelligence assets that the insurgency is on the brink of dissolution. It will be less than a year before the threat to U.S. security and to the successful function of the government of Jalal Talabani and the security forces of Iraq will be in a position to protect their citizens from the threats posed by AQI and ISIS, which is almost bankrupt and lacks manpower to mount an offensive.

- Sec/State reported a favorable political climate. The Talabani government requests further U.S. assistance for six months to a year to be able to train its military and to accumulate sufficient military materiel to see the nation through a minor anticipated reaction from the insurgency once the American forces withdraw. During the upcoming year, the security and diplomatic forces of the U.S. can identify and freeze monetary assets globally. Further, identification of recruitment centers around the world is well under way and should be fully effective in six to twelve months so that they can be fully weeded out, stymied, and eliminated.
- Sec/Def presented a detailed report confirming the readiness of Iraqi forces to defend themselves and the law-abiding citizens of the country. He argued that there should be overlap by U.S. forces for six months following formal beginning of withdrawal to ensure security.
- POTUS and his staff took the rest of the day and returned with a decision. Complete withdrawal of United States military forces will commence on July 12, 2007 and will be complete before the end of 2007. Exceptions will be marine embassy guard forces, intelligence operatives, and Delta Force rangers, who will continue training of their counterparts and to report to Sec/Def and JCOS. In the interim, U.S. military forces will stand down to a training force to complete the readiness of the Iraqi military so that Iraq can fully defend itself against any remaining threat.

Signed:

George W. Bush

George W. Bush, POTUS

CHAPTER FOUR

"Hear now this, O foolish people, and without understanding; which have eyes and see not; which have ears and hear not."
—*Holy Bible, KJV, Jeremiah*, 5:21

"None so deaf as those that will not hear. None so blind as those that will not see."
—Matthew Henry, *Matthew Henry's Commentaries*, 1708-1710

"There are three kinds of mind: the first grasps things unaided; the second when they are explained; the third never understands at all."
—Niccolò Machiavelli, *The Prince*, Chapter XXII, translated by Russell Price, Cambridge: Cambridge University Press, Cambridge, 1988)

Sinjar Village, Nineveh Province of Northern Mesopotamia, part of the disputed territories of northern Iraq, May 12, 2007

Her parents and the Yazidis of their generation closed their eyes and ears to what was happening–to the changes. Khatoon did not because she could both see and hear. She was no longer a child; she was a Yazidi woman of marriageable age—twenty-one. She was intelligent and observant. Beyond that she had a most valuable source of information; or, as Avery put it, of intelligence. The American military man, Avery Challenger, had visited her village—in reality to see her—several times a year, more often than his official duties would have required. When she was seven, she was madly in love with him—the Prince Charming of her life and world. Now, as she entered her majority, she realized that she did, indeed, love the kind man, but in the way a daughter loves a doting father or a young sister loves a protective older brother—platonic, but with something more, indefinable, but more.

His visits were a source of hope and pleasure. Her mother thought it was more than that, but she was wrong. He was a man who loved a girl, then the woman, but without the romance that Americans made so much of. By dint of long and patient visits to Sinjar Village, Agent Challenger had earned the villagers' trust and confidence. Khatoon trusted him without reservation and believed without doubt that he had the family's best interests at heart even though his requests that they find a new place to live every time he visited were somewhat annoying.

What Khatoon was seeing and hearing on her own, and what was confirmed by Avery, was that the world in her province and in her village was beginning to change–and not for the better–and with a visible level of acceleration. As evidence of the withdrawal of American troops began to be observed by the jihadists, they became bolder and to show their vertebral column of intolerance. It was an infection that spread.

Where for centuries, the minorities of Nineveh Province lived in an uneasy peace, exhibiting a level of fairness in their treatment with one another and with the majority Muslims. In the last several months, she had both witnessed and experienced unmistakable insults and slights from neighbors. She and her family now felt very uneasy about traveling to see friends and family or to do business in villages as close as Kocho and Solagh or as far away as Tawaf for fear of being accosted by arrogant young Muslim men who took it upon themselves to erect barricades on the roads and to exact a toll from nonMuslims who wished to proceed.

More disconcerting—even alarming—was that she had to endure insults about her being ugly and stinking because she was a Yazidi. She was now being called dirty names like, "whore" and "slut" and "the mother of dogs." Even in the company of her step-father, men made lewd suggestions and invitations for her to violate her sacred purity. And these were from Muslim men who would kill another man who made such comments against their wives or daughters. It was evident that she and her virtue were not regarded on the same level as their women. It was no longer rare to be called a *"kaffir"*; it was the rule. She hated going to the Muslim areas, even though she had to in order to keep the family's business going, humble as it was.

This year, 2007 or 6,757, by the Yazidi calendar–as he did most years–Agent Avery Challenger visited during the time of the great festival of the year for ordinary Yazidis called the *Cejna Cemaiya* [Feast of the Assembly] involving travel to Lališ, north of Mosul, for the seven-day pilgrimage to the tomb of Sheikh Adi ibn Musafir. The festival is celebrated annually from September 23rd to October 1st. Although there were insults and inconvenient roadblocks put up by the ever more dogmatic and unsympathetic Muslims–which now included older people and even children—the presence of the large and heavily armed American prevented any banditry or overt assaults. The family–with the conspicuous absence of the late Elias's sexy second wife (widow)–and their oldest son–the putative protector–enjoyed the festival and encountered no incidents. Avery knew in his gut that this would be the last time the festival would occur with any hope of safety.

Once again, Avery gathered up his courage to confront the Yazidis about the impending danger they faced. Their humble home was decorated with an abundance of poppies, and for the period of that joyful *eid* [celebration], the family's heirloom hand-knotted carpets appeared from their secret hiding place.

It was after the evening meal of the celebration: colored eggs; *tashrib*, a dish of long-simmered lamb; *shawi*, a barbecue of the chosen lamb's heart, kidneys, liver, and other organs; chickpeas and spices poured over flatbread; and soup with meat-stuffed dumplings.

There followed fresh salads; platters with rice, couscous, and other plates of fruits, nuts and sweets, and a special dish of chopped hard-boiled eggs and green onions sautéed in olive oil. The family and Avery were seated on the ground as was the custom for the Murid Caste—the commoners, the majority of Yazidis.

The family patriarch—Grandfather Naif Jasso Yazidi–opened the treasured *Yazidi Black Book* and the *Book of Revelations*, the two holy books of *Sharfadin* [Yazidism, in Kurdish] and read aloud from them in the Kurmanji dialect. It was almost a form of music to listen to the familiar creation myth directly from the holy books. The eyes of many members of the family glistened as venerable grandfather read to them with his full-bodied deep voice.

When the formalities and the feasting were done, Avery eased into his serious remarks with "*eida ta piroziby*" ["happy *eid*" in the Yazidi Kurdish dialect of Sinjar].

"Once again, I thank you for your hospitality. It may be some time before I see you again, since my duties call me elsewhere. I do not wish to offend, but now I beg you to let me help you move to safety in Baghdad before it is too late."

Avery's request again fell on deaf ears and was ignored, albeit politely. They knew he meant well; but he was not a Yazidi, an Iraqi, or even a Middle Easterner. How could he know what the wisdom of custom and history had ingrained in his audience?

He bade them a fond farewell with a touch of sadness. His hug for Khatoon was that of a father leaving his favorite daughter for a long journey with no surety that either would be present for another fond embrace.

University of Baghdad [Saddam University] Baghdad, Iraq, August 31, 2007

Avery Challenger rushed about the country to assess the preparedness of the Iraqi insurgency to see if he could anticipate the onset of the most severe of the savageries of which the jihadi group was capable. Everywhere he went, he saw the determined and deadly efficiency of the men released from the Camp Bucca "school of jihadists." Although they had a bewildering set of ever-changing political alliances—which lulled Washington into thinking that they would not be able to mount a unified offensive—Avery's assessment and in his reports was that the opposite was true. A massive strike was imminent, and it would most likely occur in the north where security forces were spread to their thinnest. His judgment may have been clouded by his fears for the Yazidis and especially for Khatoon's family.

His worst expectations were proved to be absolutely prescient and nearly perfectly correct, to his dismay. On August 19, 2007—which came to be known as the "Day of Death" in Nineveh Province, among the northern minorities, and throughout Iraq and even within the United States defense forces, all evidence for calm and hope disappeared. All sense of security evaporated. It had seemed that security in Iraq's central and northern provinces was improving, and the citizens and the security forces alike were beginning to believe that the naysayers like the CIA were wrong. Suddenly—and totally without warning–coordinated suicide truck bombings decimated several villages of the minority Yazidis west of Mosul. Hundreds were killed and wounded in the deadliest strike since the beginning of the Iraq war. Khatoon's brother, two cousins, and an uncle and aunt were killed; and several members of her extended family sustained shrapnel and burn wounds.

Avery did not have to say, "I told you so."

He rushed to Sinjar and found several homes and businesses still aflame. The Yazidi family lived on the outskirts of the village and had escaped this round of carnage and conflagration. Khatoon met him at the door of the house. Her mother was suffering from end-stage breast cancer; so, Khatoon was now the titular mother—and head of the family.

"Come in," she said somberly and shook Avery's hand.

He held hers for a moment, then asked, "What can I do to help?"

She shook her head.

"Not much. We need everything: enough food, clean water, animal feed, security, and weapons against looters. Our Muslim neighbors are now acting as outright enemies. Our boys are mounting around the clock armed watches against them. We are in a war. I know you predicted this, but I am sure it is no consolation to you to be right."

He shook his head and spoke softly, "Unlike when I was here in May, I can no longer move you to Baghdad and safety. The roads are either destroyed, or are under fire, or are clogged with refugees. The *Da'esh* are everywhere and seem to be winning. Do you have any family I can get you to? Any place to go?"

"Only to the mountain."

"That seems to be reasonable now. The *Da'esh* have not tried to prevent Yazidis from gathering on Mt. Sinjar. I understand that your people have stockpiled food, fodder, and military supplies up there. I can get you through with a convoy. We will have to leave tonight. It is no longer safe for you to be here. The killers will overrun the villages in a matter of hours."

This time, Khatoon believed him and acted on that belief. She ordered the family to pick up the personal items they could carry and to line up in front of the hut for evacuation. Even Grandfather submitted. He was a broken man.

Avery and ten Iraqi Army men and half a dozen Americans drove up in a cloud of dust and stopped in front of the hut. With prodding by a sergeant-major, and a determined Khatoon, the family clambered aboard the armored vehicles and made a bee-line to the sacred mountain. They drove up the winding and rutted road to as near the top as they could get. Time was essential. Avery could not linger. He sent Khatoon and her family scurrying up the incline to the top, then ordered his convoy to return the way they had come.

Avery's orders were to find out what had happened, why his and other CIA agent units had been taken by surprise, and where had the U.S. and Iraqi military forces failed. It would not make him popular; and he did not care; but he did his job with the objectivity and precision of a trained engineer, soldier, and spy. At this point in time, he was the new COS-Iraq, and the responsibility weighed heavily on his shoulders.

He pieced together a history of both the insurgency and the defenses against it. The findings and his conclusions were most sobering. The process was not as difficult as he and his fellow CIA operatives might have expected. He recalled having met an odd detainee at Camp Bucca, named Ibrahim—one of the most common names in all the Muslim world. No one could recall the man's family name off hand, but a quick perusal of the camp records revealed one Ibrahim Awad Ibrahim al-Badry, a camp secretary. Avery had to be reminded by his fellow agents that the nondescript man now strongly preferred to be known by what he grandiosely called himself—Abu Bakr al-Baghdadi. It was an obvious *nom de guerre*; but then, they all seemed to change to old Islamic names to enhance their status or just for the romance of the adventure. What did he care?

Avery did care about the fact—of which he had to be reminded—that this al-Baghdadi had been an entirely reliable snitch during his prison stay. The best thing was that he did it for money regardless of ideology. In Avery's experience, the double agents who betrayed their fellows for money were less apt to get exposed or to flip back to the other side when situations changed. Money was still money.

The CIA operatives traced al-Baghdadi down with little effort. They discovered an announcement in the student newspaper of the University of Baghdad that a man named Abu Bakr al-Baghdadi, aka Ibrahim al-Badri, was scheduled to defend his PhD dissertation in *Qur'anic* studies entitled *On Creating an International Caliphate* on August 31, 2007.

"Seems too easy to be true," said Elizabeth Tandy, the analyst who made the discovery regarding al-Baghdadi's future whereabouts.

Avery said, "I think we can rely on this tidbit in the student newspaper. They included both of his known names because his doctoral work was done under his birth and family name. The *nom de guerre* is an add-on that might not persist in the future. You know how these guys are, Lizzie."

Elizabeth preferred her given name but did not protest when they called her "Lizzie" since it signaled acceptance into the CIA old-boys-club, a barrier that took her years to penetrate.

"Probably," she said, ever the doubting-Thomas and critical thinker.

"Oh, go ahead and accept that you done good," Avery said and smiled at her. "Even for a librarian, that was good quick work. You deserve an occasional 'attaboy.'"

"I guess 'attagirl' would sound peculiar; so, okay, I accept."

The crew traveled to Baghdad, arriving two days in advance of the doctoral defense to be able to reconnoiter the university, places to stay, and how things were done. Actually, there were four doctoral defenses that day, all in the same auditorium. They made sure that they did not call attention to themselves as they found seats. They walked in with the small number of supporters and detractors who gathered with al-Baghdadi and the faculty members who were involved in his field of study—which was probably the largest area of interest in the university curriculum during that period. The auditorium was not well lit for a room of its size and showed signs of age and wear, likely because money for maintenance or improvements had been diverted to the nation's defense, as almost all infrastructure funding had. The floors and aisles had not been swept for weeks.

The auditorium hushed in deference to the professor who stood at the podium and held up his hand for quiet.

"Ladies and gentlemen, scholars, guests, and interested brothers and sisters, may it please Allah, the Merciful and all-knowing scientist for us to come to order. We are met here today for a most significant occasion and to give consideration to an important issue in our faith. In keeping with university policy, we will use the name of our defender that he used during the preparation of his dissertation so as to avoid future confusion when referencing his work. May I present our first candidate to defend his dissertation, Ibrahim al-Badri. Our candidate already holds a master's degree in a related subject; so, we should consider ourselves privileged to learn from an acknowledged expert. His dissertation is entitled *On Creating an International Caliphate*.

"Unfortunately, al-Badri's faculty advisor from Tikrit is unable to attend because of the ongoing violence throughout the country. He has sent his commentary on Mr. al-Badri's dissertation. One of my assistants will read it verbatim but will allow me to summarize his conclusions. He judged the work to be very good. He said, 'I am most pleased with my student's work.'"

The judgment of "very good" constituted the grade for the dissertation and made all the rest of the morning a formality. For the CIA officers the next hour and a half was excruciatingly boring, but they put on empty expressions and endured. Finally, the board of faculty examiners, all clothed in their formal ceremonial regalia, closeted for half an hour. They returned to the auditorium and took their places on the platform wearing faces of stolid solemnity.

The dean of religious studies stood at the lectern and announced, "By the grace of God, the Almighty and all Knowing, will the audience stand before him and receive His faithful servant, Ibrahim Awwad Ibrahim Ali al-Badri al-Samarrai."

All eyes were directed to stage right, and shortly, al-Baghdadi stepped from behind the curtains and walked sedately to stand in front of the faculty review board.

"I am Ibrahim Awwad Ibrahim Ali al-Badri al-Samarrai," he said.

The dean stepped over to the candidate, performed the turning of the tassel of his cap from right to the left, then said, "It is my great pleasure to award this certificate of achievement of the degree of Doctor of Philosophy in *Qur'anic* Exegesis and Sciences. Henceforward, Sir, you are to be addressed as Doctor al-Badri. Congratulations."

He shook al-Baghdadi's hand robustly and stepped aside to allow a brief comment from the new PhD.

There was a significant change in al-Baghdadi's look and demeanor. He had a bronzed facial tan and a very full-face beard. His facial hair was jet black, and he now wore thick eyeglasses which made the sides of his face seem narrowed when he turned his head. The spectacles were something new after his prison days. He had put on weight and looked healthier than he had done during his stay in Camp Bucca.

He began what would be a sixty minute oration serving as his public utterance in defense of his dissertation, "In the name of God, the Compassionate, the Merciful, the Guarantor of Success, and his Messenger, The Prophet, [SAWS], I give thanks for this occasion and this award. I give all credit to Him who created all things. Praise be to God the Lord of the Worlds, and prayers and peace be upon the noblest of those sent, his family, companions and whoso has followed them. Praise be to God who has fixed the causes by their causes and made faith in Him, reliance on Him, and working to obey Him the strongest cause in realizing happiness and attainment in this world and the Hereafter and for their every essence, and has granted His allies truth in dealing with Him; so, they like I, have reaped its fruits. I praise Him—the Exalted One—for the secret of His pleasures and abundances of His blessings that man cannot count; and I bear witness that there is no deity but God alone with no partner for Him in His lordliness, divinity, names, and qualities, a true complete witness by its necessities and meanings."

For the CIA agents, the speech—and indeed, the entire proceeding—was stultifying–very nearly unbearable–but bear it they did. None of them so much as allowed a facial twitch to escape, no matter how effusive, repetitive, and foreign, the manner of expression of religious fervor in comparison to their own ways. It was the worst for Avery, who was a life-long zealous atheist.

It did eventually come to an end, as did the post ceremonial congratulatory period conducted on the university grounds. At long, long last, Avery was able to maneuver unobtrusively through the remaining stragglers and to sidle up to al-Baghdadi.

"Congratulations," he said and offered his hand.

It took al-Baghdadi a moment to place the four men since they were so out of context in the present setting.

"Thank you…Agent…Challenger, I believe."

"Good memory, Dr. al-Baghdadi. We would like to have a brief word with you in private. We will not take much of your time on this important occasion for you."

Baghdadi made an effort not to display his disdain for the agents. They were all *kuffars*, after all, and workers for an enemy state...but they were also generous when they were inclined to be. They also might just be formidable enemies he could not afford to offend just yet.

"Follow me," he said, and set out towards the administration building.

They found a small conference room four doors down from the dean's office and sat around the utilitarian metal table on well-used straight back chairs.

"How can I be of assistance?" al-Baghdadi asked.

"I always like to get right down to business," Avery replied. "We are well aware of your ascension within the ranks of your organization, and we congratulate you for that. You were recently promoted to Al-Qaeda's Shura Council, we heard. That is quite a step for one so young and new to the organization."

Al Baghdadi nodded.

"We have been hearing some disturbing things about some of the senior members of AQI, especially Abu Musab al-Zarqawi and Ayman al-Zawahiri. Of course, we have a great interest in Usama, as you can well imagine."

Al-Baghdadi gave another rather disinterested shrug.

Avery continued, "Dr. al-Baghdadi, we appreciate and value the information you have provided us over the past several months. We are most grateful for the information you shared with us about al-Zarqawi's safe house in Baqubah which led to a successful airstrike on June 7, 2006. The world—your world and AQI—is a better place without al-Zarqawi, and his so-called spiritual adviser Sheik Abd-Al-Rahman. We now have additional specific needs and will pay well to get the information we want."

Al-Baghdadi's face became considerably more animated.

"Our sources confirm for us that al-Zarqawi had become a liability by his stubborn concentration on attacking Shi'ites instead of following AQ's official course of concentrating efforts against the Saudis. We are well aware–as we presume you are also–that his successor, the Egyptian Abu Ayyub al-Masri–also known as Abu Hamza al-Muhajir–has become erratic and excessively violent. That makes him a liability to

AQ's future goal of becoming a recognized political party and a force in parliament to establish an eventually accepted Islamic state. Am I not correct, thus far?"

Al-Baghdadi nodded firmly, and his face began to show real interest, not entirely certain where this was headed; but it sounded as if it might be of benefit for him personally.

"Well then–to get right to it–we need regular updates on the whereabouts and the agendas of two men and several others we will tell you about as time goes on. We recognize that getting such information and sending it on to us securely will be somewhat difficult and complicated and perhaps costly.

"We are prepared to pay for what we get, but only if what we get proves to be both true and useful. Are we tracking together, Sir?"

"Please go on."

"We offer six-figure payments in gold for information that leads to the capture of either or both of these terrorists–Ayman al-Zawahiri and al-Masri–or perhaps even better, ongoing insider information about the thinking of the decision makers. We will also wire-transfer funds of eight thousand U.S. dollars a month for you to defray costs."

"Tell me the six figures you have in mind."

"$200,000 for al-Zawahiri, and $250,000 for al-Masri."

"Not enough. There will be payments, you understand. Let us think more reasonably... about...say, $250,000 and $500,000 for the two men separately–$750,000 for both at the same time. Being suspected of betraying my brother, Abu Ayyub al-Masri, holds a personal risk for me that far exceeds anything we have dealt with together before. I can only give information on him for, shall we say, $500,000."

"We know that these scholarly credentials you received today as well as the work you have already had done to manage AQI's religious affairs have already brought you favorable attention by al-Masri. We also know that he appointed you to be supervisor of the Sharia Committee—a very serious position because you have effectively become the official enforcer of all the organization's religious policies. Just recently al-Masri also named you to the eleven-member Consultative Council. That brings you closer to the man than ever before and makes our request not only possible but something you can do without real danger to yourself."

Al-Baghdadi was very impressed that the CIA had been able to obtain such top-secret information about AQI; things he, himself, only became privy to recently.

"That is naïve, Avery. You know the danger this represents to me and to my family. I must insist on the figures I cited in order to secure a safe house well away from Iraq. That is costly."

"We can agree to that even though your request is excessive, Dr. al-Baghdadi; but it must be fairly soon; or the deal is void."

"I agree," al-Baghdadi said with finality and extended his thumb for a thumb-hook sign of full agreement, "However, I will need to acquire certain equipment to make myself useful enough to gain favor with these men and with the rest of the AQI leadership—which, incidentally, we prefer to call ISI [Islamic State of Iraq]. I know you have considerable stored military materiel like vehicles, tanks, arms, and ammunition, left over from the War in Afghanistan, and the first war in Iraq. We will need those to be released to us in less than a month."

"Only with a guarantee that none of the weaponry will be used against Americans."

"But, of course. That is easy since we are now such good friends. We will have to use force to solidify our position here in Iraq and to diminish the power and influence of other groups—those who have fallen away from the true cause and have become *takfir*."

"Do right by us, and you will find us to be very generous friends and supporters of you and your personal cause."

"Trust me, my brothers," al-Baghdadi said with feeling.

Al-Baghdadi felt it would be better not to share the fact in that in 2006 he had joined the umbrella organization—*TQJBR* [*Tanzim Qaidat al-Jihad fi Bilad al-Rafidayn*—"Organization of Jihad's Base in Mesopotamia," or AQIM, "Al-Qaeda in Mesopotamia"]–formed by al-Qaeda in Iraq to unite several jihadist groups to resist the American occupation.

CHAPTER FIVE

"Will you walk into my parlor?" said the Spider to the Fly,
'Tis the prettiest little parlor that ever you did spy; The way
into my parlor is up a winding stair, And I've a many curious
things to show when you are there."
Mary Howitt, Poem-*The Spider and the Fly*, 1829. As
a picture book, illustrated by Tony DiTerlizzi, the book,
The Spider and the Fly, was published in 2002 by Simon &
Schuster Books for Young Readers, 2002

"And, good lieutenant, I think you think I love you.
William Shakespeare, *Othello, Act II.Scene iii*—Iago speaking
to Cassio, originally published in 1622

AQI Mobile Headquarters, MND [Multi-National Defense region] Northern Iraq, particularly Nineveh, Tamim, and northern Salah ad Din provinces, September 30, 2007

Al-Qaeda was in more disarray than the public realized. Except for Abu Bakr al-Baghdadi's secret information passed to Avery Challenger–the CIA Chief of Station in Iraq–the United States would have presumed the terrorist organization to be just as strong and dangerous as it was throughout the spring and summer of 2007. The de facto leader of

Al-Qaeda, Abu Ayyub al-Masri—invited Abu Bakr al-Baghdadi to share a lunch prepared by his second wife.

The wife—a Yemeni woman–Hasna Ali Yahya, served a platter of dolma [stuffed spiced rice wrapped in grape leaves], *masgoulf* [seasoned fresh carp] skewered and cooked by barbecuing and grilling on their outside grill, iced tea, and jumbo medjool dates. She was dressed in a severe burka with only eye slits showing anything of a person beneath the shroud. Even the eye slits had a black lace covering. She was silent and efficient. She never looked up or at Abu Bakr, and she was scrupulously careful not to make even accidental physical contact with him.

"Congratulations, Brother," al-Baghdadi said, "you have the perfect wife."

"Thank you, Brother. God, the Merciful and Compassionate has been most kind to me. The woman came from a good Believer family, and she was properly trained. Her father did not spare his sons or his daughter the whip when it was required. The result is what you see today. I praise God and his Messenger (SAWS) for their gifts, for all three of my wives. They are exemplars for the *ummah*, if I may say so without seeming to be boastful."

"Indeed, it is so, my Brother. Allah, the one God, is most merciful. You can be justifiably proud. I, myself, have but one wife. She is also an obedient and hard-working woman who inspires the best in me before God."

"We have a matter of some importance to discuss, Brother. I have observed you for some time, and I have been pleased with what I have seen. You have likewise found favor in the eyes of God, the Great Observer."

Al-Baghdadi lowered his eyes deferentially.

"To further God's work, the Consultative Council and I have seen fit to appoint you to a most important position in our God Blessed endeavor. From this day forward, you are to be the adviser to Emir Abu Umar and to the brothers in all things religious. You will be the enforcer of the Islamic State of Iraq's strictures for all Believers and the scourge of all *kuffars* wherever and whenever they are found. God–who knows all things–knows what is in your heart and has let those of us in His movement know that it is good."

That appointment comforted the majority of nationalistic Iraqi jihadists who joined the coalition in support of Abu Umar, who was their countryman and the putative leader of the movement. They were restless and unsatisfied with their newly coined jihadist organization and only remained in it because of Umar. Concealed from the rank-and-file, was that the ISI was actually firmly under the control of Abu Masri, whose base of support came from his fellow *foreign* jihadists.

When al-Baghdadi joined the council, the Iraqi members were becoming restless and a schism between the Iraqi faction—basically the old Al-Qaeda–and the foreign faction was developing. One of his early appointments was to go to Damascus to ensure that AQI's propaganda adhered to the principles of ultra-conservative Islam. Under his hawk's eye scrutiny and attention to even the slightest deviations, the propaganda that left the printing press under al-Baghdadi's control was impeccable— i.e. without even the smallest spot or taint of wrongful ideas about Islam and the duties of Muslims as determined by the rapidly ascending ultraconservative wing of the organization.

Although al-Baghdadi had a measure of power and influence, he walked a tight rope, and found it taxing to avoid falling to one side or the other. On any given day, he was likely to have a serious discussion with members of both factions.

Muhammad Abd al-Ouahhab–who was something of a self-appointed representative on the council–implored al-Baghdadi to "beware of the extremists coming into our midst from the foreign lands. They are not our people, and they do not know our ways. Mark my word, good Brother, they will undermine all that Al-Qaeda has accomplished, and all that we seek to create. You know the Holy Book better than most of the lawyers, Dr. al-Baghdadi; and it is your mission to put the foreigners back on the righteous path. You will be counted as a friend of God when you do. I wish God's blessings upon you and your family for all its generations. May you always walk in the footsteps of his Messenger (SAWS). I cite one example from an undeniably reliable source of the lengths that the dissenters will go. A man in the outskirts of Midan one day during a demonstration that had turned violent sent his eight-year-old daughter to be a martyr with a bomb strapped to her small chest. She walked into the police station in Midan and tripped the mechanism."

Al-Baghdadi appropriately gasped at such cruelty and audacity; but in his heart of hearts, he tucked away the example for possible use when he became the Caliph, which he never doubted would happen.

An hour later, while attempting to rememorize a difficult passage from the *Qur'an*, "We have not sent down the *Qur'an* unto you to cause you distress, O Muhammad (SAW), but only as a reminder for those who fear [Allah]"-*Taha* 201-2, Sheikh Said Muhammad al-Tikriti happened by, and–having seen al-Ouahhab conversing with al-Baghdadi–felt it timely to speak his mind to the young council member.

He said, "Ah, Good Brother, Allah, the Great and the Merciful, the only Deity, has smiled upon me to be able to meet with you when you are not occupied with weighty matters. I wish to convey the concerns of my companions from all around the world of the Muslim true Believers. The *ummah* has gone astray, My Boy, and we must bring them back into the body of the Believers if we are ever to bring to rein the *kuffars* of the west, the Great Satan, the Little Satan, and those among us who would pervert the world of God, the innovators, and even the innocent who are misguided."

"What would you and your companions have us in the leadership of the Great Jihad movement do to further the return of the misinformed and the willful back to the true path, my Learned Friend?"

"Oh, Abu Bakr, how I hope that your father aptly named you when he gave you the sacred name of the first and best friend of the Prophet (SAWS). We must be the servants of the Almighty to usher in World War III—the ongoing war of words, ideas, and killing machines, under the banner of the only true religion–a war of correct Islam against the rest of the sinful and ignorant world. We are ISIS [*ad-Dawlah al-Islamiyah fil-'Iraq wash-Sham*]. Al-Sham is the Levant covering Syria, Lebanon, the East Bank of the Jordan River—until the desert—the west bank of the Jordan River, and Israel]."

"We see what is plain and clear, Brother: The despised *kuffars* of Iran who wrongly worship Ali have followed the pathway of *Shaytan* from the beginning; the *ummah* has drifted far from the true way mostly out of ignorance or by following fools and charlatans. Even ISIS has begun to move away from its Allah-approved hardline positions by making concessions to the reformist/dissident trend.

"We must not shy away from making war on all of those, even the People of the Book and those claiming to be Muslims but whose beliefs and practices are not in keeping with God and the Messenger (SAWS) and his great family. Our well-intentioned Islamic State leadership deviated from true monotheism when they began to grant unwarranted concessions to the dissident and reformist trend within God's jihadist movements on issues such as whether *takfir* of the idolaters is of the principles of the religion. For many of us, these concessions mark a dangerous turn towards "*Jahmism.*" Our leader, Umar al-Baghdadi, has wrongly entrusted such matters to the ignoramuses of the Delegated Committee. He is an old man with a fuddled brain who has his head in the sand. Remember the admonitions of those of the brotherhood who reside abroad. Their's is the wisdom of the Right Thinking Caliphs. Heed them."

The "foreign contingent" favored a much more militant and violent approach to jihad and were beginning to complain openly, even sometimes in public. The old Al-Qaeda of Usama bin Laden and his inner circle believed that the 9/11 attack in New York City was extremely successful, had put AQ on the world's political map, and needed not to be repeated. Instead—in the opinion of the present AQ leaders, it was time for AQ to go legit—to become a regular, albeit jihadist, political party.

Abu Bakr al-Baghdadi was an intelligent man who saw the growing shism in the ISI as one more opportunity. Much as he had done in Camp Bucca, Baghdadi quickly developed a role for himself to act as a go-between and as a respected and unbiased conciliator between the two opposing sides. Despite being a publicly unabashedly al-Masri protégé, Baghdadi earned enough of the venerable Abu Umar's trust to be get himself appointed to the Islamic State's Coordination Committee. Then, he was one of a very powerful three-man panel that could select, supervise, and fire, the Islamic State's commanders in the group's Iraqi provinces; and his sphere of influence was expanding.

To the firebrand Abu Umar, he acted as the young and energetic voice of change, the voice of Islam rising.

"My esteemed Brother in the Cause of God," al-Baghdadi said, "I will once again say to my comrades on the council that our time has come. But until we have a stronger man in the leader's seat, I fear that my message will fall upon deaf ears. Nevertheless, I will exert effort to bring those nationalists and populists around to the true cause of World Islam rising again."

He drafted messages from Abu Umar to the putative, but largely absent, great leader of Al-Qaeda—Usama bin Laden—painting a subtle picture of chaos in the leadership and a rudderless rank and file. He suggested perhaps that maybe or possibly there might be a newer, fresher, more energetic leadership appointed. He did not act or write so presumptuously as to offer suggestions about who that leader might be.

Although Abu Umar al-Baghdadi did exist and walk among the jihadists and was hailed by the leaders as the head of ISI, his role was entirely fictitious. His persona was one actually created by al-Masri to give foreign-led AQI activities the illusion of Iraq-born legitimacy. It was the duty of Abu Bakr al-Baghdadi to give credence to the mythology.

He also coordinated communication between the Islamic State of Iraq's top leaders and their provincial representatives, much of which was conducted by couriers. As such, he granted himself the latitude to inject his own–but unattributed–suggestions and began to bend the minds of the men who mattered to his way of thinking, a very conservative and authoritarian way. The implication of the one selected to author the communication conveyed something of a not-so-subtle indication of who might well be the one whom Allah had anointed to be the chief of state and the "commander of the faithful" in due time.

In the interim, the messenger had to convey to the jihadist leaders that Al-Qaeda required that all Muslims—certainly all jihadists while the war raged—to give obedience to the relatively unknown named Abu Umar al-Baghdadi and to acknowledge him. Around the jihadi world, many of them had never even heard of him. The older Baghdadi—Umar–was not just unknown, he was mysterious.

It was more than highly unusual for Muslims to call or consider a man a caliph. It was usually considered the height of hubris to claim a title reserved for historically important leaders of areas conquered and administered by Muslims. In fact–most of the time–the faithful reserved the title only for the early friends of The Prophet who became the series of four leaders of the religion and its people and territory after the Prophet's death—and they themselves have long since passed on to live in paradise with Allah and His Messenger.

Sunnis strongly believe that to be caliph, a man must be a descendant of the Quraysh tribe to which Muhammad belonged. Young Abu Bakr of 2007 quietly claimed to descend from Muhammad through ten of the twelve Shi'ite imams. Umar–the elder al-Baghdadi–could make no such claim. The younger and more aggressive one subtly allowed his childhood records and his very early family connection to God's

Messenger (SAWS) to leak out. This was an irony of the first order since the caliph to be–al-Baghdadi–hated the Shi'a and had gone out of his way to emulate his mentor, Athman al-Zawqari—and to do as much injury to them as possible. Abu Bakr al-Baghdadi claimed with an absolute and unwavering testimony to be a 44th direct descendent of the Prophet, and thus, entitled to the role of caliph. Since his prison days, he never again mentioned that he was, in fact, born Ibrahim Awwad Ibrahim al-Badri and had no legitimate claim to be the mujahid sheikh Abu Bakr al-Baghdadi al-Hussaini al-Qurashi–Abu Bakr al-Baghdadi, for short, a *nom de guerre* he chose for himself.

The choice of "Baghdad" as part of his name comes from a certain mythology held deeply in the souls of fundamentalist Muslims, not just the jihadists. The Islamic Golden Age was a period of cultural, economic and scientific, flourishing in the history of Islam which eclipsed European culture which–during the same period–was mired in its dark ages. That great period dates from the 8th century to the 14th century beginning during the reign of the Abbasid caliph Harun al-Rashid (786 to 809) with the inauguration of the House of Wisdom in Baghdad.

Abu Bakr al-Baghdadi considered himself to be a well-educated Islamic scholar among scholars, and it flattered his ego to have the place associated intimately with him as part of his very name. Furthermore, there are various *Qur'anic* injunctions and Hadith, which place values on education and emphasize the importance of acquiring knowledge that have played a vital role in influencing Muslims of all ages in their search for knowledge and the development of the body of science. That search has always seen its roots to be in Baghdad. The scholarship of the Hadith also had firm roots in Baghdad. But foremost for Abu Bakr al-Baghdadi and his fellow fundamentalists, Baghdad, Iraq lives on as the embodiment of what a caliphate was and what it will be again when the jihadists conquer the world.

Avery Challenger and his CIA agents had their hands and minds full trying to sort out the complexities of the Middle Eastern and Iraqi world of jihadism. There were dozens of factions, all committing acts of terrorism. ISI seemed to be a lesser of evils organization which–if properly groomed—it seemed, could potentially ameliorate the chaotic and apparently haphazard pattern of terrorism.

AQ had evinced an interest in legitimacy by participating as a legally recognized parliamentary political entity. After several months of discussions, the ODNI [Office of the Director of National Intelligence] sent down a succinct and blunt order to the COS-Iraq. The last sentence in the order read: "Of all the bad choices available to the U.S. government, the least problematical is AQI. There is at least some semblance of order on the part of that organization. AOI has kept its promises not to attack the U.S. during the time specified in our most recent contractual periods in exchange for receiving advanced military materiel. COS-Iraq is hereby ordered to enter into another such contract for the remainder of FY 2007 and FY 2008. There must be a written contract signed by the head of AOI before any American weapons or vehicles change hands."

When Elizabeth Tandy—the embassy's chief of intelligence analysis—read the letter, she gave a snort, "Doesn't Vice Admiral Mike McConnell know that '*qui cum canibus concumbunt cum pulicibus surgent?.*'"

Avery said, "I'm sure he would know that's Latin for 'He that lieth down with dogs shall rise up with fleas.' He got an Ivy League education same as you."

"Ummh, hmmh, but he doesn't have to go talk to al-Masri, you do."

"I can hardly wait. Can you get me an appointment with nice Mr. al-Masri, Lizzie?"

"Sure, and don't call me 'Lizzie,'" she smiled.

"I thought it was, 'how many drinks does it take to make you dizzy? With the answer being 'about two, and my name is Daisy," Avery joked, and Elizabeth laughed.

It took two days for al-Masri to agree to a secret rendezvous with the COS-Iraq. AQI was understandably as nervous about having anyone in its world know about such a meeting as the proverbial skittish cat in a room full of rocking chairs. Negotiations took place in a fine old colonial mansion in Baghdad with the United States footing the bill for champagne, steak, truffles, and chocolate soufflé. Besides al-Masri and his bodyguards, Avery was surprised to see that the only other jihadist present was the up and coming young Abu Bakr al-Baghdadi.

He was not surprised when—after twenty hours of haggling—the deal was Ayman al-Zawahiri's head on a platter ASAP and twelve others to be delivered over intervals during the next twenty-four months; no attacks on Americans in or out of Iraq by AQI; no attacks on AQI bases in Iraq or Syria by the U.S. for two years; delivery of $200 million worth of currently moth-balled 140 M-1A1 main battle tanks, and diversion from Turkey of another 150 German Leopard tanks.

Germany had provided Turkey with a fleet of 354 Leopard 2A4 main battle tanks on the condition Turkey would not sell or transfer them, 40 paramilitary M-1 Abrams tanks, 180 Humvees, 24 U.S.-made M-113 armored personnel carriers, 20 F-16s (with the provision that they not be used in Iraqi cities), and enough small arms and ammunition to arm three full militias.

The results were less than perfect overall and less than that for which Avery Challenger had contracted: CIA operatives were given the whereabouts of the Egyptian-born al-Zawahiri, a trained surgeon. He was living and well in a mud-brick compound in Karachi with his three wives and children. More importantly, Pakistan's ISI [Inter-Services Intelligence agency] effectively protected al-Zawahiri and many other evicted al-Qaeda operatives who had fled from Afghanistan in late 2001.

Acting on information Avery received from AQI, in February 2008, the CIA located the senior terrorist leader, Imad Mugniyah, in Damascus. Mugniyah died in a powerful car bomb explosion, similar to his own favorite modus operandi. Of particular interest to the U.S. National Intelligence were the bombing of the American Embassy in Beirut, which killed CIA Middle East officer Robert Ames, the kidnapping and murder of Beirut CIA station chief William Buckley, and directing the bombing of the U.S. Marine and French paratrooper barracks at the Beirut airport.

An important operative known only as "Muthanna," Al-Qaeda's emir of the Iraq/Syrian border was assassinated by Avery's agents. Finally, AQI provided a list of 500 al-Qaeda fighters from many foreign countries including: Libya, Morocco, Syria, Algeria, Oman, Yemen, Tunisia, Egypt, Jordan, Saudi Arabia, Belgium, France, and the United Kingdom. Of those, Avery's hunter-killers and their Iraqi counterparts found and eliminated 29 al-Qaeda high value targets. They were either killed or detained by Task Force 88–Multinational Forces Iraq's hunter-killer teams working with CIA agents to target senior al-Qaeda leaders and operatives.

Still, the continuing success of AQI as a terrorist organization; and the fact that his main target, al-Zawahiri, remained alive and elusive; and Abu Ayyub al-Masri survived an assassination attempt, made Avery feel as if his skin was itchy.

CHAPTER SIX

"We are not preachers of violence. Jihad [striving or holy war] in Islam is a defensive movement against those who impose violence."
   –Grand Ayatollah Sheikh Mohammad Hussain Fadlallah, quoted *in Laura Marlowe, A Fiery Cleric's Defense of Iihad, Time Magazine* (New York), Cambridge University Press, January I5, 1996

If you don't know where you're going, any road will take you there.
   –Charles Lutwidge Dodgson [pseudonym Lewis Carroll], illustrations by John Tenniel, *Alice's Adventures in Wonderland, Macmillan and Company,* London, 1865

AQI Mobile Headquarters, MND [Multi-National Defense region] Northern Iraq, particularly Nineveh, Tamim, and northern Salah ad Din provinces, September 30, 2007

Serious debates began in earnest among the jihadist community— dozens of groups—about the methods and goals of the jihadist movement. AQI was supported by a majority of activists who saw the issues to be solved as local and national instead of international. The argument was that global terroristic incidents did not seem to attract recruits, financial benefactors, and certainly did nothing to further sympathy for the cause itself. The purpose of any Islamic party had to be to improve the lot of the people–the common Muslim individual and Muslim family. Therefore, the focus should be on constructing and maintaining physical and societal infrastructure.

Imposing a severe religious culture on a society with a lengthy history of secular government and state provided services had not worked for those areas where repressive regimes had taken over countries. AQI and its sympathizers had evolved to a point where they desired peace, prosperity, opportunity, access to government officials, state supported secular schooling, and the utility and attractiveness of well-functioning infrastructure.

The more action-oriented–more foreign based groups–took an ideological approach. It was the duty of the brethren involved to make a change in the thinking and actions of Muslims' lives. It was time to return to the enlightened era of the seventh century when the Prophet and the right-thinking Caliphs ruled and imposed a righteous form of government under Islam with Allah as the recognized head of both government and religious institutions—no nonsense about separation of church and state. That goal should become a world ideal turned into a reality. All goodness, effectiveness, and progress, should be attained by compliance with the *Qur'an*, the *Hadith*, the writings of the approved scholars and lawyers, and with the imposition of Sharia law.

That could only be accomplished in a world free of the evils of democracy, capitalism, innovation, and polytheism. Since people mistakenly defended ideas so abhorrent to God, war was the only answer—holy war. Global war–World War III–required a stable and secure base, and that could only be realized by the establishment of an Islamic State. Therefore, the first battles needed to be fought in the countries where the population was a majority of Muslims. It was crucial to own and control land, enough money to have security, and to have a loyal and dedicated standing army. The only way for the people who saw a future where the true religion— strict original Islam—achieved global control was to begin the war now in the Middle East and to build God's kingdom in the promised land of al-Sham [Syria] as promised by the Prophet himself.

Opinions hardened, and it became necessary for the partisans of jihadism to take sides.

It was also necessary for the W.O.M.s in Washington to "remove the scales from their eyes" and to admit—at least to themselves—that they had been duped once again by the wily Islamists. Avery's communications with his superiors became increasingly harsh about what the various murderous groups were doing. DNI Vice Admiral Mike McConnell and a small entourage of security agents and scholarly analysts and university professors came to Baghdad to confer about strategy with the "down-in-the-trenches" agents and several army rangers who had been in-country longer than their fair share.

Adm. McConnell was not a stickler for protocol or niceties, and he did not tolerate idle chatting or fools.

They sat down in a Spartan conference room in the temporary embassy located within the safety of the Green Zone. It was a former Republican Palace of Saddam Hussein. The campus was huge, covering forty-two hectares, making it the largest and most expensive U.S. embassy in the world—almost the same size as Vatican City, and more than ten times the size of the embassy in Beijing, which is only the third largest U.S. diplomatic mission abroad. The current embassy opened July 1, 2004 in Baghdad's Green Zone as an interim campus while the grand new embassy was being built on the side of the Tigris River, west of the Arbataash Tamuz Bridge.

"We've seen your messages, Challenger. No need to repeat things here. Give us the sitrep as of today. Looks like we need to do something different."

"Yes, Sir, we do. We have been playing footsie with monsters for a long time here in hopes that—at least—they would be *our* monsters. AQI has fed us names of men who oppose their particular brand of Islamic extremism and protects the ones whom they see as important assets for their particular notion of how things should be run.

"They take a rather long view of things, sort of the way the Red Chinese do. We seem to start out with a battle plan based on 'we'll have the troops home for Christmas' optimism. We should have learned more from the War in Viet Nam. AQI has been milking us like a cow and has been willing to trade some lives they don't much care about in order to get what they want in the long term."

"And what is that, exactly?"

"An Islamic State. Iran is somewhat the model, but Iran's ambitions are pretty much self-contained. The new Islamic State AQI envisions is based on Muhammad and his original friends' idea of a world-wide Allah run mega-theocracy with the world headquarters in Baghdad eventually. My insider sources tell me that their target is Syria, or al-Sham as they call it. Syria as the location is described in the *Qur'an*; so, they are content to terrorize everyone, everywhere, and all the time, to get their particular brand of governance in place in Syria and then to spread out from there.

"I think they would be content with a centuries long process so long as the process keeps moving. I know they think that the spread will quicken as the areas they conquer get converted to the "True Church" and move into the ranks of fanatics who will go forth to do battle in the name of Allah."

"What is the process, as you understand it, Challenger?"

"In a sense, I think the enemies of AQI are their own worst enemies. AQI per se is content to achieve local political clout. The real Islamic Staters are rigid, dogmatists, a lot like the Taliban in Afghanistan. They don't really care much at all about the "state" part of their activities. They will shed anyone's blood they have to in order to impose their extremely severe theological notions on their captives.

There is excellent scholarly evidence that such attitudes ultimately fail almost every time. Since these people only read their own self-serving, self-promoting, Islamic literature; they cannot absorb the concept that success really comes from providing real government...like building good infrastructure, providing necessary services, and making their territory into a desirable place to live, to raise families, to practice their religion without being hounded, etc., etc."

"If we left AQI alone, what would be the outcome, do you think?"

"They are murderers, but they are also relatively educated pragmatists. In the short term, they will kill and terrorize the locals into submission, but only to the extent that they become a dominant party among parties making up the government. They are not really the ones we have to fear and should fight."

"This is what I came to hear. If we fight any group or coalition, are we just going to make some regime changes and then see different *ali babas* doing the same things Arabs and Islamists have been doing for the past millennium and a half with no real changes? Or do you see this group of hardnoses being an existential threat to America, and therefore someone we need to engage and to stop, even at the cost of American blood being shed, and our reputation being further tarnished?"

"There is a putative Islamic State already. It is in name only, and its very existence is on shaky ground. In the first place, they really don't control any land. They are almost nomadic Islamic hunter killers. The history is almost all about the Jordanian national Abu Musab al-Zarqawi. His religion and politics are about as far to the right as it is possible to be; he subscribes to the Saudi type Wahhabi fundamentalism which everywhere else is known as Salafism. His goal and that of his fanatical followers is the establishment and expansion of a new Islamic caliphate no matter how many people have to die. al-Zarqawi began training extremist militants in Jordan in 1999. It is almost funny, but he charged the students to be trained as his cannon fodder.

"From October, 2004 until June of 2006 he kept his group going by nominally pledging allegiance to Usama bin Laden's al-Qaeda and to al-Masri's AQI. Al-Masri sold him out to us, and we assisted him to martyrdom that June. His group was originally called *Tanzim Qaidat al-Jihad fi Bilad al-Rafidayn.* He got his so-called 'foreign insurgents' to form the Mujahideen Shura Council in January of 2006. That has now morphed into al-Qaeda in Iraq.

"There has been a philosophical and strategic falling out between al-Zarqawi's proteges and al-Masri; and in fact with bin Laden, although they all give lip service to the idea that al-Qaeda is still the grand jihadist organization. The split widened on October 15, 2006 when Tanzim and five other Iraqi insurgent groups merged to form Islamic State of Iraq—ISI. They prefer just IS, because that is their eventual goal."

"Who runs AQI and who runs IS? Does it matter? Should we move against either or both? What do you think from your time on the ground here, Challenger?"

"I think there is a monster in the background who is kind of a mysterious character, not at all well known by our military or intelligence services. He goes by the *nom de guerre* of Abu Bakr al-Baghdadi. Many of the jihadists in AQI call him either "the invisible sheikh" and "*Al-Shabah*" [the phantom or ghost]."

"Is that the guy who took al-Masri's place after he was killed?"

"No, that was Abu *Umar* al-Baghdadi. He was killed along with al-Masri. There is a hole in top management for the time being, but my sources tell me that the Shura Council is looking hard at this guy, Abu Bakr al-Baghdadi, to be the new emir. It's kind of like the old European 'the king is dead, long live the new king' except, they are slow and ponderous about decision making."

"Refresh our memories of this al-Baghdadi character, please, Challenger. Seems we will need to know him and will need to deal with him sometime down the line. Agree?"

"Yes, Sir. I'll give you a brief run-down."

Avery took an hour to fill in all the blanks he could in al-Baghdadi's dossier to the present.

Adm. McConnell asked, "Is he a crazy? I mean can he be reasoned with or does he just want to get the seventy virgins and whatever for becoming a martyr?"

"He is not crazy, nor is he stupid. He tends not to get into the thick of the battle and has no real intention of being either a hero or a martyr. He has flunkies for that. Al-Baghdadi has a PhD, and he has successfully manipulated his way from obscurity to his present position as a high kahuna in AQI. At times I think it's just a goat rope in that camp. He is going to have to show his true colors one of these days; and when he does, I predict that he will break off with his own Islamic State show.

"Then, we will have a fight with a dangerous and powerful enemy. He is going to drag down a lot of people as his legacy, I think. How much we want to be involved remains to be seen. That said, I do think we have to begin dealing with him now. And I don't think we will get anywhere with a diplomatic approach."

"I tell you, the more I learn about these terrorist people, the less I seem to understand; and the less I feel like I know what to do. Can we assassinate him? Would that help? And 'goat rope?' Did you grow up in a small town with a county fair, Challenger?"

"The answers are: Maybe, probably not, and yes, I did grow up in a small town; that's where I picked up that kind of slang. We have to thwart his progress at every step. We must not let him really establish a state. That would be like having the kluckers running the devil's own country."

"I don't think they're crazy either, Challenger. But, it doesn't seem so far-fetched that their method has no method; it is just a goat rope after all—a hectic, disorganized, and confused, situation made worse by too many people and complicated by human error."

Operation Hard Strike, Hussein Hamadi Village, Plain of Mosul, Nineveh Province, Iraq, October 29-30, 2007

Avery Challenger expanded his network of informants after Adm. McConnell's visit to Baghdad. His earliest successes came from Kurdish Peshmerga families who were pushed towards the northern border of Nineveh Province. Kurds and Sunnis never got along, and when AQI and the nascent organization of the Islamic State began to press the Kurds to take over their ancestral homelands in Mosul and northward, the Kurds pushed back every way they could.

Avery got an urgent telephone call from Behremend Rozaki, one of his Peshmerga agents who had been a CIA contract agent since 1988 and whose bona fides were beyond question. After reconciliation between the two opposing Kurdish factions was ratified by the 1998 Washington Agreement, U.S. Special Forces and the CIA deployed agents to Kurdistan. The relationship of co-operation between the Peshmerga and the U.S. solidified after 2003 when the United States linked up with Kurdistan to oust Saddam Hussein's Ba'athist Iraqi government. The role of the Peshmerga was key in that effort, and Behremend became a prominent CIA operative who worked closely with the CIA agents who came to the Plain of Mosul.

Behremend was an overweight bear of a man, a quintessential Kurdish swashbuckler with all the prejudices and intolerances that define such a man. He was tall for a Kurd, and muscular aside from his excess weight. He had large black eyebrows, tousled straight, unmanageable hair, full-face beard and mustache, and intelligent, curious eyes which studied everyone and everything that came into his view and purview. His peshmerga uniform was rumpled and unbuttoned at the top to reveal a mat of coal black curly chest hair. His skin was the color of a chestnut, sweaty, and smudged with dust and oil smears. He did not look tired despite long hours of managing fights and bearing the tensions of leadership and of being a double-agent. He had a stentorian voice.

The call came over a secure line and was encrypted.

"Behremend, it is good to hear from you, old friend. How are things with you?"

"My family and I are fine...prospering, in fact. However, I have something for you which must be acted upon as quickly as you can."

"We'll catch up another time. What do you have that is so urgent, Behremend?

"You know that al-Qaeda and its offshoot ISI has been trying to get a toehold in the Nineveh Plain in order to infiltrate and then to take over all of Nineveh Province. Our people have found a small sleeper cell in Bakhdida, or al-Hamdaniya as you might know it. The information is as good as gold, my friend. You and your fighters can capture or eliminate the cell and stop its communication with AQI in Iraq. I can't tell you how long the heathens will be in place, but I do know that they have ordered a new Toyota pickup truck for use in terrorist attacks. Once it gets to Bakhdida, we won't be able of follow them effectively because they will probably take off."

"You have never failed us, My Friend. Give me the particulars about where this cell is located, and we will do the rest. I will have one of my agents share the line with us to be sure that we get the information correct, all right?"

"Yes, is he ready now?"

"It's a she, and yes, she is right here beside me. Her name is Elizabeth Tandy. She's what we call, an analyst. She's the best of the best."

That made her blush

"I'm here, you can proceed when ready," Lizzie said.

"Good. Let me know if I talk too fast, Lizzie," Behremend said. "There are somewhere between six and ten 'freedom fighters' in the cell. They are holed up in Bakhdida Village. Check your map: it is situated in Nineveh Province about thirty kilometers southeast of Mosul and sixty km west of Erbil. The fighters are holed up in an old farm house and barn less than a kilometer from the old Dayra d'Mar Yoḥannan Daylamáyá [also known as Naqortaya and Muqurtaya—the chiseled monastery]. Europeans and the faithful Syriac Orthodox refer it as Monastery of Saint John of Dailam. Failure to stop this cell will allow the heathens to put a big unit of so called 'freedom fighters' into place with equipment to communicate with the terrorists in Iraq at will. Believe me, Avery, they are heavily armed and are looking for a fight."

"Is it easy to find?"

"Not bad. There are two roads that go past it. I will see you at the takeoff point of the gravel road and guide you the rest of the way. I plan to be part of the firefight, Avery, no arguments please."

"How many men do you think we'll need?'

"Ten to fifteen."

"I'll be there, and so will my top NCO. I think we can get there in the wee hours of Thursday morning."

"I would really like to be part of the unit that goes in, Avery. I think I've earned a spot."

"I do, too, Behremend. No problem. Come loaded for bear."

"Aye, aye," Behremend said.

CHAPTER SEVEN

"The U.S. is one of the major causes of Middle East instability which has opened the jack in the box of terror that can never be put back in. If we have to put the blame anywhere then we must blame the U.S. The U.S. starts meddling in other countries' affairs, that leads to power vacuums and instability and other western countries jump on the bandwagon, copying the U.S. like a blind monkey or are the puppets while the U.S. is the puppet master."
  –Ayatollah Ali Khamenei, Supreme Leader of Iran, quoted
    by Samuel Osborne, *Independent*, Tuesday, June 13, 2017

Dayra d'Mar Yoḥannan Daylamáyá Monastery, Bakhdida [Al-Hamdaniy], Nineveh Governorate, Northern Iraq, October 2, 2007

Bakhdida is connected to the main city of Mosul by two main roads. The less traveled of these was a gravel road for decades and then was first paved during the 1990s. It had not been maintained at all well and was full of potholes and fissures and returned to gravel in several areas. The CIA agents and Army Special Forces contingent arrived at the crossroads shortly after midnight with a convoy of very well armed and highly trained combat veterans. They had brought sufficient materiel to mount either a shock and awe assault or a protracted siege. Avery Challenger, the

CIA agent in charge, and his agents occupied an unacknowledged role, and were never listed by name. Army Special Forces Captain, Howard Cummings, was the team leader of the four CIA agents and three squads of NCOs and enlisted men—twenty total. They had been cooped up in their barracks for weeks and were itching for a real fight.

Behremend Rozaki and his sergeant-major Agir Jaf, the Sorani Kurdish Peshmergas, signaled the convoy with three quick flashlight flashes from a hiding place just off the gravel road. The small forces joined up and quickly planned how they would conduct the attack.

Avery whispered hoarsely, "Take one of them alive, if at all possible."

He received a few lackluster grunts devoid of any enthusiasm as his only reply.

"Move out," whispered Capt. Cummings, and the convoy moved ahead, lights out and on radio silence.

Behremend was seated in the shotgun position in the first truck. He tugged at the driver's arm.

"Stop here," he said. "We have to walk in, and we have to spread out. Every five minutes give two clicks of your crickets to let us keep us all in touch and coordinated."

Staff Sgt Bagley nodded his understanding, stopped the truck, got out and personally delivered Behremend's instructions. Twenty-four men stepped into the darkness wearing night-vision goggles. Two stayed with the trucks. They were on strict radio silence and no lights.

It was a two kilometer walk along the rutted road before they began to make out the form of the Syriac Orthodox monastery silhouetted in green against the surrounding darkness. Using hand signals, Behremend directed the combatants to the left—north—for another half a klick. He raised his right hand signaling "halt."

The Americans and Peshmergas had drilled for a day and a half, and each knew his assignment. At Behremend's signal, they split up to surround the dilapidated old house facing them. There were no lights coming from inside the building. As near as they could tell, there were only two sentries, both of which were talking and smoking by the front door.

Capt. Cummings tapped SSgt. Bagley on the shoulder and pointed at the two sentries. He made a throat cutting sign. The Peshmerga, SGM Jaf, joined Bagley without being asked. He pulled out a wicked curved knife whose blade had been painted black. The two men walked silently towards the sentries, moving in shallow circles so that if one of them was seen, the other would not be immediately detected.

Capt. Cummings and Avery watched and waited. In less than two minutes, both AQI fighters were on their way to Paradise and the reward of martyrs.

The two killers returned to stand at the ready by their leaders.

"We agreed to keep at least one bogey alive for questioning," urged Avery.

"And, I said we would try. Let's move in…slow and quiet. Split the team into two units, one for the front and one for the back," said Behremend.

He began a slow, efficient, and silent, hunter's walk towards the front door. Avery took the back with his half of the men. He and Cummings tried the doors, front and back. Neither was locked. They stepped in, holding their breath for fear of encountering a trip wire. The only sounds were the beating hearts of the intruders and from several snorers.

An older man from among the AQI fighters suddenly stood up and stepped away from his cot to answer a call of nature. It is said of them that there are old freedom fighters and bold freedom fighters, but there are very few old and bold ones. The old man was a very seasoned combat cadre, and he sensed the presence of the group of strangers in the room immediately. He did a tuck and roll towards his cot and extracted a handgun from beneath his pillow. He swung wildly to decide where to point his gun and managed to get off three shots before being cut down by a dozen or more American shooters.

The commotion was startling and shocked the sleepers into total awareness and instant action. Bullets began to fly everywhere. One shooter put the point of a laser sight on Capt. Cummings' chest, and Avery shot him twice in center chest and another tap to the spot between his eyes.

Cummings whispered a quick hoarse "thanks" and began to fire at the freedom fighters working their way out of slumber and numbness, and into position to fire at unseen enemies.

Most of them died during the first cacophonous barrage. Others found cover as best they could, and another five of them dropped under the withering fire seemingly coming from everywhere. One AQI was wounded in his right shoulder, and the shock of the wound put him out of commission. Another had a heavily bleeding wound in the back of his right thigh. One Peshmerga sustained a painful but not disabling wound to his left anterior thigh, but it did not even interfere his ability to walk. Peshmergas are tough.

And then it was over. Travis sent CIA agent, Clint Tucker, to strip the dead AQIs of anything of interest to the analysts, and he set out to find anyone living. There were two AQIs who lay on the floor gasping for breath and moaning at the pain from their bullet injuries. One of them saw Avery, turned prone, and clasped his hands behind his head, interlocking his fingers to punctuate the fact that he was admitting defeat and submission. The other wounded AQI squeezed his thigh in desperation to get rid of the terrible pain and to stop the bleeding. He made no attempt to reach for any of his weapons.

Avery spoke to him in Arabic, "We have a medic. He will take care of you shortly. Don't make a false move, and you will live. While the medic works on your leg, we'll talk. What you say to me will determine if you ever see your family, *fahm* [understand]?"

The terrified jihadi soldier whimpered as Avery asked him questions, pausing occasionally to cry out as the medic did something to the bullet wound that overcame his determination to be brave. The medic applied a large clean gauze Kerlex bandage.

Capt. Cunningham sneered and nodded his head at the volubly confessing and subdued prisoner.

"Well, I guess we got you a couple of decent prisoners to interrogate," he said. "Don't I get a kiss or an attaboy or at least some thanks?"

"Thanks," Avery said, barely loud enough to be audible over the background hum of voices and boxes scrapping along the floor on their way to the U.S. trucks.

"You gonna share the info you get done with the…interrogation?"

"Certainly, You and I will have more joint ventures, and I want the info as soon and as often as I can get it. So, does this count as cooperation?"

"I guess so. It has been a pleasure. I look forward to more missions, and that's the genuine truth."

Avery saluted.

As Avery and his men drove away from the insurgents' safe house, he saw the military equipment confiscated from the Islamic State rebels: Fifteen AK-47s, twenty-five full AK-47 magazines, six RPK rifles, eleven pistols, fifty-six grenades, and six heavy military vehicles. The vehicles were burning brightly after being torched by the Peshmergas.

On the way back to base, Avery and his CIA agents and the Peshmergas made a short detour into Erbil. They passed through the towns of Bartella and Karamles and on to the sprawling city of Mosul. The city was quiet, everyone going about their business. The agents noted that no one talked to anyone else. They kept their heads down.

"What's up with that?" Avery asked.

He had been in Mosul before, and it had been bustling and had a certain friendliness and a sense of life in it. This time, something had made it different.

"I know," said Agir Jaf.

"What?" asked Edgar Wright, the oldest of Avery's agents in the country.

"It's tax day. IS has been here and extorted a phony tax. They say it's for security and road work. They roam around pretending to be some sort of guards, but that's just an excuse to abuse women who aren't dressed right, or who are laughing out loud, or are talking to a man who is not their husband. They scare everyone. Us Peshmergas are the only thing that keeps them from driving right in and raping the women, stealing whatever they want, or burning the place down."

"Where are the police? The Iraqi army? Where are the men with their AK-47s out in the street hunting for the cowards who hurt and scare their women and children?" SGM Jaf asked, knowing the answer, but still so angry he had to ask.

"And the Americans are pulling out," Avery said before someone else had to.

"What can we do? It's the way things are here," observed Agent Wright.

"I know a Yazidi family up in Sinjar. I wonder how things are going for them."

"Can't be very good. Anything or anyone not a fundamentalist Muslim is fair game for IS thugs," said Edgar.

Avery began to worry, but it turned to frustration, because he had his job which was not to go to Nineveh province. It was to wreak a little havoc among the pseudoreligious fundamentalists and, especially the IS thugs before they get too strong to be dealt with.

CHAPTER EIGHT

"Now let's make two things clear: ISIL is not "Islamic." No religion condones the killing of innocents, and the vast majority of ISIL's victims have been Muslim. And ISIL is certainly not a state. It was formerly Al-Qaeda's affiliate in Iraq and has taken advantage of sectarian strife and Syria's civil war to gain territory on both sides of the Iraq-Syrian border. It is recognized by no government, nor the people it subjugates. ISIL is a terrorist organization, pure and simple. And it has no vision other than the slaughter of all who stand in its way.

–President Barack Obama, prime-time speech to the nation on the eve of the 13th anniversary of the Sept. 11 terror attacks, September 10, 2014

Diyala Governate, January–July 2008

As far back as 2006, Divala Province became important to AQI and therefore to the CIA and the military units of the United States and the Army of Iraq. At that time Abu Musab al-Zarqawi was head of al-Qaeda in Iraq. He designated Diyala Province as the capital region of the Islamic caliphate he envisioned, and began to establish Baqubah—the present capital of the province–as the capital. First, he had to subdue the province and the capital. During that period, al-Zarqawi made his headquarters in an obscure village northwest of Baqubah. Situated on the main road and rail routes between Baghdad and Iran, it became a center of trade for agricultural produce and the most important agriculture region for Iraq's commercial orange and pomelo groves.

In a setback for insurgents–but a golden opportunity for Abu Bakr al-Baghdadi–Iraqi and U.S. officials confirmed on June 7, 2006, that al-Zarqawi had been killed in an airstrike and raid eight km north of Baquba. Despite that setback, IS rebounded and–during the latter part of the year–Baqubah and most of the critical Diyala Governorate came securely under Salafi Sunni control. By January, 2007, the mayor was kidnaped; his office bombed; and the promises of the American and Iraqi military that they had the city under good law and order control proved to be as substantial as fairy dust.

The legitimate Iraqi government in Baquba toppled, and the key city became a stronghold for the insurgents fighting against the American led coalition in the overall Operation Iraqi Freedom.

In the census of 2003, the city had more than 450,000 citizens. By February, 2007, Avery Challenger's spies described the city as a "ghost town." They were able to move about Baquba without seeing a single person. Either the residents had become fleeing refugees, or they were effectively hiding in their homes or in the obscurity of the surrounding desert.

From their secure positions in the surrounding hills and wadis, IS launched a lightening-fast and well-coordinated offensive throughout the province. It seemed to Avery and his comrades in the special forces that the insurgents were attacking Muqdadiyah, Balad Ruz, Kanaan, Khalis, Khan Bani Sa'ad, and the capital Baqubah, almost at once and certainly without serious interference. They were able to control the rural areas east and southeast of Baqubah–from Balad Ruz to Turki–as supply bases for their frequent and devastating bombing campaigns in Baghdad and Diyala. IS appeared to have an unlimited number of trained recruits and sufficient foreign funding to make them almost invincible.

They expanded to develop bases in the Diyala river valley to the northeast. From there, they fought for control of Muqdadiyah, an important line of communication to Lake Hamrin, Kirkuk, and Iran. The insurgents also had control of the tribal areas of Khan Bani Sa'ad south of Baqubah to Salman Pak, south-east of Baghdad. Baghdad was almost surrounded, and its preservation for the democratic forces was in real doubt. Every indicator told of IS success and Iraqi and U.S. impotence. It was clear to every observer that something drastic had to be done and quickly if the long and difficult endeavor in Iraq was going to come back to life.

Oval Office, White House, Washington, D.C., Special Meeting, February 5, 2008

Meeting recorded and stamped "TOP SECRET, EYES ONLY, POTUS, Secy. of Defense, Secy. Of State, DNI Present: George W. Bush, POTUS; Vice Admiral John Michael "Mike" McConnell, DNI; Robert Gates, Secretary of Defense; Condoleezza Rice, Secretary of State; Chairman House Defense Appropriations Subcommittee, Rodney Proctor Frelinghuysen (R-NJ); COS-Iraq, Avery Challenger

Date: February 5, 2008.

Subject: Emergency appropriations for Operation Phantom Phoenix to secure Diyala Province, Iraq from the Islamic State

Summary:
DNI: The situation in Diyala Province is now dire. IS has taken over key provinces around Baghdad and will soon control almost the entire northern two-thirds of the country, thereby endangering Operation Iraqi Freedom. The present U.S. military presence is stretched thin and is insufficient to retake the critical provinces of Anbar and Diyala. Suggest a temporary "surge" of increased army and marines of 50,000 combat troops and necessary equipment to carry out the mission. National Intelligence deems this to be urgent and crucial.
COS-Iraq: Troops on the ground report increasing strength of IS including funding, recruiting, training, and troops in theater. The acquisition of territory, subjugation of population, and increase in military power, will likely be beyond the capability of U.S. to manage in less than a year. The options then will be to desert Iraq to IS or to mount a major world war comparable to the police action in Korea.

POTUS: We have no other viable choice. We cannot allow this Islamic terrorist organization to gain a permanent foot hold or footprint in Iraq and/or Syria. By Presidential Order, I will approve an immediate increase in military manpower of fifty-thousand active combatants from the army and marine corps with all the necessary materiel. I hereby make a formal request of the Departments of State, Defense, and House appropriations, to exercise all due haste in making this crucial request happen.

Signed:

George W. Bush, POTUS

Avery was back in Diyala Governate three days later, on the move throughout the rural hills and wadis to gain intelligence, to buoy up his assets, and for his own protection. Everything that the CIA could do was in readiness for the expected arrival of the surge reinforcements; so, all the soldiers, marines, and agents, could do was to wait.

Avery knew that the Nineveh Province was likely to be in more trouble than ever from the incursions of IS. He could not shake the sense of dread for what could be happening to the Yazidis, and particularly to Khatoon, whom he had come to have the sense of protectiveness he might have had if she were his daughter or younger sister. It had something to do with his status as an orphan whose early life had been spent in an orphanage with no one he could really count on. He knew it was irrational, but he felt that he had to have someone to care for or perhaps who might care for him.

He rounded up two assistants–contract officers–Malcolm Fortner and Devlin O'Malley–and loaded a desert camouflaged HMMWV with guns, ammunition, and food. They saw multiple small units of IS soldiers as they sped along, but no one made an attempt to interfere with their progress. In two days, they were on the outskirts of Sinjar Village. It was quiet—too quiet, as they used to say in the Western movies—and very few people were out on the dusty streets. Doors were barred, and windows were shuttered. Avery felt a growing sense of dread.

As they passed the perimeter streets, they saw several sets of black-clad IS soldiers walking around looking menacing with their heavy ammunition cross-belts and Chinese CQ 5.56 mm rifles. Several pick-up trucks passed by waving the distinctive IS black flag with its odious white inscription: "*There is only one God, Allah, and the prophet, Muhammad, is his messenger,*" in Arabic. The IS soldiers glared at the occupants of the HMMWV but made no menacing movement. It became apparent, however, that they were being followed and watched.

Avery said, "I think it's a bad idea to drive right up to the Yazidi's house; that would not be likely to help them. Drop me off, and I'll arrange for them to get a couple of trucks to collect the stuff we brought for them. Their place is less than a mile from here. I'll walk the back streets until I can be sure I don't have a tail. I'll get you on the sat phone when I have useful info. Heads up now, gentlemen. This is Indian country."

He felt like a thousand eyes were on him, but he could not detect any attempt to tail him. He dodged through backstreets, backyards, onion fields, and doubled back several times. His camo uniform probably helped, but the most realistic reason he was not seen or reported was because of the fear that kept people indoors and away from their windows. He looked in every direction before circling the last hundred meters to the Yazidi's house—a much scaled down dwelling compared to the expectations of a decade before–a simple mud brick structure with a tandoor oven, sleeping mats on the floor, and an outdoor privy, situated on north side of town. It was the time of the year when the occupants slept on roof because of intense heat and now because of threats and attacks from Muslim neighbors.

He knocked. No one answered. He saw faint rustle of a curtain behind a window; so, he knocked again.

This time, he said, "Please let me in. It's Avery, the American. I come in peace."

There was a brief pause, then the door was opened by Khatoon who greeted him with a worried smile and hurried him inside.

"What is the situation here, Khatoon? Have the *Da'esh* taken over the city?"

"Oh, Avery, it is so frightening here. They come around in their trucks and shout commands for everyone who is not part of the Islamic State to come to the *Jevat* to be registered. Almost no one goes. We are afraid that it is only an excuse to take us away, especially the women. We have heard terrible things about what they have been doing down south in Baqubah and Mosul. Are they true, Avery?"

"For the most part, yes. The *Da'esh* have taken slaves, made women sex slaves, and murdered men and boys in terrible ways. That I have seen with my own eyes. They are every bit as bad as what the rumors say. I can't really be sure why they haven't taken over Nineveh Province and called it IS territory yet."

"What can we do, Avery? We are scared and poor and defenseless."

"Khatoon, not to beat a dead cat, but I have begged you to leave here and to come with me. I don't think it is safe for you to travel to the south where I'm working now. Why don't you and your family head north to the mountain? You will probably be safe there for the time being."

"Mother is sick, Granpa is old, and we have no food or anything. We lost our truck a while back; so, we have no way to travel. I see many people walking, but it is terrible. The *Da'esh* put up roadblocks and steal the women. I am so terrified of them."

"I have a vehicle filled with food, clothes, guns, and ammunition. We can take you there. Hopefully it will only be necessary temporally. There is going to be a big battle in Diyala Province very soon, and the *Da'esh* will withdraw all their forces to concentrate them in and around Baqubah. Gather up your family and a few personal things, and let's go now. Please, Khatoon. It is no longer safe here."

She hesitated.

"Please, Khatoon. Do it for me. I would never forgive myself if something dreadful happened to you. I love you like a sister or a daughter. You are important to me."

With that, she relented.

"All right, I will persuade the family. Granpa does not like to be told what to do, especially by a female; but this time, I won't take 'no' for an answer."

Khatoon was successful, helped by a terrifying and convincing plume of smoke coming from the northeast. It ushered in the most violent time ever in Iraq and turned out to be the deadliest attack in the history of the province. The smoke and fire came from Siba Sheikh Khider and Tel Ezeir which could be seen from Sinjar and Kocho. A fuel tanker and three cars were blown up by extremists indiscriminately killing 800 people and injuring 1000.

Avery and his operatives had no illusions about what was happening. The Sinjar Village and Kocho area was were situated in a dangerous region since it was too close to the southern edge of Iraq's non-Yazidi area and the southern border of Kurdistan whose Peshmergas were in constant conflict with the Salafi Islamic State. It was an important crossing point between Syria and Iraq. The Yazidis had only settled there in the early 1950s and could not lay claim to the antiquity boasted of by the Muslims.

The relationship between Muslims and non-Muslims had always been tenuous at best but with many safe and positive interactions with Muslim doctors, merchants, boys acting something like god-parents for Muslim boys undergoing circumcision, and between employers and employees. However, during the previous ten years, even before the advent of the *Da'esh*, long suppressed prejudices became increasingly overt. Along the way, the Muslims began to call Yazidis *kuffar*—plural, or *kaffir*—singular.

Those intolerances and abuses led to blaming Yazidis for almost every ill wind, much like the Nazis blaming the Jews for all ill fortune suffered by the German nation. Those intolerances turned to outright hatred. Hatred led to violence which led to acceptance of hatred and violence becoming the norm. That normalization of violence led inexorably to terrorism. Extremists harbored in nearby Muslim villages spewed hatred against all non-Muslims and even Shi'ites and other non-Salafi Muslims. It came as no real surprise that on that day in 2008, extremists fire-bombed a village near Sinjar killing hundreds of people.

"Move out on-the-double," ordered Avery; and the heavily laden HMMWV sprang forward jouncing over the rutted and only partially paved road north towards the mountain considered to be sacred and a place of refuge by the Yazidis.

Mt. Sinjar is long, narrow, and bone dry, in summer. Man-made steppes in summer were made for growing tobacco. In winter, the top is covered with clouds and snow. On top–perched on a cliff–on the highest peak of the Sinjar Mountains is the small white *Chermera* temple. The areas around the Sinjar mountains have been mainly inhabited by Yazidis since the 1950s who venerate them and consider the highest point to be the place where Noah's Ark settled after the biblical flood. Water was scarce there, and much of it was not fit to drink. Yazidis had to fight with goats for the remaining water on the dry mountain. The only thing that could be said in the area's favor is that it was the lesser of evils—better than facing the mercies of the Islamic State in the villages below and to the south. Conditions were filthy during the best of times; but now, the mountainside and soon the people, were covered in goat droppings.

The HMMWV pulled up slowly to an IS barricaded checkpoint in the road. They did not stop, and every port hole from the American vehicle bristled with heavy machine guns. That and the fact that the Kurdistan Peshmerga controlled the road beyond that point prompted the IS to allow them passage. In fact, they were part of a force already on their way south to help defend Baqubah; and it was not in their best interest to engage in a lethal firefight with the determined Americans. There was one road up and down the mountain, and everyone in the HMMWV breathed a heavy sigh of relief that they were now under the protection of the Peshmergas.

At the disembarkation point below Mt. Sinjar's peak and the temple, Avery helped the Yazidi family out of the vehicle. Several Yazidi men rushed over to offload the precious commodities that the CIA men had brought.

Avery gave Khatoon an unexpected hug, and she flinched noticeably.

"I'm sorry, Khatoon," he said, "I forgot about the Yazidi restrictions between men and women."

"I overreacted, Avery," she said, "It is our culture, and not something I can easily overcome. That was the first time I was ever hugged by any man other than my father and brothers. I know you meant well."

Avery shook his head. He hated to have to leave, but his duty was back in Diyala Province. He was concerned about the physical condition of the family. For all her health and beauty, Khatoon was overly thin, looked weary, and her complexion was sallow—almost grey. He recognized the early signs of starvation and could only hope that she would benefit from the supplies he and his men had brought.

"Mr. and Mrs. Yazidi and family, I am sorry that we must go back. There is a battle to be fought against the *Da'esh*, and we must be there to help. I will try to get back to you as soon as I possibly can. Take care of each other."

"Go with God," Safaa Yazidi said in her native tongue.

Khatoon translated. Avery gave them a quick salute, turned and headed back down the mountain, kicking up a cloud of dust.

CHAPTER NINE

"What's clear is that ISIS and its monstrosities won't be defeated by the same powers that brought it to Iraq and Syria in the first place, or whose open and covert war-making has fostered it in the years since. Endless western military interventions in the Middle East have brought only destruction and division. It's the people of the region who can cure this disease – not those who incubated the virus."

–Kenan Malik, *Terrorism has come about in assimilationist France and also in multicultural Britain. Why is that? The Guardian*, November 14, 2015.

Diyala Governate, Iraq, March, 2008, morning

A series of battles and skirmishes preceded the battle for Diyala—Operation Phantom Phoenix. The capital, Baghdad, came under severe pressure by the insurgents with destruction of the electrical grid, suicide bombings in the major markets, and nighttime artillery attacks. Militants opened fire on U.S. and Iraqi troops near the heavily fortified Green Zone—too close for any measure of comfort. Defense forces found themselves contending with attackers armed with rocket-propelled grenades, hand grenades, and automatic rifles, on Haifa Street which led directly into the Green Zone. They engaged in open gun battles with insurgents in the Dora neighborhood south of the capital. An explosion at a Sunni mosque killed ten worshippers and wounded fifteen. Shi'a citizens suffered multiple attacks. It appeared that the entire city was going to be engulfed in flames and a hailstorm of bullets. The president ordered a curfew and conceded that a major portion of the city was controlled by the IS. When Iraqi Army and United States forces gathered to counterattack, they found only a few remaining terrorists. The rest had moved surreptitiously from the capital north towards the Diyala Governate hoping to establish their new capital base.

Avery and his CIA operatives detailed the well-planned tactical retreat and reported it with precision to the military commanders at VBC [Victory Base Complex] the cluster of installations surrounding the BIAP [Baghdad International Airport]. Camp Victory was the location of Saddam Hussein's former Al-Faw Palace, which served as the headquarters for the Multi-National Corps-Iraq initially and later as the headquarters for the United States Forces-Iraq. Per his working instructions, Avery reported directly to Commanding General Lloyd Austin at Camp Striker.

"What is so important that you had to interrupt our logistics conference, Agent Challenger," the brusque no-time-for-chatting general demanded as soon as Avery made his way past the phalanx of security guards.

"We have good evidence that IS is moving out of Baghdad and heading in small separate units to Diyala Province. Our spies tell us that they are moving their resources from Baghdad– despite it being at present more than eighty percent under insurgent control–to Al Anbar province, which is entirely under their control, and to Diyala. They plan to set up headquarters in Baqubah and to make a decisive stand there. These current skirmishes in Baghdad are something of a diversion for that plan even though they are very serious attacks."

"Numbers?"

"Tens of thousands, maybe more than a hundred thousand. They are well armed, well-fed, well-equipped; and their morale is high. They are ready for a major fight and a prolonged one, Sir."

"Thank you, Special Agent. You are dismissed."

Avery turned and left not knowing whether his information had been comprehended, appreciated, or if it would be acted upon. It was not his to question why.

He need not have worried. General Austin separately verified the CIA's information and moved decisively to put his preplanned Operation

Phantom Phoenix into immediate motion. The advance scouts from the army special forces unit met up with Avery and his agents on a mesa overlooking the fortified village of Turki. The Multinational Force in Iraq at Camp Victory was notified by the radio man, and the first battle to retake control of Diyala Province was launched.

While Avery, Malcolm Fortner, and Devlin O'Malley, watched through binoculars, American paratroopers of the 5th Squadron, 73rd Cavalry Regiment of the 82nd Airborne Division floated out of the sky, landing on the outskirts of Turki far enough away to avoid being cutdown in flight. Nevertheless, they incurred casualties amounting to half of the original force during the fierce fighting that ensued. U.S. transport planes followed with units from Iraq—the 5th Iraqi Army Division–Georgia, and the U.K.

Avery caught sight of an insurgent whom he thought could be al-Baghdadi. He became convinced when he saw that the truck he entered was heading away from the fight in Turki and was headed towards Baqubah. That was the great caliph's modus operandi; he was too important to stay with his men during a fight.

"Let's go after him," Avery told Malcolm and Devlin, "He'll get into the open road, and we should be able to spot him. We can't do anything much to help here in Turki; but, if we can arrest or kill al-Baghdadi, we will have really struck a blow."

"So, stop talking, Avery. Let's get a move on," said Devlin.

They were in their HMMWV. It was full of fuel, and the mechanics had pronounced it perfectly fit for duty the day before they settled on the hilltop overlooking Turki. They roared down the rock-strewn mountain road kicking up a choking plume of dust. The CIA agents followed an up-to-date MapAction PowerPoint rendition of rural northern Iraq which led them safely around the perimeter of Turki and onto the main road to Baqubah and the east and south.

At the junction of that road and the dirt track they selected, they encountered a squad of Army Bronco Troop 1-14 Cavalry which had detained a group of black clad IS fighters. Avery stopped the hummer, got out unarmed and with hands in plain sight, and approached the captain in charge.

"Hi, Captain, how's it going?"

"Good right now. Who's asking?"

"Oh, sorry, I'm Avery Challenger. I'm the COS/CIA Iraq, headquartered in Camp Striker."

He presented his cred-pack.

The army officer nodded and said, "I'm Will Salinger, Bronco Troop. The gentlemen on the ground there dressed in black pajamas are foreign fighters for the Islamic State. We caught them red-handed extracting an impressive load of weaponry. Somebody outside this forsaken country really likes these dudes. There must be a million bucks just in this one cache."

Arrayed on the ground behind the IS terrorists were rows of AK-47s, RPGs, grenade launchers, several Iranian-made machine guns, piles of grenades and land mines, and even one SA-7 missile meant to bring down helicopters. Of particular interest to the CIA agents was the sophistication of the weapons thus far removed from the hidden cache.

The Iranian or Russian or Chinese suppliers had been very generous and very busy. Avery counted two dozen Katyusha rockets, fifty rocket propelled grenades, forty-five TOW anti-tank missiles, machine guns from five different countries including the United States, and nearly three dozen anti-tank mines. The Broncho Cavalrymen were in the process of removing a stack of anti-personnel mines, and mortar rounds.

"Good work, Will. This has to make something of a dent in the supply train. I hope you didn't suffer any casualties."

"Thanks, we got through unscathed, almost without a fight. And, no, we had no WIA or KIA, thanks for asking. Where are you guys headed?"

"Oh, I got too engaged in looking at the cache to remember why we're here. Did you see a big, very heavily bearded IS guy in a Toyota go rushing past here? We think it may be al-Baghdadi, and we presume he's skedaddling for Baqubah."

"You know, I think we actually did. We saw the truck coming burning up the road. The guy in the shotgun seat looked a lot like the great caliph's photos, now that you mention it. We thought it was a bit queer that they didn't open fire on us. They were going too fast for us to get any decent shots off. Besides, we were protecting the cache we captured. Do you think it was really him?"

"Not certain, but we got a good look from our perch on the hill north of Turki. It looked like him, but maybe I just think they all look alike."

Will and Avery shook hands, and Avery got back in the hummer.

"Looks like we're on the right track. Move out. We might be able to catch him before he gets into the thick of Baqubah."

Abu Bakr al-Baghdadi looked back from his seat in the speeding Toyota pick-up and saw the plume of dust coming from the HMMWV. It was gaining ground on him and his soldiers.

"Brothers, by the love of Allah the Merciful and Compassionate, we must go faster. We will not be able to make it to Baqubah before they catch us. Our blessed caliphate cannot lose its caliph this early in the war. God wills our victory, and He has let me know that I must not be killed or captured. Pull onto the back road into Buhriz. Our people own the village, and we can be defended there."

"As you order, Great Caliph."

They moved at breakneck speed throwing caution to the winds, weaving and careering around corners and ruts until they were in the heart of the village. Black pajamas appeared from everywhere.

"Escort us out to the road to Baqubah, Brothers," al-Baghdadi ordered. "Allah will reward you from his palace in paradise for your struggles. Carry on the fight against the Christian Crusaders. Victory will be yours, by God."

Buhriz was tiny, no more than ten streets across. The local IS leader skillfully led the way to a dirt track leading into a jungle that had almost overgrown the narrow road.

"Go with God, the Merciful and Compassionate, Great Caliph, and with the blessings of the Prophet and his family (SAWS). You are protected, but you must hurry. We will engage the Christian Crusaders from the Great Satan; and, if we cannot kill them, at least, we can slow them down."

Avery saw the truck roar into Buhriz, almost turning over several times. He knew the dusty little track would inevitably lead him and his co-agents into a lethal trap; so, he ordered them to stop.

"If I was him, I would move as fast through the village as possible and find an escape route on the other side before we can call in an air strike. Let's follow the main road around to the far side of town and try and get a glimpse of him leaving. Check the map, Malcolm. What does it have to tell us about the terrain on that side?"

"Looks like almost solid trees, a regular jungle. Climate info says it rains there more than in any other place in all of northern Iraq."

"We're headed into the jungle, I guess," Avery commented with no particular enthusiasm.

"I found a little farm road two or three klicks from the southern perimeter of the town. It intersects with the road that goes straight out of the village. Maybe we are in for a bit of luck," Malcolm said.

"Or a big ambush," Devlin groused.

"Nobody lives forever, Devlin, remember that," Avery said.

"Thanks, that pithy bit of wisdom fills me with good feelings, Chief."

Al-Baghdadi and his truck load of killers moved as fast as they could, but the overhanging tree branches threatened to knock the men in the bed of the truck off and into the rocks and underbrush. They had to stop several times to machete down small trees that had fallen athwart the road. The caliph's famous temper was beginning to show.

"By God and His angels, you will move this infernal machine faster or I shall personally execute you and your wives when we reach headquarters. Do you understand, fools?"

"Yes, Great Caliph. We ask God, the All-Mighty to come to our aid. We count on Him as always to bless our sacred mission."

They came to open road and a cultivated area crisscrossed by irrigation ditches and barbed wire fences. A road intersected the small track they were on; and, beyond that point, the road became wider and less rutted.

"God, our Protector and the Giver of Life, has smiled down on us. We can move much more quickly now. Allah is guiding his chosen people. We will be safe, and we will prevail. This is a good omen," al-Baghdadi said almost as if he were in a trance and receiving direct revelation from the Supreme Being.

None of the other IS soldiers thought it prudent to suggest that the U.S. HMMWV following them might be similarly be rewarded with travel on the better road ahead of them both. They knew better that to contradict the Great Caliph ever, but especially when he was having one of his personal religious experiences.

CHAPTER TEN

"People who struggle to liberate themselves from foreign oppression have the right to use all methods at their disposal, even violence…they are in "the last fifteen minutes" of a long struggle…The dawn approaches. Victory is at hand."
— Mohammed Yasser Abdel Rahman Abdel Raouf Arafat al-Qudwa al-Husseini, aka Yasser Arafat, special session of the United Nations General Assembly convened in Geneva, December, 1988

Diyala Governate, Iraq, near the capital city, Baqubah, March, 2008, afternoon

Avery, Malcolm, and Devlin white-knuckled their way across the access road of the forest area below Buhriz. The gravel road was better than the dirt roads in the village itself; and the gravel surface had recently been dragged, indicative of its importance as a farm road. They were nearly at the HMMWV's maximum off-road speed top speed of 110 km/hr since they were driving a vehicle that had almost no load other than the men and their light arms. Avery was driving, and the other two were acting as lookouts. There was no telling what might lay ahead.

They were moving so rapidly that when they came to the intersection with the forest road, Avery was unable to slow down and overshot the roadway perpendicular to the gravel road they were traveling on. Part of the momentary alarm that thrilled through the three of them was that al-Baghdadi's Toyota was in the middle of the intersection; and Avery had to make choices among ramming the other truck, slamming on the brakes and probably spinning around several times and landing upside down, or making a slight swerve to miss the Toyota. In the half-second he had to think about it, Avery chose option three, even though it almost certainly would put them in a disadvantage as soon as the inevitable fire fight began.

The hummer missed the Toyota by inches and startled the terrorists as much as it spooked the Americans. Everyone in both vehicles swiveled to be able to fire at the enemy. The occupants of the HMMWV had a second or two advantage over the Toyota in terms of dealing with the surprise and were able to lay down an erratic and poorly aimed–albeit frightening–level of machine gun fire. One terrorist was killed, but the Toyota driver had the presence of mind to slam the truck into reverse to throw off the aim of the American attackers.

Avery attempted a bootleggers' turn, but that brought him a most unwelcome surprise. Coming down the farm road at top speed was another truck, an old, but sturdy, Nissan Navara D22 pickup, painted coal black and waving a huge IS black flag with white Arabic script.

Avery shouted, "Guy on the right fire at the Toyota, guy on the left fire at the Nissan. Make it a 'mad-minute.'"

Al-Baghdadi, sitting in the shotgun seat of the Toyota figured out the American's predicament in a flash of inspiration. They could not concentrate on him and also save their lives.

"Drive away!" he yelled in his guttural Arabic accent.

"But, Caliph, you want us to run away when we might stay and kill the Christian Crusaders?"

"Do as I order. It is most important that I be saved."

The driver knew he should have kept his mouth shut. He also knew that al-Baghdadi's every instinct was to flee and leave the fighting to other, lesser men. *We may yet survive, Inshallah.*

Much as three Americans would have loved to chase al-Baghdadi, the better part of valor was to live to fight another day. As the Toyota shot off to the south, Avery ordered his men to concentrate on the Nissan. They had no time to be timid; so, as the bullets came raining fairly harmlessly at the HMMWV, Malcolm took aim with one of their SMAWs [Shoulder-launched Multipurpose Assault Weapon MK153

Mod 0, 83mm multi-purpose recoilless rifle]. When he fired, the Nissan disappeared into a ball of fire, smoke, and noise.

That allowed Avery to right the HMMWV and send it after al-Baghdadi's Toyota. The road was not as good as the gravel crossroad had been, and the hummer could only get up to between ninety-six and ninety-seven km/hr. The Toyota could manage closer to a hundred ten. Every klick they went, the Toyota edged a little bit further ahead. It was maddening. They were less than twenty-five klicks from the outskirts of Baqubah. Once the terrorists crossed the perimeter defenses of the provincial capital, it would be suicide to follow them. And once they entered the city, the terrorists could easily find a safe house.

Hoping against hope for the Toyota to have a mechanical breakdown or a flat tire or two, Avery kept pushing. If he was a praying man, this would have been a good time; but there were three avowed atheists in the vehicle; and they all knew that it would be hypocritical. They drew close enough to be able to see al-Baghdadi's Toyota cross the perimeter line of waving black flags and through a throng of flag waving men in black pajamas who were shooting their AK-47s recklessly skyward.

"All right, we lost. Let's get back to Turki and see what's going on. We're done here."

"Alhamd lilah," whispered al-Baghdadi as he swept into the outskirts of Baqubah.

All the other men in the trustworthy little Toyota murmured the same, "thanks be to God."

In the city center, al-Baghdadi ordered the driver to stop in the middle of the bustling market. The market was packed with people going about their daily lives and with a veritable horde of black pajama wearing, AK-47 yielding, young men pushing the people aside as they walked about. On the west end of the square was a peculiar cinder block wall five meters tall and twenty meters long. Behind it was a heavy military plow.

"Get their attention," he ordered.

Two fighters alighted from the Toyota and fired their rifles three times in the air. That got the attention of every individual. IS fighters spread out around the square and achieved order, sometimes with the butts of their guns.

Abu al-Baghdadi stood on the hood of the truck and announced: "*Salam* to all the brothers among you. I have come to inform you that our hearts are with you, and for you to be patient and considerate, for victory is with patience, and ease with adversity. *As-salam alaykum wa rahmat Allah wa barakatuhu*. I speak by my authority as the Caliph of Allah's restored Islamic State—with the rank of the greatest imam–and by the intervention of Allah, the Merciful, the Compassionate, the All Powerful. Praise be to God the Lord of the Worlds, and prayers and peace be upon the noblest of those sent, his family, companions and whoso has followed them with *ihsan* to the Day of Judgment."

Cheering interrupted the flow of his speech. He graciously acknowledged the cheers with a slight wave of his hand. The gathered crowd immediately returned to their original reverential quiet.

"I am the one elected by the *majlis al-shura* [consultative council or Shura council], representing the *ahl al-hall wal-aqd* [lit. the people of loosing and binding, i.e. those qualified to elect or depose a caliph on behalf of the *ummah*] of the Islamic State as their caliph. The *hujjaj* [senior members of IS]—the *thiqat* [trusted ones]–with the intervention of Allah, the Merciful, and the Soldiers *Diwan* [military department] offer their protection of the caliphate and me, its caliph. I serve in the name of all the true monotheists and the martyrs, may God bless them in His realms of paradise and may they enjoy the rewards, as God wills."

Another round of cheering came from the crowd which was beginning to fidget.

"What shall this caliph do, I ask? I shall erupt the volcanoes of jihad such has never been known before. Before me, the Crusader Christians shall bow or fall. I will lead our religion of fighting to the end that all the world will bow down before Allah and His anointed caliph. Together we shall form a caliphate for all the world. I will seek out and destroy apostates, *kuffar*, those indulging in *shirk* [innovation], the nullifiers of Islam, the dogs of Shi'ism—may God fight them.

"Under Sharia law we will utilize the evidence collected by our *Diwan al-Buhuth wa al-Iftaa'* [The Investigation and Fatwa Issuing Department], and we will exact God's justice. I shall free Palestine, break the borders of Jordan and Lebanon; and I will live to see the great crusaders bow down and submit that there is but one God, that the caliphate is his government for all the world, and to pay *jizyah* [a per capita yearly tax historically levied on non-Muslim subjects–the *dhimma*–permanently residing in Muslim lands]. The *Diwan al-Amn* [security department] shall pursue the non-believers, the cursed Shia, and all the polytheists until they have paid the uttermost *dirham* for all their crimes."

Full throated cheering from the weary but animated crowd. This was all they had lived and fought for.

"I will succeed, and I will bring you along with me in this blessed jihad for God Almighty is the Guarantor of Success. We will all receive our reward and will join the great Prophet Muhammad SAWS and his blessed family in paradise.

"We shall begin the cleansing here and now. I have ordered the *Diwan al-Amn* to arrest the enemies of the caliphate in this city. They have been found guilty of all manner of crimes against God and the *ummah,* and now shall their punishment be exacted by God, the Just."

With a wave of his hand, al-Baghdadi signaled soldiers at the east end of the square, and they herded over a hundred bowed and shuffling men, women, and children, towards the middle of the square where al-Baghdadi's truck was parked.

"These are the damned," al-Baghdadi announced. "Make the dogs bow before me and admit their guilt."

The condemned received baton strikes on the back of their knees, and every knee bent into an abject *jetho* [genuflection]. For those who needed further incentive, the *Diwan al-Amn* guards prodded them in the back to achieve an adequately penitent bowed head. Guards stepped between the kneeling captives and pushed them apart far enough so that a man could comfortably stand between them.

Al-Baghdadi gave a fateful small nod of his head, and hooded men stepped into the spaces created. Each man held a large Bowie knife with serrated spines. The knives had special handles to allow a two-hand grip.

Video cameras focused on a handsome bearded man who spoke in a distinct British accent to the world, "I am the one known as Jihadi John. I have the honor to be chosen to execute the will of Allah, the Almighty and All Just."

Jihadi John was later identified as British subject, Mohammed Emwazi, who was employed as the chief killer of foreign hostages.

Without a further word, he assumed a crouched position, raised his large knife over his head and swung it down with all the force he could muster. The huge knife sliced through to the bowing man's cervical spinal process, Jihadi John having miscalculated slightly on the exact location and slant of the cut. The man screamed and bled. His executioner bent over him and began to saw vigorously at the back of his neck. He adjusted the direction of the cut and finally cut between the spinous processes, and–with a great show of strength–transected the man's spinal cord and vertebrae. Mercifully, the man died without further suffering. A few more sawing motions resulted in the head dropping to the concrete of the square into a large and spreading pool of blood. Several of the other victims waiting their turn to be similarly executed fainted and had to be revived with a series of shallow stabbings in the back.

Many of the other executioners were less adept with their knives, and the sawing off of several of the heads took longer than expected and created a cacophony of screaming which brought a smile to the Caliph's visage. The children were held in place by two executioners, and their beheadings were quicker. Two women struggled and fought back and were beaten into unconsciousness before their heads were severed from their necks. Women slaves hurriedly loaded the heads and bodies into a dump truck; and the next phase of the public shaming, executions, and mutilations began.

Several thieves were forced to assume the *jetho* position. One of the *Diwan al-Amn* guards extended the right arm of the thief and strapped the hand and forearm over a wooden block. Another guard raised a razor-sharp curved scimitar over his head and swung it down deftly across the outstretched arm neatly severing the hand from the forearm. A guard applied a tourniquet around the forearm of the now unconscious man who had fainted. A second guard dragged the punished thief away, and a third dragged another and another and another until all fifteen had suffered their just punishments.

An assortment of criminals sustained mutilation punishments as ordered by Sharia courts for such diverse crimes as smoking, women failing to wear appropriate facial and body coverings, or placing cucumbers too close to tomatoes on their vegetable carts. The punishments exacted in the town square and market of Baqubah included amputation, removal of an eye, and gouging of a knee.

Then came the highlight of the afternoon. Six men and two women were frog-walked to the west end of the square, securely bound at the ankles, knees, and across both arms around their chests. They were then placed face up the ground in front of the previously erected cinder block wall—which had been carefully built without mortar.

A *Diwan al-Amn* official read the indictments: "The punishment of the *Qur'an* for these men who have committed crimes against nature by copulation of man with man which is forbidden. The two Shi'a women you see were taken in the act of adultery. Let the punishment proceed."

From behind the wall a *Diwan al-Amn* guard moved the heavy military plow forward slowly and pushed the massive loose cinderblock wall over crushing the criminals whose muffled cries were drowned out by the crash of the fracturing blocks.

Attention was then drawn to the top of a three-story flat-topped building on the north east corner of the square by two guards who fired off their rifles. Five especially egregious homosexual men were forced to stand on the edge of the roof, then were pushed off to their deaths on the concrete below. This ended the punishments and the desired effect on the subjects of IS rule who were looking on and who would spread the word.

From his perch on the hood of his truck, al-Baghdadi smiled down on the proceedings, confident that his plan to publicize the beheadings and mutilations would successfully differentiate himself and IS from the weak-kneed AQI and would identify himself with Khalid Sheikh Mohammed–may God protect him–the al-Qaeda leader who beheaded the American journalist and achieved lasting acclaim among the faithful.

Rahim Jamaluddin–ostensibly a foreign fighter from Indonesia–moved away from the crowd in the square and walked down a narrow side street. He was nauseated, but he steeled himself not to vomit and thereby draw attention to himself. He took care to be certain that he was not being followed or observed, then entered an old two-story apartment building. He unlocked the door to his apartment on the second floor, walked in, and triple-locked the door behind him. He lifted a worn carpet from in front of his closet and placed his index finger into a metal gromet. He lifted a section of the floor, reached inside and lifted out a square old suitcase. He unlocked the case and extracted a KGB "suitcase radio" set ORIOL / P-350 *ОРЁЛ* and began hurriedly typing the Cyrillic language marked keys. The Russian machine automatically encrypted the call. It was sent to the receiver in the possession of Avery Challenger, COS-Iraq.

12 March, 2008, 1625 Zulu/UTC Standard Time/Greenwich
Top Secret, Eyes Only: COS-Iraq
From: Agt. 46177802

Message:
Caliph IS held a rally in center Baqubah, Diyala Governate, this date and time. Usual rant, but promising wide jihad events. Murdered and/or mutilated 20-30 persons, including women and children. Question sanity of caliph. Great fear and suffering in citizenry. Large conc. fighters. Appear well-trained and ready for large scale and prolonged battle.
No signature

CHAPTER ELEVEN

"All we have to do is to send two mujahedin…[and] raise a piece of cloth on which is written "Al-Qaeda" in order to make the generals race there, to cause America to suffer human, economic, and political losses."
> –Usama bin Laden, videotaped message, 2004

"Abu Mus'ab al-Zarqawi, a hotheaded terrorist, recently released from jail, insisted on launching attacks on all "nonbelievers" including especially, the Shi'a. Atiyya Abd al-Rahman, a high-ranking Al-Qaeda leader, insisted that he refrain and, instead, that he treat other Muslims with kindness, sympathy, and friendliness. Atiyya wrote to Zarqawi reminding him that the long-term goal was the establishment of the caliphate, "My brother, what use is it for us to delight in some operations and successful strikes when the immediate repercussion is a defeat for us of our call, and a loss of the justice of our cause and its logic in the minds of the masses who make up the people of the Muslim nation?…You need all of these people if you want to destroy a power and a state and erect on its rubble the state of Islam."
> –George Crile, *Charlie Wilson's War*, Grove Press, New York, 2003

Diyala Governate, Iraq, cities of Baqubah River Valley, Mid-March, 2008

The first attack by coalition forces into the Baqubah River Valley was on Turki Village. It became so protracted before victory was achieved that the ensuing campaign was dubbed the "Turki Bowl" by the Americans involved. The plan of battle was determined by the realization that the battles to gain control over the capital city, Baqubah, and eventually the national capital of Baghdad would require near complete pacification of the Diyala Province before the major cities could be approached. U.S. and Iraqi forces killed about 100 insurgents and detained 50 more during Operation Turki Bowl. The fighting was serious but not as severe as they had encountered the previous fall.

They were impressed with the weapons captured which indicated a significant and ongoing supply chain. Coalition troops found twenty-five separate weapons caches. It was sobering to realize that just those caches contained armaments to sustain a large terrorist network for several weeks or months. They logged: nearly 1,200 Katyusha rockets, 1,000 rocket propelled grenades, over 150 TOW anti-tank missiles, nearly 1,000 machine guns, thousands of anti-tank and anti-personnel mines, thousands more mortar rounds, ammunition for an assortment of lethal weapons, and rocket-propelled grenades. It was clear that the upcoming operation would be lengthy and costly in time, money, and blood.

After the costly success in Turki, the coalition forces moved south to Buhriz, a town that Avery and his agents had recently bypassed because it was too dangerous. This time, they returned with the large force of Americans and Iraqi Army and their heavy machines of war.

Heeding Avery's warning, the armies did not put boots on the ground in Buhriz until after mounting an artillery barrage and employing the support of Apache gunships firing a torrent of Hellfire missiles. It concerned officers and enlisted alike that they were inflicting considerable collateral civilian casualties; but–since IS employed the hapless citizens as human shields–it could not be avoided.

When return fire abated, the armies began to march across the defense perimeters set up by IS months previously. Initially, they met with only desultory fire; and it seemed as if the town might be deserted and that most of the insurgents had fled. They soon realized that they were wrong, at least about the insurgents. They did not stand and fight or organize anything like a set-piece conclusive battle. The coalition forces met guerilla tactic resistance. The insurgents launched hit-and-run ambushes, IEDs, and attacks by RPGs launched from building tops some distance away. Coalition forces inflicted forty to fifty insurgent casualties in the initial encounters, but it was clear that the insurgents were far from being defeated.

A meeting was held after three days of determined but inconclusive fighting to decide what should next be done. Avery was asked to attend since he and his agents were the most recent coalition members to have any kind of a battle with the defensemen of Buhriz.

When it was his turn to speak, Avery said, "All of the plans and efforts that have been used thus far are highly unlikely to move the IS out of this little burg. We keep getting caught up in their kind of fighting, and they—as defenders—have the advantage. We do not have forever, and they might as well have. They can resupply fighters and materiel at will. We need to do something different, something that might surprise them.

"What I propose is that we move straight through the city guns blazing and drive right out the back end and into the palm groves surrounding the place where they are hiding and resupplying. It is a jungle, and we need to get used to the idea that this will be the kind of battle…battles…I should say, we should expect and prepare for. I have been there, and it is hard to see more than a few feet ahead in any direction."

His argument carried the day. The coalition juggernaut roared through the town destroying houses, businesses, and several ammunition dumps. They advanced only fifty meters into the thick scrub and palm forest by the time darkness made it unsafe to continue.

Avery Challenger, Malcolm Fortner, and Devlin O'Malley, teamed up with three Delta Special Forces scouts to determine the safest and most effective directions to proceed the following day.

Even with night vision goggles, it proved to be futile. The enemy could be anywhere or everywhere on a moment's notice. A soldier could walk within a few feet of an enemy and not be aware of his or her presence.

The agents and scouts gave their report to Lt. Col. Bruce Antonia, commander of Task Force Regular. The brass made the decision the next morning to consolidate the entire task force and to begin clearance operations of the palm groves surrounding Buhriz which destroyed acres of beautiful old growth palm trees. The palm grove in Buhriz–like many throughout Iraq–are ancient and have grown in Iraq for thousands of years. There are some 450 varieties or cultivars which vary in size, shape, and color, and many of those different cultivars were visible before the armies moved through the grove.

The nightmare of close-quarters jungle warfare ensued with the resilient insurgents moving constantly around the determined coalition soldiers.

Avery commented to one of the older noncoms, "I have spent my military and intelligence time in the desert, and I thought it was pretty tough. However, this seems like the jungle warfare my father described during his time in Viet Nam. I'm pretty sure that I prefer the desert."

"Me, too," said SSgt. Jenkins. "But we still have to get the job done."

The IS guerrilla forces employed a tedious ambush, hit, and run, strategy. Coalition soldiers faced snipers hidden in the top of the palms, mines hidden in the ground, and prepositioned ambush sites hidden everywhere. Avery, Malcolm, and Devlin, were assigned to map escape routes and that proved to be crucial because the coalition forces were then able to use the information obtained to cut off the looping escape trails which allowed the American and Iraqis to mow down several squads of insurgents. In the fight, both sides used SA-7 missiles, thousands of rounds of machine gun ammunition, boxes of grenades, and countless output of ammunition for AK-47s; and the insurgents used Iranian 81 mm high explosive mortar rounds to their advantage.

Insurgent forces were also confirmed to have fired several SA-7 missiles at Apache attack helicopters, resulting in one being brought down and one altogether too close a near miss. In the aftermath, several caches were discovered containing large supplies of Iranian munitions. The materiel included explosive devices of various sizes designed to penetrate armor-hulled vehicles which had stopped two coalition tanks, shaped charges, machine guns, one Mauser rifle, two Dragonov sniper rifles, two RPG launchers and twenty Iranian manufactured RPG warheads.

The yanks and Iraqis won the skirmish by any measuring stick, and the insurgents were no longer able to operate openly in Buhriz. For weeks thereafter, there were still a small number of hit and run attacks; and they included the use of mines, small arms, and snipers throughout Buhriz. One such sniper attack killed a rearguard American soldier.

Operation Turki Bowl moved on. The forces split with one headed east towards the Iranian border, and the other headed south and east towards the belt of cities and towns that surround the capital–from Falluja south and east to Mahmudiyah, Iskandariyah, Salman Pak, then looping north to Balad Ruz and Baqubah, west to Tikrit and Balad and thence back to Falluja over the next several months. The focus of the coalition's attack was against the Baqubah Sunni foreign fighters' well-established network operating between Iran and the Iraqi towns of Khanaqin, Mandali, Balad Ruz, and Baqubah.

The other thrust was to form a serial attack line headed directly towards Baqubah and on towards Baghdad which is located about two-or-three hours' automobile drive from Baqubah. American, coalition, and Iraqi forces, engaged in coordinated raids and strikes something like the theory behind Pacific Island hopping during the War in the Pacific. The plan was to disrupt terrorist, insurgent, and militia, networks–of which there were scores–all with diverse reasons to fight the lawful government of Iraq and the Great Satan.

Among the first and most important obstacles between Turki and Baqubah was a medium sized town called Balad Ruz. The town and its environs were a well-established strong hold and staging area for the insurgency. There was a large military force of Wahhabist/Salafist extremist jihadis closely linked to Al-Qaeda operating in the southern outskirts of the city. Balad Ruz is located about an hour's drive north of Baghdad and about thirty-five miles east of Baqubah, making it a crucial choke point in the drive to Baghdad. Balad Ruz sits upon the secondary roads that link Muqdadiyah with Baqubah and southeastern Baghdad. Terrorists use the secondary roads to circumvent U.S. and coalition forces which made the interdiction of those roads a priority in the allied drive.

Avery and his co-agents were summoned to Lt. Col. Antonia's tent the evening before the main attacks were to commence.

"Avery," Antonia said, using the familiarity they enjoyed as working partners, "I want the three of you and three special-ops guys to reconnoiter the roadways leaving Balad Ruz and heading towards the town of Mandali, the last town before the Iranian border thirty-eight and a half klicks west of Balad Ruz. Mandali is not a border crossing and is not your final destination. More importantly, there's a secondary road that runs from Mandali to the major border crossing at Khanaqin, another seventy-seven or so klicks north. The road is important—we know that from satellite photos—because it is one of the main thoroughfares for bringing resupplies from Iran to the strongholds, caches, and armed forces, in the Baqubah River Valley. You've already seen the extent of that contribution. You need to collect the intel that lets us destroy the route and all the supplies we can hit, okay? Also, it would be useful to get any and all evidence you can that this Iraq war is an Iran backed operation."

"Sure, glad to help."

"Look, Avery, it's Indian country up there. Be careful. Avoid engaging, if at all possible. I think your chances of escaping detection would be best if you found some black pajamas, but you'll have to calculate the risks of being caught as spies. It would not be a good thing."

"To say the least. But the mission is crucial, and we are going to take the risk. Oh, that reminds me, do you have a captured pick-up we can use? Might as well look the part—in for a penny, in for a pound."

"You'll have your coms. Keep radio silence unless it's a real emergency. We'll send in air cavalry for you if we have to, but that would scrub all hopes of a surprise attack along the road."

"Copy that, Colonel. We'll do our best."

"You always do. Thanks in advance."

The reputation for cruelty and torture was well known for the Sunni extremists who controlled the secondary access roads. Iraqi soldiers and police were reluctant in the extreme to venture anywhere near the area. Avery's intel informed him that the previous week, the monsters kidnapped several families from local Shi'ite tribes, tortured and killed every single man and boy over the age of fourteen–thirty-nine civilians in all. The younger children were sold into slavery or farmed out to Sunni families in need of farm help. The women were taken captive to serve as sex-slaves. The 3rd BCT, 1st Cavalry Division, conducted deliberate, small-scale raids and air assaults to try and help them, but to no avail.

It was no problem to obtain IS "uniforms" because hundreds of them had been taken from dead IS fighters. Avery and SGM Rudi Tomlinson of the 3rd Battalion, 10th Special Forces Group worked through the night to get everything ready. Rudi and his partner, SSgt. Dewayne Michaelson, were chosen for the mission not only for their remarkable skill sets but because they could pass for Iraqis in a pinch, as could Avery with his now nut-brown face.

With only two hours sleep, the group of spies set out on a circuitous route to get to the road to Mandali.

CHAPTER TWELVE

WASHINGTON, Sept. 19 - Secretary of State Colin L. Powell and Defense Secretary Donald H. Rumsfeld have raised sharp complaints in recent days that Iran is providing support for the insurgency in Iraq, expressing concerns over what they say are Iran's attempt to shape Iraq's future. Pentagon, State Department, and military officials, describing intelligence reports that are fueling those concerns, say money, weapons, and even a small number of fighters, are flowing over the border from Iran to assist Shi'ite insurgents commanded by Moktada al-Sadr, a rebel cleric. But there is no consensus on the exact scale of Iranian activities.

–Thom Shanker and Steven R. Weisman,
Iran Is Helping Insurgents in Iraq, U.S. Officials Say,
New York Times, September 20, 2004

Khanaqin, Iraq, major border crossing between Iraq and Iran, March 20, 2008

Travel the first morning—more specifically, the first two hours of the morning—was uneventful; and Avery and Rudi and their men made good time. The ravages of the war were evident everywhere along the way. At outposts, bunkers lined with Hesco [short for the name of the company that produced them, HESCO Bastion], prefabricated boxes of heavy wire with synthetic mesh liners, each filled with gravel, sand, and/or dirt were commonplace. The abandoned bunkers had served the coalition as fighting positions and for blast protection, now sat as silent reminders of the struggles that took place months and years ago. The Hesco crates came in several different sizes and were quick to apply to non-engineer based construction. Small wooden B-Huts had served as housing on mid-sized and larger bases were now vacated. The box protectors enclosed troop bunkers, fuel depots, ammunition bunkers, mortar pits, artillery batteries, and blast shelters, for protection against incoming rocket or mortar fire.

The Hesco bunkers created neighborhoods—Hesco Villages–on bases with: guard towers, rows of portable toilets, crude latrines, and acres of gravel and crushed stone, for heli landing zones. PVC pipes angled through the Hesco walls or under the ground to serve as open-air urinals–"piss tubes." During quiet periods these "villages" had small gyms with shipped in exercise equipment, and burn pits producing acrid mixed odors from organic material, fecal material, diesel fuel, and smoldering piles of tobacco.

In the dry seasons—like Avery and Rudi's present journey–the Hesco Villages were coated with fine, dry dust–"moon dust," as the soldiers dubbed it—which settled over, around, and inside everything: cameras, shoes, socks, gun barrels, in nostrils, and between men's teeth. In these ghost villages, soldiers and local helpers had talked, smoked—including hashish—and crunched over the heavy packed sand to endure attacks. One of the problems for the occupants of the makeshift fortresses was the walls were too high and obstructed vision and allowed insurgents to lob grenades over the top. In time, the armies moved on to greater battles and to safer and more secure billeting.

The spies stopped occasionally to relieve themselves, but they ate sandwiches, drank coffee, and had small bars of chocolate, to celebrate their successful progress while still in motion. When they reached Mandali, the geography changed. Not the look of the desert or its scrub trees, but the people. Every woman they saw—and that was precious few—had a heavy black burka with only eye slits to reveal that behind the stiflingly hot cloak was a human being. No woman glanced in their direction as they passed through the dismal little town. The opposite was true with the men. Every man had an AK-47 and crossed bandolier bullet belts. Every man had a cell phone, and it seemed to Avery and Rudi that they were all talking about the spies' old Toyota truck.

This was probably going to become the testing place for their costumes, their knowledge of IS small talk, and their facility with Arabic. Both men were confident, but neither could help but feel the tension. All the occupants of the Toyota fingered their handguns.

Although Mandali was populated by a majority Southern Kurdish-speaking Shi'ites and minority Sunni Arabs, there were no Shi'ites evident in the town as they moved cautiously through the town. Mostly, the townspeople—other than the IS soldiers—ignored them. Of the regular 30,000 citizens, only a handful had dared to venture out into the streets.

Finally, a gruff looking Egyptian held up his hand for them to stop.

"In the name of God, the Merciful, and Compassionate, and may blessings be upon his Prophet SAWS—[*sallallahu alayhi wa salaam*]– may God's prayers and peace be with him, what is your business here, Brothers, I have not seen you before?"

"*As-salamu alaykum*, Brother," Avery replied. "We come in peace with orders from the Caliph himself, may God protect him and move forward his great work. He has ordered us to Khanaqin to act as security for the caravans of…goods…he requested for his work in Baqubah."

"*Wa aleykum as salam*. What direction will you take from Kanaqin, Brothers?"

"We will receive our orders from Kanaqin."

"Who gives those orders?"

"It is above my pay grade, as the Christian Crusaders would say."

The IS soldier laughed, "Well said, Brother. It is good that you do not divulge secure information. Allah will bless you."

"And you, Brother. Go with God's protection for you and the great work."

The soldier stepped back satisfied that he had done his duty, and these men could be some of the new foreign fighters the movement so sorely needed.

Avery and the other Americans tipped their heads and gave a small wave with their right hands in respectful gestures and drove on.

The road improved the closer they got to Khanaqin. It became a hardpack gravel throughway which hardly even plumed dust as the traffic rolled over it. Now, the spies were moving at speed along the Alawand, a tributary of the Diyala River. They were in a flat, fertile, and intensively cultivated, area along the river. Huge green pastures stretched out for miles, interlaced with irrigation canals and occasional fences. Kanaqin has a long border with Iran and serves as a local trade center for agricultural produce and livestock. The roadway was busy with people minding their own business—largely the business of agricultural commerce. Occasionally they passed or were passed by the common Toyota filled IS squads who seemed to accept them as much a part of the landscape as they were. At the gates of the city, there was a sign which read, "CITY OF TOLERANCE."

At Avery's orders, Malcolm Fortner and Devlin O'Malley took copious notes about the geography, road conditions, amount and type of traffic, and some semblance of a count of the number of enemy vehicles and insurgents they saw. This was all relayed via computer to a satellite link overhead. One thing they noted as they came nearer to Kanaqin was that inhabitants of the surrounding areas of Khanaqin were abandoning their villages and moving to safer towns like Kifri and Kalar. The CIA agents took this to be sure evidence that the number of the Islamic State insurgents and their attacks were increasing significantly, and confirmed the intel they had that over the past several weeks. In excess of twenty Kurdish and Sunni Arab villages had been evacuated around Khanaqin and Jalawla due to the increased activities of the jihadis.

At a point on the road five klicks southeast of Khanaqin, they took note of a substantial oil field and of a large refinery located at Alwand Village. Tanker trucks by the dozens entered and departed the filling pump areas forming an apparently endless supply chain which reached like a monster octopus tentacle in the direction of Turki.

The spies entered the city which was ordinarily a busy customs station located on the Iranian border with a rail terminus in Kanaqin itself. On another day, the place would have been a chaos related to the strong rural agriculture society. Today, it was very busy; but today, the business was war. Thousands of IS soldiers offloaded railroad cars of foodstuffs, boxes and boxes of ammunition, crates of lethal weaponry, and barrel after barrel of fuel. The offloading and reloading onto the long convoys of IS trucks was under the stringent watching eye of senior—nonforeign—insurgents. Any attempt at sabotage would be suicidal. All of this was relayed to the watching satellite.

It was apparent that virtually all traffic and the road itself belonged to the Islamic State. On a day in the less ruthless past, the area's roads would have been filled with farmers and livestock herders moving their produce through the customs station destined for the Iran border eight kilometers to the south. Other contributors would have been pilgrims traveling to and from the Shi'ite holy sites in Iraq and the Arabian holy cities. All of this had been displaced by a bustling and determined war industry. The CIA and Iraqi intelligence knew that Iraq was awash with captured or donated Ba'athist-era automatic rifles and domestic military ordnance. It was apparent that Kanaqin was also a major smugglers' crossing from Iran.

In the heart of the city there were no women or children. The markets were closed and boarded up. The administration and city security and fire departments were likewise inoperative. The Islamic State owned the city, lock, stock, barrel, and person. Malcolm Fortner kept the reports rolling; and Avery, Devlin, SGM Rudi Tomlinson, and SSgt. Dewayne Michaelson, kept itchy and sweaty fingers very near the triggers of their Colt M-16s. No weapon was on safety.

"We need to know what's in those tankers," said Avery. "Flip a u-eey and move closer to the road coming out of Alwand."

"You're kidding," said Malcolm. "Why don't we just paint a sign on the truck reading "MULTI-NATIONAL FORCE-IRAQ"?

"I admit that there's risk, but we really need to know. So, buckle up; it may be a bumpy ride."

They got the information Avery wanted and more. They were able to photograph signs on the freight cars and the trucks detailing the contents. Even IS could not keep track of their massive cargoes without some factual designation on the vehicles and on the cargoes themselves. Malcom worked as quickly as his fingers could fly to transmit the intel to the spy satellite.

"Can you imagine how tough this would be without computers. Imagine what just happened. I sent copy and photographs to an eye in the sky. Pretty Buck Rogers stuff!"

Malcolm's moment of appreciation ended abruptly.

Two parked IS troop trucks started up and began speeding towards them. The enemy would be upon them in a matter of minutes. Avery had a decision to make: run, hide, and maybe be safe; or make a fighting stand here and now and even with a small victory, their mission would be hopelessly compromised, or—it came to him in a burst of serendipity—they could lead the killers on a goose chase while the satellite could get them help. He chose his burst of inspiration.

"Move it! Swing off road and head back towards Kanaqin. Turn at the first perimeter road and head towards the general direction of Turki. Remember all that stuff we learned at sabotage school and at the Farm about "escape, evade, and engage." This is the time to remember everything we learned."

SGM Tomlinson was driving, and it was obvious that he was at the top of his class at defensive drivers' school. Avery's memory of the roads was good. They made a dangerously rapid left turn onto the narrow frontage road that ran parallel to the main road from Kanaqin to Turki—a road which heretofore the Multi-National Force-Iraq commanders had not known about. Malcom communicated frantically with the satellite, and hopefully with Lt. Col. Antonia in Balad Ruz.

"May-day, May-day!" he signaled over and over, each time including the changing GPS location, all in the day's specific code.

After a frantic five minutes of jouncing on a rutted dirt path, and after ten repeat messages, a similarly coded reply came through.

"Cavalry on the way! Repeat, cavalry on the way! The Peshmergas are coming. Hang on."

The good thing about the flight from fight situation they found themselves in was that there were still only two IS vehicles in pursuit. The bad thing was that the enemy was gaining on them.

"Must have gotten a better batch of Toyotas than we did. Try a short evasive trip off-road, Rudi. We have to buy some time!" Avery shouted.

There was a small clearing in the trees immediately ahead on the left. Rudi swept over the tall grass and into the clearing. From there, he maneuvered the Toyota around and through narrow—but passable—spaces between the trees. The going was slow, and the IS killers were hot on their trail. They could not have missed seeing where the Americans drove off road.

"Avery, this is it. I can't find any way through the trees. We have to turn back."

"Can you do that?"

"Not really; it's too narrow even to turn around. I'll have to back up."

"Stop. Everybody out. This is our last stand. Bring every weapon you can carry and hide around in the trees here. I don't think they will expect us to stop and to start a fight."

"Let's pray that's so," said Devlin.

"Yeah. I guess this is as good a day to die as any," SSgt. Michaelson said with resignation.

It was only minutes before the Americans could hear the IS platoons stopping, clambering out of their trucks, and shouting and arguing orders. It sounded something like a Chinese fire drill, and it would have been funny if the situation were not so serious.

Suddenly, gunfire erupted from the frontage road, sounding like every man in the two trucks was firing his AK-47 skyward like they enjoy doing during celebrations.

Avery and his men gave each other quizzical looks.

The answer came within seconds. The unmistakable roar of two F-14 Tomcat fighter planes sounded almost directly overhead.

"Peshmergas!" whispered Avery *soto voce*.

The Peshmerga army had captured the planes from IS secret airfields. The aircraft were made in Iran for IS use. The Zeravani [military police] unit—loyal to the Kurdistan Democratic Party—were responsible. Iran returned 100 fighter planes to Iraq that Iran had captured during the Iran/Iraq war of Saddam Hussein in 1991. It was no great feat of detection to locate the Americans in trouble and the IS trucks which were the source of the trouble.

The Tomcats made a beeline directly at the two pickup trucks stopped on the road and surrounded by IS soldiers. Each Tomcat co-pilot aimed then fired two Soviet-made–and modified for the Tomcats to fire–air to ground missiles at the IS trucks parked within a few feet of each other. The result was virtual erasure of the trucks and their drivers in a fireball—two fireballs, technically. More than a dozen IS fighters standing near the trucks were killed instantly, and fifteen more were critically wounded.

The Tomcats curved away in opposite directions to avoid allowing the IS ground crews to be able to fire off missiles at them. Each Tomcat waggled its wings as if to say "this is thanks for the Western countries'— American, German, French, Australian, Canadian, Albanian, Croatian, Danish, Italian, Spanish, and United Kingdom–officers in Iraqi Kurdistan."

Avery and Rudi were instantly sure of what had just happened.

"Attack," Avery shouted. "Follow me. We have to finish off every last one of them. If we don't, we're toast, and so is our mission. Move it!"

The stunned IS fighters could not muster a defense against the howling banshees who rushed out of the trees and mowed them down with machine gun fire. Avery made a quick runaround to check for survivors but found none and no blood trails. He and Rudi checked the flow of traffic on the main road and decided that the attack had occurred in a screen of dust from both the main and the frontage roads and amidst the din of the heavy truck traffic.

"I think we got away with it," Rudi said with more optimism than he really felt.

"Hope so," said Avery, "but we have to get our tails out of here. Go back and get the truck, please; and the rest of us will start dragging bodies into the brush."

"Will do," said Rudi. "When I get back, I have an idea to share."

"Okay."

They could not clear the debris from the destroyed trucks, but Avery and the others were able to move the bodies out of obvious sight. It was the best they could do in the time allotted.

After they collected the rest of their weaponry, loaded up the truck, and were again underway, Rudi told the rest his plan.

"I noticed that these convoys go along in groups of seven or eight vehicles with fifteen or so minutes of space between them. Probably because of the time needed to offload the goods from the train. I think we can dig a few holes for IED placement in front of and behind a column, explode them in series to disrupt an entire column and to slow down the whole convoy."

"Don't you think that will give away our involvement?" Avery asked.

"I don't. This is a war. All sides employ IEDs all the time. They'll wonder who the saboteurs were; but I think they'll conclude the most likely candidates are unconverted locals, probably Kurds."

"Maybe wishful thinking, but what the hey, let's do it."

They raced to a crossing which was shrouded by trees and waited until the last truck lumbered past. Then, they divided up into teams and placed IEDs on both sides of the main road and a hundred meters apart. SSgt. Michaelson was the unit's explosives expert, and he set the IEDs up on timers so that the rear explosives would detonate three minutes after the forward bombs and create a complete blockage of the road both in front of and behind the luckless convoy.

Trusting Michaelson's expertise, the spies traveled full speed ahead down the frontage road towards Turki. They barely heard the explosions behind them. Devlin scrutinized the map carefully, looking for a turnoff. As it turned out, it could not have been more obvious. They came to a fairly wide crossing with signs pointing west that read, "BALAD RUZ, BAQUBAH, BAGHDAD." They turned in that direction and raced towards the teeth of the battle they knew was already well under way.

CHAPTER THIRTEEN

"No soldier ever really survives a war." "And freedom is what
America means to the world."

> –Audie Leon Murphy (1925-1971) was the most decorated soldier
> that survived WWII. No known attribution.

Balad Ruz, Iraq, March, 2008

The Battle of Balad Ruz commenced on a decidedly negative note
for the coalition forces. Any hope of secrecy was dashed when the
signals officers intercepted a commercial radio broadcast from the Balad
Ruz Arabic radio station Al Noor ["the light"]. The station was very much
pro-coalition and anti-Islamic State but exercised the worst of judgment.
It announced that the "Battle to end all battles, and to drive out the
anti-Islamic Islamic State" was about to begin, and the end of the vicious
occupation was at an end. The result was a capable enemy being alerted
to the need to shore up security and to prepare a guerilla-type defense.

Before the Multi-National Force-Iraq reached the outskirts of Balad
Ruz, a suicide bomber wearing an explosive belt attempting an attack
against an eastern checkpoint, tried to approach the eastern checkpoint.
Checkpoint security was able to stop the bomber before he could reach the
checkpoint itself, but he was able to kill himself and an American Army
advisor. Over the next eight hours–as the multi-national forces advanced–
eight U.S. soldiers acting as advance scouts were killed by ambushers.

About fifty IS operatives lay in wait at three different locations. They camouflaged themselves and hid in trenches and behind earthen berms on both sides of the main road into the city. The guerillas were armed with AK-47 assault rifles, rocket-propelled grenades, heavy machine guns, a new weapon—highly accurate mortars which could be fired from as far away as six-seven kilometers. In the early afternoon, a member of the 278th Regimental Combat Team from the Tennessee National Guard and another U.S. soldier from Minnesota were killed by snipers in fierce fighting that followed a surprise attack on the mixed force of U.S. and Iraqi troops by hidden insurgents. Witnesses called it "driving into a shooters' alley."

Finally, it was learned from Avery Challenger and his fellow CIA agents that the coalition forces were about to engage the Iranian Army in addition to IS—a twist that made clear that war creates strange bedfellows. It was especially surprising because Balad Ruz since 2006 had been the site of frequently recurring sectarian violence separately involving Sunni and Shi'ite militias.

Lt. Col. Bruce Antonia, commander of Task Force Regular–upon receiving Avery's intel—recognized that he lacked adequate forces to clear the city without incurring excessive casualties. He requested and received additional forces to assist in that task. The Battle of Balad Ruz–instead of being a short stop in an "island hopping" operation–became a major campaign.

Antonia was directed to move his entire force to Forward Operating Base Caldwell–the second largest U.S. Base in Iraq—to shore up defenses there and unite as a reinforced unit. The entire facility covered just under half a kilometer square and had several medium size groups of semi-permanent buildings called pods. Troop living quarters were a long line of temporary trailer complexes—hundreds of trailers of dubious local construction. Most of those were single-wide trailers separated into two or sometimes even three parts known to the soldiers as "hootches."

Joint Base Balad–as it was known officially—historically was under multiple different names: including Balad Air Base—by the U.S. Air Force, Al Bakr Air Base, Camp Anaconda or LSA [Logistical Support Area Anaconda]. The men serving there knew it as "Life Support Area Anaconda" or the "Big Snake."

As Lt. Col. Antonia's force moved into the base, they found it in a fever of activity. The 69th Engineer Battalion was running cable. The 69th's cable dogs were hurriedly installing a variety of cables for different kinds of communication systems in anticipation of a major communication requirement during the upcoming battle. They were repairing old lines and installing more permanent cable lines. The eventual job—once the imminent battle was over–was to put in miles of fiber cable to create a way to connect a variety of communication—was part of the critical infrastructure for the entire Sunni Triangle of Central Iraq. A large concrete pad had been poured the day before to support a tall communication tower—a sign of permanency and a signal to the insurgency that the Iraq government and its supporters were there to stay.

Runways were being reinforced, and supplies were being placed along them for rapid repairs after the expected mortar attacks—which happened almost daily even before the significant battle in the offing. HAS [Hardened Aircraft Shelters] were being inspected and hardened further with addition of more re-bar and specially imported hardened concrete. The properties which determine the quality of the hardened concrete fall into the following three groups: strength, durability, and dimensional stability. The Anaconda Base concrete was the best combination of all those factors that American industry could produce. Simply put, the strength of concrete is the maximum amount of load which it can handle and force it can withstand. The strength of concrete is determined by the compressive strength and tensile strength. The HAS shelters were meant to survive the impact of mortars, artillery, and bombs.

Mortar attacks were part of daily life at Joint Base Balad; so much so, that the soldiers and airmen assigned there referred to their base as "Mortaritaville" and as "The most attacked base in the country." Camp Balad had a joint army/CIA black site jail, euphemistically titled U.S. Military Detention Camp Balad or TSF [Temporary Screening Facility] to interrogate high-value detainees. Despite the euphemistic titles, Avery and his co-agents had used the prison to hold prisoners in wooden crates, too small to stand in or lie down, and who were subject to constant white noise. Avery assumed command of the facility and ordered a tripling of the guards and perimeter sentries from the Garrison Support Unit Jolly Roger because of the importance of the detainees and the information they had.

384

At first light—while the muezzin sounded the *aazan* [Eng. "to listen"] for the *salat* [the call to prayer], the coalition forces launched the all-out Battle of Balad Ruz. F-16s were launched from the base and the well-trained pilots were able to spot IEDs on the ground before they were detonated and warned the soldiers below of the explosive's location. As opposed to the day before, IEDs were only a minor problem on the day of the major launch. It was slow and difficult going. IS fighters blasted holes through the walls of houses to permit them to move unseen from house to house. The coalition soldiers and military police had to resort to door-to-door inspection and house raids and arrests.

They were backed by the use of Abrams tanks which removed even the most recalcitrant of the insurgents. The early morning quiet was pierced by the screams of the wounded, the whistle of whizzing bullets, and the loud explosions from mortars, artillery, and tanks. The city became a hellfire, brimstone, and cordite, nightmare. For most of the IS fighters who were unfamiliar with what the American military might was capable it was a serious–usually brief–educational experience. Many of the IS commanders would have agreed with Japanese Naval Marshal General Isoroku Yamamoto's comment about his attack on Pearl Harbor in 1941, that "I fear all we have done is to awaken a sleeping giant and fill him with a terrible resolve."

The boots-on-the-ground offensive was truly a demonstration of shock and awe. Large, well-trained, and firmly disciplined, units from the 100th Infantry Battalion, Task Force 34, the Combat Heavy 864th Engineer Battalion, G Btry 202 ADA, 30th Heavy Brigade Combat Team, Early Warning Team 4, 278th Armored Cavalry Regiment, 1-32 Cavalry, 5-32nd Cavalry, 2nd Squadron, 3rd Armored Cavalry Regiment, 1st Cavalry Regiment 5th Squadron, B Btry 2/4 FA, MLRS, 5th Iraqi Army MiTT, and a unit of Shi'ite civilian militia aching for revenge, flooded the City. They moved from east to west and north to south like a horde of locusts. They devoured the enemy as they went.

The after-action searches revealed caches of weapons and money, larger caches containing hundreds of assorted types of rockets, IED-making materials, thousands of small arms munitions, and several dozens of anti-tank weapons. Labels on munitions boxes supplied firm evidence that the extremist enemy smuggled Iranian weapons into and through Diyala province. Iraqi Police and coalition forces also discovered a cache of explosively formed projectiles (EFPs) imported from Iran. It is unclear whether the cache belonged to the Iranian terrorist military group JAM [*Jaysh al-Mahdi*], Al-Qaeda, or another insurgent group of the more than eighty extant in the Iraa region; but it was abundantly clear from the labels that the groups hiding the caches were funded, trained, and armed by the Iranian Quds Force, part of the Islamic Revolutionary Guard Corps.

More grimly, locals directed the searchers to mass grave sites and torture complexes, some containing piles of skeletons of women which confirmed the suspicions of human trafficking being carried on by IS units. As the investigation expanded beyond the Balad Ruz borders, a mass grave holding well over two hundred bodies was found in an orchard just north of Baquba, a harbinger of things to come as the coalition began its powerful movement in the direction of the capital city of the governate. The searchers discovered and mapped out an insurgent supply line running from several Iranian entry points through Muqdadiyah and into northern Baqubah. The American and Iraqi leaders of the Multi-National Force Iraq did not for a moment underestimate their enemy and braced themselves for a severe battle.

CHAPTER FOURTEEN

"It struck me that such analyses had it backward. It's the American public for whom the Iraq War is often no more real than a video game. Five years into this war, I am not always confident most Americans fully appreciate the caliber of the people fighting for them, the sacrifices they have made, and the sacrifices they continue to make. After the Vietnam War ended, the onus of shame largely fell on the veterans. This time around, if shame is to be had when the Iraq conflict ends–and all indications are there will be plenty of it–the veterans are the last people in America to deserve it. When it comes to apportioning shame, my vote goes to the American people who sent them to war in a surge of emotion but quickly lost the will to either win it or end it. The young troops I profiled in *Generation Kill*, as well as the other men and women in uniform I've encountered in combat zones throughout Iraq and Afghanistan, are among the finest people of their generation. We misuse them at our own peril."

–Evan Wright, *Generation Kill: Devil Dogs, Iceman, Captain America, and the New Face of American War*, G.P. Putnam's Sons, a member of Putnam Group (USA) Inc., 2004

Baqubah, Capital of Diyala Governate, Iraq, Late March, 2008

The early morning wind began kicking up puffs of dust even before the armada began to move against Baqubah and its occupying terrorists. As the HUMMVEES, tanks, and armored troop transport vehicles, hit the open road between Balad Ruz and the capital city, dust began to envelope them in a vision obscuring cover that made it difficult to nearly impossible for an enemy to distinguish an individual vehicle. After an hour, an actual sandstorm moved from north to south turning visibility for the drivers to near zero. They had to rely on their GPSs to follow the otherwise quite good road.

The lead vehicles were driven by reconnaissance forces who had the most thankless jobs in the army. They traveled at considerable speed in lightly armored HUMMVEES ahead of the following better equipped and protected main force. They were charged with the frightening task of eradicating IS ambush sites by driving at breakneck speed directly into the oncoming danger. Everyman in every vehicle fired his assigned weapon almost machine-like as they passed an occupied ditch, a mosque manned with insurgents, or a canyon wall of buildings with snipers on both sides and in almost every window.

They had been trained never to flinch about making direct contact with a determined and well-trained enemy. The catch phrase used by the enlisted was, "Hail, Caesar. We who are about to die, salute you!" They used up prodigious amounts of expensive ammunition, unlike the research that indicated that a large percentage of WWII marines hitting Pacific beaches who were found in after-battle assessments to have failed to fire even a single round; and they were not even aware of it.

A little beyond the line of the reconnaissance spearpoint, overhead a flotilla of Cobra gunships whump-whumped, occasionally unleashing a deadly salvo at a concentrated nest of IS fighters. Even before the main body of attackers pushed their way through the narrow streets of Baqubah, the sights, sounds, confusion, and stench, of war were enveloping the city. Sewer mains were disrupted, and small rivers of sewage flooded the roads. Whole blocks of residential and commercial buildings were systematically being blown to pieces. The older two-and-three story buildings that had dried out in the sun for eons crumbled and fell as if some giant dinosaur had kicked over a dust pile. Even over the noise of the vehicles and the guns, the haunting sounds of screaming, cursing, and crying, could be heard. The term, "fog of war" applied in spades.

The soldiers in the spearpoint HUMMVEES and those who followed pumped out grenades at passing buildings reducing them to rubble and dumping IS insurgents out like so many broken rag dolls. Rhythmical bursts from .50 Cal. machine guns and from the roof turret heavy machine guns were enough to discourage even the most intrepid IS fighters, and many of them began to retreat further into the heart of the city through the tunnels they had created by blasting out holes in the walls of peoples' homes.

Behind the spearpoint reconnaissance forces came the main body of the Multi-National Force Iraq, a truly daunting spectacle. HUMMVEES, armored troop transport trucks, jeeps, and helicopters conducting air assaults, all ferried "ground-pounders" [infantry soldiers] into the combat zone. The force's massive firepower was irresistible. IS gunmen concealed behind windows, in mosques, office buildings, and homes began to fall like scythed wheat, as if the protective walls were not even there. The fury of the sandstorm seemingly bowed to the superior power of the war machine and began to abate, although a forty to fifty MPH wind persisted.

Visibility improved and presented ever more targets. The juggernaut began in slow motion but was now moving as fast as the vehicles could maneuver around the wreckage on the main streets. Sections of buildings, piles of mudbricks, destroyed cars, carts, and trucks, abandoned weapons, downed trees and light poles, and dead animals and human corpses, were now litter to be circumvented. Snipers fired from rooftops, from behind boxes and barricades in alleys, and from behind doorways of buildings where human shields were being held hostage. Smoke and fire were all around. The stench of burning bodies mixed with that of human waste permeated every man and woman's nostrils and could not be ignored.

Rarely, an RPG would be fired with accuracy and destroy a coalition vehicle and even one tank, killing all occupants. Otherwise, very few coalition casualties occurred, and the coalition armada moved as if a well-oiled and dehumanized machine was moving through Baqubah as an irresistible force, oblivious to the pinging of machine gun bullets bouncing harmlessly off the well-armored vehicles.

By the time the armored juggernaut traversed the city from north to south, the place was largely in ruins. Then, the coalition field artillery and attack Cobras began to pound known concentrations of enemy soldiers and military materiel caches. Hardly a neighborhood in Baqubah went unscathed.

Despite all the destruction, IS was not yet finished. They saved up a surprise for the coalition helicopters which served as a sobering reminder that they were still there. Experiences in the Soviet-Afghan War formed a significant part of Al-Qaeda's and IS's military thinking. They learned from the experience of that insurgency about the vulnerable areas in America and its allies' defenses. Fairly early in the Soviet offensive against Afghanistan, the Soviets launched a series of effective operations designed to bring a basic level of security to the country and control by the communists.

These operations relied heavily on the use of Hind helicopters both to transport infantry and to bring to bear mobile firepower since the terrain in Afghanistan made the use of ground weapons and carriers very difficult. In one of its greatest mistakes, the United States government and military allowed Charlie Wilson and his cooperative CIA agents to supply the Afghan mujahideen with Stinger surface-to-air missiles. That produced a major turning point of the Soviet war. The missiles brought down numerous previously thought to be invincible Soviet helicopters and occasional transport aircraft. After the introduction of the Stingers, Soviet pilots began to refuse to fly combat missions in contested areas, and the Soviet offensive ground to a halt. Like dominoes, the Soviet war machine began to crumble to defeat and then retreated in ignominy. AQI and IS learned from the Afghanistan experience that a Stinger missile or two could dissuade even the most intrepid of coalition pilots from venturing too close.

Amidst all the smoke, sand in the air, and the haze of war, two Stingers were fired from a hardened concrete silo with deadly accuracy bringing down two Cobra helicopters in spectacular fireballs which caused a pause in the coalition advance.

Lt. Col. Antonia ordered Avery and his CIA spies, Malcolm Fortner and Devlin O'Malley, and his friends in the special forces, SGM Rudi Tomlinson of the 3rd Battalion, 10th Special Forces Group and his partner, SSgt. Dewayne Michaelson, to locate any remaining Stinger missile launching sites and either destroy them or signal the air corps the position; so, they could get rid of them.

"It's like driving in Berlin must have been during the last great battle of the European Theater in World War II," Avery observed as they bobbed and weaved about along the rubble strewn streets.

"I can't even imagine what that must have been like," Rudi said, "despite everything I've seen in my career. No wonder they call those guys, 'The Greatest Generation.'"

"Amen," echoed Devlin, who was an aficionado of World War II history.

"What's that…over there on the left? Is that a bunker, or just some ruins?" asked Dewayne, pointing in the direction of a large semi-conical cement mound.

"Suspicious, at least," said Avery. "Lock and load, and let's check it out."

No sooner had he said that than they began to take on machine gun fire. Bullets ricocheted off the HUMMVEE like a nasty hailstorm. Avery drove at full speed around the emplacement to try and get a location of the machine-gunners.

Dewayne called out, "See one," and fired a grenade at his target hitting it straight on.

Body segments and parts of two machine guns rained down on the passing HUMMVEE harmlessly, but with gruesome impact which was not lost on the occupants. Avery bobbed and weaved, made frightening and rough bootlegger about faces, and rushed areas of interest. The machine gun fire had died down. As they slowed down to get their bearings, another fusillade began, this time centered on the three-inch thick plastic windows of the hummer. Everyone fired a weapon at the place he understood the machine gun fire to be coming from, but none of them hit a target of value.

Avery made a dizzying, looping, traverse around the emplacement twice, drawing fire, but sustaining no real damage. Finally, Devlin and Malcom yelled at the same time.

"Got him!," and they began logging grenades from their launchers in a steady pounding thrum, thrum, thrum, until their presumed targets lighted up in a massive bonfire. One victim ran out, his body engulfed in flame, and Rudi killed him with a mercy shot. The sounds of war became distant; and after a time, Avery stopped the hummer and got out.

"Let's have a look," he said.

As soon as all the Americans alighted from their vehicle, half a dozen IS fighters poured out of a nearby copse of trees with their hands up.

Malcolm ordered them in Arabic to put their hands in the air and to kneel down. Rudi—the noncom with the most experience in battle of any of them—walked briskly to where the enemies were kneeling and quaking.

"Where are other Stinger emplacements?" he demanded in Arabic.

He put his AR-16 barrel against the head of one of the bearded and bowed enemies and repeated his demand, this time with full threatening emphasis.

The IS fighter made an imploring gesture and blurted out directions to where two more emplacements were maintained.

"Are there still missiles in them unfired?" Rudi asked, this time more quietly, but with equal malevolence.

The response was a vigorous head nodding by all six.

Then, Rudi surprised everyone–American and Middle Easterner–by putting his rifle on full auto and shooting all the IS fighters in the face. He turned and walked back to the HUMMVEE and calmly recited the Stinger locations verbatim.

Avery gave him a rather shocked quizzical look.

Rudi said, "Just 'dead-checking," the Marine term for extrajudicial execution of wounded combatants.

The American spy unit raced to each Stinger missile site in its turn and found both of them to be unmanned and the missile still intact. Rudi, Dewayne, and Malcolm, rigged explosives in a ring around the protruding missile's cone and told Avery to move the HUMMVEE a hundred yards away. Rudi tripped the electrical detonator switch and blew the missiles at each location into a million pieces. They reported to Lt. Col. Antonia about their successes but left out the 'dead-checking' incident.

It was dusk when operations–other than desultory mop-up and reconnaissance for caches–ceased. Antonia ordered the army to dig in, and entrenching tools were removed from several thousand backpacks. Shallow holes were hacked and jammed out of the hard-scrabble desert surface; and the bone weary, filthy, and sated, soldiers bedded down for satisfying slumber despite the lumps of rocks and rubble beneath them.

Reveille was sounded at 0500; MRE [Meal Ready to Eat] breakfasts where choked down with bottled water; and a day of search and destroy ensued. Right off the bat, a patrol of thirty coalition troops who were searching for a suspected weapons and money cache came under ambush attack from insurgents hiding in canals and ditches under tree branches for cover. The hidden IS insurgents attacked using small arms, rocket-propelled grenades, and mortars. Five Iraqis and one American were killed in the initial foray and the rest of the patrol was pinned down. The patrol called in an air strike and a Cobra flew past strafing the ditch killing all the insurgents. It was now 0530.

An early reconnaissance unit started to pass through a hamlet called Khan Bani Saad just south of Baqubah when a frightened and very excited elderly Shi'ite imam flagged them down. None of the men spoke Farsi. They tried Arabic and English, but to no avail. The imam waved to them to follow him. They drove half a klick to the south with nerves on edge fearing a trap. The old man began to weep as he pointed at the destination. A young man—an English speaker–explained the obvious: A female suicide bomber blew herself up near his mosque. An even dozen people–mostly elderly and many of them infirm–were killed outright and twenty or so others were lying on the ground gravely wounded. Another five or six walking wounded shambled around the destroyed mosque in turmoil and confusion.

The patrol sergeant in charge called into base for help and requested medics, several ambulances, and graves registry. He and his men began doing the best they could to treat the people's physical and even their serious psychological traumas. They remained there for half an hour until help from the base arrived before hurrying on to the next problem area. It was 0645, and the sun was just above the horizon. It was not yet hot, but the men all knew they were in for a scorcher.

Presuming that they would inevitably lose the battle and have to move on, the leaders of the Islamic State forces had the forethought to set up mine fields, booby traps, weapon and ammunition caches, and carefully hidden ambuscade sites. They had feverishly developed a complex system of signals; fortified irrigation ditches; and had hollowed out spider holes in them. They hid motorcycles in large culverts to allow fleeing insurgents to move along through the canals in relative safety. The leaders set aside reserve squads of a dozen or so fighters with orders for them to fight to the death, even to resort to suicide bombings.

Avery and Malcolm were passengers in a surveillance Cobra helicopter when Avery spotted several bands of men on motorcycles driving along in canal beds. He alerted the pilot, who immediately gave the GPS coordinates and called in artillery and close air support because there were so many insurgent motorcyclists. Avery kept the enemy constantly in his vision. He was alarmed to see one of the insurgents park his bike and begin to assemble an RPG-7 to fire at his helicopter.

He shouted to the pilot to make a hard bank to the right while he readied his own rocket launcher. He fired two seconds before the insurgent below and blew him and two of his comrades to pieces. The industrious IS soldier had armed his rocket launcher; so, when the blast hit him, his rocket shot parallel to the ground for fifty meters and mowed down another ten fighters. Avery patted himself on the back for having made such a great shot. Malcolm just laughed at him.

The Islamic State fighters also mined almost every road in the areas surrounding Baqubah, especially those headed in the direction of Baghdad. They even slipped in behind the coalition vehicles after they demined a road and remined it to catch unsuspecting Iraqis or Americans. It was the American pattern to make a swift forward sweep, stopping to clear mine fields identified by specialists and after going a set distance forward, to make a convoy about face and return back the same way they had come, presuming that it would be safe. It took only a couple of examples to enlighten the soldiers and the brass.

Avery had something of a turkey shoot from his shotgun seat. He and the pilot made nearly a dozen passes along canals, sometimes dodging RPGs, and more often being able to spray a group of hiding insurgents or to destroy a cache of motorcycles or arms. Devlin O'Malley and Dewayne Michaelson took the ground route. They moved from house to house and were pleasantly surprised when they found the citizens to be affable, even grateful. They called them liberators and friends. Some of the townspeople were happy to help. They hated the Islamic State; some had lost family and friends to forced conscriptions.

A few Shi'ites remained, and they wept over the loss of daughters to the IS sex-slave trade. They were enthusiastic to inform Devlin and Dewayne about what they knew of weapons, money, and drug caches, where motorcycles were hidden, maps of escape routes and safe havens, and the most recent maps of mine fields they had. They willingly turned over maps of the myriad irrigation canals and ditches and marked where contraband or killers could be found.

The help from the townspeople proved to be invaluable and hastened mopping-up operations considerably. The capturing of potential informants and the killing of the rest took three full days. The coalition army lost count by the end of the first day.

CHAPTER FIFTEEN

Oval Office, White House, Washington DC, PDB [President's Daily Briefing], May 3, 2008

Meeting recorded and stamped "TOP SECRET, EYES ONLY; POTUS, George W. Bush; DNI, Daniel Coats; Secy. Of State, Condoleezza Rice; Chairman of the Joint Chiefs of Staff, Admiral Michael Glenn Mullen

Present: POTUS, DNI, Secy. of State; CJCS; General David Petraeus, commander of multinational forces in Iraq; Ambassador Ryan Crocker, U.S. ambassador to Iraq; Senator John McCain R-Az, ranking Republican on the United States Senate Committee on Armed Services; Senator Barack Obama, member of the United States Senate Committee on Foreign Relations, COS-I, Special Agent Avery Challenger

Date: May 3, 2008

Subject: Withdrawal of all U.S. military forces in Iraq

Summary:
- CJCS summarized the situation at present in Iraq. Iranian agents and weapons are fueling the ongoing strife in Iraq and are helping the insurgency to spread. Further U.S. troop withdrawals will have to wait

until at least stability is achieved. Although the last of the additional U.S. combat brigades dispatched in 2007 is scheduled to leave in June 2008, Gen. Petraeus and all the COS recommend against further withdrawals for at least 45 days. I concur, except that period should be at least 60 days. Future troop levels should be based on conditions on the ground as reported regularly by military intelligence and CIA agents in place. In the seven months since our last appearance before Congress, U.S. and Iraqi forces made progress toward tamping down the violence but the progress has been "fragile" and "reversible." Furthermore, he stated, "while the current situation in Afghanistan is both precarious and urgent, the 10,000 additional troops needed there would be unavailable "in any significant manner" unless withdrawals from Iraq were made. CJCS stated that "my priorities given to me by the commander-in-chief are: Focus on Iraq first. It's been that way for some time. Focus on Afghanistan second. It will be there forever, always at war."

- Secy of State stated that he reluctantly agreed with CJCS despite the expectation that initial American public response will be negative and as well, initial world-wide criticism will almost certainly result. That outcome would likely be relatively short term—most likely a matter of months but would be preferable to having to return to shore up the currently shaky government and military of Iraq. The Secy stated—for the record—that it was his studied opinion that there exists no option of withdrawal "with honor" or that the fragile peace now extant would persist.

- Sen. McCain spoke only briefly. He emphasized that his opinion has been presented formally to Congress, to the White House, to his contacts in the military, and to the American public, that "I was a leading advocate of the 2007 troop increase, and I point out for the record that the United States is no longer staring into the abyss of defeat as a result. Premature removal of troops would be to court disaster."

- Sen. Obama stated the contrarian opinion that, "I question whether the conditions set by U.S. commanders for withdrawal would lead to a war that could last until 2028 or 2038. The invasion of Iraq was a massive strategic blunder that allowed Al-Qaeda and Iran to spread their influence into Iraq. I am of the strong opinion that the United States should pressure Iraqi officials to settle the war by threatening to leave. "If the definition of success is as high as the conservatives demand, i.e. that there be no traces of Al-Qaeda and no possibility of reconstitution of a highly-effective Iraqi government, a democratic multi-ethnic, multi-sectarian functioning democracy with no Iranian influence, at least not of the kind that we don't like, then that portends the possibility of us staying for 20 or 30 years, which is not just my personal opinion. If–on the other hand–our criteria amounts to a messy, sloppy, status quo but there's no huge outbreaks of violence, there's still corruption, but the country is struggling along, but it's not a threat to its neighbors and it's not an Al Qaeda base, that seems to me an achievable goal within a measurable timeframe. I strongly recommend the latter course."

- COS-I stated that he returned from the battle front in Diyala Province in Iraq, and that it was his observation that–if anything–our troops are being stretched to or even beyond their limits. Instead of a troop withdrawal, he said, "I firmly recommend that there be a troop surge to see our operations through the summer to gain control of the north, the Diyala Province, and the Baghdad region. That would be eminently capable of accomplishment with twenty-to-fifty thousand more troops present until at least through June. Please do not desert our troops or the loyal Iraqis who have suffered so much to accomplish our mutual aims. Thank you."

- POTUS stated that he was convinced that it would be premature to order a troop withdrawal, however much the liberals in the United States and abroad would applaud such an action. "I have studied the issue at length, have held numerous discussions with our military, and State Department people, and have called our real allies around the world. Therefore, it is my decision to order a so-called "surge" of 25,000 more troops to leave for Iraq immediately, and an addition 25,000 to be deployed in two months. I agree with Adm. Mullen that we will have to leave Afghanistan for another day. Would that we had never allowed ourselves to be seduced into an endless war there."

Signed:

[signature]

George W. Bush, POTUS

CHAPTER SIXTEEN

Baghdad was the seat of the Abbasid caliphs from the eighth century. In 1248, however, Genghis Khan's grandson Möngke became great khan of the Mongols and resolved to extend his sway to the Middle East and beyond that, if possible, to Syria and Egypt. Ten years later Mesopotamia was overrun by a Mongol horde under his brother Hülegü. The Mongols advanced on Baghdad and demanded the city's surrender.

Confusion reigned in the Caliph al-Musta'sim's capital and it was said that his wazir, or principal minister, was a Shi'a who betrayed his Sunni master and had treacherously reduced the size and strength of Baghdad's garrison. It seems significant that after the Mongol victory, he was confirmed in his office by Hülegü.

It was clear that the city had no hope of resisting the Mongol army. When it surrendered, the Mongols looted it and slaughtered thousands of the inhabitants – more than 200,000, according to Hülegü's own estimate. They also killed the Caliph, though exactly how is uncertain. David Morgan in his book on the Mongols suggests that the most likely story, told by Marco Polo among others, is that the Caliph was wrapped in a carpet and kicked or stamped to death. The Mongols did not like to execute anyone of noble blood by any method that involved shedding that blood. As Morgan says, the Caliph probably did not appreciate the compliment. Hülegü founded his own kingdom. The line of

Abbasids as accepted heads of the Sunni Muslims was ended after five centuries.

–Richard Cavendish, *Baghdad Sacked by Mongols, History Today Volume 58 Issue 2*, February, 2008

"The most basic barrier was language itself, very few Americans in Iraq whether soldiers or diplomats or newspaper reporters could speak more than a few words of Arabic. A remarkable number of them didn't even have translators. That meant for many Iraqis the typical 19-year-old army corporal from South Dakota was not a youthful innocent carrying America's good will, he was a terrifying combination of firepower and ignorance."

–Dexter Filkins, *The Forever War*, Vintage Books, A Division of Random House Books, Inc., New York, 2008

Haifa Street, Karkh neighborhood, Baghdad, Iraq, May 9, 2008

Baghdad—anciently, *Madinat al-Salam* [Arabic: "City of Peace," a misnomer] has had a long and bloody history of attacks, being severely damaged and rebuilt, changes of governments and status, and religious trends. Nevertheless, the old city has persevered since 762 C.E. and had been the capital of Iraq since 1920. Through it all, Baghdad maintained a mystique and allure equaled by few of the world's cities. Many Muslims—especially fundamentalists–revere the old city as the seat of the last legitimate caliphate and others–more secular–as the cosmopolitan center of the Arab and Islamic worlds when they were at the height of their grandeur.

As Avery surveyed the outskirts of the capital city of Iraq, he pondered whether this time, the Islamic State would actually win, make it their capital, and condemn the population to a slavery under a hideous interpretation of Sharia law. According to Abu Bakr al-Baghdadi's interpretation, the new and lasting Islamic State–as based on the prophesies of Muhammad and his original friends; the world-wide mega-theocracy under Allah–would have its world headquarters in Baghdad when all the conquering was finished.

Avery looked at the map with colors designating the different entities in control of this part of the Baghdad Province. It was readily apparent that IS had taken over the key provinces around Baghdad City and—if not defeated in the upcoming campaign–would soon regain strength and return to control the northern two-thirds of central Iraq, and Anbar Province. Yes, he knew, coalition forces had just taken much of Diyala Province; but if history held true, it was certainly not impossible that IS would recoup and move right back into the position it had just vacated.

This would endanger Operation Iraqi Freedom and all that America, its allies, and the decent people of Iraq, had sacrificed so much for. He knew that the U.S. government had its head stuck in the sand and would not admit how puny the hold was on the gains of the recent victory. Given the wild history of Baghdad, it might well be that either al-Baghdadi or some other Mongol like Hülegü might spring out of history. Or maybe, Avery had been studying Baghdad history too much, he thought. The present U.S. military presence was stretched thin and was insufficient to retake the critical province of Anbar and to hold Diyala. The stakes resting on the impending attack on Baghdad could hardly be higher.

Avery and Dewayne were eating breakfast, talking very little, as each man made a quick inventory of his life, as men do before what might turn out to be their last battle. After the "dead-checking" incident, neither man wanted to be around SGM Rudi Tomlinson.

"You seem to be someplace else, Avery," Dwayne said. "What's up?"

"Probably something I ate last night. Didn't sit quite right. If I was out drinking, this would be a hangover…you know the feeling—just kind of crappy."

"I know the feeling—kinda like you know it's gonna be bad day when you wake up face down on the concrete."

"Yeah, that kinda thing. I'll shake it. Let's saddle up."

The battle for Baghdad was going to be the biggest yet in the Operation Phantom Phoenix operations. Plans included more than two thousand Multi-national Force Iraq troops from a dozen countries; and, this time, it was going to include five-hundred battle-hardened U.S.

marines. The four CIA agents, Dwayne, and Rudi, were assigned to be in the spearhead reconnaissance unit that made the first sortie up Haifa Street.

The choice of the Karkh neighborhood and Haifa Street came about from a specific request by the Iraqi Security Forces trying to achieve an IS free law-and-order condition in the capital city—a very difficult security problem. They were overwhelmed by the large force of insurgents who now controlled the principle throughway into the Green Zone. Haifa Street ran for about three miles through the center of Baghdad following the west bank of the serpentine Tigris River. Most buildings on either side of the street were high-rise apartments—many twenty-stories high—which meant that the planned battle zone would be in what amounted to a box canyon. The IS forces held the high ground above the "canyon floor" because of their positions on the roofs and top floors of the tallest buildings and their central location which gave a commanding view up and down the street and of the sky above.

They had a long established and fortified position which threatened the Green Zone. Their goal was eventually to defeat the Multi-national Force Iraq, to occupy Baghdad, and to recreate the 13th Century kingdom [caliphate] of Hülegü. Almost everything about the impending battle was in favor of the Islamic State. The buildings on Haifa Street constituted dominant urban terrain and were highly defensible. Abu Bakr al-Baghdadi had promised his soldiers that they need only hold out in order to prevail; since the Crusaders lacked endurance; they wanted it all to be over by Christmas. He made the promise just before taking a small security force and leaving for the Anbar Province, conveniently just before everyone else knew that the battle was about to commence.

The previous January, Iraqi troops on patrol in the Karkh neighborhood had discovered a fake checkpoint in the neighborhood, manned by insurgents in Iraqi Army uniforms. A brief but fierce battle took place; a small force of American soldiers was requested; and the combined troops killed thirty insurgents. The troops—satisfied that their work was complete—left only a token force of Iraqis to protect the site of the battle. During the middle of that night, insurgent commandoes returned to the far end of the neighborhood and dumped twenty-seven corpses of Shi'ites whom they had tortured, mutilated, and executed.

The day after the small American force left, IS returned; and the battle scenario repeated itself. The next chapter in the Haifa Street scenario found more significant American reinforcements–the 1st Battalion, 23rd Infantry Regiment–equipped with Stryker light armored vehicles, to join the battle as a strike force. The American numbers and materiel were insufficient for a major attack; so, they went around the neighborhood—staying close to the throughway to the Green Zone—eradicating one hotspot after another. It was highly unsatisfactory; everyone on both sides knew full well that all the Americans had done was to improve local force ratios temporarily.

Once again, Americans had to return later in the month. This time, a larger and better equipped force—code named Operation Arrowhead Strike III—entered the city and carried out "clear and control" operations dedicated to remove all enemy forces and to eliminate remaining forces of organized resistance—to maintain a physical presence in the neighborhoods to interdict any enemy return to utilize the area as a staging or defensive site.

A force of about 1,000 crack troops of the 1-23 Infantry Battalion joined forces with the Iraqi Security forces in Tala'a Square, on the north end of Haifa Street in the middle of the night. Together–after a brief but very violent skirmish–the Americans and Iraqi government forces occupied several strategic buildings and rounded up suspects. As this operation was taking place, the insurgents launched a pre-planned ambush and began firing on U.S. and Iraqi troops and their vehicles from well-hidden sniper positions on the roofs and the doorways of buildings. They coordinated mortar fire indicative of a surprisingly high degree of training, cunning, cohesiveness, and courage. Unlike previous skirmishes with insurgents using guerilla tactics, they continued to fight, rather than running away from American forces. In a serious mistake, the U.S. and Iraqi forces had not cordoned off the area before or during the fight.

The insurgents occupied temporary positions in successive buildings, then they moved swiftly and with considerable effect from building to building requiring the American and Iraqi forces continually to play catch-up, a less than favorable situation. The battalion from the Stryker Brigade called for close air support from Apache helicopters and F-18s, which targeted the snipers on the building roofs for three or four hours. The U.S. battalion on the ground fought for another nearly twelve hours. After dark settled in, the security forces—which had learned from their previous error–patrolled the area with heavy armored vehicles. Iraqi soldiers took over vacated positions on the rooftops. Almost miraculously, no U.S. troops were killed in action; and they killed fifty-one insurgents, and captured over twenty, including a number of foreign fighters who—under interrogation—supplied substantial military information.

According to intelligence obtained by Avery and his team of spies, insurgents had reinfiltrated the area again by late January, a scant two weeks after the 1-23 Infantry Tomahawk Battalion moved out, leaving the responsibility for security to the Iraqi government contingent.

A new and larger—and hopefully more definitive and long-lasting operation—was to take place on this otherwise pleasant day in May. The 1-23 Infantry therefore returned to clear the area of insurgents once again. Together, the units brought a large force of infantry—upwards of 3,000 men—four U.S. M1A1 tanks, 8X8 eight-wheeled IAV Stryker light armored vehicles, and this time, BFVs [Bradley Fighting Vehicles]–the more heavily armored fighting vehicles with tracks rather than wheels, to the fight. The fight this go around was planned to be more methodical and geared not just to win the day and to drive out the IS for a time. They intended to drive them away altogether and permanently.

The battle began with rapidly executed searches by RSTA Squadrons [Reconnaissance, Surveillance, and Target Acquisition units] and the 3rd Stryker Brigade Combat Team, 2nd Infantry Division outside of Baghdad which found and confiscated huge stockpiles. This action was followed by the CIA/ranger agents, Dwayne, and Rudi, being assigned to the spearhead reconnaissance unit that made the first actual sortie up Haifa Street from south to north. The spearhead consisted of two stripped down HUMMVEEs with eight men in each and an Apache and a Cobra combat helicopter overhead.

They moved as fast and as recklessly as possible, purposefully drawing fire to be able to pinpoint enemy positions. It was unnerving to listen to the pings and thunks of bullets hitting their vehicle's armored plates and not to be able to fire back except occasionally when they encountered a target they could hit on the run. With that, they were moderately successful. Dewayne made a record—a sort of 3-D map—of the high-rise buildings and the locations of enemy snipers and squads. At one point, something caused a fire at the rear of their HUMMVEE which brought on momentary alarm; but the flames died out of their own accord. They stopped in Tala'a Square, on the north end of Haifa Street and made a defensive position for themselves as they waited for the main force to meet them after a successful drive.

The amassed assault force consisted of Multinational Division Iraq North, five hundred 3rd Battalion, 3rd Marines, a fully Iraqi Army Brigade, 700 Iraqi police officers—seeking revenge–along with members of the 2-505th 82nd Airborne Division. The assault force included the full complement 1-23 combat division, 4,500 American support troops from the F.O.B. [Joint Base Balad], and a 3,000 man Shi'ite militia eager to demonstrate their loyalty and to exact revenge on the radical Sunnis, bringing up the rear.

The offensive assault was launched with a quick-strike air assault, with thirteen 155 mm Howitzer Field Artillery support. From the beginning there was an almost continuous Apache and Cobra attack helicopter presence, American and British close air support, and the fearsome Stryker and Bradley Fighting Vehicles. To military observers, it looked like a World War II set piece battle in microcosm; and the attackers meant business.

Firing from the armored vehicles was proving to be too dangerous; so, the commanders reluctantly ordered a dangerous and tedious alternative of moving from building to building floor to floor, and room to room, clear and control operation following the artillery and air assault first strikes. The din was deafening; the acrid smell of cordite smoke was sickening; the fear and apprehension palpable. For the predominately under age twenty-five-year-old young men, it was a terrifying, exhilarating, exhausting, and dehumanizing, experience.

They moved methodically killing, maiming, and executing, IS soldiers. It was a brutal "no quarter asked, and none given" exercise of inhumanity towards fellow men. Avery, Malcolm, Devlin, Dewayne, and Rudi, discovered a major weapons cache at Karkh High School and destroyed it—which also destroyed four adjacent buildings where IS fighters had established an ambush site, killing in all fifty-three insurgents.

During the inconclusive battles leading up to the major attack on the insurgency in June, 2,008, insurgents shot down six U.S. helicopters in a two-week period as part of a concerted strategy patterned after the AQ success in Afghanistan with Stinger missiles. Military intelligence documented that insurgents were increasing their attacks on U.S. helicopters and were well supplied with Iranian Misagh-1 SAMS–a knockoff the Chinese QW-1 Vanguard. Commanding General Odierno of the current attack had no intention of allowing a replay of IS successes. Heavy artillery, fighter jet rockets, and tank building buster rounds, were employed with shattering effect. As a result, only one helicopter crashed; and that was attributed to possible mechanical failure.

The assault moved inexorably south to north on Haifa Street towards the heavily defended Green Zone. Enemy losses were massive; coalition forces were losing a handful of KIA and WIA—serious and sad, but an acceptable loss of men considering the scope of the engagement and its importance. One Bradley fighting vehicle was destroyed by enemy rocket fire. A very large and deeply buried land mine exploded destroying a Stryker and killing all six American marines aboard.

Avery and his crew found an IS torture center in an old bank building about halfway up Haifa Street. They rescued twelve battered hostages and killed the torturers and their security detail with an average of fifty rounds per man. They considered the overkill to be justified under the circumstances. In the after-action report, Rudi Tomlinson was asked why he and his men put fifty rounds into each insurgent.

"Because we ran out of bullets," Rudi answered simply.

After eight hours of almost continuous fighting, the Multinational forces going from building to building found that they were discovering fewer and fewer insurgents still in the buildings and in the battle. Avery noted the same thing and came to a conclusion: the insurgents were retreating out of the back of the buildings. He had his men take hundreds of photographs of the exodus which was moving west in the direction of Anbar Province and the Euphrates River and northeast towards the wild areas along the border with Iran.

Raymond Odierno, the four-star Commanding General of III Corps was the overall commander and decision maker for the battle. His major priorities in order of importance were: protect the lives of American and coalition soldiers and marines, subdue and defeat the Islamic State insurgency in Baghdad once and for all, establish an effective and permanent security force of Iraqi Army forces, and to prevent further loss of massively expensive and important American war materiel, especially to prevent American arms falling into the hands of the insurgency.

He and his senior officers–relying on Avery's spies–decided that the battle was over at dark after the twenty-seventh day of fighting along a two-mile street. The Multinational Force slowly and carefully backed out of the war-torn street. A number of weary fighters gathered around their torn-up HUMMVEES to talk about what had gone on for the past month. Many were agitated and hyped up. Some looked like they might cry or had developed the thousand-yard stare; and some laughed and joked about their killing spree with the ultimate of machismo. All of them were covered with dust, fine sand, gun oil, and blood.

The force remained on Baghdad's perimeter for two weeks to discourage reentry by IS forces as they had previously done. Avery and his men ranged very widely around the province and found that there were only small pockets left, and that the bulk of the insurgency had moved on to al-Anbar Province, preparing to fight another day. Elements of the 6th Iraqi Army Division were assigned to patrol the sector of the battle, and they reported a satisfying state of calm with a cautious return of commerce, outdoor café gatherings, and resumption of haggling—the favorite sport of Arab men and women.

The security forces reported that there were almost no Shi'ites left in Baghdad; almost all of them had migrated south to the protection of the Mahdi Army under Iraqi Shi'ite cleric Muqtada al-Sadr, the Badr Organization, and Iran backed militias, including the Qods Force. Sadr City and the region south of Tikrit were strengthening the dominance of the Shi'ites with the liberal help of Shi'a militias like Hezbollah Battalions and League of Righteous Forces.

The U.S. government–in its wisdom–decided to provide Iraq with 140 M-1A1 main battle tanks. That had to be another one of those problems for another day. In fact, a large number of those tanks ended up under the control of Shi'ite militia or quiet Iranian control and were used against the Americans and its allies ten years later during engagements in the Syrian Civil War.

Avery wanted to return to Sinjar as soon as his duties were completed in Baghdad. While he waited, he shared his boredom with American soldiers and marines. They were amazingly candid and less predictable than one might have believed for young farmers from Iowa, ranchers from Utah, former gangbangers from Los Angeles, Chicago, and New York City, some born-agains from the old Confederate South states, current pot-blowers, and former heavy-duty illicit drug abusers from all around the country.

Once he established his bona fides as a brother combat veteran and as a brother-in-arms, Avery was able to ask probing questions. Many of the men were actually eighteen-year-old boys, who the previous week had been furious and relentless killers.

"What do you all think about serving here in the Middle East? Are we doing good?"

"Look," one eighteen-year-old answered, "I'm just a hick from Coeur de Alene, Idaho. I believed everything I was told about the righteousness of our bringing Christianity and the goodness of Jesus to these heathen Muslims. I volunteered. It didn't take me any time at all to learn that all this stuff out here in the desert is a big American lie and is as much a part of America as the IRS. I just want to do my stint and get out of here and back to my family and my girl."

Another one, a marine, said, "I would like to see real normal again. I hate to look in the mirror at myself and to realize that my feeling right now is that killing and eating dust and being abusive to people is what normal is. I remember a time when I didn't think that all."

"Since you mentioned abuse," a soldier interrupted, "I hate myself for what I've become, for what me and my buds have done. I had to kill people; but I know that most them were just farm boys like me, attended to their religion like I did. That doesn't bother me, doesn't make me ashamed nearly as much as how unfair and plain mean it all is. There are plenty of innocent people here, but we kick in the doors of their houses, point guns at them and terrify their children; we mock their religion, insult their women for wearing what they consider to be modest clothes, and generally go out of our way to treat them with dishonor. They value honor more than their own lives. We need to get out of here and leave them alone."

The next man continued, "Yeah, I'm gonna regret what I've done here for the rest of my life. I have nightmares."

A corporal took his turn, "It's a total waste. I read that we've had 4,000 guys killed so far in Iraq, and it isn't even near over. This is the fifth year of the war, and it's costing the American taxpayers twelve billion dollars a month…A MONTH!. My dad told me that so far in five years we have spent a whopping total of six-hundred billion—that's BILLION—dollars. I can't even imagine what a billion dollars would look like, let alone six-hundred of them. I'm from New Jersey; and I agree with my senator, Bob Menendez. He said something I wrote down, 'George W. Bush took us to war on the wings of a lie.' It's a big fat lie, I say."

Near midnight, an older sergeant commented, "I think war is tough, and all of you guys are tired and want to go home. I can see that. But, I'm gonna re-up. I still believe in America. The jihadi monsters here need to be stopped. You guys must not be reading about the atrocities, murders, rapes, and all of that the IS and all the other extremists are doing. I want to make a difference. I want to help, not just gripe and moan about myself. I tell you that I'd re-up just to catch the creeps who looted the treasures from the Baghdad Museum and are smuggling them out of the country to sell to rich sociopaths around the world."

CHAPTER SEVENTEEN

"Nevertheless, there are two groups of Muslims preaching tolerance in the West. First, many Muslims have grown up with Western values, and they prize freedom of speech and freedom of religion just as their Western neighbors do. Since these Muslims believe that peace and tolerance are to be prized, they assume that Muhammad must have prized peace and tolerance. Hence, when these Muslims read the *Qur'an* and the Hadith, they are drawn to Muhammad's teachings from the early Meccan period, and they ignore his more radical teachings. In other words, these Muslims really believe that Islam is a religion of peace."

–David Wood, *Nadir Ahmed, Jihad, and Taqiyya,*
Islamoblog of Acts 17 Apologetics,
Wednesday, January 9, 2008

"Terrify the enemies of Allah and seek death in the places where you expect to find it," he said. "Your brothers, on every piece of this earth, are waiting for you to rescue them."
Abu Bakr al-Baghdadi, audio message, *A Message to the Mujahideen and the Muslim Ummah in the Month of Ramadan,* article for *Huff Post* by Yara Bayoumy (*Reuters*), July 1, 2014

Hit [also Heet] City, Al Anbar [also Al-Dulaim] Governate, Iraq, September 29, 2008

Abu Bakr al-Baghdadi arrived in Anbar Governate on May the twenty-second with Iraqi Army forces close at his heels. The province was a decidedly unwelcoming place for the government, and they reluctantly turned back to continue the mop-up fighting in Diyala Governate. He sought out his people and immediately began to consolidate his power. He did not dwell on the battles going on in Diyala Governate, nor did he mention that once again he had escaped the scene of lethal action leaving his underlings in the crossfire.

"By God, the Merciful and Compassionate, we shall see the entire Anbar Governate under Sharia law and as willing subjects of the caliphate," he said. "We shall convene the *Majlis Shura al-Mujahideen fi al-Iraq* on the next day of prayer. Arrange it."

He was speaking to Sulaiman Abdullah al-Anbar, headman of the al-Sharayida clan and recently appointed military leader of the *Saray al-Jihad* Group. Family and members of the clan spoke to Sulaiman with something akin to reverence. He had never taken orders from anyone in his life other than his father who died young. He sucked in his gut, gritted his teeth, and replied with due deference.

"Yes, my Caliph. *Inshalah*, it shall be done. Do you want the rest of the tribal leaders as well?"

"Of course, Headman. All of them. It is time for them to know their leader and to learn their responsibilities. I fear that Sharia has been applied loosely here, and that must cease. The treatment of women is not proper, not proper at all. I see some as I drove by who wear only a scarf, an insult to the Prophet SAWS and his blessed family. You will see serious changes in the province, mark my words."

"I always do, Caliph. You are the caliph, the leader of the Islamic State—the emir–and the *Amir al-Mu'mineen* [Commander of the Believers]. I swear my allegiance to you and speak for the al-Sharayida clan and the *Saray al-Jahid* Group. By God, the Merciful and Compassionate and the Prophet SAWS and his blessed family, we will serve until all the world bows before you."

"Well said, my good and faithful servant. You will sit at my side in the courts of heaven, *inshalah*."

Headman Sulaiman Abdullah al-Anbar scheduled the important Sunni meeting on the following Friday, after *dhuhr* [noon prayers] in the Abdul al-Aziz al-Anbari Mosque. On the caliph's orders, Sulaiman had required worshippers to be checked for weapons before al-Baghdadi's sermon, which did not sit well with some of them.

Abu Bakr al-Baghdadi was the *khatib* who presented the *Khutbah* [sermon, address] that day by no coincidence.

He stood regally straight in the *minbar* and fervently intoned the *hamdala*, "*al-hamdu li'llāh*" [Praise belongs to Allah], as prescribed by tradition.

Since the *khatib* must be in a state of ritual purity; al-Baghdadi's formal black clothing was in accord with the prescriptions. He fidgeted from the delay of having to wait through the mandatory preliminaries: the *hamdala*, the *salawaat* [invocations of peace and blessings on Muhammad], the *Qur'anic* recitation, and the admonitions to piety and the *dua* [prayer]. The *Khutbah* is ordinarily brief, but al-Baghdadi had no intention of being brief. This was to be one of the key addresses of his tenure as caliph, and a necessary oration of his beliefs and intentions. He wanted to get on with it.

Finally, all attention was turned to the caliph as he started the *Khutbah*.

"To *ahl as-sunnah wa l-jamā'ah* [the people of the sunnah and the community]" he announced formally in his deep formal preaching voice.

The men gathered to hear him had been carefully selected. They included the most significant Sunnis in the only province of Iraq where Sunnis were in the majority over the Shi'ites: The tribal leaders of the Dulaim [the largest tribe in Anbar], the Zoba, the Al-Jumeilat, and Al-Bu Issa fighters were dutifully in their assigned seats.

Per al-Baghdadi's orders, Headman Sulaiman Abdullah al-Anbar had invited the notables, Abu Omar al-Shishani, leader of the JMA [*Jaish al-Muhajireen wal-Ansar*] who had been the first to swear an oath of allegiance to al-Baghdadi; and the heads of the six Sunni Islamic insurgent groups already taking part in the Iraqi insurgency against U.S., coalition, and Iraqi forces. They included the *Tanzim Qaidat al-Jihad fi Bilad al-Rafidayn* [al-Qaeda in Iraq]; *Jaish al-Ta'ifa al-Mansurah*; *Katbiyan Ansar Al-Tawhid wal Sunnah*; *Saray al-Jihad* Group; the *al-Ghuraba* Brigades; the *al-Ahwal* Brigades; the *Mutayibeen Coalition* consisting of MSC [Mujahideen Shura Council] There were six loyal Anbar Sunni tribes accounting for 300,000 members; and three smaller independent insurgent groups–the Shura Council of the Jihad Fighters in Iraq; *Jaysh Al-Fatihin* [The Army of the Conquerors]; *Jund Al-Sahaba* [The Army of the Companions]; *Kataib Ansar Al-Tawhid wal-Sunna* [The Monotheism and Sunna Brigades].

This was to be less a sermon and more a political and military address; however, no such communication could be given unless it was couched in Islamic religious language.

"Holy warriors," al-Baghdadi said and spread his arms wide to be all encompassing. "*Salam* to all of you, my brothers. It is my fond desire and responsibility to inform you that our hearts are with you, and for each of you to be patient and considerate, for victory is with patience, and ease with adversity. The greatest of the Sharia obligations in this time is jihad in God Almighty's path in order to support the religion of God the Exalted and save the *Ummah* from degradation and humiliation, and to establish the Islamic Caliphate–that obligation by whose absence the Muslims all sin on account of the words of the Messenger of God (SAWS).

"Praise be to God, the Merciful, the Compassionate and the Exalted. I have all praise for Him, as should all the brothers. I exhort you to make faith in Him, reliance on Him, and work to obey Him always and every day. I bear witness that there is no deity but God alone with no partner for Him in His lordliness, divinity, names, and qualities. He has no son, and no equal. Allah is the true complete witness by divine necessity and all meaning.

"And I bear personal witness that the Prophet Muhammad is His servant and Messenger who broke the capitalist system of profits and usury and democracy by his miracles. The Exalted one's signs appeared in the revelation of the great *Qur'an* and the *Mi'raj*: splitting of the moon, giving life to inanimate things. Even the pebbles know the glorification of God. Oh, Beloved God, bless Your servant and Messenger Muhammad— blessed and mighty is he–his family and companions, the people of truth and resolve in matters, and who went about straightening what was bent from the path, and making clear its customs and obligations. And may He grant many salutations on them. We are with you, oh our brethren in every time and occasion by the help of God–Blessed and Almighty is He; and we do not see the difference between our group and your group, our jihad and your jihad. We all proceed on the path of the Book and

Sunna; and our aim is to make supreme the word of God over the face of the Earth; and our desire is to seek the contentment of God–Exalted and Almighty is He.

"Oh God, we pray, destroy the usurping Jews, the hateful American Crusaders, the secularists, hypocrites and apostates, adulterers, and thieves, and those most abhorrent to God who in filth cling to the unnatural. Oh God, destroy them, for they cannot incapacitate You.

"Oh God, count them in number and assist us to kill them and send them into dispersal. We pray, thee O' Great God—and there is no other–do not let any of them escape. See to justice by burning the homes of the *muharibeen* [Christians at war]. Oh God, help us to destroy democracy, the foreign schools, and the rest of the houses of corruption, *ya Jabbar*. Oh God, tear up the man-made laws of *kuffar* and those who put them in place and implement them against the Muslims.

"Remember the sins of the Americans, the Europeans, and all Christians. *Ya Aziz, ya qahar*: oh God, defeat every government that does not rule by Your Holy Book and the Sunna of Your Prophet, oh Lord of the Worlds. Oh God, establish the Islamic State, and its development with the banner of Tawheed, and protect it through Your mujahideen servants, and make it beautiful with the Sunna of al-Mustafa, *ya aziz, ya hakim*. Lead us to heaven on the day of *Yawm al-Qiyamah, Yawm al-Din*, Day of Judgment!

"*As-salam alaykum wa rahmat Allah wa barakatuhu.* May God accept from us and from You the justness of deeds. May your *Eid* be blessed and your days be happy, *wa kull aam wa intum bi-khayr.*"

The men could no longer restrain themselves, and they began to cheer, "*Allah Akbar! Allah Akbar! Allah Akbar!*"

Caliph al-Baghdadi gave a small nod of his head to recognize the adulation being shown him. He did so with a demeanor of utmost humility.

When the near frenzy of spirit died down, al-Baghdadi moved on to business.

"We have come as the Islamic State to make real the purpose of the Shura Council: to manage the struggle in the battle of confrontation with the invading *kuffar* [infidels] and their apostate stooges from near to our world; we will unite the word and deed of the *mujahideen* and close with them in their ranks; and we will determine and share with you a clear position toward developments and incidents so that people can see things clearly and the truth will not be confused with falsehood, and *shirk*, and wrong thinking.

"All shall obey the Committee for the Promotion of Virtue and Prevention of Vice whose divine purpose with God's help is to enforce the strict Islamic code of the Wahhabis and the Islamic state. The council and the committee were formed to resist efforts by the American and Iraqi authorities to win over Sunni supporters of the insurgency. We shall be managing the struggle in the battle of confrontation to ward off the invading infidels and their apostate stooges. Be with us in uniting the word of the mujahideen and closing their ranks—let those ranks be our ranks, under God, the Almighty creator and conqueror.

"Be attentive and obedient as we determine the clear position toward developments and incidents so that people can see things clearly and the truth will not be confused with falsehood. From time to time, we will send you messengers with papers and word; so, you can always be of a right mind with God, with Muhammad, and with the Holy Caliphate.

"Together–under the orders of the Caliphate and the Sharia judges— we will stone the adulterers and even the accused adulterers, whip the drinkers of the demon alcohol, amputate the hands of thieves, and execute the vile apostates."

He paused, and the quiet was disturbed by more cheering. He raised his right hand for quiet; and the room fell silent, such was the power of his presence—a fact he did not take for granted.

Six masked men wearing white hoods and gowns entered from the wings of the mosque and stood in front of the assembled mujahideen.

Al-Baghdadi raised his voice saying, "These brothers represent us in an oath to the *hilf al-mutayyabin* [scented ones]. This is the oath:

"We swear by God almighty and the blood of martyrs that the Safavid army will not enter our city, our province, or our country, except over our dead bodies. We will give all we have and can do to implement God's sharia. We swear by God, the Almighty and Blessed One, to do our uttermost to free the prisoners of their shackles, and to rid or brother Sunnis from the oppression of the rejectionists [Shi'ites] and the Christian Crusader Occupiers, to assist the oppressed, and to restore all rights to the Believers even at the price of our own lives, to make Allah's word supreme in the all the world starting in this place and at this time, and to restore the glory of Islam. Let all tribal leaders and the brothers join the sacred

Islamic state to protect our religion and our people, to prevent strife and so that the blood and sacrifices of your martyrs are not lost."

Al-Baghdadi went through the written oath phrase by phrase and had the entire assemblage repeat each phrase after him. He ended with, "so help me, God."

The thoroughly aroused Sunni fundamentalist jihadis cheered until their throats were parched. They left the mosque rejoicing and began that very day to accelerate the work of God in Anbar Governate. Al-Baghdadi made himself busy with Allah's holy work with equal zeal. He met with the former Saddam officers and Ba'athist sympathizers. They provided IS with guns and ammunition looted from nearly a hundred munitions sites in the province. They acted as armed robbers to steal weapons stockpiles from local armories and police stations around the huge province. Sympathetic Ba'athists and escaped Saddam officials in exile around the world gladly sent in money to finance foreign insurgent soldiers. They provided safe sanctuary for the mujahideen in Anbar, throughout Iraq and the Middle East, and sometimes in Europe and the Americas. Anbar became a huge sanctuary and stockpile of materiel, food, and necessities for all anti-occupation holy warriors.

Avery's spy in al-Baghdadi's camp–Rahim Jamaluddin–kept him and the CIA apprised of developments despite the peril of his own life in so doing. His information was very sobering.

CHAPTER EIGHTEEN

Oval Office, White House, Washington DC, PDB [President's Daily Briefing], August 1, 2010

Meeting recorded and stamped "TOP SECRET, EYES ONLY; POTUS, Barack Obama; DNI, Dennis C. Blair; Secy. Of State, Hillary Rodham Clinton; Chairman of the Joint Chiefs of Staff, Admiral Michael Glenn Mullen

Present: POTUS, DNI, Secy. of State; CJCS; Army Gen. James N. Mattis, commander, U.S. Central Command; Army Gen. Raymond T. Odierno, commander, MNF-Iraq; Ambassador James F. Jeffrey, U.S. ambassador to Iraq; Joseph Lieberman (I-Conn) Chairman, Senate Armed Services Committee; Special Agent Avery Challenger, COS-I

Date: August 1, 2010

Subject: Establishment of a date for withdrawal of all U.S. military forces in Iraq

Summary:
Adm. Mullen-brief history of war in Iraq and troop deployments. Sirs, by way of bringing us up to date, this is a synopsis of U.S. Military involvement in Iraq to date:

- March 20, 2003–U.S.-led coalition forces invaded Iraq from Kuwait to oust Saddam Hussein. 125,000 U.S. and British soldiers and Marines were deployed.
- April, 2003—An additional 100,000 troops deployed to the invasion force.
- May 1—Then President George W. Bush declared hostilities to be over.
- February 22, 2006–Bombing of Shi'ite shrine in Samarra sparked widespread sectarian slaughter, raising fears of civil war.
- February 14, 2007–Prime Minister Nuri al-Maliki launches U.S.-backed crackdown in Baghdad aimed at pulling Iraq back from brink of civil war. Five U.S. combat brigades plus supporting troops–about 30,000 soldiers–sent to Iraq between February and mid-June 2007.
- June 15 - U.S. military completes its troop build-up, or "surge," to around 170,000 soldiers.
- From April to June 2007, 331 U.S. soldiers were killed, the deadliest quarter of the war for the U.S. military.
- September 10–U.S. commander in Iraq, General David Petraeus, recommended cutting troops by more than 20,000 by mid-2008.
- July 22, 2008–the last of five extra combat brigades sent to Iraq in 2007 were withdrawn, leaving under 147,000 U.S. troops in Iraq.
- November 17, 2008–Iraq and the United States signed an accord for Washington to withdraw its forces by the end of 2011. The pact gave the government of Iraq authority over the U.S. mission replacing a U.N. Security Council mandate. Parliament approved pact after negotiations 10 days later.
- Secy. Clinton—stated that her canvass of world leaders indicates near total agreement with expeditious total withdrawal.
- Amb. Jefferies—stated that the Iraq government is pressing for immediate withdrawal but asks for a force of advisors to be maintained in place until order is more fully restored.
- Gen. Odierno—troops are anxious to leave but fear reprisals against Iraqis who sided with the U.S. It is recommended that a phased withdrawal over the next year accompanied by continued training of the Iraqi army be employed.
- Spec. Agt. Challenger—IS is not defeated. They have moved to Syria, Lebanon, other Middle Eastern Muslim countries, and to Europe where they are recruiting soldiers and raising funding which

is effective. Withdrawal in less than a year will result in a massacre of minorities in the region including Christians, Yazidis, and Shi'ites, to name but a few.

- POTUS—Although I have previously said that we would withdraw U.S. forces by 2009--then revised that to 2010–I am now convinced that the complete withdrawal should be postponed until 2011. That is a final date. Lest it seem that politics or public opinion has influenced this decision, I hereby order all U.S. combat operations in Iraq to cease by August 31, 2010. All U.S. combat units will begin immediately to withdraw from Iraq's urban centers and to redeploy to safer rural areas until they are ordered to leave the country. There are currently 88,000 American troops still in the country. I also order 50,000 troops to remain deployed until August 31 for training, equipping, and advising, Iraqi Security Forces as long as they remain non-sectarian. Our troops will supervise but not participate in conducting targeted counter-terrorism missions and will protect our ongoing civilian and military commitments within Iraq. Thereafter, Iraq will be on its own. I wish it to be known that there has been far more than enough American blood and treasure expended in Iraq and the Middle East. The U.S. Congressional Budget Office reports that the cost of Iraq operations totals around $752 billion—a very conservative number–since 2003. Although estimates of casualties vary, somewhere near 111,000 violent deaths of combatants and between 184,000 and 206,000 violent civilian deaths. More than one in four U.S. troops have come home from the Iraq war with health problems that require medical or mental health treatment, according to The Pentagon. Forty percent of Iraq's middle class has fled the country. Mind you, these are only estimates; and the total numbers will probably be much higher before all of this is over. Enough is enough.

Signed:

Barack Obama, POTUS

"The American combat mission in Iraq has ended. Operation Iraqi Freedom is over, and the Iraqi people now have lead responsibility for the security of their country."

  –President Barack Obama, Speech in the Oval Office, August 31, 2010

CHAPTER NINETEEN

"The Battle of Fallujah was not a defeat—but we cannot afford many more victories like it.."
*—Keiler, Jonathan F., "Who Won the Battle of Fallujah?."
Proceedings. The Naval Institute, January, 2005.*

"The IS has fallen, but it will return just as the Taliban returned in Afghanistan after its defeat at the hands of the Americans. The American withdrawal from Iraq will be the time to act. When the Americans withdraw within two years…the situation will be strongest politically and militarily for the Islamic plan to prepare to completely seize the reins over all Iraq." They noted that other factions were planning to do the same.
—Mufakkirat al-Fallujah communique in Arabic to
worldwide jihadists, 2010

It [U.S. government] stopped short of a formal break in diplomatic relations with Syria but was considered a strong signal that Obama administration officials believe there is nothing left to talk about with Mr. Assad. Though more isolated than at any time in the four decades since Mr. Assad's family took power, the government was emboldened by the vetoes of Russia and China on Saturday of a United Nations Security Council resolution backed by Western and Arab states supporting a plan to end the bloodshed. The vetoes appeared to end–for the moment–any concerted diplomatic efforts.
*—Anthony Shadid, U.S. Embassy in Syria Closes as Violence
Flares, New York Times*, February 6, 2012

Damascus, Syria, March, 2011

For simplicity's sake, it is easiest to conclude that the trouble began in the impoverished drought-stricken rural province of Dara'a a few days before the commonly recognized date of the troubles. A teenage boy and fifteen of his friends in the city of Dara'a–were arrested by the security officers under President Bashar al-Assad's cousin Rami Makhlouf, for writing graffiti on building walls, "The people want the fall of the regime." There were protestors in the streets over the arrests, and security forces opened fire on them. Bashar al-Assad's Ba'ath government forces detained six of the boys.

There was an important juxtaposition of events occurring at the same time; a series of antigovernment uprisings were underway in various countries in North Africa and the Middle East. The tumultuous changes that began in Tunisia in December, 2010 were sweeping the Arab world a year before the protests in Dara'a. Protests in Tunisia became the Tunisian Revolution. It spread quickly to five other countries: Libya, Egypt, Yemen, Bahrain, and finally to Syria in what became known as "the Arab Spring."

Three CIA agents—Avery Challenger, Malcolm Fortner, and Devlin O'Malley were having a late brunch in the embassy patio with Robert Stephen Ford, the new U.S. Ambassador Extraordinary and Plenipotentiary, on a clear bright March day which promised to be a hot one. The hulking building including the large diplomatic compound was surrounded by high concrete walls topped with coils of razor wire. The embassy chef was renowned, and his brunch was a good example.

"These are troubled times, my friends," Ambassador Ford said, "enjoy a full Syrian breakfast while you still can. The vibes are that we may not be here much longer."

Waiters laid out a buffet on the large lazy-susan center of the mahogany table wafting the scents of centuries' worth of flavors starting in Turkey: *maghdoos* [pickled eggplant in olive oil], *labneh* [tart, strained yogurt eaten as a spread with olive oil and mint on the top], multiple types of cheeses and olives. The meal was intended to be a long course of bites, nibbles, and cup after cup of teas and coffees, to set the scene for hours-long conversation. The waiters set small trays of *mezza*, and pita bread, replaced with pastries later. On the lazy-susan there were eggs—both fried and hard-boiled—fresh vegetables, a variety of cheeses. This variety included the chef's special 'Syrian cheese'—a hard cheese placed into a dripping cup that shapes it, then salted—*foul mudammas* [a fava bean dip], *manakish* [pastry pies topped with *za'atar* and cheese], and *borek* [feta-filled phyllo pies].

Their conversation had hardly begun when a crowd began to gather, then to multiply, then to fill the upscale Mansour neighborhood from the major traffic circle to embassy row. The embassy sat back from Abo Jafaar Al Mansour and Ataa al-Aiyouby Streets, and the four men watched from their table set on the second story of the embassy. At first the gathered demonstrators were peaceful, but their faces were full of hate and vengeance.

They began to shout a choreographed slogan "*Ash-sha'b yurīd isqāṭ an-niẓām* [the people want to bring down the regime!].

Ambassador Ford asked the agents to remain in their seats as a show of courage and indifference to the rowdy crowd, to demonstrate that this was not an American issue. That rapidly altered as the crowd changed from chanters, to screamers, to enraged rioters. They began to throw rocks and pieces of brick into the compound. From somewhere, a few young men put up scaling ladders on the perimeter walls intending to enter. The marines repelled them.

"If we have to employ our marines, then, gentlemen, I guess it's time to retire to the smoking room," Ford said with an air of insouciance he did not really feel.

The CIA agents were not altogether taken by surprise by the angry demonstrators. Their assets in the entire Arab region where reporting similar outbreaks in Libya, Egypt, Yemen, Syria and Bahrain, in Morocco, Iraq, Algeria, Iranian Khuzestan, Lebanon, Jordan, Kuwait, Oman and Sudan. Regimes were toppling along with major uprisings and social violence taking place, including riots, civil wars, or insurgencies. Sustained street demonstrations took place or minor protests were occurring in Djibouti, Mauritania, the Palestinian National Authority, Saudi Arabia, and the Moroccan-occupied Western Sahara. The global situation was well beyond the usual five-day-news-cycle importance.

The sustained street demonstrations were obviously pre-planned and well-organized. The regime had to crackdown on rioting in the suburbs of Damascus, in a rugged northern region around the nearby town of Idlib, and in the sacred city of Homs. The newspapers—*Tishreen and*

Al-Thawra [official dailies], and *Al-Watan* [Independent daily] reported that the Khalidya neighborhood in Homs was one of the hardest-hit areas in Syria and the actions there the most vociferously condemned by the Assad government. By the end of the day, the violence had a name: "Syrian Day of Rage." The rage was given a symbol.

In Dara'a, a thirteen-year-old boy demonstrator was arrested by the intelligence services. Four days later, his body was returned to his parents at their home. It was photographed with all its evidence of torture—cigarette burns over most of it, and the boy's penis had been amputated. Publicly, Walid Bey Jumblatt, president of the Progressive Socialist Party of Lebanon described his conversation with Bashar after world outrage became a daily news feature. Jumblatt reported that Bashar denied the torture by saying that the boy's body was rotten; it just fell to pieces. Jumblatt asked President al-Assad if he had killed the boy, and al-Assad said, simply, "yes." The persona of mild-mannered former ophthalmologist and father of the citizens crumbled as his true, behind-the-scenes persona of the tough despotic murderer—like his father, Hafez, before him–was revealed.

The ambassador took Avery aside and ask him, "What does the agency think about all of this? Is it a flash-in-the-pan? or is it something that will last and be important?"

"I don't think we know a lot more than you do, Sir. What we do know is that it is very violent and not slowing down. It is bringing a lot of crazy groups out of the woodwork. The main difficulty is trying to figure out which of them will come out on top once this kaleidoscopic nightmare burns itself out."

"Who do you think will, Agent?"

"Like most revolutions, it is likely to be the most violent and the most ruthless—probably AQI or maybe even the IS which is gaining ground now that the U.S. has withdrawn all combat troops. They are gathering tons of donations and an amazing number of fresh recruits from all over the place, including the U.S."

"God save us if the final winners of this "who's-the-king-of-bunker-hill-I-can-fight-and-I-can-kill" are either of those bunches of fanatics."

"Amen to that, Mr. Ambassador. I remember that old game from when I was a kid. I remember a lot of bruises and scrapes and a few broken bones all around. We'll probably see plenty of that by the time the dust settles here in the wild west—Syrian west."

It was only a matter of days before declaration by the International Committee of the Red Cross on July 15, that the fighting had become so widespread that the situation should be regarded as a civil war—a severe calamity for a nation that was barely a hundred years old. Within days after that, it was clear to the entire world that the sporadic Syrian uprisings were an out-and-out full-scale civil war with foreign fighters from around the region and from widespread countries around the world joining in just as they had done during the Russian and Spanish civil wars. It was anyone's guess as to who was fighting whom, why, and for what.

Probably the most concerned and confused was the United States. President Obama was absolutely loathe to get involved. He took the position that the U.S. had always taken which was to oppose Bashar al-Assad and his totalitarian regime. What was difficult for him and his advisors was to which—if any—of the warring groups the U.S. should give support and aid.

Avery, his agents, and the Firm, had no serious difficulty with that decision. It was the Kurds, the only real allies of the United States in the region other than Israel. It was a diplomatic nightmare for Obama. Turkey was a sometimes and quasi-ally which had allowed U.S. bases to be established on its soil over the protests of the U.S.S.R. and the Arabs. He could hardly come to the aid of the Kurds, who were considered terrorists against Turkey. The official decision on the part of the government was to waffle.

Behind the scenes and in secret, the CIA sought out the Kurds and offered them as much aid as they could get away with. Avery began to reinforce his personal friendships with the Kurdish warlords and was able to establish working military relationships that held the Islamic extremists at bay out of mutual self-interest. His long time friend and agent-asset Behremend Rozaki proved once again to be most beneficial.

The three CIA agents were flown by Air America to a field in northern Nineveh Province where they obtained a jeep and provisions for a desert trip towards the Iraqi-Syrian border. Their goal was to reach Al Tanf, a border town a few kilometers from the Iraqi-Syrian-Jordanian tripoint. The intelligence coming to them from the area was sketchy, and they were unsure about whether IS had overtaken Al Waleed–the Iraq-side border town–through which they were going to have to pass. Accordingly, they loaded up serious weaponry as part of their provisioning.

They would have to cross the *Badiyat al-Sham*—[Syrian desert]–which accounts for half of the land mass of Syria–in late March. The land is open—lacking obvious landmarks–rocky or gravel-strewn desert hard-pack, largely devoid of plant life, and is cut with occasional nondescript wadis. It merges with the great Arabian desert and its ever-shifting sands. As a consequence of the inadequate and sparse grass, the agents were unlikely to encounter wildlife, except perhaps the golden hamster. It is not a place for the careless or the faint-of-heart because—in addition to its seemingly endless wars—it is inhabited by several tribes whose economy is based on banditry.

Avery and his agents had excellent topographical maps complete with good GPS listing. Their end-point was near 33.3747°N 38.7936°E. To get there, they had a several day jaunt across the middle of the desert—[the Hamad Plateau], a flat, featureless, uninviting, stony semi-desert. They were going to have to rely on their jeep's water supplies because the plateau receives very little rain, most of which flows uselessly into salt flats. There are no rivers or streams, ponds, lakes, or oases. The last water they would see was the Euphrates River, along whose banks IS held sway.

Remarkably, that stretch of desert is almost never hot. The recorded high temperatures rarely exceed, 87 °F, the lows 53°F, and the mean temperature is an easy to live in 70°. They made good time and conserved their water supplies until they reached the Hamad Plateau. They met roving bands of blue-masked Bedouin bandits who would as soon slit their throats as share tea. Four separate times they had to conduct running fights followed by two or three days of hiding in one wadi or another. Their water supplies were beginning to look quite low; so, they had to resort to rationing.

When they arrived in the high country around Al Waleed, their worst fears were realized. Not only would they be unable to replenish their water supply, but they might have to have a running battle with any number of Islamic State fighters who obviously occupied the town.

They stopped to reconnoiter.

"Okay, boss, this is what they pay you the big bucks for. What's the plan?" Malcolm asked with his patented wry smile.

"Good question, Mate," Avery responded.

He squatted on the rocky sand, templed his fingers on the bridge of his nose, and began to think.

Malcolm and Devlin recognized that this was not a time to interrupt Avery, because out of this kind of semi-trance, he usually came up with something worthwhile.

Three minutes later, Travis looked at his two comrades, smiled, and began to present his thoughts.

"We put on our IS black pajamas again and drive around the perimeter of the town. We stop to resupply our water wherever we can. If we get challenged, we tell the brothers that we are on our way to reinforce our comrades in Rojava Syria."

"Why Rojava?"

"It's not Al Tanf. Wouldn't do to let the brothers know where we're actually heading, now would it?"

Malcolm and Devlin shook their heads.

"If they press us, we can tell them that we are to meet up with some Hamas brothers in the Al Tanf Palestinian camp, who will go with us. It's enough of the truth to seem plausible, and not too much so that we seem to be laying it on too thick."

And if they don't buy it, or they don't like us that much, then what?"

"What we do best, I guess," said Avery knowing that he needn't explain.

"Lock and load, my friends. It's time to go."

CHAPTER TWENTY

KOBANI, Syria (Reuters). Almost three years after Kurdish fighters defeated Islamic State in the Syrian town of Kobani, residents still mourn the dead and feel abandoned by their foreign allies as they struggle to rebuild… But much of the town near the border with Turkey was destroyed, leaving it facing a huge reconstruction challenge and in need of help from the allies that had supported the fight to defeat Islamic State, including the United States.

Electricity still works only a few hours a day and regularly cuts out. The internet, using a Turkish communications signal, is expensive and unreliable.

That, local officials say, is because aid quickly dried up, and the town's problems could soon be replicated across parts of northern Syria as Islamic State cedes ground.

–John Davison, *Syrian town struggles to cope alone after key victory over Islamic State,*
Reuters *WORLD NEWS*, October 15, 2017

No Man's Land between Al Waleed and Al Tanf, Syria, March 28, 2011

Their beat-up old U.S. Army jeep was right in style among the hodge-podge of vehicles from Russia, Iran, Iraq, Syria, and the United

States. They paused long enough to steal an IS flag from among the hundred or so set up along the way—a rutted and seldom used back way–as it turned out. They proudly let it flutter from the right front bumper, like all the rest of the motor vehicles they saw. The masquerade held well until they stopped at a gasoline and water depot.

For reasons unclear to the agents, an IS guard—one of three—stopped them.

"Password, Brothers," he ordered.

The agents had dreaded having to manufacture an answer to that very question. Avery improvised, and Malcolm and Devlin held sweaty forefingers on handgun triggers.

"*Allah Akbar*, Brother," Avery ventured and held his gun at white-knuckled readiness.

"Not right. That was yesterday's," the frowning self-important guard—who was all of seventeen-years-old–declared haughtily.

"Sorry, we have traveled across the Hamad for the past four days. We have seen no one but bandits."

"Step out of the vehicle, Brothers. We will need your IS IDs and travel permits."

"Please, Brother, we are very tired and thirsty. Can you not provide gasoline and water; so, we can go on with our important work for the cause."

"Out of the jeep," the officious young guard demanded, abandoning any semblance of comradeship or courtesy.

Avery gave a shrug of resignation, nodded to his companions, then threw open the jeep door and placed a bullet between the young guard's eyes. Malcolm and Devlin dispatched the other two guards with one bullet each.

"Throw on two barrels of water and two of gas, and let's boogie," Avery ordered.

The barrels were fifty gallons steel drums and weighed a ton. It took all three men to muckle each one of the barrels into the back of the jeep.

Their hearts were beating over time, and their breathing was coming in short gasps from the exertion.

"Pray that nobody heard the shots," Devlin said soberly.

"Think we have time to throw the bodies somewhere, Boss?" Malcolm asked.

Avery took a second or two to look around then—seeing no one coming—said, "Yeah. Let's dump them in the trash and cover them up. Get a move on."

Each of the three hefted one IS corpse and carried him to the far side of the dump. There was abundant trash to cover them.

"Check for anything that might tell us the password or passwords. This isn't over."

Malcolm found a list of the coming weeks rotation of codes stashed with one of the guard's credentials.

"We're good to go, then," Avery said, and they jumped into the jeep and sped away as fast as they dared.

They saw more and more fighters the closer they got to the border crossing point. Most of them gave the CIA jeep the fish-eye, but no one challenged them until they were on the asphalt portion of the road leading up to the crossing stations. Two IS soldiers stood in the middle of the road with their AK-47s pointed directly at the jeep, a clear suggestion that the driver should stop.

"What to do? What to do?" sing-songed Malcolm.

All three knew that there was no way they could talk their way out of this one. Avery slowed the jeep down to a crawl looking for all the world like he was about to stop. The IS guards started walking forward towards them. The slow-down apparently indicated either that they were co-combatants, or that they were about to submit to IS justice.

Avery put the pedal to the metal and roared forward. The dumb-founded guards could not think fast enough to get out of the way, and the jeep got near identical dents in its two front fenders. The guards died.

The guards at the border lowered the barrier arm gates and dropped into defensive positions, their guns aimed at the oncoming speeding jeep. Since the jeep was not slowing down and had already killed two guards, the remaining border security officers felt no need to capture and imprison the anti-IS criminals. One of the guards dropped to one knee and aimed a heat-seeking RPG at the hurtling jeep.

"Incoming!" shouted Devlin.

Avery already had his right foot pressing against the floor. He began zig-zagging as quickly and sharply as he could without turning over. His mind was computing exactly where the jeep should be when the rocket reached their position. It was a fraction of a second kind of decision. He suddenly jerked the wheel hard to the right as the rocket roared by, its fiery tail throwing sparks all over the jeep, and the smoke that followed the flames obscuring the jeep's position for a few precious seconds.

The rocket missed its primary target, but its velocity and lethality were undiminished. Its computer locked onto the large troop carrier that was chasing the jeep. The driver might have made a similar defensive maneuver to the one executed by Avery; but, even if he had done so, it would have been to no avail. Turning that bulky old Russian BTR-152–essentially a Zis truck covered with five tons of armor–was slow and difficult under optimal circumstances. The truck had a turning radius the equivalent of a battleship. The RPG hit it dead center in the front windshield and penetrated three meters through the cab before exploding. That made fourteen less IS terrorists in the world to rape and pillage and murder.

Avery and his men did not have the luxury of enjoying their near miss. They came out of the rocket smoke within four meters of the barrier gate. Avery leaned out the driver side window and fired forward with his M-16 A1 rifle with the A2 configuration on full-automatic. Malcolm and Devlin leaned out of opposite side windows and fired their automatics in a mad-minute fusillade with only minimal aiming. They were so close to the security guards at the border post that they could have been shooting a shotgun. They mowed down the ill-prepared IS youths. The jeep was peppered so full of holes that it was nothing short of miraculous that it was still running, and none of its occupants was wounded.

Each of them took a fraction of a moment to thank his lucky stars, etc. for having just escaped another near miss—several hundred of them, as a matter of fact. Again, they had no time to savor the moment. They were now in the no-man's land between the two sentry gates. Despite the intel they had been given and upon which they depended, as soon as they crashed through the barrier gate, the first thing they saw was a building in Al Tanf with a huge Islamic State flag fluttering in the breeze from its top. That discouraging sight was compounded by the presence of several IS troops manning the Syrian side gate. Al Tanf was supposed to be in Syrian Army hands and–at this point–supposed to be on reasonably good terms with the U.S.

"I won't be able to pull another stunt like I just did again. We're toast," Avery said resignedly. "But, I don't know about you guys; I am gonna go down fighting and not spend my last days in an Arab torture chamber."

"Right on, Boss," Malcom and Devlin chorused. "We gonna stop and fight or have a suicide crash into the barrier?"

"I'll stop about three or four meters from the barrier gate. Be ready to jump out, take cover behind the jeep, and fire at will. We'll take down more of them than they do of us."

CHAPTER TWENTY-ONE

"In 1982, Albania held an election which Communist Party chief Enver Hoxha won by 1,627,959 votes to 1. A decisive victory. It suggested to me at the time a key to what political philosophers had long been seeking: a reliable tyranny index."

–Charles Krauthammer, article that discusses a Tyranny Index related to the margin of victory in an "election."

"A few weeks ago, the Tirana Index met yet another challenge. In the midst of a severe food and energy shortage, Romania held a referendum. The result: 17,699,772 Romanians voted yes, no one voted no. A shutout. A perennial contender for the honor of most repressive regime on Earth (in Romania, typewriters must be registered with the police) had conducted what may be the most perfect election yet."

– *Chicago Sun Times*, Jan 12, 1987

"Assad wins "election" with 97% of the "vote."
DAMASCUS, Syria, July 17: Syrian President Bashar al-Assad officially began his second seven-year term Tuesday. Assad, who in May won 97 percent of the vote as the sole candidate, was sworn in Tuesday in Damascus, *Alalam Satellite News* reported

–Elder of Ziyon, Tuesday, July 17, 2007

[Author's note: Walid Jumblatt, Lebanese Politician asked Bashar how it could be that he won the election by 97% when he was the only candidate running. Bashar replied, "It's because they love me."]

432

Al Tanf, Syria, March 28-30, 2011

They were brave men, but Avery, Malcolm, and Devlin were afraid to die. As soon as Avery skidded to a stop, they each jumped from the jeep, did a tuck and roll, and landed prone in a firing position. Before they could begin automatic firing, however, they became aware that the border guards were now facing away from them and towards the town. The first hint of what was going on came when the red, white, and green colors of the KDP [Kurdistan Democratic Party] flag beginning to show as a force of armored vehicles came steadily into view from the direction of Al Tanf. The heavily outnumbered IS border guards threw down their weapons and raised both arms above their heads as far as the arms could stretch.

"Kneel, *Kuffars*," a megaphone ordered, and the guards complied with alacrity.

Eight assorted kinds of troop carriers and one old M1-Abrams tank pulled up to the border gate and fanned out in a semi-circle.

One of the guards picked up a radio, and the peshmerga colonel shot him.

"Open the gate," the colonel said quietly.

The gate was opened.

The colonel gave a hand motion to invite the CIA agents into Syria. They hopped back into the jeep and moved promptly through and away from the Iraq-side border gate. Avery got out, came to attention, and gave the KDP colonel a stiff salute. It was returned with a more casual and friendly salute and a broad gap-toothed smile.

"Let me be the first to welcome you to sunny Syria, Avery, my friend," said Col. Behremend Rozaki.

Avery said, "My friend, once again you come to our rescue. Last time was on the Plain of Mosul. We are doubly grateful and indebted."

"Just part of the service," Behremend said.

He was one of Avery's prime assets in Iraq, and they had developed a warm personal relationship over the years of war.

"My intel was lousy, Behremend. We had it that Al Tanf was in Kurdistan control. The Kurdistan politicos told us that the KDP and the PUK put aside their differences and were working together. At least, the military wings are. How strong is the Islamic State? They're in the driver's seat here, it would appear. Give me your assessment, please."

"This is not the time or the place for a chitchat, Avery. The IS army will be here in strength in less than an hour. They would give a right arm to capture the two of us. Hop in one of the T18 Armored Personnel Carriers. They're old, but they're good. We need to get to the east before IS can break free a search and destroy unit out of their positions on the west side of the city."

The town of Al Tanf was now a besieged fortress with Iraqi Kurdish peshmerga fighters and moderate Syrian anti-Assad rebels moving west to east bombarding Islamic State positions on the east.

When they were settled in, Behremend gave Avery, Malcolm, and Devlin, more bad news.

"The battles in Kobani and Al Tanf—which seem to be going well for the Kurds and the U.S.—are being touted as big wins, but the news is biased and is deflecting attention from how well IS is doing in Syria everyplace else. The Islamic State just took over two big gas fields last week. It was a blow for Assad's Syrian Arab Army Forces. It was as much a psychological blow as it was a physical and economic loss. All of this happened because your Obama removed the U.S. troops too fast and too soon. It does not look good."

"All we can do is to concentrate on winning back Al Tanf for now. The big civil war will have to wait," Avery said.

"Yes, my friend, that is true. The militias and armies appear and disappear almost weekly, and their allegiances change about as often. All I can assure you of now is that Kurdistan stands with the United States. Please do whatever you can to get the U.S. to stand with us. We need boots on the ground, food, resupply, ammunition, guns, tanks, planes… you name it. I'm afraid that the peshmerga will go under and soon if Obama doesn't send us a big load of what we need. We cannot keep up with what Iran is supplying the insurgency in Iraq. Right now, it looks like they will move Hezbollah troops in to side with al-Assad; but who knows what will go on next week," Behremend said.

Behremend found foxholes behind a berm; so, the CIA agents could have some semblance of a night's sleep before joining the peshmerga in its next day of battle. Behremend, himself, repaired to his large and well-appointed tent and enjoyed his evening smoking Arguile and drinking strong Turkish Mehmet Efendi coffee.

Just before they went to their often-interrupted sleep, Malcolm commented, "Gentlemen, welcome to Syria, the Prophet's site for the Islamic State. God help us."

Dawn was rent by the first salvos of Kurdish artillery—only a few, because ammunition was scarce and precious. It was more than enough to arouse the CIA agents from wherever their dreams had been taking them. IS artillery responded—but, like the Kurdish attempts—was well short of the mark. Men scrambled from their makeshift beds, threw on their camo uniforms and boots, and mustered in front of the mess tent.

Col. Rozaki introduced his friends, the CIA agents, outlined briefly the day's attack plans, and shooed everyone off to a sumptuous breakfast, given the circumstances. The united PUK/KDP peshmergas recognized from the offerings of meat that this was going to be a tough day. The busboys ran around the mess tent serving from platters of lamb and chicken, flat bread, cheese, honey, sheep yogurt, hard-boiled eggs, and steaming glasses of sweetened black tea.

The colonel sought out Avery and invited the CIA cadres to come with him to the hilltop observation on the northwest side of Al Tanf. They watched the battle-hardened peshmergas running towards the direction of the firing.

"They are my pride and reason for going on," Behremend said.

He watched them through his binoculars, giving each agent a turn to get a good view of the battleground and of the developing battle.

"The goal is to retake the communications center this morning, and to retake the police station by mid-afternoon. We will take some losses in order to gain that much territory. Do you know what the word "peshmerga" means, Agents?"

"No, Sir," Devlin answered, "can't say we do."

"It means, 'before death' or 'those who face death.' These brave men take a certain well-earned pride in being so designated. They are my pride and joy, and it is an honor to lead them."

"And we salute you and them, Behremend. How can we help?"

"I hate to risk you, Avery."

"We are risk takers, but it is true that our main mission is to gather useful intelligence. In this case, I think we need to get into the thick of it to be able to assess the sources of threat, the level of resistance, and the capacities of the enemies. Frankly, we need to know which group is friend? which is enemy? and which is frenemy?"

"Frenemy," echoed Behremend with a low chuckle, "that is a good term in a place with such shifting allegiances."

"Point out the police station, Colonel," Avery put the question formally to make it a professional query.

Behremend drew a hasty diagram in the sand.

"This is the main avenue in Al Tanf. It passes in front of the police station about here. The intersecting street is called, "8 March, 1963 Street" which is Revolution Day to commemorate the take-over of Syria by the Ba'ath Party."

"Not quite so popular nowadays, I guess," Avery commented.

"Right. The main avenue is named simply, '1946' in honor of the year Syria officially became an independent country—maybe the only thing Syrians can mutually honor in these troubled times.

"If you are really hell-bent on becoming a peshmerga, then now is the time to do it while most of the enemy's attention is focused on our attack around the communications center. You don't have to do it, you know."

"Consider us volunteers."

"Do you know the American army mantra, Colonel?" Malcolm asked with a smile.

"No, what is it?"

"Salute everything that moves; paint everything that doesn't; and never, never volunteer!"

Behremend laughed, "But you do anyway."

"It's in our DNA," Devlin said, "so, give us some pointers on how to get to the police station."

"Walk carefully down the hill. Mind the flagged path to avoid mines. At the bottom of the hill walk over to that small mosque and follow the alley out to 1946 Street. Head southwest towards the wrecked area of town. You can't miss it."

They all laughed.

"Keep your heads down and hug the walls. Slip into alleys. Look all directions for enemy positions, including up. When you get to '8 March, 1963 Street, you are looking at the police station. It will probably be heavily guarded unless they have released some of the garrison to come this way to defend the communications building."

"Aye, aye, Sir," Avery said, and hefted his backpack and the carrying strap of his M-16 A1 rifle over his right shoulder. "Off we go, you new peshmergas," he said to Malcolm and Devlin.

CHAPTER TWENTY-TWO

"Terrify the enemies of Allah and seek death in the places where you expect to find it," he said. "Your brothers, on every piece of this earth, are waiting for you to rescue them."
Abu Bakr al-Baghdadi, audio message, *A Message to the Mujahideen and the Muslim Ummah in the Month of Ramadan*, article for *Huff Post* by Yara Bayoumy (*Reuters*), July 1, 2014.

"Men never do evil so completely and cheerfully as when they do it from religious conviction."
–Blaise Pascal, *Pensées [Thoughts]*, Published posthumously as *Pensées de M. Pascal sur la religion et sur quelques autres sujets*, 1670.

Al Tanf, Syria, April 4, 2011, morning

The three agents gingerly made their way down the rocky slope. Scree made the going tense, because frequently flat rocks slipped out from under the men's feet, knocking them off balance. The mine-free path was well marked and zig-zagged down the hill. There were no plants that might provide shade or cover. It was already hot, and the three broke into light sweats in the first fifty meters.

Apparently, they were not seen by IS fighters or sympathetic towns-people before they got to the alley by the mosque. An older lady–bent over from the kyphosis of osteoporosis so common in the poverty-stricken areas of the country—stepped out of her back door and into the alley as the agents reached the mid-point.

Avery put his finger to his lips and gave a little friendly nod. The *alsayidat aleajuz* [old lady] looked at the three men with interest but with remarkably little fear. She gave them a toothless smile of welcome.

"*Sabah el khair* [good morning]," Avery said in his softest and most pleasant voice.

"*Sabahu An-Nur*," she replied and shuffled back into her house.

"Think she'll rat us out?" Malcolm asked matter-of-factly.

"Color me an optimist, but I don't. I think these citizens have probably had enough of the kindly Islamic State treatment and think of us peshmergas as liberators. Besides, this is more-or-less Kurdistan country."

"We'll see."

Devlin was walking point when they came to '1946' Avenue, a rather grandiose name for a dusty rutted one lane road. He put his head out and looked each of the three ways, then ducked back in.

"Looks clear, Boss."

"Okay, I'll go first," Avery said, and moved quickly out onto the street hugging the dun brick wall.

Nothing happened; so, the other two followed him. They moved in quick bursts, ducked into every alley, and waited a minute or two to see if anyone was following or putting the barrel of a sniper rifle out of a broken window.

The first shot in anger came just as they got to 8 March, 1963 Street. It was of some little comfort to see that the street sign was written in Arabic and Sorani Kurdish. A sniper dispelled that miniscule bit of joy. The bullet ricocheted off a mud brick a meter about Malcolm's head, and the agents flattened themselves on the ground. It was the only shot fired.

Avery elbow crawled to the boardwalk and quickly over to cover behind a dumpster. He peaked out briefly enough for safety but long enough to see the glint of a gun barrel from the rooftop of the police station.

He spoke in *soto voce*, "Malcolm, go around the block and come up on the rear of the police building. See if you can find a fire escape to get to the top. Get rid of the sniper on top. We can't do anything useful with him there."

"Copy that," Malcolm said.

It took almost an hour—a tense and sweaty one—until Avery watched Malcolm dispatch the IS sniper from behind. He gave a thumbs-up signal. The station windows were boarded up, and they could not see any movement; so, Avery and Devlin made a mad dash across the narrow street and rolled to their knees in front of the door.

"Now what, Boss?" Devlin whispered.

"Malcolm will try and find a way in from the back. Let's wait about ten minutes to give him a chance, then we'll knock a hole in the boards over the window and toss a couple of grenades in. Any better suggestions?"

"Nope. Your plan seems good as any."

Devlin knocked a hole in one of the two front window plankings with the butt of his rifle. Machine gun fire poured out through the hole and through the planks, largely destroying them. Devlin reached up from his one knee down position and banged another hole, this time between a mass of machine gun bullet holes. Despite the automatic fire, Avery flipped off a grenade's clip, counted four seconds, then lobbed it in through the larger of the two holes in the window's cover. The CIA agents rolled away from the building as fast as they could for the remaining two seconds; and the grenade exploded, blowing the front of the building away. Among the debris were several body parts. Inside the station, the agents could hear coughing and some moaning. A few seconds later, the distinctive sound of an M-16 A1 rifle sounded from behind the main room. Then there was silence.

"Malcolm!" Avery shouted.

"Yeah, Boss, all clear."

He said it so deadpan that both Avery and Devlin started to laugh.

"Street seems clear, too," Avery responded.

"C'mon in, the air's foul," Malcolm said.

Avery and Devlin climbed through the hole in the front wall of the police station and into the acrid smell and fog of cordite smoke.

Avery coughed a few times then said, "Probably safer than hanging around outside."

"I'll go upstairs to see if there are any boogeymen and to see if I can find any coming from the streets around us," said Devlin.

The staircase was still architecturally sound but had some missing steps, balusters, and a splintered guard rail and base rail in two places. Devlin moved cautiously with his finger on the trigger of his rifle. Then, he quick-stepped onto the second floor and moved swiftly, throwing open doors and making a cursory check.

"Clear," he yelled.

"We got six bodies, more or less," Malcolm said.

Avery called up to Devlin, "Post yourself at the window. We'll checkout this main floor and the basement below. Yell if you see something."

"Avery," Malcolm said, "We either have to get outta here PDQ or get reinforcements. Let's call Col. Rozaki."

"I thought of that, but my coms aren't working—just static."

Malcolm tried as well and came up with nothing as well.

"I'll go up to the top of the building and see if I can get a line-of-sight with the hilltop. Should be clear up that far."

Five minutes later, he returned and informed Devlin, then Avery, what had transpired.

"Talked to Rozaki, himself. The cavalry's on the way. We are to hold out until we have enough peshmergas to hold the building, then we can go make mischief someplace else."

Devlin took the stairs three at a time to report that he was seeing a few IS soldiers coming along both 1946 and 8 March, 1963 streets.

"They don't seem to be in any great hurry, and there aren't very many of them."

"Keep me posted, Devlin. Malcolm, give the colonel another update. This is likely to turn hinky pretty soon if we have to defend this place all by ourselves," Avery said.

Devlin reported a full platoon of insurgents coming down 8 March. No sooner had he made his report than a second large platoon headed towards their building from 1946 Street.

"Okay, guys, prepare for a hot Mexican standoff. We need to buy time."

"And not get killed while we do it."

Two IS soldiers appeared at the hole in the front wall. The agents shot them and made the others think better of marching single file to their deaths.

Someone out there tried and failed to start the old stone building afire, but to no avail.

"It's sweaty. And I don't mean the 86°ambient temperature," griped Devlin.

A grenade rolled through the hole in the wall and exploded in the middle of the floor on the main floor. The three agents were watching from the second floor. Black pajama clad men began to rush into the main room and trying to clear the smoke. Before they could get their bearings and the necessary visibility, the CIA agents opened fire and decimated the platoons. A man—presumed to be the last survivor—began crawling towards the hole in the wall. He was dragging his right leg and was also bleeding from his left arm. He was struggling.

"Should I shoot him, Boss," Devlin said, hoping fervently that he would hear a 'yes.'

"No, he's worth more to us alive. His squad has to slow down to treat their man. And, besides, he can spread the good word that this place is not safe for the them."

Ayatollah Ali ibn Abu Bakr, cautioned his unit of Hezbollah fighters against moving in.

"We will be picked off like ravens trotting into a tunnel. We can always come back. They know they can't leave. It's too unsafe. Let's go around and come in back of the communications center. They'll never know what hit them," the Ayatollah said.

The best laid plans of mice and men gang aft agley…

Within five minutes of walking away from the police station, the two platoons of Party of Allah insurgents met with twice as many Sunni peshmergas coming towards them down the main road as the Iranian contingent had to protect themselves. The commanding Ayatollah ordered a speedy retreat. Several fell from rifle wounds, but the main body of the platoons made it to safety. The peshmergas relieved the CIA agents and proceeded to fortify the police station as a peshmerga stronghold.

Avery, Malcolm, and Devlin made an indirect and circuitous traverse of the city back towards the battle underway at the communications center. They surprised three separate IS squads with their backs to them who were firing at attacking peshmergas. They engaged in brief sequential firefights and killed eight or nine insurgents to secure their way to the battle lines near the communications building.

Col. Rozaki was there directing his peshmerga fighters and was glad to be reinforced by the CIA agents. The fighting continued until it was too dark to be sure they wouldn't kill each other; so, the peshmergas made a carefully planned retreat. The battle had proceeded to a lethal draw and would be fought again another day.

The day's fighting was not a failure, however. The peshmerga and Syrian Arab Army had pushed the insurgents six streets further east and into a narrower defensive zone in the city. The insurgents did not have the capacity to attack; so, they would just have to wait for the inevitable. Capture of the police station created a strong base within the center of the city from which to launch tomorrow's attacks.

The entire battle lasted a full month and resulted in Assad's Syrian government resuming control. What disturbed Avery was the presence of several platoons of very unfriendly Russian Red Army troops who reinforced the Syrians. Northeast of the city, several MIGs landed and made a home base there. The CIA agents were now persona non grata and left in the night to move farther north into the Syrian Desert to see if the Al Tanf example was what was to be the order of force in the country.

Avery was able to radio-phone to the ODNI, Washington. The DNI, Lt. Gen. Jim Clapper, himself talked to his COS-Iraq.

"Come back here, Avery. Bring your agents. They deserve some R&R. We have to have a rethink with the president. We have to decide who's on who's side, who we're going to support, if anybody, and what official and even unofficial U.S. policy should be. Get here as soon as you can. Call me for any help, you need. We have to be right on this, Avery. This is not for public consumption, obviously, but we're floundering at the moment."

It was going to be a daunting task. Avery knew that.

CHAPTER TWENTY-THREE

Oval Office, White House, Washington DC, PDB [President's Daily Briefing], April 18, 2011

Meeting recorded and stamped "TOP SECRET, EYES ONLY"; POTUS, Barack Obama; Director National Intelligence, Lt. Gen. James Robert Clapper, Jr.; Secy. of State, Hillary Diane Rodham Clinton; Secy. of Defense, Robert Gates; Chairman of the Joint Chiefs of Staff, General Martin Dempsey

Present: POTUS, DNI, Secretary of State, Secretary of Defense, CJCS, Special Agent, COS-I [Chief of Station, Iraq], Avery Challenger

Date: March 28, 2007

Subject: The conundrum of Syria

Summary:
- Secy. of Defense and Secy. of State—deferred to DNI, and CJCS. We have made a study of the current and evolving situation in Syria. We have consulted foreign allies, all military departments, professors from Yale, Harvard, UCLA, and Stanford, to formulate a cogent presentation, Mr. President. In the past, presidents have sought

to overturn regimes in Syria for various reasons and have publicly pronounced "red lines" over which our enemies must not venture. For all of that, Syria remains an enigma and a conundrum—one we must at least come to understand if not truly conquer. Our data have been reviewed by our premier asset in the field, COS-Iraq, Avery Challenger. He will present the current and most up-to-date information available with the slant his personal experience affords.

- COS-Iraq: The situation in Syria is confoundingly complex, conflicting, and in constant evolution. Today's enemies are tomorrow's friends, and who and what the United States should support or fight is becoming increasingly unclear. The study referenced by the DNI divides the belligerents according to its supporters as of this week. This is a summary; and it is probably incomplete, and will likely change next week:

- Syrian Arab Republic and allies: SAA [Syrian Arab Army, official al-Assad Government of Syria, Armed Forces—including a mix of volunteers and semi-organized local militias], NDF [National Defense Force, made up of several salaried militia forces], "*Lionesses of National Defense*" [NDF women's wing which operates checkpoints.], Syrian Christian Militias, Shabiha [unofficial pro-government militias drawn largely from Syria's Alawite minority group], *Jaysh al-Sha'bi* [organized official militia, with assistance from Iran and Hezbollah], Hezbollah [sometimes fighting with and sometimes fighting against extremist Sunni Islamists], Iran Army and Revolutionary Guard [including Lebanese Hezbollah fighters backed by Tehran, battlefield support forces, and Islamic Revolutionary Guard Corps Quds Forces in charge of President Assad's security portfolio and oversees the arming and training of thousands of pro-government Shi'ite fighters], Foreign Shi'a militias [including Shi'a fighters from Afghanistan and Pakistan which are far more numerous than Sunni non-Syrian fighters. For example-*liwa' fatimiyun* [Fatimiyun Brigade of Afghanistan], and Pakistani *liwa' zaynabiyun* [Zaynabiyun Brigade], and Russia [a bit confusing because a Russian general joined to represent Russia at the joint information center in Baghdad set up by Russia, Iran, Iraq, and Syria, to coordinate their operations "primarily for fighting IS" (Islamic State)].

- Syrian opposition and allies: Syrian National Coalition and Interim Government, Free Syrian Army and affiliate groups, Syrian National Army, Syrian Salvation Government [alternative government of the

Syrian Opposition seated within Idlib Governorate], YPG [Kurdish People's Protection Units], Syriac Military Council Islamist militias independent of IS and other Salafist forces, and the SNC [Syrian National Coalition, formally, the National Coalition for Syrian Revolutionary and Opposition Forces—recognized as the legitimate government of Syria by numerous Persian Gulf states], Syriac Military Council; United States of America [$123 million in nonlethal aid to Syrian rebels through FSA, reportedly, the Free Syrian Army was joining an alliance and common front with Kurdish militias including the YPG to fight IS], and Christian militias [such as Khabour Guards, Nattoreh, and Sutoro].

- Salafist factions [frequently shifting alliances]: Al Nusra Front, Islamic State, Ahrar ash-Sham, Suqour al-Sham Brigade, Al-Tawheed, Faylaq Al-Sham—a coalition of Muslim Brotherhood-linked rebel groups—and Suqour al-Sham Brigade.

- Rojava [The Autonomous Administration of North and East Syria (NES), is a de facto autonomous region in northeastern Syria]: Syrian Democratic Council, Syrian Democratic Forces, U.S.-led coalition against ISIL [ISIS, AQI, AQ, IS].

- Foreign involvement: TFSA [Turkish-backed Free Syrian Army, a group of defecting Syrian Army officers. TFSA'S main interest is to occupy northern Syrian land, bordering Turkey, and attacking the SDF and Kurdish people, including those fighting IS]; the Combined Joint Task Force, set up by the US Central Command to coordinate military efforts against ISIL pursuant to their collectively undertaken commitments. Those who have conducted airstrikes in Syria include: the United States—especially under the aegis of the CIA which affords certain Syrian rebels training from the CIA and Special Forces at bases in Qatar, Jordan, and Saudi Arabia, at a cost of a billion dollars a year. Sunni states—most notably Turkey, Qatar, and Saudi Arabia, are contributing more than three billion dollars a year—Australia, Bahrain, Canada, France, Jordan, The Netherlands, the United Arab Emirates, and the United Kingdom. Both the Syrian government and the opposition have received support—militarily and diplomatically—from foreign countries leading the conflict to be accurately described as a proxy war. The major parties supporting the Syrian Government are Russia—including the GRU—Iran, and Hezbollah. The main Syrian opposition body–the so-called Syrian coalition–receives political, logistic, and military support from the United States, Britain, and France. Some Syrian rebel groups are—from time-to-time–supported by Israel and the Netherlands. The Islamic State–with more than 3,000 foreign jihadists–receives private donations from the Gulf states. The Shi'ite militia of Iraq, Mahdi al-Harati, has joined the opposition in defiance of Hezbollah; and radical Sunni groups have entered Syria to oppose al-Assad.

- Former Belligerents: several tens of thousands of defectors ± involvement on either or both sides depending on shifting circumstances.
- Not to belabor the point, Mr. President, but the complete study lists several hundred more separate groups, which probably makes this the most complex–even kaleidoscopic—civil war in history. I must conclude with a partial list of confounding factors:
- The Shabiha is a notorious Alawite paramilitary, who act as unofficial enforcers for Assad's government. They are referred to as "gunmen loyal to Assad."
- The leader of the FSA has acknowledged that the rebel opposition is badly fragmented and lacks military skill. He acknowledged to our CIA operatives having had common operations with Islamist group Ahrar ash-Sham but denied any cooperation with Islamist group al-Nusra Front.
- The Islamic State has stated that many of the FSA members who had been trained by United States,' Turkish, and Arab, military officers were actually redefecting and joining IS.
- After the Russian intervention, many fighters defected to other rebel groups–including the Democratic Union Party–left in 2011 to join the Kurdish National Council.
- Relations among Syrian political opposition groups are generally poor. The Syrian Revolution General Commission, the Local Coordination Committees of Syria or the Supreme Council of the Syrian Revolution, oppose the NCC calls to instigate dialogue with the Syrian government. The NCC [National Coordination Committee for Democratic Change] is an opposition bloc consisting of thirteen left-wing political parties and what they call "independent political and youth activists" with ± violent activity.

- The Mujahideen's strict religious views and willingness to impose sharia law disturbed many Syrians. Some rebel commanders have accused foreign jihadists of "stealing the revolution," robbing Syrian factories, and displaying religious intolerance in the extreme.
- The al-Nusra Front renamed itself to JFS [*Jabhat Fateh al-Sham*] and later became the leading member of HTS [*Hay'at Tahrir al-Sham*]. The implications are unclear.
- Our CIA informants tell us that the IS has not been targeted by the Syrian government "with quite the same gusto" as have other rebel factions. IS fights more battles against Turkish-backed rebel groups, SDF [Syrian Democratic Forces—an alliance of mainly Kurdish but also Arab, Syriac-Assyrian, and Turkmen militias] For a time, IS supported the al-Assad regime which was remarkably tolerant of them. Currently, IS is approaching a control of almost a third of Syria. IS is clearly now the dominant force of Syrian opposition. It has defeated Jabhat al-Nusra and now controls most of Syria's oil and gas production—a situation that al-Assad cannot tolerate and have his regime persist. Nor can the U.S. tolerate it because it will fuel the terrorist activities of the group for as long as we can project.
- Some Syrian rebels signed a non-aggression agreement with IS in a Damascus suburb because of their inability to deal with both IS and the Syrian Army's attacks at the same time.
- The Syrian Democratic Council was intended to be the political wing of the Syrian Democratic Forces originally. The council includes more than a dozen blocs and coalitions that support federalism in Syria, including the Movement for a Democratic Society, the Kurdish National Alliance in Syria, the Law–Citizenship–Rights Movement, and the Syria's Tomorrow Movement—all ostensibly non-military entities. However, the SDC is actively engaged in the shooting war against al-Assad.
- Generally opposed to the al-Assad regime, *The Female Protection Forces of the Land Between the Two Rivers* is an all-female force of Assyrian fighters in north east Syria fighting IS alongside other Assyrian and Kurdish units.
- Some members of the Joint Task Force are involved in the conflict beyond combating IS and at times actively assists IS: Turkey fights against Kurdish forces in Syria and Iraq as a priority, and CIA reports

indicate that they collaborate on intelligence operations at times. The DIA [Defense Intelligence Agency] and the Joint Chiefs of Staff in a secret memo stated that Turkey has effectively transformed the secret U.S. arms program to support of "moderate rebels"–who no longer exist–into an ill-defined program to provide technical and logistical support for all elements of the opposition, including Jabhat al-Nusra and Islamic State.

Such is the state of affairs in Syria, Mr. President. I regret having to convey such intelligence to you and add to your burdens.

POTUS: Thank all of you for your careful and thorough work. Frankly, I don't see the Syrian situation to be as much of a problem or conundrum as you or the nation's press does. This is not our war, any more than the Iraq situation. We are going to exit. I do not see the Islamic State as much of a threat to us, despite their murderous program in their own area. With regards to Bashar al-Assad and his Syrian Army, I will say just this: the use of chemical weapons is a "red line" for me that will prompt military intervention by the United States. Our issue from the beginning has been to see that Bashar al-Assad and his terrible family are ousted; so, Syria can rejoin the family of nations…so we can have peace. I was not awarded the Nobel Peace Prize for nothing. It was because it is one of my two most important issues and hopefully my legacies: Peace in our time, and a sensible approach to conservation, global warming, and the like. That way, we can rejoin our allies, be apologetic for our war crimes and willing to be real friends. We do not need to be the world's policemen, and we don't want their oil. We want peace. Russia and China vetoed a U.N. Security Council resolution last year that would call for an immediate halt to the crackdown in Syria against opponents of Assad. So be it. We will back off. Make peace your goal. Back off from the belligerents—I don't want to hear any more talk about, "extremist Islamic or Muslim jihadi terrorists"—it is inflammatory; let them destroy themselves if they must. It is not our war; we have more important issues to deal with.

Signed:

Barack Obama, POTUS

CHAPTER TWENTY-FOUR

"Sember Occultus."—Always Secret.
–Motto of the SIS [MI-6, British Secret Intelligence Service]

"It's part of a writer's profession, as it's part of a spy's profession, to prey on the community to which he's attached, to take away information–often in secret–and to translate that into intelligence for his masters, whether it's his readership or his spy masters. And I think that both professions are perhaps rather lonely."
–John le Carre, *John le Carre Quotes. (n.d.). BrainyQuote. com., from BrainyQuote.com Web site: https://www.brainyquote.com/quotes/john_le_carre_471074,* May 21, 2019

Caravanserai near The Citadel, Aleppo, Syria, July 19, 2012

A very and his two spy companions walked from the old caravanserai where they were staying for a week or two to observe the level of disturbance caused by the civil war in Syria's largest city, Aleppo. The city was controlled by Bashar al-Assad's SAA [Syrian Arab Army], and law and order were fairly well maintained. The CIA agents were dressed as Afghan traders [loose, long-sleeved shirts reaching to the knees, baggy dun colored trousers with a drawstring at the waist, and *chapans* [long quilted robes] despite the dry heat of the day. They had on well-made heavy-duty shoes–a luxury—for most rurals, which set them apart from country bumpkins. Their head coverings were heavy turbans which—along with their heavy beards–obscured their faces better than the more common skullcaps or Afghan Caps.

They sauntered into the old city of Aleppo and made their way to the Al-Madina Souq where they browsed around the labyrinthine alleyways. They stopped at a tobacconist's shop where they talked rather more loudly than usual, haggling, telling jokes, and sharing plum juice. To passers-by, it did not look out-of-the-way for the men to adjourn to the back room, presumably for more serious business talk.

The hail-fellow-well-met façade was dropped as soon as they were out of sight and ear-shot of the teeming shoppers in the popular old souk, to which Arabs flocked from all over the world for a chance to experience the old Arab haggling and the incense-scented smoky atmosphere.

The shop owner, Elias Omar al-Aleppo, was a fourth-generation citizen of the city, a devout Sunni Muslim who openly supported the sitting government in Damascus, a secret member of Jabhat al-Nusra, and a paid CIA informer. He was of indeterminate age, had a salt-and-pepper full-face beard, and the deep topographical bronzed skin of a desert denizen. He was a small, quick man whose eyes flitted about nervously. He had a valid reason for being anxious–in fact perpetually–owing largely to being a triple-agent. His clothing was simple and cheap—long-sleeved Islam green shirt buttoned up to the neck, a pair of faded black sweatpants with a *New York Yankee* logo on the left front pocket. He wore common thin silk slippers like most of his competitors. In short, he fit in well.

"Elias, my friend," Avery began, "we hear rumors that an attack is on its way. What can you tell us? If only for our personal protection."

He looked about nervously, as if he suspected peekers or that his cloth enclosure was bugged.

"Listen, do not let this get back to me. It is more than my life is worth. Al-Nusra Front–Jabhat al-Nusra—is planning something big and right away, maybe even today. It will be in one of the suburbs, probably somewhere in the southwest. I am just a very minor foot soldier, and no one tells me the details. Security, you know. Al-Nusra Front is nuts about security, and they kill at the drop of a hat anybody they even suspect. It's "kill all the suspects and let Allah sort them out after.""

"Not in the main city of Aleppo itself?"

"Not yet, but it is going to happen. Aleppo is too important. It is the financial capital of al-Sham [Syria]; and because of that, it is more important than Damascus. I suggest you get away while you can. It will be very *albashiea* [ugly] when God wills it."

Avery was always impressed with just how deeply the vein of religion ran in the Muslim world. It seemed fatalistic to him—*inshalah* governed all thinking, decisions, and explanations.

"Who will be involved? How many? What kind of weapons?"

The only group I know for sure is al-Nusra. But I presume some IS and some foreign fighters will be part of it. Gambling is forbidden; but if I were to bet, I would say that there will be six or seven thousand, and a heavy assortment of big guns, maybe even planes."

"Thank you, Elias. Remember to get the secret offshore account like we talked about. You and we can't afford to have the insurgency or the regime discover your accounts. Have you been getting your money regularly?"

"I have. I have come to trust the CIA; more than my Sunni Arab so-called friends."

"Always remember to count your fingers after you shake hands, my friend. Trust God, and me. Nobody else."

Avery and his agents believed Elias. They hurried back to the caravanserai, packed their few things, paid their bill, and drove their "technical" [Hilux armored car with a 50 caliber machine gun mounted in the truck bed] towards the mountainous area in the southwest above the town of Salaheddine, which seemed to them to be a likely target. The technical did not attract attention; such vehicular precautions were commonplace.

They made the right choice. A fierce cacophony of gunfire began at 2200 that evening—July 19, 2012–which started what would become the massively destructive and prolonged Battle of Aleppo. The rebel forces of Jabhat al-Nusra poured artillery fire into the town, which was well known to favor the regime, even more than Aleppo proper, which was largely loyal to al-Assad. Casualties were very high on both sides, and no clear winner could be determined by body-count alone. The CIA agents were spell-bound as they watched through their high-power binoculars at the slaughter. Corpses littered the streets, and no one dared to venture out to clear them away. In a few days the stench carried even up to the agents' position. They could only imagine what it was like in Salaheddine itself.

For ten days, the battled seesawed back-and-forth with no real change in control of the city itself. However, the insurgents were beginning to get the upper hand outside the city limits. During the last two days of July, al-Nusra and the FSA captured an important—a crucial—town north of Aleppo, which established for them a direct route between Salaheddine and the Turkish border where they maintained one of their most important supply bases.

Shortly thereafter, they overran and captured the Al-Bab army base northeast of the city. Next to fall was the air base at Minakh, northwest of Aleppo. The crucial element of that battle was that the arms and tanks captured at the checkpoint were taken away from the regime and used against them. The insurgent forces were a succeeding juggernaut. They gained serious territory in Aleppo and early on came to control most of eastern and southwestern districts. Salaheddine succumbed completely as did parts of Hamdaniyeh.

The insurgents and Syrian rebels against the regime targeted military security centers and police stations. One of the most significant clashes was with the Air Force intelligence headquarters in Aleppo's northwestern district Zahraa. The rebellion was increasingly successful as the month went on. Rebels over-ran multiple police stations and security posts in the central and southern districts of Bab al-Nerab, Al-Miersa and Salhain, seizing a significant quantity of arms and ammunition, which lessened the al-Assad's forces' abilities to defend its hold on Aleppo, and strengthened both the resolve and capacities of the anti-Assad coalition.

It was too dangerous and chaotic for the CIA agents to get close to the tumultuous and ruinous battles raging in the ancient city. They depended on Elias Omar al-Aleppo, their Jabhat al-Nusra contact. Avery, especially, was dubious about the veracity of al-Nusra since other informants were telling him that they were a breakoff of the Islamic State and were in the process of being subsumed by the rapidly growing terrorist jihadi extremist organization.

Elias reported the details of what news outlets were describing. The FSA doggedly continued its rapacious offensive in Aleppo, and the SAA continued its indiscriminate retaliation against the citizens, the buildings, and the architecture of what was once a thriving metropolis and a good place to live and work.

"Incidentally," he added, "Outside news. I saw on the Telly that the foreign ministers from nineteen Arab League countries have voted to impose economic sanctions against the Syrian regime for its part in a bloody crackdown on civilian demonstrators."

33,500 buildings were either damaged or destroyed by shelling, demolition, looting, and occupation, by uncaring insurgents. An extensive conservation work took place in the early 2000s by the Aga Khan Trust for Culture in collaboration with Aleppo Archeological Society. All of that became piles of the debris of war. The Great Mosque of Aleppo's minaret tower sagged to the side and toppled during shelling. Its roof caved in, and a wall was blown apart by RPG shelling destroying priceless heirlooms and sacred objects.

The marvelous old Al-Madina Souq—the world's largest covered historic market—was utterly destroyed by shelling and ground fighting and reduced to charred rubble by fire. 1,000 shops were destroyed by the fire and looting. Sahat Al Hatab square and the buildings around it were devastated. Many historical heritage sites were destroyed. They included the Carlton Citadel Hotel which was destroyed down to its foundations as were the madrasas of al-Sharafiyya and Khusruwiyah.

Al-Assad's Syrian Arab Army perpetrated air and ground strikes against hospitals, schools, markets, water and sewage facilities, and bakeries—commonplace occurrences. The Russian and Syrian government offensive cut off eastern Aleppo from food and humanitarian supplies. They executed hundreds of people and dumped them in pits or left them to rot in the streets. Syrian army aircraft dropped thousands of barrel bombs, claiming the lives of many thousands of people, even after the enactment of United Nations Resolution 2139 which ordered the end of using barrel bombs in the battle. The government never admitted to using barrel bombs, despite all evidence to the contrary. The SAA and the Russians used chlorine gas and incendiary bombs which were also declared to be a violation of international law.

The Citadel of Aleppo–a large medieval fortified palace in the center of the old city of Aleppo, considered to be one of the oldest and largest castles in the world—was heavily damaged in a series of bombardments. Usage of the Citadel hill dates back at least to the middle of the 3rd millennium B.C.E.. According to the Sunnis, the hill upon which it was built was once the land where the Prophet Abraham milked his sheep. The street plan on the south area of Aleppo retained the ancient Hellenistic grid street plan until the battle.

Thereafter it became unrecognizable as such. A bomb set off in a tunnel under one of the outer walls caused extensive damage to the citadel. During the conflict, the SAA used the Citadel as a military base. The walls acted as cover for shelling surrounding areas and the ancient arrow slits in walls were used by snipers to target rebels. The rebels did extensive damage to the citadel in their attempts to occupy the fortress. Avery mused that should the civil war ever end, no amount of repair and restoration could ever bring back what was lost in the wonderful and historic city.

In January–beginning the second year of the siege–the rebels seized the Umayyad Mosque; and during the battle, the mosque's museum caught fire, its ceiling collapsed, and Jabhat al-Nusra fighters detonated explosives inside the minaret, destroying it. The mosque was a UNESCO historic site, beloved by Muslims because it served as home to the remains of Zechariah, the father of John the Baptist. The original building was one of the earliest in Islamic history. It was built in the beginning of the 8th century CE, about a hundred years after the advent of the Prophet's adulthood. The building destroyed in the Battle of Aleppo dated to the 11th through 14th centuries. Its minaret was built in 1090. It toppled and was destroyed during the savage fighting.

The estimated costs to reconstruct Aleppo after the urbacide were estimated at between $35–40 billion. No such funding has been forthcoming.

31,000 people were killed. Civilians told of the rebel forces using private homes for shelter and the occupants as human shields. Elias's sources estimated that the population of rebel-held Eastern Aleppo had been reduced to 300,000. Elias provided intel that rebel forces had nearly 7,000 fighters in eighteen battalions involved in what they described as the "Mother of all Battles."

Initially, a substantial minority of the citizens of Aleppo sympathized with the rebellion, in principle at least. However, as the siege dragged on, and the rebels used indiscriminate tactics against civilians such as improvised artillery, including "hell cannons" [makeshift mortar firing gas cylinders packed with explosives and shrapnel], which were, as the IS commanders said, "primarily to terrorize the inhabitants of western

Aleppo," the realities of war resulted in the rebel occupiers losing most of its previous sympathizers. One of the clinchers that resulted in widespread dissatisfaction was that the Kurds produced unequivocal evidence that IS used weaponized gas on civilians living in a Kurdish neighborhood.

IS established Sharia law in the areas they controlled, imposing torture, abductions, hostage-taking, arbitrary detention, other mistreatment of prisoners, and summary public executions. Although denial of water and sanitation is a war crime, water supplies in the city for tens of thousands of people were deliberately cut by the Jabhat al-Nusra group. Jaish al-Islam prohibited civilians from receiving food and other necessary supplies.

Rebel fighters were crude, and ill-disciplined. It was common for them to leave the fighting to go looting for supplies—and most often from the beleaguered townspeople. They were fickle and greed-driven; many deserted or switched their loyalties to groups that had more to offer. This deteriorating approach led to the killing of at least one rebel commander following a dispute.

Elias reported from secret Jabhat al-Nusra war councils that supposedly fanatic and religiously committed fighters retreated with as much loot as they could carry. This caused a serious loss of a frontline position advantages. In one instance, it directly led to the failure of an attack on a Kurdish neighborhood. The looting cost the rebel fighters the majority of popular support. It persisted even though the rebel commanders inflicted executions on looters. Aleppo descended into hell.

Both sides suffered a high level of casualties, and the unfortunate men, women, and children, in Aleppo were rapidly becoming refugees and a problem for the rest of the world. Rebel commanders of all stripes announced from the beginning that their main aim was to capture the city center, and it appeared that they were on the cusp of doing so. In the end, it was a rather futile and dreadful war of attrition. It was highly questionable what the definition of "winning" was.

Avery communicated with the ODNI on a regular basis regarding the Aleppo situation and the general to-and-fro nature of the civil war. Midway into the four-year-long siege of Aleppo, Director Clapper gave his COS-Iraq sobering news: the Russian government announced through back channel diplomats that it was going to become directly involved in the war unless America bowed out. President Obama and Secy. of State Clinton gave a polite but firm reply that it would look upon such an intervention with the gravest of misgivings. Gen. Clapper's own intelligence informants in Russia assured him that President Putin was deadly serious, and that the Russian Air Force would join the Battle of Aleppo shortly.

"The United States just closed its embassy in Damascus. The prime minister of Syria just defected. The place is going to hell in a handbasket. Get out, now, Avery. That is an order. Are we clear?"

"Aye, aye, Sir. It is a terrible shame what is happening here, but it is completely beyond anything we can do to help or hinder. We will head down to Baghdad forthwith."

CHAPTER TWENTY-FIVE

"To infuriate and terrorize the infidels, we renew our pledge of loyalty to the commander of the faithful and the caliph of the Muslims, the mujahid sheikh Abu Bakr al-Baghdadi al-Hussaini al-Qurashi may God preserve him."

–Statement posted on their social media groups by Islamic State militants announcing formation of the Islamic State caliphate headed by Caliph Shaykh Abu Bakr al-Baghdadi, Mosul, June 29, 2014

"The army is engaged in a crucial and heroic battle ... on which the destiny of the nation and its people rests ..."

Syrian President, Bashar al-Assad, said on the occasion of the 67th Anniversary of the Syrian Arab Army, *Syria army in 'crucial and heroic battle,' says Bashar al-Assad, The Daily Telegraph, London, August 1, 2012.*

Mosul, Nineveh Governate, Iraq, June 29, 2014

The Islamic State began to come back to life shortly after the U.S. President ordered the withdrawal of all American forces from Iraq which was begun in December, 2007 with the end of the Iraq War troop surge of 2007 and was completed in December 2011. Recruits to IS flocked into Iraq and Syria; billions in donated or stolen funds enriched the State's coffers; until in early 2014, the IS insurgency was stronger than ever. They launched their Northern Iraq Offensive and moved inexorably through the northern provinces. In January, IS regained control of Fallujah and Ramadi which brought most of Anbar Province under their control. Abu Bakr al-Baghdadi was not in the province at the time, but his ardent supporters reported that he cheered them on "from the sidelines."

Avery, Malcolm, and Devlin, were ensconced in Mosul in April, posing as reporters from Reuters, and had genuine passes validated by both the Iraqi army and the IS press relations unit. As a result, they were close observers when–at 0230 hours–IS military convoys of pickup trucks–each truck carrying four fighters–entered the perimeter areas of Mosul shooting successfully at the city's checkpoints. Avery's informants told him that Mosul's first line of defense contained a robust 2,500 soldiers, but the reality was that the defenders numbered less than five hundred. In another miscalculation, Mosul's Iraqi Army commanding officer lost all of the city's tanks to the outlying areas of Anbar province. The CIA officers were witness to the fact that the city was left with very little to combat the IS fighters. It was little short of a medieval massacre. The insurgents hanged, burned, tortured, and crucified, many Iraqi soldiers in the path of their attack.

Within six days of fighting, the outlying districts, the city itself, and Mosul International Airport with all of its helicopters, fell to the marauders. 500,000 civilians fled from the city. During the early days of the conflict, Iraqi security forces killed the IS military chief Abu Abdulrahman al-Bilawi. The rank and file of IS dubbed their eventually successful military operation "Bilawi Vengeance" in honor of their late commander's alias.

Within the city, the Iraqi army had 30,000 soldiers and 30,000 federal police stationed as defenders. The IS attacking force was greatly outnumbered—only 1,500 soldiers, 15 to 1—but they had different advantages over the defenders. First, they had the element of surprise, which was owing to exceedingly poor intelligence coming into the SAA and Iraqi commanders, and their poor decisions when faced with the common knowledge that the Islamic Army was advancing on them from the north more rapidly than any of them could have imagined.

Second, the weaponry—both large and small arms—possessed by IS far exceeded the army's materiel. During its Northern Iraq Offensive IS had made significant territorial advances in neighboring southern Syria. That gave them access to city and governate treasure—gold and cash obtained by theft—and provided them with a major stockpile of weapons which further strengthened their drive. They were far better prepared as attackers by the time they had looted Fallujah and Ramadi and better than the poorly supplied and resupplied national army.

The fighting was intense, and the government ordered a strict curfew. Iraqi army helicopters dropped bombs on the IS forces and also caused numerous instances of collateral damage to buildings, vehicles, and citizens. IS sent in five suicide bombers who blew up a government arsenal. The next day, IS intensified their attack from the northwest. They bombed the Patriotic Union of Kurdistan party office, then launched a hundred vehicles into the city. At the same time, sleeper cells hidden in several neighborhoods numbering in the hundreds revealed themselves after being ordered into activation. As the planners had expected, whole neighborhoods rallied to them, especially in the eastern portion of Aleppo. The sleepers carried out dozens of assassinations which removed the heads of Mosul leadership.

Throughout the day, IS fighters bombed police stations, executed captured security force officers, and commandeered an old building for headquarters. Then, as rapidly as they had entered the city, they left. Some retreated to hideouts in the surrounding desert and changed clothes to camouflage themselves and move about in plain sight among the local population. Avery and the CIA agents had maneuvered around the crowded city most of the day witnessing atrocities from both sides of the conflict. Mostly, however, they were looking for al-Baghdadi. Devlin waited in a watching post close to the IS check station near the northwest perimeter. A long convoy of undamaged, and recently washed pickup trucks stopped at the request of the sentries. Al-Baghdadi and two body-guards stepped out of one of the trucks and shook hands with the sentries.

He asked for directions, then had his men recheck their guns. Devlin was in a nondescript old Toyota and followed the convoy at a safe distance. He had a $3,000 Nikon D850 DSLR camera with a $13,500 Nikon AF-S NIKKOR 180-400mm f/4E TC1.4 FL ED VR lens—the best the CIA could provide. The photos he got turned out to have a depth of focus and a degree of definition and clarity beyond anything he had ever seen. What he did see was not fit for anyone to see except those who absolutely had to do so. Baghdadi had turned into a vicious and psychopathic killer, delighting in violence.

He had a raucous and fiendish laugh as he had his lackies blow up children in ice cream parlors and on playgrounds. He forced parents—usually Shi'ites—and their children to watch as he blew up kittens, gerbils, and garden snakes, in family pet shops. Not satisfied with his near lunatic frenzy against defenseless small animals, his convoy—acting with foreknowledge of locations—traveled about blowing up family weddings, then coming back the following day and blowing up the resultant funerals.

Al-Baghdadi had a personal mercenary motive as well. During the two days Devlin shadowed him and his convoy, he committed more serious crimes on numerous occasions. Even Devlin knew that the leader was committing one the most serious crimes under Islamic law: *hirabah* [defined in Sharia law as brigandage, banditry, terrorism, insurrection]. He and his men shot Shi'ites at random from the windows of their vehicles. His blood lust and avarice were insatiable.

IS fighters armed with machine guns and rocket-propelled grenades stormed several Nineveh provincial headquarters that same day. That took away almost every security official in the city and a great many throughout the province. The Iraqi Army Fourth Battalion was among the last of the local police fighting the attackers. The rest of the defense forces either deserted their posts and ran into the desert or joined the opposition. Iraqi Army soldiers fled the city while it was under attack.

The Iraqi army crumbled in the face of the militant assault, the U.S. and Iraqi brass concluded in after action reports which is evidenced by the fact that many soldiers abandoned their weapons and dressed as civilians to blend in with the noncombatants. It was determined that many of the Iraqi army men either did not fire their weapons at all or during the battle, they were firing their weapons into the air, despite the fact that no one was shooting at them.

This dismal performance allowed the militants to control much of Mosul by midday on the 10th of June. Immediately, Aleppo began to transform. Black flags appeared on the front of government buildings and on their tops. They were ubiquitous. The Black Banner or Black

Standard [banner of the eagle] was one of the flags flown by the Prophet Muhammad according to popular Muslim tradition. The white Arabic script *shahada* on a black banner was an inscription used as a military ensign as long ago as the 18th-century Hotak dynasty. It was adopted by the Taliban, and then by Al-Qaeda in the 1990s. This usage was widely adopted by jihadists in the early 2000s. In the 2010s, the Islamic State of Iraq and the Levant, and after declaring the Islamic State, it was for the IS what the swastika was for the Nazis. Avery and other western observers called it "the black flag of jihad."

Elias Omar al-Aleppo–the secret member of Jabhat al-Nusra, and even more secret CIA asset, and Col. Behremend Rozaki–ranking peshmerga officer and CIA spy in al-Baghdadi's camp–quietly sidled up to Avery, Devlin, and Malcolm, to watch the promised major announcement on the twenty-ninth of June. It was very warm, and everyone in the square was fidgety. They followed the congregation into the Central Mosque of Mosul—"herded" would be more accurate. The congregation at the mosque in the video had been ordered to come to that Friday Prayer, and no one in the city dared to refuse.

Worshipers were directed through a check-point as they neared the mosque; there, they were searched thoroughly by armed ISIS fighters. Beyond the check-point, IS soldiers pushed the entering Muslims to one side or another, to the front or the back, and into whichever row and seat they wanted the congregant to sit. They were not altogether pleasant about it, either.

"Sit like this," each soldier said and demonstrated a very straight right-angle sitting stance, head up, eyes forward, and hands folded on the lap. "No slouching; no talking; no laughing; no facial gestures; no moving about."

As the disguised CIA agents neared the entryway into the mosque, Abu Bakr al-Baghdadi, his well-armed guard unit, and a large convoy of Japanese support pickup trucks, pulled into the center of the square surrounding the handsome old building. The fighters cleared a space around the mosque; snipers perched themselves on the rooftops; and a special guard unit lined a route into the mosque. The disguised CIA agents wedged their way into the mosque and ended up having to find standing room near the *minbar*. Al-Baghdadi was escorted to the stairway leading to the platform of the *minbar*, where he stood quietly until everyone was in his or her place and following instructions.

Silence descended over the room; then, Abu Bakr al-Baghdadi began to speak. His manner was a surprise to Avery who had expected to be greeted with bombast, fire, and brimstone. Instead al-Baghdadi spoke in what seemed to be a humble and pious tone.

"*As-salam alaykum wa rahmat Allah wa barakatuhu* [May God accept from us and from you the justness of deeds, and unto you, peace]. May your *Eid* be blessed and your days be happy. W*a kull aam wa intum bi-khayr.*"

A responding chorus from the congregation came almost as if from one person, "*Wa-alaykum as-salam!*"

"May it please God, the Merciful and Compassionate, who has sent me to you. I declare, by God, the All Wise and All Powerful, that in this place and from this da**y**–*Ramadan* 2, 1435 [*Umm-Al-Qura* calendar]– forward, we live in the restored Caliphate with me, His humble servant having the rank of the greatest imam. I shall be known as Ibrahim in honor of the great prophet who milked his sheep on Aleppo's hill and as the *Khalifa* of Islam, in the name of Allah, the Entirely Merciful, the Especially Merciful. All praise is to Allah, Lord of the worlds, I was placed as your wali and caretaker, and I am not better than you," he said, "I am the teacher appointed to show you the right way and the *Amir al-Mu'mineen* [Commander of the Believers], *inshalah.*

"So, if you found me to be right, then help me; and if you found me to be wrong, then advise me and make me right. I do not promise you– as the kings and rulers promise their followers and congregation–luxury security, and relaxation; instead, I promise you what Allah promised his faithful worshipers," he said.

His voice grew a little hoarse at this point and he had to clear his throat before continuing.

"I say—as we should all say at all times–praise be to God. I praise Him; and we praise Him, seek His help, and His forgiveness. And we seek refuge in God from the evils of ourselves and evils of our deeds. Whomsoever God guides, there is nothing to mislead him; and whoso is misled, there is no guide for him. And I bear witness that there is no deity but God alone with no partner for Him, and I bear witness that Muhammad is His Servant and Messenger: God's blessings and salutations be upon him and his family.

"And more I say, 'praise be to God, the Lord of the Worlds, and prayers and peace be upon the seal of the Prophets and those sent to aid our Prophet Muhammad SAWS. And I bear witness that Muhammad is His servant and Messenger who broke the system of profits by his miracles whose signs appeared in the revelation of the Great Holy Book, the *Qur'an*. and the Mi'raj. It was Allah who split off the moon and made life of inanimate things. Oh God, bless your most humble servant Ibrahim and your Servant and Messenger Muhammad, his family and companions, the people of truth and resolve in matters, and the *thiqat* [trusted ones]. May God straighten what was bent from the path and make clear life's true customs and obligations. And may He grant many salutations on them and us as we serve Him.

"Learn gratitude for God who gave your mujahideen brothers victory after long years of jihad and patience; so, they declared the caliphate and placed your grateful caliph in charge," he said.

"Let me repeat what you already know from the Holy *Qur'an*. Remember with me the verse that says, 'Give Glad Tidings to the Patient.' It is drawn from a beautiful verse of the *Qur'an* that promises 'glad and good 'tidings' in Paradise to those who remain steadfast on the path of faith in life. Speaking as Khalifa Ibrahim, I praise the ferocious resistance by our Islamic State warriors in Damascus this year. I tell you that our Islamic State, willed to us by God, the Merciful, and Rememberer of his martyrs, is the only shield for the Sunnis against the genocidal regime of Bashar al-Assad and his Shi'ite lap dogs from Persia."

"It is required of you to read the *Qur'an*. It is hoped of you that you will memorize it and become a respected *Hafiz* [one who memorizes the *Qur'an*, and often travels to recite for audiences]. You must have a working knowledge or our Holy Book, because often our code words are taken from its *Surahs* and *ayahs*. From the *Qur'an* comes all truth and all you need to know.

"Forget the professors and teachers, the philosophers and scientists. They are often wrong; their thinking is too often western; and you can rely only on your *Qur'an*. Those corrupted by the West talk of evidence. You have no need of evidence; you have the *Qur'an*, for all the explanations you need are contained in it. God made it clear, that when it comes to evidence, He is the reckoner. He knows all things and imparts them in his Holy Book.

"Real wisdom comes from His scripture, but only after long study. You may become wise enough to discern *mutatis mutandis*—the ability to make comparisons of two or more cases or situations and be able to make such alterations in thinking as necessary while not affecting the main point at issue. Now, I say the last thing about our Book today: when a knowledgeable one abandons what he has come to know from the Book of God and the Sunna of His Messenger, he immediately becomes a disbelieving apostate who deserves the punishment in this world and in the Hereafter."

Al-Baghdadi's hoarseness was increasing. He paused to take a few sips of water before resuming.

"Now, let us talk of enemies. We Sunnis have many, and there are many who have made themselves enemies of God. Consider the idolators: Almighty Allah has said: 'Oh you who have believed, fight those who are nearest to you of the disbelievers and let them find in you harshness' (*al-Tawba* 123). This is true jihad against the disbelievers, the enemies of God and His Messenger, for all whom there has reached the call of the Messenger of God to the religion of God with which he was sent but they do not respond to it. I speak here of wrong minded Muslims such as the accursed Shi'ites, the Alawites, and the Kharijis. It is thus *obligatory* to fight them 'until there is no more *fitna*, and religion belongs entirely to God' (*al-Anfal* 39). And the Almighty has said even more pointedly, 'Slay the idolaters wherever you find them' (*al-Tawba* 5).

"Think of the al-Nusra when you consider who is an example of idolatry. Consider as examples, Abu Musab al-Zarqawi, and Ayman al-Zawahiri, may God punish them.

"And know what awaits those godless Christian Crusaders and the stupid and wicked Jews. By God, we will cut off their heads after mere moments. Let them know, by God, our fire will not be extinguished except by displaying you before the court and before men—you contemptible scum, you slaves of money. You will see and finally learn from us everything, oh traitors…so our enmity towards you is until the Day of Judgment…you and whoso is loyal to you. To be clear, we mean the Americans, the Jews, the Christian Europeans, the Hindus, the Buddhists, the Atheists, and the unrepentant men—all the dogs and contemptible scum–who wrongly call themselves Muslims and Believers.

"What shall we see done to them. By God, and through His Sharia, "We shall inflict the punishments of *Hudud, Diyya* and *Ta'zir*, all of the punishments for offenses at the discretion of the *Qadi* [judge] or ruler of the state—which at this blessed time is me, Caliph Ibrahim. We will see the worst of them lose limbs, suffer the humiliation of public lashing, be hanged, die by crucifixion, be burned, be mutilated. Our enemies in each of the cities we have conquered already know of our godly fury.

"Allah holds a special place in His mind for the Jews.

"We ask God to aid us in exposing those loathsome persons indulging in innovation or *shirk*—those arrogant, misguided, and foolish ones who associate partners with God. Here we speak of polytheism, idolatry, the deification or worship of anyone or anything besides the singular God, Allah. We know from God in His Holy Book that the denial of monotheism is of *shirk* entirely. For every new invention is an innovation and every innovation is an error so it disavows the errors and innovations of the sects that deviate from the direction of the prophets entirely.

"Consider as examples, the Christian dogs who believe in a Son of God, as if the Oneness of God would permit such a travesty. We Believers have faith in prayer to the One God. The loathsome Christians—those idolators—believe in having angels be intermediaries between man and God—a wrongful idea cursed by the One God. Kill them whenever the opportunity arises. Eliminate all the sects and those that adhere to them that deviate from the direction of the prophets entirely: such as the Khawarij, Mu'tazilites, Rafidites, Jahmis, Qadaris, Murj'ites, Asha'irites, Maturdites, Karamites, Sufis, and others besides them, from sects of error and paths of innovation.

"There is no discussion, truce, reconciliation, or *dhimma* pact with the apostates. The Messenger of God said: 'Whoso changes his religion, kill him. The Prophet said, 'I was sent with the sword before the Hour so that God alone may be worshipped with no partner for Him.

"Oh God," al-Baghdadi prayed, looking skyward, "destroy the usurping Jews and the hateful Americans, and Europeans, and the secularists, the hypocrites, and the apostates. Oh God, destroy them, for they cannot incapacitate You. Pray do not let them have a chance to incapacitate we weak fighters in Your cause.

"Oh God, count them in number and as individuals and kill them in dispersal. Let not any of them escape. Oh God, destroy the hated democracy, the foreign schools, the banks, the houses of usury, and the rest of the houses of corruption, *ya Jabbar*. Oh God, all around the world, tear up the man-made laws of *kufr* and those who put them in place and implement them against the Muslims. *Ya Aziz, ya qahar*: oh God, defeat every government that does not rule by Your Holy Book and the Sunna of Your Prophet, oh Lord of the Worlds.

"We shall, with the help of Almighty God, find the people of innovation and whims. We will condemn them and oppose them according to their state and their innovation. The Islamic State in my person as Khalifa consider the state institutions of the world outside the Islamic State, from governments, ministries, courts and popular, consultative and parliament councils, army, gendarmerie and police, to be apostasy institutions that must have *takfir* declared on them. We declare them now to be legally incompetent, and they are hereby disavowed. Their people must also be disavowed and disowned, and one must show hatred and hostility towards them. This, we humble servants pray. Lead us to do thy will in this killing and destruction.

"Oh, Great God, remember this day of history. Oh God, Most Merciful and Compassionate, establish the Islamic State, and its development with the banner of Tawheed, and protect it through Your mujahideen servants, and make it beautiful with the Sunna of al-Mustafa, *ya aziz, ya hakim*.

"And now, let us speak of jihad, of our blessed jihad. Praise be to God the Lord of the Worlds. God Almighty is the Guarantor of Success. *Salam* to all the brothers among you. May God protect them. I, your Khalifa, do inform them that our hearts are with them, and for them to be patient and considerate, for victory is with patience, and ease with adversity. We shall shortly have our *qisas* [retaliation]. By God, we will cut off their heads in moments. Our fire will not be extinguished—you, the contemptible scum–you slaves of money and usury, you hypocrites. You will soon see from us from everywhere and in everything, oh traitors. Our enmity towards you is until the Day of Judgement–you and whoso is loyal to you. God, the Almighty, shall, through our holy jihad remove from our people all things loathed: prison, striking, threats, and shackles, placed on them by the *kuffars*.

"For hundreds of years, the Khawarij were a source of insurrection against the Caliphate, and still are to this day. Let us deal with the Khawarij on the basis of the words of the Prophet who said, .'..Kill them wherever you find them, for in killing them is a reward with God for the one who kills them on the Day of Judgment. If I were to find them, I would certainly kill them and kill them again.' And I say that I will publish abroad a *fatwa* against those whom we declare jihad against: The polytheists, the transgressors, the horrid Jews, the murderous Christian Crusaders, those Shi'ite Dogs, apostates, traitors, Ayman al Zawahiri, may God ruin him and those who seek common ground with al-Qaeda, and all who fight against us. Oh, mujahideen brothers in particular and Muslims in general, may God make us and you among those He loves because they fight in His path as one rank in our blessed jihad.

"And now as I close, I—as his *Khalifa*—give you counsel from Allah, the Merciful and Compassionate. To you doctors and nurses, Sharia judges, experts in Islamic jurisprudence, and Muslim engineers, I call on you to remain steadfast with us and to help develop the caliphate. To all Muslims, support the man, your *Khalifa, ashab al-manhaj al-salim* [the owner of the curriculum, the one having the sound *manhaj,* which is to say, the man who knows the clear path set by God, the Sovereign in the Day of Recompense]. Know from the *Sacred Qur'an* that is the word of Allah: '*Li kulli* only' *minkum syir'an wa manhaajan*' meaning, for every *ummah,* we give a rule and a clear path in contrast to the extremists, the innovators, the ignorant, and the unqualified.

"The new and everlasting Islamic State shall begin today to ensure that all Muslims have correct belief in and testify to our six crucial articles of faith—the six pillars of *iman.* I shall do away with the crimes so rife around us. There will be no discussion, truce, reconciliation, or *dhimma* pact with the apostates. The Messenger of God said: 'Whoso changes his religion, kill him.'

"We shall enforce the treatise on the Shi'a sects which make clear that they are apostates and original disbelievers. The apostate/original disbeliever distinction is important for the issue of taking women as concubines/sex slaves: IS permits women from the original disbelievers to be enslaved as well as the nonbelievers. Others in the past have refrained from enslaving women of the apostates, but this is in error. We shall hold slave auctions beginning tomorrow morning.

"We shall adhere with deep faith to the definitions of *huddud* divine punishments and will exact the proper punishments for such crimes as: *zina* [unlawful sexual intercourse such as fornication], unfounded accusations of *zina,* drinking alcohol, highway robbery, and some forms of theft. We shall be strict about the Islamic laws of *tazir* and will punish offenses at the discretion of the *Qadi* [judge or ruler of the state]. There will be financial compensation paid to the victim or heirs of a victim in the cases of murder, bodily harm, or property damage. At times, *tazir* will be an alternative punishment to *qisas* which is the solemn right of a murder victim's nearest relative or *wali* [legal guardian] to—if the court approves—take the life of the killer.

"No detail is too small for the scrutiny of our *wahdat al'amn* [security unit]. If you play the popular game of table football in the Caliphate as it is now played, it is a sin. If want to play, then, you will need to behead the players. As you well know, you must cut of the heads of the figurines lest they resemble idols for worship. The Committee for the Promotion of Virtue and Prevention of Vice will be everywhere. Women—hear and obey the voice of your husband and master. Dress modestly in the hijab as required by the Islamic State. Show an ankle or a wrist or a wisp of the hair of your head, and you will pay dearly. Hear this and heed my word!

"Do jihad in the cause of Allah, incite the believers and be patient in the face of this hardship. If you knew about the reward and dignity in this world and the hereafter through jihad, then none of you would delay in doing it.

"I will say more when the need arises. This is enough for now."

With that he began to descend the stairway of the *minbar*.

The congregation—with instruction by the *wahdat al'amn*—began a spontaneous outburst of chanting, "We renew our pledge of loyalty to the commander of the faithful and the caliph of the Muslims—the mujahid sheikh Abu Bakr al-Baghdadi al-Hussaini al-Qurashi—may god preserve and keep him; may God protect him; may God have mercy on him," over and over.

At first, it was clumsy and discordant; but, once the faithful learned the script, it became a well-coordinated and stirring rallying call.

Finally, out of the stifling heat and humanity of the mosque, Avery looked about to be sure he was not overheard, and whispered, "Now that was a world-level diatribe—a fine sleeping pill with all its repetition. I hope you guys noted that it took place with an audacity that even Usama bin Laden never tried."

Beginning that afternoon, IS forces executed at least 4,000 Iraqi Security Force prisoners and dumped their bodies in the single largest known mass grave in Iraq yet, at what locals called the "Khafsa Sinkhole." This mass grave was not discovered until later in 2017 at the end of the second battle of Mosul. As they hurried away from the Hadean city, the CIA agents were witness to corpses of men who had been crucified; men, women, and children who had been beheaded, and—littering the streets—the bodies of people who had been tortured and murdered. The Islamic State was now a reality, and a night of endless darkness settled on Mosul and every other piece of territory they captured.

CHAPTER TWENTY-SIX

"No one slept that night. A few hours before, ISIS had launched surprise attacks on several nearby villages, driving thousands of Yazidis out of their homes and toward Mount Sinjar, in a dizzying, panicked mass that soon thinned to a frail march. Behind them, the militants killed everyone who refused to convert to Islam or who was too stubborn or confused to flee; and they chased down those who were slow on their feet, shooting them or cutting their throats. The trucks—when they got close to Kocho—sounded like grenades in the quiet rural air. We flinched in fear and moved closer to one another."

–Nadia Murad, with Jenna Krajeski, *The Last Girl: My Story of Captivity, and My Fight Against the Islamic State,* Tim Duggan Books (Penguin Random House), New York, 2017

"But Nadia's spirit is not broken nor is her voice muted."
–Amal Clooney, barrister, Op cit.

Sinjar Village, Nineveh Governate of Northern Mesopotamia, part of the disputed territories of northern Iraq, August 3, 2014

Relations between local Muslims and all the minorities—Nineveh plain has small enclaves of Yazidis, Christians, Turkomen, Kaka'i,

Shabak, Roma, Chaldeans, Mandaeans, Armenians, Shi'ites, even a small community of Iraqi Jews—especially the Yazidis, deteriorated to its nadir during the summer of 2014. Relations reduced to barely tolerable after Abu Bakr al-Baghdadi and his fighters declared the existence of the Islamic State in Mosul on June the twenty-ninth. Muslims would not hire Yazidis, buy their products, sell them goods, and eventually, even speak to them. There were sporadic relatively minor acts of racism and gross intolerance but no outright violence.

The day before the IS came was a holiday in Sinjar district; Khatoon and the other Yazidis gathered to celebrate the end of a fasting period. The wheat had been harvested leaving the fields stubbly and reflecting the severe heat–40°C. The sky was pale blue as if the heat had drained it of color, and the sun radiated rippling heat waves over the parched countryside. People slaughtered sheep and gathered with their relatives to celebrate the holiday, handing out sweets and exchanging news and gossip. In the past, they would have invited their Muslim neighbors to join the celebrations; but more recently, a distance had grown between them, leading the villagers to keep mostly to their own and to understand that the past was gone.

The social atmosphere was restless, and the high temperature was relentless. The top of sacred Mount Sinjar, just north of the town shimmered disturbingly in the heat—almost as if a bad omen was developing. The people living below the mountain mostly avoided travelling until after the sun had set; but the mood had darkened. On this holiday, the streets were filled with neighbors trading frightening rumors. Many of the Yazidi men were now patrolling with guns which further dampened the holiday spirit. Late that night, a large contingent of Yazidi family members and friends from nearby Siba Sheikheder began pouring into the slightly larger Sinjar, telling anyone who would listen that the IS terrorists had taken over their town.

On the following day, August the third, that all changed—for the worse. By then, things had deteriorated to the point that the Yazidi family stayed indoors almost twenty-four hours a day and slept on the top of their mud brick home to find some relief from the oppressive desert heat and for security. One member of the family was on lookout at all times in four-hour shifts; so, the rest could get some sleep. Sleep was difficult because of the snoring of their grandfather, Naif Jasso Yazidi, the cloying heat, and the noise of the carousing IS fighters, and occasional screaming. It was also difficult because twenty-eight-year-old Khatoon–the last family member to have a job—was fired by her kindly old Muslim mullah employer, and now they faced the specter of starvation which stared at them constantly and heard the pangs of their stomachs.

The mullah asked Khatoon to come to his house, where he could tell her to her face, "My dear, I am afraid. The extremists have come to my place of business–and last night to my very home—to threaten me with terrible things—things a young virgin girl like you should not hear. They told me that if by tomorrow I had any employees who were not Sunni Muslims, they would burn down my house and business building and feed me to the dogs. And some other things I cannot say. I am sorry, dear girl, I can no longer allow you to work with me. *Adhhab mae allah, Najlat Adam* [Go with God, Daughter of Adam]. I have a daughter of my own. I fear for her. She is called, Mahbooba."

That was more credit than her father had ever given her, or her mother had, for that matter. Societal changes are strongly resisted by the Yazidi and Muslim cultures which interfere with any masculine area of privilege and importance. Birth of a boy in Northern Iraq and Kurdistan is considered a success. He is a *bacha,* a child. Birth of a girl is a failure. She is called *dokhtar* [other], a daughter. Khatoon had had to accept that low class position throughout throughout her life, like it or not.

She had long since recognized that her stepfather, Abdul, was worthless as a man. He lost his job because he had once flirted with joining the local Yazidi militia. He performed no work for the family or in the house. He did complain and nag the rest–especially Khatoon–for failing to provide for him in the manner to which he had become accustomed while living with his young first wife, Hanush. She was wise to him in less than a year and forced through a divorce and left him for another, younger man. Abdul and her mother, Safaa, married out of perceived mutual desperation. That made Safaa's desperation worse. Abdul hated the Muslims passionately, but felt emasculated because he could not fight them or even stand up for his family.

Khatoon was still pretty even though she was gradually getting thinner, and her complexion was becoming more sallow each week. She seldom smiled or joked now. Life was simply too somber for anyone to understand or appreciate humor. She was fully a young woman now, who should have been in the bloom of her life. She was tall for a Yazidi woman, willowy, but becoming too thin to be considered just svelte. Her hair had been a fine auburn brown conditioned with the best extra-virginal olive oil and done up in two braids in the Kurdish fashion. Now, she had no soap and little time to primp. That and her poor nutritional status made her hair an unkempt limp brown color with no luster. Poor girls and women like Khatoon were reduced to wearing one dress until it fell apart. Hers had once been a bright flower print calico made in India. Now it was dirty, had holes, and a frayed hem. Her condition was such that she no longer cared.

Undoubtedly, something important was about to happen. For the first time since 2003 when America invaded Iraq, Khatoon began to see a number of coalition forces planes flying over Kocho village and Sinjar on their way to Baghdad. The day it did happen started as a fairly benign day. Khatoon took a number of neighborhood children to the school ground for a lesson in Yazidi history and to play. The school building was decidedly unimpressive—dull dun in color, built of sandstone colored concrete. It was decorated with children's innocent posters. There were no toys like balls to play with. None of the children's families could afford such luxuries.

Spontaneously, the young ones began to play one of their favorites, a game that did not require toys or any manufactured items of any consequence. It was called *bin akby* [lit. in the dirt]. Enterprising and clever girls ran about hiding small items around the school yard. Someone let out a shrill whistle, and all the other girls ran about and dug in the dirt to find the fun but–for practical purposes–worthless things. They could keep the things they found; so, there was a certain cache to collect a larger number than the other girls. Shortly, every girl's fingernails were filled with dirt, just as the fingernails of their mothers and grandmothers had been generations before. Being that dirty was a small guilty pleasure that made them giggle, as little girls like to do. For a few minutes, they could forget the pain of hunger, the fear of the soldiers of IS, and the uncertainties of their future.

The fun and pleasure came to an abrupt end. Khatoon sighted a convoy of IS soldiers in old trucks advancing up to the walls of the city. The Yazidi men of the town rushed to the walls and the gate with their pitiful armaments—a few pistols and old World War I and II rifles. At first, the Yazidis were able to fend off the sporadic attacks by the Islamic

State insurgents who came at them in two or three trucks loaded with four or five men. That positive situation was short-lived; and after about an hour, IS soldiers swarmed the walls and gates looking for vulnerable spots. More than a dozen IS men died in their attempts to come over the walls; but soon, they were too much for the poorly armed and ill-trained Yazidis. The defenders retreated to their houses; now, it was every family for itself; and after a short while, it was every man for himself.

Abdul and his two eldest sons, Suliaman and Morteja, knew things were hopeless. They could now only fight and die to prove their courage and the worth of the Yazidi people. The Yazidi men fought to the last to protect their daughters and wives, and to save their innocence. It was futile. The battle for Sinjar lasted less than four hours before the extremists began to enter every home in the town and to go on to unleash their savagery on the neighboring towns of Kocho, Dohuk, and Solagh.

The three grown men abandoned the girls, women, and younger boys, to their fates and left by night to join the hastily thrown together Yazidi militia. The militia formed small guerrilla units and made small swift "lightening strikes" then faded away into the darkness and the desert. Theirs was a lost cause since the Islamic State ruled the darkness and infested the desert like an organized army of Australian Bulldog Ants. In less than a week, ninety percent of the militiamen were killed or captured, the latter being the worst of fates. Abdul, Suliaman, and Morteja, were among the captured. The family had no information about the capture of the men. And they had worse things to worry about and to deal with.

CHAPTER TWENTY-SEVEN

"He asked, 'Croesus, who told you to attack my land and meet me as an enemy instead of a friend?'

The King replied, 'It was caused by your good fate and my bad fate. It was the fault of the Greek gods, who with their arrogance, encouraged me to march onto your lands. Nobody is mad enough to choose war whilst there is peace. During times of peace, the sons bury their fathers; but in war, it is the fathers who send their sons to the grave."

–Herodotus, Greek Historian 484 BC-425 BC, in
Histories

Sinjar Village, Nineveh Governate of Northern Mesopotamia, part of the disputed territories of northern Iraq, August 6, 2014

From time to time, Khatoon and her mother, Safaa, risked peeking out of the rough-hewn windows of their mud brick house to see what the invading IS men in black were doing. They told each other white lies that the killers were not interested in a hut such as theirs, or that the killers had found all they wanted and were beginning to leave for more lucrative areas of the governate, or—when they could see none of the marauders–that the coast was clear; and the only question facing them was when could they leave the house to obtain food and water. Both of them had to become very harsh with the young children. When they cried, the two adult women slapped them and hissed, "silence" at them until they feared Khatoon and Safaa more than they did the Islamic State monsters or the gnawing hunger pangs in their stomachs. They had to know that it was too dangerous to attempt to go out even to find food for their little tandoor oven. This was their life now—fear, the specter of starvation, the omnipresence of the murderous Islamists who had no room in their hearts for love of children or innocent girls, or of respect for anyone else's customs or traditions.

The two women compounded the trauma for the young ones by snatching up all of their toys, clothing—except that being worn at the moment—all of the family valuables like the girls' meager stashes of jewelry, religious paraphernalia, and—worst of all—the family photographs. They dug a hole in the floor and saved everything of any monetary value, and they burned the rest. The consumption of the treasured family photos erased their pasts, and everyone in the family huddled together and wept.

Safaa stopped her crying first and said sharply, "We cannot allow those monsters to find anything about our lives or that we ever lived here. They will destroy it and joke about what we were like as if we were never human beings. That's what they do, and we will keep them from having that little pleasure at our expense."

"Mama, my friend, Rokhsana, told me that the men in black will spare us if we convert to their religion. We should do that, or at least pretend to do it, shouldn't we?" Seven-year-old Nisreen asked in her innocence.

Safaa answered with facts she had wanted to avoid, "Nisreen, my pretty little one, Rokhsana is a Christian girl. I have heard that the criminals have made such offers to the Christians, but I have also heard that it was a lie. Even the ones who agreed to convert were taken away to God knows where."

That made Nisreen cry.

Safaa made an angry face and told Nisreen and everyone else, "You have to grow up now. The Muslims hate us. They always have, and these are the worst of the worst. You must do anything you can to survive: lie, run, beg, agree to anything they demand, pretend to be one of them. You cannot be a Yazidi and live, sweet girl. You must become someone or something else. Khatoon, tell them the truth about what the Muslims think of us."

She was reluctant, but Khatoon realized that the shock of the bitter truth was necessary to convince the little girls and boys to do whatever was necessary to save themselves.

"They hate us because we are different, because we are not Muslims like them. They refuse to believe in our Tawusi Melek, and they say that he was sent to hell because he would not obey Father Adam and would not bow to him. That is not true; we know that; but they purposely or ignorantly misinterpret our doctrine. They say our Yazidi religion is not a real religion because we don't have a sacred book like their *Qur'an* or the Christians with their Bible. The regular Muslims use that idea to be unfair and mean to us, but the Islamic State killers use that idea as an excuse to kill us, to exterminate our whole race; and that is what is happening. There is even a name for it—genocide.

"Some special days we don't shower or bathe; so, they say we are ignorant and dirty and that we stink. That makes us less than humans. Because when we pray, we face the sun, they say we are pagans and polytheists. It is not true; we are monotheists and have only one God just like them; but it doesn't matter. They use any excuse to hate us, to hurt our girls, and to kill us like we were some sort of diseased dogs. I am sorry you have to hear such things; but you have to know that they do not have mercy like we do; and they will do you terrible harm. They have to be avoided if it is at all possible for you to do it. Starting today, we are all going to dress like the Muslims."

Safaa pulled out some faded and dirty dresses that looked fairly similar to what the town's poor Muslim girls wore and handed them out to the daughters. The two little boys got baggy pants and shirts that extended below their knees. All of them were given old silk shoes with upturned toes. She had not been able to procure burkas; so, the girls had to make do with plain cloth head scarves. The children looked like Yazidis trying to look like Muslims, Khatoon thought; but her mother was trying her best; and Khatoon did not want to undermine her.

That night, just before the family was to start up the ladder to the roof to lie down on their sleeping mats, the world as they knew it came to an end.

The low door to the house was kicked in and four hairy faced snarling men stomped their way into the room.

"Bow to us, Dogs," the youngest man in black demanded.

Every member of the family dropped to his or her knees and pressed their faces to the dirt floor.

"You pretend to be Muslims, but God knows you lie. You will sign these documents stating that you agree to convert to the true religion, or you will die or meet a fate worse than death."

"Sign," Safaa whispered, which got her a hard kick in the ribs from one of the home invaders.

The two youngest children could not yet write their own names; so, Safaa had them make an X mark. The others hated to do so, but they signed the papers without even having a chance to read them.

"Get up and walk to the truck. This place belongs to the Islamic State now, Dogs. We will take you and your conversion papers to the *jevat* and line you up at the courthouse; so, the judges can determine if you are sincere."

The men were rough. They pushed, hit, and kicked the Yazidis in head of them and forced them into the back of an old troop truck with a dozen other women and children whom Khatoon recognized from their neighborhood. Their truck and nearly two dozen others converged on the town square and slammed to a stop in front of the courthouse. Hanging over the large doors of the judicial building was a huge jihadist Islamic State flag—called "The Eagle"–black background and white Arabic inscription of the *shahada*: "*la 'ilāha 'illā llah muḥammadun rasulu llah.*" [There is no god but God. Muhammad is the messenger of God.]. As she looked around, she realized that the black flags adorned almost every building of any size in the town.

Khatoon and her mother were jerked into the court room, which had been converted to handle large numbers of defendants at once. It was not strictly a Sharia court, since most of the defendants were non-Muslims being tried for crimes related to being non-Muslims. More than two-thirds of the people standing before the bar of justice were women, and none of the "defendants" were Muslims. There were no chairs or benches for the defendants. Most of them were less defendant than applicant. They were required to stand in silence to await a pronouncement from the judge regarding a proceeding about which they were largely uninformed. Some were actually there for crimes, such as prostitution, adultery, lasciviousness, theft, and for rather vague charges related to "crimes against religion" and "crimes against the state."

Safaa's turn came first. She learned that she was charged with adultery, a charge that came from the fact that her husband had left her to remarry, then returned to her without there having been a divorce. Safaa was then fifty-four years old, thin and haggard. Because of the abruptness of her arrest, she was unkempt. She was found guilty of the crime for which she was charged and for failing to wear the hijab. Immediately upon hearing her verdict, two burly IS guards hustled her out of the room before she and Khatoon could even say goodbye.

Khatoon and twenty-two relatively young and fairly attractive women were required to stand for another two hours until all of the regular criminals were found guilty. The judge placed all the papers relating to the reason for the women having been brought to the courtroom together in one stack. He gave each document a cursory glance then pressed his stamp in the upper right-hand corner of the document.

"You are now Muslims. You will be taught how a Muslim woman is to behave. By the action of this court, you are now citizens of the Islamic State and subject to its laws. You will obey all orders of the commander of the faithful and the caliph of the Muslims, the mujahid Shaykh Abu Bakr al-Baghdadi al-Hussaini al-Qurashim, may God preserve him. Your allegiance is now to this flag," here, he pointed to the large black banner on the wall above his head. "All of you repeat after me, 'We will not lay down this flag until we present it to Jesus–the son of Maryum–and the last of us fights the Deceiver. We will remain faithful–by the permission of God, the Merciful and Compassionate–until the arrival of the Hour and the last of us remains to fight the Deceiver. We ask God–praised be He–to make this flag the sole flag of all Muslims, we are certain that it will be the flag of the people of Iraq when they go to the aid of the Mahdi at the Holy House of God.'"

The women stumbled through the lengthy oath with the help of IS soldiers who prodded them painfully when they faltered.

The judge made the women recite the *shahada* in God's language and would not let them leave the courtroom until everyone of them got it word perfect, "*La 'ilāha 'illā llah muḥammadun rasulu llah.*"

The exhausted women were speaking a foreign language mouthing what to them was a detestable phrase, while under terrible stress; so, they had to endure more than an hour of practice before unforgiving men.

"Keep this record of your conversion to the only true religion on the earth with you always. You will be asked to repeat the *shahada*. If you cannot, the punishments will be severe."

With that, the court appearance was over, and the terrified women had had their first taste of what Sharia law entailed. There were no lawyers in the room; no defense was permitted; no one spoke in their behalf; no evidence was presented; and no witnesses were allowed. The religious imam in front of them was the prosecutor, judge, jury, and deliverer of the religious dicta.

They were pushed from the courtroom and outside into the clutches of IS guards who laughed at their documents.

"*Kuffars*," the men pronounced, as they separated the women by age groups into different trucks.

Khatoon was segregated into a group of women and girls who ranged in age from fifteen to about thirty. They were taken via a very crowded bus which smelled of body odor, urine from girls who could no longer avoid the humiliation, and fear, to the school yard in Tal Afar.

CHAPTER TWENTY-EIGHT

"Abu Bakr al-Baghdadi, also known as Abu Du'a, also known as Ibrahim 'Awwad Ibrahim 'Ali al-Badri, is the senior leader of the terrorist organization Islamic State of Iraq and the Levant (ISIL)...Under al-Baghdadi, ISIL has been responsible for the deaths of thousands of civilians in the Middle East, including the brutal murder of numerous civilian hostages from Japan, the United Kingdom, and the United States. Al-Baghdadi has taken credit for numerous terrorist attacks in Iraq since 2011, killing thousands of his fellow Iraqi citizens. The threat that al-Baghdadi poses has increased significantly since the Department of State's initial $10 million reward offer for information leading to his location, arrest, or conviction was announced in 2011..."

U.S. Department of State offered a reward of up to $25 million for information leading to the capture or death of mujahid Shaykh Abu Bakr al-Baghdadi al-Hussaini al-Qurashi. Al-Baghdadi is designated by the Department of State as an SDGT [Specially Designated Global Terrorist] under Executive Order 13224. He is also listed at the United Nations Security Council ISIL [*Da'esh* and al-Qaeda] Sanctions Committee.

Baghdad to Sinjar Village, Iraq, August 6, 2014

Avery, Malcolm, and Devlin, had been very busy since President Obama ordered the withdrawal of United States military forces from Iraq and Syria—except for a small caretaker force of special forces. The rapid exodus of the U.S. troops had undermined the coalition forces and left the Iraqi Army and police to deal with the increasingly vicious insurgency. The Islamic State had capitalized to the maximum in the absence of an effective deterrent force. Abu Bakr al-Baghdadi and his rabidly fanatical international fighters had returned to Iraq and Syria in division size forces and with billions of dollars in funding from sympathizers—including armed bandits acting in the name of IS–from all over the world.

It was all the three CIA agents and their subordinate contract agents could do to keep up with troop movements. Because they were powerless to do anything about the influx of men, military machinery flowing in from the excess armaments left behind by Americans leaving Afghanistan, and the seemingly endless funding sources, the agents could only bemoan and report their observations about the northward movement of jihadist fanatics and mercenaries towards the Diyala Governate, Sinjar Province, and Kurdistan. Their worst fear was that the jihadists would regain their foothold in Baghdad after the Iraqi Army and U.S. coalition forces had struggled so hard, for so long, and at such an enormous human and monetary cost, to make the capital city livable for decent people.

Avery had been seriously troubled by the difficulty of communicating with the northern Mesopotamian provinces. He knew he was kidding himself when he mused that maybe "no news is good news."

At 0410 hours on August 6, 2014, Avery's radio man woke him up.

"Boss, I have Rahim Jamaluddin on the horn. He says its urgent."

"If Rahim says it's urgent it is. He never exaggerates or embellishes. Switch him over to me. Thanks for the heads-up."

There was some static and to start with only muffled voice transmission. Then, Rahim moved to a different position; and the transmission was perfect.

"Boss, sorry to wake you; but o-dark-thirty is the only time I can safely transmit. I can only be on for fifteen seconds. The message is: Sinjar and Kocho in Nineveh Governate have been overrun by the bogeys. Happened on the third. Both villages have been cleared out of all non-Muslims. I don't think there is a single Yazidi left. They get help pronto or the jihadists will accomplish a complete genocide. Copy?"

"Copy. Don't take chances. We'll do what we can. Thanks Rahim."

The communication terminated abruptly. Avery summoned his two agents and informed them of the new development.

"Boss, I presume we're going to head up there and take on the IS army, that about right?" Devlin asked.

"A bit exaggerated, but not completely. We have to get there to get an up-close-and-personal reconnaissance; so, we can give the ODNI an accurate sit rep. I propose that we tippy-toe around up there and keep our heads down. I don't underestimate the IS fighters or their intelligence services. Let's pack up and get the flock out of here."

The CIA unit had its own small—but highly useful fleet of military vehicles—and all the supplies to sustain them for six weeks in the field. The agents rounded up three trusted Iraqi army intelligence officers and made a quick weapons inventory. Malcolm brought out a large two arm loads of IS uniforms, flags, and phony IS identification papers. Less than thirty minutes had elapsed since Avery hung up on his call from Rahim.

It was still inky black on a starless night when they set off in two beat-up looking Russian Antonov-12 troop transporters–shipped over from Afghanistan as a brotherly gesture from the American CIA and then the mujahideen—and two vintage, but souped-up–HMMVEEs bearing Afghan war lord markings. They were as prepared as they would ever be to set out on the five hundred plus kilometer journey on route 1 to Sinjar. The closer they were to Baghdad and its perimeter, the safer they were, and the faster they could go. They encountered no checkpoints or impediments from Baghdad to the outskirts of Baqubah, capital of the Diyala Governate.

The signals officer got a coded call for Avery.

"Boss, this is coming from Kurdistan."

Avery picked up the receiver, "Avery here."

"Is this a secure line?"

"It is. Proceed."

"This is Col. Behremend Rozaki, peshmerga. If this is Avery, give me your code ID."

His code was his birth date July 30, 1990. The code was a numerical book code based on the KJV of the Bible and was expressed in military style as 30-06-90 Frisco, easy for Avery to remember because his birthplace was San Francisco.

Avery recited his ID and asked, "What's up, Behremend?"

"Bad news, as you might expect. The monster squad has retaken Baqubah and has committed a massacre in Sinjar and Kocho. The survivors are trying to make it to Mt. Sinjar; but it is a terrible ordeal, my friend. I know you have connections there, but maybe it's not worth it to go there. I hate to say it, but they are probably dead or enslaved by now. The IS monsters captured the towns and trucked off almost everyone who is not a Salafi Muslim believer. My peshmergas have not been able to get back to either town or to Solagh to see what happened."

"Thanks, Behremend. Do you think we can get through in IS uniforms and with what I think are pretty nearly genuine documents?"

"Probably, Avery. You've done it before. Your Arabic is good, but the most important thing is that the IS army is rapidly on the move north to take over as much of Syria as they can grab while the civil war is still raging. I think they will be gone in two weeks except for a garrison maintenance unit. Maybe your contacts there are worth it to you. You realize that no sane man or coward would go anywhere near those pitiful towns."

"I guess I'm more crazy than coward; so, we'll go on. I'll give Malcolm and Devlin and the contractors the option of going or not. I appreciate the warning. Hopefully, I can find a way to see you in Erbil or Sulaymaniyah before all of this is over."

"I'll keep an eye open for intel and to be able to communicate when you get near us."

"Good. Over."

"And out."

Every man agreed to go with Avery which touched him. They were brothers, and he hated to put them at risk. He knew he had an irrational attachment to a Yazidi woman who was ten years younger than him and would never be more than a sort of stepdaughter. But she represented a people facing genocide, and that struck at his core value system. No religion or ideological credo can be given a pass when it comes to their plan to exterminate innocents just to further their onerous agenda. He would have pushed on, if he had to do it all by himself.

Col. Rozaki had been right about the activity the agents were going to encounter. There was a mass exodus of IS soldiers, support forces, imams, camp followers, and enslaved prostitutes, headed north into Kurdish country towards the several crossings into southern Syria. The CIA operatives looked like and acted like the rest of the black pajama soldiers. They inserted themselves into a long convoy, made mental and physical notes, and traveled on to Sinjar with their black flags of jihad flying just like all the rest of the vehicles in the convoy. At the intersection with a back road into Sinjar, they turned right and away from the convoy. There was a small checkpoint manned by thoroughly bored young men, some barely teenagers. The CIA agents–who looked every bit the part of IS fighters–breezed through and into the town.

Sinjar had transformed almost completely since Avery had last been there. Black flags waved in the light breeze everywhere—on almost every roof top, storefront, and several from every municipal building. Those buildings shown in the sun reflecting off the fresh shiny black paint that transformed Sinjar into an Islamic State enclave. Most of the streets were devoid of life; a few of them were still littered with corpses which were unmistakably Yazidi men, women, and children, by their clothing and hair styles.

Devout men lay face down on the gravel roads or hung from poles, identified by their having hair in long braids and faces covered with white cloth. Women—some still clutching dead babies—lay in grotesque and some in obscene positions, scattered along the roads. Most of the women wore gauzy white dresses, veils, and headscarves, as had their mothers and grandmothers for many generations.

Some of the women had been disemboweled; many were spread-eagled indicative of their having been the victims of gang-rape. There were children who had been decapitated and showed evidence of torture and mutilation. Even the battle hardened agents–whose experience in the Middle East had exposed them to almost every form of inhumanity–were sickened by the Francisco Goya-like dark and bleak outlook seen in his prints and drawings—real sights and stench that permeated the once vigorous and relatively tolerant little city.

Abdul and Safaa's little mud house was empty and showed signs of brutality. Avery was saddened to find the little nooks and crannies where the little children had secreted away their precious little treasures now vandalized. There was nothing in the house that told him what had happened to the adults or where they might be.

That knowledge came to the agents less than an hour later. They found a long shallow pit site. A cursory bit of digging revealed hundreds of bodies in varying states of decomposition. It was the worst thing any of them could remember, and it was proof of genocide. A worse sight was yet to come.

Just over the top of the low hill where the wadi containing the body dump was located, they came upon a sight that would have made lesser men weep. There were twelve poles fixed upright near the crest of the hill. On each pole hung crucified men and a few women, their faces still contorted in their death agonies. Later, when the burial pit was excavated, it was found to contain mostly women and a few small children, some of whom had not been dead when they were covered with dirt and rocks.

The ghastly hellish scenes were even worse in Kocho and Solagh. It was abundantly evident that a genocidal massacre had taken place. An even larger body dump site was discovered in Solagh with the eventual discovery of hundreds of murder victims.

A fury seethed in Avery's chest. He fought to contain it as he made contact with the ODNI. Because the world's press had already published *forme frustes* of what had transpired in those Yazidi towns and speculated on what those hints pointed towards, the DNI himself took the call.

Avery gave his code ID, then said tersely, "We have nothing short of a genocide in progress here. The Yazidi survivors are making their way through a gauntlet of IS murderers to try and get to the top of their sacred Mount Sinjar. Without our help, they will starve, die of thirst or their Wounds; and we will be responsible for having turned away when these human beings were in their worst extremis."

"How many dead and wounded do you estimate, Avery?"

"Thousands at least. Who knows how many captives and slaves are out there in the clutches of the Islamic Jihadist terrorists?"

"Listen, Avery, we can't say Islamic or jihadist or even terrorists. The president forbids any reference to religion connected to such calamities as intolerance. He wants us all to get along."

"I've never known you to be a man who jokes about serious things, Director Clapper. Is that a real policy?"

"Afraid so. You need to get to Washington ASAP, and—a word to the wise—Avery, ixnay on the adistjay and micIslahay."

"I'll do my best: no jihadist or Islamic. I'll be a verbal pretzel before the day is over trying to find enough euphemisms."

They both laughed.

Avery and his agents were exfiltrated by marine Bell OH-58D Kiowa Warrior helicopters late that night.

CHAPTER TWENTY-NINE

Oval Office, White House, Washington DC, PDB [President's Daily Briefing], August 11, 2014

Meeting recorded and stamped "TOP SECRET, EYES ONLY"; POTUS, Barack Obama; Director National Intelligence, Lt. Gen. James Robert Clapper, Jr.; Secy. of State, Hillary Diane Rodham Clinton; Secy. of Defense, Robert Gates; Chairman of the Joint Chiefs of Staff, General Martin Dempsey

Present: POTUS, DNI, Secretary of State, Secretary of Defense, CJCS, Special Agent, COS-I [Chief of Station, Iraq], Avery Challenger, and Senate Majority Leader, Mitch McConnell (R Ky), Senate Minority Leader, Harry Reid (D-Nev)

Date: March 28, 2007

Subject: The impending genocide of the Yazidi people of Iraq

Summary:
- DNI: Our intelligence sources inform us that the Islamic State insurgency has grown from almost nothing to a major political, ideological, and military, power in the Middle East since its nadir in

2011. Terrorist attacks in the region and around the western world have increased at a significant and unpredicted rate. Presently, they are in the process of establishing their Islamic State with headquarters in Mosul, Iraq; and they are on the move to establish their final state in Syria, which I believe was prophesied in the *Qur'an*. They have had serious recruitment, fund raising, and propaganda, successes in the region and among emigres in Europe.

The most pressing immediate problem is that of the ongoing genocide of the Yazidi minority in northern Iraq. The issue is what–if anything–should we do to help them? Should we return with a military force? Should we provide drone, fighter, and bombing support? Should we attempt to resurrect the coalition that all but disbanded in 2011 when we withdrew? We are faced with a human, political, military, and diplomatic, catastrophe of existential proportions in the region with repercussions throughout the world for us.

- Secy. of Defense: We cannot—in good conscience—allow these defenseless people to be annihilated on our watch. I can speak for my department and for the JCOS. We must strike militarily while there is still time to save a significant portion of the Yazidis and other minorities who are being hounded to extinction much like Hitler's progressive attacks against the Jewish people before and during World War II.

- Secy. of State: I agree with Secy. Gates. We are already in poor standing among civilized nations for having abandoned our allies and the minorities in Iraq. We would appear to be craven now, if we do not mount at least a rescue mission supported by air force and humanitarian aid. It is not too late, but it soon will be.

- CJCS: I am strongly against reopening the war in Iraq. The Iraqis must sink or swim on their own efforts and will. However, they are not prepared to give anything like adequate assistance to the Yazidis and other minorities, including our allies, the Kurds. The COS-I has been in-country for more than a decade. No one knows the on-the-ground conditions better than he does. I think a sit-rep is in order; and I, for one, would welcome his conclusions.

- COS-I: Mr. President, Lady and Gentlemen, thank you for inviting me. Like the situation in Syria, the overall situation in Iraq is a Gordian knot we will never untie satisfactorily. However, the condition of the

Yazidis is at once simple, terrible, and fixable. It is simple because the IS is in the process of exterminating them, and we can make that stop. It is terrible because there is a genocidal holocaust beginning to take place in full view of the press corps of the world. To do nothing is unconscionable, and we Americans will lose all credibility as the leader of nations if we continue to turn a blind eye. It is fixable because we have air power, drone power, political and economic, power aplenty to make IS change its present course. It is my recommendation and that of every American in service in that poor country that we send bombers and strafing fighter jets to wipe out the advancing murderers. We send a secret contingent of special forces to penetrate the IS defenses, and finally, that we freeze the assets of every malignant group who supports IS, including Saudi Arabia. There is a political necessity to get Russia to cease and desist in its support of our enemies and even to give material support to the Yazidis.

- POTUS: The White House is united and adamant in opposing any reintroduction of regular military personnel into Iraq. It is a quagmire we must avoid so long as it is at all possible. I am finally convinced that we cannot just sit by and watch a defenseless people fall as prey and to extinction by a conscienceless group of bullies and killers. Therefore, it is my order as of today that the CJCS and the Secretary of Defense commence a forceful response to help the Yazidi people to defend themselves. The Secretary of State will take charge of a humanitarian operation of sufficient size and strength to prevent starvation, severe thirst, exposure to the elements, and lack of medical aid, which is beginning to decimate the population on Mount Sinjar. I direct the Department of Justice and our intelligence services to track down and to eliminate the tyrant behind all this suffering. Use whatever measures are necessary short of torture to accomplish that end. Good day, lady and gentlemen.

Signed:

Barack Obama, POTUS, August 11, 2014

CHAPTER THIRTY

"Sometimes the Bible in the hand of one man is worse than a whisky bottle in the hand of (another)... There are just some kind of men who - who're so busy worrying about the next world they've never learned to live in this one, and you can look down the street and see the results."

–Harper Lee, *To Kill a Mockingbird*,
J.B. Lippincott & Co., Philadelphia, 1960

"Remember that all through history, there have been tyrants and murderers–and for a time–they seem invincible. But in the end, they always fall. Always."

–Mohandas [Mahatma] Karamchand Gandhi, Mahadev
H. Desai (Translator), *Gandhi:
An Autobiography, The Story of My Experiments with the Truth*, written in weekly installments and published in his journal *Navjivan* from 1925 to 1929.

Tal Afar Village, Nineveh Governate, Iraq, August 12, 2014

The school in Tal Afar was not much different than the school of her youth in Sinjar. Not much changed in the rhythms of life in northern Iraq day to day or even year to year. Except for this day when nothing in the world was the same, as if her flat earth had been turned over on its face. Khatoon had been a good girl her entire life—an example of the purity of manners, obedience, and most importantly in matters of personal and private things, the things that were not talked about. She had had girlish fantasies of having a life like the American or the Bollywood stars and sometimes of having her first kiss.

All that sweet pure fantasy had been ruined on the bus ride. Men she did not even know walked by and squeezed the private area of her chest. They laughed when she cried out in pain. A ten-year-old girl she had met once in the market had begun to cry uncontrollably when two men tore at her clothes. She was totally uneducated in what goes on between men and women; and the men thought that naiveté to be hilarious, so much so, that they would not leave the girl alone. No one dared to speak out about such terrible behavior—not even Khatoon—let alone try to defend her.

It was growing dark, and the black clad soldier figures looked more ominous than ever in the gathering dusk. The buses caused a swirl of dust with every turn of their large wheels making all the girls dirty. Khatoon could taste the grit in her mouth which was already parched from lack of water. She was almost beyond hungry. She was dizzy and felt like she might faint. Older men began milling around the crowds of girls and young women. Sometimes they grabbed an unsuspecting girl and made her cry out. Several of the men stood face-to-face with one of the girls and held their noses.

"You stink, filthy Yazid! You won't fetch even five dollars at the auction."

The men did stink. They obviously had not bathed for weeks and were proud of it. It was one more thing they could have to torment the girls. They were sex-starved; but more than that, the brain-washed zealots could hardly wait for a full chance to humiliate and to cause pain in a girl that had never even been kissed before. Many girls curled into balls, screamed, and thereby invited severe slappings.

Mention of the "auction" struck fear into Khatoon. She had indulged her curiosity for learning occasionally and read about the Arab slavers and the Atlantic triangle of African, Caribbean, and American; slave trade. She had seen drawings of the terrible slave auctions. She had had to turn her face away even from the pictures. How would she ever endure the actual auction, she wondered. She began a process of steeling herself not to cry and to shame herself.

The young women of Khatoon's age range were pushed, shoved, and bullied up to the third floor of the schoolhouse and told to go to sleep on the floor. The night was hot, and the closed off room was airless, dusty, and had a fetid smell. She laid on the floor between two girls younger than her who cried all night. It was impossible to sleep, and the crying carried with it a grim portent of things to come.

It was not yet quite light out when the Muslim men began to stir. At the sound of the muezzin's call to prayer, every man dropped to the floor facing Mecca and began the sing-song mechanics of rote prayers. The older men demanded that any women who had been converted to Islam—however unwillingly—assume the position and to mimic the motions and sounds which were strange and incomprehensible to the simple Yazidi girls. Many of them failed to perform well and felt the sting of a leather strap across their backs until they could do the motions of the strange prayers with the minimum of acceptability.

A bucket was passed around, and every girl gulped down as much as she could get before the bucket was yanked out of her hands and passed to the next girl. Then, perhaps just to cause revulsion in the minds of the previously entirely private young women, a second bucket was passed for use as the most primitive of toilets. The stench and textures in the buckets were almost unbearable, but the need to eliminate overrode feelings of modesty. They learned to hold their breath until their turn was over, and the bucket mercifully moved on.

A third bucket—this one filled with grey water from the laundry—was passed around with instructions for the girls to wash their hands, faces, arm pits, and between their legs. It did feel better to be somewhat cleaner. They were each given a small bowl of cold water into which a handful of coarsely ground millet was dropped. By the time the pasty gruel could be swallowed, it had the consistency and general taste of mucilage. It did fill a portion of their empty stomachs and eased the hunger pangs, but only briefly because millet is almost entirely devoid of nourishment. The breakfast was about as savory and nutritious as a hair-ball.

"'Ajlis [sit down]! ordered the main guard and threatened slow girls with his well-worn strap.

Khatoon assumed a reasonably comfortable cross-legged position and settled in for a long wait. That wait consumed nearly two hours. Every ten or fifteen minutes a dozen girls and women were ordered to their feet and shoved out of the room and down the stairs. When it was Khatoon's turn, she stepped out into the blazing sun of midday and immediately began to sweat profusely. She was ordered to walk up three steps to a meter-wide platform and to stand over a heavy steel ring attached to the planks under her feet. A gnomish little man stepped up to each woman and handcuffed her wrists and attached the cuffs by a chain to the steel ring. The chain only allowed about half a meter of movement, and no sitting was permitted.

After what seemed like an eternity–but in reality, was only half an hour—a group of black pajama-clad IS soldiers gathered all around the platform and ogled the women. Several of the girls vomited. The gathered men whistled and made catcalls which were laced with obscenities and scatological references, which jarred the sensibilities of even the roughest of the farm women. Any woman or girl who cried received a hard slap in the face. Soon, the women were silent and resigned to whatever fate awaited them in their powerless state. None of the women dared to try and comfort any other woman for fear of reprisal. They shared their fear and misery in an anguished silence where every passing second was like dying a bit more. Some of the younger, more nubile girls, had their dresses ripped off; so, their salability could be better demonstrated. Men spat on their hands and rubbed them in unfeigned glee.

The slave sellers assured the waiting men that all the women were virgins, checked by IS doctors. All the slave selling activity was pre-planned by the IS. The seller passed out pamphlets telling all who could read that all women on display were property and "fit for intercourse."

One by one, all the women were purchased by men who pawed and slathered over them. The younger men—who did not have the full ten-dollar slave rental fee—were given a discount, which made them whoop and dance around with enthusiasm and sickened the women. Several men haggled over Khatoon, who was taller, stronger, and more buxom, than any of the other women. Finally, the ante became too high for two younger suitors; and she was sold outright for forty dollars to an old pock-faced man who cackled as he groped her. He did not speak to her, just shoved her down the stairs and pulled on her arm until he could force her into his automobile. She showed him her papers verifying that she had converted, but he ignored her with a sardonic laugh.

"Not only are you a subhuman, a polytheist, and an enemy of God, but you are stupid to think that those papers mean anything. You are a nothing, a mere woman, a *musbrik* [a polytheist who is to be enslaved], and now my *sabah* [sexual servant], my property to be used as I please."

She opened her mouth as if to protest, and the angry slave owner reached back and ripped off her head scarf and struck her face with a vicious back hand slap which dazed her.

To add insult to injury, Khatoon discovered that she was seated in the back seat by a young boy and a girl of about twelve; and in the front seat was seated a dour middle-aged woman in a full face burka with only eye slits to look out at the world. The conversation between the old man and the woman made it clear that she was the wife, and she was going to have to agree to have the much younger and prettier woman as her husband's second wife. Khatoon was afraid she was going to throw up.

She learned later that her immediate fate was not as terrible as it was for some 400 other Yazidi women who were bused to Mosul for the great slave sale. They all had to be raped first; so, no virgins would be sold. That was considered to be against Sharia law, but raping a slave was not a sin. Yazidis are infidels. The rapes were particularly brutal and left the girls dazed and in pain. Many made suicide attempts after being raped. Along the way and in Mosul, many were burned with cigarettes, slapped, whipped, and spat upon, after being informed that this was the place where they were to be sold or given away to brave soldiers as rewards.

Khatoon's first night in the slave owner's house was the stuff of nightmares. Kahled Umr al-Sham, the fat, wrinkled, and extremely hirsute old brute who owned her, made her shower and to have the first wife scrub her all over with a stiff brush which left her skin raw. The wife told Khatoon over and over that she deserved it because she was a filthy *kaffir* and a *sabah* and could not be made clean with just a soap and water bath. Then the bear of a man strode into the bedroom and threw off his dishdasha to expose himself in all his presumed glory as a virile man.

That was not altogether a true picture; so, he became enraged and beat her before and after an especially brutal object rape which left Khatoon bruised, bleeding, and in severe pain. Because he could not perform well enough—and that was blamed on the *sabah's* poor performance—he had his male servants, a brother, and two soldiers complete an eminently successful gang rape. Mercifully, Khatoon passed out; and the last three men were left with an unconscious and defenseless semi-corpse.

She was aroused in time for the first prayer of the day by the son of the family who expected to get his share; but when he saw what she looked like, he fled in revulsion. After the compulsory prayers, she was forced to limp around and do the dishes, sweep the carpets, and scrub the slate tile floors before being given a small bowl of watered-down canned tomato soup and yesterday's rice. The only good thing that happened that first week was that the old man was so humiliated that he did not visit her again for a full seven days.

CHAPTER THIRTY-ONE

"The war of Islam and its followers against the crusaders and their followers is a long one," Baghdadi told a group of followers sitting with him on the floor of a bare, whitewashed room. An AK-47 rifle was perched by his side. "Our battle today is a war of attrition to harm the enemy, and they should know that jihad will continue until doomsday."
–Robin Wright, *Baghdadi Is Back—and Vows That ISIS Will Be, Too. The New Yorker*, April 29, 2019

Nineveh Governate, Iraq, August to October, 2014

Avery, Malcolm, Devlin, and four more seasoned paramilitary CIA cadres–dressed in IS uniforms–began to search the Nineveh Governate for any possible survivors, the wounded in need of care, and to capture or kill any lingering IS soldiers. They located less than twenty living Yazidis in the six villages they visited, but they found multiple mass graves. Most of the victims were Yazidi men and young children, older women, and a minority of Muslims whom they presumed to have been unwilling to convert to Abu Bakr al Baghdadi's particular brand of Islam. There was abundant evidence of torture and mutilation including amputations, signs of crucifixion, headless corpses, and separate heads. One such body dump was at the Shingal Technical Institute's fish pond. Shallow pits held eighty-nine corpses of people who had been forced to kneel while a fighter walked behind them and put a bullet in the back of their heads.

The men were over being sickened by then; now, they were consumed with rage. They killed every man or woman who was clad in IS pajamas they could find. From some of the few survivors, they learned that under the only true religion practiced in the Islamic State, women were erased from public life. They were told of beatings and starvation. Worse, decent women told the CIA agent about girls who were raped until their young bodies broke. One girl—who had escaped from her captors–said that she told her would-be rapists that she had cancer of her genitals and that he should not touch her. She was taken back to the slave market and resold, raped into unconsciousness, and left for dead in the back seat of an old car. She sneaked away.

Other girls, less fortunate, or maybe less plucky, were known to have entered into a recurring cycle of being sold, raped, beaten, then resold, over and over again. Signs around the governate advertised a five-thousand-dollar reward—which turned out to be a lie–for turning in a runaway slave. Some of the girls killed themselves or cut their genitals to avoid being raped. Others—like Khatoon in Tel Afar—felt less than human; something inside them had died; and, for survivors, was never to be regained.

The CIA cadres moved farther north towards Mount Sinjar. Avery hoped against hope that he would be able to find Khatoon alive and relatively well, or–absent that salutary event—that he could locate some of her family who could tell him where she was or what had happened to her.

They fought a few isolated skirmishes with IS soldiers at hastily improvised check points on the way to the mountain, but nothing very serious. They made radio contact with a unit of ten army rangers [Green Berets] who had been sent to the region to interfere with the IS attacks on the mountain. They hatched a loose plan to mount guerrilla attacks to keep the insurgency off balance. They were not unaware of the enemy they were about to annoy.

The IS fighters were receiving funding support from the Arab Gulf States of Kuwait, Qatar, and Saudi Arabia. CIA and NSA intel reported that they had accumulated more than $40 million and operated 350 oil wells in Iraq and Syria producing 80,000 barrels a day. The oil sold at $30-$40 a barrel. The IS economy received several million dollars a month in taxes levied on individuals and companies in Mosul alone and a great deal more than that from their other occupied territories. The CIA estimated that IS took in ten million dollars a month from kidnapping alone.

Their thriving sex-trade industry–managed like a Western corporation–"employed" nearly 4,000 Yazidi women who were sold at ten to twenty-five dollars each as a recruiting tool. Each sex slave could service as many as twenty Muslim militants a day. The income was staggering. The promise and delivery of money and sexual incentives kept reinforcements pouring in, and the majority were gathering at the base of Mount Sinjar in northern Mesopotamia for the final genocide of the Yazidi people.

By the end of August, 2014, the Islamic State had an estimated twenty to thirty thousand militants under its flag–of which two-thirds were operating in Syria and at least partially available for the attack in the Sinjar Mountains [Jabal Sinjar]. Fifteen thousand foreign militants traveled in from eighty countries to join the insurgency. That number included 3400 westerners and twelve American citizens. IS used a slogan from other times and places to describe the impending "Mother of All Battles."

The genocidal IS actions against the Yazidi population had already resulted in something on the order of 500,000 refugees, and several thousand more killed, kidnapped, and sold into slavery and eventual total obscurity. The early efforts to achieve genocide led to the expulsion, flight, and effective exile, of the Yazidis from their ancestral lands in Iraq. The Yazidis also had their human rights violated by a myriad of other terrorist organizations which followed the IS example and their twisted reasoning to kill Yazidis.

Fifty thousand Yazidi were–by the time the CIA agents and Green Berets entered the fray–besieged by IS fighters on Mount Sinjar and waiting for their genocidal enemies to reach the top of the mountain. Any succor or defense now depended on the Western coalition because the Kurdish Peshmerga had fled from the IS back into their safe havens in Kurdistan leaving the Yazidis defenseless.

The CIA agents, Green Berets, the western world's information outlets, and—not least—the Yazidis on the mountain and in front of their television sets in the North America and Europe, were deeply relieved to see the planes of a multinational relief effort flying in close to the top of the mountain and making humanitarian drops of food, winter clothing, water by the five hundred gallon reinforced steel drumful, and weapons to the beleaguered people. It was all to the good, but nowhere near enough. The enemies were still in place, and their plans undeterred by the "Christian Crusaders" whom they derided as fools and cowards afraid to fight.

As late as October–contrary to the intel Avery had forwarded to his CIA and NI leaders—there were 2,000 Yazidis–mainly volunteer fighters–who had remained behind to protect the scattered villages–and noncombatant civilians. The civilians were seven hundred families who had hidden or were trapped and unable to escape; so, they were still in the Sinjar provincial area. In the end, most were forced by ISIL to abandon the last villages in their control–Dhoula and Bork–and to make a very painful retreat to the Sinjar Mountains, adding to the crisis already unfolding.

In this mass exodus–combined with the effects of two previous ones–two-hundred Yazidi children died from thirst, starvation, heat, and dehydration, while fleeing to Mount Sinjar. The elderly, weakened, sick, and those recovering from wounds, died and fell to the wayside, leaving their corpses to rot in the dry heat of the desert. IS fighters ignored them except to move away towards the mountain to avoid the cloying and increasing stench.

On the mountain, the intensely crowded and nearly helpless Yazidis watched with mixed horror as the Islamic State hordes gathered and fired at them, and with joy as the supply drops began. They watched in horrified fascination beheadings by IS on their few remaining cell phones. On the top of the mountain, days were insufferably hot, and the nights were freezing cold. The Yazidis began dying of starvation and dehydration. In desperation, the elders slaughtered all the sheep for what might be a last small taste of meat for everyone. Some men loaded a tractor with wheat which was boiled on the top and everyone got one cup of unflavored wheat.

The battle—such as it was—began in August when President Obama ordered a massive humanitarian airlift. Contrary to his original orders of early August, the president now ordered military air strikes, and a real battle got underway. He stopped short of allowing any U.S. troops to set foot in Iraq to battle IS to save the Yazidis. After the airstrikes, the United States airdropped 3,800 gallons of water and 16,128 MREs to the thirsty and starving defenders. Impressed that America was at last standing up to the Islamic State, the United Kingdom and France also began to contribute airdrops.

Heartened by the presence of allied aircraft with their guns and bombs, Yazidi defenders began to contribute. They made det cord out of braided cotton rope soaked in axel grease, stuck the cords into fifty-gallon drums of gasoline as wicks, and set fire to the wicks. Then, with great courage, the men exposed themselves to gunfire and sent the barrels rolling down the mountainside. They were able to get the timing just right to have the fire reach the full barrel just as it entered a group of unsuspecting jihadists.

Not all the improvised incendiary bombs found a good target, but those that did struck the fear of God into the intended victims and the witnesses. No one hardens enough to watch several of his friends and comrades-in-arms turn into a living human torch. The screaming and violent contortions of the men on fire ignited intense and psychologically disabling fear in the IS witnesses.

Women and boys rolled large stones down the mountain side and resulted in some severe injuries, and a great deal of fear, because none of the IS fighters could predict when a great stone would come his way. When they ran out of large stones, men, women, boys, and girls began throwing smaller rocks. That was ineffective as predicted, but it developed a sense of comradery that made everyone on the mountain feel as if he or she was contributing something to the defense of the Yazidi people.

Despite the outside help, the Yazidis on the mountain were losing. Power supplies gave; out; the clean water supply failed, and there was no rain in sight; filthy clothes and bodies and disease—especially among the weak children and the elderly; and hunger and thirst–were taking a dreadful toll. Even during the best of times, relief from Kocho—the nearest village to Mt. Sinjar—took four hours. Now, if there were no IS soldiers or roadblocks, the trip would take ten hours because of the great damage done to the roadway. But the reality was that IS owned the road, and nothing could get through at all.

Life was at its darkest, both physically and figuratively. There were not even enough candles to light the way of a sentry at night. The United States Air Force took full advantage of that mine shaft level darkness and two hours past midnight, they carried out five precise surgical airstrikes. The bombing and shelling destroyed several dozen IS armed vehicles and several strategically placed mortar positions causing a retreat of a hundred meters on the part of the IS military units.

Avery and his CIA agents, Sergeant Major Erwin Phelps and his Green Berets, along with Air Force special operations commandoes from the 1st Special Operations Wing out of Hurlburt Field, Florida, did HALO parachute drops on the top of Mt. Sinjar right in front of the temple. There was a dozen of them; and their commander, Chief Master Sergeant Colon Perez-Rodriguez, handed Avery a plan devised in the Pentagon. All the secret agents dropped what they were doing to keep the Yazidis alive, and began to execute the top-secret directive.

Before dawn's light, and without anyone from the Islamic State being the wiser, almost 50,000 Yazidis out of the now 150,000 stranded on the mountain—the strongest and most able to travel—were evacuated down the back—northeast—side of the Sinjar Range. An army of triumphant Kurds—men from the YPG [People's Protection Units. *Ḥdoywotho d'Sutoro d'Amo*, a mainly Kurdish militia in Syria, and the primary component of the Democratic Federation of Northern Syria's Syrian Democratic Forces], the PUK [Patriotic Union of Kurdistan], the PKK [Kurdish Workers Party], and the Peshmerga [the standing military of Iraqi Kurdistan], swarmed the starving Yazidis. They handed them loaves of bread, goatskin bags of milk, and baskets of the Yazidis' favorite food and grapes in celebration. The Kurds–in an extraordinary demonstration of Kurdish unity–broke the Islamic State's siege on the backside of the mountain range. The Yazidis showed worshipful gratitude to the Kurds and were provided a military escort to Erbil, the capital of Kurdistan—where they could begin a new and safe life.

There was additional great news that busy night: The United States Central Command made a seventh airdrop completing an addition of nourishment totaling 114,000 meals and more than 35,000 gallons of potable water that had been airdropped to the displaced Yazidis on the mountain during the preceding seven days.

The commandoes–with an addition of a twenty-five man unit of KDP [Kurdistan Democratic Party] combat hardened Kurds under the command of Col. Behremend Rozaki, ranking peshmerga officer, CIA spy, and old personal friend of Avery Challenger–began to make tactical plans to undermine the IS army on the front side of the mountain. The Peshmergas insisted on carrying a huge red, white, and green colored of KDP flag to taunt the extremists whom they hated.

Everyone who could stand or walk gathered to show gratitude to the commandoes and to celebrate their thanksgiving in the proper Yazidi way at the temple. Many could not. All the children suffered from severe diarrhea. People with wounds–even common, everyday wounds–of feet injured by broken glass, or less common ones such as old shrapnel injuries were incapacitated by the infections growing to severe levels without proper wound care bandages, antibiotics, or capable nurses and doctors. At least 500 people had died, mostly children. So, it was part celebration and part funereal mourning that early morning.

Mt. Sinjar is long, narrow, bone dry, and has only a few trees in good times. Most of them had been cut for fires and to build combat shelters. Man-made steppes were created from narrow stretches made from growing tobacco. In winter, the top was covered with clouds and snow, and that day was not far off. The people knew that they would all perish if they were still there when winter set in.

On top–perched on a cliff, on the highest peak of the Sinjar Mountains–stands the small white *Chermera* temple. That point is considered by the Yazidis to be the place where Noah's Ark settled after the biblical flood. Water was scarce there all the time, and much of it was not fit to drink in the best of times. Yazidis had to compete with goats for the remaining safe water. After the Islamist siege was well under way on the dry mountain, the water supply dwindled down to an amount where rationing yielded only a cup and a half full of the life-giving fluid per person per day. Goats—valuable as they were–could no longer be allowed to use the precious water; and they all had to be slaughtered. There was very little wood left for fuel and cooking; so, much of the valuable meat was wasted. Before entering the temple for what many feared would be the last time in their lives, they were provided with a pleasant meal of okra and tomatoes, bread, dried chicken, and strong sugary tea.

CHAPTER THIRTY-TWO

"We are not preachers of violence. Jihad [striving or holy war] in Islam is a defensive movement against those who impose violence."
–Grand Ayatollah Sheikh Mohammad Hussain Fadlallah, quoted *in Laura Marlowe, A Fiery Cleric's Defense of Jihad, Time* (New York), Cambridge University Press, January 15, 1996

"The IS media bewitch the perceptions and eyes of the masses with flashing visuals, slogans, and the like. They are similar to the sorcerers of Pharaoh. Meanwhile, the security department instills fear and is on the lookout for those on the inside with proper insight into the system. Thus, the media department and security department constitute the pillars of a classic tyrannical system. The media department has been a hub of extremism. Since IS insists that the media department is its official voice, then extremism is regrettably the official *manhaj* of IS which we must disavow…

"In drawing on the story of Qaroun from the *Qur'an*, Masri draws a parallel with the present situation in that the 'masses' of people are dazzled by superficial displays of splendor whereas a minority have proper insight and understand the reality. The people Masri is talking about in drawing on the story of Qaroun are the 'masses' of IS fighters and sympathizers with its cause."
–Aymenn Jawad Al-Tamimi, *Opposition to Abu Bakr al-Baghdadi: Sheikh Abu Eisa al-Masri's Critique of Islamic State Media,* May 27, 2019

Nineveh Governate, Iraq, October, 2014

Khatoon was not a good fit in the household of Kahled Umr al-Sham, his shrewish wife, and his surging hormone bearer of a son. After a ten-day sojourn in hell—inaccurately called the al-Sham home—Kahled decided that the Yazidi woman was not worth the bother. She was dirty, smelly, and seemed to be sweaty all the time. That was altogether true, and it was entirely on purpose. Khatoon early on reasoned that if she neglected herself entirely, let her fingernails grow long with grease and grime under them, and often raised her arms when in the presence of the slave-owner, Khaled, to give him a heady waft of her hairy, dirty, armpits, and apocrine gland secretions, she would largely be left to herself. She was truly thankful that—during her week in hell—she started the female time when she should have been left at peace in the Red Tent.

Much as she had longed to be free of the odious old man and his unbearable and extended family, she quaked with fear of the unknown when Kahled came to her room on Friday morning and announced, "You filthy stinking *kaffir* dog, it is time for you to make me a profit. We go to the capital of the Islamic State, Mosul. Bring only your two chadors and slippers. You will not need more where we are going."

She was forced into a chicken wire enclosure in the back of Kahled's pick-up like a sheep or goat going to market and driven in a serpentine course generally headed south towards Mosul. Kahled speculated that the journey would take five hours or less. His confidence came from his previous life before the Islamic State when he was a traveling salesman for a shoe company. He shared the information that he was originally from Sinjar and knew back roads and shortcuts like he knew the wrinkles on his face. Most of the time they drove on a minor road that twisted through the desert scrub of the Nineveh plains. Khatoon had to pull her chador around her face to keep out some of the dust being kicked up. She had less comfort and protection than a dog would have had. The already long and tedious trip was lengthened by mandatory stops at multiple checkpoints situated as a network around Sinjar.

Several of the checkpoints were nothing more than several empty barrels standing across the road with a long 2X4 laid across their tops. They were also little more than excuses for underpaid young IS fighters to extort the travelers. Khaled kept a small metal container filled with cash under his feet to pay the "customs fees." Finally–in the distance further down highway 47–Khaled and Khatoon could see the impressive Mosul dam beginning to come into view, as if it were rising out of the desert sands. They crossed over the dam which traversed the Tigris where it spanned across from one low hill to another leaving a fairly good-sized reservoir.

Just before the bridge there was no checkpoint; but almost immediately on the other side, they had to stop at a cinder-brick building festooned with Islamic State flags strategically placed to cover bullet holes and missing areas in the walls. The two occupants of the truck were ordered out and hurried along to the door of the building.

The interior of the building was a single room with only a few pieces of furniture: a single military issue metal desk and an uncomfortable straight-backed metal chair. There was a sink and faucet on the north side standing over a partially covered latrine which had a nasty uriniferous odor misting up from it. A wood box on the opposite side of the room had a coil hot plate, which served as a primitive grill for cooking. There were two sofas and a soft cushion chair, all of which were seriously grimy. One of the sofas had an exposed broken spring sticking up out of its cushion. All the walls and the concrete floor were scuffed and had trails of grease and unidentifiable fluid trails down them. The only place where a person might be able to try to sleep was an army cot against the west wall. It had no mattress, sheets, or blankets. Men who needed to sleep badly enough had to supply their own bedclothes and pillows. No decent person would even think of sleeping where another person had slept for fear of the omnipresent fomites.

There were two soldiers in the room; one was sitting at the desk with piles of paperwork on the desk in front of him. He was smoking a hookah pipe and looked dreamy and completely disinterested in the newcomers. The second soldier was attempting to wash off a little of the baked-on grime coating the windows to let in a little light and to facilitate being able to see a little something of the outside. They waited more than an hour until the ranking soldier put down his hookah pipe and seemed to recognize the presence of other people.

"Papers," he slurred.

"Here," said Khaled and handed his and Khatoon's documents to the man, apparently an IS military sergeant.

"Not good," the sergeant said without even looking at them.

"I think they are completely correct," said Khaled, and handed the documents back to the sergeant with a small pile of dinars tucked in among them.

This time, the sergeant reached for the papers, took a short look–at the money but not the documents themselves–and pronounced, "Papers good," and affixed an official IS stamp.

He waved Khaled and Khatoon out with a curt wave of the back of his hand.

Things began to improve after that. There were attractive and undamaged ranch houses with small, neat, farm plots where the dam's Iraqi and Italian engineers lived. There was a well-kept little one-room schoolhouse and an inviting playground for their children. Just inside the perimeter fence of the IS capital city, they encountered their last check point–a makeshift and probably quickly mobile place–consisting only of some old boxes blocking the road and two young boys leaning against the wall of a mud-brick former store. They had Kalashnikovs slung carelessly from their right shoulders.

One of the boys looked in the window of the truck at Khaled.

"Purpose?"

"Business," Khaled said without making eye contact.

"Papers."

Once again, the slave owner passed over his and Khatoon's documents which were given only a cursory once over.

"Any food?"

"Just some lunch for me and my *sabah*."

Without bothering even to look at Khatoon, the other boy put down the truck bed gate and took hold of the wooden box sitting next to Khatoon's wire enclosure. He pried off the top with his k-bar knife and looked in. He scooped up all the bananas, grapes, plums, onions, and artichokes, he could carry in his two hands and took his booty to his friend for him to share. That food would have been lunch for Khatoon who had not eaten all day, but now it was gone. A small handful of dinars changed hands, and the truck was again on its way.

Khaled was animated now. He had always become excited when a commercial transaction was about to come to fruition, especially if he anticipated making a decent profit. That is why he loved his visits to the souk for the haggling, the conversation, the give-and-take, and finally the consummation of the deal. He was an excellent bargainer, and it stimulated him to participate. Today was no different. He had thoroughly enjoyed the auctions before, but this was important to him. He had to win; it was necessary for him to make a profit; and it was crucial for him to get rid of the haughty Yazidi she-dog. She humiliated him, and she had to suffer for it. It was part of his manhood to make that happen.

He held his small Mosul city map in his right hand and steered the truck with the left. He had visited the area of the auction numerous times; so, he knew the way even without the map. He had to admit that the situation—the no-good woman—had set his nerves on edge. The streets of Mosul were none too good before all the warring started, and now there was a conspicuous absence of street signs. Some streets were in terrible condition, and Khaled had to turn back from them. Some streets were barricaded or otherwise blocked.

Finally, however, they drove into a large clearing which was beginning to fill with dozens—and soon would be hundreds–of men in black. They were beginning to surround a sturdy chain-link wire fenced enclosure topped with five strands of new barbed wire. Steel struts had been placed as upright supports. There was a single, narrow gate that served as an entry point which was guarded by four bulky IS military police. Another fifty guards stood rigidly around the perimeter, Kalashnikovs at the ready. Khaled was relieved; this was most certainly the place.

As Khaled and Khatoon moved forward in their truck, guards had him stop and directed him to a parking area sixty meters from the enclosure.

"Move out quickly, soldier. The *sabahs* are beginning to enter the corral," one of the guards urged.

Indeed, strings of women and girls wearing metal rings around their necks and attached to each other by stiff hemp ropes were being pulled along by their masters and hired slavers to take their places inside the enclosure. Khatoon feared that she would faint, soil herself, or start to sob, or in some other hideous way humiliate herself. She fought the urge.

There was a short exchange between Khaled and a huge black man dressed in the distinctive all-black jacket and trousers with balaclava and black ammunition belt uniform assigned to senior officers, *wahdat al'amn* [security unit] officers, and *istishhad* [martyrdom] suicide bombers—all considered to be men of distinction.

"Buying, selling, or looking?" the security officer asked brusquely, not one to suffer delays.

"Selling."

"This one?"

"Yes. She is my legal *sabah*, one of the accursed Yazidi *kuffars*."

"Get a collar on her and put her in the corral."

Khaled nodded. He pushed Khatoon to the gate. There a man whose sole task was to do so, sized up Khatoon's neck, chose an open metal collar, and snapped it in place. He put a padlock on the connection point and handed Khaled the key."

"Collars come back after buyers get *sabahs* to their quarters. You must pay for the lock."

Khaled waited.

"One dollar, American."

Khaled paid the man, and the collar man pulled Khatoon into the enclosure. It was a secure pen for donkeys, oxen, sheep, and goats. Khatoon tried to figure out whether she was worth as much as one of those. She would soon find out.

The *wahdat al'amn* officer saw that there were no more slaves waiting to get it; so, he closed and padlocked the gate.

An announcer gave instructions over a sound system:

"All *sabahs* have a card with a number on it. Watch for that number to come up. I will give the signal for the bidding to begin. One bid at a time, Brothers. All sales are final; however, there is no problem with re-sales at any future auction. Before you leave the auction center, you must pay the sales tax. To do that, you must have your identity papers in hand to verify that you are one of the Islamic State's brothers. Any questions?"

There were none. The only voices heard were from overly anxious soldiers, usually the young ones making catcalls and pretending to beg a certain girl to pay attention to them.

Khatoon was not able to tune out the background of evil voices. She heard herself and the other girls called every filthy name she had ever heard and then some.

The sounds settled into a kind of human white noise:

"Today is distribution day, God willing," they joked with one another.

They flashed lascivious grins and said, *"You can sell your slave, or give her as a gift. She's your property and you can do whatever you want with your share."*

"I heard that you can buy any woman for three banknotes or a pistol."

"I know the Qur'an—IS mujahideen [holy warriors] are promised by God, the Merciful and Just, that it is so."

"Yes, Brother. Our Holy Book requires of us that we sanction their genitals as a sign of realization and dominance by the sword of the mujahideen. It is blessed in the Qur'an by The Prophet, himself, SAWS, may God bless and keep him and his holy family."

"The Islamic texts say that you can beat your woman or your slave, but there are instructions not to hit the slave's face."

"Who do you think will enforce any of that?"

Generalized laughter.

Khatoon clutched her number card—46—nervously as the sales began to move according to numbers. Around her Yazidi and Shi'ite women and girls began to scratch and bloody themselves in an attempt to make themselves unattractive to potential buyers. Inside the slave prison, the women had had to share a few filthy, overflowing toilets, forcing them to stand in raw sewage.

"Number eighteen."

Their bodies were crawling with sand flies, and they all had lice in their hair. Early in their incarceration, women sat on bags or clothes to try and avoid touching the filthy ground; but soon they determined that the stench, the lice, and the sewage on their feet and legs, made them less attractive; and maybe that would save them. Others coated their faces with ashes to achieve an even more convincing end. Some cried that they had converted—were forced to convert, and they had papers to prove it. They were roundly ignored, even by their supposed co-religionists.

"Number twenty-one."

The girls should have known by now that it did not matter a fly's hair's worth whether she had converted or not. All of them had been sold into slavery, and there was no hierarchal system. They were all equally cast down to the depths.

"Number twenty-five."

Through the spaces in the fencing, Khatoon caught sight of five busloads of fighters unloading. She had thought her despair could not get worse; but, she now knew that was untrue. Among the women, there was no comradery, no smiling, no little jokes—just faces of despair.

"Number forty."

Khatoon looked around to see what the remaining men looked like. They were of different ages, skin colors, heights, weights, and degrees of ugliness; but to her, they all looked the same—repulsive and evil.

"Forty-three."

She watched a ten-year-old girl be dragged screaming and weeping and be placed in the clutches of two men who had divided up their shares to be able to bid high enough to have a chance to get a virgin.

"Forty-five."

Khatoon looked out at the men. Only half of them were gone. A particularly loathsome creature ogled her. He looked more like a gorilla than a man.

"Forty-six."

CHAPTER THIRTY-THREE

"Some of those women and girls have had to watch 7-, 8-, and 9-year-old children bleed to death before their eyes, after being raped by ISIS militia multiple times a day. ISIS militias have burned many Yezidi girls alive for refusing to convert... Why? Because we are not Muslims..."

–Mirza Ismail, chairman of the Yezidi Human Rights Organization-International.

"I remember a man who looked at least 40 years old coming and taking a ten-year-old girl. When she resisted him, he beat her severely, using stones, and would have opened fire on her if she had not gone with him. Everything against her will. They used to come and buy the girls without a price, 'I mean, they used to tell us Yazidi girls, you are *sabiya* [spoils of war, sex slaves], you are *kuffar* [infidels], you are to be sold without a price,' meaning they had no base value. Some Yazidi girls were sold for a few packs of cigarettes."

–Quoted by Middle East scholar Raymond Ibrahim during the partially successful escape efforts after the putative defeat of the Islamic State.

Sinjar, Nineveh Governate, Iraq, December, 2014

The Battle of Sinjar was actually conducted in several locations, including Sinjar Village, Sinjar Mountain, and in the desert areas of

Nineveh Governate. It was finally not worth sustaining any more losses, and Abu Bakr al-Baghdadi sent a message to his commanders from his safe location in the desert of Anbar. His commanders knew that the caliph does not come to the areas targeted by the coalition. They knew that the great caliph's safety was crucial to the ongoing existence of the Islamic State. It was never suggested that he lacked courage.

The jihadi fighters moved on to their new stronghold and now the de facto capital of the caliphate—Raqqa, Syria. After all the fighting in Iraq, the group still maintained a strong presence in the Syrian desert and remote areas along the border. With similar thinking, the coalition and Iraqi forces did not think that the risk/benefit ratio was in their favor to pursue the Islamic State forces further for the time being.

With the shooting fairly quiet for the present, Avery and his CIA agents began to assist the exhausted and hungry survivors on top of the mountain to get back to their homes. The main rescue operations and what fighting was necessary was being successfully carried out by the several U.S. backed Kurdish forces. The three agents had talked occasionally about the horrors of war and how they were going to handle the emotionally wrenching experiences of bringing back survivors to veritable ghost towns. The conversations were generally upbeat towards a mutual goal of maintaining composure and the good old British "stiff-upper-lip." However, when they began moving shell-shocked and life-defeated civilians to see their old home towns of Kocho, Sinjar, and Solagh, the grief and distress were overwhelming.

Their searches yielded fifty-four mass graves, and almost everyone presumed that there would be more as time went on. There were no resources to facilitate the exhumation of remains; so, the distraught families could know the fates of their loved ones. Despite the fraction of people saved from the mountain, the Yazidi families documented at least 3,000 women, girls, and children, as missing and their whereabouts unknown. Best estimates from the families, from city, provincial, and national governments, and military sources, were that over 400,000 Yazidis were displaced—many to foreign countries and to wretched displacement camps in wide-spread and hostile Middle East locations.

The CIA agents, accompanied by a unit of KDP [Kurdistan Democratic Party] combat hardened Kurds under the command of Col. Behremend Rozaki, a detachment of Iraqi regulars, and a scary unit of the Kurdish trained all female YJS [Sinjar Women's Units] militia, formed a protective cordon for the families who wanted to return to assess what had become of Sinjar in the north and Kocho in the south of the governate. Those two areas had sustained the most terrible attacks during the August massacre.

Avery spoke briefly with the YJS commander, "What are your goals, now, Ma'am?"

"We are still at war and will be until every Islamic State soldier and sympathizer is dead or gone. They raped and destroyed the lives of countless women in this province and everywhere else their presence polluted. Men who gang-raped innocent children and girls, who burned women at the stake, who buried women alive, and who stole the childhoods of boys by sending them to Raqqa to become child-soldiers should not share the same planet as decent human beings."

She was earnest and determined but had used up her tears and rage long ago. Now, there was a job to be done; and she and her sisters were doggedly ready to live and to die–if necessary–to get that job done.

"Is it revenge that drives you?"

"Yes, it is," she said looking him straight in the eyes. "But revenge is not the only or the most important thing. Our girls out there are waiting for us to come and save them. They need a great deal of medical and psychiatric care to give them some semblance of normal life again. The criminals must be brought to justice—real justice, not the twisted Sharia kind. Maybe not in our lifetimes; but sometime in the future, we must see the Yazidi community back in its homelands secure and happy, free to practice our religion in our own way. The militia members have sworn an oath to see these things come to pass. There are 10,000 women in total ready to fight on the front lines as part of the Kurdish forces in Syria and Iraq, which have been the most efficient ground troops in curbing the jihadis' territorial expansion. By all that is decent and holy, we will succeed."

Seeing the villages through the eyes of the people who had lost their families, their homes, and their belongings, was more heart wrenching than Avery had anticipated. Several times he had to turn his eyes away from the profound grief. Kocho was a dead city. Not even a dog ran in the empty streets. Every building had been toppled, burned, or bombed, into rubble. Row upon row of skeleton houses looked out of empty eyes upon puffs of dust kicking up in the idle streets. Not a single *Husseiniya* [Shi'a congregation place] remained as what could even be described as a building. What were once the beloved homes of decent people, were now hulks which had been pounded by bombs, peppered by machine-gun fire, and made dangerous by booby-traps, and left by the angry and devilish IS terrorists when they had to retreat.

In Sinjar, the returnees asked to be able to see the old school. The walls were lined by photographs of some of the thousands of killed and missing citizens. Far more women than men had their pictures on those bare walls. Otherwise, the schoolhouse was as empty as the neglected streets. The civilians in the party frankly told their protectors that many former citizens could no longer bear to see where their lives had once taken place and where their loved ones had greeted them with affection—a gesture now largely lost in the bitter land.

The dismal circumstances stirred some of the returnees to begin telling their stories. A woman who said she was twenty-four but looked fifty, told of the horrors of being a sex slave. She had been a virgin until August 3, 2014 at four-ten in the afternoon. Somehow, she escaped from a hellhole where she was imprisoned in Raqqa, Syria and made her way to a house in Mosul—still under IS's murderous control. She was desperate and hoped for some bit of kindness. The people who opened the door were strangers and were dressed in Muslim clothing. Her heart sank. However, although the people were not altogether welcoming, they had enough left of human decency to take her in and to keep her for several days while they negotiated with the girl's family for a ransom that could satisfy the greed of the IS government.

Over a protracted period of time, the family and their friends collected tens of thousands of dollars, made arrangements with equally greedy smugglers, and finally allowed her to be sold back to her family. When she returned to Sinjar, her family considered her to be unclean and no longer a virgin, both severe taints on any person of their faith. The women in the family procured some blessed water and ritually washed every part of her scarred body. That allowed her to be considered to be clean from her terrible sins of the past and to be accepted back into the community.

A girl of ten—who had not spoken since returning–told the assembled guardians that–when she was six–she was captured with the rest of the girls of the three towns. All of them were murdered, but she was kept alive to become a kidney donor. They took her to Turkey and made her ready for surgery. Everyone but the doctor left the room. Seizing his chance, he swept up the terrified little girl into his arms; and they became fugitives. They moved from safehouse to safehouse until they finally ran into a unit of Kurdish soldiers who took them in.

The YJS militia commander asked the little girl what she planned to do for the rest of her life.

The child replied, "I cannot go back to my own village of Kocho; there is no hope that there will ever be life in my village. There are only bones of the dead here."

"Would you like to come and live with me and my sisters in the militia, dear one?"

The girl silently cried and nodded her head.

Avery had to step away lest his insistent hot tears be noticed.

Mosul, al Anbar Governate, Iraq, late December, 2014

As far ahead as Khatoon could see, life was hopeless. Each morning when she arose to wash herself and to find a little food left over from her master's supper, she recited to herself what had become her mantra: '*I will survive. I will return to my homeland with honor. I will punish the monsters.*' It was becoming increasingly harder to say the lines with conviction as the days and weeks passed. One problem for her was that her memories were too exact, too vivid, and too emotionally charged.

When she—number 46–was finally purchased, it was by a man who almost did not look like a man. He was not even six feet tall, but his weight exceeded 300 pounds and was all muscle. It was not the muscle of a slender, well-defined, and cut, athlete; but instead he looked like one of those "strongest man in the world" types that she and her sisters loved to watch on the television. He was barrel-chested, had upper arms as big around as her waist; and he could lift a small car, pull tractor out of a mud bog better than a horse, and—as he loved to demonstrate—he could unscrew a lug nut from a wheel with his bare hands. His abdomen was ponderous but not fat; in fact, he had no more than two percent body fat. His face was round, almost Asian; and he had squinty narrow eyes that looked mean. His beard was so large that it surrounded his face giving him a distinct bearlike visage. His skin was dark from the sun and dirt. He was a frightening personage. His presence in a battle caused consternation each time he encountered a mano-a-mano opponent.

He was not truly a mean man for all his power and frightening visage. However, he was a true Islamic believer—the Islamic State Salafi brand of Islam believer. Women were hardly more than things; she was his property; and he was not even obligated to ask her nicely for lovemaking. He had a prodigious libido, and great stamina. He raped her at least twice a day, sometimes three times. He never attempted anything like foreplay. Rape–for him–was just the woman's opportunity to enjoy his great endurance. He left her alone in his house except for the rape times.

His house was the finest she had ever seen, let alone lived in. His name was Ismail. She never heard a last name, and she was required to call him, *al-raisi* [master]. He had acquired the home the same day as he bought her at the Mosul auction. He drove an old Russian *Zaporozhets* car purchased at a ridiculous discount from a Muslim auto enthusiast who was fleeing from the Islamic State invasion of Baghdad at the time. He got a sensational bargain, especially since the man had treated this favorite automobile with loving care, seldom drove it, and kept it gleaming and impeccably clean. Ismail loved the car, in part because it had large bench seats front and back. The seats were large enough for him to ride in comfort. His preference was similar to that of old fat westerners who buy Ford Crown Victorias ["Crown Vics"] for the same reason.

Ishmail ordered Khatoon to "stay in the car. Keep your burka on properly; so, your face does not show; and do not make sounds. Do you understand my order?"

"Yes, Master."

Burka or not, she could still see out the large vehicle's windows. The scene transpiring before her was heart wrenching. First, three crying children were literally kicked out of the house and down the five front steps. They sat forlornly on the neat lawn as a woman—obviously their mother—was dragged out of the house and down the steps by two of Ishmail's underlings. One of the men swatted her across her back and sent her sprawling beside her children. Ishmail stepped out onto the porch carrying a horse whip. He snapped it once over the heads of the three people being evicted. The woman was bare headed, her long auburn hair flying in the easy breeze of the not yet scorching day. She painfully stood up, made the sign of the cross twice and kissed her large Armenian

[Siroun, "lovely"] cross. Khatoon had not seen that type of cross before. It was more intricate and more attractive than the traditional crosses she had seen people wear. She squinted to see that it was adorned with floral embellishments. The forlorn woman fondled her cross with her left hand and led her children away from the house with her right. Khatoon wept silently along with the three dispossessed Christians.

Ishmail gestured to one of his two minions. He trotted down the stairs and out to the car. He banged his large fist on the window and gestured with his finger for Khatoon to get out. She wiped her eyes, smearing her heavy eye shadow, and obediently got out of the shiny polished automobile. She walked behind the IS soldier. Ishmail took her hand and pulled her into the house. The two guards stayed behind. Ishmail was in a good mood; it was time for another rape.

CHAPTER THIRTY-FOUR

"For the first time since being punished by Hajii Salman, I thought about escaping. The torture at the checkpoint and the promise that I was going to Syria reignited the urgency to flee. I contemplated climbing out of the kitchen window, but before I did, I walked to the front door to see if the militant had, by some miracle, left it unlocked. The door was heavy and wooden. I turned the yellow handle, and my heart sank. It wouldn't budge. He wouldn't be so stupid as to leave it unlocked, I thought. But, for good measure, I gave it one more pull and nearly fell over when it swung open."

–Nadia Murad, with Jenna Krajeski, *The Last Girl: My Story of Captivity, and My Fight Against the Islamic State*, Tim Duggan Books (Penguin Random House), New York, 2017

Sinjar, Nineveh Governate, December, 2014 to Mosul, al Anbar Governate, Iraq, January, 2015

Avery received two different sets of intel from his favorite informants, Rahim Jamaluddin in al-Baghdadi's camp, and Col. Behremend Rozaki, ranking peshmerga officer and CIA spy—the same information from two highly valued and trusted assets. Both told Avery that the Sinjar and Kocho girls and women had been moved to Mosul, and that al-Baghdadi and his Islamic State was preparing to leave Iraq for Syria within the month. Avery rationalized that his work was largely done in Sinjar; so, he could indulge his obsession of protecting and taking care of the attractive Yazidi girl who had taken on the persona of his daughter over his years in Iraq. He could not let her get lost in the desert of Syria, never to be returned to her home like thousands of other girls.

"Malcolm, Devlin, I'm sorry, I can't let this go. Try and understand, but this girl, Khatoon represents something deeply personal and profoundly important to me. I have to go and find her if it is at all possible. Maybe we can find more girls and save them. Whatever, I have to go to Mosul to see if anyone has seen her or knows about her. You have no obligation to go with me, but I would value your company more than you could know, if you do."

"We are done here, Boss. Let's do something good. We're with you," the two agents said. "And, we're sure that our entire field unit will want to go with us."

That promise resulted in the addition of six more very capable fighters to Avery's unauthorized travel plan: CIA contract agents Carl Johnson, David Wade, Richard Erickson, and Tom Wright, and—to his surprise and great pleasure–Behremend Rozaki and his sergeant-major, Agir Jaf, the Sorani Kurdish Peshmergas. For all of them, the crusade was a personal one, a chance to do some harm to the militants and some good for their victims, albeit miniscule in the cosmic order of things.

They left the next morning over war torn and pot-holed roads south towards al-Anbar province in a convoy of three heavily armed and well-provisioned HMMVEEs. The region was barren. The only green plants were those by the riverbank. Other plants scattered on the dusty hillsides were dead and dry, and the hostile desert stretched into the distance. Anbar is one of the driest governorates in Iraq's western desert climate, and portions of the governate are contiguous with the Syrian Desert. Most of Al Anbar is considered as a topographical continuation of the Arabian Peninsula plateau region.

The CIA agents were traveling through the area whose geographical qualities largely included steppe and desert terrain. As they moved farther north and east, they began to encounter some small hills and wadis where much of the land had long been exposed to the elements and showed the effects of severe erosion. What farms still persisted in the drought dried desert were managing to grow some potatoes and a few patches of wheat, barley, and maize.

Along the way, the saw the wreckage of previous battles—burned out cars, trucks, oil pumps, and burned down Iraqi checkpoints. Even without war, the road winding through the desert, was narrow and famous for accidents. Trucks spatter rocks and gravel along the way chipping the windshields of cars and trucks going the opposite ways. Further along was an area of sand dunes, some uprising land that became cliffs, then stretched out into sand again. There were occasional mud-brick villages—residential areas of a god-forsaken country in the minds of the spies passing by. There were what passed for small restaurants widely separated along the road. Those restaurants separated men from women behind plastic screens, of course. They stopped once to eat kabab and bread among men wearing white dishdashas instead of black pajamas, which gave them some sense of security.

They encountered a few hostile checkpoints which they obliterated, multiple fleeing squads of IS soldiers headed north which they ignored, and long columns of wretched refugees headed in every direction away from al-Anbar province where the fiercest fighting was currently taking place.

Mosul, itself, was still heavily and successfully protected by its Islamic State militant insurgents who were not showing any suggestion that they were being defeated or were ready to join other fighters moving towards Raqqa, Syria where Abu Bakr al-Baghdadi was rumored to be hiding.

Mosul, Iraq, December 25, 2014

Khatoon overheard Ishmail and his goons discussing plans for the army to abandon Mosul and to take all the slaves to Syria where the strength of the cause exceeded their current status by several times over. During the next few days, she pieced together the plans of Ishmail to sell his house to an IS banker and to leave by mid-January, 2015. Her sense of urgency to escape heightened since she was sure that—once in Syria—she would live out the rest of her days as a slave until she became so unattractive that she was either worked to death in the fields or murdered.

There was increased activity on the streets of Mosul; more people were out walking and busying about than usual. Fewer of the men were staying in their houses; and more women were to be seen out walking in groups of two or three to do errands, shopping, and visiting. She sat on the stoop of Ishmail's house when he and his goons left each morning and made a subtle effort to attract the attention of some of the women. She gleaned the difference between slave and more or less free women from the way they walked. The free women walked briskly, talking and laughing quietly. The slaves trudged along with their heads down, never looking from side-to-side, and keeping their trajectory straight and free of deviation. They never looked in shop windows or at advertisements.

Khatoon got up the courage to venture as far as the front fence where she finally attracted the attention of two apparent slaves shuffling along to accomplish some duty or other. They looked about carefully, then—they too—dredged up a little courage and walked closer to the wall where Khatoon was standing.

"*Al-akhwat* [sisters]," she hissed hoarsely as they drew close. "I am from Sinjar, are you?"

The girls looked around frantically for a moment, then ventured a quick reply, "No, from Kocho."

Khatoon took a leap of faith, "May I walk with you? Today and for the next several days, *Al-akhwat?*"

They nodded. Khatoon had already tested the front gate and had discovered to her surprise that it was unlocked. It was evident that Ishmail had no fear that Khatoon would or could escape. There was no place to go and no one to help her.

She took her first step towards freedom. She walked onto the street and formed a threesome with the two other black shrouded nondescript ghosts. They joined the many other burka clad women and walked along the main street, turned around and returned in less than an hour. It was mildly exhilarating to be away from her prison; but what was best, was that she dared to speak frankly; and the other two women were receptive.

After some innocuous chit-chat about Yazidi life in the Nineveh Governate, the conversation slowly turned to their condition and lives as slaves. Khatoon watched the women's eyes and saw no hint of anger or betrayal. She was guessing out of hope and desperation.

Finally, when they were nearly back to Ishmail's house, Khatoon threw caution to the winds, "Sisters, I have heard that the capital is going to move to Raqqa in al-Sham. We will be taken there, and I think we will never get free without much money for ransom. My family—if any are still alive—have no money. I am going to escape this week. Would you like to leave with me? It would be safer and more likely of success if we left in a group."

The two other women had no one else to trust and no hope for a future with the Islamic State. They both considered that it would be better to be executed on the run than to die a thousand deaths from rape, torture, and neglect as slaves.

"How would we do it, Sister?"

"I am unsure, of course, but I have seen a few houses that don't have the evil black flag on their front doors. Maybe those people would be willing to help sister women in trouble."

"And maybe they would turn us in to the *Diwan al-Amn* in a minute for the rewards."

"Better executed than tortured for life," said Khatoon with finality. "I am going. Come with me or not, but I beg you not to betray me."

The two women looked at each other earnestly then replied, "We'll come, too. When?"

"Three days. Every day we will do this same walk. Every day we will return to our masters. On the fourth day, we will just keep walking."

"Agreed. We need to get some provisions. Hide them under our burkas and find places to stash them along our escape route," the girl named Masuda offered.

Her friend Ruhasva nodded her agreement and added, "I can steal some steak knives from my master's house. He stole them from the Christians who used to live there."

"All of that is better than nothing," Khatoon said, buoyed up by at least having some sort of plan—however flimsy. "Next Friday, when the men are at mid-day prayers would be a good time to go."

"We are agreed," said both Ruhasva and Masuda.

For three days, the three women established a routine. Ishmail told Khatoon that he knew she was out walking with other women.

He said with a little menace, "I give you permission. Be gone no more than two hours and only if your chores are done. If I hear that you have visited another man, you will be whipped to death. Understand?"

"Yes, Master. I will obey."

"Good," he said.

His complete mastery—as demonstrated in that conversation—was so satisfying that he considered it an occasion for another trip to the upstairs bedroom which he enjoyed and Khatoon hated. However, this time, she did everything she could to please him and repeated the same phony enjoyment performance every time every day including Friday.

The muezzin bellowed out the sing-song call to mid-day prayer. Usually Khatoon ignored the five daily calls out of over-familiarity. This time, the call was a signal that her time had come. It was the same with Ruhasva and Masuda.

Khatoon walked through the gate as soon as the other two approached. She never looked back.

The muezzin intoned the monotonous call as they hurried along:

Allahu Akbar
God is Great
(said four times)
Ashhadu an la ilaha illa Allah
I bear witness that there is no god except the One God.
(said two times)
Ashadu anna Muhammadan Rasool Allah
I bear witness that Muhammad is the messenger of God.
(said two times)
Hayya 'ala-s-Salah
Hurry to the prayer (Rise up for prayer)
(said two times)
Hayya 'ala-l-Falah
Hurry to success (Rise up for Salvation)
(said two times)
Allahu Akbar
God is Great
[said two times]
La ilaha illa Allah
There is no god except the One God

No one paid any attention to the three women as they walked. The men were at prayer, and the women were either at home resting from the orders from their men or were busily hurrying about complying with their man's orders. Khatoon, Ruhasva, and Masuda, kept on walking northward through the entire length of the city and out into the desert beyond. They were hungry, tired, frightened; but on they went well into the night.

Mosul, Iraq, December 25, 2014, time of Dhuhr [noon prayer]

Once again, the CIA agents—now nine of them—including Behremend and Agir, the peshmergas, donned their well-used IS security forces uniforms and began walking through the streets of Mosul as soon as the *Dhuhr* was over. They acted and spoke with typical IS security men's authoritative manner and speech. Everywhere they went, they demanded of passers-by, shopkeepers, women walking, IS soldiers, and businesspeople, whether they had seen the woman in the photograph they showed. The implication was that they were looking for an escaped *sabah*.

One woman in a burka–who was definitely not a slave–thought she might have seen three suspicious women walking north towards the edge of the city. It was odd she thought, because it was during the *Salat al-'asr* [late afternoon prayer]. Other than that one flimsy lead, they had no luck in finding Khatoon. Mentioning her name caused every person they asked to draw a blank. Khatoon is a Yazidi name, and one with which they were not familiar.

They split up and began knocking on doors. Carl, Richard, and Tom, took the right side; and Avery, Malcolm, and Devlin, the left. Behremend and Agir walked up the center of the street. All of them had their AK-47s nervously at the ready. They traversed the city to its northern edge then doubled back taking a different road to where their HUMMVEEs were hidden.

"Boss, I guess we must be wrong about Mosul being where the Yazidi girl is being kept," said Malcolm.

"I'm not so sure, myself," said Devlin. "Mosul is the only place where we have any intel about her being held."

"We've only hunted for a day," Avery said. "Let's give it at least one more day before giving up. I don't know where we would go if we do quit in Mosul."

That proved to be an excellent choice. They started walking and asking again after the following morning's *Salat al-fajr* [dawn prayer]. Almost immediately they began to see posters on telephone poles and business fronts of Khatoon Yazidi by name and with her photograph—a grainy open face picture without a burka. The other two posters alongside Khatoon's were for women in burkas, as identifiable as individual fence posts standing like sentinels.

A charge of excitement enlivened the nine coalition hunters. That was leavened by the presence of more than a dozen similar groups of IS security officer clad soldiers going door-to-door. The search for the CIA contingent took on increased urgency now they knew they were in the right place. The concern was that the real IS *wahdat al'amn* would find her first.

CHAPTER THIRTY-FIVE

"Be extremely subtle, even to the point of formlessness. Be extremely mysterious, even to the point of soundlessness. Thereby you can be the director of the opponent's fate.
    –Sun Tzu, Bingfa, [*The Art of War*], 5th century B.C.E.

"It is essential to seek out enemy agents who have come to conduct espionage against you and to bribe them to serve you. Give them instructions and care for them. Thus, doubled agents are recruited and used...All warfare is based on deception."
    –Sun Tzu, *Bingfa*, [*The Art of War*], 5th century B.C.E

Road from Mosul, Iraq to Duhok, Kurdistan ["Mosul Dam Road"] late January, 2015

The three young Yazidi fugitive women had been walking at night, hiding during the day, and trying to sleep in ditches, hay-stacks, old burned-out vehicles, and abandoned dwellings, all the while evading a veritable army of IS hunter "police." It was nothing short of a life and death quest. They were filthy almost beyond recognition, starving, parched, and weakened, from long arduous hiking, exposure to the elements, and hordes of insects. The one thing they had going for them was their nearly absolute protection from incidentally encountered men owing to the fetid and filthy odor they emanated. One of the three was in the middle of her "curse" and could not even find rags to clean herself. Khatoon had stopped menstruating as soon as the rapes started.

Masuda and Khatoon were somehow able to force themselves up with the onset of darkness, but Ruhasva was very nearly at the end of her tether.

Masuda licked her dry, chapped, and split lips wincing, "My dear friends. We must take a chance and try and find a woman somewhere along this God-forsaken road who can give us a little help. Surely, not everyone has lost their humanity."

"How could we possibly discern the human from the wives who accompany the monsters out of conviction?" Khatoon responded.

Ruhasva wept quietly. She was beyond her ability to control herself.

"I have taken my last step, Girls. Hide me in the trash pile; so, the torturers can't get at me, and let me die in peace," the frail girl moaned.

It was no idle threat. Khatoon knew she had only one more day left in her to continue their march of death. Masuda had less than that. The two of them racked their brains for a solution.

Finally, Khatoon volunteered, "I am not far from deciding that Ruhasva's plan is all that may be left for us. Tonight, I am going to go down to the highway and find a little village or collection of huts and see if there is a lone woman in a house. I will take the risk of being betrayed and turned over to the slavers or executioners. It is hard to imagine anything worse than this. One more night and not being able to swallow even if water becomes available."

No one objected. They were at their nadir, and no one had a better plan.

Khatoon made her way down the rocky slope towards the highway hampered by trash and debris and a moonless dark night. She squinted in each direction trying to be sure she did not walk into a checkpoint by mistake and destroy herself. She looked intently to see if she could see campfires or a glow of light coming from a dwelling. To turn left was the general direction of Duhok and Kurdistan; so, she arbitrarily elected to struggle along in that direction. Her feet had calluses upon calluses and were cut and bleeding. Like Ruhasva, she had run out of rags, and her feet were now bare.

It occurred to her that it was her birthday—the least pleasant of her entire life. She allowed herself to shed a few tears then slogged on. Two kilometers and an hour further along, she saw a small cluster of lights in the distance, no more than another half kilometer away. The moment of truth would be soon upon her. No vehicles with men in black pajamas drove by and neither did any white knights on horses stop to help.

She came to the camp which was hardly even a hamlet. It consisted of ten buildings, seven of which seemed likely to be living quarters. She slunk around and peered into windows. To her relief, she saw only women. Evidently, the men were out killing or whoring; but whatever they were doing had to be beneficial for her and her two worn-out friends.

Her good fortune–based on serendipity–increased. In the third hut from the road, she looked in and saw a woman with a crimson scar of a brand on her forehead—"KAFFIR SABAH"–it read. The brand had not had time to heal fully. Only terror would force this girl–not so different from herself—to betray her.

She tapped lightly on the only door. It had leather hinges and latch. There was no response. She tapped more loudly. Finally, the door opened a crack; and a frightened girl—who could not have been more than fourteen—peaked out. She was bareheaded and was wearing a worn calico dress; she was—in all probability a Yazidi like Khatoon.

"Sister," Khatoon said quietly, "please help me and my three friends. We are fugitives. If the killers find us we will be tortured and killed."

"Go away. You make danger for me."

"Please, Sister, we cannot go farther. We are dying of thirst. Even a dog deserves a little help. I am Khatoon Yazidi from Sinjar. Which was your village?"

"Kocho," the girl said timidly and sheepishly.

"Let me come in. Someone will see me, and both of us will be in bad trouble."

The girl reached out and took Khatoon's hand and pulled her inside. She double locked the flimsy door and looked intently at the older girl.

Khatoon studied her as well. She had something of an epiphany.

"Are you...the mullah's daughter, Sister? Let me try to remember your name...isn't it Mahbooba? I remember your father telling me that that means 'moonlight?'"

"I remember you. You are Khatoon, the teacher from Sinjar."

"I worked for the mullah. He had to let me go because of threats from the terrorists."

"My *bābā*," she cried. "Oh, my poor *bābā* was killed by the fiends from *al-jahim* [hell]."

It was as if the teenager had been struck by lightening. She dropped to the dirt floor on her hands and knees and sobbed.

"How can it be?" she said over and over. "Have you come to save me, Khatoon? Is it a miracle from Allah?"

"Maybe we can save each other, Mahbooba. Let us work together and work quickly. How long is your slave master going to be gone?"

"All I know is that they are fighting on the road to Kurdistan. The men talked about three or four days and warned us girls not to open the doors to anyone. If a man crossed into the house, he and I would die a thousand deaths."

"I must hurry. I need to eat and drink; so, I can have strength. I must go back to my friends and bring them here. Then, dear Mahbooba, we all must escape to Kurdistan tonight."

"*Inshalah*," Mahbooba said as a fervent prayer not the usual perfunctory Arabic slogan.

She hurried about the kitchen to find left-overs. There was *tashreeb* [bread-and-meat-soup] from breakfast, *biryani* [rice and meat] from the midday meal just before her slaver had left for the fighting, and a little *masgouf* [barbecue fish—one of the national Iraqi dishes]. It was generally considered to be lower class type food, but for Khatoon, it was ambrosia and God's banquet.

Mahbooba found a pair of her man's old boots. He was a small man, and the boots became comfortable enough for Khatoon with three layers of heavy cotton socks. She filled a rucksack with water, food, and shoes, for Ruhasva and Masuda and hurried out into the night to fetch her fugitive friends.

Food, water, a little rest, and renewed hope refreshed Khatoon; and she was able to force her fatigued and stiff legs to do their duty. Because she knew where her friends were, there was nothing tentative about her return. She could not actually run, but she moved quickly—a sort of fast walking like the race that Mexicans win in every Olympics. She scrambled up the rocky incline and found the two girls to be in tough shape—weak, slack muscles, sunken eyes, and sallow complexions. Neither had the energy to do more than to nod their heads and give Khatoon a small girlish wave.

"Girls," she said, "you cannot just lie here and die. I have found food, water, help, and hope. You have to summon up energy enough for a kilometer and a half walk. That's all. I found a sister and a temporary safe heaven. Get up! Please!"

From somewhere down deep–based on trust in Khatoon–Ruhasva and Masuda struggled to their knees. They placed their thin hands on their slack thighs and pushed up to a stooped position. Then–with Khatoon's help–they finally stood upright. She helped Ruhasva to get down the uneven ground of the hillside and sat her down on the road. Then, she helped Masuda. She let them rest for a couple of minutes then—feeling the urgency of time pressure and fear—she pushed, pulled, and prodded them to walk. One foot in front of the other; repeat. Repeat, repeat... There was no concept of destination beyond the next step.

After a night's journey that seemed like half a lifetime, Khatoon led them up to the flimsy makeshift door of Mahbooba's door and gave three soft raps on the wood.

Two minutes elapsed, then Mahbooba's quiet quavering voice asked, *"Min ealaa albabb?"* [Who is at the door?]

It was almost a whisper, and Khatoon answered in kind, "Khatoon, your friend. I have two other friends who are having real difficulty. Please let us in."

The door opened a crack letting out a small ray of light into the inky night.

Mahbooba's hand shot out and took Khatoon's wrist and pulled her inside. Khatoon held Masuda's wrist with her other hand, and Masuda pulled on Ruhasva's until they were all inside and the door was closed and relocked. Mahbooba was overjoyed and almost faint with relief. She embraced Khatoon as fervently as a sister; then, to the surprise of the two exhausted newcomers, she hugged them. They whispered their horror stories, a bonding based on mutually shared humiliation, torture, destitution, and rape. Things no one else would ever fully understand. Mahbooba's story was entirely reminiscent of all of theirs:

"Many times when the men were about to rape me," she said, "even three or four of them, they would kneel and pray before the raping, to convince themselves that is was sanctioned by their awful god and their vicious religion."

Through the bonding of their tears, the three frightened women squeezed each other's hands. From that moment on, they were a sisterhood—through what may come, life or death.

Northeastern Outskirts of Mosul, on the Mosul Dam Road, the same day and the same time in January, 2015

"Let's palaver, Avery," Malcolm said. "We either turn back and brave zombie city again, or we go on with no real destination. Seems like we're flailing around."

"Let's all get out of the vehicles and talk. We should take a vote about whether to go back or to go ahead."

The nine coalition hunters were glad to get out and to stretch their cramped legs and aching backs.

Avery put it to them simply and directly: "I am going to find the girl, no matter what. You can do what you need to do, and I won't make a judgment. If you are going to stay with me, vote. Otherwise, you should probably take one of the HUMMVEEs back north to something like civilization."

All nine of the others showed their loyalty be staying put. It came to a vote for going forward or turning around, and it was unanimous to slog on towards Kurdistan, looking for Khatoon all along the way.

Avery said, "It's still dark night. I'm sure that—if she's still able—she be traveling by night. Keep your eyes peeled."

They mounted their vehicles and moved at a constant but barely moderate rate of speed. They did not see a soul or a sign of life until they caught sight of a hamlet with a few fires burning off to their right.

"Let's get out and have a sneaky peak," Avery said.

They were half a kilometer from the lights. The first hut with any hint of light was the third hut in from the main road. The men surrounded it and listened intently to catch any hint of what kind of people were in there. Tom Wright squinted through a crack between two planks of the door.

He whispered, "Almost certain, they're all women. Don't see firearms. They look like they are packing for a journey."

"Lock and load. Be ready. Let's go in; I'll go first."

He tapped on the door as Tom watched what movement he could. One of the women–maybe a young girl–slid quietly up to the door.

"*Min ealaa albabb?*" she asked in a timid voice.

"*Iinaa sadiq,*" Avery said as softly and unthreateningly as possible. "I am a friend, a friend of Khatoon's. I have come to help her."

Over the pounding of her heart and the staccato rhythm of her respirations, Khatoon recognized Avery Chamber's voice and exulted at his message. Ignoring Mahbooba's protests, she flung open the door and pulled him into the room.

CHAPTER THIRTY-SIX

"Thus, what enables the wise sovereign and the good general to strike and conquer, and achieve things beyond the reach of ordinary men, is foreknowledge. That is, knowledge of the enemy's dispositions, and what he means to do. Now this foreknowledge cannot be elicited from spirits; it cannot be obtained inductively from experience. Knowledge of the enemy's dispositions can only be obtained from other men."
–Sun Tzu, *Bingfa*, [*The Art of War*], 5th century B.C.

"In 1962, when [John A.] Scali was a diplomatic reporter for ABC News, President Kennedy disclosed the existence of offensive missile sites in Cuba and warned that if any were fired at the United States, the United States would retaliate against Moscow, not Havana. Two days later, Scali was contacted by Alexandr S. Fomin, a KGB official in Washington and a personal friend of Khrushchev.

"Is Kennedy serious? Would he really do that?" Fomin asked Scali.

"You're goddamn right he would," Scali said, according to a friend, Warren Rogers.

[Kennedy would not allow Scali to submit his report. Scali was reported by friends to have asked Khrushchev why he gave in to Kennedy. The Soviet premier replied that, "Americans are strange people. They will absorb insults, put up with betrayals, endure injuries. Then, they will shoot you in the heart. That's why."]
–Harry F. Rosenthal, *Washington AP*, October 9, 1995

Last IS Checkpoint before Duhok, Kurdistan, just before first light, late January, 2015

However surprising and serendipitous, emotional and joyful, the reunion was, they all realized that there could not be any waste of time. The darkness of the night was waning, and it would not be very long before all the occupants of the hamlet would be able to see clearly a hair in the new dawn's light. They would be arising for the *Salat al-fajr*, the first prayer of the day. The young women had to be well away from the hamlet before the local muezzin began his call to prayer. Most believers arose early enough to wash and to ready themselves for their appearance before God.

The escape party was now swollen to thirteen people—nine men to four women. The decision was to carry on the charade that the men were good IS soldiers conducting slaves to sell to the brokers who gathered at the major checkpoints—including the border crossing into Kurdistan. It was common to unload merchandise that would be frowned upon before entering the land of the Kurds. IS soldiers had enough trouble convincing the border guards on both sides that they had legitimate business and that their business was not a threat to the Kurds in general or the peshmerga in particular.

The men did all the work. The women were all too fatigued to be able to move quickly and efficiently enough. Khatoon joined the men in urging the women to hurry, even though she—like her sisters—was teetering on the brink of exhaustion. It was still dark—but just barely—when the HMMVEEs were all loaded, and the passengers dragged themselves aboard. As quietly as HMMVEEs can be, they moved slowly out of the hamlet's cluster of huts and pock-ridden dirt-track roads and onto the Mosul Dam highway.

They moved along at moderate speed for almost an hour before encountering the first sign of human activity, and this was a lone man.

"Keep going?" Carl asked Avery.

"Maybe we should have a chat with our nice friend and co-worker in the pajamas. We don't know enough about the checkpoint coming up to be able to protect ourselves. Let's find out what he knows."

Avery slowed his—the lead—hummer to a stop, and the rest of the three stopped behind and to the side of him.

He called out to the IS soldier, probably a sentry, "*Sabaah alkhayr,* [Good morning] Brother, may God, the Merciful and Compassionate, see you through the day."

"*Kayf hi ahwalk?*" [how are you?], the young man responded unsuspecting of the men in U.S. vehicles he presumed had been purloined from the careless Americans.

"*As-salam alykum.* [I am well, praise be to God]" answered Avery.

He and Richard walked nonchalantly up to the soldier.

The boy responded perfunctorily, "*Wa-alaykum as-salam.*"

Carl Johnson was a big man—a very big man–who had been a defensive tackle for the Dallas Cowboys before deciding to make a real contribution to America by joining the rangers.

They avoided reaching out to shake hands, an American affectation. Instead, Carl moved to his right side, and Avery to his left. A slight nod by Avery and the two of them overpowered the IS soldier and silenced him with Carl's massive hand over his mouth.

"Do not make sounds," Avery said. "Struggling is futile. We will kill you if you do."

The frightened jihadist nodded his submission and acquiescence. His eyes were bulging, and his respirations were so deep and rapid that Avery worried that he might die of a heart attack for a moment.

"My nice friend here will remove his hand; so, we can talk. If you make a peep, he will break you. *Tafahm*? [understand]."

The boy now fully understood the predicament he was in and realized his own foolishness. More than anything at the moment, he wanted to survive. He showed enthusiasm in his understanding and surrender.

Carl slowly removed his hand and the boy tightened his lips to demonstrate his commitment to silence.

"*Maa ismuk*?" [What is your name].

"*Ismii Ibrahim.* [My name is Ibrahim]. Like the *Kalipha*."

"We will not harm you, Ibrahim," said Avery, "all we want is a little information. Give it to us truthfully, and we will let you go."

The boy nodded his head. He was guileless and trusted the three men even though they were his avowed enemies.

How many men at the Dohuk checkpoint?

"*Dah*, [ten]" Ibrahim said without hesitation.

"How many during *dhuhr*? [noon prayers].

"*Du*," [two].

"Where do the men go for prayers?"

Ibrahim had to think a moment.

"Into the guard house. They drink their coffee during that time and sometimes have a short nap."

"How long, Ibrahim?"

"They are not supposed to, but often an hour or more."

"You have done well, Ibrahim. We will let you go free now. Do you promise not to make a noise."

"*'Aedak!*" he said, and his promise seemed genuine even though it had been coerced.

Avery smiled and nodded at Ibrahim, turned and started walking back to the HUMMVEE. Carl moved silently behind the boy and broke his neck.

"It is war, and I hate it," was his only comment to Avery when they got back in the vehicle.

"What's the plan, Boss?" Devlin asked.

"Go through the checkpoint at noon, maybe a minute or two after. There'll only be two guards then. It has to be silent. We can't stir up the Kurds; they would likely kill us just to be sure."

The girls had watched the entire proceedings and had mixed feelings: shock at witnessing a killing right in front of them, and exhilaration at the thought of a little revenge at last. Khatoon's feelings about Avery became even more mixed than they already were.

Ibrahim's predictions were correct. Islamic *salat* times are core beliefs and are rigid in the Islamic State. All Muslim schools of thought agree that any given prayer cannot be performed *before* its stipulated time. The time interval for offering the *Zuhr* or *Dhuhr* prayer starts from immediately after the sun passes its zenith and lasts until about twenty minutes before the call for the *Asr* [late afternoon] prayer is to be given. For most Muslims, this is a rather long period of time within which this prayer can be offered. However–under the caliphate–the time required is immediately after the sun is at its highest; and they are very scientific about it. They use sophisticated cameras to record the position according both to local time and to the universally agreed upon analemma.

An analemma is oddly shaped figure-of-eight diagram, smaller on the top, that shows the annual variation of the sun's position on the celestial sphere. The Muslim guard in charge carried a folder of photographs. An analemma can be shown by superimposing photographs taken at the same time of day, a few days apart for a year. It is also expressed as a graph of the sun's declination, plotted vertically, against the equation of time, which is plotted horizontally. Usually, the scales are chosen so that equal distances on the diagram represent equal angles in both directions on the celestial sphere. Precisely 3 minutes, 56 seconds in the equation of time, are represented by the same distance as 1° in the declination, since earth rotates at a mean speed of 1° at that rate, relative to the sun.

An analemma is drawn as it would be seen in the sky by an observer looking upward. If north is shown at the top, then west is to the *right*. This is usually done even when the analemma is marked on a geographical globe, on which the continents, etc., are shown with west to the left.

Some analemmas are marked to show the position of the sun on the graph on various dates, a few days apart, throughout the year. This enables the analemma to be used to make simple analog computations of quantities such as the times and azimuths of sunrise and sunset. Educated Muslims long ago stopped using sun dials, because they have very little practical usefulness. The process used by the guard was quick, efficient, and sufficient for the men's needs, despite slight imperfections in the process. For practical purposes, the guard merely had to check his photo of the day against the ones printed for that day in the folder he carried.

Avery and his men estimated that they were looking at the checkpoint in the distance approximately twenty minutes before the sun was exactly overhead. They backed the HUMMVEEs into a narrow wadi pointing outwards to the Mosul Dam road, ready for a hasty retreat if that became necessary. They left the women in the vehicles to have a siesta and to catchup on their sleep debt. They loaded their backpacks and belts with knives and ammunition and put on their Kevlar vests. It was oppressively hot—the hottest time of the day.

They divided into two units and made a wide arc out around the approach to the checkpoint. They were far enough away to avoid being heard, and they were in tall brush which gave them protection from being seen. They moved double-time to be in place as soon as the guards moved into the guardhouse for prayers and—hopefully—for a snooze.

At the checkpoint, the senior guard took his photo of the sun relative to the horizon. He wore heavy blackened eye protectors which made him blind to his surroundings for a few minutes as he made the photo. Avery and his men crept to within a meter of the place where the guard was standing and hid in the underbrush while he was concentrating. He signaled his men to follow him into the dark and cooler interior of the guard house. The two men who had drawn the punishing duty in the sun would only be relieved after the *Dhuhr* and siesta. They began a desultory back-and-forth march across the opening of the checkpoint barrier arm gates.

Richard and Malcolm were stationed where they could see into the dim light of the guardhouse. They gave a thumbs-up signal when the men inside laid themselves out for their naps—the best and most tranquil part of the day.

Tom and Carl slowly crawled on their bellies to within half a meter of the guard posts and lay there like logs until their man came up to the point where he would make his about-face. In the heat and boredom, the two jihadists were rather like sleepwalkers. With the suddenness of a viper strike, Tom and Carl brought down their quarries with a single direct stab wound through the bifurcation of the common carotid artery. The maneuvers were silent. They moved the bodies off to the side; so, they would not attract the attention of the Kurds in the opposite check-point, then joined their fellow commandoes at the guard house.

Each man attached a baffle-suppressor to his gun barrel. Avery gave a silent signal for the entry by counting down from five to zero by ticking off five fingers.

They burst through the doors and windows with numbing speed and surprise. Most of the guards were dead before they realized what was happening. No jihadist was able to reach his gun. No Muslim left that room in the guardhouse that noon. Fifteen seconds had elapsed.

CHAPTER THIRTY-SEVEN

"It's a lot like the Wild West out here... just with tea shops instead of saloons. Wild West Sahara, that is."
                    —T.K. Naliaka, *A Difficult Damsel to Rescue:*
                                           The Decaturs, 2014

"While we still remain among human beings, let us cultivate our humanity."
                    —Lucius Annaeus Seneca, *Moral and Political Essays,*
                    De Ira (On Anger) III,43, mid-1st century, C.E.

Last IS Checkpoint before Duhok, Kurdistan, noon, the same day.

No one came out from the Kurdish guard house to look in their direction. Avery presumed they were also having prayer or a nap or both in the only remotely cool place on their side of the militarily established border. He pondered his group's options for a couple of minutes. They could wait until dark and sneak around. That was a poor choice, he decided. They could not presume that no one else would come to the border crossing for the rest of the day. In fact, the corpses would begin to smell in the bake oven that the guard house was becoming. The outdoor thermometer hanging catawampus on the side of the guard house read 41°C in the sun. There was no shade anywhere.

He did a quick calculation: "*106° American,*" he said to himself.

The corpses were a source of insistence that they move more quickly.

He dispensed with thoughts of a nighttime sneak. Next, he considered pretending to be IS soldiers and their wives on a quick temporary errand inside Kurdistan. That would work if the peshmerga guards were high on drugs, were morons, or could be bribed. It took less than a second to discard that notion. He came to the only even remotely rational choice. It was particularly crazy; they could give the truth a try, even though it was unspylike.

"Get over behind the brush for a little conference," he asked everyone. They moved like slugs. Sweaty slugs.

"We have to get out of here. Someone has to get here and smell or see the dead bodies, and we will have to fight. We can't just keep fighting. So, let's all change clothes into civvies. We can lend the girls clothes enough to keep them decent, and we can explain it all to the Kurds. I am hoping they will believe that we are allies, accept our plea for sanctuary for the girls, and decide not to jail the rest of us."

"A lot of ifs, there, Avery," Malcolm posited. "I have another one. What if no one there speaks English or Arabic? Any of you guys speak Kurdish?"

SGM Agir Jaf, the Sorani Kurdish peshmerga, volunteered, "I do. If I get a chance to speak before they shoot us, I think I can convince them. Hope they're peshmerga, not regular army. We don't always get along so well."

Khatoon spoke up, "I speak Kurdish well. My family and I did a lot of business with Kurds in the old days. We lived there for a while."

"All good," said Avery. "Anybody have a better idea?"

Richard Erickson seldom talked—the strong silent type–but he wanted everyone to agree to getting out of there as soon as possible. The psychological image of the corpses was beginning to gnaw away at his nerves.

"Sounds good to me. We have a plausible set of players and some half-decent costumes for our little production. I say, let's make it happen."

Twenty minutes later, everyone looked their assigned parts—more or less. The girls took off their *niqabs* [full body overhead black abaya prayer garments] and reveled in the freedom to be dressed like women again–not black ghosts–even though their dresses were tattered and filthy. They were all pouring sweat. The temperature had risen a degree, if that was even possible. They were all champing at the bit.

"Okay, mount up," Avery said. "It could be a bumpy ride; so, buckle up. Let Agir and Khatoon do all of the talking until something happens to have someone else chime in."

They retrieved the HUMMVEEs from the hiding place behind the bushes and moved slowly and directly up to the IS barrier gate. Devlin jumped out and held it open, and the three vehicles passed through into no-man's-land.

They drove the short distance over to the lowered barrier on the Kurdish side. No one was outside to hail or to stop them.

"Wanna chance it?" Carl Johnson asked, certain of what the answer would be.

"No, let's try and act like what we are trying to be. Agir and Khatoon, come with me and do your thing. Be convincing."

He gave Agir a quick salute and Khatoon a soft squeeze on her upper arm and was pleased when she did not flinch.

Avery exhaled with relief that his decision was right when six fierce looking peshmergas stepped out from the guard house where they had been watching the occupants of the hummers.

Agir gave a proper peshmerga salute and was pleased when it was reciprocated. It portended a good start, he thought.

"Brothers," he said, "we have come a very long way. These women are Yazidi, and they have been very badly treated by the *kuffars* of the Islamic State as they dare to call themselves. The men are Americans who have volunteered to help and protect these poor girls."

The sergeant of the guard looked at the girls with a serious critical eye.

"Where are you from?" he asked, sweeping his eyes over them all.

"Sinjar," Khatoon said and nodded to the other girls who did not understand the Kurdish but did recognize 'Sinjar.'

"Kocho," the rest chorused.

"You look very thin and very tired. Were you very badly treated?" Khatoon translated.

Mahbooba began to cry softly and slowly removed the cloth from her forehead to reveal the hideous brand. It was not necessary for her to speak.

The sergeant lowered his eyes and clenched his fists.

"Yet one more reason to hate the jihadist monsters," he spat. "We have seen enough. You may pass. Do you have anyone in Kurdistan to help you, to feed you, to give you a place to stay, Sisters?"

Again, Khatoon translated.

All the girls shook their heads.

"Usually, we do not permit anyone to pass through who does not have support in the province. However–among us–we know good people who will help you. You will go to Erbil to the "Yazidi Humanitarian Center." It is run by the U.N. and many Yazidis and good Kurdish friends will welcome you with open arms. Private Moradi is our secretary. He will prepare papers for you. Do not lose them. That would be dangerous."

As soon as they crossed into Kurdistan out of the checkpoint, every person in the hummers breathed an audible sigh of relief. If it could have been done, they would have gotten out of the vehicles and kissed the free earth.

The small caravan of HMMVEEs set off again—this time trying to avoid friendly fire. Kurds were friendly to the U.S., and unfriendly to the IS; but in this wild west land, the distinction was often unclear. The Kurds were tense and inclined to shoot first and to let God sort out the dead. Their fairly short journey took them on a decent paved road past green mountains—some reaching 1,900 meters in height–criss-crossed by lush valleys, occasional snowcapped peaks, large and small canyons— some with beautiful waterfalls. To the four girls it was as if they were heading into heaven.

Their first view of Duhok City was from the mountain road leading down into it. The Duhok Dam formed the background of the view. The city was surrounded by a wide belt of green farmland. Owing to its latitude and altitude, this part of the Assyrian homeland is cooler and much wetter than the rest of Iraq. Due to its relatively wet climate, the region is rich in plant species. Some seen by the newcomer girls for the first time included: firs, oaks, conifers, platanus, willow, olive trees, poplar, hawthorn, oriental plane, and mountain ash poplar. The rich farmland held large pastures, huge plowed sections, and commercial cherry plum, rose hips, pistachio, and pear trees. After the deserts of their homeland and their suffering in the hell of al Anbar province, this was heaven, indeed.

They stopped at a small, neat, clean, café for lunch, a unique experience for all three girls. Their apprehension was slowly changing to anticipation and perhaps, even happiness. They had had enough sleep during the ride to be refreshed and ready for nonthreatening new adventures. An important element of Duhok—which added to the joy of being there—

was that it is known to the locals as Duhok of Dassini, meaning "Yazidi village." They saw men, women, and children, who were reasonably recognized by their faces and traditional costumes as Yazidi. Each girl took heart at being reminded that the Yazidi culture lived on.

Another sign of normalcy was noted as they passed the bus station in the center of the city: Americans, Shi'ites, and Kurds, greeted each other as old friends. Boys hawked silver bags of chips, plastic bottles of water, and candy bars. Everyone was seen to be haggling over price. There were towers of cigarette packs and stacks of cans of

something called "Diet Coke." Yellow taxis with signs for destinations printed on their tops passed them intent on getting to their destinations quickly. There was not a single niqab or burka in sight. It looked like the world the girls remembered, or perhaps, fantasized about.

On the way from Duhok to Erbil, the girls became animated and took delight in seeing the remarkable fauna of the region, which had not been decimated to near extinction by war. Khatoon saw a striped hyena and a golden jackal. Mahbooba saw her first goitered gazelle, crested porcupine, and Persian fallow deer, although she had no idea what they were. For her, they might have inhabited Mars—a place she had barely heard about. Masuda saw a wild boar and a gray wolf chasing a hare. She saw a new bird to her—a masked shrike. Ruhasva's main interest was in birds, and she squinted intently. Finally, her efforts were rewarded by seeing a see-see partridge, a squacco heron, and a hooded crow.

There were remarkable contrasts between ancient and modern in the fields they were passing. On one field, there would be a bent bearded man in a long flowing shirt plowing the land walking behind two mules holding onto a primitive wooden plow; and on the next farm, modern agricultural machinery such as tractors and harvester-thresher-reapers doing the work of ten such men. Some fields now bristled with oil drilling rigs. The kilometers passed very quickly for the girls which made Avery relax along with them.

They came to their first checkpoint inside Kurdistan, about three kilometers from the capital, Erbil. It was a neat white stucco building flying a large red, white, and green, tricolor with a sun emblem flag of Kurdistan which was a welcome relief after seeing the thousands of ominous IS flags in Iraq.

Avery and the other drivers started to get out of their hummers, but heavily armed peshmergas in camouflage uniforms held up their right hands to have them remain in place. A fiftyish officer carrying a swagger stick walked up to the first hummer and bade Avery to lower the side window.

His insignias indicated him to be a lieutenant colonel in the Kurdish intelligence agency, *Asaish*.

He stood looking Avery in the eyes for a full minute before politely requiring, "Papers, please."

Avery handed him all the papers for all the occupants of the three vehicles, neatly stacked. At the top of the stack were the documents prepared by Private Moradi at the Duhok border crossing.

The officer read the Duhok papers with care, then riffled through the passports more quickly.

"CIA?" he asked looking Avery directly in the eyes.

This was the moment of truth. Avery decided to trust in the truth because he believed that the Kurds were genuine friends.

He produced his cred-pack for a hidden pocket and held it open for the officer.

"Others, too?"

"Yes, I will ask the agents to step out and show their credentials as well."

"Please do."

Avery stepped out of his hummer slowly and carefully, taking care to keep his hands in plain sight at all times. He walked to each HUMMVEE and asked the drivers—Malcolm and Devlin—to step out and to follow him back to where the intelligence officer was standing stiffly but patiently.

"Gentlemen, please show the lieutenant colonel your cred-packs. It's okay, he's a friend of America's."

When the three men had certified the genuineness of their identities, the Kurdish officer spoke again, "What about the other men?"

"Military," Avery answered laconically.

"The women?"

This was likely to be the sticking point. The women, the soldiers, and the agents, had all been counseled not to admit that a woman with them was a fugitive slave from the Islamic State. He gritted his teeth.

"Escaped slaves from the jihadists. They have been treated as no person—no woman–should ever be treated. They are all Yazidis and seek to regain their dignity in the safety of Erbil. Please treat them with respect, Sir."

The officer ordered the women out of the vehicles. They were shivering with fear. The officer took note of Mahbooba's forehead branding scar, then looked long and hard at Khatoon. Suddenly, his face registered a look of recognition.

"You are Khatoon Yazidi–fugitive Islamic State slave–is that not true, young lady?"

Khatoon felt faint. She took a moment to gain composure.

"Yes, Sir. I have gone through hell and worse to get here to find my people. I will find a way to take my own life rather than to go back to the monsters."

She said it in a matter-of-fact but steely resolute way.

"You misunderstand me, Khatoon. I got your information from a poster found in Erbil's bus station. My men and I have been on the look-out for you in order to give you protection. You and your friends are safe now. The government of Kurdistan and the peshmerga are at your service. We will no longer tolerate any attempts to recapture our girls. Kidnappers face very serious charges here. You will have to be careful; but here is my card. You may call any time to get help. Welcome to Kurdistan, Sister. We are your family now."

Khatoon looked at the colonel in consternation, then awe, then—to her surprise and humiliation—she began to weep. For the first time since the massacre in Sinjar, she gave in–albeit involuntarily–to her pent-up anger, frustration, pain, fear, horror, and surpassing relief. It was a cathartic and revivifying cry—one that women only occasionally experience. The colonel waited patiently until the tidal wave was over and the floodgates closed. It was one of the best experiences of his military career, and he thanked Allah for letting him be the instrument of the true God to help a defenseless woman and her equally traumatized companions.

Even the men who had traveled with the girls and had risked much to save and protect them were touched to their cores. Most of them had to turn aside and to pretend to remove something from their eyes. It was a moment of rare, sublime, and memorable, joy.

Avery said, "Colonel, you can scarcely imagine what you have done. I speak for everyone here to express our everlasting gratitude to the good people of Kurdistan."

He and the rest of the men came to rigid attention and gave crisp salutes.

CHAPTER THIRTY-EIGHT

"While we still remain among human beings, let us cultivate
our humanity."

–Lucius Annaeus Seneca, *Moral and Political Essays,*
De Ira (On Anger) III,43, mid-1st century, C.E.

Ergil, Kurdistan, late afternoon, the same day, January 2015

As soon as the convoy of HUMMVEES departed from the waving Kurdish soldiers, Avery realized that some urgent housekeeping measures were in order. They were nearly out of gas, for one serious thing. Unlike the present condition in northern Iraq with the ongoing battles between coalition forces, the Iraqi army and the northward migrating Islamic State forces, the environs of the capital of the Kurdistan Autonomous Region was civilization. There was a BP service station to their right that looked as if it could have been transplanted from Sheboygan. A Yazidi boy rushed out to serve them, filled the huge hummer tanks, scrubbed the bugs off the windshields, and offered them a carwash. They had to pay in Iraqi dinars which was no problem since they had brought bagsful of the colorful paper.

When they returned to the main road into Erbil, the sound of music filled the vehicles—the spontaneous melodious soprano outbursts of women laughing and giggling together, sharing secrets that gave them pleasure.

Malcolm turned to Avery and said, "Warms the cockles of your heart, don't it, Boss?"

"It does."

Erbil was a mixture of old, fairly recent, and new and modern, architecture. The city had changed in the past twenty years, especially in the last decade. In past visits, Avery and his agents had moved about quite freely among the many villages dotting the periphery of the capital. They saw a local preference for mud huts early on, then brick, then stone. On this trip, every new building in the outskirts was built of concrete blocks. They passed unfinished concrete skeletons and empty storefronts dotting the city's middle bands. Since their last visit, Erbil had devised a Green Belt of parks, farms, and wooded areas hopefully to control urban sprawl and to exploit Kurdistan's naturally rich—but largely neglected—agricultural economy.

Even in the city—which was making a determined effort to modernize—concrete blocks were becoming the majority of building materials. The checkpoint *Asaish* officials had warned them that there were still tensions in the city, and they would need to watch their backs—not to be paranoid, but vigilant. Displaced and discouraged Muslim youths were attacking the "*kuffars*"—Yazidi and Christian—businesses and their religious meeting places. They often disrupted funerals. The peshmerga had their hands full to keep order while keeping the rabid jihadists at bay.

Erbil is 350 km north of Baghdad—the national capital—and borders the Al-Hasakah Governorate of Syria. It lies on a rich fertile plain between two rivers, the Greater Zab and the Lesser Zab. The local Kurds—for as long as anyone could remember—have called their city Hewlêr. It is shaped like a large, uneven circle. It is the most populated and best protected city in the Kurdish inhabited areas of Iraq. It is located near the center of Iraqi Kurdistan region and north of Iraq proper.

The HUMMVEEs moved through the improving streets towards the heart of the city where the ancient Citadel of Erbil stands as a reminder of the city's illustrious and dominant past. They stopped for a look and a bathroom stop and a brief foot tour. It was disappointing to discover that the only religious structure currently surviving in the Citadel was the Mulla Afandi Mosque. The hammams were still there. The men—and even the women—looked wistfully at the location of such delightful hot baths. The Citadel is a round structure, almost thirty-two meters high.

Even in the modern era it dominates the old city. On top of the Citadel stood an enormous *Alaya Rengîn* ["Colorful Flag"]–red, white, and green, tricolor Kurdish flag with its bright yellow twenty-one ray central sun.

The formidable battered old fortress sits on what—at first glimpse-would appear a remarkably symmetrical mound. But the current Citadel has been built upon seven layers of civilization and is a monument to thousands of years of history. The mound itself is not natural but has been formed by successive layers of settlements: Assyrian, Akkadian, Babylonian, Persian, Greek, and now Kurdish.

By this point in the journey, Avery had gladly relinquished study of the metropolitan maps to the girls. Khatoon–the natural leader–became the spokesperson.

"Turn right at the next paved street; go five or six kilometers (she now used the military lingo, "klicks") and turn left. The Yazidi Humanitarian Center should be almost next door to the bus station and across the main boulevard from the United Nations building. We should be able to see a large blue UN flag or two as we approach."

Avery drove the lead hummer and followed Khatoon's directions. It took less than fifteen minutes to reach the humanitarian center.

"Everybody out," ordered Khatoon jauntily.

She was enjoying her new-found leadership position and talked conspiratorially with the other girls as if what they were doing was a usurpation from the men. It felt good to both sexes. The battle toughened men remained wary. The area of the bus station was a notorious kidnapper hangout, and jihadi spies were said to be everywhere. It was a surprise to see that they were the only men packing weaponry more substantial than the traditional Kurdish belt knives every man past puberty in Kurdistan carried.

They formed a loose circle around "their women" as they had come to regard the girls. The girls warmed to the attention and the security these big men represented. They walked into the center like a large multi-legged creature and went directly to the information desk.

Travis took charge at this point, "Are you the person we see to get these four refugees settled and taken care of?"

"This is where it all begins, Sir. We will need to have all of you–even the men—fill out some papers. You can sit at those desks to the left."

"It can't be this easy," Devlin whispered to Avery. "There must be somebody we have to shoot."

"I hardly dare think it, let alone say it out loud; but I think we are at the end of the rainbow; and things are going to work out."

"Nirvana," Devlin agreed.

It was not entirely easy; there was a pile of papers each man and woman had to attend to. When they were done, each girl had an assigned room in the "new-arrivals" building, and an application to process for a permanent placement in a fairly prosperous and secure section of the city, Ankawa district. Ankawa was a predominantly Assyrian suburb to the north of the city which was now the residential district for a diverse set of professionals who have moved in from around Erbil. The district maintained its Christian history but was doggedly serious about the section being a safe haven for Yazidis.

Each girl had acquired a starter job, and each of them was thrilled at the prospect of being on her own and free of the degradation of the jihadi life and even the domination of Yazidi culture. They were going to make their own ways. Khatoon was the only one with educational aspirations, and she was provided with an application for admission and recommendation papers for entrance into the prestigious AUK [American University of Kurdistan]. Avery considered that gift of the government of Kurdistan to be little short of a miracle, and Khatoon was as speechless with wonderment as if she might have been stepping out onto a different inhabited planet.

The university was founded that same year by Masrour Barzani, the leader, with generous American help. It was a sister to the American University in Washington, D.C. It was a not-for-profit liberal arts university with a growing number of colleges. Khatoon was advised to matriculate in the liberal arts education program and then to get a college job in cross-disciplinary research. She elected to live in the housing of the College of Business and to do her university work in the Department of Business Management.

With nothing better to do during their few days left in Erbil, the men decided to accompany "their women" on a small sight-seeing tour and to take in the great covered Erbil Qaysari Bazaars, lying below the main entrance to the citadel. The girls were in need of stocking up on the plentiful household goods, foods, and tools to be found in the dizzying maze of alleys and shop stalls.

Getting there was half the fun—or annoyance, if you are a glass half empty sort of person. From flags to statues to street names, to shop titles, the city of Erbil deliberately embraced Kurdish culture to such an extent that it almost seemed to have become a spectacle for tourists. However, the intended audience was the Kurds themselves. In the city's downtown, everything celebrated Kurdish figures. There was a plethora of streets named after Mustafa Barzani–historic leader of the Kurdish independence movement and father of the current President Masoud Barzani–and Salahaddin, a Kurd who led successful campaigns against the Crusaders in the middle ages. Roads and houses spread out from the ancient citadel like the spokes of a wheel—for as far as they could see. There was still the familiarity of men in traditional Kurdish salwar pants and turbans sipping tea in cafes.

Avery could scarcely navigate his way through the teeming and intensely busy city—a far cry from his previous visits. A wave of traffic—oddly, an inordinate number of large white SUVs everywhere–oil firms, property developers, chain stores, tall buildings, hotels, supermarkets, and consulates, had invaded the city, reshaping its character, erasing old landmarks, and pushing its borders out into the surrounding plains and scrubland beyond the old, high, sand-colored, city walls. New chrome and glass skyscrapers and a considerable number of new malls and hotels lined the streets fronting onto the pavement of narrow sidewalks. There was construction almost everywhere, much of which interfering with traffic. They were in no real hurry; so, the language in the hummers remained appropriate for polite society.

The agents, soldiers, and girls, were open-mouthed at the United Nations level of diversity they were encountering in the bustling and teeming crowds milling about in the bazaar. In addition to the majority Kurds, the visitors could make out the clothing, mannerisms, and dialects of Armenians, Chaldeans, Assyrians, Syriacs, Kurdish Yezidis, Shabakis, Sunnis, Shi'ites, Christians, and Mandaeans. Strange as they all were, the place seemed quite welcoming to their diverse qualities and to the girls who thought they were going to fit right in among the rest of the different looking people.

Each girl was deposited at her new address. There was no hugging; the girls were neither culturally nor emotionally ready for such contact with a man, even a member of the family. Khatoon thanked Avery effusively as he walked her to her apartment and new life.

Avery had one more task to accomplish before he and his agents left Erbil and Kurdistan. He had them follow him to the Finnish Consulate on 400 Ishtar Road in Ankawa. He found them places to relax in the consulate lobby then moved quickly to find a friend who was the reason he had stopped at the consulate.

A very attractive, very blond, and pleasingly willowy, young, receptionist greeted him in Finnish.

"*Hyvää iltapaivää,*" [good afternoon] she said with her patented full-face Finnish smile.

Avery, of course, did not understand a word of the passingly strange Finno/Ugric language.

"Please, do you speak English?"

"But, of course, Sir. How may I be of help?"

"*Oh, good,*" thought Avery, "*something easy.*"

"I need to speak to one of your diplomats, Dal Järvinen; it is a matter of some urgency."

"I will see if the military attaché is in house. Please take a seat; it may take a few minutes. Whom shall I say is asking?"

"Avery Challenger from Washington, D.C."

He was not altogether sure that Dal would remember him.

He was wrong in that. Captain Järvinen was standing at his side in a quarter of an hour and clapping him on the back.

"Avery–you invisible old spy master–what brings you to Kurdistan—to the remotest part of Kurdistan, this little bit of Finland in Erbil?"

"Spy stuff, but also some important humanitarian stuff. There is a girl I would like you to kind of look after."

"So, the world's most confirmed bachelor just might be developing a chink in his armor; is that the case here?"

"No, my friend, this girl is more like a daughter to me."

He described Khatoon's history and present situation in Erbil. He ended with a statement that surprised even him:

"I retire in three or four years, and I am going to try to convince her to come to the U.S. to expand her life. She is just coming out of shock for the time being; so, I am not about to press her. I just want her to stay safe."

"If she means that much to you; she means that much to me," Dal said.

Avery returned to the lobby of the consulate, gathered up his comrades-in-arms and took them all out to dinner in the Abu Shahab City Restaurant on 60 Metres Road at the junction with Ainkawa road—the best Kurdish food the city had to offer. He had telephoned for reservations the day before and had arranged a special menu as a token of gratitude for his loyal and eminently courageous friends.

As soon as they were seated, the restaurant owner greeted them effusively and announced: "*Çêştî Kurdî*–enjoy!"

With a small hook of his right forefinger, a dozen white aproned waiters surrounded the hungry foreigners and began removing a plethora of small plates of Kurdish cuisine from large pewter platters: deep-fried Kurdish *kubbeh* liberally covered with fresh local herbs, *berbesel, biryani, dokliw, kellane, kullerenaske, kutilk, parêv tobouli*. In addition to that vegetarian fare, there was *kuki* [meat and vegetable pies], *burgul pilaf, tapsi* [aubergines, green peppers, *courgettes,* and potatoes in a slightly spicy tomato sauce], *tashreeb* [layers of naan in a sauce of green pepper, tomato, onions and chilies], *pide* [a crusty white loaf], and *dolma*.

Alcohol was strictly forbidden; so, the Americans tried *sorani* [yogurt and salt mixed with water] and Turkish coffee strong enough to allow a spoon to stand up in it.

A group of local boys and girls in a folkloric club danced the *halperke*, a traditional Kurdish dance. The men talked for a little while about everything but their combat experiences and the current war. At 2200, Avery begged off. They all had different new assignments in other locations and had to get going to be on time and in starched uniforms with all documents in order. They shook hands heartily; these men were not huggers.

Avery paid the bill and left a good tip. His last action in country was to see Khatoon in her new apartment to say goodbye. He had made sure in advance that she had a chaperone. Her hotel's windows were covered with gauzy curtains and had grey tile on the floor. In the hotel lobby, most people were Yazidi women wearing flowing white dresses and patterned silk head scarves.

He overheard one girl say to another, "We Yazidi don't have anyone or anything but God."

"*Sad, but true,*" he thought. "*I can make things better for at least one Yazidi.*"

Khatoon came to the lobby dressed the same as all the other girls. They were all thin and trying to regain their pre-massacre musculature and figures.

"I will come back for you, Khatoon. I want you to meet my family and to see America. If, by then, you want to become an American, I can make that happen."

"I will give it great thought, Avery. You are most kind."

CHAPTER THIRTY-NINE

"President Trump revealed highly classified information to the Russian foreign minister and ambassador in a White House meeting last week, according to current and former U.S. officials, who said Trump's disclosures jeopardized a critical source of intelligence on the Islamic State. The information the president relayed had been provided by a U.S. partner through an intelligence-sharing arrangement considered so sensitive that details have been withheld from allies and tightly restricted even within the U.S. government, officials said.

"The partner had not given the United States permission to share the material with Russia, and officials said Trump's decision to do so endangers cooperation from an ally that has access to the inner workings of the Islamic State. After Trump's meeting, senior White House officials took steps to contain the damage, placing calls to the CIA and the National Security Agency."

–Greg Miller and Greg Jaffe, *Trump revealed highly classified information to Russian foreign minister and ambassador, The Washington Post*, May 10, 2017

"President Trump's national security adviser said Tuesday that the president's decision to reveal highly classified information during a meeting with Russian officials last week was 'wholly appropriate'–the latest attempt by the White House to contain the explosive disclosure that Trump potentially jeopardized a crucial intelligence source on the Islamic State. H.R.

McMaster–the president's top security adviser–repeatedly described the president's actions in a press briefing just a day after a *Washington Post* story revealed that Trump had shared deeply sensitive information with Russian Foreign Minister Sergei Lavrov and Ambassador Sergey Kislyak during an Oval Office meeting last week.

–Ashley Parker, *McMaster: Trump's sharing of sensitive intelligence with Russia was 'wholly appropriate,'* The *Washington Post,* May 16, 2017

Langley, Virginia, May 10, 2017, early evening

Avery was instructed to return to Washington early in 2016 because the civil war in Syria and the final stages of the defeat of the Islamic State were creating such a degree of chaos and danger that it was considered the better part of valor to bring senior officers back to the United States. They were to await developments not nearly so confusing or fraught with hazard. That gave him a brief chance to use agency communication systems to check in with Dal Järvinen in the Erbil Finnish Consulate. He was reassured that everything was peaceful in Kurdistan; the action was all in Syria; and who knew what was happening there? Avery asked Dal to get Khatoon to agree at least to come to Washington for a couple of weeks; so, he could have a chance to persuade her to emigrate.

He had another request, "Dal, I don't know how feasible it is, but I would like you to get hold of my spy in al-Baghdadi's camp–Rahim Jamaluddin. I just told you a very serious top-secret piece of information. I need to know if he is all right. I have not been able to get hold of him for a while. You should be able to contact him through Peshmerga Colonel Behremend Rozaki. I think we need to put a rush on it. I have a kind of an unpleasant premonition."

"Thanks for trusting me. I'll get right on it. I remember how prescient your hunches were when we were working together in Operation Odyssey Lightning in Libya, back in the day. I'll get back to you as soon as I have something."

"Thanks, Pal. I'll owe you one."

Avery leaned back in his chair to have a drink and to finish his delivery Chinese General Cho's Chicken and the mixed sea food and vegetables dishes he liked. He was just about to take his first swallow from a long neck bottle of *Stella*–a light lager from Egypt which had become his favorite–when the call came.

His heart skipped a beat—as it always did—when he saw the red bulb flashing on the secure phone.

"*Nothing good ever came on that thing*," he muttered to himself and picked the receiver up after two rings.

"This is a secure line," he said.

"COS-I Chambers. Put down the receiver and wait for a call from the DCIA."

No hello, please, or good-bye. The secure line was always like that.

In less than a minute, the secure line buzzed again.

"Agent 12ABG2323," he said.

"Do you recognize my voice?"

It was that of DCIA Gina Haspel. This was serious.

"Yes, Ma'am."

"Drop what you're doing and get to my office as fast as you can without attracting attention. *Capiche?*"

"I *capiche*. I'm on my way."

He was staying in a Company apartment in McLean within seven minutes of the George Bush Center for Intelligence—the "CIA Building."

He did not bother to change his clothes or to enjoy his nice cold Egyptian beer. He ran to the garage and made as much as a beeline as possible.

Avery drove as much above the speed limit as he dared: northwest on Old Dominion Drive to Chain Bridge Road, took a right then another slight right to Dolley Madison Boulevard, then a left onto Georgetown Pike for a mile and a half. Then it was left onto Colonial Farm Road where he made a right onto the restricted usage road. On that deserted stretch, he made another right, then a short left, another right, and the formidable building loomed up on his left.

He was expected. The receptionist noted his creds and waved him to the elevator. He took the express to the seventh floor—the holy of holies—where the gods of the Central Intelligence Agency dwelt.

The ADCIA was directing the last of four senior agents and NIA administrators into the conference room. The DCIA was standing at the far end of the long cherry-wood table waiting for the stragglers to arrive. Her face was somber and angry. This was a definite tel.

"Take your seats, Gentlemen and Ladies. I am going to warn you now—and especially SAC Challenger that this is horrific. I would not expose anyone to this if it didn't hit too close to home."

The lights dimmed, and a large screen descended from the ceiling. Immediately, a crisp clear movie began. Its production qualities gave it high clarity, excellent sound projection, and true-to-life color. An IS flag was spread across the rear wall as a backdrop. Three recognizable men stood behind a simple right-angle steel chair. The chair faced a rudely debarked eight-foot long pole which appeared to be about eight inches in diameter. Showing from the bottom, six feet apart, were two screw rings.

The three men were: Tarad Muhammad al-Jarba [pseudonym Abu Muhammad al-Shimali, the key logistician of foreign fighters on the left]; Abu Bakr al-Baghdadi, the Caliph, in the prominent center position; and Abi al-Hassan al-Muhajer, spokesman for the Islamic State on the right.

"I guess that settles the question about whether or not al-Baghdadi is still alive," Director Haspel said before any voices were heard coming from the movie.

A masked man in black walked from the left side and placed an empty large rectangular metal basin in front of the pole, then exited the way he had come in.

A fourth—entirely recognizable man to all the intelligence officers— stepped into the frame from the right side. He was known to everyone as Jihadi John—real name Mohammed Emwazi, a British Arab, who was the main figure in multiple televised beheadings. He was holding a very large serrated knife—similar in size to a Bowie knife—and apparently honed to razor sharpness. He held the knife calmly in his right hand against his chest, blade upward.

No one in the conference room took a breath.

Shortly after the main players had taken their places, Abu Bakr al-Baghdadi gave a short angry speech in Arabic. Avery understood it perfectly; many in the room did not; but the meaning was still as malevolent as if they could translate fluently. It was couched in his usual grandiose and flowery religious language and was more than tinged with vitriol.

He sat down, and from the left, a man in chains was dragged forward. His arms were affixed to the screw bolts under the pole, and his buttocks were jammed down onto the steel chair. It was obviously a very uncomfortable position which caused him to squirm violently. Three vicious strikes with a large wooden bat quieted him down. He sagged into the desired position.

Avery put his hands over his face. The poor man was Rahim Jamaluddin, once Avery's most trusted and top-secret agent, and one of the men he respected the most among the many men he admired. His face was battered; all the fingers on both hands had been selectively broken after the fingernails had been pried off. His ears were gone.

Al-Baghdadi read from a scroll. Avery understood every word; it was a formal death sentence. Without changing expression, the caliph nodded to Jihadi John who walked over to the nearly inert victim. In a gesture of complete defiance, the executioner removed his face covering and flashed a toothy grin at the camera, his straight white teeth and jet-black beard giving strong contrast for his handsomely boned face.

He raised the knife above his head, adjusted its angle, and took the handle in both of his large hands. Quicker than the spectators could follow, the knife blade descended down on Rahim's vulnerable neck slicing it down to the posterior cervical spinal processes but not through the bone. Rahim's screams pierced the watchers and listeners to the marrow. The three Islamic State observers did not flinch or change expression. Jihadi John tried again, harder. One of the bony processes shattered off; but his aim was still off a fraction; and the sharp edge did not reach the soft spinal cord. Blood poured into the receptacle on the floor.

Deciding that his modus operandi was not working, the Islamic State executioner tried a new tack. He began to saw the large knife back and forth. Finally, he found the right place and penetrated. Rahim gave one last agonal breath and slumped to a limpness akin to having been deboned.

Avery was afraid he would vomit and humiliate himself. He was glad he had missed lunch and supper. Once through the bone, the arrogant Britisher Mohammed Emwazi triumphantly held the severed and dripping head aloft; so, no one could miss his accomplishment. The movie faded to black with a message telling the world that this was the fate of traitors, *Inshalah*!

Avery had never felt such fury and had to fight to regain control of his tormented emotions.

"I'm so sorry, Avery," DCIA Haspel said.

She meant it sincerely.

"Frankly, Colleagues, that is not the worst of it. Have you all read the *Post* from this morning?"

Everyone silently nodded; most of their faces were now contorted with difficult to contain fury, shock, anger, and determination.

"Let me rehash, lest anyone here think there is some gross reporting coincidence or error—'Fake News'—as it were."

Disdain dripped with every syllable.

"These are the facts. Late this morning—10, May, 2017–the President of the United States, Donald John Trump, met in the Oval Office of the White House with two very senior Russian diplomats and a photographer from Russian News Agency TASS. All other media reporters were escorted out. The Russian dignitaries were Russian Foreign Minister, Sergey Lavrov and the Russian Ambassador to the United States, Sergey Kislyak. The American president disclosed secret information providing sufficient details (including the city where the threat was detected) that could be used by the Russians to deduce the source of the information and the manner in which it was collected, according to current and former government officials we have contacted. The disclosures were codeword-classified."

There was a unanimous sharp intake of breath.

"Meaning—as everyone in this room knows full well–that its distri- bution was restricted only to those who were explicitly *cleared* to read it. Certainly not the Russians. That classification means that the secrets were of such a crucial nature and sensitivity that they were not intended to be shared beyond the United States and *certain allies*. Let me be perfectly clear as a former federal prosecutor and a long-time intelligence agent. Donald Trump revealed code word intelligence, the highest layer of classification. Mind you, it is even higher than the 'top secret' classification. These are facts, not opinions; and they have been thoroughly and quickly evaluated. They have an unequivocal "1" rating by every officer who was in on the investigation.

"Furthermore, the details of the disclosures were such that it was easy for the Russians to make a quick deduction that the source was Israel. I cannot tell you how furious the cousins in Israel are. They told me that *Ynetnews*–an Israeli news website–had previously reported that U.S. intelligence officials had advised Israeli Mossad and other intelligence officials to "be careful" when transferring intelligence information to the Trump White House and administration until the possibility of Russian influence over Trump has been fully investigated. They are going to publish that information. It will take a very long time for us to regain Israel's trust. The *Washington Post* will publish a tell-all within the week."

Avery raised his hand, making an heroic effort to control his facial expression, "Director, was Rahim Jamaluddin outed as a result of the disclosure?"

"We'll never be able to prove it, but you can bet both the farm and the house that he was."

Someone spoke up, "That has to be grounds for impeachment doesn't it?"

"And who is going to divulge what we know? We are caught between a rock and a hard place. Our only option going forward is to be extraordinarily careful about what we share and wait for this administration to become history."

"Avery, you are too much of an optimist. When this regime in Washington and the ones in the Middle East go away, others–altogether similar–will take their place. Look on the bright side of that: we will always have a job."

EPILOGUE

"Sometimes the dragon wins."
        —Ancient Asian proverb. There is a popular poster that portrays a fire-breathing dragon about to deliver the *coup de gras* to a fallen medieval knight which makes the point.

"Look, you're already dead. If you'll just quit fighting, I'll make it easy for you."
        —Robin Barefield, *The McCarthy Massacre of 1983*,
        AuthorMasterminds, Alaska, 2019

Langley, Virginia, May 16, 2017, morning.

Khatoon Yazidi finally telephoned Avery Chambers to let him know that she did not want to be seduced by all of America's delights, freedoms, and opportunities. He had enticed her to come for a visit to America, an enticement which included a Harlequin Opal pendant with gold backing on back—an heirloom from his grandmother. It contained a new inscription gold plate attached to the back: "Love forever, you can depend on me."

Her place was with her people. She had joined the Kurdish trained all female YJS [Sinjar Women's Units] militia. She wanted to fight for herself—for revenge—for her people—to guarantee them a future in the homeland of their choice, and for the coalition of fighters who had come to the Yazidis' rescue—to show her great appreciation for them. She had been offered great employment opportunities in Kurdistan when she graduated from the American University; she had received the very high honor of accompanying the Yazidi hero and recipient of the Nobel Peace Prize on a global speaking tour. But, she always came back to her wish to fight, to rid herself of the memories of being helpless and defenseless against the monsters of the Islamic State. She pledged to keep in touch.

As a side note, she reported that—since they had last seen each other—she and the other girls had been invited to the Chermera Temple on top of Mount Sinjar. They passed through the lovely little pristine town of Lalish to begin a purification process. They and more than a thousand other girls gathered, removed their shoes, and began to walk barefoot in buildings, and on streets.

Those streets were immaculate. Every day volunteers cleaned the town and the temples and replenished the sweet smelling olive oil for the lamps from olives grown in the valley. The girls and their chaperones were cautioned to be entirely respectful—no spitting or stepping on entranceways. Each girl was directed to kiss the doorframes and entrance way before entering temple. They then tied knots in colorful silk representing prayers and wishes and were directed to wish to become virgins once again.

The Baba Sheikh [Baba Chawish] came in his white robes to greet them and welcomed them home. He supervised their baptisms in the pools beneath the tomb of Sheikh Adi. When they arose from the waters of baptism, Baba Chawish pronounced each of the girls individually to be a virgin once again. There was not a tearless eye among the thousands of girls and their well-wishers.

American and Iraqi volunteers invited several thousand Yazidi and Shi'ite girls to Baghdad for re-virginization surgery. Khatoon had the procedure done along with the other two girls who had fled with her. They all agreed that it was good, and that they were once again accepted into Yazidi society. Still, not all the memories or scars had been washed away or removed by Baba Chawish. Those were forever.

Idlib, Syria, February, 2018.

Caliph Abu Bakr al-Baghdadi was reported by *Al Jezeera* and the government-run *al-Sabah* daily to have suffered very severe leg wounds in an air raid in Syria but is still alive and hiding in Syria's Jazeera desert, west of Deir Az Zor. The official sources said that he was being treated in northeastern Syria. Other reports indicate that the leader suffers from injuries, diabetes, and fractures to the body and legs, that prevent him from walking without assistance. Al-Baghdadi has achieved the dubious status of being one of the world's most-wanted men with a $25m U.S. bounty on his head. It appears to most Western intelligence observers that al-Baghdadi's days of fighting and leadership are over.

Langley, Virginia, CIA Building, January 12, 2019.

COS-Iraq Avery Chambers attended the ceremonial awarding of the intelligence services black star for Rahim Jamaluddin's death in the service of his country and the Central Intelligence Agency. President Trump pushed Congress to have the hero awarded full naturalized citizenship posthumously.

After the ceremony, Avery met with DCIA Haspel in her office for five minutes.

He said, "Madam Director, I wanted to tell you in person. I'm done. This is my formal resignation."

He placed a sealed envelope on her desk.

"It has been an honor to serve my country and the Agency. It has been a pleasure to work with you. Thank you."

"We will all hate to see you go, but we understand. What are your plans?"

"Find a good woman; change my name; discover where Margaritaville is and go there and raise a family and catch fish; I'm still young enough, I think. No more fighting, lying, hiding, or playing politics. I have seen too much, done too much, and turned my face away from too much, to be able to live with myself in this capacity any longer."

"Well, *vaya con dios, Amigo*. Have fun."

Erbil, Kurdistan, July 8, 2019

Finnish Consular Military Attaché Dal Järvinen received a formal warning from Mossad that an Islamic State fatwa had been distributed naming Col. Behremend Rozaki, ranking peshmerga officer and CIA spy in al-Baghdadi's camp, as a traitor to the Islamic State's cause; and all Muslims everywhere were authorized to kill him on the spot if or when he was sighted. It remained a mystery who had betrayed him. Col. Rozaki was not an easily frightened or timid man. He had been fighting peshmerga battles since he was thirteen-years old, and he was tired. Bone tired. He obviously could no longer keep up his double-agent charade. He decided it was time to quit.

He came in from the cold, not to his peshmerga friends and allies, but to new friends in the Finnish Consulate. He did so during the middle of a hot summer's night when most people were trying to get cool in the darkness of their thick-walled homes. Dal supervised his exfiltration and his transformation into a new man: a citizen of Finland, a teacher of history at the University of Helsinki specializing in Middle Eastern modern history and catering to foreign students getting their higher education in Finland. He was a different man; plastic surgery gave him a new, younger face and new, perfect white teeth. His own mother would not have recognized him. He dyed his hair brown, shaved his face every day, and lost weight by diet, exercise, and liposuction. Per Dal's and Avery's instructions, he never talked of his life in Kurdistan or with the peshmerga, and he cut off all previous contacts as he entered his new and excitingly different life.

National Hospital for Neurology and Neurosurgery, University College, Bloomsbury, London, England, October 13, 2019

Sister Marie, head nurse on Neurosurgery 1, stopped by Daniel Pathmarajah's private room to be sure that all was in order for his release from the hospital and that his outpatient care instructions were well understood. He had had a rather extensive series of operations done in two separate admissions.

"How is your back today, Mr. Pathmarajah? Ready for the big day?"

"Thank you, Sister, I am most grateful to say that I have only a twinge or two of pain every now and again. No leg pain, although I still have the limp in the right one; and I can tell that some weakness persists.

But, I am most satisfied with the results. Please thank the surgeons, Mr. Howard and Mr. Nesbit-Curtiss, for all of their kind attentions and their expert care."

"I will do that, Sir. It has been a pleasure to work with you towards your improvement. Now, my man, you know that it is not over. You are expected to appear at the Bloomsbury Rehab Clinic thrice each week to get those limbs strengthened and limbered up. Six months from now, you will be fit as a fiddle—able to leap tall buildings in a single bound, as they say in the *Superman* movies."

As always, Mr. Pathmarajah resisted having the sister nurses assist him to dress. Today he intended to look particularly natty. It was a grey day in London, like most days; so, he chose a nice three piece tweed, a matching Scottish country gentleman cap, Thistle shoes–leather Ghillie Brogue Kilt shoes, the traditional Scottish Piper and Highland Outfit foot ware–featuring extra-long laces and leather tassels, and a custom made gold handled cane. The cane was more of an affectation than a real aid to walking, he told himself; but he liked the sense of security it provided.

It annoyed him a little when Sister insisted that he had to be taken to the release door by wheelchair. It made him look something of an invalid, something he definitely was not. He needn't have concerned himself about being recognized. He looked nothing like the man he was seven months ago. Now, he was very much an English businessman of Pakistan origin.

He continued to be a bit surprised when he caught himself in the mirror. No more heavy full faced black beard, thick nose, heavy eyebrows that could make passersby think him to be an Afghan or a Middle Easterner. The plastic surgery had been rather painful and tediously slow to heal, but the result was worth it. Lazar surgery corrected his myopic vision; so, he was no longer obliged to wear eyeglasses. He had been the star patient in rehab; all the physical therapists said so. He lost three-stone in weight and had tightened his muscles so that they were well defined, unlike the roundness of his musculature previously.

He resolved to work even harder on his Pakistani accent; he knew it was not quite second nature to him; and he most certainly did not want to sound like an uneducated speaker of Paklish or Pinglish. He practiced his new accent as often as he found it to be safe to do so.

Mr. Pathmarajah was helped into a waiting black taxi—actually yellow in color, but all London cabs are called "black cabs"–by ever helpful Sister Marie, then they waved goodbye.

As he sat down in the back seat, Mr. Pathmarajah asked, *"Aapko English ati hai?"* [Do you know English?]

The cabbie said, "A bit of a moment, Kind Sir. I'll open the meter, and we'll be off. Where to, Guv?"

That cleared up the concern about which language to use.

"Tower Hamlet—East Ham, if you please."

"Got a number?"

Mr. Pathmarajah fumbled for a paper in his front suit pocket.

"481 Grangewood Street; it's near Priory Park."

"Ah, yes, I know the place. We'll be there in two shakes of a dead lamb's tail. Sorry, though, can't go over the speed limit; there's Kojacks with a Kodak everywhere these days."

The cabbie was chatty. Daniel liked that because it kept him from having to talk much and incur the risk of divulging too much inadvertently.

"I've been hired by the company to work in the office, be on parade from come next Monday."

"Congratulations. That's a real step for a man so young as you."

"Lots of jealousies about. The rest of the lot think I've been made a direct Sergeant; you know, got be promoted out of turn and given too much responsibility and authority too soon. I rather think they might be right, you know. Maybe I should just keep on movin' me Black Hack. But I'm going to do all in my pan to prove them wrong."

"Good for you; I like to see our people get ahead," Daniel said.

"Ah, I thought you was a Paki. Can't quite trace the accent, though. Peshawar?"

"No, Lahore—born and bred."

"Hmmh, *Theek Hai.*" [Okay]

The cabbie went on, "Tough what's been happening to the Islamic State of late. The Crusaders seem to be bringing 'em down. Hate to see that coming about. There was real promise there for us."

"I don't suppose we should count them down and out just yet. By God, they have the true way on their side."

"*Inshalah.* Do you think Sir is still among us?"

"Last I heard, he was. He gave a speech on BBC telly April 30 this year."

"Didn't catch it. What did Sir have to say?"

"The Caliph told us that he and the leadership have had pledges of allegiance from militants in Burkina Faso and Mali, and that there are IS protests in Sudan and Algeria. He said by God, the Merciful and Compassionate, jihad is the only solution to 'tyrants.' That is even though both of those countries have seen their long-term rulers overthrown this month. Although Iraq and Syria rightly continue to account for the lion's share of IS attacks; Afghanistan, Somalia, the Philippines, Nigeria, and Egypt's Sinai Peninsula also regularly have their share. The jihad is not over and will not be until every last Crusader and *kaffir* is gone. That's what he said."

Daniel worked to school his tongue. He was saying too much, too soon.

The cabbie enthusiastically agreed.

"Well, Sir, we're in East Ham on Grangewood. What was the number again?"

"481."

"We're right here by Barkley's Bank. I'm afraid to take you any farther into the section; high crime here, you know. And, Sir, if you don't mind me saying so, you should mind your "P"s and "Q"s out here. Look over your shoulder and no dark alleys, if you get my meaning. *Khuda Hafiz*," [May God be your protector-Goodbye."].

Daniel paid the cabbie the metered fare and a tip and stepped out onto the crowded sidewalk. It was quite similar to a big city in the Middle East, but one which had opened up to full diversity a long time ago. He liked the familiarity—Indians, Malays, Turks, Egyptians, Syrians, Iraqis; turbans, kaftans, dishdashis, skull caps, hijabs, burkas–he especially like to see that–and the rough-wear of workmen.

In the better kept-up areas, there are several pleasant green spaces intermingled with the more prominent bustling and urbanized area of East Ham. Following the instructions he had memorized, Daniel passed the graveyard of the old Norman St Mary's church–now maintained as a nature reserve. His apparent–but actually quite purposeful—meanderings led him along Central Park Road past the park itself, and for a nice morning's exercise stroll through Plashet Grove Park. The two parks were large with highly enjoyable open space, playgrounds for children, and a variety of cafés. At Priory Park and Flanders Field, he paused to get his bearings and took a 360° look-around.

From verbal memory, he turned left off Grangewood into a wide busy alleyway named "Gilgitbazar" which was packed with shops, most of which were Pakistani—foods, including potatoes, beans, chilis, carrots, celery, bananas, oranges. There were meats of all kinds, limes, buffalo butter, dried meats and fruits, dairy, grains, oils, herbs, fresh figs, cherry tomatoes, avocadoes, kale, banana peppers, mushrooms, organic honey, and fresh cheeses.

There were brass, copper, tin, pewter, and ceramic ware, stalls—each shop owner shouting his or her wares louder than the stall before. There were myriad street foods: stews in gravy bubbling in huge cauldrons, *halawa puri* [somewhat sweet chickpea stew], and paya+charsi tikka. At the end of the blind alley there were vendors of prepared products such as salads, chutneys, beauty, and skincare products.

Daniel paused at a retail handmade knife and knife sharpening stall and pretended to look at the beautiful cutting instruments with avid interest.

"Do you find something of interest, Effendi?" the owner asked, looking closely at Daniel's face.

"Perhaps not here. Do you have another showroom?"

"Who sent you?"

Daniel whispered the code words, "The Caliph."

The vendor looked at the well-dressed gentleman standing in front of him with awestruck eyes.

"Enter the door behind me, Great Sir."

Daniel looked about quickly, saw nothing suspicious—no bobbies or obvious plain clothes agents—and quickly walked around the stall, pushed open the heavy metal door and walked in. The hallway was dark, and it took his eyes a few minutes to accommodate to the diminished light. When they did, he saw two large men in IS uniforms—men he recognized, and who had been expecting him.

"Ahmed and Muhammad, how good it is to see, my brothers. Take me to the meeting room."

He followed the two powerful guards through a minor maze of halls, stairways, and up two sets of elevators to the southern half of the buildings' topmost rooms. They entered a room lit by large candles and filled with incense smoke. Six well-dressed Muslim men sat cross-legged on cushions eating from a delicacy covered revolving tabletop.

Every man leaped to his feet as soon as Daniel walked into view. They each dropped to one knee and gave a deep bow as if greeting an eighth century caliph.

The senior of the men spoke for the rest, "Oh, mighty *Kalipha* Ibrahim, may God, the all-powerful and his servant, Muhammad, be praised for bringing you through your trials. God is great; God is good; and his caliph is back among his faithful. The true jihad lives!"

Abu Bakr al-Baghdadi nodded to the now standing men and acknowledged their obeisance with genuine humility.

"Be seated, Brothers in the jihad. Let us plan. Indeed, the jihad lives; and we will make ourselves known so that no one in the accursed world of the unbelievers will ever again doubt it."

The men arranged themselves as the caliph always wanted them to do. He looked at each man in a way that made each one of them feel specially chosen of God and his caliph on earth. He looked into their souls with his searing brown eyes for a moment before speaking.

"Let us break bread together before God and speak of His work. Give me the current report on manpower, funding, *esprit de corps*, and faithfulness among the Brothers."

Each of them gave a succinct and highly positive report.

"Brothers, you have carried on the work of Allah extremely well during the time when I was recovering and changing my appearance. I have work to do that requires that I meet people who would otherwise recognize me and would betray the cause. I now give you your assignments: Achmed, the funding coffers showing four billion Crusader dollars is excellent. Double it in two years. Muhammad, the ready reserve of manpower of two million fighters waiting in reserve is likewise a great asset. Secure the communication links; continue to proselytize as if there were no tomorrow; we must act as if that were God's truth revealed to us. Double the ranks over two years and increase the readiness by continual, but secret, drills. Be relentless. Dragan, you will work in Asia; I will take Europe; and Mahrouz, you take America and get funding at a fever pitch to assist Brother Achmed. Finally, Zag, begin a blitz of news and propaganda. Let all the world know that we are back, and that we will be seen very soon.

"A note of caution: there are traitors to our cause—wolves in sheeps' clothing—the so-called pro-IS 'dissident' outlet named *Mu'assasat al-*

Turath al-'Ilmi, seeks to destroy our Islamic State and each of us true believers. May God bring ruin upon them. I hereby issue a fatwa against them: kill them on sight; take no prisoners. Remember, we do God's work. We will see victory in His good time. I hail the jihadi victory which has restored the caliphate after centuries. God gave your mujahideen brothers victory after long years of jihad and patience. This is a duty on Muslims that has been lost for centuries. Our Muslims brothers feel theologically, metaphysically, and emotionally, humiliated because they can no longer humiliate the Jews, whom we all deem to be inferior—*dhimmis* (humbled)"

"Now be on your way. I will contact you for an update in three months' time. *Adhhab mae Allah!* [Go with God!]."

Note: that statement came from a man–mujahid Shaykh Abu Bakr al-Baghdadi al-Hussaini al-Qurashi–for whom the U.S. Department of State has offered a reward of up to $25 million for information leading to capture or his death.

–THE END–

"Islamic State (ISIS) leader Abu Bakr al-Baghdadi was reported by Syrian media to have been killed on June 10 in a U.S.-lead coalition artillery strike. Syrian state television said the terror group's leader–the world's most wanted terrorist–was killed in an artillery strike on the group's headquarters in Raqqa
–*WorldTribune Staff*, June 11, 2017

"He was known for a series of high-profile speeches, including one from the central mosque in Mosul during the height of the Islamic State group's reign. The subsequent conflict was marked by multiple reports of his death, including a Russian assertion with 'high probability' that its airstrikes killed Baghdadi outside Raqqa…The elusive leader remains a dangerous symbol of an increasingly global extremist network."
–Paul D. Shinkman, Senior National Security Writer, *After ISIS' Defeat: Where is Abu Bakr al-Baghdadi? U.S. News and World Report*, March 25, 2019.

"The war of Islam and its followers against the crusaders and their followers is a long one," Baghdadi told a group of followers sitting with him on the floor of a bare, whitewashed room. An AK-47 rifle was perched by his side. "Our battle today is a war of attrition to harm the enemy, and they should know that jihad will continue until doomsday."
–Robin Wright, *Baghdadi Is Back—and Vows That ISIS Will Be, Too. The New Yorker*, April 29, 2019.

φ φ φ φ

"Whenever the Crusaders think they have spread their influence and usurped an abode of the Muslims, the conquerors appear in another region, in a war the builders of the Caliphate and its leadership have desired-after God granted success to them-should be characterized by challenging the enemy and vying with him in every place and inch of the earth, and bleeding his powers and capabilities. And this is what requires the sons of the Caliphate to work persistently and do all they can."
–Islamic State spokesman Abu al-Hassan al-Muhajir, with reference to *Qur'an* 9:29, 2014

Islamic State officials named Abu Ibrahim al-Hashimi
al-Qurayshi as al-Baghdadi's successor.

APPENDICES

APPENDIX I

AUTHOR'S COMMENTARY ON TERRORISM AND TERRORISTS

109 definitions of terrorism have been put forth by credible academic institutions, law enforcement agencies, and careful individual researchers, with no consensus among them. For working purposes, we will consider only two:

Definition from U.S. Code Section 2656 (short abstraction): Terrorism is premeditated, politically motivated, violence, against noncombatant targets by subnational groups or clandestine agents, usually intended to influence an audience.

Definition from the FBI: Terrorism is the unlawful use of force or violence against persons or property to intimidate or coerce a government, the civilian population, or any segment thereof, in the furtherance of political or social objectives.

Terrorism is largely a political concept—not just an act of violence, but about power and use of power to achieve political changes. It is the use of violence or threat of violence or coercive intimidation as a calculated means to destabilize. It is propaganda by deed.

The history of terrorism is as long as history itself. In this commentary, we will focus on relatively recent history and almost entirely on terrorism from radical Islamic jihadists. A fair history would be impossibly long and tedious, and scarcely exists. By the definitions above, terrorism can be attributed to such diverse organizations as the Zealots of Judea and the Zionists, the Shi'a Assassins, Sicarii, and the Hashhashin, the Indian Thuggies, the American revolutionaries, the French revolutionaries under Robespierre, the Jacobins, the Israeli Irgun and the Lehi, Russian Narodnaya Volya and the Bolsheviks, Anarchists, IRA [Irish Republican Army], Ku Klux Klan, the Black Hand, Nazis and Fascists, the Mau Mau, Basque ETA, FARC of Colombia, Tamil Tigers of Sri Lanka, the American Weathermen, German Baader-Meinhof Group, Italian Red Brigades, the Greek Revolutionary Struggle, and the Peruvian Shining Path, to name only a few of the thousands of terrorist organizations.

There are multiple different reasons given for using terrorism; but in this commentary, we will only consider those applicable to the Islamic jihadist terrorists, another narrow focus. There are several underlying and even seemingly incompatible explanations given by Islamic terrorists for their actions that most of humanity considers to be heinous:

1. Allah is the One God; Islam is the only true religion (voiced by both Sunnis and Shi'ites), and there is a duty to defend Islam against invaders, crusaders, occupiers, and corrupters. Deadly measures may well be required.

2. True Islam has been usurped by organizations other than the one committing the terrorism, and the religion must be cleansed and revivified by the purists. This is especially true as professed by the Wahhabists, and Salafists, who demand that Islam return to The Prophet's seventh century original form.

3. To aid in the global spread of Islam.

4. The enemies of Islam must be defeated and eradicated—including Jews, Christians, Hindus, and any other nonIslamic religions extant today. This reason is about hatred—against the United States and its allies for supporting the near enemies–the corrupt, reprobate, and authoritarian antiIslamic regimes in the Middle East.

5. Altruism: Islamist terrorist grievances can be considered as perceptions of relevant threats and the terrorist acts with altruism to defend against an intergroup (or even intragroup) threat.

6. A means of directing attention to the cause—usually as directed outside the home country borders or against the perceived fomenters of harm against the religion, its practitioners, or the country

giving assistance to the terrorist organization. Terrorism is psychological, and it is theater.

7. The terrorist as a freedom fighter, a defender of truth and right and above all, Allah and Islam, against existential enemies. To fight against those who would enslave Muslims by forcing them to deny or betray their religion for any reason.

8. The more crass and venal reason: for personal gain through crime and extortion.

This author finds the reason behind the acts of terrorism to be far secondary to the acts themselves. It is the acts that must be countered and prevented. Many argue that violence is not germane in the big picture, but rather that its underlying causes–misery, privation, bad government, frustration, etc. that produce the violent acts are what is important: the nature of the act, not the perpetrator. There are root causes which may be improved which cause the perceptions of victimhood, and therefore the desire for terrorism to diminish significantly. They will be addressed separately below.

For the sake of clarity, let us dispense with the commonly held misconception that terrorists–especially suicide bombers–are lunatics. After all, you would have to be crazy to want to commit suicide and mass homicide to further some strange grandiose idea, no? Adam Langford, University of Alabama professor, makes the informed observation (summarized here): After 9/11, there was a rush to explain the psychology of suicide terrorists. They were described as crazy, lunatics, inherently bad people. This ignored the influence of social and situational factors. Langford doubts that. His opinion is that mental illness, suicidal motives, and personal crises, are the qualities of the terrorists who do *not* commit suicidal/homicidal acts, in general.

Reasonable and objective commentators described the terrorists as being "influenced by religious fundamentalism with a fanatic ideology and a commitment to martyrdom... or that they had come into being because of "institutional manipulation, group indoctrination, collective loyalty and commitment, willingness for self-sacrifice, murderous intent, shared altruism, collective group identity, charismatic leadership, deindividuation, and affection for their in-group and enmity towards others in the out-group—essentially normal psychology, stable with no personal socially dysfunctional attributes. Like other dedicated persons such as heroic soldiers."

His conclusion is that suicide bombers share more general personality and psychological traits with people from the general population who commit suicide and murder-suicide than those who commit suicide for a collective cause.

The role of religion—of Islam, or of a corrupted form of Islam, if you prefer—cannot be denied. There is an overwhelming preponderance of young Arab Muslim males among the terrorists, and a zero representation among blue-haired old Christian ladies from Poughkeepsie. The role of the religion can be attributed to any or all the above listed explanations. The number of Muslims in the world is estimated by a number of sources to be about 1.8 billion—just under 25% of the population of the world. They are the majority population in forty-nine countries.

There is very considerable disagreement about what percent of the Muslim population is either actively involved in terrorism or is significantly supportive (funding, recruiting, arranging, hiding, etc.). The range for true extremists is about 0.01%–100,000—as calculated by apologists because they discount the true religiosity of the extremists or their religious literacy. They are deemed to participate for political, other ideological, or for purely local reasons such as to install Sharia law in a region by force, which is not a religious reason, the apologists assert.

Other estimates range from 3.0% to as high as 33%, taking into consideration the helpers as well as the actual trigger pullers and beheaders. Those numbers would give a range of 3 million to 330 million—a number equal to the population of the United States. The ability of the Islamic State to recruit and to deliver reinforcements and its ability to put troops into battles over and over again suggest that the range is not as low as 0.01% even if it is not as high as even 3.0%. Whatever the truth is, there are a considerable number of extremists, insurgents, and enablers, prowling the earth and committing heinous crimes.

There is no dispute over the sad fact that the vast majority of victims of the extremist jihadi murderers are their own co-religionists, their fellow Muslims. It is also true that violence attends every country that borders on a majority Muslim nation, whatever the exact motivation may be on the part of the extremists. It is the opinion of this author that women who live in areas controlled by terrorist groups or who are associated by birth or marriage are subjected to what most westerners would consider a form of terrorism: Radio Sharia [Taliban outlet]—lists rules against women such as wearing clothing that rustled, laughing in public, or talking too loudly. Male tailors could not measure women. Women are forced to enter the back door of buses and to sit in the rear. Women are not allowed to go out on streets during times of prayer. It is unsafe for them to do so anyway because Kalashnikov wielding *Amr bil-Maroof* [Taliban guards of virtue and suppression of vice] are on the prowl and have no supervision.

Drawing, such as a sketch of a design for a dress, is illegal. Women are beaten, even starving beggars. Some are beaten for being outside without a *mahram* [male escort, original meaning "forbidden" as in not legal and proper for them to have intercourse with]. Three laws currently govern women: women will stay at home; are not permitted to work; and must wear chadri in public. Women can only go out in public for important reasons—as determined by men or the *Amr bil-Maroof*-and must be accompanied by a male family member.

Under the Taliban and Islamic state, women and girls are banned from attending schools; girls' schools were physically closed down or turned into schools for males with all-male faculties. Overnight, women vanished from the streets of Kabul and Mosul, and forced to lead useless, boring, and frustrating, lives cooped up in their homes. This is especially terrible for families headed by widows—30,000 families. Around the world, 160 million female babies were aborted throughout Asia. Potential consequences of a world of men only are daunting. In Kabul, there is a thriving industry of ultrasound machines and secret late abortions of females.

According to the World Health Organization, "It is estimated that more than 200 million girls and women alive today have undergone female genital mutilation in the countries where the practice is concentrated. Furthermore, there are an estimated 3 million girls at risk of undergoing female genital mutilation every year. The majority of girls are cut before they turn 15-years-of-age."

The *Qur'an* is quoted for both the peaceful and for the murderous violent extremists. The *Qur'an* contains 109 verses [*ayahs*] that speak of war with nonbelievers, usually on the basis of their status as non-Muslims. Some are graphic and truly violent, with commands to chop off heads and fingers and kill infidels like Jews wherever they may be hiding.

Muslims who do not join the fight are called 'hypocrites' and warned that Allah will send them to Hell if they do not join the slaughter. Two examples will suffice: *Qur'an* 2:216, "Fighting is prescribed for you, and ye dislike it. But it is possible that ye dislike a thing which is good for you, and that ye love a thing which is bad for you. But Allah knoweth, and ye know not.," and *Qur'an* 5:33, "The punishment of those who wage war against Allah and His messenger and strive to make mischief in the land is only this, that they should be murdered or crucified or their hands and their feet should be cut off on opposite sides or they should be imprisoned; this shall be as a disgrace for them in this world, and in the hereafter, they shall have a grievous chastisement."

It is true that the Bible–especially the Old Testament–contains violent verses. There is a fundamental difference in the violence recommended in the two religious books. The violence in the *Qur'an* is not limited to a time or a place usually; so, it can be interpreted by extremists to extend to any time—even now. Most OT verses are local, limited, and temporary.

Examples of peaceful *Qur'anic* verses are present, but in a lesser number than the violent ones. Here are two examples: *Qur'an* 18:29, "And say, 'The truth is from your Lord, so whoever wills, let him believe; and whoever wills, let him disbelieve." And *Qur'an* 21:107, "Oh, Prophet, we have sent you as a mercy to all creatures." It is as possible to gerrymander the *Qur'an* as it is the Bible, but the choice of violence from the Holy Book of Islam has very serious consequences when used as an excuse. The superficial reader or listener may be fed a pablum of peace sura, but a deeper look indicates either the violence, or the hypocrisy, or both.

Religion, per se, is not as significant a driving force of terrorism as is usually believed. It is, however, the cause of terrorism with more indiscriminate violence—attacks on people whose views differ from those of the fanatical religious organization. Countering violence does not require an attack on the religion of the terrorists. Instead, it is necessary to counter the club networking qualities of the organization, to provide better services and security, and to provide better opportunities outside the organization, even outside its benign service structure. The principle problem over which religious terrorism leaders obsess is not theology but the issue of defection.

In fact, there are mundane business factors that play a role at least as great as fanaticism. Like any corporation, a terrorist organization needs to have corporate officers and employees. The leaders determine how business is to be conducted, and the employees do the bidding of the leaders. That requires communication, bookkeeping, security, accountability, and the imposition of consequences. Unlike a regular business corporation, terrorist organizations must carry on in secret to avoid being found out by law enforcement, government officials, and other state actors.

While communication is critical, the more communication, the less security exists for the terrorist organization. Security of communication and obedience on the part of the employees—the regular terrorists—requires accountability and even punishment to keep the terrorists in line. Each organization has a "corporate" mission statement to maintain. When a terrorist away from headquarters decides to go on his own, that poses problems. If the goal of the organization is eventual recognition by the populace and government as a legitimate group—even a certified political party—then the level of violence must not be more than the state or the populace will tolerate before lashing out with military violence.

An uncontrolled sadist or excessively violent member or clique undermines the leadership and its goals. Terrorist organizations cannot at the same time be reliable, resilient, secure, and under perfect control of their leadership. That is their dilemma and their Achilles heel.

The leadership must make important decisions that require a certain sensitivity. They hold the power of life and death over the regular terrorist, especially including the miscreant. The choices are counseling, a reprimand, termination of employment, physical punishment, and even execution. Execution would seem to be the simplest answer. However, if the other terrorists see execution as excessive, or to be applied capriciously, or unfairly, they may rebel, mutiny, or form a new organization which either becomes a competitor, or a violent enemy. To allow misdeeds to go unpunished, undermines the authority of the leadership. These conundrums constitute the Terrorists' Dilemma. Terrorists–including the leaders–are people like other people in the world. They are venal, self-important, cruel, overbearing, disobedient, unforgiving, and often unreliable. One dilemma is intermarriage between and within groups which leads to loyalties that can expose partners to coercion when one is compromised. A terrorist organization is difficult to control from the inside, and even relatively minor fissures in the system may lead to failure.

A cursory look at the history of terrorism reveals that in the long run, virtually all terrorist organizations either burn out, fail, or transform into less virulent groups and take a place in the body politic, or simply fade away. There is a dilemma for the opposition groups who are determined to keep the terrorists from disrupting the daily ebb and flow of commerce and enjoyment of life on the part of the citizenry. The two main sources of disagreement within terrorist groups relate to resources and tactics and methods to mitigate exposure of the group to security forces. Tighter control leads to compromise of security—a conundrum.

Should government forces crack-down in such a fashion as to try and eliminate by killing, incarcerating, or driving out, members of the terrorist group? Or should law enforcement and the government allow a certain leniency so as to allow the terrorists a measure of self-expression and protest, but within definite bounds. There have been some instances where direct contracts have been approved and abided by both parties. Other terrorist organizations evolve into political parties on their own and cease the violence. More often, the terrorists have to make major concessions to achieve enough trust and harmony to rejoin society. Nonviolence is not the rule, however; and that is a dilemma for both parties.

Strategies based on a determination to kill or imprison as many high-level leaders of terrorist groups have not gone well. The efforts have ended in inability of mid-level leaders to control operatives who killed more people and more capriciously. That kind of strategic thinking empowers more militant factions and the more moderate groups are less able to negotiate. Putting maximal pressure on terrorist factions has proved not to be the optimal solution.

Because terrorist groups cannot afford to reduce communications, investments by anti-terrorist governments towards intercepting terrorist communications can pay great dividends at low cost, especially in human loss terms. Governmental investment in infrastructure, maintenance, and services has been money well spent whenever it has been tried. Note that no small terrorist group has ever succeeded in taking over a functioning state. The "club model" is seen among religious radicals with larger families. They send their children to religious schools that give poor secular educations but strong religious binding. It is imperative that the population ripe for radicalization be taught market principles and democratic ideas. Opportunity to encounter and experience such salutary concepts tends to cause people to leave the terrorist groups, to stress different thinking and ways of behaving, and to disrupt the mutual aid society type of life in a closed and tight society.

It is likely that an incremental process will succeed better than efforts at cataclysmic eradication. A place to start can be negotiation with terrorists to have both sides to agree that some weapons and tactics are simply unacceptable and beyond the bounds of even the terrorist policies if the terrorist group is to gain its goals eventually. Both sides need to agree on facts such as that there is a fundamental qualitative difference between state armed defense and terrorist launched murder and that the horrors of war have produced rules and norms to prohibit certain types of weapons and policies from being employed: dum-dum bullets, chemical gas, biological agents, and torture.

Certain noncombatants are to be considered immune from attack: civilians and aid workers as hostages or as targets. Belligerents agree to decent treatment of captured, to the prohibition of reprisals against civilians or POWs, to recognize neutral territory and rights of citizens of neutral countries and to the inviolability of diplomats and accredited representatives.

Terrorist groups generally exist to correct perceived problems and inequities such as poverty, bad roads, polluted water, or disputes. Sometimes, they come into being to defend against invaders or true enemies of their customs, traditions, or religion. The Islamic State proved to be different: it existed to command unswerving obedience to a particular Islamic ideology, to establish Sharia law as an absolute, and to revert society back fifteen hundred years to the perceived golden age when The Prophet and his immediate friends and followers reigned with Allah giving day to day direction for all thoughts and actions. Improvement of physical issues in a community has never been any kind of priority for the Islamic State, and that is why they had no chance to survive as a caliphate.

The vast majority of Muslims–even of fundamentalists–do not want to see the imposition of Sharia law as the law of the land in their countries. They do not vote in parties that espouse the idea, nor do they welcome outsiders–like the Islamic State terrorists–into their midst even if they share mutual hatreds of the West. Why not? Is Sharia law so different from jurisprudence as it is practiced in the West?

The answer is yes, and the differences are such that it is highly unlikely that any Muslim community in the world will willingly accept Sharia over Western common law without being forced to do so. Terrorists try and fail over and over again, despite committing all manner of terroristic acts, murders, and atrocities, to enforce their will on the citizens.

The nature of Sharia law is diametrically opposite to, and openly in opposition to, the Western concept of how a legal system should proceed. Sharia has the idea that God controls righteous lawyers and judges, and they will judge righteously under His control. To understand terrorists, Muslims in general, and the legal system, one must realize that the idea of God being in control absolutely permeates the thinking of Muslims. *Inshallah*—"as God wills" dominates the rather fatalistic way of perceiving the world and all human action and interaction. Other religious sects–however fundamentalist–seldom adopt such an all-pervading hands-on interaction of man and God. The imam, mullah, or ayatollah, has great latitude in determining just what it is that God has in mind under the practicalities of Sharia.

This author is a strong advocate of tolerance of differing opinions and customs so long as those opinions are not threatening to people whose beliefs differ. The great majority of Muslims around the world deserve the protections afforded by liberal democracy and fair judicial systems. However, not every belief and practice is acceptable; and Sharia law is one of those, because of its illiberal core nature. Sharia represents and functions as an antithesis to democracy, equal rights under the law; and its proponents among the terrorists would deny such rights to all who do not agree with their extreme point-of-view. Sharia is one camel's nose that should never be allowed to push under the tent flap.

In a Sharia court, no defense attorney is permitted; the defendant is not afforded the opportunity to speak or to mount a defense, and contrarian evidence is not permitted, because God and the judge know all; and judgment will come from the religion, not the civil authority and its laws. No non-Islamic state can afford to allow even a determined fraction of its population to practice such law and to prevent even select and acquiescing citizens from having access to governmental judicial systems. To allow such a fraction to succeed is to invite the camel all the way into the society which owns the tent and would be foolhardy in the extreme. The large majority of Muslims–even in the Middle East–are in agreement with that opinion and are at the present time fighting those who would impose Sharia on them.

The crises in the Middle East as they relate to the United States are not over; in fact, we may be about to see a new beginning. Militant Islam came to believe that under Allah it was invincible and would eventually prevail over all the rest of the world. A terrible truth is that an entire generation of young militants swelled the ranks of the jihadists flushed with the belief that the future was theirs and that they could do whatever they wanted to do; and it would be as God willed. The epilogue cannot yet be written, because there is a chapter or chapters that will need to be composed yet, unfortunately.

603 U.S. troops have been killed by Iran-backed militias during Operation Iraqi Freedom—one out of every six combat fatalities are attributable to Iran and its proxies. Most of those casualties were the result of explosively formed penetrators [EFPs], IEDS, improvised rocket-assisted munitions [IRAMs], rockets, rocket-propelled grenades [RPGs], mortars, sniper and small arms attacks.

Recently, Iran shot down an unmanned U.S. drone over international waters; on July 17, 2009, Iran ambushed and seized an oil tanker in the Straits of Hormuz; and on July 18, 2019, the amphibious warship, the *USS Boxer* shot down an unmanned Iranian drone which was menacing the U.S. ship of the line. The U.S. president has sent additional troops to Saudi Arabia. Hezbollah continues to contribute funding, military materiel, and troops, to shore up al-Assad's Syrian Army. Fighting against IS and other jihadists continues in the Idlib area of Syria. The world is collectively holding its breath to see what Iran will do next, and how the American president will respond. American military might is poised in the Straits of Hormuz of the west coast of Iran in readiness.

Within the select world of Muslim fundamentalists who contend with better educated and generally peaceable Muslims, the contention will persist. There exists to the present day a huge pool of suicide terrorists, available truck bombs, explosive belts, and other deadly weapons hidden in stockpiles ready for use when required. There is a scattered but easily available coordinated network of operatives which recruits, raises funds, motivates armies, directs, covers tracks, takes credit, publicizes, and even compensates families. IS is not gone, just hiding in the shadows.

That is a Muslim problem, not a Western one, until or unless violence passes over borders into nonMuslim areas. The United States has meddled in such affairs uninvited and for purposes of regime change for well over a century, and it is time posthumous that We the People call a halt to such poorly thought out military/diplomatic misadventures. The battles still rage in Syria. Bashar al-Assad still rules Syria and has won the Civil War. Russia and Iran will remain involved whether or not the U.S. ups the ante and runs the risk of igniting World War III.

We all need to understand the full situation in Syria and in the Middle East. The running conflicts between the Sunni and the Shi'ite is a civil war and a chasm that has been going on for more than 1,400 years. Furthermore, the CIA has a dark and dirty history of wanting to overthrow regimes but none is more notorious then its constant plans to want to overthrow the Syrian regime. It isn't just the current Assad government; the CIA has been trying to overthrow various Syrian presidents throughout history from as far back as March of 1949, when Syria was under the rule of President Shukri al-Kuwatli. [*BuzzFeed*, 2017]. According to a report in *Businessinsider.com*, Dec. 15, 2017, *A new report sheds light on the origins of the weapons ISIS militants use in Iraq and Syria.* "An investigation revealed that the Central Intelligence Agency may have purchased anti-tank missiles, which eventually fell into the hands of ISIS militants."

"A year into the Syrian rebellion, the US and its allies weren't only supporting and arming an opposition they knew to be dominated by extreme sectarian groups; they were prepared to countenance the creation of some sort of "Islamic state"–despite the "grave danger" to Iraq's unity–as a Sunni buffer to weaken Syria."

–a recently declassified secret US intelligence report, written in August 2012

> "Isis [sic] is a direct outgrowth of al-Qaeda in Iraq that grew out of our invasion. Which is an example of unintended consequences. Which is why we should generally aim before we shoot."
>
> –President Obama.

The CIA, together with Saudi Arabia, elected to move billions of dollars into arming the mujahideen fighters in Afghanistan to thwart the

Soviet Union. That led to the creation of the terror group al-Qaeda. In turn, that led to the 9/11 terror strikes, the invasion of Afghanistan and Iraq by the U.S., and the eventual creation and arming of the Taliban and ISIS.

It is this author's opinion that there will always be a strong-man tyrant looming in the Middle East, and the liberal democrats of the Middle East should deal with the problem. It is silly to the point of madness to keep repeating the same pattern: tyrant takes over a country and refuses to bend to U.S. demands; U.S. secretly and then overtly creates a war to obtain regime change; U.S. succeeds in ousting the criminal dictatorship; and the circle closes with a new tyrant filling the power vacuum. The U.S. repeats the pattern ad infinitum. Madness.

Has the present author exaggerated the intolerance and determination of the fundamentalist, jihadist, Islamist terrorists? Consider this formal statement:

- **The fundamentalists value argumentative wisdom only for extracting truth out of the holy Book and traditions and only in limited instances;**
- **They are followers of religious stipulations and traditions;**
- **They are loyal to sharia law and jurisprudence;**
- **They consider the above instances as being unchangeable and eternal;**
- **They aim to establish a society where sharia law and jurisprudence are enforced in their most complete forms;**
- **Since non-religious governments are an obstacle to realization of the above goals, they try to overthrow such governments;**
- **They endeavor to establish governments based on sharia law;**
- **They do not believe in religious and political plurality;**
- **They consider religion as having answers to all human needs both for this world and the Hereafter.**
- **No other source, but Salafi and Wahhabi jurists, are qualified to issue fatwas and pass laws to run social**

affairs. Also, making laws on the basis of human wisdom is rejected;

- Freedom of conviction cannot be accepted because it would lead to blasphemy;
- Rulers derive their legitimacy from God and leaders of different societies should be authorized by religion;
- Freedom of expression is not acceptable because it may lead to insult against God and divine rules;
- Religion is not separate from politics and government;
- Political parties are not supported by Islam because they pave the way for activities of non-religious elements.
- It is not allowed (by Muhammad) for a Believing man to be killed except for three offences: fornication after chastity, apostasy from Islam, or killing a Believing life without a life.
- The most deserving of people in wealth are the mujahideen in the path of God so that sufficiency may be realized even if infants, children and the hungry die, because preserving the religion is of greater priority than preserving life.

–Statement of the Armed Islamic Group

"Four things greater than all things are: Women and Horses and Power and War. We spake of them all, but the last the most.

–Rudyard Kipling, *The Ballad of the King's Jest, The Collected Works of Rudyard Kipling: Departmental Ditties and Barrack-Room Ballads,* vol. 25, p. 234, 1941

APPENDIX II

CAST OF IMPORTANT CHARACTERS, BY REGION AND ERA

From PROLOGUE I, BANANA WARS 1:
North Americans

1903 Enlisted men—jarheads, gyrenes–of the United States Marine Corps, GCE of the II Marine Expeditionary Force, 8th Regiment, 2nd battalion, eighth marines, Delta Battery, 3rd Platoon, 6th rifle squad–Sergeant Mark E. Snyder, Private First Class Rodney Wayne Carter, Pvt. Glen Gabler, Lance Corporal Nephi Muhlestein, and attached medic Corporal Danny NMN Broadhead

Sgt. Rickie Sanchez, marine fighter and translator; Corporal Emil John Franklin, machine gunner who was awarded the Congressional Medal of Honor; Private Harry Cohen, a Jewish boy from Crown Heights, Brooklyn, who learned how to make the sign of the cross to give last rites to a dying comrade

NCOs–Master Gunnery Sergeant Orville Cramer from Berryville, Arkansas; Sergeant Major Jethro Amos Rider from Tuscaloosa, Alabama; navy MCPO [Master Chief Petty Officer] Joe X. Tyler from Norfolk, Virginia; and CMDCM [Command Master Chief Petty Officer] Neal Bradley Dastrup from San Francisco, California

Officers—Bullard Henry Lewis, Major-General USMC; Joseph Newton Hemphill, Captain, USN; George "Bully" Breckinridge, Colonel, USMC; Hiram Smith, Lieutenant, USMC; Robert Jacobsen, Captain, USMC/MC

Sympathizers–Alby Prentiss, out of work railroad construction man; Don Hipolito Antonio Ricardo Guitáin-Doloraso, governor of Panama for the nation of Colombia

Enemies–Guillermo Rodriguez, *Capitaine* Colombian Army, commander of Colon garrison

ψψψψψψ

From PROLOGUE 1, BANANA WARS II:
North Americans
1915 Enlisted men–Harry Chandler, Sergeant USMC, HQ Third Regiment aide de camp to Gen. Price; Henryk Zimbrowski, Sergeant, USMC, 3rd of the 3rd

Officers–Stephen Morgan Price, Brigadier General USMC, commanding officer of the 3rd of the 3rd; Oscar W. Peterson, Colonel, USMC and commander of the attack force against the entrenched *cacos* in Fort Rivière Haiti

Major Smedley Darlington Butler, First Sergeant Ross Iams, and Private Samuel Gross, were awarded Medals of Honor for actions taken during this engagement.

ψψψψψψ

From PROLOGUE I, BANANA WARS III:
North Americans
1954 Enlisted men—Ed Campbell, Jackie Hendricks, Henry Zslowskiwiez, and Tom Dastrup, CIA enlistees for Operation PBSUCCESS

Officers–General Carlos Castillo Armas for CIA Operation PBSUCCESS; Goeffery Lander Ryan, Lieutenant USMC

Nonmilitary movers and shakers–Andrew W. Preston, President of the United Fruit Company; Bradley Palmer—the corporate attorney and director—the face and controller of United Fruit

ψψψψψψ

From PROLOGUE I, MIDDLE EAST I

North Americans

1949 Enlisted men and nonmilitary—Danny Wiseman, detective third grade in the LVMPD; Abu Bakr ibn Haq, Sergeant-Major, Syrian Arab Army Special Forces

Officers—Miles Weston Howard II, COS-Syria for the CIA; Marcus Denali, CEO Arabian-American Oil Company [ARAMCO];

Syrians–Shukri al-Quwatly, President of Syria; Mohamed Ibriham al-Sham, Major General, Syrian Arab Army; and Colonel Abdullah Faid ibn Nagib, Colonel of the Syrian Arab Army Special Forces; Sami Hinnawi, Colonel Syrian Arab Army, and successor as president to al-Sham; Adib Shishakli, Colonel Syrian Arab Army, and successor to Hinnawi in Syria's third coup in nine months.

ψψψψψψ

From PROLOGUE II, Viet Nam I: The 1st Indochinese War [the French War; Franco-Vietminh War, the Anti-French Resistance War]

Americans

1945-1954 CIA cadres—Glen Gabler, Neal Dastrup,

Officers—Parker Leary Granston, Lieutenant Colonel, USAF, and COS-VN for the CIA.

Vietnamese–Ho Chi Minh, overall leader of the Viet Minh and later president of the DRVN [Democratic Republic of Viet Nam–North Viet Nam]; Ngo Dinh Diem, President of the RVN [Republic of Viet Nam–South Viet Nam]; Vo Nguyen Giáp, Commanding General Viet Minh, and later of the PAVN/NVA [People's Army of Viet Nam/NorthVietnam Army]

French– Henri Navarre, *Général de corps d'armée* [France]; Charles Piroth, *Général d'armée*, artillery commander at Dien Bien Phu; Generals Jean Gilles and Jean Dechaux–the ground and air commanders at Dien Bien Phu; Christian de Castries, Colonel and overall commander at Dien Bien Phu

ψψψψψψ

From PROLOGUE II, Viet Nam II: Second Indochina War, The American War; CIA Phoenix Program

Americans

1965 CIA cadres—Barbara Robbins; Manolo Jesús Antonio Visayas, Lieutenant Commander, USN; Y'Yool, Montagnard PRUC; Le Duc Bach, former Kit Carson and current PRUC; Nguyen Van Xuan, Rallier and current PRUC; Binh, Chi, Duc, Tuan, Vien, Vu Caden, PRUCs; Nguyen Dai Xuan, CIA operative; Dao Xander, PRUC.

Officers—David Broadhead, COS-VN and PRUC/O; Karl Isaacson, PRUC/O

Vietnamese—Nguyen Giang, Viet Cong contact; Nguyen Van Bac, Region VCI Commander; Pham Pierre Do, half French-half Vietnamese planter;

From PROLOGUE III, War in Afghanistan

Americans

1981 Cadres and minor officers— Bill Edward Campbell known as "Ball"; Jonathon C. (NMN); Hendricks was "Crank"; Harvey Edward James O'Dwyer, was "Three," and Robert Emmanuel McDonald, was "Bob"' Umar Muhammad bin Khost, and Ibrahim

Senior Officers–U.S. Congressman Charlie Wilson, Democrat, of the 2nd District of Texas and his man in Afghanistan and Pakistan, GS-12 Gust Lascaris Avrakotos; Mike Vickers, COS-A and second-in-command to Charlie Wilson

Pakistanis–Awan al Malik, Colonel Pakistan Army and head of the ISI [The Inter Services Intelligence Agency of Pakistan]; Tim Osman, the "Tactician" [UBL-Usama bin Laden]; General Muhammad Zia-ul-Haq, General of the Pakistan Army and eventual president of Pakistan, and defense minister Abu Ghazala, General of the Pakistan Army; Ahmad Ahmad Chagharzai, Colonel Pakistan Army in charge of the Pakistan special forces

Afghans–Jalaluddin Haqqani and Yunis Khalis, Afghan Generals of the Soviet supported DRA Army; Aymenn Hafs al'Aishat Shindand City Militia Commander, Ismail Khan-mujahideen general

Soviets– Soviet commander of the DRA Shindand Airforce base, Ivan Abramovich Yekenovoral, General Lieutenant of the Army of the U.S.S.R. (Red Army); Yvgeni Nikoliavich Sammarand, Soviet Airforce Colonel and commandant of the Shindand Airforce Base and its security forces

ψψψψψψ

From BOOK III, THE RISE AND FALL OF THE FIFTEENTH CALIPHATE: The CIA Giveth, and the CIA taketh away…

Americans

1993 Lower ranks— Al Lee, CIA Officer; Elizabeth Tandy–the embassy's chief of intelligence analysis, who was affectionately referred to as Lizzie, and as "the librarian"; Agir Jaf, Sergeant-major of the Sorani Kurdish Peshmergas, who operated under Behremend Rozaki; Malcolm Fortner and Devlin O'Malley, Avery Challenger's two assistants—CIA contract officers; Rahim Jamaluddin, CIA spy embedded in Islamic State; SGM Rudi Tomlinson, and SSgt. Dewayne Michaelson, Army Special Forces; Elias Omar al-Aleppo, a secret member of Jabhat al-Nusra, and a paid CIA informer in Syria; Sergeant Major Erwin Phelps, Sergeant Green Beret Special Forces; Chief Master Sergeant Colon Perez-Rodriguez, Air Force special operations commando from the 1st Special Operations Wing; Carl Johnson, David Wade, Richard Erickson, and Tom Wright, CIA contract agents;

Senior officers—Avery Daryl Challenger CIA agent, COS-I; Dwight R. Cunningham, Jr., who preceded Avery as COS-I; Behremend Rozaki, Colonel of the Kurdish Peshmerga and a CIA contract agent; Howard Cummings, Army Special Forces Captain; Muhammad Zia-ul-HaqJ General of the Pakistan and president; Abu Ghazala, defense minister of Pakistan; Ahmad Ahmad Chagharzai, colonel in charge of the Pakistan special forces; Bruce Antonia, Lieutenant Colonel, commander of Task Force Regular; Dal Järvinen, Captain, Finnish Army, military attaché in Erbil, Kurdistan;

Iraqis—Yazidi family: Khatoon, daughter who was kidnapped by the Islamic State; father, Elias, who abandoned the family; Mother, Safaa; Abdul, Khatoon's step-father; grandparents—Grandfather and patriarch of the family, Naif Jasso Yazidi, and Grandmother Lydia; Mahbooba, Masuda, and Ruhasva, fugitive slave girls;

Islamic State–Ibrahim Awwad Ibrahim Ali Muhammad al-Badri al-Samarrai, aka Abu Bakr alBaghdadi, Caliph of the Islamic State–many of the jihadists in AQI call him either "the invisible sheikh" and "*Al-Shabah*" [the phantom or ghost], aka Daniel Pathmarajah; Ayman al-Zawahiri, an ophthalmologist who helped found the Egyptian militant group *Islamic Jihad* who would live to become AQ's chief ideologue; Abu Mus'ab al-Zarqawi, a Jordanian hothead; Jihadi John later identified as

Mohammed Emwazi, who was employed as the chief killer of foreign hostages; Sulaiman Abdullah al-Anbar, headman of the al-Sharayida clan and recently appointed military leader of the *Saray al-Jihad* Group in al-Anbar Governate; Kahled Umr al-Sham and Ishmael, IS slave owners.

APPENDIX III

GLOSSARY OF TERMS [NOTE— FOREIGN WORDS ARE ITALICIZED AND A NOTATION OF THE LANGUAGE OF THE WORD IS INCLUDED]

- Abbasaids: Dynasty of Muslim caliphs whose seat was in Baghdad. Governed most of the Islamic world from the 8th to the 11th century when it was conquered by the Seljuqs.
- Afghan: An Afghan tribal person or citizen of Afghanistan. Afghani is the name of the colorful blue, rose, and green colored currency of Afghanistan.
- *Akhi:* Arabic for brother
- Alawites: Members of the Alawite offshoot of the *Shi'a*. Founded in the 9th century. Currently live in Syrian coastal mountains.
- *Alhamdulillah:* Arabic for "thanks be to God" or "praise God."
- *Amir al-Mu'mineen* (Commander of the Believers'): Title taken by Abu Bakr al Baghdidi when he was appointed caliph. Equivalent of commander-in-chief, especially of the armed forces.
- AQ/al-Qaeda/*al-Qaeda al-Subah*: Arabic for a vanguard of the strong, refers to the safe house in Pakistan where the first recruits were housed and influenced each other. Bin Laden used the term "the list"

for Al Qaeda, meaning the list of recruits who stayed at the house and became the strongest of his supporters._

- Al-Qaeda in Iraq: *Tanzim Qaidat al-Jihad fi Bilad al-Rafidayn_*
- *Amir al-Mu'minin:* Arabic for leader of the faithful—originally only used for the four Rashidun Caliphate—but the title has come to be used for Abu Bakr al-Baghdadi by IS faithful.
- *Amr bil-Maroof wa Nahi al Munkir* [Taliban Ministry for the promotion of virtue and suppression of vice].
- Al Sham, or Bilad Al Sham: Arabic for Syria.
- Amu Darya: Central Asian river which forms part of Afghanistan's northern border.
- *Ansar:* Arabic for helpers. The early Muslims from Medina are called the Ansar. Also, locals in Iraq and Syria.
- *Aqeeda:* Arabic for creed.
- Aramaeans: Semitic-speaking people who ruled several kingdoms beginning in 1,200 BCE. Some remain in Syia as Aramaic-speaking Christians.
- Aramaic: Semitic people and languages of very ancient origin. Remain in Christian communities of Syria, Iraq, southeast Turkey, and northwest Iran.
- Armenians: Ancient ethnic group which held power in Turkey and Armenia from 321-428 BCE. Currently, most live in urban areas. Many reside in Aleppo.
- Ayatollah: Farsi. In *Shi'a* Islam, a high-ranking title given to clerics.
- *Ashab al-manhaj al-salim* ("having the sound *manhaj*"), in the sense of language is, "clear /clear path."
- Ayyubids: Sunni Muslim dynasty founded by Kurds which ruled Egypt and Syria during the 12th and 13th centuries CE.
- *Baas:* Arabic for bus.
- *Bab:* Arabic for door or gateway, including the gates of a walled city.
- *Bacha:* Child—a boy. Birth of a boy is a success. Birth of a girl is a failure. She is called *dokhtar* "other," a daughter.
- *Bachbek:* Arabic for little baby.
- *Badiya:* Arabic for desert.
- *Baksheesh*-Persian for bribe money, alms, or a tip
- *Bay'a:* Arabic for allegiance.
- *Bayanat:* Arabic for leaflets.

- *Bebejan*: Arabic for grandparents, or "my sweet dear" or *babakalan*, "dear older father."
- *Begherat:* Arabic for coward.
- *Bibi-jan*: Yazidi for grandma.
- *Bimaristan/Maristan*: Arabic for hospital or treatment center.
- *Birinj*: Arabic for rice.
- Black Tulips: Soviet planes that carried dead Soviet soldiers home from the Russian war in Afghanistan.
- *Bujul-hazi*: a popular game in Afghanistan resembling marbles which is played with sheep's knuckles.
- *Bukbari*: Arabic for a type of wood burning stove.
- Burn notice: An official statement issued by an intelligence agency to other agencies. It states that an asset or intelligence source [spy] is unreliable for one or several reasons–often fabrication–and must be officially disavowed. This is essentially a directive for the recipient to disregard or "burn" all information derived from that individual or group. The result for the spy is that his or her assets and ability to work are frozen.
- *Buzkashi:* (goat pulling, in Dari–Iraq) is extremely popular. Like polo. The two teams circle around the goat or calf's body at the start of the game. Opposing teams try to gain control of and drop the dead body of a goat or calf into the designated scoring area at the end of the game.
- *Buliis*: Arabic for police.
- *Cacos*: Haitian peasants who revolted against American occupation of their country.
- Caliphate: Properly, a Muslim state, sometimes applied to an organization. Requires a leading figure with a valid claim to be a successor to Muhammad, with a valid and accepted claim to be an authentic leader of the entire Muslim community, and which can claim actual land and property.
- Camp Bucca, Iraq: Infamous U.S./Iraq prison camp for insurgents and recalcitrant Ba'athists. Known as the "Academy" because it was a learning ground for future major insurgents including Abu Bakr al-Baghdidi.
- *Chaka*: Arabic for yogurt cheese.
- *Chai*: Arabic for tea. Tea without sugar is *chai bebi shakir.*

- CPSU-Communist Party of the Soviet Union
- Crusades/Crusaders: A series of brutal, bloody, and violent invasions of Muslim territories in the Middle East with the intent to ensure Western Christian domination of the region and protection of Christian pilgrims. Since the beginning—11th through 13th centuries— Muslims have regarded any invaders, Christian proselytizers, Christian run businesses, media, education, and thinking to be contaminated by crusader intent to extinguish Islam.
- *Dariha*: Arabic for mausoleum.
- *Da'esh*: Arabic for Islamic State. Used by other Muslims and insurgents as a somewhat derogatory term.
- Days of the week: (Arabic)—Dushama, Seshama, Chwaarshama, Penshama, Juma, Shama, Yekshama, corresponding to (English)— Monday, Tuesday, Wednesday, Thursday, Friday, Saturday, Sunday.
- *Dawla mubaraka*: Arabic for the blessed revolution. *Dawla* is the Islamic State.
- *Deir*: Arabic term for a Christian monastery or convent.
- *Dhimmis* (humbled) or humiliated. Used as Muslims humbled by being unable to carry out the *Qur'an's* curses on the Jews.
- *Diwan al-Buhuth wa al-Iftaa'*: *Islamic State* Investigation and Fatwa Issuing Department.
- *Dokhtar zai*: a mother who only brings daughters– mother is dismissed as a "mother who only brings daughters. Entirely childless woman is known by the insulting, "*sanda, or "khoshk*" or "dry" in Dari, and the woman is regarded as fundamentally flawed.
- *Dushman*: Arabic for enemy.
- Durand Line: An artificial boundary line imposed by the British in 1893 to separate Afghanistan from British India.
- DRA: Democratic Republic of Afghanistan. Proper name for the country when the communists controlled it and were defended by the army of the U.S.S.R.
- Druze: People of the Druze religious group, a breakoff sect from Ismailism, which developed in the 13th century CE. Significant minority in Syria, especially around Damascus, and the Israeli-occupied Golan Heights.
- *Diwan al-Amn:* Islamic State Security forces.

- *Eid/Eid al-Adha-*"Festival of Sacrifice" /*Eid al-Fitr*–two Islamic holidays celebrated worldwide each year.
- *Farhud*: Arabic for breakdown of law and order.
- Fatimids: another Ismaili Muslim dynasty which ruled Egypt for the 11th-13th centuries CE. Most Fatimids in Syria live in the southern portions of the country.
- *First name-jan:* Yazidi-to a child-first name, then jan=my beloved or dear.
- *Fatwa/Fatawah*. Arabic for judicial opinions.
- *Fedayeen*: Arabic for commandoes.
- *Fitna/Fitnah*: Arabic for division, temptation, trial, sedition, civil strife (as in creating divisiveness). *Fitan* is tribulations or civil wars.
- *Funduk*: Arabic for hotel.
- Free Syrian Army (FSA): opposition group to Bashar al-Assad's Syrian Army.
- *Gharib* (sing) *ghuraba (pl):* Arabic for stranger(s). Jihadist foreign fighters in Syria call themselves, "The Strangers." The term "Strange" is used because they adhere to the true Islam. Strangers are a saved group from foreign lands—"tribes"—who come in end times to fight for pure Islam. The mujahideen who come from all over the world to fight, are the best–the chosen people. They came to Syria to fight Bashar al-Assad, but also to fight against anyone who does not share their concept of Islam. The "strangeness" of the concept is that ninety percent of all attacks on Assad's *enemies* came from its Islamic State competitors.
- *Ghazni*: Commercial center city in east-central Afghanistan.
- *Ghurfa*: Arabic for room.
- *Gosht*: Arabic for meat.
- *Gringo*: Mexican/Latino derogative term for Yankees/American soldiers and marines. Origin of the term is uncertain: some Mexicans said it was because the U.S. soldiers wore green uniforms, and when the fights began, they ran away. The Mexicans derisively called after their backs: "Green go, green go," and it stuck. Another version of the origin is that the U.S. Army sang when they marched a favorite song *Green Grow the Lilacs;* the chorus was, "Green grow the lilacs; all sparkling with dew; I'm lonely my darling since parting with you. But by our next meeting, I hope to change the green lilacs to the red, white, and blue..." The Mexicans said they could hear the U.S.

armies from miles away yelling, "Gringo, gringo." Music historians worldwide disagree about the origins of this song. Many think that it is Irish in origin while many others think it was composed during the American-Mexican War in the 1840's. I like the latter explanation.

- *Hadith/Ahl al-sunnah wa 'l Hadith*: "Followers in the path laid out by the Prophet himself." The hadith is a compilation of the direct sayings of Muhammad, and as such is considered hallowed within the Tradition, second only to the *Qur'an* in sacred correctness. The hadith was compiled by al-Bukhari after he winnowed down 600,000 such sayings to 4,000 which seemed to have authenticity after a sixteen year of searching the world through writings on papyrus, leaves, pieces of bark. Still, it remains rather incredible to non-believers that such a vast number of utterances could have been made by a single individual. The current hadith contents were eventually ratified by *ijima*, a principle of consensus among Islamic scholars and lawyers.
- *Hafiz*: Arabic for preserver, a title awarded to one who has memorized the entire *Qur'an*, often by attending a special course for the purpose; the *imam khatib* of a mosque is frequently (although not always or necessarily) a *hafiz*.
- *Halal*: Arabic for food—especially meat—that has been certified to meet Islamic standards. Comparable in principle to Jewish Kosher.
- *Hamas, al-Ikharon al-Moslemoon, or al-Ikhwan [The Islamic Resistance Movement]*: Terrorist Palestinian political party. Muslim Brotherhood had to reinvent itself; so, it established a militia called Hamas. Very deadly against Israel. Hamas. The *Harakat al-Mugawama al-Islamiya* (Arabic for "zeal"), the Islamic Resistance Movement, headquartered in Palestine. Gassam Brigades-terror squads of Hamas.
- *Hamam*: Arabic for toilet.
- *Hammum*: Arabic for traditional public bathhouse.
- *Hangwin*: Arabic for honey.
- *Harbiyah:* Arabic for irregular troops.
- Head coverings for women: black abayas, niqabs—veils worn by some Muslim women in public, covering all of the face apart from the eyes. However, it may be worn with a separate eye veil. It is worn with an accompanying headscarf.
  - *Hijab* describes the act of covering up generally but is more often used to describe in general the headscarves

worn by Muslim women. These scarves come in many styles and colors in different places and under differing levels of tyrannical fundamentalism discriminating against women. The type most commonly worn in the West covers the head and neck but leaves the face clear.

- The *burka* is the most concealing of all Islamic veils. It is a one-piece veil that covers the face and body, often leaving just a mesh screen to see through so that no part of the female anatomy is visible, nor even the female form is identifiable because of the voluminous folds of the covering.
- The *niqab* is a whole body cover which is pulled over the head, something like a poncho, but it covers from scalp to feet.
- The *al-amira* is a two-piece veil. It consists of a close-fitting cap, usually made from cotton or polyester, and a tube-like scarf.
- The *shayla* is a long, rectangular scarf popular in the Gulf region. It is wrapped around the head and tucked or pinned in place at the shoulders.
- The *khimar* is a long, cape-like veil that hangs down to just above the waist. It covers the hair, neck and shoulders completely, but leaves the face clear.
- The *chador*, worn by many Iranian women when outside the house, is a full-body cloak. It is often accompanied by a smaller headscarf underneath.

— *Helke ron*: Arabic for fried eggs.
Hezbi Islami, the *Hezb-e Islami Khalis*, *Harakat-i-Inqilab-i-Islami* and the *Mahaz-e-Melli*: Mujahideen groups fighting under the authority of regional DRA commander Jalaluddin Haqqani.
— *Hijrah*: migration for the purpose of jihad. First *hijrah* was Muhammad's travel to build up the *Ummah* (people) and to return to destroy Mecca.
— *Hirabah*: Arabic from the *Qur'an* for the action of a group or an individual by which property is seized or destroyed and people are killed or kidnapped. The *Qur'an* condemns it as *"fasad fil ard"*–war against God and his Messenger and as "spreading mischief" (disorder).

- *Hudud*: In Muslim law–divine punishments for the category of crimes most egregious and therefore most severely punished, including theft, highway robbery, drinking alcohol, unlawful sexual intercourse, false accusation of unchastity. Hudud punishments range from public lashing to publicly stoning to death, amputation of hands, and crucifixion. Related terms in Islamic law are—*ta'zir*, punishment for offenses at the discretion of the judge—*Qadi*–or ruler of the state. It is one of three major types of punishments or sanctions under Sharia Islamic law—*hudud, qisas*—equal retaliation–and *ta'zir. Diya/Diyat* is the financial compensation paid to the victim or heirs of a victim in the cases of murder, bodily harm, or property damage.
- *Hukm*-Arabic for ruling.
- *Inghimasi*-style (attack): Arabic for martyrdom seeker [commando-plunging into enemy lines operations.]
- *Imam*: Arabic for the person who leads prayers in a mosque, a title of various Muslim leaders, especially of one succeeding Muhammad as leader of *Shi'ite* Islam.
- *Iman*: Arabic for faith.
- *Insha'allah*: Arabic for "God willing."
- ISIS/ISIL/IS: Islamic State of Iraq and Syria, Islamic State of Iraq *Dawa'esh/dea'sh* and the Levant, and Islamic State. The Islamic State is also known as *Da'esh* (by IS detractors), and *al Dewala(t) al-Islamaya(h)* in Arabic—previously *ad-Dawlah al-Islāmiyah fī 'l-'Irāq wa-sh-Shām*. The followers are known as *Dawa'esh/Da'esh* in Arabic.
- Ismailis: Offshoot *Shi'ite* religious sect that developed in the 8th century and persisted in power until the 11th century in the Fatimid period in Syria. Currently, mainly found in Salamiyeh and Masyaf towns of the Hama province of Syria.
- *Iwan/Ivan*: Arabic and Persian term for a rectangular room, building, or enclosure, usually with vaulted walls. The walls are closed on three sides with a fourth opening into a courtyard. A common residential and religious Arab architectural style.
- *Islam*: An Abrahamic monotheistic religion which teaches that there is only one God, that an Arabian trader of the Qurash tribe, named Muhammad/Mohammed, became the Prophet and messenger of God, that accepts a book called the *Qur'an/Koran*—the "recitations" as exact word of God, having been dictated word for word by the

Archangel Gabriel/Jibril to Muhammad, who was illiterate. To its followers, Islam is the true religion of "Allah"/the God; and as such, its name represents the central principle of Allah's "God's" religion; the total submission to the will of Allah. In fact, the Arabic word Islam means the submission or surrender of one's will to the only true god worthy of worship—Allah—and anyone who does so is termed a "Muslim." The word also implies "peace" which is the natural consequence of total submission to the will of Allah according to Muslims, and it is—therefore—not a new religion brought by Prophet Muhammad in Arabia in the seventh century, but is the true religion (*iuqui*) of Allah re-expressed in its final form. *Islam* is the second largest religious sect in the world with nearly a billion and a half adherents. There is violent controversy regarding the successors to Muhammad which divides Islam into a majority of *Sunnis* and a minority of *Shi'ites*. Defense of the religion Islam and its captured territories has plunged the sects into a seemingly interminable series of conflicts ever since Muhammad announced his great spiritual experience. Muslims—true believers/submitters—have hated Jews ever after one of those early battles.

The doctrines are fairly simple: the only prerequisite to becoming a Muslim is to recite aloud and with conviction that (in Arabic) *"la ilaha illa'llah* (there is no god but God), and *Muhammadun rasul Allah."* (in English) There is no God but God, and *"wa Muhammadan rasula l-lah."*—and Muhammad is the messenger of God." One must not commit *shirk*—innovation, to introduce anything new or different to the religion which is tantamount to denying the monotheism of Allah (God). Abraham is considered to the first Muslim, and he is revered. Muslims believe in a coming apocalypse, satan/devil, and *jinns*/evil demon spirits, angels, prophets (with Muhammad being the last and greatest), resurrection, and the afterlife; practice the five pillars of Islam, follow the Islamic commandments, revere the *Qur'an*, a short book that is frequently memorized in its entirety and is considered to be the only wholly correct book of scripture.

— *Izzat*: Arabic for glory/honor/dignity.
— *Jama'at al-Muslimeen*: Arabic for group of the Muslims, i.e. the wider Muslim community, not merely any group that requires its members to pledge allegiance to its *amir/emir*.

- JAM [*Jaysh al-Mahdi*]: Iranian terrorist military group.
- *Jevat*: Arabic term for city governmental area.
- *Jihad*: Several meanings—for the individual Muslim, it means striving and a struggle of the self, communicating one's faith, and obedience to God. For Muslims as a whole, it is holy war when necessary to defend attacks against the religion, or less often to propagate Islam. It is at the same time a struggle to be a better person and to be religiously holy and the jihad of the sword to defend the faith or to fight against efforts to interfere with the ability of Muslims to practice their faith. Shi'a doctrine favors the jihad of the sword definition of the word. There are three levels of Jihad: <u>Heart</u>-Every Muslim must hold this anger and hatred of nonMuslims in their heart; <u>Word</u>-Muslims may engage in *Da'Wa* (Islamization of knowledge; changing things like history so that the history is all right for Muslims). They can engage in politics in an attempt to destroy the government from within, engage in debates, lie. <u>Supporting</u>-Canadian Muslims send $1.5million to Islamic Relief. A Muslim Brotherhood charity is a good friend of Hamas. <u>Hot</u> Jihad–action such as a Muslim man drove into a policeman in Edmonton and tried to stab him and others.
- *Jinn*: Arabic word (in Arabian and Muslim mythology) for an intelligent, usually fearful and evil, spirit of lower rank than the angels, able to appear in human and animal forms and to possess humans.
- *Jizya*: Arabic for welfare. Also, to have nonMuslims care for and provide for Muslims (as in European refugee in migration).
- *Jali/Jaali*: Urdu term for net, is the word for a perforated stone or latticed screen, usually with an ornamental pattern constructed through the use of calligraphy and geometry.
- *Jawwaaz safer*: Arabic for passport.
- *Jebel*: Arabic term for mountain.
- *Jirga/Jirgah/*the circle: Pashto word for a tribal assembly for group decision making. *Loya Jirgah* is the Pashto word for a grand assembly–a special type of *jirga* that is mainly organized for choosing a new head of state in case of sudden death of a primary leader, adopting a new constitution, or to settle national or regional issue such as war.
- *Kaffir/Kifr/Kufr* (sing.)/*kuffar* (pl): Arabic for infidel, meaning rejector, disbeliever, unbeliever, or nonbeliever. In Islam, Kaffir means a person who rejects or disbelieves in Allah, God as described by Islam

according to the teachings of the Islamic prophet Muhammad–a strictly pejorative descriptor, especially as applied to South African blacks by Afrikaanners.

— *Khastegari:* Afghan pre-marriage process where one family courts another for their daughter. The daughter's only currency is her virginity.

— *Khawarij:* Arabic for oppressive, corrupt, dishonest, love money, declare *takfir* on people they don't like, dealers in blood and money, liars.

— *Khidmat al-'alam:* Arabic for obligatory service.

— *Khatib:* Arabic for preacher. Imam khatib is a common combination of two elementary offices: leader (*imam*) of the congregational prayer, which in most mosques is performed at the times of all daily prayers; and preacher (*khatib*) of the sermon or *khutba.*

— *Khalq:* one of the two main factions of the PDP'A, People's Democratic Party of Afghanistan, lit. people/masses. Parcham is the other faction— "flag or banner." The PDPA is the Afghan Communist Party founded in 1963 with the goal of changing the feudal Afghan society into a socialist state.

— *Khan/Caravanserai:* A large inn to provide accommodation for trade caravans and their animals which has a large central courtyard and a large variety of necessary provisions.

— Kurds/Kurdistan: an ethnic group and their chosen homeland in northern Syria located between northern Iraq, northwestern Iran, and southeastern Turkey. The Kurds speak their own Kurdish language and are largely Sunni Muslims with both Christian and Yazidi minorities.

— Levant/Greater Syria: A broad region which includes the modern states of Syria, Lebanon, Jordan, Israel, and Palestine.

— *Madrasa/Madrassa/Madrasah:* Arabic for school, usually meaning religious school, especially an Islamic university.

— *Mahram:* Arabic for male escort; originally "forbidden" as in not legal and proper for them to have intercourse with the woman being escorted.

— *Majdal/burj:* Arabic for tower.

— *Majlis/Mejlis:* Arabic for "a place of sitting" or council, a special gathering of men, especially in Saudi Arabia with Islamic ties and usually involving a great leader—sheikh—meeting with petitioners.

— *Mak-hah:* Arabic for café.

- *Maktab al-bariid*: Arabic for post office.
- *Malik:* Arabic for head man in an Afghan village,
- "*Ma'lim Sahib*": Arabic for teacher, sir.
- *Manhaj*: Arabic for ideological program, direction, and *aqeeda* (creed or doctrine)–the methodology of receiving, analyzing and applying knowledge. *Ashab al-manhaj al-salim* means having the sound *manhaj*. In the Islamic States's narrative, the people of sound *manhaj* contrast with 'extremists'/'innovators,' 'ignorant,' 'unqualified' and otherwise unjust individuals who are portrayed as playing a disproportionate role in the Islamic State today. The Armed Islamic Group and other fundamentalists embrace the *manhaj* of the Prophet in knowledge and deed
- *Marja' at-taqlid*: Persian for a complex title used in Twelver Shi`ism, namely. *Marja'* (pl. *maraji'*) means "source," and *taqlid* refers to religious emulation or imitation. On several occasions, the *Marja'iyyat* (community of all *maraji'*) has been limited to a single individual, in which case his rulings have been applicable to all those living in the Twelver *Shi'a* world. Of broader importance has been the role of the *mujtahid*, a cleric of superior knowledge who has the authority to perform *ijtihad* (independent judgment). They are few in number, but it is from their ranks that the *maraji' at-taqlid* are drawn.
- *Masbagha*: Arabic for laundry.
- *Mashhad*: Arabic for a religious shrine, usually a tomb containing the relics of an important *Shi'ite* religious leader.
- *Masi*: Arabic for fish.
- *Masjid*: Arabic for mosque.
- *Mast*: Arabic for yogurt.
- *Mataar*: Arabic for airport.
- *Medina*: Arabic for the commercial center of a city. Also one of the two holiest cities in Saudi Arabia.
- Mesopotamia: The historical area of the Tigris-Euphrates River systems—most of which now is found in modern Iraq.
- *Mihrab*: Arabic for the central niche in the prayer hall of a mosque which indicates the direction pointing towards Mecca.
- *Minaret*: Arabic for the tower of a mosque from which the muezzin sounds the call to prayer.
- *Mirishik*: Arabic for chicken.

- Mosque: Arabic for a place of communal worship, not necessarily a building. Typically, it has features of a minaret *mihrab, minbar,* and courtyard where a fountain is maintained for ablutions preceding prayers.
- *Moz*: Arabic for banana(s).
- *Muezzin/Mu'adhdhin*: Arabic for an official who calls from the high platform of the minaret of a mosque when it is time for Muslims to pray.
- *Mufti*: Arabic for a Sunni cleric–a scholar who has completed an advanced course of study which qualifies him to issue judicial opinions or *fatawah/fatwas.*
- Mughal/Mongol Empire: Dynasty founded by Turko-Mongol invader Babur in the 1500s that persisted for 300 years with heavy handed occupation of India and Middle Eastern territories.
- *Muharibeen:* Arabic for Christians at war.
- *Mujahideen*: Arabic for loosely connected tribal-based alliances of Islamists. One engaged in jihad. Within the IS, distinctions are made between *muhajireen* (foreigners) and *ansar* (locals of Iraq and Syria).
- *Muhajirun*: in Urdu and Arabic, it is a term used in Pakistan to describe the mostly Urdu-speaking Muslim refugees and their descendants who migrated from India and settled in Pakistan after the partition of India into India and Pakistan. In Arabic, they are known as The Emigrants, who were the first converts to Islam and the Islamic Prophet Muhammad's advisors and relatives, who emigrated with him from Mecca to Medina; the event known in Islam as The *Hijra.* The early Muslims from Medina are called the Ansar ("helpers").
- *Mullah*: Persian for master–commonly translated "cleric" in the West– is a title of address for any educated or respected figure, not even necessarily (although most frequently) religious.
- *Murtadd* (pl. *murtaddeen*): Arabic for apostate.
- *Musbriks: Mujahideen* Arabic for polytheists who are to be enslaved, especially the women (e.g. Yazidis). According to the terrorists' interpretation of the *Qur'an*, it is all right to make such women into sex slaves, even prepubertal girls. Those who do not comply can choose to be punished by whipping or by the biter—applied to a breast. Many women who join IS are no less bloodthirsty and participate in beheadings (patterned after Khansa) and stand by as guards as their men rape the defenseless women slaves.

– *Muslim*: Arabic for a believer/ "one who voluntarily submits" to God/ Allah in Islam. To become a Muslim—a qualifier–and to convert to Islam, it is essential only to utter the *Shahada*, one of the Five Pillars of Islam, a pillar of faith and trust that professes that there is only one God/Allah and that Muhammad is God's messenger. It is a set statement recited in Arabic: "*lā 'ilāha 'illā-llāhu muḥammadun rasūlu-llāh*" "There is no god but Allah, (and) Muhammad is the messenger of God."

In Sunni Islam, the *shahada* has two parts: *la ilaha illa'llah* (there is no god but God), and *Muhammadun rasul Allah* (Muhammad is the messenger of God), which are sometimes referred to as the first *shahada* and the second *shahada*. A convert must only recite the first *shahada* at least.

Required religious practices for all Muslims are called the Five Pillars of Islam: 1. the declaration of faith (*shahadah*), 2. daily prayers (*salat*), 3. fasting during the month of Ramadan (*sawm*), 4. almsgiving (*zakat*), and 5. the pilgrimage to Mecca (*hajj*) at least once in a lifetime.

The *Shi'ite shahada* includes a phrase concerning Ali, the first Shia Imam and the fourth Rashid caliph of Sunni Islam: «*wa 'alīyyun walīyyu-llāh*," "Ali is the wali of God."

– Muslim Brotherhood/*al-Ikhwān al-Muslimūn*, is a transnational Sunni Islamist organization founded in Egypt by Islamic scholar and school teacher Hassan al-Banna in 1928. The MB spread far beyond Egypt and throughout the Muslim world, influencing various Islamist movements from charitable organizations to political parties even to the present day. It is now a legal political party in Egypt. MB has been implicated in terrorism directly and indirectly throughout its existence.

– *Mustashfa*: Arabic for hospital.

– *Muttafiq alayhi*: Arabic for one who leaves his religion and separates from the group.

– *Nan/Naan*: Arabic for bread. *Naan-bayee*=naan bread bakery.

– *Naqis-ul-aq*: Baby girls are called "stupid by birth."

– *Nekah:* Afghan wedding ceremony.

– *Nom de guerre*: French for a pseudonym, an assumed fictitious name under which a person engages in combat or some other activity or enterprise.

- Numbers 1-10: (Arabic)—Yek, Du, Se, Chwaar, Penj, Shash, Hawt, Hasht, No, Dah, corresponding to (English)—One-1, Two-2, Three-3, Four-4, Five-5, Six-6, Seven-7, Eight-8, Nine-9, Ten-10.
- Ottomans: A Turkish Muslim multinational empire founded in 1299. It reached its height in the 16th-17th centuries CE when it had governance over the Levant, North Africa, and the Balkans. The Ottomans were defeated and its caliphate disbanded in 1923 after the end of WWI.
- *Pahlwani*: Wrestling, especially in Pakistan. Not allowed to touch opponent's legs.
- *Pashtunwali*: unwritten laws and codes followed by most Afghans and almost all Pashtuns. Code of honor, courage, self-pride, and respect. Hospitality is extremely important since it enables individuals to uphold personal and family honor. Food, drink, and shelter are available to all who seek it. Must avenge any insult against themselves, their families, or their tribe. Many feuds run from generation to generation.
- PAVN, VC, DRVN, RVM, ARVN: Peoples Army of Viet Nam (NVN), Viet Cong, Democratic Republic of Viet Nam (NVN), Republic of Viet Nam (SVN), Army of Viet Nam (SVN).
- *Penir*: Arabic for cheese.
- *Peshmerga*: Kurdish word meaning "before death" or "those who face death." The Peshmerga are the military forces of the federal region of Iraqi Kurdistan. Because the Iraqi Army is forbidden by Iraqi law to enter Iraqi Kurdistan, the Peshmerga–along with their security subsidiaries–are responsible for the security of the regions in Iraqi Kurdistan. *Zeravani* (military police).
- Phoenix Program: Secret capture and turn organization of American and South Vietnamese forces which also turned former Viet Cong (ralliers) to serve the South Vietnamese government. Employed educational, persuasional, and torture techniques. Highly successful in achieving its goals.
- PRUC, PRUC/O: Provincial Reconnaissance Unit Cadre/Officer, became part of the Phoenix Program in Viet Nam.
- *Qawwal*: Kermanji word for traveling Yazidi religious teachers.
- *Rallier*: French for a person who switches sides, implying a switch from the wrong to the right side. Used by Phoenix Program for VC who switched to the government side.

- *Riban/maslaha:* usury (charging interest) is illegal/a sin in Islam.
- *Ribat:* Arabic for manning of frontline points.
- *Risala/risalah/risalat/resalah*: Arabic word for "message." Often refers to: Risalah (fiqh), a summary of religious prescriptions in Islamic jurisprudence.
- *Rote:* Arabic for a cookie for special occasions, like Eid
- SAWS: Arabic acronym for the Arabic words *"sallallahu alayhi wa salaam"* (may God's prayers and peace be with him—The Prophet). Muslims often use these words after his name to show respect to Allah's Prophet when mentioning his name and honoring him as the Messenger of God. They also often use just the acronym.
- *Shabab*: Somalian terrorist organization.
- *Shakir*: Arabic for sugar.
- Salafi/Salafi movement/Salafist movement/Salafism is a reform branch or revivalist movement within Sunni Islam that developed in Egypt in the late 19th century as a response to European imperialism, with roots in the 18th-century Wahhabi movement that originated in the Najd region of modern-day Saudi Arabia. *A salafi is* a member of a strictly orthodox Sunni Muslim sect advocating a return to the early Islam of the *Qur'an* and the Sunna.
- *Sharia*: Arabic for street.
- Sharia Law/*Fiqh*/The Path: A very important element of Islamic Tradition which is the law of the land in strict Islamic states such as Iran. It is divine law with God as the drafter, legislator, explicator, forbidder, rewarder, and punisher, of the law. *Fiqh* is understanding in the legal sense—God speaks; God commands; and man must submit and obey and must do so actively, not passively, joyfully, not grudgingly, and with exactitude.

There are four officially accepted schools of Sharia law and every Muslim must subscribe to one of them: The Hanafi, Maliki, Shafi'I, and Hanbali which keep the official books governing mankind's conduct toward God. Saudi Arabia, under Wahhabi fundamentalism, insists on strict Hanbali law, remaining as only one of two Islamic states requiring amputation of the hand of a thief. The other is the Islamic State. Other sets of Sharia laws deal with the laws governing human relations such as marriage, divorce, fosterage, polygamy, proper slaughter of animals, governance in the Islamic community, including establishment of an inspector of public morals. Sharia law prohibits consumption of alcohol, eating pork or hyena meat, gambling including playing chess, dice, allowing a polytheist to enter a mosque, or any other games involving gambling.

— *Shu'bat al-Mukhabarat al-'Askariyya*: Syrian intelligence service.
— *Sabah or sabiyya (plural):* Arabic for slave, esp. sexual slave.
— *Sifaara*: Arabic for embassy.
— *Sharif/Shareef/Alsharif/Alshareef*: Traditional Arabic title meaning noble or highborn.
— *Shi'ites*: an adherent of the *Shi'a* branch of Islam—found mostly in Iran, Iraq, and Gulf island state of Bahrain. *Shi'a* Muslims—in contradistinction to Sunnis–believe that just as a prophet is appointed by God alone, only God has the prerogative to appoint the successor to his prophet. They believe God chose Ali to be Muhammad's successor, infallible, the first caliph (*khalifah*, head of state) of Islam. Sunnis believe that the Muslims choose the successor by vote of the faithful accompanied by God's inspiration. The Sunnis believe that Muhammad had no rightful heir, and they believe that Muhammad's followers chose Abu Bakr, Muhammad's in-law, close friend, and advisor, as his successor. The schism between the two sects began after the death of Muhammad in 632 A.D., at which point a dispute over the identity of Muhammad's religious successor caused the followers of Islam to divide into Sunnis and Shi'ites.

Another contentious religious difference between *Shi'ite* and Sunni Muslims relates to the belief in the Mahdi, Arabic for "guided one." While both sects perceive the Mahdi to be the sole ruler of the Islamic community, the Sunnis hold that the Mahdi has not yet been born and anticipate his arrival sometime in the future, and the Shi'ites believe that the Mahdi was born in 869 A.D. and will return to Earth under Allah's orders.

— *Shirk*: Arabic for–in the most literal form–associating partners with God, i.e. polytheism, idolatry etc. which is tantamount to denying the unique oneness of God. Promoting change.
— *Siyasa*: Arabic for politics/policy.

- SOG: Studies and Observations Group (MACV-SOG=Military Assistance Command- Studies and Observations Group) a highly classified, multi-service United States special operations unit which conducted covert unconventional warfare operations prior to and during the Vietnam War. Also known as Special Ops Group.
- *Souq/bazaar*: Arabic for market.
- *Sufi*: Offshoot branch of *Shi'ite* Muslims who accept a mystical interpretation of the faith, its literature, and its practices. Sufis are generally ascetic in lifestyles, practice dances including whirling—whirling Dervishes—poetry, and music particular to the faith. There are several different orders, but all have grandmasters who claim a direct chain of succession of teachers all the way back to the Prophet Muhammad.
- *Sultan*: Arabic for a tribal chief or sovereign Muslim ruler.
- *Sunnis/Sunnites/Ahlus Sunnah*: the larger and most prominent of the two main branches of Islam, which differs from the *Shi'a* in its understanding of the *Sunnah*, its conception of religious leadership, and its acceptance of the first three caliphs. It accounts for the vast majority—90%–of Muslims around the world and is second only to Roman Catholicism in terms of numbers of adherents. Both *Sunnis* and *Shi'ites* have large majorities of peaceful religious people and minorities of violent terrorists. Both groups export terrorism. The *Sunnah (ahl as-sunnah wa l-jamā'ah)*—from which the descriptor of Sunni—arises, relates to the behavior of the Prophet Muhammad.
- *Sura*: Arabic for *Qur'anic* scriptural verse. There are 114 *surrahs* in the *Qur'an*.
- *Taliban*: =*talib* or student, "the men from Kandahar." The organization started at least in 1898, recruited from Pashtuns in *Qur'anic* schools, educated by illiterate mullahs in refugee camps in Afghanistan and Pakistan and came into power in 1994. Taliban established the Islamic Emirate of Afghanistan in 1996, a violently repressive fundamentalist Islamic sect that was particularly abusive to women. Leader was Mullah Omar. Utilized Kalashnikov wielding *Amr bil-Maroof* [Taliban guards of virtue and suppression of vice] as enforcers. Early on, they were supported financially and militarily by the United States through the CIA.
- *Takfir*: Arabic for pronouncement that someone is an unbeliever, a kafir.
- *Tạm dung lại!*: Vietnamese for halt.

- *Tawheed/Touheed/Tevhid*: Arabic for oneness [of God], the indivisible oneness concept of monotheism in Islam. *Tawhid* is the religion›s central and single-most important concept, upon which a Muslim›s entire faith rests.
- *Tawusi Melek:* Yazidi angel who came to his earth in the form of a peacock, hence the Yazidi reverence for the peacock.
- *Tayara*: Arabic for airplane.
- *Tayeb*: Arabic for good.
- *Tazkiya*: Arabic–vouching for someone to join the group.
- *Tel*: Arabic for hill.
- *Tet Mau Than Tong Cong kich/Tong Khoi Nghia:* Vietnamese for General Uprising, specifically for the Tet Offensive of 1968]
- *Thiqat*: Arabic for trusted ones. Also known as *Hujjaj'* (singular: *Hajji*), a term in Islamic State parlance for senior members of the group; also a term for one who has made the *haj*—the pilgrimage.
- Terrorism: There are at least 109 different quasi-official definitions of the term. Only three will be presented here, since they seem to be fairly broad, logical, and inclusive: Definition from US Code Section 2656: "Terrorism is premeditated, politically motivated, violence against noncombatant targets by subnational groups or clandestine agents, usually intended to influence an audience."

  FBI Definition: "Terrorism is the unlawful use of force or violence against persons or property to intimidate or coerce a government, the civilian population, or any segment thereof, in the furtherance of political or social objectives."

  OED (Oxford English Dictionary Definition): "Terrorism is a political concept—not just an act of violence, but about power and use of power to achieve political changes. Violence or threat of violence or coercive intimidation. "Propaganda by deed." Calculated means to destabilize."

  Although there is no clear consensus of the definition, the vast majority of scholars and law enforcement personnel agree that "terrorism is theater."
- Tiradores Battalion: Unit of the Colombian army which fought the U.S. Marines in 1903 after the marines took over Panama and created Panama as a separate state.
- *Turba*: Arabic for tomb or burial site.

- Turkmen: Ethnic group of Turkic origins found mainly in northern Syria, Iraq, Iran, and Turkey. They speak their own language.
- *Qalaa*: Arabic for castle or fortress.
- *Qasr*: Arabic for palace.
- *Qala*: Arabic for fortress-like compound, usually with high walls around the compound
- *Qur'an/Koran*: Arabic for recitation. It is the Holy Book of Islam, the final book of divine revelation. It was dictated by the Angel Gabriel and recorded verbatim by the Prophet Muhammad,
- *Ummah/ummat al-Islām*: Arabic for the Islamic community and it is commonly used to mean the global collective community of Islamic people.
- Umayyids: First Islamic caliphate based in Damascus. They persisted in Cordoba Spain until 1031 CE.
- VC/VCI: Viet Cong/Viet Cong Infrastructure
- *Wadi*: Arabic for valley or watercourse.
- Wahhabism/Wahhabis: Saudi Arabian extremely strict fundamentalist Sunni religious organization.
- *Wajib*: Arabic for obligatory.
- *Wakh*! or *Akh-Allah*!: Arabic outcry when hurt.
- WOMs: Wise Old Men (referring to the leaders in Washington who do not get down and dirty like the foot soldier).
- Yazidis/Yezidis/Ezidis: Kurmanji speaking religious minority people of an ancient Zoroastrian linked sect practiced by a small minority of Kurds in Iraq, and a few in Syria. Yazidism is an ancient monotheistic religion which is something of a mixture of similarities to Judaism, Zoroastrianism, Mithraism, and Islam.
- *Zahir*: Arabic term meaning literal or apparent. Fundamentalist/traditionalist theological belief holds that the strict meaning of the *Qur'an* and the hadith have sole authority in matters of belief and law; and that the use of rational disputation—considered to be "shirk"–is forbidden even if it verifies the truth. These traditionalists insist on a literal reading of the *Qur'an*, as opposed to one engaged in *ta'wil* (metaphorical interpretation). They do not attempt to conceptualize the meanings of the *Qur'an* rationally, and believe that their realities should be consigned to God alone (*tafwid*) rather than by reason or seeking evidence—which in and of itself is considered

to be nonIslamic. The texts of the *Qur'an* and Hadith are in accepted with simple faith without asking, "*Bi-la kaifa?*" [how?].

— *Zalat*: Arabic for salad.
— *Zaybah/Jamila:* Arabic for beautiful.

APPENDIX IV

NAMES AND ACRONYMS OF GROUPS AND SOME FRIENDLIES

*Abu Hafi al Masri
*Abu Khabab (al Qaeda Factions)
*Abu Sayyaf & MILF (Morro Philippine Islamic Liberation Front)
*Al Qaeda training camps Khaldun&Darunta
*Al Qua'ida-Al Qaeda
*AMB (al-Aqsa Martyrs Brigade)
*Ansar al-Shari'a (Libya)
*Ahrar al-Sham, Syrian rebel group
*Badr Brigades
*Brigades for the Defense of the Holy Shrines
*Egyptian Islamic Jihad
*Fatah & Fatah Black September Movement
*Fedayeen-commandoes
*GIA (Armed Islamic Group—Algerian)
*Hamas
*Hashd Sha'abi (Popular Mobilization) in Iraq "Islamic Resistance." An adherent of an Islamic movement originating in India and seeking to revive the practices and theological and legal interpretations of early Islam.
*Hezbollah
*Indonesian Jamaiya Islamia

*IM (Indian Mujahiden)
*IMK (Islamic Movement in Kurdistan)
*Irgun (Israeli)
*ISU (Islamic Jihad Union (2010)
*Jamaah Islamiyah (SE Asian Militant Islamist Group)
*Lashkar-e-Taiba
*Lashkar-e-Tayyaba (Army of the Pure)
*LeT-violent wing of Jamaa-ud-Dawa an Islamist polit/educ movement among poor Palestinians.
*Machtevet (Israel underground terror)
*Mahdi Affiliates: Divine Wrath Brigades
*Mujahideen (loosely connected tribal-based alliances of Islamists)
*PFLP (Popular Front for Liberation of Palestine)
*PLO (M-19) Palestine Liberation Organization
*Shahiba (Palestinian)
*SSNP—Syrian Socialist Nationalist Party
*Taliban

Other Acronyms:
*AFSOAD-Air Force special operations air detachment, AFSOF-Air Force Special Operations Forces
*AMD-Air Mobility Division
*Beach Party-The Navy component of the landing force support party under the tactical control of the landing force support party commander
*C-day-The unnamed day on which a deployment operation commences or is to commence
*CJCS-Chairman, Joint Chiefs of Staff. JCOS-Joint Chiefs of Staff, CNO-Chief of Naval Operations
*Classified information-Official information that has been determined to require, in the interests of national security, protection against unauthorized disclosure and which has been so designated. *Classified information can be designated Top Secret[Sensitive Compartmented Information (SCI) or special access program (SAP)], Secret, Restricted, Official, or Confidential.
*Complex catastrophe-Any natural or man-made incident, including cyberspace attack, power grid failure, and terrorism, which results in

cascading failures of multiple, interdependent, critical, life-sustaining infrastructure sectors and caused extraordinary levels of mass casualties, damage, or disruption severely affecting the population, environment, economy, public health, national morale, response efforts, and/or government functions. See also, snafu

*CONUS-Continental United States

*COS-Chief of Station (CIA), see also SAC [Special Agent in Charge]

*DA-double agent. Agent in contact with two opposing intelligence services, only one of which is aware of the double contact or quasi-intelligence services

*DCIA-Director CIA, DDCIA-Deputy Director CIA

*DOD-Department of Defense

*DNI-Director National Intelligence. ODNI-Office of the Director of National Intelligence

*FOB-forward operating base. An airfield used to support tactical operations without establishing full support facilities

*HALO-Parachute term. High Altitude (jump), Low (altitude) Opening.

*HUMINT-human intelligence. Intelligence derived from information collected and provided by human sources.

*Intelligence-1. The product resulting from the collection, processing, integration, evaluation, analysis, and interpretation of available information concerning foreign nations, hostile or potentially hostile forces or elements, or areas of actual or potential operations. 2. The activities that result in the product. 3. The organizations engaged in such activities

Intelligence asset-Any resource utilized by an intelligence organization for an operational support role

*Law of war-That part of international law that regulates the conduct of armed hostilities. Also called the law of armed conflict, also rules of engagement.

*MACV-Military Assistance Command Vietnam

*Materiel-All items necessary to equip, operate, maintain, and support military activities without distinction as to its application for administrative or combat purposes.

*MC-Medical Corps, as in Capt. USN/MC/AD (Active Duty)

*NATO-North Atlantic Treaty Organization

*Need to know-A criterion used in security procedures that requires the custodians of classified information to establish, prior to disclosure, that

the intended recipient must have access to the information to perform his or her official duties.

*POTUS-President of the United States

*POW-Prisoner of war. A detained person (as defined in Articles 4 and 5 of the Geneva Convention Relative to the Treatment of Prisoners of War of August 12, 1949) who, while engaged in combat under orders of his or her government, is captured by the armed forces of the enemy.

*Rangers-Rapidly deployable airborne light infantry organized and trained to conduct highly complex joint direct action operations in coordination with or in support of other special operations units of all Services.

*SEAL team-[Sea, Air, and Land] United States Navy forces organized, trained, and equipped to conduct special operations with an emphasis on maritime, coastal, and riverine environments.

*USMC-United States Marines, USN-United States Navy, etc.

*USOM [United States Operations Mission].

*USS-United States Ship

APPENDIX V

TIMELINE OF IS (ISLAMIC STATE) TERRORISM

Modern international terrorism:

- Origin in *Wahhabism*—the ultraconservative sect of Islam in Saudi Arabia–created in the 1730s by an alliance between Abd al-Ouahhab and a tribal leader of the Arab peninsula, Ibn Sauod. This led to the formation of the ultraconservative and terroristic state ruled by the religious Wahhabis, and the militarily powerful Saud family. Wahhabism spread the doctrine of extreme fundamentalism and intolerance throughout the Muslim world, and fostered connections to the Salafi School of the Arab league established in Mecca in 1962 which came to be the founding and persistent doctrine of the Islamic State.
- Iranian Islamic Revolution: Started an increase in religious groups transporting terrorism to fifty percent of all international terrorism (January, 1978-February 1979 to 1995).
- Collapse of Soviet Bloc with sudden massive increase in availability of military weaponry, December 26, 1991.
- Taliban established the Islamic Emirate of Afghanistan in 1996.
- Advent of global terrorism: Started when PFLP [Popular Front for the Liberation of Palestine] hijacked Israeli El Al commercial air flight from Rome to Tel Aviv. 12th incident in 1968 alone. Earlier

ones were for revolutionaries to get to Cuba. El Al hijacking was a *political statement* to trade hostages for Palestinian prisoners in Israel.

Thereafter, terrorists began traveling on commercial airlines to commit terror in multiple countries. Intent was to sew shock, fear, alarm, and thereby to attract attention to themselves and to their cause. (July 22, 1968.)

- Global War on Terror was declared September 16, 2001.
- U.S.-led invasion of Iraq (2003)
- Ibrahim Awwad Ibrahim al-Badri–otherwise known as mujahid sheikh Abu Bakr al-Baghdadi al-Hussaini al-Qurashi—(aka Amir al-Mu'mineen Abu Bakr al-Baghdadi), Abu Bakr al-Baghdadi for short, a *nom de guerre* he chose for himself, was born in 1971 in Samarra, Iraq. Although Baghdadi claimed to be a 44th direct descendent of the Prophet–and thus, entitled to the role of caliph–he has no verifiable link to the Prophet.
- U.S. forces arrested Baghdadi in Falluja, Iraq and sent him to a detention facility at Camp Bucca, Iraq where he was held for ten months (February, 2004-December, 2004). There, he learned how to be a dangerous and merciless terrorist from the masters.
- AQI (Al-Qaeda in Iraq—also called AQIM, al-Qaeda in Mesopotamia) established in Iraq (2004).
- Abu Ayyub al-Masri, head of AQ (al-Qaeda), outwardly dissolved AQI (al Qaeda Iraq) and founded the Islamic State in Iraq (ISI). The group continued to pledge allegiance to al-Qaeda privately and secretly (October, 2006)
- The new black IS flag called the eagle was formally shown by the media/propaganda arm, *al-Fajr.* (January, 2007)
- AQI was severely weakened in 2007 after Sunni tribes paid by the United States began to form militias known as "Awakening Councils" to expel al-Qaeda in Iraq from their territories (2007). By the end of 2007, AQI was one among dozens of groups contributing to Iraq's violence, prompting some to criticize the Bush administration for over-emphasizing the group's role.
- AQI, facing backlash from the community because of its brutality and increased pressure from U.S. and Iraqi forces, the group declined until 2011, when it found a great regrowth through its involvement in the Syrian Civil War (2007-2011). The prophecy of the 12,000

man Army failed, however; and many insurgent groups announced that the IS collapsed in 2012 before it could become fully a state. At most, it was looked upon as a proto-caliphate.

- The Arab Spring—equated with The End of the World by jihadists— was a series of anti-government protests, uprisings, and armed rebellions that spread across the Middle East. It began in response to oppressive regimes and a low standard of living beginning with protests in Tunisia. The Arab Spring—which began late 2010— became the Arab Winter by 2016.

- Al-Sham/the Levant (ISIS/ISIL) announced by its leader, mujahid sheikh Abu Bakr al-Baghdadi al-Hussaini al-Qurashi, that al-Nusra was part of ISI (Spring, 2013)

- al-Qaeda's leader Ayman al-Zawahiri expelled ISIS from al-Qaeda (February, 2014).

- IS quickly took over territory in Syria and Iraq, had enormous success as it revived with recruitment and obtaining funding. IS made large territorial gains beginning in January 2014, when it first defeated Iraqi forces and took control of Fallujah. In June, the group captured Mosul. The funds seized in the occupations, combined with income from foreign donors and from criminal activities such as smuggling and extortion of local businesses, gave ISIS an estimated $2 billion in assets. ISIS's oil revenues alone brought in between $1 million and $2 million per day (September, 2014).

Further, IS gained attention and support from the global jihadi community and began preparing governing structures to take control after the U.S. and coalition withdrawal from the country as a first step toward creating a caliphate to rule in the Middle East. The U.S. led Coalition withdrawal effectively rescued AQ, and the government of Iraq's lack of inclusiveness and security failures expedited AQI's return to prominence (2011).

However, in addition to its rapid expansion, the group also drew attention for its suicide bombings that killed civilians, for its campaign of assassinations and gruesome beheading videos that it released on the Internet after kidnapping and killing non-Arabs, Western, and Muslim, captives in Iraq public beheadings, and for its large, alarming, and growing contingent of foreign fighters. On the ground, IS fought the Assad Regime and allied Shi'ite forces,

Syrian opposition groups, the Iraqi military and militias ,the Kurdish peshmerga, and the Russian Army (2013 and 2014).

- The Islamic State of Iraq and the Levant [ISIL] with Abu Bakr al-Baghdadi as its self-proclaimed caliph was formally announced in Mosul, Iraq (2014-the present). Al-Baghdadi declared himself caliph and assumed the simple title of Caliph Ibrahim for everyday use.
- The U.S., under President Obama, began airstrikes against the IS (Fall, 2014).

To bring the reader briefly up to the present regarding the IS: The group *Tanzim Qaidat al-Jihad fi Bilad al-Rafidayn (Al-Qaeda in Iraq)* formed as an affiliate of Al-Qaeda network of Islamist militants during the Iraq War after considerable contention with AQ proper. The group eventually expanded into Syria and rose to prominence as the Islamic State of Iraq and the Levant (ISIL) during the Syrian Civil War. The group declared itself a caliphate under Abu Bakr al-Baghdadi on June 29, 2014 in Mosul, Iraq and renamed itself simply as the "Islamic State" This claim has been widely rejected. No prominent Muslim scholar has supported its declaration of being the caliphate; even Salafi-jihadist preachers whose philosophy IS centers on, accused the group of engaging in political showmanship and bringing disrepute to the notion of Islamic state and shame to Muslims everywhere.

ISIL has been at war with a wide-spread loose alliance of military and diplomatic forces including the Iraqi Army, the Syrian Army, the Free Syrian Army, Al-Nusra Front, Syrian Democratic Forces, Russian Armed Forces, and Iraqi Kurdistan's *Peshmerga* and People's Protection Units (YPG) along with a sixty nation coalition headed by the United States in its efforts to establish itself as a *de facto* state on Iraqi and Syrian territory with the ambition to spread that "state" worldwide under Sharia law. In 2016, the U.S. Department of State offered a reward of up to $25 million for information leading to the capture or death of mujahid Shaykh Abu Bakr al-Baghdadi al-Hussaini al-Qurashi.

- October 17, 2017: ISIS lost control of its self-declared capital, Raqqa.
- Nonetheless, IS considers itself to be the worldwide and final Islamic state, and has shattered so many lives, structures, political institutions, and shed so much blood, that it deserves to be counted as a caliphate—

apparently, a dubious honor, at least among the majority of Muslims and almost everyone else in the world at the present time.

Therefore, the historical count of caliphates comes to something on the order of fifteen–a highly arguable number–but it suits the interests and the title of this novel.

TIMELINE OF THE CALIPHATES

The Caliphates:

- Muhammad: –the prophet and founder of Islam. Born Abu al-Qasim Muḥammad ibn Abd Allah ibn Abd al-Muttalib ibn Hashim ibn Abd Manaf ibn Qusai ibn Kilab in Mecca in 570 CE. At age 40 (c610), he began to have revelations from Allah that became the basis for the *Qur'an* and the foundation of Islam. In 613, he took his message public, these would later become the *Qur'an*, Islam's sacred scripture. By 630 he had unified most of Arabia under a single religion. He died in 632 and was buried in Medina.

  The succeeding leaders or stewards of Islam–the caliphs—were persons considered to be a religious successor to the Prophet Muhammad and a leader of the entire ummah (body of the Muslims). A caliphate is an Islamic state under the leadership the caliph, counting Muhammad as the leader of the first caliphate in the present reckoning.

- Rashidun Caliphate: the empire that was controlled by the first four successors of Muhammad—the four "Rightly Guided" caliphs (The empire was founded after Muhammad's death on June 8, 632 CE at the age of 62 and and lasted until 'Ali's death in 661 c.e.). During the early period of Islam, four major caliphates succeeded the Prophet and each other. The four friends of the Prophet who led the caliphates were: Abu Bakr, Umar ibn al-Kattah, Uthman ibn Affan, and Ali ibn Abi Talib. Ali was a member of Muhammad's clan–the only one of the companions to be so related. The Shi'ites hold the belief that Ali was the first rightful caliph and Imam. A civil war occurred between his ardent followers and the supporters of Uthman, the previous caliph who was assassinated. That war led to the establishment of the Umayyad Caliphate

- Abbasid Caliphate (750–1258) associated with Muhammad's family through Hashim—a great grandfather, and Abbas, an uncle of Muhammad–and the Abbasid Revolution from 746–750, which primarily arose from non-Arab Muslim disenfranchisement. The Abbasid Caliphate capital was established in Baghdad in 750. The Buyid and later, the Seljuq, Turks gained control of the Abbasid Caliphate (945-1157)

- Ottoman Caliphate (1517-1917)

  The next recognized caliphate came about following the Ottoman Turk successful conquest of the ruling dynasty of Islam, previously under control of the military slave caliphate of the Mamluks in Egypt in 1517. The Ottoman control included Mecca and Medina. It persisted until the Ottomans were defeated in World War I by nonMuslims. On March 3, 1924, Mustafa Kemal Atatürk, the first President of the Turkish Republic, abolished the institution of the caliphate as part of the new Turkish constitution.

- Throughout the long history of Islam, several Islamic states—most of them hereditary monarchies, claimed to be caliphates after the Abbasid dynasty lost effective power over much of the Muslim realm by the first half of the tenth century. The claimants to caliphate status were convinced of their rights, but most of those caliphates were not generally accepted throughout the Muslim world. Because of their claims–and despite the contentions–this author counts them in the final number of caliphates, especially if the Islamic State of Iraq and the Levant can also thus be counted. The less well accepted caliphates include: the Isma'ili Fatimid Caliphate in Tunisia, Northeast Africa (909–1171) with Cairo as its capital; the Umayyad Caliphate of Córdoba in the Iberia Peninsula (929–1031) which revolted and separated from the Umayyids and was headed by Caliph Abd al-Rahman III; the Berber Almohad Caliphate in Morocco–(1121–1269) when most of the Iberian Peninsula fell to the Christians; the Fula Sokoto Caliphate in present-day northern Nigeria (1804–1903), and the Parallel Caliphates to the Ottomans–Yogyakarta Indonesia Caliphate (1755-2015) and the Sokoto Caliphate (1804–1903);

the Khilafat Movement in British India (1919–24), founded by the Sharifian Caliphate rulers of Hejaz (1924–25). Since it never had any real ruling or territorial power, it will not be numbered in the overall count of the caliphates of Islam.

The non-political caliphates: the Sufi Caliphates–In Sufism, tariqas (orders) are led by spiritual leaders (*khilafah ruhaniyyah*). Since Sufism is not accepted by mainstream Islam, their caliphates should not contribute to the overall count of historical caliphates; and the Amadiyya Calipphate (1908-the present day). The Ahmadiyya Muslim Community is an Islamic revivalist movement founded in 1889 by Mirza Ghulam Ahmad of Qadian, India, who claimed to be the promised Messiah and Mahdi, awaited by Muslims. He also claimed to be a follower-prophet subordinate to Muhammad, the Prophet of Islam. Ahmadi Muslims believe that the Amadiyya Calipphate established after the passing of the community's founder is the re-establishment of the Rashidun Caliphate. Many Islamic texts–including several ahadith, sayings of the Prophet–state that the Mahdi will be elected caliph and rule over a caliphate.

After Ahmad's death in 1908, his successor–Hakeem Noor-ud-Din–became the accepted caliph of the community and assumed the title of *Khalifatul Masih* (Successor or Caliph of the Messiah). The successors—five of them–have maintained their caliphate until the present time. The current caliph–based in London–is Mirza Masroor Ahmad. The Ahmadiyya Caliphate claims ten to twenty members in over 200 countries and territories of the world. Because of its persistence, relative wealth, land ownership, and fairly significant population, this author has elected to include the Ahmadiyya Caliphates as one of the counted caliphates or at least a serious contender. Since the Ahmadiyya is widely viewed as a heterodox movement by the mainstream of Sunni and Shi'ite Islam, most Muslims outside the movement do not recognize Ahmadi claims to a caliphate as valid.

SUGGESTED READING

Max Abrams, *Are Terrorists Really Rational?: The Palestinian Example,* Orbis 48, no. 3, 2004

Farah Ahmedi, with Tamim Ansary, *The Story of My Life: An Afghan Girl on the Other Side of the Sky,* Simon Spotlight Entertainment, Simon Schuster, New York, London, Toronto, Sydney, 2005

Abdel Bari Atwan, *The Secret History of al-Qaeda,* University of California Press, Berkeley, 2006

John Ayoto, *The Wordsworth Dictionary of Foreign Words in English,* Wordsworth Reference, Wordsworth Editions, Ltd., Hertfordshire, 1995

Noel Barber, David Kings, David Donovan, *War of the Running Dogs, How Malaya Defeated the Communist Guerrillas 1948-1960,* William Collins, Sons, London, 1971

Gabriel Ben-Dor and Ami Pedahzur, *The Uniqueness of Islamic Fundamentalism and the Fourth Wave of International Terror, in Religious Fundamentalism and Political Extremism,* ed. Leonard Weinberg and Ami Pedahzur, Frank Cass, 2004

Eli Berman, David O. Laitin, *Religion, Terrorism, and Public Goods: Testing the Club Theory, 1942-1967, Journal of Public Economics, no. 10-11,* October, 2008

Mia Bloom, *Dying to Kill: The Allure of Suicide Terror*, Columbia University Press, New York, 2005

Vahid Brown, *Cracks in the Foundation: Leadership Schisms in al'Qaida from 1989-2006*, West Point, New York, Combating Terrorism Center, 2007

Jason Burke, *Al Qaeda: Casting a Shadow of Terror,* I.B. Tauris, London, 2003

Richard Clarke, *Against all Enemies: Inside America's War on Terrorism,* Free Press, New York, 2004

Colby, William, *Lost Victory*. Contemporary Books, Chicago, 1989.

Cooper, Chester L. *The Lost Crusade: America in Viet Nam,* Dodd, Mead, and Company, New York, 1970.

Kim Cragin and Sara A. Daly, *The Dynamic Terrorist Threat: An Assessment of Group Motivations and Capabilities in a Changing World,* RAND Corporation, Santa Monica, California, 2004

Martha Crenshaw. *How Terrorism Declines, Terrorism and Political Violence 3, no 1,* Spring 1991

George Crile, *Charlie Wilson's War: The Extraordinary Story of How the Wildest Man in Congress and a Rogue CIA Agent Changed the History of Our Times,* Grove Press, New York, 2003

Audrey Kurth Cronin, *How Terrorism Ends: Understanding the Decline and Demise of Terrorist Campaigns,* Princeton University Press, Princeton and Oxford, 2009

Chris Dickman, *Terrorism, Crime, and Transformation: Studies in Conflict and Terrorism, 24, no. 1,* 2001

R. Hair Dekmejian, *Islam in Revolution: Fundamentalism in the Arab World,* Syracuse University Press, Syracuse, New York, 1995

Alan Dershowitz, *The Case for Peace: How the Arab-Israeli Conflict Can be Resolved, John Wiley,* Hoboken, 2005

Carl Douglass, *Last Phoenix, A Story of the CIA's Phoenix Program*, Publication Consultants, Anchorage, 1997

Fall, Bernard B, *The Two Viet-Nams: A Political and Military Analysis*, Frederick A Praeger, Publishers, New York, 1963.

David P. Fridovich and Fred T. Krawchuk, *Winning the Global War on Terrorism in the Pacific Region: Special Operations Forces' Indirect Approach to Success, Joint Forces Quarterly 44, 1ˢᵗ Quarter, 24-27*, 2007

P. Fritsch, *Religious Schools in Pakistan Fill Void, and Spawn Terror*, Wall Street Journal, October 2, 2001

Morton Halperin, *The Lawless State: The Crimes of the U.S. Intelligence Agencies*, Viking/Penguin Press, New York, 1976.

Lindsay Heger, *In the Cross-Hairs: The Targets of Terrorism*, doctoral dissertation draft, UC San Diego, Chaps 1 and 4, San Diego, California, 2008

Edward S. Herman, *Atrocities in Vietnam: Myths and Realities*, Pilgrim Press, Philadelphia, 1970.

Seymour Hersh, *Cover-up*, Random House. New York, 1972.

Michael Howard, *What's in a Name?: How to Fight Terrorism*, Foreign Affairs 81, no. 1, January-February, 2002

Yateenda Singh Jaffa, *Defeating Terrorism: A Study of Operational Strategy and Tactics of Police Forces in Jammu and Kashmir, India, Police Practice and Research 6, no. 2*, Kashimir, India, May, 2005

Brian Michael Jenkins, *Countering al-Qaida*, RAND Corporation, Santa Monica, California, 2002

Mark Juergensmeyer, *Terror in the Mind of God: The Global Rise in Religious Terrorism*, Berkeley, 2000

Stanley Karnow, *Viet Nam - A History: The First Complete Account of Viet Nam at War*, The Viking Press, Chicago, Illinois, 1983.

Evan F. Kohlmann, *State of the Sunni Insurgency in Iraq*, Report, NEFA Foundation, 2008

David Kretzmer, *Targeted Killing of Suspected Terrorists: Extrajudicial Execution or Legitimate Means of Defence?*, European Journal of International Law, 16, no. 2, 2005

Alan B. Krueger, *Jitka Maleckova, Education, Poverty, and Terrorism: Is There a Causal Relationship?* Journal of Economic Perspectives, 17, no. 4, 2003

Timur Kuran, *Islam and Economic Underdevelopment, in Islam and Economics, University of Southern California, 1999* as quoted in Eli Berman, *Radical, Religious, and Violent: The New Economics of Terrorism*, MIT Press, Cambridge, Massachusetts, 2009

Lester D. Langley, *The Banana Wars: An Inner History of American Empire, 1900-1934*, University Press of Kentucky, Lexington, 1983

Edward Lansdale, *In the Midst of Wars*, Harper and Row, New York, 1972.

Gayle Tzemach Lemmon, *The Dressmaker of Khair Khana*, Harper Collins Publishers, 2011

Gideon Levy, *The Twilight Zone: A Dead Man Walking, Ha'Aretz, Relates to the manhunt by Israel for Zakaria Zubeidi, al-Aqsa Martyrs' Brigade commander, for suicide attacks from 2003-2007.* March 26, 2004.

Terrence Maitland, Peter McInerney, *The Vietnam Experience (6 Vols)*, Boston Publishing Company, Boston, 1983.

Gabriel García Márquez. *Cien años de soledad [One Hundred Years of Solitude]*, by Editorial Sudamericana, Buenos Aires, 1967

William McCants, *The ISIS Apocalypse: The History, Strategy, and Doomsday Vision of the Islamic State*, Picador, St. Martin's Press, New York, 2015

Mark Moberg, *Crown Colony as Banana Republic: The United Fruit Company in British Honduras, 1900-1920*, Journal of Latin American Studies, Vol. 28, No. 2, May, 1996

Nadia Murad, with Jenna Krajeski, *The Last Girl: My Story of Captivity, and My Fight Against the Islamic State*, Tim Duggan Books (Penguin Random House), New York, 2017

Ivan Musicant, *The Banana Wars: A History of United States Military Intervention in Latin America from the Spanish–American War to the Invasion of Panama,* New York City, Macmillan Publishing Company, August, 1990

Abu Bakr Naji, *The Management of Savagery*, Translated by William McCants, Combating Terrorism Center, West Point, New York, 2006

Peter Neuman, *Negotiating with Terrorists, Foreign Affairs 86, no.1,* January-February, 2001.

Keith William Nolan, *Battle for Hue: Tet, 1968*, Presidio Press. Novato, California, 1983

Jenny Nordberg, *The Underground Girls of Kabul: In Search of a Hidden Resistance in Afghanistan*, Broadway Books, an imprint of Crown Publishing Group, a division of Random House LLC, New York, 2014 and 2015

Robert A. Page, *Dying to Win: The Strategic Logic of Suicide Terrorism*, Random House, New York, 2005

David Petraeus, James Amos, *Counterinsurgency, Field Manual*, Department of the Army, December, Washington D.C., 2006.

Daniel B. Pickard, *Legalizing Assassination?: Terrorism, the Central Intelligence Agency, and International Law*, Georgia Journal of International and Comparative Law, 30, no.1, 2001

John Prados, *Presidents' Secret Wars: CIA and Pentagon Covert Operations Since World War II*, William Morrow, New York, 1986.

David C. Rapaport. Ed., *Inside Terrorist Organizations*, Columbia University Press, New York, 1988.

Ahmed Rashid, *The Taliban: Militant Islam, Oil, and Fundamentalism in Central Asia*, Yale University Press, New Haven, Connecticut, 2000

John Roth, *Monograph on Terrorist Financing: Staff Report to the Commission, National Commission on the Terrorist Attacks upon the United States*, Washington D.C., 2004

Saeed Shafqat, *From Official Islam to Islamism: The Rise of Dawat-ul-Irshad and Lashkar-e-Taiba*, in Christophe Jaffrelot. Ed., *Nationalism Without a Nation: Pakistan Searching for its Identity*, New Delhi, Zed Books, New Delhi, India, 2011

Neil Sheehan, *A Bright Shining Lie: John Paul Vann and America in Vietnam*, Random House. New York, 1988.

Nadav Shragai, *Two out of Five, Ha'Aretz*, September 26, 2003

Ronald H. Spector, *After Tet: The Bloodiest Year in Viet Nam*, The Free Press, 1993.

Ehud Sprinzak, *Rational Fanatics,* Foreign Policy, Issue 120, September-October, 2000

Rodney Stark and William S. Bainbridge, *Secularization, Revival, and Cult Formation*, Berkeley University of California Press, 1985.

Jessica Stern, *Terror in the Name of God: Why Religious Militants Kill,* Ecco, New York, 2003

Robert Taber, *War of the Flea: The Classic Study of Guerrilla Warfare*, The Citadel Press, New York, 1965

United States Counterinsurgency Initiative, United States Counterinsurgency Guide, January, 2009.

Douglas Valentine, *The Phoenix Program*, William Morrow and Company, Inc. New York, 1990.

Ronald Wintrobe, *Rational Extremism: The Political Economy of Radicalism,* Cambridge University Press, New York, 2006

Evan Wright, *Generation Kill: Devil Dogs, Iceman, Captain America, and the New Face of American War*, G.P. Putnam's Sons, a member of Putnam Group (USA) Inc., 2004

Marilyn B. Young, *The Viet Nam Wars - 1945-1990*, Harper Collins Publishers, New York, 1991.

SOME OF THE COSTS OF
TERRORISM IN THE MIDDLE EAST

Of the past 3,400 years, humans have been entirely at peace
for 268 of them, or just 8 percent of recorded history.
                    –Chris Hedges, *New York Times*, 2003

The current wave of terrorism began in 2012 and has been largely
concentrated in *Iraq, Syria and Afghanistan*. There has been a 650%
increase in the number of terrorist deaths in the OECD countries since
2012. The cost of terrorism is indeed high, but it is minor in comparison
to the total economic impact of violence: $13.6 trillion in 2015,
equivalent to 13.3% of the *global* GDP. [The monetary cost amounts to
17.3% of Iraq GDP, 16.8% of Afghanistan's, and 8.3% of Syria's]

In the first five years of the *Syrian Civil War*–which began in 2011–an
estimated 5.7 million have fled the country; and 6.1 million are displaced
internally, creating a world-wide humanitarian and immigration crisis.

More than 1,000 children have been killed or injured in 2018 across
Syria. A U.N. envoy stated that the U.N. estimates that there have
been at least 7 million killed during the seven year long civil war with
unverified reports putting the number at more than 20,000. Another
view: The Violations Documentation Center in Syria assessed the overall
death toll as of December 2016 at 22,633 adult male deaths, 2,849 adult
female deaths, 3,773 child male deaths, and 1,775 child female deaths.
23,604 or 76% of all fatalities were civilians with 7,406 or 24% being

636

military deaths. Causes of death were explosions, shelling, field execution, shooting, warplane bombardment, chemical and toxic gas attacks.

In 2013, Bashar al-Assad had about 22% percent of Syrian territory but had 70% of population. By 2019, the majority of Syrian land and population was under al-Assad's control, and most observers believe that the war has turned completely in Assad's favor.

The United States has suffered about 7,000 casualties, has spent roughly $1.6 trillion between 2001 and 2014 including *costs of Iraq and Afghanistan*, military bases, an assortment of other defense expenditures not associated with Iraq and Afghanistan per se, contrary to the $6 trillion reported by one government official. $1.6 trillion is for baseline operations costs but also adds in counterterrorism costs. The Pentagon states that the war in Afghanistan costs American taxpayers $45 billion per year, and there is no end in sight. We the People may will have to keep paying that bill for years to come. Adding in Pakistan and Syria and extending to timeline out to 2016 brings the total to $4.36 trillion. To get to the $6 trillion, the cost of future veterans' care must be factored in, but it is certainly a real factor for the legislature to deal with. Nation building raises costs by about a billion dollars. An additional $1 trillion has been necessary to pay the huge interest costs because combat in the Middle East [still ongoing] is financed with borrowed money.

The *War in Afghanistan* began in 2001 and has cost the U.S. $975 billion, as of 2019. As of 2018, there have been 2,372 U.S. military deaths with 1,856 of these deaths being the result of hostile action. 20,320 American service members have also been wounded in action during the war.

The *Vietnam War* cost $168 billion or [$1 trillion in 2019 dollars]. That included $111 billion in military operations and $28.5 billion in aid to South Vietnam. The Vietnam Conflict Extract Data File of the Defense Casualty Analysis System (DCAS) contains records of 58,220 U.S. military fatal casualties of the Vietnam War. Out of 2,594,000 personnel who served in Viet Nam–besides those killed–there were 153,300 wounded, more than 23,000 armed forces personnel who suffered 100 percent disability, and there are 1,643 still MIA.

The financial costs of the *Banana Wars* are unknown because so many of the actions were secret, and because the overall risk/benefit ratio was so highly favorable to the United States and its companies that dollar costs were scarcely noted. The casualties were low, relative to other U.S. military actions: For Nicaragua—KIA 159, WIA 290, Total Casualties 449. For Haiti—KIA 148, WIA 26. Santo Domingo—KIA 1, WIA 1, Total 2.

www.ingramcontent.com/pod-product-compliance
Lightning Source LLC
Chambersburg PA
CBHW071330020726
47502CB00001B/33